The Dark Reflections

TRILOGY

INCLUDES *THE WATER MIRROR,*
THE STONE LIGHT, AND *THE GLASS WORD*

KAI MEYER

Translated by Elizabeth D. Crawford

Margaret K. McElderry Books

New York   London   Toronto   Sydney

MARGARET K. MCELDERRY BOOKS

An imprint of Simon & Schuster Children's Publishing Division

1230 Avenue of the Americas, New York, New York 10020

The Water Mirror English language translation copyright © 2005 by Elizabeth D. Crawford

Die Fliessende Koenigin text copyright © 2001 by Kai Meyer

The Water Mirror original German edition © 2001 by Loewe Verlag GmbH, Bindlach

The Water Mirror originally published in German in 2001
as *Die Fliessende Koenigin* by Loewe Verlag

The Stone Light English language translation copyright © 2007 by Elizabeth D. Crawford

Das Steinerne Licht text copyright © 2001 by Kai Meyer

The Stone Light original German edition © 2002 by Loewe Verlag GmbH, Bindlach

The Stone Light originally published in German in 2002
as *Das Steinerne Licht* by Loewe Verlag

The Glass Word English language translation copyright © 2008 by Elizabeth D. Crawford

Das Gläserne Wort text copyright © 2002 by Kai Meyer

The Glass Word original German edition © 2002 by Loewe Verlag GmbH, Bindlach

The Glass Word originally published in German in 2002
as *Das Gläserne Wort* by Loewe Verlag

All published by arrangement with Loewe Verlag

For information about special discounts for bulk purchases, please contact Simon & Schuster
Special Sales at 1-866-506-1949 or business@simonandschuster.com.

The Simon & Schuster Speakers Bureau can bring authors to your live event.
For more information or to book an event, contact the Simon & Schuster Speakers Bureau
at 1-866-248-3049 or visit our website at www.simonspeakers.com.

Book design by Russell Gordon

The text for this book is set in Stempel Garamond.

Manufactured in the United States of America

This Margaret K. McElderry Books paperback edition October 2010

2 4 6 8 10 9 7 5 3 1

Library of Congress Control Number 2009942507

ISBN 978-1-4424-0938-5

These titles were previously published in the United States individually
by Margaret K. McElderry Books.

Contents

The Water Mirror

Contents

1

Mermaids

THE GONDOLA CARRYING THE TWO GIRLS EMERGED FROM one of the side canals. They had to wait for the boats racing on the Grand Canal to pass, and even then, for minutes afterward there was such a jumble of small rowboats and steamboats that the gondolier chose to wait patiently.

"They'll be past pretty soon," he called to the girls as he grasped his oar with both hands. "You aren't in a hurry, are you?"

"No," replied Merle, who was the older of the two. But actually she was more excited than she'd ever been in her life.

People in Venice had been talking about nothing but the regatta on the Grand Canal for days. The promoters had advertised that the boats would be drawn by more mermaids at once than ever before.

Some people disparaged the mermaids as "fishwives." That was only one of the countless abusive terms they used for them, and worst of all was the claim that they were in league with the Egyptians. Not that anyone seriously believed such nonsense—after all, the armies of the Pharaoh had wiped out untold numbers of mermaids in the Mediterranean.

In today's regatta there were to be ten boats at the starting line, at the southern end of the Grand Canal, at the level of the Casa Stecchini. Each would be pulled by ten mermaids.

Ten mermaids! That had to be an all-time record. *La Serenissima*, most serene lady, as the Venetians liked to call their city, had never seen anything like it.

The mermaids were harnessed in a fan shape in front of the boats on long ropes that could withstand even needle-sharp mermaid teeth. The people were gathered to watch the show on the right and left sides of the canal wherever its banks were accessible and, of course, on all the balconies and in the windows of the palazzos.

But Merle's excitement had nothing to do with the regatta. She had another reason. A better one, she thought.

The gondolier waited another two or three minutes

before he steered the slender black gondola out into the Grand Canal, straight across it, and into the opening of a smaller canal opposite. As they crossed, they were almost rammed by some show-offs who'd harnessed their own mermaids in front of their boat and, bawling loudly, were trying to act as if they were part of the regatta.

Merle smoothed back her long, dark hair. The wind was making her eyes tear. She was fourteen years old, not big, not small, but a little on the thin side. That was true of almost all the children in the orphanage, though, except of course for fat Ruggiero, but he was sick—at least that's what the attendant said. But was it really a sign of illness to sneak into the kitchen at night and eat up the dessert that was to be for everyone else?

Merle took a deep breath. The sight of the captive mermaids made her sad. They had the upper bodies of humans, with the light, smooth skin that many women probably prayed for every night. Their hair was long, for among the women of the sea it was considered shameful to cut it off—to such an extent that even their human masters respected this custom.

What differentiated the mermaids from ordinary women was, for one thing, their mighty fish tails. The tails began at the level of their hips and were rarely shorter than six and a half feet. They were as agile as whips, as strong as lions, and as silvery as the jewelry in the treasury of the City Council.

But the second big difference—and it was the one that humans feared most—was the hideous mouth that split a mermaid's face like a gaping wound. Even though the rest of their features might be human, and strikingly beautiful as well—innumerable poems had been written about their eyes, and not a few love-smitten youths had voluntarily gone to a watery grave for them—still it was their mouths that convinced so many that they were dealing with animals and not with humans. The maw of a mermaid reached from one ear to the other, and when she opened it, it was as if her entire skull split in two. Arising from her jawbone were several rows of sharp teeth, as small and pointed as nails of ivory. Anyone who thought there was no worse bite than that of a shark had never looked into the jaws of a mermaid.

Actually, people knew very little about them. It was a fact that mermaids avoided humans. For many of the city's inhabitants, that was reason enough to hunt them. Young men often made a sport of driving inexperienced mermaids who'd gotten mixed up in the labyrinth of the Venetian canals into a corner; if one of them happened to die as a result, people thought that was too bad, certainly, but no one ever reproved the hunters.

But mostly the mermaids were caught and imprisoned in tanks in the Arsenal until a reason for keeping them was found. Often it was this boat race, more rarely fish soup—though the taste of their long, scaled tails was legendary, surpassing even delicacies like sea cows and whales.

"I feel sorry for them," said the second girl, sitting next to Merle in the gondola. She was just as under-nourished and even bonier. Her pale, almost white blond hair hung way down her back. Merle knew nothing about her companion, only that she also came from an orphanage, though from another district of Venice. She was a year younger than Merle, thirteen, she'd said. Her name was Junipa.

Junipa was blind.

"You feel sorry for the mermaids?" Merle asked.

The blind girl nodded. "I could hear their voices a while ago."

"But they haven't said anything."

"Yes, under the water," Junipa countered. "They were singing the whole time. I have quite good ears, you know. Many blind people do."

Merle stared at Junipa in astonishment, until she finally became conscious of how impolite that was, whether the girl could see it or not.

"Yes," said Merle, "me too. I feel they always seem a little . . . I don't know, melancholy somehow. As if they'd lost something that meant a lot to them."

"Their freedom?" suggested the gondolier, who had been listening to them.

"More than that," Merle replied. She couldn't find

the words to describe what she meant. "Maybe being able to be happy." That still wasn't exactly it, but it came close.

She was convinced that the mermaids were just as human as she was. They were more intelligent than many a person she'd learned to know in the orphanage, and they had feelings. They were *different*, certainly, but that didn't give anyone the right to treat them like animals, to harness them to their boats or chase them through the lagoon whenever they pleased. The Venetians' behavior toward them was cruel and utterly inhuman—all the things, really, that people said about the mermaids.

Merle sighed and looked down into the water. The prow of the gondola was cutting through the emerald green surface like a knife blade. In the narrow side canals the water was very calm; it was only on the Grand Canal that stronger waves came up sometimes. But here, three or four corners removed from Venice's main artery, there was complete stillness.

Soundlessly the gondola glided underneath arching bridges. Some were carved with grinning stone imps; bushy weeds were growing on their heads like tufts of green hair.

On both sides of the canal the fronts of the houses came straight down into the water. None was lower than four stories. A few hundred years before, when

Venice had still been a mighty trading power, goods had been unloaded from the canal directly into the palazzos of the rich merchant families. But today many of the old buildings stood empty, most of the windows were dark, and the wooden doors at the water level were rotten and eroded by dampness—and that not just since the Egyptian army's siege had closed around the city. The born-again pharaoh and his sphinx commanders were not to blame for all of it.

"Lions!" Junipa exclaimed suddenly.

Merle looked along the canal to the next bridge. She couldn't discover a living soul, to say nothing of the stone lions of the City Guard. "Where? I don't see any."

"I can smell them," Junipa insisted. She was sniffing at the air soundlessly, and out of the corner of her eye Merle saw the gondolier behind them shake his head in bewilderment.

She tried to emulate Junipa, but the gondola must have gone on for almost another two hundred feet before Merle's nostrils detected something: the odor of damp stone, musty and a little mildewed, so strong that it even masked the breath of the sinking city.

"You're right." It was unmistakably the stench of the stone lions used by the Venetian City Guard as riding animals and comrades-at-arms.

At that very moment one of the powerful animals appeared on a bridge ahead of them. It was of granite, one of the most common breeds among the stone lions of the lagoon. There were other, stronger ones, but that made no difference in the long run. Anyone who fell into the clutches of a granite lion was as good as lost. The lions had been the emblems of the city from time immemorial, back to the days when every one of them was winged and had been able to lift itself into the air. But today there were only a few who could do that, a strictly regulated number of single animals, which were reserved for the personal protection of the city councillors. The breeding masters on the island of the lions, up in the north of the lagoon, had bred out flying in all the others. They came into the world with stunted wings, which they bore as mournful appendages on their backs. The soldiers of the City Guard fastened their saddles to them.

The granite lion on the bridge also was only an ordinary animal of stone. Its rider wore the uniform of the Guard. A rifle dangled on a leather strap over his shoulder, pointedly casual, a sign of military arrogance. The soldiers had not been able to protect the city from the Egyptian Empire—instead, the Flowing Queen had done that—but since the proclamation of siege conditions thirty years before, the Guard had gained more and more power. Meanwhile they were surpassed in their arrogance only by their commanders, the city councillors, who managed affairs in the captive city as they saw fit. Perhaps the councillors and their soldiers were only trying to prove something to themselves—after all, everyone else knew that they weren't in a position to defend Venice in an emergency. But so long as the Flowing Queen kept the enemy far from the lagoon, they could rejoice in their omnipotence.

The guardsman on the bridge looked down into the gondola with a grin, then waved to Merle and gave the lion his spurs. With a snort the beast leaped forward. Merle could hear all too clearly the scraping of its stone claws on the pavement. Junipa held her ears. The bridge quivered and trembled under the paws of the great cat, and the sound seemed to career back and forth between the high facades like a bouncing ball. Even the still water was set in motion. The gondola rocked gently.

The gondolier waited until the soldier had disappeared into the tangle of narrow streets, then spat into the water and murmured, "The Ancient Traitor take you!" Merle looked around at him, but the man looked past her down the canal, his face expressionless. Slowly he guided the gondola forward.

"Do you know how far it is now?" Junipa inquired of Merle.

Before she could answer, the gondolier replied, "We're there now. There ahead, just around the corner." Then he realized that "there ahead" was not information the blind girl could use. So he quickly added, "Only a few minutes, then we'll be on the Canal of the Expelled."

11

❖

Narrowness and darkness—those were the two qualities that impressed themselves on Merle most strongly.

The Canal of the Expelled was flanked by tall houses, one as dark as the next. Almost all were abandoned. The window openings gaped empty and black in the gray fronts, many panes were broken, and the wooden shutters hung aslant on their hinges like wings on the ribs of dead birds. From one broken door came the snarling of fighting tomcats, nothing unusual in a city of umpteen thousand stray cats. Pigeons cooed on the window ledges, and the narrow, railingless walks on both sides of the water were covered with moss and pigeon droppings.

The only two inhabited houses stood out clearly from the rows of decaying buildings. They were exactly opposite one another and glared across the canal like two chess players, with furrowed faces and knitted brows. About three hundred feet separated them from the mouth of the canal and from its shadowy dead end. Each of the houses had a balcony, that of the one on the left of stone, that of the one on the right wrought of intertwining metal grill-work. The balustrades high over the water were almost touching.

The canal measured about three paces wide. The water, though still a brilliant green, looked darker and deeper here. The spaces between the old houses were so narrow that hardly any daylight reached the water's surface. A few bird feathers rocked languidly on the waves caused by the gondola.

Merle had a vague notion of what lay ahead of her. They had explained it to her at the orphanage, repeatedly mentioning how grateful she should feel that she was being sent here to apprentice. She would be spending the next few years on this canal, in this tunnel of greenish gray twilight.

The gondola neared the inhabited houses. Merle listened intently, but she could hear nothing except a distant murmur of indistinguishable voices. When she looked over at Junipa, she saw that every muscle in the blind girl's body was tensed; she had closed her eyes; her lips formed silent words—perhaps those she was picking out of the whisperings with her trained ears, like the movements of a carpet weaver, who with his sharp needle purposefully picks out a single thread from among thousands of others. Junipa was indeed an extraordinary girl.

The building on the left housed the weaving establishment of the famed Umberto. It was said to be wicked to wear garments that he and his apprentices made; his reputation was too bad, his quarrel with the Church too well known. But those women who allowed themselves to secretly order bodices and dresses from him swore behind their hands as to their magical effect. "Umberto's clothes make one slender," they said in the salons and streets of Venice. *Really* slender. For whoever wore them not only looked slimmer—she was in fact so, as if the magical threads of the master weaver drew off the fat of all those who were enveloped by them. The priests in Venice's churches had more than once thundered against the unholy dealings of the master weaver, so loudly and hatefully that the trade guild had finally expelled Umberto from its ranks.

But Umberto wasn't the only one who had come to feel the wrath of the guilds. It was the same with the master of the house opposite. There was also a workshop housed in that one, and it too devoted itself in its way to the service of beauty. However, no clothing was woven there, and its master, the honorable Arcimboldo, would doubtless have protested loudly at any open suggestion of a connection between him and his archenemy, Umberto.

ARCIMBOLDO'S GLASS FOR THE GODS was written in golden letters over the door, and right beside it was a sign: MAGIC MIRRORS FOR GOOD AND WICKED STEPMOTHERS, FOR BEAUTIFUL AND UGLY WITCHES, AND EVERY SORT OF HONEST PURPOSE.

"We're there," Merle said to Junipa, as her eye traveled over the words a second time. "Arcimboldo's magic mirror workshop."

"How does it look?" Junipa asked.

Merle hesitated. It wasn't easy to describe her first impression. The house was dark, certainly, like the whole canal and its surroundings, but next to the door stood a tub of colorful flowers, a friendly spot in the gray twilight. Only at the second look did she realize that the flowers were made of glass.

"Better than the orphanage," she said somewhat uncertainly.

The steps leading up to the walk from the water surface were slippery. The gondolier helped them both climb out. He had already been paid when he picked the girls up. He wished them both luck before he slowly glided away in his gondola.

They stood there a little lost, each with a half-full bundle in her hand, just under the sign offering magic mirrors for wicked stepmothers. Merle wasn't sure whether she should consider this a good or a bad introduction to her apprenticeship. Probably the truth lay somewhere in between.

Behind a window of the weaver's workshop on the other bank, a face whisked past, then a second. Curious apprentices, Merle guessed, who were looking over the new arrivals. *Enemy* apprentices, if you believed the rumors.

Arcimboldo and Umberto had never liked each other, that was no secret, and even their simultaneous expulsion from the trade guilds had changed nothing. Each one blamed the other. "What? Throw me out and not that crazy mirror maker?" Umberto was said to have asked loudly. The weaver asserted, on the other hand, that

Arcimboldo had cried at his own expulsion, "I'll go, but you'd do well to bring charges against that thread picker, too." Which of these accusations matched the truth, no one knew with utter certainty. It was clear only that they had both been expelled from the guilds because of forbidden trafficking with magic.

A magician, Merle thought excitedly, though she had been thinking of scarcely anything else for days. *Arcimboldo is a real magician!*

With a grating sound, the door of the mirror workshop was opened, and an odd-looking woman appeared on the pavement. Her long hair was piled up into a knot. She wore leather trousers, which emphasized her slender legs. Over these fluttered a white blouse, shot through with silver threads—Merle might have expected such a fine item in the weaver's workshop on the opposite bank of the canal, but not in the house of Arcimboldo.

But the most unusual thing was the mask behind which the woman hid a part of her face. The last Carnival of Venice—at one time famous the world over—had taken place over four decades ago. That had been 1854, three years after the Pharaoh Amenophis had been awakened to a new life in the stepped pyramid of Amun-Ka-Re. Today, in time of war, distress, and siege, there was no occasion to dress up.

And yet the woman was wearing a mask, formed of paper, enameled, and artfully decorated, doubtless the work of a Venetian artist. It covered the lower half of her face right up to her nostrils. Its surface was snow white and shone like porcelain. The mask maker had painted a small, finely curved mouth with dark red lips on it.

"Eft," the woman said, and then, with a barely noticeable lisp, "that's my name."

"Merle. And this is Junipa. We're the new apprentices."

"Of course, who else?" Only Eft's eyes betrayed that she was smiling. Merle wondered whether the woman's face could have been disfigured by illness.

Eft ushered the girls in. Beyond the door was a broad entrance hall, as in most of the houses of the city. It was only sparely furnished, the walls plastered and without hangings—precautions against the high waters that struck Venice some winters. The domestic life of the Venetians took place on the second and third floors, the ground floors being left bare and uncomfortable.

"It's late," said Eft, as if her eye had happened to fall on a clock. But Merle couldn't discover one anywhere. "Arcimboldo and the older students are in the workshop at this hour and may not be disturbed. You'll get to meet them in the morning. I'll show you to your room."

Merle couldn't repress a smile. She had hoped that she and Junipa would share a room. She saw that the blind girl was also happy to hear Eft's words.

The masked woman led them up the steps of a curving flight of stairs. "I'm the housekeeper for the workshop.

I'll be cooking for you and washing your things. Perhaps in the first few months you'll be giving me a hand with it; the master often requests that of newcomers—especially as you are the only girls in the house."

The only girls? That all the other apprentices could be boys hadn't occurred to Merle at all until now. She was all the more relieved that she was beginning her apprenticeship with Junipa.

The blind girl wasn't very talkative, and Merle guessed that she hadn't had a very easy time of it in the orphanage. Merle had only too often experienced how awful children can be, especially to those they consider weaker. Certainly Junipa's blindness would frequently have been a reason for mean tricks.

The girls followed Eft down a long hallway. The walls were hung with countless mirrors. Most were aimed toward each other: mirrors in mirrors in mirrors. Merle doubted that any of these were Arcimboldo's famous magic mirrors, for she could discover nothing unusual about them.

After Eft had explained all the rules about eating times, going out, and behavior in the house, Merle asked, "Who buys Arcimboldo's magic mirrors, anyhow?"

"You're curious," stated Eft, leaving it open as to whether this displeased her.

"Rich people?" Junipa queried, absently running her hand over her smooth hair.

"Perhaps," Eft replied. "Who knows?" With that she let the subject drop, and the girls probed no further. They would have time enough to find out everything important about the workshop and its customers. *Good and wicked stepmothers,* Merle repeated to herself. Beautiful and ugly witches. That sounded exciting.

The room that Eft showed them to was not large. It smelled musty, but since it was on the fourth floor of the building, it was pleasingly bright. In Venice you saw daylight only above the third floor, to say nothing of the sunshine, if you were lucky. However, the window of this room looked out over a sea of orange tiles. At night they would be able to see the starry heavens, and all day they would be able to see the sun—provided their work left them time for it.

The room was at the back of the house. Far below the window, Merle could make out a small courtyard with a round well in the center. All the houses opposite appeared to be empty. At the beginning of the war with the Pharaoh's kingdom, many Venetians had left the city and fled to the mainland—a disastrous mistake, as it later turned out.

Eft left the girls, telling them she would bring them something to eat in an hour. And then after that they should go to bed, so that they would be rested for their first workday.

Junipa felt along the bedposts and gently let herself

down on the mattress. Carefully she stroked the bedcover with both hands.

"Look at the blankets! So fluffy!"

Merle sat down beside her. "They must have been expensive," she said dreamily. In the orphanage the blankets had been thin and scratchy, and there were all kinds of bugs that bit your skin while you were asleep.

"It looks as though we've been lucky," Junipa said.

"We still haven't met Arcimboldo."

Junipa raised an eyebrow. "Anyone who takes a blind girl from an orphanage to teach her something can't be a bad man."

Merle remained skeptical. "Arcimboldo is known for that—taking orphans as pupils. Anyway, what parents would send their child to apprentice in a place that calls itself the Canal of the Expelled?"

"But I can't see, Merle! I've been nothing but a millstone around people's necks all my life."

"Did they make you think that at the home?" Merle gave Junipa a searching look. Then she took her narrow white hand. "Anyhow, I'm glad you're here."

Junipa smiled in embarrassment. "My parents abandoned me when I was just a year old. They left a note in my clothes. They said that they didn't want to raise a cripple."

"That's horrible."

"How did you land in the home?"

Merle sighed. "An attendant in the orphanage once

told me that they found me in a wicker basket floating on the Grand Canal." She shrugged her shoulders. "Sounds like a fairy tale, huh?"

"A sad one."

"I was only a few days old."

"Who would throw a child into the canal?"

"And who would abandon one because it couldn't see?"

They smiled at each other. Even though Junipa's blank eyes looked right through her, Merle still had the feeling that her glances were more than an empty gesture. Through hearing and touching Junipa probably perceived more than most other people.

"Your parents didn't want you to drown," Junipa declared. "Otherwise they wouldn't have taken the trouble to lay you in a wicker basket."

Merle looked at the floor. "They put something else in the basket. Would you like to—" She stopped.

"—see it?" Grinning, Junipa finished the sentence.

"I'm sorry."

"You don't have to be. I can still touch it. Do you have it with you?"

"Always, no matter where I go. Once, in the orphanage, a girl tried to steal it. I pulled all her hair out almost." She laughed a little shamefacedly. "Oh, well, I was only eight then."

Junipa laughed too. "Then I'd better put mine up in a knot for the night."

Merle touched Junipa's hair gently. It was thick and as light as a snow queen's.

"Well, so?" Junipa asked. "What else was in your wicker basket?"

Merle stood up, opened her bundle, and pulled out her most prized possession—to be precise, it was her only one, besides her sweater and the simple patched dress she had for a change of clothes.

It was a hand mirror, about as large as her face, oval and with a short handle. The frame was made of a dark metal alloy, which so many in the orphanage had greedily eyed as tarnished gold. In truth, however, it was not gold and also not any other metal anyone had ever heard of, for it was as hard as diamond.

But the most unusual thing about this mirror was its reflective surface. It wasn't made of glass, but of water. You could reach into it and make little waves, yet never a drop fell out, even when you turned the mirror.

Merle placed the handle in Junipa's open hand and carefully closed the blind girl's fingers around it. Instead of feeling the object, she first put it to her ear.

"It's whispering," she said softly.

Merle was surprised. "Whispering? I've never heard anything."

"You aren't blind, either." A small, vertical furrow had appeared in Junipa's forehead. She was concentrating. "There are several voices. I can't understand the words, there are too many voices, and they're too far away. But they're whispering with each other." Junipa lowered the mirror and ran the fingers of her left hand around the oval frame. "Is it a picture?" she asked.

"A mirror," Merle replied. "But—don't be scared—it's made of water."

Junipa betrayed no sign of astonishment, as if this were something entirely ordinary. Only, when she stretched out a fingertip and touched the water surface, she flinched. "It's cold," she said.

Merle shook her head. "No, not at all. The water in the mirror is always warm. And you can put something in it, but when you pull it out again, it's dry."

Junipa touched the water once more. "To me it feels ice-cold."

Merle took the mirror out of her hand and stuck her index and middle fingers in. "Warm," she said again, now almost a little defiantly. "It's never been cold, as long as I can remember."

"Has anyone else ever touched it? I mean, except you."

"Nobody so far. Just once, I gave permission to a nun who came to visit us in the orphanage, but she was terribly afraid of it and said it was a work of the Devil."

Junipa pondered. "Maybe the water feels cold to any-one else except the owner."

Merle frowned. "That could be." She looked at the

surface, which was always slightly in motion. Distorted and quivering, her reflection looked back.

"Are you planning to show it to Arcimboldo?" Junipa asked. "After all, he knows all about magic mirrors."

"I don't think so. At least not right away. Maybe later sometime."

"You're afraid he might take it away from you."

"Wouldn't you be?" Merle sighed. "It's the only thing that I have left of my parents."

"*You* are a part of your parents, don't forget."

Merle was quiet for a moment. She considered whether she could trust Junipa, whether she should tell the blind girl the whole truth. Finally, after a cautious glance toward the door, she whispered, "The water isn't everything."

"What do you mean?"

"I can stick my whole arm into the mirror and it doesn't come out on the other side." In fact, the back side of the oval was of the same hard metal as the frame.

"Will you do it now?" asked Junipa in astonishment. "I mean, right now this minute?"

"If you want." First Merle let her fingers slide into the interior of the water mirror, then her hand, finally her entire arm. It was as if it had vanished completely from this world.

Junipa reached out her hand and felt from Merle's shoulder to the rim of the mirror. "How does it feel?"

"Very warm," Merle reported. "Comfortable, but not

hot." She lowered her voice. "And sometimes I feel something else."

"What?"

"A hand."

"A . . . hand?"

"Yes. It grasps mine, very gently, and holds it."

"It holds you fast?"

"Not *fast*. Just . . . oh, well, it just holds my hand. The
way friends do. Or—"

"Or parents?" Junipa was looking at her intently. "Do
you believe that your father or your mother is in there
holding your hand?"

It was uncomfortable for Merle to speak about it.
Nevertheless, she felt that she could trust Junipa. After a
brief hesitation, she overcame her shyness. "It could be
possible, couldn't it? After all, they were the ones who put
the mirror in the basket with me. Maybe they did it to stay
in contact with me, so that I'd know that they are still . . .
somewhere."

Junipa nodded slowly, but she didn't appear to be
completely convinced. Rather, understanding. A little
sadly she said, "For a long time I imagined that my father
was a gondolier. I know that the gondoliers are the hand-
somest men in Venice. I mean, everyone knows that . . .
even if I can't see them."

"They aren't *all* handsome," Merle objected.

Junipa's voice sounded dreamy. "And I imagined for

myself that my mother was a water carrier from the mainland."

People said that the water carrier women who sold drinking water on the streets from huge pitchers were the most attractive women far and wide. And as in the case of the gondoliers, this story did possess a kernel of truth.

Junipa went on, "So I used to imagine that my parents were both these two very beautiful people, as if that would say something about me. About my true self. I even tried to excuse them. Two such perfect creatures, I said to myself, couldn't see themselves with a sick child. I talked myself into thinking it was their right to abandon me." Suddenly she shook her head so hard that her pale blond hair flew wildly around her. "Today I know that's all nonsense. Perhaps my parents are good looking or perhaps they're ugly. Perhaps they aren't even alive anymore. But that has nothing to do with me, you understand? I'm me, that's the only thing that counts. And my parents did wrong because they simply threw a helpless child out onto the streets."

Merle had listened, perplexed. She knew what Junipa meant, even if she didn't understand what that had to do with her and the hand in her mirror.

"You mustn't fool yourself, Merle," said the blind girl, and she sounded much wiser than her years. "Your parents didn't want you. Therefore they put you in that wicker basket. And so if someone is reaching out a hand to you in your mirror, it doesn't necessarily have to be your father or your mother. That thing you are feeling is magic, Merle. And with magic you have to be careful."

For a moment Merle felt anger rising in her. Wounded, she told herself that Junipa had no right to say such a thing, to rob her of her hopes, all the dreams she had when the other person in the mirror held her hand. But then she understood that Junipa was only being honest and that honesty is the most beautiful gift that a person can give to another at the beginning of a friendship.

Merle shoved the mirror under her pillow. She knew that it wouldn't break and that she could press the pillow as hard as she wanted onto the surface of the water without it becoming wet or sucking up the liquid. Then she sat back down next to Junipa and put her arm around her. The blind girl returned the hug and so they held each other like sisters, like two people who have no secrets from each other. It was such an overpowering feeling of closeness and mutual understanding that for a while it even surpassed the warmth of the hand in the mirror and its calm and strength, with which it had won Merle's trust.

When the girls released each other, Merle said, "You can try it sometime, if you want."

"The mirror?" Junipa shook her head. "It's yours. If it wanted me to put my hand in, the water would have been warm for me."

Merle felt that Junipa was right. Whether it was the

27

hand of one of her parents that touched hers inside there or the fingers of something entirely different, it was clear that they accepted only Merle. It might even be dangerous if another person pushed so deeply into the space behind the mirror.

The girls were sitting there together on the bed when the door opened and Eft came in. She was bearing the evening meal on a wooden tray, substantial soup with vegetables and basil, along with some white bread and a pitcher of water from the well in the courtyard.

"Go to sleep when you've unpacked," lisped the woman behind the mask as she left the room. "You'll have all the time in the world to talk with each other."

Had Eft been eavesdropping? Did she know of the mirror under Merle's pillow? But, Merle told herself, she had no reason to mistrust the housekeeper. Eft had so far been very friendly and welcoming. The mere fact that she hid the lower part of her face behind a mask didn't make her an evil person.

She was thinking again about Eft's mask as she began to fall asleep, and half-asleep she wondered whether everyone didn't wear a mask sometimes.

A mask of joy, a mask of sorrow, a mask of indifference. A mask of you-can't-see-me.

2

Mirror Eyes

IN A DREAM MERLE MET THE FLOWING QUEEN.

It seemed as if she were riding through the waters of the lagoon on a being of soft glass. Green and blue phantoms beat against them, millions of drops, as warm as the water inside her mirror. They caressed her cheeks, her neck, the palms of her open hands as she held them against the current. She felt that she was one with the Flowing Queen, a creature as unfathomable as the sunrise, as the power of thunder and lightning and the storm, as incomprehensible as life and death. They dove down under the surface, but Merle had no trouble breathing, for the

Queen was in her and kept her alive, as if they were two parts of one body.

Swarms of shimmering fish traveled along beside them, accompanying them on their journey, whose destination became less and less important to Merle. It was the journey alone that mattered, the oneness with the Flowing Queen, the feeling of comprehending the lagoon and sharing in its beauty.

And although nothing else happened, other than her gliding along with the Flowing Queen, it was a dream more marvelous than any Merle had dreamed for months, for years. In the orphanage her nights had consisted of cold, the bite of the fleas, and the fear of theft. But here, in the house of Arcimboldo, she was finally safe.

Merle awoke. In the first moment she thought that a sound had snatched her from sleep. But there was nothing. Complete silence.

The Flowing Queen. Everyone had heard of her. And yet no one knew what she really was. When the galleys of the Egyptians had tried to enter the Venetian lagoon, after their campaigns of extermination all over the world, something unusual had happened. Something wonderful. The Flowing Queen had put them to flight. The Egyptian Empire, the greatest and most horrific power in the history of the world, had had to withdraw with its tail between its legs.

Since then, the legends had twined about the Flowing Queen.

It was certain she was not a creature of flesh and blood. She was in and throughout the waters of the lagoon, the narrow canals of the city, as well as the broad expanses of water between the islands. The city councillors maintained that they had regular conversations with her and acted according to her wishes. If in fact she had ever begun to speak, however, it was never in the presence of the simple folk.

Some said she was only as big as a droplet that was sometimes here, sometimes there; others swore she was the water itself, some just a tiny swallow. She was more power than creature, and for many even a deity, who was in every thing and every creature.

The campaigns of the tyrants might sow grief, death, and desolation, Amenophis and his Empire might subjugate the world—but the aura of the Flowing Queen had protected the lagoon for more than thirty years now, and so there was no one in the city who did not feel obligated to her. In the churches Masses were held in her honor, the fishermen sacrificed a portion of every catch, and even the secret guild of the thieves showed her gratitude by keeping their hands to themselves on certain days in the year.

There—again a sound! This time there was no doubt about it.

Merle sat up in bed. The tendrils of her dreams still

lapped at her senses like the foaming tide at one's feet during a walk on the beach.

The sound was repeated. Metal grating on metal, coming up from the courtyard. Merle recognized that sound—the lid of the well. It sounded the same way all over Venice when the heavy metal covers over the wells were opened. The cisterns existed all over the city, in every open piazza and in most courtyards. Their round walls were carved with patterns and fabulous creatures of stone. Gigantic semicircular covers protected the precious drinking water from dirt and rats.

But who was busying himself about a well at this time of night? Merle got up and wiped the sleep from her eyes. A little wobbly on her legs, she went over to the window.

She was just in time to see in the moonlight a form climb over the edge of the well and slide into the dark well shaft. A moment later hands reached out of the darkness, grasped the edge of the lid, and pulled it, grating, over the opening.

Merle emitted a sharp gasp. Instinctively she ducked, although the form had disappeared into the well long since.

Eft! There was no doubt that she had been the shadowy figure in the courtyard. But what would make the housekeeper climb into a well in the middle of the night?

Merle turned around, intending to wake Junipa.

The bed was empty.

"Junipa?" she whispered tensely. But there was no corner of the small room she could not have seen from there. No hiding place.

Unless . . .

Merle bent and looked under both beds. But there was no trace of the girl.

She went to the door. It had no bolt that the girls could have slid closed for the night, no lock. Outside in the hallway it was utterly quiet.

Merle took a deep breath. The floor under her naked feet was bitterly cold. Quickly she pulled her dress and sweater on over her nightgown and pushed her feet into her worn-out leather shoes; they reached beyond her ankle and had to be tied, which at the moment required much too much time. But she couldn't possibly go looking for Junipa and run the danger of tripping over her own shoelaces. Hastily she laced and tied them, but her fingers trembled, and it took twice as long as usual.

Finally she slipped out into the passageway and pulled the door closed behind her. An ominous hissing came from somewhere in the distance. It didn't sound like an animal, more like a steam engine, but she wasn't sure whether it was coming from here in the house. Soon after, she heard it again, followed by a rhythmic pounding. Then silence again. Only as she was already on her way down the stairs did it occur to Merle that there were only two inhabited houses on the Canal of the Expelled—

Arcimboldo's workshop and that of the weaver on the other side.

The whole house smelled strange, a little of lubricating oil, of polished steel, and the acrid odor she knew from the glass workshops on the lagoon island of Murano. She had been there one single time, when an old glassmaker had contemplated taking her to work for him. Right after she arrived, he ordered her to scrub his back in the bath. Merle had waited until he was sitting in the water and then run as fast as she could back to the landing point. Stowing away in a boat, she'd managed to get back to the city. Such cases were not unknown at the orphanage, and although the authorities weren't at all happy to see her again, they had enough decency not to send her back to Murano.

Merle reached the landing on the third floor. Until then she'd met no one and discovered no sign of life. Where might the other apprentices be sleeping? Perhaps on the fourth floor, like her and Junipa. She knew at least that Eft was not in the house, but she avoided giving too much thought to what the odd woman was looking for in the well.

There remained only Arcimboldo himself. And, of course, Junipa. What if she'd only had to go to the bathroom? The tiny chamber, in which a round shaft in the floor ran straight down to the canal, was on the fourth floor too. Merle hadn't thought to look there, and now she cursed herself for it. She'd forgotten the most obvious thing—perhaps because in the orphanage it was always a bad sign when one of the children disappeared from his or her bed at night. Only a few of them ever reappeared again.

She was about to turn around to look, when the hissing started again. It sounded even more artificial, machine-like, and the tone made her shudder.

She thought she heard something else, too, very briefly only, soft in the background of the hissing.

A sob.

Junipa!

Merle tried to make out something in the dark stairwell. The area was pitch-black, only a touch of moonlight falling through a high window beside her, a vague suggestion of light that scarcely sufficed to make out the steps under her feet. In the hallway to her left ticked a grandfather clock, alone in the shadows, a monstrous outline like a coffin that someone had leaned against the wall.

Meanwhile she was certain: The hissing and the sobbing were coming from the interior of the house. From farther below. From the workshop on the second floor.

Merle hastened down the steps. The corridor that branched off from the staircase had a high, arching ceiling. She followed it, as softly and quickly as she could. Her throat was tight. Her breathing sounded as loud to her as the wheezing of one of the steamboats on the Grand Canal. What if she and Junipa had jumped out of the frying pan into the fire? If Arcimboldo had planned some horror similar to that of the old glassblower on Murano?

She recoiled as she perceived a movement next to her. But it was only her own reflection, flitting across the innumerable mirrors on the walls.

The hissing was coming more often now, and sounded nearer. Eft hadn't shown them exactly where the entrance to the workshop was. She'd merely mentioned that it was on the second floor. But here there were several doors, and all were high and dark and closed. There was nothing for Merle to do but follow the sounds. The soft sobbing had not been repeated. The thought of Junipa being helplessly delivered to an unknown danger brought tears to Merle's eyes.

One thing was certain in any case: She would not let anything happen to her new friend, even if it meant both of them being sent back to the orphanage. Of the worst she didn't want to think at all. Nevertheless, the bad thoughts stole into her mind like the buzzing of small gnats:

It's nighttime. And dark. Many people have disappeared into the canals already. No one would care about two girls. Two fewer mouths to feed, nothing more.

The corridor made a bend to the right. At its end glowed the outline of arched double doors. The crack between the two doors shimmered golden like wire that has been held in a candle flame. A strong fire must be burning inside the workshop—the coal boiler of the machine that was uttering the primeval hissing and snorting.

When Merle approached the door on tiptoe, she saw that a layer of smoke lay over the stone flags of the corridor like a fine ground fog. The smoke was coming from under the door, emerging in a fiery shimmer.

What if a fire had broken out in the workshop? *You have to remain calm*, Merle kept drumming into herself. *Very, very calm.*

Her feet stirred the smoke on the floor, conjuring up the outlines of foggy ghosts in the darkness, many times enlarged and distorted as shadows on the walls. The only light was the glow of the crack around the doors.

Darkness, fog, and the glowing doors directly in front of her—it seemed to Merle like the entrance to Hell, so unreal, so oppressive.

The acrid odor that she'd noticed in the upper stairwell was even more penetrating here. The lubricating oil stench was also stronger. It was rumored that messengers from Hell had visited the City Council in the past months and offered it the help of their master in the battle against the Empire. But the councillors had ruled out any pact with Old Nick. So long as the Flowing Queen was protecting them all, there was no reason for it. Ever since the National Geographic Society expedition under the famed Professor Charles Burbridge in 1833 had proven Hell to be a real place in the interior of the earth, there had been several meetings between the ambassadors of Satan and representatives of humanity. However, no one knew any of the details, and that was probably just as well.

All this shot through Merle's head while she walked the last paces up to the door of the workshop. With infinite caution she placed her hand flat on the wood. She'd expected it to feel warm, but that proved to have been wrong. The wood was cool and in no way different from any of the other doors in the house. Even the metal door handle was cold when Merle ran a finger over it.

She considered whether she should enter. It was the only thing she could do. She was alone, and she doubted there was anyone in this house who would come to her aid.

She'd just made her decision when the latch was pressed from the other side. Merle whirled around, meaning to flee, but then she sprang into the protection of the left-hand door, while the right one swung to the inside.

A broad beam of glowing light splashed across the smoke on the floor. Where Merle had just been standing, the swirls of smoke were swept aside by a draft of air. Then a shadow crossed the light stripe. Someone walked out into the corridor.

Merle pressed herself as deeply as she could into the protection of the closed side of the door. She was less than six feet away from the figure.

Shadows can make people menacing, even if in reality

they aren't at all. They make midgets large and weaklings as broad as elephants. So it was in this case.

The mighty shadow shrank, the farther the little old man got from the source of the light. As he stood there, without even noticing Merle, he looked almost a bit comical in his much too long trousers and the smock that had become almost black with soot and smoke. He had disheveled gray hair that stood out on all sides. His face glistened. A droplet of sweat ran down his temple and was lost in his bushy side whiskers.

Instead of turning around to Merle, he turned back to the door and extended a hand in the direction of the light. A second shadow melted with his on the floor.

"Come, my child," he said, his voice gentle. "Come out."

Merle didn't move. She hadn't imagined her first meeting with Arcimboldo like this. Only the calm and serenity in the old man's voice gave her a little hope.

But then the mirror maker said, "The pain will stop soon."

Pain?

"You needn't be afraid," Arcimboldo said, facing the open door. "You'll quickly get used to it, believe me."

Merle scarcely dared breathe.

Arcimboldo took two or three steps backward into the passageway. As he moved, he held both hands outstretched, an invitation to follow him.

"Come closer . . . yes, just like that. Very slowly."

And Junipa came. With small, uncertain steps she walked through the door into the hallway. She moved stiffly and very carefully.

But she can't see anything, Merle thought desperately. Why was Arcimboldo letting her wander around without help in a place that wasn't familiar to her? Why didn't he wait until she could take his hand? Instead he kept moving backward, farther from the door—and in fact at any moment he was going to discover Merle, hiding in the shadow. Spellbound, she stared at Junipa, who was falteringly stepping past her in the hallway. Arcimboldo, too, only had eyes for the girl.

"You're doing very well," he said encouragingly. "Very, very well."

The smoke on the floor gradually dispersed. No new clouds came from the depths of the workshop. The glowing firelight bathed the hallway in flickering, dark orange.

"It's all so . . . blurry," Junipa whispered miserably.

Blurry? Merle thought in astonishment.

"That will improve soon," said the mirror maker. "Just wait—early tomorrow, by daylight, everything will look very different. You must only trust me. Come just a little closer."

Junipa's steps were more confident now. Her careful progress was not because she couldn't see. Quite the contrary.

"What do you recognize?" asked Arcimboldo. "What exactly?"

"I don't know. Something is moving."

"Those are only shadows. Don't be afraid."

Merle couldn't believe her ears. Was it possible, was it actually possible that Arcimboldo had given Junipa sight?

"I've never seen before," said Junipa, baffled. "I was always blind."

"Is the light that you see red?" the mirror maker wanted to know.

"I don't know how light looks," she replied uncertainly. "And I don't know any colors."

Arcimboldo grimaced, annoyed with himself. "Stupid of me. I should have thought of that." He stopped and waited until he could grasp Junipa's outstretched hands. "You'll have a lot to learn in the next weeks and months."

"But that's why I came here."

"Your life will change, now that you can see."

Merle could no longer stay in her hiding place. Unmindful of all consequences, she leaped from the shadows into the light.

"What have you done to her?"

Startled, Arcimboldo looked over at her. And Junipa blinked. She strained to make anything out. "Merle?" she asked.

"I'm here." Merle walked up to Junipa and touched her gently on the arm.

"Ah, our second new pupil." Arcimboldo had quickly recovered from his surprise. "A quite curious pupil, it seems to me. But that doesn't matter. You would have found out early tomorrow morning in any case. So you are Merle."

She nodded. "And you are Arcimboldo."

"Indeed, indeed."

Merle looked from the old mirror maker back to Junipa. The realization of what he'd done found her unprepared. At first glance and in the weak light the change hadn't caught her attention, but now she asked herself how she could have overlooked *that*. It felt as though an ice-cold hand were running its fingers up her back.

"But . . . how . . . ?"

Arcimboldo smiled proudly. "Remarkable, isn't it?"

Merle couldn't speak a syllable. Dumbly she stared at Junipa.

Into her face.

At her eyes.

Junipa's white eyeballs had vanished. Instead of them, silvery mirrors glittered under her lids, set into her eye sockets. Not rounded like eyeballs, but flat. Arcimboldo had replaced Junipa's eyes with the splinters of a crystal mirror.

"What have you—"

Arcimboldo gently interrupted her. "Done to her?

Nothing, my child. She can see, at least a little. But that will improve from day to day."

"She has mirrors in her eyes!"

"That is so."

"But . . . but that's . . ."

"Magic?" Arcimboldo shrugged his shoulders. "Some might call it so. I call it science. Besides humans and animals there is only one other thing in the world that is able to see. Look in a mirror, and it will look back at you. That is the first lesson in my workshop, Merle. Mark it well. Mirrors can see."

"He's right, Merle," Junipa agreed. "I actually can see something. And I have the feeling that with every minute it's getting to be a little more."

Arcimboldo nodded delightedly. "That's wonderful!" He grabbed Junipa's hand and did a little dance of joy with her, just carefully enough not to pull her off her feet. The last remnants of the smoke flew up around them. "Say it yourself, isn't it fantastic?"

Merle stared at the two of them and couldn't quite believe what was taking place before her eyes. Junipa, who'd been blind since she was born, could see. Thirteen years of darkness had ended. And for that she had to thank Arcimboldo, this little wisp of a man with the disheveled hair.

"Help your friend to your room," said the mirror maker, after he'd let go of Junipa. "You have a strenuous day ahead of you tomorrow. Every day is strenuous in my workshop. But I think it will please you. Oh, yes, I really think so."

He held out his hand to Merle and added, "Welcome to Arcimboldo's house."

A little dazed, she remembered what they'd hammered into her in the orphanage. "Many thanks for having us here," she said politely. But in her confusion she hardly heard what she was saying. She looked after the gleeful old man as he hastened back into his workshop with dancing steps and pulled the door closed behind him.

Merle shyly took Junipa's hand and helped her up the stairs to the fourth floor, anxiously asking every few steps whether the pain was really not too bad. Whenever Junipa turned toward her, Merle shivered a little. She wasn't seeing her friend in the mirror eyes but only herself, reflected twice and slightly distorted. She reassured herself with the thought that it was certainly only a matter of getting used to Junipa's appearance until it looked completely normal to her.

But still, a slight doubt remained. Before, Junipa's eyes had been milky and unseeing. Now they were as cold as polished steel.

"I can see, Merle. I can really see."

Junipa kept murmuring the words to herself long after they were back in their own beds again.

Once, hours later, Merle awakened from tangled

dreams when she again heard the grating of the well cover, deep in the courtyard and very, very far away.

The first few days in Arcimboldo's mirror workshop were tiring, for Merle and Junipa were left to do all those jobs that the three older apprentices, boys, didn't want to do. So, many times a day Merle had to sweep up the fine mirror crystals that were deposited on the workshop floor like the desert sand that in some summers was driven across the sea as far as Venice.

As Arcimboldo had promised, Junipa's vision improved from day to day. She still perceived hardly more than ghostly images, but she was already able to differentiate one from another, and it was important to her to find her way around the unfamiliar workshop without help. However, they gave her easier jobs than Merle's, even if not much pleasanter ones. She was allowed no real recuperation after the stresses of that first night, and she had to weigh out endless quantities of quartz sand from sacks and put it into measures. What exactly Arcimboldo did with it remained a puzzle to the girls for the time being.

Actually, the mirror workshop under Arcimboldo appeared to have little to do with that long-standing tradition of which people in Venice had been proud since time out of mind. Earlier, in the sixteenth century, only the select were initiated into the art of mirror making. They all lived under strict watch on the glassblowing island of

Murano. There they lived in luxury, lacking for nothing—except freedom. For as soon as they had begun their training, they might never again leave the island. And for those who tried anyway, it was death. The agents of La Serenissima hunted down renegade mirror makers throughout Europe and killed the traitors before they could pass on the secret of mirror production to outsiders. Murano's mirrors were the only ones to adorn all the great houses of the nobility of Europe, for only in Venice was this art understood. As for the city, the secret could not be weighed in gold—well, except in the individual instances. Finally some mirror makers did succeed in fleeing from Murano and selling their secret art to the French, who then repaid them by killing them. Soon afterward the French opened their own workshops and robbed Venice of its monopoly. Mirrors were soon produced in many lands, and the prohibitions and punishments for Murano's mirror makers receded into oblivion.

Arcimboldo's mirrors, however, had as much to do with alchemy as with the art of glass making. After only the first few days, Merle sensed that it might be years before he would initiate her into his secrets. It was the same with the three boys. The eldest, Dario, though he'd already lived in the house for more than two years, had not the slightest glimmer of how Arcimboldo's art worked. Certainly they observed, even eavesdropped and spied, but they did not know the true secret.

Slim, black-haired Dario was the leader of Arcimboldo's apprentices. When the master was present, he always displayed very good behavior, but on his own he was still the same lout he'd been when he came from the orphanage two years before. During their short free periods he was a braggart, and sometimes domineering, too, though the two other boys had to suffer more from that than Merle and Junipa did. In fact, to a large extent he preferred to ignore the girls. It displeased him that Arcimboldo had taken girls on as apprentices, probably also because his behavior toward Eft left much to be desired. He seemed to be afraid that Merle and Junipa would take the housekeeper's side in arguments or might betray some of his little secrets to her—such as the fact that he regularly sampled Arcimboldo's good red wine, which Eft kept under lock and key in the kitchen. She didn't know that Dario had laboriously made himself a copy of the key to the cupboard. Merle had discovered Dario's thieving by accident on the third night, when she'd met him with a pitcher of wine in the dark in the passageway. It never occurred to her to use this observation to her own advantage, but obviously that was exactly what Dario feared. From that moment he had treated her even more coolly, with downright hostility, even if he didn't dare start an overt quarrel with her. Most of the time he gave her the cold shoulder—which, to be precise, was more notice than he bestowed on Junipa. She seemed not to exist at all for him.

Secretly Merle asked herself just why Arcimboldo had taken the rebellious Dario into his house. But that also raised the uncomfortable question of what he had found in *her*, and to that no answer had occurred to her as yet. Junipa might be an ideal subject for his experiment with the mirror shards—the girls had learned that he'd never dared anything like that before—but what was it that had prompted him to rescue Merle from the orphanage? He'd never met her and must have relied entirely on what the attendants could report about her—and Merle doubted that Arcimboldo had heard too much good about her from them. In the home they had considered her uncooperative and cheeky—words that in the vocabulary of the attendants stood for intellectually curious and self-confident.

As for the other two apprentices, they were only a year older than Merle. One was a pale-skinned, red-haired boy, whose name was Tiziano. The other—smaller and with a slight harelip—was named Boro. The two seemed to enjoy finally not being the youngest any longer and being able to boss Merle around, although their behavior never deteriorated into meanness. When they saw that the delegated work was getting to be too much, they readily helped, without being asked to. Junipa, on the other hand, they seemed to find uncanny, and Boro, especially, preferred to give her a wide berth. The boys accepted Dario as their leader. They didn't have the doglike devotion to him that Merle had sometimes seen with gangs in the orphanage, but they clearly looked up to him. Anyway, he'd been apprenticed to Arcimboldo a year longer than the two of them had.

After about a week and a half, shortly before midnight, Merle saw Eft climbing down into the well a second time. She briefly considered waking Junipa but then decided against it. She stood motionless at the window for a while, staring at the well cover, then uneasily lay down in her bed again.

She'd already told Junipa of her discovery on one of their first evenings in the house.

"And she really climbed into the well?" Junipa had asked.

"I just told you so!"

"Maybe the rope had come off the water bucket."

"Would you climb down into a pitch-black well in the middle of the night just because some rope was broken? If it really had been that, she could have done it in the daytime. Besides, then she would have sent one of us." Merle shook her head decidedly. "She didn't even have a lamp with her."

Junipa's mirror eyes reflected the moonlight that was shining in through their window that night. It looked as though they were glowing in the white, icy light. As so often, Merle had to repress a shudder. Sometimes at such moments she had the feeling that Junipa saw more with her new eyes than just the surface of people and things—almost as if she could look directly into Merle's innermost thoughts.

"Are you afraid of Eft?" Junipa asked.

Merle thought about it briefly. "No. But you must admit that she's strange."

"Perhaps we all would be, if we had to wear a mask."

"And why does she wear it, anyhow? No one except Arcimboldo seems to know. I even asked Dario."

"Maybe you should just ask her sometime."

"That wouldn't be polite, if it really is an illness."

"What else would it be?"

Merle said nothing. She'd been asking herself these questions. She had a suspicion, only a very vague one; since it had come into her mind, she couldn't get it out of her head. Nevertheless, she thought it was better not to tell Junipa about it.

Merle and Junipa hadn't spoken about Eft again since that evening. There were so many other things to talk about, so many new impressions, discoveries, challenges. Every day was a new adventure, especially for Junipa, whose vision was fast improving. Merle envied her a little for how easily she became enthusiastic about the smallest things; but at the same time she rejoiced with her over the unexpected cure.

The morning after Merle saw Eft climb down into the

well the second time, something happened that once again turned her thoughts from the housekeeper's secret activities: the first meeting with the apprentices on the other bank of the canal, the apprentices of Master Weaver Umberto.

Merle had almost forgotten about the weaving workshop during the eleven days that she'd been living in the mirror maker's house. There'd been no trace of the well-known quarrel between the two masters, which had once been the talk of all Venice. Merle hadn't left the house at all during this period. Her entire day was spent mainly in the workshop, the adjoining storerooms, the dining room, and her room. Now and again one of the apprentices had to accompany Eft when she went to the vegetable market on Rio San Barnaba, but so far the housekeeper's choice had always fallen on one of the boys; they were bigger and could carry the heavy crates without any difficulty.

So Merle was caught completely unprepared when the students from the other side brought the quarrel forcefully to mind. As she later learned, it had been a tradition for years among the apprentices of both houses to play tricks on each other, which not infrequently ended with broken glass, cursing masters, bruises, and abrasions. The last of these attacks had been three weeks before and was credited to Dario, Boro, and Tiziano. The weaver boys' retaliation was long overdue after that.

Merle didn't find out why they'd chosen this morning,

and she was also not sure how they'd succeeded in getting inside the house—although later it was suspected they'd laid a board across the canal from one balcony railing to the other and so had balanced their way to the mirror maker's side. That they did all this in broad daylight, and during working hours, was a sign that it had been done with Umberto's blessing, just as earlier trespasses by Dario and the others had taken place with Arcimboldo's agreement.

Merle was just about to begin gluing the wooden frame of a mirror when there was a clatter at the entrance to the workshop. Alarmed, she looked up. She was afraid Junipa had stumbled over a tool.

But it wasn't Junipa. A small figure had slipped on a screwdriver and was staggering, fighting for balance. Its face was hidden behind a bear mask of enameled paper. With one hand it flailed wildly in the air, while the bag of paint it had held in the other burst on the tiles in a blue star.

"*Weavers!*" Tiziano bellowed, dropping his work and jumping up.

"Weavers! Weavers!" Boro, in another corner of the workshop, took up his friend's cry, and soon Dario also thundered in.

Merle got up from her place in irritation. Her eyes traveled uncertainly around the room. She didn't understand what was going on, ignorant of the competition among the apprentices.

The masked boy at the entrance slipped on his own paint and crashed on the seat of his pants. Before Dario and the others could laugh at him or even go for him, three other boys appeared in the corridor, all wearing colorful paper masks. One in particular caught Merle's eye: It was the visage of a splendid fabulous beast, half man, half bird. The long, curving beak was lacquered golden, and tiny glass gems glittered in the painted eyebrows.

Merle didn't have a chance to look at the other masks, for already a whole squadron of paint bags was flying in her direction. One burst at her feet and sprayed sticky red, another hit her shoulder and bounced off without bursting. It rolled away, over to Junipa, who'd been standing there with a gigantic broom in her hand, not quite knowing what was happening all around her. But now she grasped the situation and quickly bent, grabbed the paint bag, and flung it back at the invaders. The boy with the bear mask sprang to one side, and the missile hit the bird face behind him. The bag burst on the point of the bill and covered its owner with green paint.

Dario cheered, and Tiziano thumped Junipa encouragingly on the shoulder. Then the second wave of attacks followed. This time they didn't get off so lightly. Boro, Tiziano, and Merle were hit and spotted over and over with paint. Out of the corner of her eye, Merle saw Arcimboldo, cursing, close the door of the mirror storeroom and bar it from inside. His students might break heads, so long as the finished mirrors remained unharmed.

The apprentices were left to their own devices. Four against four. Really even five against four, if you counted Junipa—after all, in spite of her weak eyes, she'd scored the first hit for the mirror makers.

"It's the student weavers from the other bank," Boro called to Merle as he grabbed a broom, wielding it like a sword with both hands. "No matter what happens, we have to defend the workshop."

Typical boy, thought Merle, as she patted a little helplessly at the paint on her dress. But why did they constantly have to prove themselves with such nonsense?

She looked up—and was hit on the forehead with another paint bag. Viscous yellow poured over her face and her shoulders.

That did it! With an angry cry she grabbed up the glue bottle, whose contents she'd been using to glue the mirror frame, and hurled herself at the first available weaver boy. It was the one with the bear mask. He saw her coming and tried to grab another paint bag from his shoulder bag. Too late! Merle was already there. She hurled him over backward with a blow, fell on him with her knees on his chest, and shoved the narrow end of the glue bottle into the left eye opening.

"Close your eyes!" she warned and pumped a strong jet of glue under the mask. The boy swore, then his words

54

were lost in a blubber, followed by a long drawn-out "Aaaaaaaahhhhhhh!"

She saw that her opponent was out of action for the moment, pushed herself off him, and leaped back up. She now was holding the glue bottle like a pistol, even if it didn't make much sense, for most of the contents had been sprayed out. Out of the corner of her eye she saw Boro and Tiziano scuffling with two weaver boys, a wild fight. The mask of one of the boys was already demolished. Instead of joining in, however, Merle ran over to Junipa, grabbed her by the arm, and pulled her behind one of the workbenches.

"Don't move from that spot," she whispered to her.

Junipa protested. "I'm not as helpless as you think."

"No, certainly not." Merle glanced at the boy with the bird mask. His upper body was green from Junipa's paint bag. "Nevertheless, better stay under cover. This can't last much longer."

As she sprang up, she saw that her triumph had been too early. Tiziano's opponent had gained the upper hand again. And there was no sign of Dario anywhere. Merle first discovered him when suddenly he was standing in the doorway. In his hand gleamed one of the knives Arcimboldo used to trim the whisper-thin silver sheets for the backs of the mirrors. The blade wasn't long, but it was razor sharp.

"Serafin!" called Dario to the boy with the bird mask. "Come on, if you dare."

The weaver's boy saw the knife in Dario's hand and took up the challenge. His three companions retreated to the entrance. Boro helped Tiziano to his feet and then pushed Merle to the edge of the workshop.

"Have they gone crazy?" she gasped breathlessly. "They're going to kill each other."

Boro's frown betrayed that he shared her concern. "Dario and Serafin have hated each other since they first laid eyes on each other. Serafin's the leader of the weavers. He cooked up this whole thing."

"That's no reason to go at him with a knife."

While they were speaking, Dario and Serafin had met in the center of the room. Merle noticed that Serafin moved with light feet, like a dancer. He skillfully avoided the clumsy attacks of Dario, whose knife cut silvery traces in the air. Before Dario realized it, the weaver boy had extracted the knife from his fingers. With a cry of fury, Dario rushed at his opponent and landed a treacherous punch on his Adam's apple. The yellow bird face flew to one side and revealed Serafin's face. His cheekbones were finely cut, a few freckles sprinkled the bridge of his nose. He had blond hair, not so light as Junipa's; the green paint had clumped it into strings.

The weaver's bright blue eyes were squinting angrily. Before Dario could avoid it, Serafin landed a punch that flung the student mirror maker against the workbench behind which Junipa had taken shelter. Dario made one leap over the bench to put it between himself and his opponent. Junipa moved back a step in fear. But Serafin followed Dario around the bench and was about to grab him again. Dario's nose was bleeding; the last blow had weakened him. Instead of facing his antagonist, he whirled around, grabbed the surprised Junipa by the shoulders with both hands, pulled her roughly in front of him, and gave her a powerful push, which sent her stumbling in Serafin's direction.

Merle uttered a scream of rage. "That coward!"

The weaver boy saw Junipa flying toward him and saw Dario as well, just behind her, ready to use his chance. Serafin had a choice: He could catch Junipa to keep her from plunging into a rack of glass bottles—or he could sidestep her and attack his archfoe.

Serafin made a quick grab. He caught Junipa and held her for a moment in an embrace that was intended to protect her as well as to reassure her. "It's all right," he whispered to her, "nothing happened to you."

He'd scarcely spoken the words when Dario rammed his fist over Junipa's shoulder into Serafin's face.

"No!" bellowed Merle furiously. She leaped past Boro and Tiziano, ran to the workbench, and pulled Dario away from Junipa and Serafin.

"What are you doing?" yelped the older boy, but she'd already pulled him over backward to the floor.

Very briefly she caught Serafin's look as he carefully

pushed Junipa to one side. He smiled through green paint and blood, then hurried back to his friends at the entrance.

"We're clearing out," he said, and a moment later the weavers were gone.

Merle paid no attention to Dario but turned to Junipa, who was standing, dazed, in front of the bottle rack.

"Everything all right?"

Junipa nodded. "Yes . . . thanks. All right."

Behind Merle's back Dario began to curse and scold; she could sense that he was approaching her threateningly. She abruptly whirled around, looked deep into his small eyes, and gave him a box on the ear as hard as she could.

Before Dario could rush at her, Eft was suddenly between them. Merle felt the powerful grip when the housekeeper grasped her by the shoulder and pulled her away from Dario. But she didn't hear what Eft said, didn't hear the crude raging of Dario, which couldn't touch her. She was looking pensively out into the corridor into which Serafin had vanished with his friends.

3

Eft's Story

"AND WHAT, PRAY, AM I SUPPOSED TO DO WITH YOU NOW?"

The master's voice sounded more disappointed than angry. Arcimboldo was sitting behind his study desk in the library. The walls of the room were covered with leather book spines. Merle wondered whether he'd actually read all those books.

"The damage the weaver's apprentices have caused with their paint is hardly worth mentioning, in light of what the two of you have done," Arcimboldo continued, letting his eyes travel from Dario to Merle and back again. The two were standing in front of the desk and looking sheepishly at the floor. Their anger at each other was in no way cooled, but even Dario seemed to understand that it was appropriate to restrain himself.

"You have kindled strife among the students. And you have led others to take sides. If Eft hadn't intervened, Junipa, Boro, and Tiziano would have had to choose for one of you." An angry spark appeared in the old man's eyes, so that he now seemed stern and unapproachable. "I cannot allow my apprentices to be divided. What I insist on is cooperation and avoidance of all unnecessary conflicts. Magic mirrors require a certain harmony in order to mature into what they are. In an atmosphere of hostility a shadow is laid over the glass that will make it grow blind."

Merle had the feeling that he was making it up. He wanted to talk them into feeling guilty. It would have suited that purpose better if he hadn't referred so plainly to "unnecessary conflicts": After all, it had been the childish quarrel between him and Umberto in the first place that caused this whole upset.

Sooner or later it would have come to a break between her and Dario anyhow, she'd felt that on the very first day. She surmised that Arcimboldo had foreseen it too. Did he regret taking her from the orphanage? Would she have to go back to the dirt and the poverty now?

Despite her fears, no feelings of guilt troubled her. Dario was a whining coward, as he'd just demonstrated twice: once when he went for Serafin with the knife, and the second time when he'd taken cover behind the defenseless Junipa. He'd richly deserved his box on the ear and, if it had been up to her, a good beating right afterward.

Clearly Arcimboldo saw it very similarly. "Dario," he said, "for your unworthy and unrestrained behavior you will clean the workshop by yourself. I don't want to find one single spot of paint tomorrow morning early. Understand?"

"And what about her?" Dario growled, pointing angrily at Merle.

"Did you understand me?" Arcimboldo asked once more, his bushy eyebrows drawing together like two thunderclouds.

Dario lowered his head, though Merle did not miss the hateful look he sent her secretly. "Yes, Master."

"Dario will need a quantity of water. Therefore, you, Merle, will get ten pails full from the well, carry them upstairs, and take them to the workshop. That will be your punishment."

"But Master—," Dario flared.

Arcimboldo cut him short. "You have shamed us all by your behavior, Dario. I know you are rash and hot-tempered, but you are also my best student, and therefore I intend to let it go at this. As far as Merle is concerned, she has only been here for two weeks and must first get used to the fact that here, unlike the orphanage, a dispute is not settled with fists. Have I expressed myself clearly enough?"

Both bowed and said in unison, "Yes, Master."

"Any objections?"

"No, Master."

"So be it." With a wave, he indicated that they could go.

Outside the door of the library Merle and Dario exchanged black looks, then each turned to the appointed task. While Dario prepared to remove the residues of the paint attack in the workshop, Merle ran down into the courtyard. Beside the back door a dozen wooden pails sat lined up. She snatched up the first one and went to the well.

Strange creatures were carved in the stone of the wall around the well, fantastic creatures with cat's eyes, Medusa heads, and reptilian tails. They were strung out in a stiff procession around the well. At their head went a creature, half human, half shark, with arms whose elbows pointed in the wrong direction; in its hands it carried a human head.

The metal lid was heavy. Merle succeeded in opening it only with groaning and straining. Below, there was nothing but blackness. Way deep, deep down, she saw a shimmer of light, the reflection of the sky over the courtyard.

She turned around and looked up. The view was only a little different from the one inside of the well: The walls of the old houses rose up around the courtyard like the stone wall of the well. Perhaps the water wasn't so far down as she'd thought. The reflection of the courtyard added that much more height, and so the well shaft seemed to be more than double its actual length. It would be less trouble to climb down to the surface than Merle had thought—at least now she could see metal handholds going down the inside of the well into the abyss. What could it be that Eft kept doing down there?

Merle tied the bucket to the long rope lying ready beside the well and let it down. The wood scraped against the stone of the wall as it went. The sound reverberated in the depths and rose up distorted into the daylight. Except for Merle there was no one else in the courtyard. The scraping of the bucket was thrown back by the facades of the surrounding houses, and now it almost sounded like whispers murmuring down from the gaping windows of the buildings. The voices of all those who no longer lived here. Ghost whispers.

Merle couldn't see when the bucket reached the surface. It was too dark down there. But she did see that suddenly the reflection of the sky in the depths was set in motion; the bucket was probably just now dipping into the water. Only it was strange that she felt no slackening of the pull and also that the scraping of the bucket on the stone wall sounded unchanged. If it wasn't the bucket that stirred the surface of the water, what was it?

She'd scarcely framed the question when something

appeared down there. A head. It was much too far away for her to be able to make out the details, and yet she was certain that dark eyes were looking up at her.

In her fright Merle let go of the rope and took a step backward. The rope whizzed over the well wall into the depths. It would have been lost, together with the bucket, had not a hand unexpectedly grabbed it.

Eft's hand.

Merle hadn't noticed the housekeeper walking up to her in the courtyard. Eft had grabbed the end of the rope just in time and was now pulling the bucket up into the daylight.

"Thank you," Merle stammered. "That was clumsy of me."

"What did you see?" asked Eft behind her half mask.

"Nothing."

"Please don't lie to me."

Merle hesitated. Eft was still busy pulling up the bucket. Instinctively Merle had a fleeting impulse to turn around and run away. She would have done that a few weeks ago in the orphanage. Here, however, she was reluctant to demean herself. She had done nothing wrong or forbidden.

"There was something down there."

"Oh?"

"A face."

The housekeeper pulled the full bucket over the edge

and placed it on the wall. Water sloshed over the edge and ran down on the grimacing faces of the stone reliefs.

"So, a face. And you are quite sure?" With a sigh Eft answered her own question. "Of course you are."

"I saw it." Merle didn't quite know how she should behave. The housekeeper seemed uncanny to her, but she felt no real fear of her. Rather, a kind of uneasiness at the way she looked over the edge of her mask and seemed to read Merle's thoughts from each movement, each tiny hesitation.

"You've already seen something before, haven't you?" Eft was leaning against the rim of the well. "The other night, for example."

There was no point in lying. "I heard the sound of the cover. And then I saw you climbing into the well."

"Did you tell anyone about it?"

"No," she lied, in order not to draw Junipa into it.

Eft ran her hand through her hair and sighed deeply. "Merle, I have to explain some things to you."

"If you want to."

"You aren't like the other apprentices," said the housekeeper. Was that a smile in her eyes? "Not like Dario. You can handle the truth."

Merle stepped closer to Eft, until she would only have needed to stretch out her hand to touch the mask with the red lips. "You want to trust me with a secret?"

"If you are ready for it."

"But you don't know me at all."

"Perhaps better than you think."

Merle didn't understand what Eft meant by that. Her curiosity was awakened now, and she wondered if that wasn't precisely what Eft intended. The more interested Merle was, the more deeply she would be drawn into the business, and the more Eft could trust her.

"Come with me," the housekeeper said, and she went from the well to the back door of an empty house. The entrance wasn't locked, and after Eft had pushed the door open, they came into a small hallway. Apparently it was the former servants' entrance to the palazzo.

They went past an abandoned kitchen and an empty storeroom, until they came to a short flight of stairs going down—unusual in a city whose houses were built on pilings and only rarely had cellars under them.

A little later Merle realized that Eft had led her to an underground boat landing. A walkway ran alongside a water channel, which disappeared into semicircular tunnels on both sides. At one time goods were loaded onto boats here. It smelled brackish, the air tasted of algae and mold.

"Why don't you go into the water this way?" Merle asked.

"What do you mean?"

"You climb into the well because you want to get somewhere through it. Of course, there could be a secret passageway branching off the well shaft, but I don't

66

believe that. I think that it's the water itself that draws you." She paused briefly and then added, "You're a mermaid, aren't you?"

If Eft was surprised, she didn't show it. Merle understood very well what she was saying—and also how unreasonable it was, basically. Eft had legs, well-shaped human legs, utterly in contrast to all known mermaids, whose hips transmuted into a broad fish tail.

Eft reached both hands behind her head and carefully took down the mask that covered the lower half of her face day and night.

"You aren't afraid of me, are you?" she asked with her broad mouth, whose corners ended a finger's breadth in front of her ears. She had no lips, but when she spoke the folds of skin pulled back and exposed a mouth of several rows of small, sharp teeth.

"No," Merle replied, and it was the truth.

"That's good."

"Will you tell me?"

"What would you like to know?"

"Why you don't take this way here, if you go at night to meet with other mermaids. Why do you run the risk of someone seeing you when you climb into the well?"

Eft's eyes narrowed, which in a human had the effect of an unspoken threat, but with her it was only an expression of distaste. "Because the water is polluted. It's the same in all the canals of the city. It's poisonous, it kills us. That's why so few of us come willingly to Venice. The water of the canals kills us, stealthily, but with absolute certainty."

"The mermaids pulling the boats—"

"Will die. Any of us caught by you humans and caged or misused for your races will die. The poison in the water first corrodes the skin and then the mind. Not even the Flowing Queen can protect us from it."

Merle stood silent with horror. All the people who kept mermaids for fun, like house pets, were murderers. Some might even know what the imprisonment in the canals did to the mermaids.

Ashamed, she looked Eft in the eye. She had trouble bringing out any sound at all. "I've never caught a mermaid."

Eft smiled, showing her needle-sharp teeth. "I know that. I can feel it. You have been touched by the Flowing Queen."

"I?"

"Didn't they fish you out of the water when you were a newborn?"

"You were listening to me and Junipa that first night in our room." With anyone else she would have been indignant, but in Eft's case it didn't seem important.

"I listened," the mermaid admitted. "And because I know your secret, I will reveal mine to you. That's only fair. And so, as I will talk to no one about your secret, you will keep silent about mine."

Merle nodded. "How did you mean that before—that the Flowing Queen has touched me?"

"You were set out on the canals. That happens to many children. But extremely few survive. Most drown. But you were found. The current carried you. That can only mean that the Flowing Queen adopted you."

To Merle's ears it sounded as though Eft had been there, so strong was the conviction resonating in her words. It was obvious that the mermaids revered the Flowing Queen as a goddess. Merle spun the thought further and got goose bumps: What if the Flowing Queen wasn't protecting the people of the lagoon at all? After all, the mermaids were creatures of the water, and if you were to believe some theories, the queen *was* the water. An incomprehensible power of the sea.

"What is the Flowing Queen?" She had no real hope that Eft knew the answer to this question.

"If it was ever known, it's long forgotten," replied the mermaid softly. "The way you and I and the Queen herself will one day be forgotten."

"But the Flowing Queen is revered by all. Everyone in Venice loves her. She has saved us all. No one can ever forget that."

Eft left it with a silent shrug of her shoulders, but Merle was very much aware that she was of a different opinion. The mermaid pointed to a slender gondola lying moored on the black water. It looked as if it were floating in nothing, so smooth and dark was the surface around it.

"Down into that?" Merle asked.

Eft nodded.

"And then?"

"I want to show you something."

"Will we be gone long?"

"An hour at most."

"Arcimboldo will punish me. He told me to take the buckets—"

"Already done." Eft smiled. "He told me what he had in mind for you. I've already put ten full buckets in the workshop."

Merle wasn't convinced. "And Dario?"

"Won't say a word about it. Otherwise Arcimboldo will find out who's swiping his wine at night."

"Then you know about that?"

"Nothing happens in that house without my knowing about it."

Merle hesitated no longer and followed Eft into the gondola. The mermaid loosed the rope, placed herself in the stern of the boat, and steered it with the long oar to one of the two tunnel openings. It became pitch-black around them.

"Don't worry," Eft said, "there's a torch in front of you and there are flints next to it."

It wasn't long before Merle had the pitch of the torch

lit. Yellow and flickering, the firelight flitted over an arching tile ceiling.

"May I ask you something else?"

"You want to know why I have legs and no *kalimar*."

"Kali—what?"

"Kalimar. That's what we call the fish tail in our language."

"Will you tell me?"

Eft let the gondola glide deeper into the darkness of the tunnel. Sheets of moss had loosened from the ceiling and hung down like tattered curtains. It smelled of decaying seaweed and corruption.

"It's a sad story," Eft said finally, "so I'll make it short."

"I like sad stories."

"It could be that you will be the heroine in one yourself." Merle turned to the mermaid and looked at her.

"Why do you say such a thing?" Merle demanded.

"You have been touched by the Flowing Queen," Eft replied, as if that were explanation enough. "Once, a mermaid was washed onto the shore of an island by a storm. She was so weak that she remained lying there, helpless among the rushes. The clouds parted, the sun burned down from the heavens, and the body of the mermaid became dry and brittle and began to die. But then a young man appeared, the son of a trader, whose father had given him the thankless task of trying to trade with the handful of fisherfolk who lived on the island. He'd passed the entire day with the poor families, who'd shared water and fish with him, but they bought nothing, for they had no money and nothing for which it would have paid to trade. Late in the day the merchant's young son was on the way back to his boat, but he didn't dare to face his father after this lack of success. He was afraid of a tongue-lashing, for it wasn't the first time that he'd returned to Venice without success, and even more he feared for his inheritance. His father was a stern, hard-hearted man, who had no understanding of the poverty of the people on the outer islands—really he had no understanding of anything in the world, except making money.

"The young man was now sauntering along the shore of the harbor to put off his return home. As he wandered lost in thought through the reeds and high grass, he stumbled on the stranded mermaid. He knelt down beside her, looked into her eyes, and fell in love with her on the spot. He didn't see the fish tail below her hips, nor did he see the teeth that would have inspired fear in anyone else. He only looked into her eyes, which looked back at him helplessly, and he made up his mind at once: This was the woman he loved and would marry. He carried her back into the water, and while she gradually regained her strength in the billows of the waves, he spoke to her of his love.

The longer she listened to him, the more she liked him.

From liking grew affection, and from affection grew more. They swore to see each other again, and so on the next day they met on the shore of another island, and on the day after that on another, and so it went.

"After several weeks the young man pulled all his courage together and asked if she would follow him to the city. But she knew how it went for mermaids in the city, and so she said no. He promised to make her his wife so that she could live at his side like a human. 'Look at me,' she said, 'I will never be like a human.' And so they were both very sad, and the young man saw that his plan had been nothing but a beautiful dream.

"But the following night the mermaid remembered the legend of a powerful sea witch who lived far out in the Adriatic in an undersea cave. So she swam out, farther than she or any of her companions had ever swum, and found the sea witch sitting on a rock deep in the sea and watching for drowned people. For sea witches, you must know, prize dead meat, and it tastes best to them when it's old and bloated. On the way the mermaid had passed a sunken fishing boat, and so she could bring the witch an especially juicy morsel as a tribute. This put the old one in a gracious mood. She listened to the mermaid's story and decided, probably still intoxicated from the taste of the corpse, to help her. She said a spell and ordered the mermaid to return to the lagoon. There she should lie on a shore of the city and sleep until dawn. Then, the witch promised, she would have legs instead of a tail. 'Only your mouth,' she added, 'that I cannot take from you, for without that you would be silent forever.'

"The mermaid attached no importance to her mouth, for after all, that was part of her face, with which the merchant's son had fallen in love. So she did as the sea witch instructed her.

"On the morning of the next day she was found in a landing place. And in fact, she now had legs where once her fish tail had been. But the men who found her crossed themselves, spoke of the Devil's work, and beat her, for they had recognized her by her mouth for what she really was. The men were convinced that the mermaids had found a way to become human, and they feared that soon they would take over the city, murder all the humans, and steal their wealth.

"What foolishness! As if any mermaid ever cared anything for the riches of humans!

"While the men were beating and kicking her, the mermaid kept whispering the name of her beloved, and so they soon sent for him. He hurried there, in the company of his father, of course, who suspected a conspiracy against him and his house. The mermaid and the young man were brought face-to-face, and both looked into each other's eyes long and deeply. The young man wept, and the mermaid also shed tears, which mixed with the blood on her cheeks. But then her lover turned away, for he was weak and feared his father's anger. 'I don't know her,' he said. 'I have nothing to do with this freak.'

"The mermaid grew very still and said nothing more. She remained silent when they beat her harder, even when the merchant and his son kicked her with their boots in her face and in the ribs. Later they threw her back in the water like a dead fish. They all took her for that too: for dead."

Eft fell silent and for a long moment gripped the oar tightly in her hand, without dipping it in the water. The torchlight shone on her cheeks, and a single tear ran down her face. She wasn't telling the story of some mermaid or other, she was telling her own.

"A child found her, an apprentice in a mirror workshop, whose master had taken him from an orphanage. He took her in, hid her, gave her food and drink, and then kept giving her new spirit when she wanted to put an end to her life. The name of that boy was Arcimboldo, and the mermaid swore in gratitude to follow him her life long. Mermaids live much longer than you humans, and so the boy is an old man today and the mermaid is still young. She will still be young when he dies, and then she will be entirely alone again, a lonely person between two worlds, no longer a mermaid and also not a human."

When Merle looked up at her, the tears on Eft's cheeks had dried. Now it seemed again as if she had told someone else's story, someone whose fate was distant and unmeaning.

Merle would have liked to stand up and throw her arms around her, but she knew that Eft didn't expect it and also wouldn't have wanted it.

"Only a story," whispered the mermaid. "As true and as untrue as all the others that we would rather never have heard."

"I'm glad you told me."

Eft nodded slightly, then looked up and pointed forward beyond Merle. "Look," she said, "we're there."

The torchlight around them paled, although the flame still burned. It took a moment for Merle to realize that the walls of the tunnel were behind them. The gondola had glided soundlessly into an underground hall or cave.

Ahead of them an incline rose out of the darkness. It ascended as a steep slope out of the water and was covered with something that Merle couldn't make out from a distance. Plants perhaps. A pale, intertwined branching. But what plant of that size could thrive here underground?

Once, while they were crossing the dark sea that was the floor of the hall, she thought she saw movement in the water. She told herself that they were fish. Very large fish.

"There's no mountain around here," she said, voicing her thoughts. "So how can there be a cave in the middle of Venice?" She knew enough about the behavior of reflections to be sure that they could not be *under* the sea. Whatever this hall was, it was located in the city, among splendid palazzi and elegant building facades—and it had been artificially constructed.

"Who built this?" she asked.

"A friend of the mermaids." Eft's tone indicated that she didn't intend to speak about it.

Such a place in the middle of the city! If it actually was located above ground it must have an outside. What was it camouflaged as? A decaying palazzo of a long-forgotten noble family? A huge warehouse? There were no windows to give access to the outside, and in the darkness neither the ceiling nor the side walls were discernible, only the strange incline, which came closer and closer.

Merle realized now that her first doubts had been right. There were no plants growing on the incline. The branching structure was something else.

Her heart suddenly missed a beat as she realized the truth.

It was bones. The bones of hundreds of mermaids. Twining over and under and into one another, forged together by death, aslant and in a jumble. With racing heart she saw that the upper bodies looked like human ribs, while the fish tail resembled a supergigantic fish bone. The sight was as absurd as it was shocking.

"They all came here to die?"

"Of their own free will, yes," said Eft as she steered the gondola to the left so that the starboard side faced the mountain of bones.

The torchlight gave the illusion of movement in the branched bones where none was. The thin shadows twitched and trembled, they moved like spider legs that had been detached from their bodies and now were flitting among one another on their own.

"The mermaids' cemetery," Merle whispered. Everyone knew the old legend. The cemetery had been thought to be far out on the edge of the lagoon or on the high sea. Treasure-seekers and knights of fortune had tried to track it down, for the bones of a mermaid were more precious than elephant tusk, harder, and in olden days they were feared as weapons in the battles of man against man. That the cemetery lay in the city, under the eyes of all the inhabitants, was hard to grasp—and in addition, that a human must have helped to establish it. What had prompted him to do it? And who had he been?

"I wanted you to see this place." Eft bowed slightly, and only after a moment was it clear to Merle that the gesture was meant for her. "Secret for secret. Silence for all time. And the oath upon it of one who has been touched."

"I should swear?"

Eft nodded.

Merle didn't know how else to do it, so she raised a hand and said solemnly, "I swear an oath on my life that I will never tell anyone of the mermaids' cemetery."

"The oath as one who has been touched," Eft demanded.

"I, Merle, who was touched by the Flowing Queen, swear this oath."

Eft nodded, satisfied, and Merle gave a sigh of relief.

The hull of the gondola scraped over something that lay under the surface of the water.

"Still more bones," Eft explained. "Thousands." She turned the gondola and sculled back in the direction of the tunnel entrance.

"Eft?"

"Hmm?"

"You really think I'm something special, don't you?"

The mermaid smiled mysteriously. "That you certainly are. Something very special."

Much later, in the dark, in bed, Merle slipped her arm into the water mirror under the bedclothes, enjoyed the comfortable warmth, and felt for the hand on the other side. It took a while, but then something touched her fingers, very gentle, very reassuring. Merle sighed softly and fell into a restless half sleep.

Outside the window the evening star rose. Its twinkling was reflected in Junipa's open mirror eyes, which stared, cold and glassy, across the dark room.

4

Phantoms

"HAVE YOU EVER LOOKED INTO IT?" JUNIPA ASKED NEXT morning, after they'd awakened to the sound of Eft's ringing the gong in the hallway.

Merle rubbed the sleep from her eyes with the knuckle of her index finger. "Into what?"

"Into your water mirror."

"Oh, sure. All the time."

Junipa swung her legs over the edge of the bed and looked at Merle. Her mirror fragments flared golden from the sunrise behind the roofs.

"I don't mean just looked in."

"Behind the water surface?"

Junipa nodded. "Have you?"

"Two or three times," Merle said. "I've pushed my face in as far as possible. The frame is pretty narrow, but it worked. My eyes were underwater."

"And?"

"Nothing. Just darkness."

"You couldn't see anything at all?"

"I just said that."

Thoughtfully Junipa ran her fingers through her hair. "If you want, I'll try it."

Merle, who was just about to yawn, snapped her mouth shut again. "You?"

"With the mirror eyes I can see in the dark."

Merle raised her eyebrows. "You didn't tell me about that at all." She hastily considered whether she'd done anything at night to be ashamed of.

"It just began three days ago. But now it's getting stronger from night to night. I see the same as by daylight. Sometimes I can't sleep because the brightness even penetrates my eyelids. Then everything gets red, as if you were looking at the bright sun with your eyes closed."

"You have to talk with Arcimboldo about that."

Junipa looked unhappy. "And what if he takes the mirrors away from me?"

"He would never do that." Concerned, Merle tried to imagine what it would be like to be surrounded by light day and night. What if it got worse? Could Junipa sleep at all then?

"So," Junipa quickly changed the subject, "how about it? Shall I try it?"

Merle pulled the hand mirror out from under the covers, weighed it in her hand for a moment, then shrugged her shoulders. "Why not?"

Junipa climbed up beside her on the bed. They sat opposite each other, cross-legged. Their nightshirts stretched across their knees and both were still tousle-headed from sleep.

"Let me try it first," Merle said.

Junipa watched as Merle brought the mirror right up to her eyes. Carefully she dipped her nose in, then—as far as possible—the rest of her face. Soon the frame was pressed against her cheekbones. She could go no deeper.

Merle opened her eyes underwater. She knew what to expect, so she wasn't disappointed. It was the same as always. Nothing but darkness.

She removed the mirror from her face. The water remained trapped in the frame, not the finest trace of dampness gleaming on her skin.

"And?" Junipa asked excitedly.

"Nothing at all." Merle handed her the mirror. "As usual."

Junipa gripped the handle in her narrow hand. She

looked at the reflecting surface and studied her new eyes. "Do you really think they're pretty?" she asked suddenly.

Merle hesitated. "Unusual."

"That's no answer to my question."

"I'm sorry." Merle wished that Junipa had spared herself the truth. "Sometimes I get goose bumps when I look at you. Not because your eyes are ugly," she added quickly. "They are just so . . . so . . ."

"They feel cold," said Junipa softly, as if she were deep in thought. "Sometimes I feel cold, even when the sun is shining."

Brightness at night, cold in the sunshine.

"Do you really want to do it?" Merle asked. She remembered how reluctant Junipa had been to put her hand in the mirror; how the water had felt ice-cold to her.

"Really, I don't want to, I know that already," Junipa said. "But if you say so, I'll try it for you." She looked at Merle. "Wouldn't you like to know what's back there, where the hand comes from?"

Merle only nodded mutely.

Junipa pushed the mirror up to her face and dipped it in. Her head was smaller than Merle's—as all of her was more petite, slender, vulnerable—and so it vanished up to the temples in the water.

Merle waited. She observed Junipa's thin body under the much-too-large nightshirt, the way her shoulders stuck out underneath it and her collarbones protruded over the edge of the neckline, outlined as sharply as if they lay over the skin instead of under it.

The sight was strange, almost a little mad, now that for the first time she was seeing another person working with the mirror. Mad things could be quite normal, so long as you were doing them yourself. Watching someone else doing them, you wrinkled your nose, turned around quickly, and walked away.

But Merle kept on watching, and she wondered what it was that Junipa was seeing at that moment.

Finally she couldn't stand it any longer and asked, "Junipa? Can you hear me?"

Of course she could. Her ears were above the surface of the water. But all the same, she didn't answer.

"Junipa?"

Merle was uneasy, but she still didn't interfere. Very slowly visions welled up in her, pictures of beasts that were gnawing on her friend's face on the other side. Now, when she pulled her head back, it would just be a hollow shell of bone and hair, like the helmets of the tribes that Professor Burbridge had discovered during his expedition to Hell.

"Junipa?" she asked again, this time a bit more sharply. She grasped her friend's free hand. Her skin was warm. Merle could feel the pulse.

Junipa returned. It was just exactly that: a return. Her face had the expression of a person who has been very far away, in distant, inconceivable lands, which perhaps existed on the other side of the globe or only in her imagination.

"What was there?" Merle asked uneasily. "What did you see?"

She would have given a lot if Junipa at this moment had had the eyes of a human. Eyes in which a person could read something—sometimes things you might rather not have known, but always the truth.

But Junipa's eyes remained blank and hard and without any feeling.

Can she still cry? ran through Merle's mind, and at the moment the question seemed more important than any other.

However, Junipa was not crying. Only the corners of her mouth twitched. But it didn't look as though she wanted to smile.

Merle bent toward her, took the mirror out of her hand, laid it on the covers, and gently grasped her by the shoulders. "What *is* in the mirror?"

Junipa was silent for a moment, then silvery glass turned in Merle's direction. "It's dark over there."

I know that, Merle wanted to say, before it became clear to her that Junipa meant a different darkness from the one Merle had seen.

"Tell me about it," she demanded.

Junipa shook her head. "No. You can't ask me about it."

"What?" Merle cried.

Junipa shrugged Merle off and stood up. "Never ask me what I saw there," she said tonelessly. "Never."

"But Junipa—"

"Please."

"It can't be anything bad!" cried Merle. Defiance and despair welled up in her. "I've felt the hand. The hand, Junipa!"

Outside the window a cloud moved in front of the morning sun, and Junipa's mirror eyes also darkened. "Let it be, Merle. Forget the hand. Best forget the mirror altogether." With these words she turned, opened the door, and walked out into the hall.

Merle sat transfixed on the bed, incapable of thinking clearly. She heard the door slam, and then she felt herself very alone.

That same day, Arcimboldo sent his two girl students on the hunt for mirror phantoms.

"I want to show you something quite unusual today," he said in the afternoon. Out of the corner of her eye Merle saw Dario and the other two boys exchange looks and grin.

The master mirror maker pointed to the door that led to the storeroom behind the workshop. "You haven't been in there yet," he said. "And for good reason."

Merle had assumed he was afraid for his finished magic mirrors, which were stored there.

"The handling of the mirrors as I produce them is not entirely without danger." Arcimboldo leaned with both hands on the workbench behind him. "Now and again one must clear them of certain"—he hesitated—"of certain elements."

Again the three boys grinned, and Merle slowly became angry. She hated it when Dario knew more than she did.

"Dario and the others stay here in the workshop," said Arcimboldo. "Junipa and Merle, you come with me."

Then he turned and went to the door of the storeroom. Merle and Junipa exchanged looks, then followed him.

"Good luck," said Boro. It sounded sincere.

"Good luck," mimicked Dario and murmured something after it that Merle didn't catch.

Arcimboldo let the girls in and then closed the door after them. "Welcome into the heart of my house," he said.

The sight he presented to them warranted the ceremony of his words.

It was hard to say how big the room was. Its walls were covered over and over with mirrors, and rows of mirrors also stretched down its center, placed behind one another like dominoes just before they are knocked down. Sunlight shone in through a glass ceiling—the workshop was in an addition that wasn't nearly so high as the rest of the house.

The mirrors were secured with braces and chains that

anchored them to the walls. Nothing would topple here, if Venice were to be struck by an earthquake or if Hell itself were to open under the city—as it was said to have done under Marrakesh, a city in North Africa. But that had been more than thirty years before, right after the outbreak of the war. Today no one talked about Marrakesh. It had vanished from the maps and the language of men.

"How many mirrors are there?" asked Junipa.

It was impossible to estimate their number, to say nothing of counting them. They reflected each other again and again in their glassy surfaces, mutually adding and multiplying themselves. Merle had a thought: Was a mirror that existed only in a mirror not just as real as its original? It fulfilled its role just as well as its counterpart—it reflected.

Merle couldn't think of anything else that was able to do this: to do something without itself being. For the first time, she asked herself whether all mirrors were not always magic mirrors. *Mirrors can see,* Arcimboldo had said. Now she believed him.

"You are now going to make the acquaintance of a very singular kind of nuisance," he explained. "My special friends—the mirror phantoms."

"Mirror phantoms? What are they?" Junipa spoke softly, almost fearfully, as though the images of what she had seen behind Merle's water mirror still danced before her eyes and made her afraid.

Arcimboldo stepped in front of the first mirror in the

center row. It reached almost to his chin. Its frame was of plain wood, like the frames of all the mirrors from Arcimboldo's workshop. They not only served as ornament but also prevented cut fingers during transport.

"Just look in," he demanded.

The girls walked to his side and stared at the mirror. Junipa noticed it first. "There's something in the glass."

It looked like shreds of mist that moved fleetingly over the mirror surface, amorphous, like ghosts. And there was no doubt that the pale outline was *under* the glass, inside the mirror.

"Mirror phantoms," said Arcimboldo matter-of-factly. "Annoying parasites who settle into my mirrors from time to time. It's the apprentices' job to catch them."

"And how are we supposed to do that?" Merle wanted to know.

"You'll enter the mirrors and drive out the phantoms with a little aid that I shall give you to take with you." He laughed aloud. "My goodness, don't look so flabbergasted! Dario and the others have done it countless times. It may seem a little unusual to you, but basically it's not very difficult. Just tiresome. Therefore, you apprentices are allowed to experience it, while your old master puts his feet on the desk, smokes a good pipe, and doesn't worry about a thing."

Merle and Junipa exchanged looks. They both felt apprehensive, but they were also determined to get through this business with dignity. After all, if Dario had already done it, they probably would be able to as well.

Arcimboldo pulled something out of a pocket of his smock. Between thumb and forefinger he held it in front of the girls' noses: a transparent glass ball, no bigger than Merle's fist.

"Quite ordinary, eh?" Arcimboldo grinned, and for the first time, Merle noticed that he was missing a tooth. "But in fact, it's the best weapon against mirror phantoms. Unfortunately, it's also the only one."

He said nothing for a moment, but neither girl asked any questions. Merle was certain that Arcimboldo would carry on with his explanation.

After a short pause, while he gave them a chance to look at the glass ball more closely, he said, "A glassblower on Murano produced this captivating little thing according to my specifications."

Specifications? Merle asked herself. *For a simple ball of glass?*

"When you put it next to a mirror phantom, you must just speak a certain word, and he'll immediately be trapped inside the ball," Arcimboldo explained. "The word is *intorabiliuspeteris.* You must imprint it in your minds as if it were your own name. Intorabiliuspeteris."

The girls repeated the strange word, becoming tongue-tangled a few times, until they were sure they could keep it in their heads.

The master pulled out a second ball, handed one to each girl, and had them step up to the mirror. "Several mirrors are infested, but for today we'll let it go with one." He made a sort of bow in the direction of the mirror and spoke a word in a strange language.

"Enter," he said then.

"Just like that?" Merle asked.

Arcimboldo laughed. "Of course. Or would you rather ride in on a horse?"

Merle ran her eye over the mirror surface. It looked smooth and solid, not yielding like her hand mirror. The memory made her briefly look over at Junipa. Whatever she'd seen this morning, it had made a deep impression on her. Now she seemed to be afraid to follow Arcimboldo's instructions. For a moment Merle was tempted to tell the master everything and ask for understanding for Junipa to remain here and Merle to go alone.

But then Junipa took the first step and stretched out her hand. Her fingers broke through the mirror surface like the skin on a pan of boiled milk. She quickly looked over her shoulder at Merle; then, with a strained smile, she stepped inside the mirror. Her figure was still recognizable, but now it looked flat and somehow *unreal*, like a figure in a painting. She waved to Merle.

"Brave girl," murmured Arcimboldo with satisfaction.

Merle broke through the mirror surface with a single

step. She felt a cold tickling, like a gentle breeze at midnight, then she was on the other side and looking around.

She had once heard of a mirror labyrinth that was supposed to have been in a palazzo on the Campo Santa Maria Nova. She knew no one who had seen it with his own eyes, but the pictures that the stories had conjured up in her mind bore no comparison with what she now saw before her.

One thing was clear at first glance: The mirror world was a kingdom of deceptions. It was the place under the double bottom of the kaleidoscope, the robbers' cave in the *Tales from a Thousand and One Nights,* the palace of the gods on Olympus. It was artificial, an illusion, a dream dreamed only by those who believed in it. And yet at this moment it seemed as substantial as Merle herself. Did the figures in a painting also think they were in a real place? Prisoners who were not aware of their imprisonment?

Before them lay a room of mirrors: not like Arcimboldo's storeroom, much more a structure that from top to bottom, from left to right, consisted of mirrors and mirrors alone. Yet the first impression was deceptive. If you took a step forward, you bumped up against an invisible glass wall, while there, where the end of the room appeared to be, was nothing but emptiness, followed by other mirrors, invisible connecting passageways, and fresh deceptions.

It took a moment for Merle to realize what was really troubling about this place: The mirrors reflected only each other, not the two girls who were standing in their middle. So it happened that they could walk straight up to a mirror and bump against it without being warned by their own reflection. On all sides, the mirrors reflected themselves to infinity, a world of silver and crystal.

Merle and Junipa made several attempts to move deeper into the labyrinth, but again and again they bumped against glass.

"This is pointless," Merle protested and stamped her foot in anger. Mirror glass creaked under her foot without splintering.

"They're all around us," Junipa whispered.

"The phantoms?"

Junipa nodded.

Merle looked around. "I can't see any."

"They're afraid. My eyes scare them. They're avoiding us."

Merle turned around. There was a sort of door at the place where they'd entered the mirror world. There she thought she could perceive a movement, but perhaps that was only Arcimboldo, waiting for them in the real world.

Something whisked past her face, a pale flicker. Two arms, two legs, a head. Close up, it no longer looked like a patch of fog but rather like the blur caused by a drop of water in the eye.

Merle raised the glass ball, feeling a little foolish. "Intorabiliuspeteris," she cried, and immediately felt even more foolish.

There was the sound of a soft sigh, then the phantom shot right at her. The ball sucked him to its inside, which soon flickered and grew streaky, as if it were filled with a white, oily fluid.

"It works!" Merle gasped.

Junipa nodded but made no attempt to use her own ball. "Now they're terribly afraid."

"You can really see them all around us?"

"Very clearly."

It must have to do with Junipa's eyes, with the magic of the mirror pieces. Now Merle also saw other blurs at the edge of her vision, but she couldn't make out the phantoms as clearly as Junipa seemed to be able to.

"If they're afraid, that means that they're living beings," she said, thinking aloud.

"Yes," Junipa said. "But it's as if they weren't really here. As if they were only a part of themselves, like a shadow that's separated from its owner."

"Then perhaps it's a good thing if we get them out of here. Perhaps they're prisoners here."

"Do you think in the glass ball they aren't?"

Of course Junipa was right. But Merle wanted to get back into the real world as fast as possible, away from this glassy labyrinth. Arcimboldo would only be satisfied when they'd caught all the phantoms. She was afraid otherwise he'd send them right back into the mirror.

She no longer paid any attention to what Junipa was doing. Merle stretched out her arm with the ball, waved it in different directions, and called the magic word over and over: "Intorabiliuspeteris . . . intorabiliuspeteris . . . intora-biliuspeteris!"

The hissing and whistling became louder and sharper, and at the same time the ball filled with the swirling fog until it looked as if the glass were being steamed up on the inside. Once, in the orphanage, one of the attendants had blown cigar smoke into a wine glass, and the effect had been very similar: The layers of smoke had rotated behind the glass as though there were something living inside try-ing to get out.

What sort of creatures were these that infested Arcimboldo's magic mirrors like aphids in a vegetable gar-den? Merle would have loved to know more.

Junipa was grasping her ball so tightly in her fist that it suddenly cracked and shattered in her hand. Tiny splinters of glass rained onto the mirror floor, followed by dark drops of blood, as the sharp edges cut into Junipa's fingers.

"Junipa!" Merle stuffed her ball into her pocket, sprang to Junipa's side, and anxiously examined her hand. "Oh, Junipa . . ." She slipped out of her sweater and wrapped it around her friend's forearm. That made visible the upper edge of the hand mirror, stuck into her dress pocket.

Suddenly one of the phantoms whizzed in a narrow spiral around her upper body and disappeared into the surface of the water mirror.

"Oh, no," Junipa said tearfully, "that's all my fault."

Merle was more concerned about Junipa's well-being than about the mirror. "I think we've caught all of them anyway," she said, unable to take her eyes from the blood on the floor. Her face was mirrored in the drops, as if the blood had tiny eyes that were looking up at her. "Let's get out of here."

Junipa held her back. "Are you going to tell Arcimboldo one of them went—"

Merle interrupted her. "No, he'd just take it away from me."

Stricken, Junipa nodded, and Merle reassuringly laid an arm around her shoulders. "Don't give it another thought."

She gently urged Junipa back to the door, a glittering rectangle not far from them. Arms tightly wrapped around one another, they walked out of the mirror into the storeroom.

"What happened?" asked Arcimboldo, when he saw the wrapping around Junipa's hand. Immediately he unwrapped it, discovered the cuts, and ran to the door. "Eft!" he bellowed out into the workroom. "Bring bandages. Quickly!"

Merle also appraised the cuts. Happily, none of them

seemed to be really dangerous. Most of them weren't very deep, just red scratches on which very thin clots were already forming.

Junipa pointed to the blood spots on Merle's wadded-up sweater. "I'll wash that for you."

"Eft can take care of that," Arcimboldo interposed. "Instead, tell me how this happened!"

Merle told in a few words what had occurred. Only, she kept to herself the flight of the last phantom into her hand mirror. "I caught all the phantoms," she said, pulling the ball out of her pocket. The bright streaks in its interior were now rotating hectically.

Arcimboldo grasped the ball and held it up to the light. What he saw seemed to please him, for he nodded in satisfaction. "You did very well," he praised the two girls. Not a word about the broken ball.

"Now rest," he advised them after Eft had treated the cuts. Then he waved to Dario, Boro, and Tiziano, who'd been lurking at the storeroom door. "You three take care of the rest."

As Merle was leaving the workshop with Junipa, she turned once more to Arcimboldo. "What happens to them now?" She pointed to the ball in the master's hand.

"We throw them into the canal," he replied with a shrug. "Let them settle into the reflections on the water."

Merle nodded, as if she'd expected nothing else, then led Junipa up to their room.

❖

The news spread around the workshop like wildfire. There was going to be a festival! Tomorrow it would be thirty-six years to the day since the army hosts of the Egyptian Empire were massed at the edges of the lagoon. Steamboats and galleys had crossed the water and sunbarks were standing ready in the skies for the attack on the helpless city. But the Flowing Queen had protected Venice, and since then this day had been celebrated throughout the entire city with festivals of rejoicing. One of them would be taking place very close by. Tiziano had heard about it that morning when he went with Eft to the fish market, and he immediately told Dario, who told Boro and, a little reluctantly, passed it on to Merle and Junipa.

"A festival in honor of the Flowing Queen! Right around the corner! There'll be lanterns up everywhere and beer barrels tapped and wine corks popping!"

"Something for you children too?" Arcimboldo, who'd been listening, wore a sly smile as he spoke.

"We aren't children anymore!" flared Dario. Then, with a scornful sideways glance at Junipa, he added, "At least most of us."

Merle was about to leap to Junipa's defense, but it wasn't necessary. "If it's an expression of adulthood," Junipa said with unwonted pertness, "to pick your nose at night, scratch your behind, and do lots of other things, then you're of course *very* grown-up. Right, Dario?"

Dario turned scarlet at her words. But Merle stared at her friend in amazement. Had Junipa slipped into the boys' room at night and observed them? Or could she, thanks to her new mirror eyes, even see through walls? This thought made Merle feel uncomfortable.

Dario was swelling with indignation, but Arcimboldo settled the argument with a wave. "Settle down now, or none of you will go to the festival! On the other hand, if you've finished your jobs punctually by sundown tomorrow, I see no reason—"

The rest of his words were lost in the cries of the apprentices. Even Junipa was beaming all over. It looked as though a shadow had lifted from her features.

"However, one thing you should all keep in mind," said the master. "The students from the weaving workshop will assuredly be there. I want no trouble. Bad enough that our canal has become a battlefield. I will not permit this quarrel to be carried elsewhere. We've already drawn enough attention to ourselves. So—no insults, no fighting, not even a crooked look." His eyes singled out Dario from the other apprentices. "Understand?"

Dario took a deep breath and nodded hastily. The others hastened to murmur their agreement as well. Actually, Merle was grateful for Arcimboldo's words, for the last thing she wanted was a new scrap with the weaver boys. Junipa's wounds had been healing well over the last three days; she needed some peace now to heal completely.

"Now, then, all back to work," the master said, satisfied.

To Merle the time till the festival seemed endless. She was excited and could hardly wait to be among people again, not because she'd had enough of the workshop and its inhabitants—Dario being the one exception—but because she missed the untamed life in the streets, the chattering voices of the women and the transparent boastings of the men.

Finally the evening arrived, and they all left the house together. The boys ran ahead, while Merle and Junipa followed slowly. Arcimboldo had made a pair of glasses for Junipa with dark glass that was supposed to keep anyone from noticing her mirror eyes.

The small troop turned the corner where the Canal of the Expelled opened into the wider waterway. Even from afar they could see hundreds of lanterns on the house fronts, lights in the windows and doors. A small bridge, hardly more than a pedestrian crossing, linked their side to that place. Its railings were decorated with lanterns and candles, while the people sat on the sidewalks, some on stools and chairs they'd brought out of their houses, others on cushions or on the bare stone. In several places drinks were being sold, although Merle realized with a trace of malicious pleasure that Dario was sure to be disappointed: There was hardly any wine or beer, for this was a poor people's festival. No one here could afford to pay fantastic sums for grapes or barley, which had to be smuggled into the city by dangerous routes. After all these years, the Pharaoh's siege ring was just as tight as at the beginning of the war. Even though the siege was imperceptible in daily life, still no one doubted that hardly a mouse, not to mention a smugglers' boat, could sneak past the Egyptian army camps. One could certainly find wine—as Arcimboldo did—but it was usually difficult, even dangerous. The poor people drank water ordinarily, while at festivals they had to be content with juices and various home-distilled liquors of fruits and vegetables.

Up on the bridge, Merle saw the weaver's apprentice who'd been the first to lose his mask. There were two other boys with him. One's face was very red, as if he were sunburned; clearly it hadn't been easy for him to wash off the glue Merle had sprayed under his mask.

Their leader, Serafin, was nowhere to be seen. Merle realized with surprise that she'd involuntarily been watching for him and was almost disappointed not to see him.

Junipa, on the other hand, was a completely changed girl. She couldn't get over her amazement. She kept whispering to Merle, "See him over there?" and "Oh, look at her!" and giggling and laughing, occasionally so loudly that some people turned around and looked at them in surprise and were especially interested at the sight of her dark glasses. Only the rich dandies usually wore such things, and they rarely mixed with the common people. On the other hand, Junipa's worn dress left no doubt about the fact that she had never seen the inside of a palazzo.

The two girls stood at the left end of the bridge and sipped at their juice, which had been watered down too much. On the other side a fiddler was striking up a dance; soon a flute player joined in. The dresses of the young girls whirled like colored tops.

"You're so quiet," Junipa declared, not knowing where to look next. Merle had never seen her so animated. She was glad, for she'd been afraid all the hurly-burly might make Junipa anxious.

"You're looking for that boy." Junipa gave her a silvery look over the top of her glasses. "Serafin."

"Where'd you get that idea?"

"I was blind for thirteen years. I know people. When people know you don't see, they get careless. They mix up blindness with deafness. You just have to listen and they tell you everything about themselves."

"And what have I betrayed about myself?" Merle asked, frowning.

Junipa laughed. "I can see you now, and that's enough. You're looking in all directions all the time. And who could you be looking for except Serafin?"

"You're just imagining that."

"No, I'm not."

"You are so."

Junipa's laugh rang bright and clear. "I'm your friend, Merle. Girls *talk* about a thing like that."

Merle made a move as if to hit her, and Junipa giggled like a child. "Oh, leave me alone," cried Merle, laughing.

Junipa looked up. "There he is, over there."

"Where?"

"There, on the other side."

Junipa was right. Serafin was sitting a little back from the edge of the pavement and letting his legs dangle over the canal. The soles of his shoes were dangerously close to the water.

"Now, go on over to him," Junipa said.

"Not on your life."

"Why ever not?"

"He *is* a weaver apprentice, after all. One of our enemies, or have you forgotten already? I can't just . . . it's bad manners."

"It's even worse manners to act as if you're listening to a friend when in fact your thoughts are somewhere else entirely."

"Can you also read thoughts with those eyes of yours?" asked Merle with amusement.

Junipa shook her head earnestly, as if she'd actually taken the possibility into consideration. "A person just has to look at you."

"You really think I should talk to him?"

"Certainly." Junipa grinned. "Or are you a little afraid?"

"Nonsense. I really just want to ask him how long he's worked for Umberto," Merle said.

"*Very* poor excuse!"

"Ninny!—No, you aren't. You're a treasure!" And with that Merle grabbed Junipa around the neck, hugged her briefly, and then ran across the bridge to the other side. As she went, she looked back over her shoulder and saw Junipa looking after her with a gentle smile.

"Hello."

Shocked, Merle stopped in her tracks. Serafin must have seen her, for suddenly he was standing directly in front of her.

"Hello," she replied, sounding as though she'd just swallowed a fruit pit. "You here too?"

"Looks like it."

"I thought you were probably home hatching plans for splashing paint in other people's faces."

"Oh, that. . . ." He grinned. "We don't do that every day. Would you like something to drink?"

She'd left her cup beside Junipa, so she nodded. "Juice. Please."

Serafin turned and walked to a stand. Merle watched him from the back. He was a handsbreadth taller than she, somewhat thin, perhaps, but so were they all. After all, anyone born during siege conditions never had the embarrassment of having to worry about his weight. Unless you were rich, of course. Or, she thought cynically, you were named Ruggiero and secretly ate up half the orphanage kitchen.

Serafin came back and handed her a wooden cup. "Apple juice," he said. "I hope you like it."

To be polite, she immediately took a sip. "Yes, very much, in fact."

"You're new at Arcimboldo's, aren't you?"

"You know that very well." She immediately regretted her words. Why was she being so snippy? Couldn't she give him a normal answer? "Since a few weeks ago," she added.

"Were you and your friend in the same orphanage?"

She shook her head. "Uh-uh."

"Arcimboldo did something to her eyes."

"She was blind. Now Junipa can see."

"Then it's true, what Master Umberto said."

"And that was?"

"He said Arcimboldo knows his way around magic."

"That's what others say about Umberto."

Serafin grinned. "I've now been in his house for more than two years, and he's never showed me a single magic trick."

"I think Arcimboldo will keep that to himself till the bitter end too."

They laughed a little nervously, not because they'd discovered their first thing in common, but because neither one knew quite how to take the conversation further.

"Shall we walk on a little bit?" Serafin pointed down the canal where the crowds of people were thinner and the lanterns shone on empty water.

Merle grinned mischievously. "It's a good thing we don't belong to fine society. Otherwise it would be improper, wouldn't it?"

"I don't give a hoot about fine society."

"Thing in common number two."

Close beside each other, but without touching, they ambled along the canal. The music became softer and soon was left behind them. The water lapped rhythmically against the dark walls. Somewhere over them pigeons cooed in the niches and carvings of the houses. They turned a corner and left the light of the shoals of lanterns.

"Have you had to chase mirror spirits yet?" Serafin asked after a while.

"Spirits? Do you think it's spirits living in the mirrors?"

"Master Umberto said it's the spirits of all the people Arcimboldo's cheated."

Merle laughed. "And you believe that?"

"No," Serafin replied seriously, "because I know better."

"But you're a weaver, not a mirror maker."

"I've only been a weaver for two years. Before, I was sometimes here, sometimes there, all over Venice."

"Have you still got parents?"

"Not that I know of. At least they've never introduced themselves to me."

"But you weren't in an orphanage too?"

"No. I lived on the street. As I said, sometimes here, sometimes there. And during that time I picked up a lot of stuff. Things that not everybody knows."

"Like how to clean a rat before you eat it?" she asked derisively.

He made a face. "That, too, yes. But I didn't mean that."

A black cat whisked past them, then made a turn and came back. Without warning it leaped onto Serafin. But it wasn't an attack. Instead it landed purposefully on Serafin's shoulder and purred. Serafin didn't even jump but raised his hand and began to stroke the animal.

"You're a thief!" Merle burst out. "Only thieves are so friendly with cats."

"Strays together," he confirmed with a smile. "Thieves and cats have much in common. And share so much with each other." He sighed. "But you're right. I grew up among thieves. At five I became a member of the Guild, then later one of its masters."

"A master thief!" Merle was dumbfounded. The master thieves of the Guild were the most skillful pilferers in Venice. "But you aren't more than fifteen years old!"

He nodded. "At thirteen I left the Guild and went into the service of Umberto. He could well use someone like me. Someone who can climb through ladies' windows on the sly at night and deliver them the goods they've ordered. You probably know that most husbands aren't happy to see their wives doing business with Umberto. His reputation is—"

"Bad?"

"Oh, well, more or less. But his clothes make them slender. And very few women want their husbands to learn how much plumper they actually are. Umberto's reputation may not be the best, but his business is doing better than ever."

"The husbands will find out the truth, at least when their wives . . ." Merle blushed. "When they get undressed."

"Oh, there are tricks and dodges there, too. They turn off the light, or they make their husbands drunk. Women are cleverer than you think."

"I *am* a woman!"

"In a few years, maybe."

She stopped indignantly. "Serafin Master Thief, I don't think that you know enough about women—aside from where they hide their purses—to express yourself about such things."

The black cat on Serafin's shoulder spat at Merle, but she didn't care about that. Serafin whispered something into the cat's ear and it calmed down at once.

"I didn't mean to insult you." He seemed quite taken aback by Merle's outburst. "Really, I didn't."

She gave him a piercing look. "Well, then I'll excuse you this one time."

He bowed, so that the cat had to dig her claws firmly into his shirt. "My most humble thanks, madam."

Merle looked away quickly to hide her smile. When she looked at him again, the cat had vanished. Spots of red blood showed through the fabric of Serafin's shirt where its claws had dug into his shoulder.

"That must hurt," she said with concern.

"Which is more painful? Being scratched by an animal or by a human?"

She chose not to answer that. Instead she walked on, and again Serafin was right next to her.

"You were going to tell me something about the mirror phantoms," she said.

"Was I?"

"You ought not to have started about it otherwise."

Serafin nodded. "You're right. It's only —" He stopped speaking suddenly, stood still, and listened into the night.

"What is it?"

"Shh," he said, and gently laid a finger on her lips.

She strained to hear in the darkness. In the narrow alleys and canals of Venice you often heard the strangest noises. The close spacing between houses distorted sounds beyond recognition. The twisting labyrinths of alleyways were empty after dark because most people preferred to use busier main ways. Robbers and assassins made many districts unsafe, and usually cries, whimpers, or rushing footsteps rebounded from the old walls and were transmitted as echoes to places that lay far from the source of the sound. If Serafin had in fact heard something to arouse concern, it might mean everything or nothing: The danger could be lurking around the next corner, but it also might be many hundreds of yards away.

"Soldiers!" he hissed. He grabbed the surprised Merle by the arm and pulled her into one of the narrow tunnels that ran between many houses in the city, built-over alleyways in which utter darkness reigned at night.

"Are you sure?" she whispered very close to his cheek, and she felt him nod.

"Two men on lions. Around the corner."

At that moment they saw the two of them, in uniform, with sword and rifle, riding on gray basalt lions. The lions bore their riders past the mouth of the passageway with majestic steps. It was astonishing with what grace the lions moved. Their bodies were of massive stone and nevertheless they glided like lithe house cats. Their claws, sharp as daggers, scraped over the pavement and left deep furrows.

When the patrol was far enough away, Serafin whispered, "Some of them know my face. So I'm not keen to meet them."

"Anyone who was already a master thief at thirteen certainly has reason for that."

He smiled, flattered. "Could be."

"Why did you leave the Guild?"

"The older masters couldn't stand it that I made bigger hauls than they did. They spread lies about me and tried to get me thrown out of the Guild. So I chose to leave voluntarily." He walked out of the passageway into the pale shine of a gas lantern. "But come on—I promised to tell you more about the mirror phantoms. To do that, I have to show you something first."

5

Treachery

Merle and Serafin walked farther through the
maze of narrow alleys and passages, here turning right,
there left, crossing bridges over still canals, and going
through gateways and along under clotheslines that
stretched between the houses like a march of pale ghost
sheets. They did not meet one single person along the way,
another characteristic of this strangest of old cities: You
could walk for miles without seeing a soul, only cats and
rats on their hunt for prey in the garbage.

Before them the alley ended at the very edge of a canal.
There was no sidewalk along its banks, the walls of the

houses reached right down into the water. There wasn't a bridge to be seen.

"A dead end," Merle grumbled. "We have to go back again."

Serafin shook his head. "We're exactly where I wanted to be." He bent over the edge a bit and looked up at the sky. Then he looked across the water. "See that?"

Merle walked up next to him. Her eyes followed his index finger to the gently swelling surface. The brackish smell of the canal rose into her nose, but she hardly noticed it. Strands of algae were drifting about, far more than usual.

An illuminated window was reflected in the water, the only one far and wide. It was in the second floor of a house on the other side of the canal. The opposite bank was about fifty feet away.

"I don't know what you mean," she said.

"See the light in that window?"

"Sure."

Serafin pulled out a silver pocket watch, a valuable piece that probably came from his thieving days. He snapped open the lid. "Ten after twelve. We're on time."

"So?"

He grinned. "I'll explain. You see the reflection on the water, don't you?"

She nodded.

"Good. Now look at the house over it and show me the window that's reflected there. The one that's lit."

Merle looked up at the dark house front. All the windows were dark, not a single one lit. She looked down at the water again. The reflection remained unchanged: In one of the reflected windows a light was burning. When she looked up at the house again, that rectangle in the wall was dark.

"How can that be?" she asked, perplexed. "In the reflection the window is lit, but in reality it's pitch-black."

Serafin's grin got even wider. "Well, well."

"Magic?"

"Not entirely. Or maybe yes. Depending on how you look at it."

Her face darkened. "Couldn't you express yourself a little more clearly?"

"It happens in the hour after midnight. Between twelve and one at night the same phenomenon appears at several places in the city. Very few know about them, and even I don't know many of these places, but it's true: During this hour, a few houses cast a reflection on the water that doesn't tally with the reality. There are only tiny differences—lighted windows, sometimes another door, or people walking along in front of the houses while in reality there's nobody there."

"And what does it mean?"

"Nobody knows for sure. But there are rumors." He lowered his voice and acted very mysterious. "Stories about a *second* Venice."

"A second Venice?"

"One that only exists in the reflection in the water. Or at least lies so far away from us that it can't be reached, even with the fastest ship. Not even with the Empire's sunbarks. People say that it's in another world, which is so like ours and yet entirely different. And around midnight the border between the two cities becomes porous, perhaps just because it's so old and has gotten worn over the centuries, like a worn-out carpet."

Merle stared at him, her eyes wide. "You mean, that window with the light . . . you mean, it actually exists— only not *here*?"

"It gets even better. There was an old beggar who sat at this spot for years and watched day and night. He told me that sometimes men and women from this other Venice managed to cross the wall between the worlds. What they don't know, though, is that they're no longer human beings when they arrive here. They're only phantoms then, and they're caught forever in the mirrors of the city. Some of them manage to jump from mirror to mirror, and so every now and then they also stray into your master's workshop and into his magic mirrors."

Merle considered whether Serafin might perhaps be playing a joke on her. "You aren't just trying to put something over on me, are you?"

Serafin flashed a phony smile. "Do I really look as though I could swindle anyone?"

"Of course not, top-notch master thief."

"Believe me, I've actually heard this story. How much of it's the truth, I can't really say." He pointed to the illuminated window in the water. "However, some things support it."

"But that would mean that I was catching human beings in that glass ball the other day!"

"Don't worry about it. I've seen Arcimboldo throw them into the canal. They get out again somehow there."

"And now I understand what he meant when he said that the phantoms could settle into the reflections on the water." Merle gasped. "Arcimboldo knows! He knows the truth!"

"What are you going to do now? Ask him about it?"

She shrugged her shoulders. "Why not?" She didn't have a chance to pursue the thought further, for suddenly there was a movement on the water. As they looked down more attentively, a silhouette slid over the surface of the canal toward them.

"Is that—" She broke off as it became clear to her that the reflection was no illusion.

"Back!" Serafin had seen it at the same time.

They whipped into the alleyway and pressed tight against the wall.

From the left, something large glided over the water without touching it. It was a lion with mighty wings of feathers; like the entire body, they were also of stone.

Their tips almost touched the walls of the houses on both sides of the canal. The lion flew almost soundlessly, only its unhurried wingbeats producing subtle whishing like the drawing of breath. Their draft blew icily into Merle's and Serafin's faces. The enormous mass and weight of that body were deceptive; in the air it held itself as featherlight as a bird. Its front and back legs were bent, its mouth nearly closed. Behind its eyes sparkled a disconcerting shrewdness, far sharper than the understanding of ordinary animals.

A soldier sat grimly on the lion's back. His uniform was of black leather and trimmed with steel rivets. A bodyguard of the City Council, assigned to protect one of the big bosses personally. You didn't encounter them very often, and when you did, it usually meant nothing good.

The lion bearing its master floated past the opening of their alleyway without noticing the two of them. Merle and Serafin didn't dare breathe until the flying predator had left them far behind. Carefully they leaned forward and watched the lion gain altitude, leave the narrow canyon of the canal, and make a wide loop over the roofs of the district. Then it was lost to sight.

"He's circling," Serafin stated. "Whoever he's watching can't be far away."

"A councillor?" Merle whispered. "At this hour? In this district? Never in your life. They only leave their palaces when it's absolutely necessary."

"There aren't many lions that can fly. The few that are left never go any farther than necessary from their councillors." Serafin took a deep breath. "One of the councillors must be very close by."

As if to underline his words, the growl of a flying lion came out of the nighttime darkness. A second answered the call. Then a third.

"There are several." Merle shook her head in bafflement. "What are they doing here?"

Serafin's eyes gleamed. "We could find out."

"And the lions?"

"I've often run away from them before."

Merle wasn't sure if he was boasting or telling the truth. Perhaps both. She simply didn't know him well enough. Her instinct told her that she could trust him. *Must* trust him, it looked at the moment—for Serafin had already made his way to the other end of the alleyway.

She hurried after him until she came even with him again. "I hate having to run after other people."

"Sometimes it helps to get decisions made."

She snorted. "I hate it even more when other people want to make my decisions for me."

He stopped and held her back by the arm. "You're right. We both have to want this. It could get quite dangerous."

Merle sighed. "I'm not one of those girls who gives up easily—so don't treat me like one. And I'm not afraid of flying lions." *Of course not,* she said silently to herself, *I've never been chased by one either—yet.*

"No reason to be offended now."

"I'm not at all."

"You are so."

"And you keep picking a fight."

He grinned. "Occupational disease."

"Boaster! But you aren't a thief anymore." She left him standing and walked on. "Come on. Or there won't be lions or councillors or adventure tonight."

This time it was he who followed her. She had the feeling that he was testing her. Would she go in the same direction that he'd chosen? Would she interpret the distant wingbeats against the sky properly to lead them to their goal?

She'd show him where to go—literally, in fact.

She hurried around the next corner and kept looking up at the night sky between the edges of the roofs, until she finally slowed and took pains to make no more sound. From here on they ran the danger of being discovered. She just didn't know whether the danger threatened from the sky or from one of the doorways.

"It's that house over there," Serafin whispered.

Her eye followed his index finger to the entrance of a narrow building, just wide enough for a door and two boarded-up windows. It seemed to have once been a ser-vants' annex to one of the neighboring grand houses, in days when the facades of Venice still bore witness to wealth and magnificence. But today many of the palazzi stood just as empty as the houses on the Canal of the Expelled and elsewhere. Not even tramps and beggars squatted there, for in winter the gigantic rooms were impossible to heat. Firewood had been a scarce commodity since the beginning of the siege, and so the stripping of the abandoned buildings of the city had begun long ago, breaking out their wooden floors and beams in order to heat the woodstoves in the cold months.

"How do you know it's this particular house?" Merle asked softly.

Serafin gestured to the roof. Merle had to admit that he had astonishingly good eyes: Something peeked over the edge of the roof, a stone paw, which scratched the tiles. It was impossible to see the lions from the street. Nevertheless, Merle did not doubt that watchful eyes were staring down out of the darkness.

"Let's try around back," Serafin suggested softly.

"But the back side of the house is right on the canal!" Merle's sense of direction in the narrow alleyways was unbeatable. She knew exactly how it looked behind this row of houses. The walls there were smooth, and there was no walk along the edge of the canal.

"We'll manage anyhow," said Serafin. "Trust me."

"As friend or master thief?"

He stopped for a moment, tilted his head, and looked

at her in amazement. Then he stuck out his hand. "Friends?" he asked carefully.

She took his hand firmly in her own. "Friends."

Serafin beamed. "Then I say to you as master thief that somehow we are going to get inside this house. And as friend—" He hesitated, then went on, "as friend I promise you that I will never let you down, no matter what happens tonight."

He didn't wait for her reply but pulled her with him, back into the shadows of the alleyway out of which they had come. Unerringly they made their way through tunnels, across a back courtyard, and through empty houses.

It seemed almost no time until they were edging their way along a narrow ledge that ran along the back of a row of buildings. The pitch-dark water rocked below them. About twenty yards farther, vague in the faint moonlight, the curved outline of a bridge was discernible. And at its highest point stood a lion with an armed rider. If he were to turn around, he would surely be able to spot them in the darkness.

"I hope the lion doesn't sense us," Merle whispered. Like Serafin, she was pressing herself flat against the wall. The ledge was just wide enough for her heels. She had trouble trying to keep her balance and at the same time keep her eye on the sentry on the bridge.

Serafin had less difficulty negotiating the ledge. He was accustomed to getting into strange houses in the most unusual ways, first as a thief, then as Umberto's secret courier. Still, he didn't give Merle the feeling she was holding him back.

"Why doesn't he turn around?" he burst out through clenched teeth. "I don't like that."

Since Merle was a little smaller than he was, she could see a little farther under the bridge. Now she saw that a boat was approaching from the opposite direction. She reported her discovery to Serafin in a whisper. "The guard doesn't seem bothered by it. It looks as though he's been waiting for the boat."

"A secret meeting," Serafin guessed. "I've seen those a few times—a councillor meeting one of his informants. They say the councillors have spies everywhere, in all sorts of people."

Merle had other concerns at the moment. "How much farther is it?"

Serafin bent over a fraction of an inch. "About ten feet, then we're at the first window. If it's open, we can climb into the house." He looked around at Merle. "Can you tell who's in the boat?"

She blinked hard, hoping to be able to see the figure in the bow more clearly. But, like both the oarsmen sitting farther behind him, he was wrapped in a dark hooded cloak. No wonder, considering the time and the cold, and yet Merle shivered at the look of him. Was she mistaken, or did the lion on the bridge paw the ground nervously?

Serafin reached the window. Now they were no more than ten yards away from the bridge. He looked carefully through the glass and nodded to Merle. "The room's empty. They must be waiting somewhere else in the house."

"Can you get the window open?" Merle wasn't really subject to dizziness, but her back had begun to hurt and a tingling was creeping up her outspread legs.

Serafin pressed against the glass, first gently, then a little harder. A slight crack sounded. The right window swung inward on its hinges.

Merle sighed in relief. Thank goodness! She tried to keep her eye on the boat while Serafin climbed into the house. The dinghy had tied up on the other side of the bridge. The lion bore its rider to firm ground to receive the hooded and mantled figure.

Merle saw flying lions in the sky. At least three, perhaps more. If one of them should swoop down again and fly along the canal, it would discover her immediately.

But then Serafin reached his hand to her through the window and pulled her inside the house. She gasped as she felt wooden planks under her feet. She could have kissed the floor with relief. Or Serafin. Better not. She felt her cheeks flush red.

"Are you all right?" he asked.

"I was working hard," she replied quickly and turned away. "What next?"

He took his time answering. At first she thought he was still staring at her; then she realized that he was listening, quite like the way Junipa had listened during their journey along the Canal of the Expelled—highly concentrated, so that not the slightest sound escaped him.

"They're farther front in the house," he said at last. "At least two men, possibly even three."

"With the soldiers that makes it roughly half a dozen."

"Afraid?"

"Not a bit."

He smiled. "*Who's* the boaster here?"

She couldn't help returning his smile. He could see through her, even in the dark. With anyone else that would have made her uncomfortable. "Trust me," he'd said, and in fact, she did trust him. Everything had gone much too fast, but she had no time to worry about it.

Quiet as mice, they slipped out of the room and felt their way down a pitch-black hallway. At its end lay the front door. A shimmer of candlelight was falling through the first corridor on the right. On their left a flight of stairs led up to the second floor.

Serafin brought his lips very close to Merle's ear. "Wait here. I'm going to look around."

She wanted to protest, but he quickly shook his head. "Please," he added.

With heavy heart she looked after him as he quickly tiptoed to the lighted hallway. At any moment the front door could open and the man in the hooded cape come in, accompanied by the soldiers.

Serafin reached the doorway, looked carefully through it, waited a moment, then turned back to Merle. Silently he pointed to the stairs to the upper floor.

She followed his instruction noiselessly. He was the master thief, not she. Perhaps he knew best what to do, even if it was hard for her to admit it. She was usually unwilling to do what others told her to—whether or not it was in her own best interest.

The stairs were of solid stone. Merle went up and on the second floor made her way to the room that lay over the candlelit room on the ground floor. There she understood what had drawn Serafin upstairs.

A third of the floor had fallen in a long time ago. Wooden beams were scattered and splintered away from the edges, framing a wide opening in the center of the room. From below, candles sent a faint light. Low voices could be heard. Their tone sounded uncertain and apprehensive, even though Merle couldn't make out the exact words.

"Three men," Serafin whispered in her ear. "All three city councillors. Big bosses."

Merle peeked over the edge. She felt the warmth of the light rising to her face. Serafin was right. The three men standing next to one another down there in the light of the candles wore the long robes of Council members, golden and purple and scarlet.

In all of Venice there was no higher authority than the City Council. Since the invasion by the Empire and the loss of all contact with the mainland, they had jurisdiction over the affairs of the besieged city. They had all powers in their hands and they maintained the connection with the Flowing Queen—at least that's what they said. They posed to the public as men of the world and infallible. But among the people, there were guarded whispers of misuse of power, nepotism, and the decadence of the old noble families, to which most of the city councillors belonged. It was no secret that those who had money received preference, and anyone who bore an old family name counted more than ordinary folk.

One of the three men on the ground floor was holding a small wooden box in his hands. It looked like a jewel casket made of ebony.

"What're they doing here?" Merle mouthed silently.

Serafin shrugged his shoulders.

There was a grating sound down below. The front door was opened. There were footsteps, then the voice of a soldier.

"My lords councillor," he announced respectfully, "the Egyptian envoy has arrived."

"For heaven's sake, shut your mouth!" hissed the councillor in the purple robe. "Or do you want the entire district to hear of it?"

The soldier withdrew and left the house, and his

companion entered the room. It was the man from the boat, and even now he wore his hood drawn deep over his face. The candlelight wasn't enough to illuminate the shadows under it.

He dispensed with a greeting. "You have carried out what you promised?"

Merle had never heard an Egyptian speak. She was surprised that the man's words showed no accent. But she was too tense to evaluate the significance of the situation right away. Only gradually did its enormous import sink in: a secret meeting between City Council members and an envoy of the Egyptians! A spy, probably, who lived in the city undercover, or otherwise his Venetian dialect wouldn't have been so perfect.

Serafin was chalk white. Drops of sweat beaded his forehead. In shock he peered over the edge into the room below.

The councillor in gold bowed respectfully and the two others did the same after him. "We are glad that you have agreed to this meeting. And certainly, we have carried out what you requested."

The councillor in scarlet nervously clasped his fingers. "The Pharaoh will show himself grateful, won't he?"

With a jerk, the black opening of the hood turned toward him. "God-Emperor Amenophis will learn of your request to join with us. What happens then lies in his divine hands alone."

"Certainly, certainly," the purple councillor hastened to appease him. He cast an angry look toward the man in the scarlet robe. "We do not intend to question any decision of His Divinity."

"Where is it?"

The councillor in gold held the jewel casket out to the envoy. "With most humble greetings to Pharaoh Amenophis. From his loyal servants."

Traitor, thought Merle in utter contempt. *Traitor, traitor, traitor!* It made her really sick to hear the groveling tone of the three city councillors. Or was it just the fear that was turning her stomach?

The envoy took the jewel casket and opened the catch. The councillors exchanged uneasy looks.

Merle bent over farther to better see the contents of the box. Serafin, too, tried to see exactly what was in there.

The casket was lined with velvet, on which lay a little vial of crystal, no longer than a finger. The envoy carefully lifted it out, heedlessly letting the casket fall. It crashed on the floor with a bang. As one, the councillors jumped at the sound.

Between thumb and forefinger the man held the vial up to the opening of his hood, directly against the light of the candles.

"Finally, after all these years!" he murmured absently.

Merle looked at Serafin in amazement. What was so valuable in such a tiny vial?

The councillor in purple raised his hands in a solemn gesture. "It is she, truly. The essence of the Flowing Queen. The charm you placed at our disposal has worked a true wonder."

Merle held her breath and exchanged alarmed looks with Serafin.

"The Pharaoh's alchemists have worked on it for twice ten years," said the envoy coolly. "There was never any doubt that the charm would be effective."

"Of course not, of course not."

The councillor in scarlet, who'd already made himself unpleasantly conspicuous, was rocking excitedly from one foot to the other. "But all your magic wouldn't have helped you if we hadn't declared ourselves ready to perform it in the presence of the Flowing Queen. A servant of the Pharaoh would never have gotten so near her."

The envoy's tone turned wary. "So, are you then *not* a servant of the Pharaoh, Councillor de Angeliis?"

The other's face went white. "Certainly I am, certainly, certainly."

"You are nothing but a whining coward. And of those the worst kind: a traitor!"

The councillor wrinkled his nose defiantly. He shook off the hand that the councillor in purple tried to place soothingly on his arm. "Without us you'd never—"

"Councillor de Angeliis!" scolded the envoy, and now he sounded like an angry old woman. "You will receive recompense for your service of friendship, if that is your concern. At the latest when the Pharaoh makes his entrance into the lagoon with his armies and confirms you as his representative in office. But now, in Amenophis's name, will you be quiet!"

"With your permission," said the councillor in purple, paying no attention to the wretched-looking de Angeliis. "You should know that time is pressing. Recently a messenger from Hell has arrived to offer us a pact against the Empire. I don't know how long we can continue to resist that. Others on the City Council are more receptive to this messenger than we are. It won't be possible to hold them in check indefinitely. Especially as the messenger has said that next time he'll appear in public so that *all* the people will learn of his demands."

The envoy expelled his breath in a wheeze. "That must not happen. The attack on the lagoon is imminent. A pact with Hell can bring it all to nothing." He was silent a moment as he considered the situation. "If the messenger actually appears, make sure that he can't get to the people. Kill him."

"And the vengeance of Hell—," de Angeliis began in a subdued voice, but the third councillor motioned him to silence with a wave.

"Certainly, sir," said the councillor in gold, with a bow in the direction of the envoy. "As you command. The Empire will protect us from all consequences when it once has the city under its control."

The Egyptian nodded graciously. "So shall it be."

Merle's lungs desperately demanded air—she couldn't hold her breath one second longer. The sound was soft, barely audible, but still loud enough to alert the councillor in scarlet. He looked up at the hole in the ceiling. Merle and Serafin pulled their heads back just in time. So they only heard the envoy's further words but couldn't see what was going on.

"The desert crystal of the vial is strong enough to hold the Flowing Queen. Her regency over the lagoon is ended. An army of many thousands of soldiers stands ready on land and on the water. As soon as the Pharaoh holds this vial in his hands, the galleys and sunbarks will strike."

Merle felt a movement at her right side. She looked around, but Serafin was too far away. However, something was moving at her hip! A rat? The truth first hit her when it was already too late.

The water mirror slid out of her dress pocket like something alive, with jerky, clumsy movements like a blinded animal. Then everything went at breakneck speed. Merle tried to grab the mirror, but it shot underneath her hand, skidded to the edge of the hole in the floor, slipped out over it—and fell.

In a long moment, as if frozen in time, Merle saw that the surface of the mirror had become milky, fogged by the presence of the phantom.

The mirror plunged past Merle's outstretched hand

into the depths. It fell exactly on the envoy, missed his hood, struck his hand, and knocked the crystal vial out of his fingers. The man howled, with pain, with rage, with surprise, as the mirror and the vial landed on the floor almost at the same time.

"No!" Serafin's cry made the three councillors leap away from each other like drops of hot fat. With a daring bound he swung himself over the edge and sprang into the middle of them. Merle had no time to consider this sudden chain of catastrophes. She followed Serafin over the edge, her dress fluttering around her, and with a loud bellow that was intended to sound grim but was probably anything but.

The envoy avoided her. Otherwise her feet would have hit his head. Hastily he bent and tried to pick up the vial. But his fingers reached past the vial and brushed across the water mirror. For a fraction of a second his fingertips furrowed the surface, vanished under it—and were gone when the envoy pulled back his hand with a scream of pain. Instead of fingertips there were black slivers of bone, which stuck out of the remainders of his fingers, smoking and burned, as if he'd stuck his hand in a beaker of acid.

A mad shrieking came from under the hood. The sound was inhuman because no face appeared to give it; the screaming poured from an invisible mouth.

Serafin did a cartwheel on both hands, almost too fast for the eye to see. When he came to a stop by the window, he held the vial in his right hand and Merle's mirror in his left.

Meanwhile the councillor in purple, the traitors' spokesman, had grabbed Merle by the upper arm and tried to pull her around. With balled fist he raised his arm to strike her, while the two other councillors ran around like frightened hens, bellowing loudly for their bodyguards. Merle dodged him and was able to shake his hand off her arm, but as she did so her back thumped against black stuff. The robe of the envoy. There was a stench of burned flesh around him.

A sharp draft whistled through the cracks of the boarded-up windows: Flying lions had landed outside in front of the house. Steel scraped over steel as sabers were withdrawn from their sheaths.

Someone placed an arm around Merle from behind, but she ducked away under it as she had in so many scraps in the orphanage. She'd had practice in fighting, and she knew what she had to hit so that it hurt. When Councillor de Angeliis put himself in her way, she placed a well-aimed kick. The fat man in the scarlet robe bellowed as if he'd been spitted, holding his lower abdomen with both hands.

"Out!" cried Serafin, holding the two other councillors in check by threatening to smash the vial on the floor—whatever that might bring about.

Merle raced over to him and ran at his side to the exit.

They turned into the corridor at the very moment the front door burst open and two bodyguards in black leather thundered in.

"By the Ancient Traitor!" Serafin cursed.

Nonplussed, the soldiers stopped in their tracks. They had been expecting a trick by the Egyptian, with men armed to the teeth, worthy opponents for two battle-hardened heroes of the Guard. Instead they saw a girl in a ragged dress and a boy who held in his hands two gleaming objects that looked not at all like knives.

Merle and Serafin used the moment of surprise. Before the guards could react, the two were on their way to the back room.

There, in front of the open window, the envoy was waiting for them. He had known that there was only one way of escape. At the back, out to the water.

"The mirror!" Merle called to Serafin.

He threw it over to her, and she caught it with both hands, grabbed it by the handle, and hit at the envoy with it. He avoided it skillfully, but that also left the way to the window free. His singed fingertips still smoked.

"The vial!" he demanded in a hissing voice. "You are setting yourselves against the Pharaoh!"

Serafin let out a daredevil laugh that surprised even Merle. Then he somersaulted past the envoy, between his outstretched hands. He landed safely on the windowsill and sat there like a bird, with both feet on the frame, knees drawn up, and a wide grin on his lips.

"All honor to the Flowing Queen!" he cried out, while Merle used the moment to spring to his side. "Follow me!"

With that he let himself fall backward out the window into the waters of the still canal.

It wasn't really his hand that drew Merle after him: It was his enthusiasm, his sheer will not to give up. For the first time in her life she felt admiration for another person.

The envoy screeched and grabbed the edge of Merle's dress, but it was with the fingers of his eroded hand, and he let go again with a yelp of pain.

The water was icy. In a single heartbeat it seemed to pierce her clothes, her flesh, her entire body. Merle could no longer breathe, nor move, nor even think. She didn't know how long this condition lasted—it seemed to her like minutes—but when she surfaced, Serafin was beside her, and life came back to her limbs. She couldn't have been under for more than a few seconds.

"Here, take this!" Underwater he pressed the vial into her left hand. In the right she was still holding the mirror, which lay between her fingers as if it grew there.

"What shall I do with it?"

"If worse comes to worst, I'll steer them away," said Serafin and spat water. The waves slapped at his lips.

Worse comes to worst, Merle thought. Even worse?

The envoy appeared in the window and shouted something.

Serafin let out a whistle. It only worked on the second try; the first just spewed water from his lips. Merle followed his eyes to the window, then saw black silhouettes slip down, four-legged shadows that sprang from holes and drainpipes, screeching and meowing, with unsheathed claws, which they sank into the robe of the envoy. One cat came up on the windowsill, immediately launched again, and disappeared completely into the dark of the hood. Screaming, the Egyptian staggered backward into the room.

"Harmless thieves' trick!" observed Serafin with satisfaction.

"We have to get out of the water!" Merle turned and let the mirror slide into the pocket of her dress, together with the vial, to which she gave no further thought for the moment. She swam a few strokes in the direction of the opposite bank. The walls came down to the canal there, and there was no hold for pulling oneself to dry land. All the same, she had to do something!

"Onto land?" Serafin said, looking up at the sky. "It looks as though that's going to take care of itself."

Breathlessly Merle turned around, much too slowly, because her dress hindered her in the water. And then she saw what he meant.

Two lions, wings outspread, were diving steeply down at them out of the black of the night.

"Duck!" she screamed and didn't see whether Serafin followed her command. She held her breath and glided underwater, felt the salty cold on her lips, the pressure in her ears and nose. The canal must be about nine feet deep, and she knew that she needed to get at least half of that between her and the lions' claws.

She saw and heard nothing of what was happening around her. When she was deep enough, she turned herself horizontal, and plunged along the canal with a few strong strokes. Perhaps she could make it if she could reach one of the old loading doors.

At one time, when Venice had been an important trading city, the merchants had been able to bring their wares into their houses from the canals through doors that lay at surface level. Today many of these houses stood empty, their owners long dead, but the doors still existed, usually rotten, eaten away by water and by salt. Often the bottom third was rotted away. For Merle they offered an ideal chance for escape.

And Serafin?

She could only pray that he was behind her, not too far above, where the lions' claws could grab him out of the water. Stone lions are shy of water, have always been, and the last flying examples of their kind are no exception. They may put their claws into the water, but they themselves will never, ever dip into it. Merle knew this weakness of the lions and she hoped with all her might that Serafin did too.

Gradually she grew starved for air and in her need she sent a fervent prayer to the Flowing Queen. Then it occurred to her that the Flowing Queen was in a vial in the pocket of her dress, imprisoned like a genie in a bottle and probably as helpless as she was.

The essence of the Flowing Queen, the councillor had said.

Where was Serafin? And where was there a door?

She was losing consciousness. The black around her seemed to turn, and she felt as if she were falling deeper and deeper, while in truth she was struggling toward the top, to reach the surface.

Then she broke through. Air flowed into her lungs. She opened her eyes.

She had come farther than she'd hoped. Very close by there was in fact a door, slanting and ragged, where the water had licked at the wood over and over and finally rotted it. The upper half hung undamaged on its hinges, but under it gaped a dark maw into the interior of the house. The rotted wood looked like the jaw of a sea monster, a row of sharp teeth, cracked and green with algae and mold.

"Merle!"

Serafin's voice made her whirl around in the water. What she saw numbed her from head to toe. She almost went under.

One of the lions was hovering over the water and

holding the kicking Serafin in its front paws, like a fish that it had grabbed and plucked out of the stream.

"Merle!" Serafin bellowed once more. She knew now that he hadn't seen her at all, that he didn't know where she was and if she were still alive. He was afraid for her. He feared she had drowned.

Her mind screamed to answer him, to draw the notice of the lions to herself in order to give him a chance to get away. But she was only fooling herself. No lion lets go of what it has caught.

Already the beast completed a turn with a well-aimed wingbeat, moved away, and rose in the air, the defenseless Serafin firmly pressed under its body.

"Merle, wherever you are," bellowed Serafin in a voice growing fainter, "you must flee! Hide yourself! Save the Flowing Queen!"

Then lion, rider, and Serafin vanished into the night like a cloud of ash dispersed on the wind.

Merle ducked under again. Her tears became one with the canal, became one with it as did Merle herself. On and on, as she dove through the wooden, toothed maw, through the rotted door into still deeper darkness; as she pulled herself to dryness in the dark, curled up like a little child, simply lay there, and wept.

Breathed and wept.

6

End and Beginning

THE FLOWING QUEEN WAS SPEAKING TO HER.

"*Merle,*" said her voice. "*Merle, listen to me!*"

Merle started up, her eyes quickly searching the darkness. The old storeroom reeked of dampness and rotten wood. The only light came in through the broken door from the canal. There was a shimmer and shining in the air—someone was searching the water surface with torches out there!

She had to get out of here as quickly as possible.

"*You are not dreaming, Merle.*"

The words were in her; the voice was speaking between her ears.

"Who are you?" she whispered, leaping to her feet.

"You know who I am. Do not be afraid of me."

Merle pulled the mirror out of her pocket and held it in the flickering torchlight. The surface was clear, the phantom nowhere to be seen. But she also felt that it wasn't he who was speaking to her. She quickly slid the mirror back into her pocket and took out the vial. It fit comfortably into her hand.

"You?" If she only spoke in single words, not in entire sentences, maybe it wouldn't be apparent how very much her voice quavered.

"You must get away from here. They are going to search through all the houses that border on the canal. And after that, the rest of the district."

"What's happened to Serafin?"

"He is now a prisoner of the Guard."

"They'll kill him!"

"Perhaps. But not right away. They could have done that already, in the water. They are going to try to find out who you are and where they can find you."

Merle shoved the vial back into her pocket and felt her way through the darkness. She was miserably cold in her wet dress, but her goose pimples had nothing to do with the temperature.

"Are you the Flowing Queen?" she asked softly.

"Do you want to call me that? Queen?"

"First of all I just want to get away from here."

"Then we should attend to that."

"We? I see only one person here who has legs to run away with."

In the dark she found a door that led back into the house. She slipped through it and found herself in a deserted entry hall. Floor and banisters were covered with thick dust. Merle's feet left tracks in the dust as if it were a blanket of snow. Her pursuers wouldn't find it hard to follow her trail.

The front door was nailed shut from the outside, like many doors in Venice these days, but she found a window whose glass she was able to break with the fallen head of a statue. By some miracle she climbed out without cutting either hands or knees.

What now? Best go back to the Canal of the Expelled. Arcimboldo would know what to do. Or Eft. Or Junipa. Someone or other! She couldn't carry this secret around with her alone.

"If your friend talks, they will look for you there first," warned the voice suddenly.

"Serafin will never betray me!" she retorted, annoyed. And in her thoughts she added: *He swore never to let me down.*

On the other hand, she had watched passively as the lion carried him away. But what could she have done anyway?

"Nothing," said the voice. *"You were helpless. You are still."*

"Are you reading my thoughts?"

She got no answer to that, which was answer enough.

"Stop that," she said sharply. "I saved you. You owe me something."

Further silence. Had she angered the voice? So much the better; maybe it would leave her in peace then. It was hard enough to think for one person alone. She needed no inner voice, questioning her every decision.

Cautiously she ran down the alleyway, stopping again and again, listening for pursuers and suspicious sounds. She even kept her eye on the sky, although it was dark enough that a whole pride of lions could have been romping around high up there. It was still hours till sunrise.

Soon she knew where she was: only a few corners away from Campo San Polo. She'd covered half the distance back to the workshop. Not much farther and she would be safe.

"Not safe," contradicted the voice. *"Not as long as the boy is a prisoner."*

Merle exploded. "What is this?" she shouted, her voice resounding loudly from the walls. "What are you? My voice of reason?"

"I will be that, if you want."

"I only want you to leave me in peace."

"I am only giving you advice, not orders."

"I don't need advice."

"But I am afraid you do need it."

Merle stopped, looked angrily around, and found a gap in a boarded-up wall between two houses. She had to settle this business once and for all, here and now. She squeezed herself through the opening, drew deeper back into the dark canyon between the house walls, and sank down with her knees drawn up.

"You want to talk with me? Well, then, we'll talk."

"As you wish."

"Who or what are you?"

"I think you already know that."

"The Flowing Queen?"

"At the moment, only a voice in your head."

Merle hesitated. If the voice really belonged to the Queen, wouldn't it then be polite to deal with her a little more respectfully? But she was still full of doubt. "You don't talk like a queen."

"I talk like you. I speak with your voice, with your thoughts."

"I'm only some girl."

"Now you are more than that. You have undertaken a task."

"I have undertaken nothing at all!" Merle said. "I didn't want all this. And don't talk to me now about fate and such nonsense. This isn't a fairy tale."

"Unfortunately, it is not. In a fairy tale, matters are simpler. You go home and find that the soldiers have

burned down your house and carried off your friends, you become angry, recognize that you must take up the battle against the Pharaoh, meet him finally, and kill him through a trick. That would be the fairy tale. But unfortunately we have to deal with the reality. The path is the same one and yet different."

"I could simply take the vial and tip whatever's in it into the nearest canal."

"No! That would kill me!"

"Then you aren't the Flowing Queen. She's at home in the canal."

"The Flowing Queen is only what you wish her to be. At the moment, a fluid in a vial. And a voice in your head."

"That's confused nonsense. I don't understand you."

"The Egyptians drove me out of the canal by laying a spell on the water. That is the only reason the traitors succeeded in imprisoning me in this vial. The magic still permeates the water of the lagoon, and it will last for months before it has evaporated. Until then my essence cannot be combined with the water."

"We all thought that you were something . . . something different."

"Sorry to disappoint you."

"Something spiritual."

"Like God?"

"Yes, I guess so."

"Even God is only always in those who believe in him. Just as I am in you now."

"That's not the same. You left me no choice. You talked to me. I must believe in you, otherwise . . ."

"Otherwise what?"

"Otherwise it would mean that I'm crazy. That I'm only talking to myself."

"Would that be so bad, then? To listen to the voice inside you?"

Merle shook her head impatiently. "That's hairsplitting. You're only trying to confuse me. Perhaps you really are only that dumb phantom who went into my mirror."

"Put me to the test. Leave the mirror lying somewhere. Separate from it. Then you will see that I am still with you."

"I will never give up the mirror voluntarily. I treasure it, as you know very well."

"It is not going to be forever. Only for a moment. Put it down at the end of this little alley, come back here, and listen to see if I am still there."

Merle thought it over briefly, then agreed. She carried the mirror to the farthest corner of the alleyway, about fifteen yards from the entrance. She had to step over all sorts of trash that had collected there over the years. She drove away rats with her feet, and they snapped at her heels. Finally, leaving the mirror, she ran back to the front end of the alleyway.

"Well?" she asked softly.

"*Here I am,*" responded the voice with amusement.

Merle sighed. "Does that mean you continue to claim that you're the Flowing Queen?"

"*I never claimed that. You said it.*"

Merle hurried back to the mirror and picked it up. Quickly she dropped it into her dress pocket and buttoned the pocket closed. "You said you used my words and my thoughts. Does that also mean that you can influence my will?"

"*Even if I could, I would not do it.*"

"I guess I have to believe you, huh?"

"*Trust me.*"

It was the second time tonight that someone had asked that of her. She didn't like it at all.

"Nevertheless, it could be that I am only imagining all this, couldn't it?"

"*Which would you prefer? An imaginary voice that speaks to you or a real one?*"

"Neither one."

"*I will enlist your services no longer than necessary.*"

Merle opened her eyes wide. "My *services*?"

"*I need your help. The Egyptian spy and the traitors will stop at nothing to get me into their power. They will hunt you. We must leave Venice.*"

"Leave the city? But that's impossible! There's been a siege for more than thirty years, and they say it's just as tight as on the first day."

The voice sounded stricken. *"I have given my best, but at last I also have fallen victim to the enemy's tricks. I can no longer protect the lagoon. We must find another way."*

"But . . . but what about all the people? And the mermaids?"

"No one can keep the Egyptians from invading. At the moment they are still not certain what has happened to me. That helps us with a delay. But there is only a little time left before they find out the truth. And the city is only safe until they do."

"That's nothing but a temporary reprieve."

"Yes," said the voice sadly. *"Nothing more and nothing less. But when the Pharaoh's fist closes around the lagoon, he will be looking for you. The envoy knows your face. He will not rest until you are dead."*

Merle thought about Junipa and Serafin, about Arcimboldo and Eft. About all those who meant something to her. She should just leave these people behind and flee?

"Not flee," contradicted the voice. *"But go on the quest. I will never give it up. If it dies, I die as well. But we must leave the city to find help."*

"There's no one left outside anymore to help us. The Empire has ruled over the whole world for a long time."

"Perhaps. Perhaps not, too."

Merle had had enough of these enigmatic hintings, even though she was gradually losing any doubt that the voice in her head actually belonged to the Flowing Queen. And although she'd grown up in a city in which the Queen was venerated exceedingly, she wanted to show no reverence. She hadn't asked to be drawn into this mess.

"First I'm going back to the workshop," said Merle. "I have to speak with Junipa, and with Arcimboldo."

"*We will lose valuable time.*"

"That's my decision!" Merle retorted angrily.

"*As you will.*"

"Does that mean you aren't going to try to talk me out of it?"

"*Yes.*"

That surprised her, but it gave her back a little of her self-confidence.

She was just about to climb out of the space between the boards to the alley when the voice spoke again.

"*There is still one thing.*"

"And?"

"*I cannot remain much longer in this vial.*"

"Why not?"

"*The desert crystal numbs my brain.*"

Merle smiled. "Does that mean you'll talk less?"

"*It means that I will die. My essence must bind with living organisms. The water of the lagoon is full of them. But the vial is only cold, dead crystal. I am going to wither like a plant that is withdrawn from the soil and the light.*"

"How can I help you?"

"*You must drink me.*"

Merle made a face. "Drink . . . you?"

"*We must become one, you and I.*"

"You're already in my head. And now you want my entire body, too? Do you know the saying about someone to whom you give your little finger and instead he takes the whole—"

"*I will die, Merle. And the lagoon with me.*"

"That's blackmail, you know that? If I don't help you, everyone will die. If I don't drink you, everyone will die. What comes next?"

"*Drink me, Merle.*"

She pulled the vial out of her pocket. The facets of the crystal sparkled like an insect's eye. "And there's no other way?"

"*None.*"

"How will you . . . I mean, how will you get out of me again, and when?"

"*When the time for it has come.*"

"I thought you'd say something like that."

"*I would not ask you to do it if we had a choice.*"

Merle thought for a brief moment about the fact that she very much did have a choice. She could still throw away the vial and act as if this night had never taken place. But how could she lie to herself about all that had happened? Serafin, the fight with the envoy, the Flowing Queen.

Sometimes responsibility sneaked up on you without your seeing it coming, and then, very suddenly, it wouldn't let you go anymore.

Merle pulled out the stopper of the vial and sniffed at it. Nothing, no smell.

"How . . . umm, how do you taste, actually?"

"Like anything you want."

"How about fresh raspberries?"

"Why not?"

After a final hesitation, Merle put the opening to her mouth and drank. The fluid inside it was clear and cool, like water. Two, three swallows, no more, and then the vial was empty.

"That didn't taste like raspberries!"

"What, then?"

"Nothing at all."

"Then it was not as bad as you thought, was it?"

"I can't stand it when people trick me."

"It will not happen again. Do you feel any different now?"

Merle listened within, but she could find no change. The contents of the vial might just as well have been water.

"Same as before."

"Good. Then throw away the empty vial now. They must not find it on you."

Merle put the stopper back in the little crystal vial and shoved it under a heap of garbage. Gradually she realized what had just happened.

"Do I really now carry the Flowing Queen inside me?"

"*You always have. Like anyone who believes in her.*"

"That sounds like churches and priests and religious twaddle."

The voice in her head sighed. "*If it reassures you: I am now in you. Really in you.*"

Merle frowned, then shrugged. "Guess it's too late to change it."

The voice was quiet. Merle took that for reason to finally leave her hiding place. As quickly as she could she ran through the alleys to the Canal of the Expelled. She kept close to the walls of the houses so that she couldn't be seen from the sky. Perhaps the heavens were now swarming with the lions of the Guard.

"*I do not think so,*" countered the Flowing Queen. "*There are only three city councillors who betrayed me, and they have to be content with their share of the bodyguards. No councillor commands more than two flying lions. That makes six altogether, at the most.*"

"Six lions with nothing else to do but hunt me?" Merle exclaimed. "And that's supposed to reassure me? Thanks very much!"

"*Don't mention it.*"

"You don't know much about us humans, right?"

"*I have never had the opportunity to find out more about you.*"

Merle shook her head dumbly. For centuries now the

Flowing Queen had been honored, there were cults dedicated entirely to worshipping her. But the Queen herself knew nothing of it. Knew nothing about humans, nothing about what she meant to them.

She was the lagoon. But was she also therefore a god?

"Is the Pharaoh a god because the Egyptians honor him as a god?" asked the voice. *"For them he may be one. For you not. Divinity is only in the eye of the beholder."*

Merle was not in the mood to think about that, so instead she asked, "Before, that business with the mirror, that was you, wasn't it?"

"No."

"Then was it the mirror itself? Or the phantom in it?"

"Have you considered that you yourself could have thrown it at the envoy?"

"I would certainly have known about that."

"You are listening to a voice in your head that is perhaps only your own. It is possible that you also do things without being conscious of them—only because they are right."

"Nonsense."

"As you will."

She wasted no more words on it, but the thought wouldn't let go of Merle. What if she really was only imagining the voice of the Flowing Queen? What if she had been talking the whole time with a hallucination? And worse yet, what if her own actions were no longer under her control and she was talking with supernatural powers that in truth didn't exist at all?

This idea frightened her more than the fact that something strange had established itself in her. On the other hand, she didn't feel this stranger at all. It was all so terribly confusing.

Merle reached the mouth of the Canal of the Expelled. The festival hadn't ended yet—a few stalwarts sat on the bridge talking softly or staring silently into their cups. Junipa and the boys were nowhere to be seen. Probably they'd made their way home long since.

Merle ran along the small path at the edge of the canal until she reached Arcimboldo's workshop. The water lapped, whispering, against the stone. One last time she looked up at the night sky and imagined the lions were up there circling, beyond the shine of all the gaslights and torches. The soldiers on their backs might be blind in the dark, but weren't cats nocturnal animals? In her mind she saw the yellow predator eyes, which stared full of bloodlust into the depths, on the lookout for a girl in wet, worn clothes, with stringy hair and knowledge that might mean death.

She knocked on the door. No one answered. She pounded again. The blows sounded louder than usual to her; they must be audible throughout the whole district. Perhaps a lion was already on the way here, just now diving straight down through the layers of cold air, then through the smog over the city, the smoke of fires and chimneys, the weak shine of the lanterns, straight at Merle. She looked up in alarm, above her in the dark, and perhaps there actually was something there, gigantic wings of stone, paws as large as puppies and—

The door opened. Eft grabbed her by the arm and pulled her into the house. "Whatever were you thinking of to just run away?" The mermaid's eyes were glowing with anger as she slammed the front door behind Merle. "I had really expected more sense from you than—"

"I must speak with the master." Merle looked anxiously back at the door.

"There was no one there," said the Queen reassuringly.

"With the master?" asked Eft. Obviously she couldn't hear the voice. "Have you any idea how late it is?"

"I'm sorry. Really. But it's important."

She held Eft's gaze and tried to read the mermaid's eyes. You are touched by the Flowing Queen, she had said to her. In hindsight the words sounded almost like a prophecy that had been fulfilled this night. Could Eft feel the change that had taken place in Merle? Did she sense the strange presence in her thoughts?

Whatever reason she might have, she stopped scolding Merle. Instead she turned around. "Come along."

Silently they went to the door of the workshop. Eft left Merle standing there. "Arcimboldo is still at work. He works every night. Tell him what you have to tell." With that she disappeared into the darkness and soon Merle could no longer hear her steps.

Alone, she hesitated before the door. It cost her great effort to raise her hand and knock. What could she say to Arcimboldo? Really the whole truth? Wouldn't he say she was crazy and throw her out of the house? And even worse: Mustn't she make clear to him at once what a threat she presented to the workshop and its inhabitants?

Nevertheless she felt a remarkable certainty that it was right to speak with him about it instead of with Eft. The mermaid worshipped the Flowing Queen. Merle's story would sound like blasphemy to her ears, the talk of a girl who wanted to make herself important.

Steps sounded on the other side of the door, then Arcimboldo's face appeared in the crack. "Merle! You're back!"

She hadn't expected him to have been aware of her disappearance at all. Eft must have told him of it.

"Come in, come in!" Hastily he waved her into the workshop. "We've been very worried about you."

That was something new. Merle hadn't experienced someone in the orphanage ever worrying about anyone else. If one of the children vanished, he or she was looked for halfheartedly, usually without success. One burden less, one more place free.

It was warm in the workshop. Steam puffed in little white clouds from Arcimboldo's apparatus, which were linked together with a network of pipes, tubing, and glass globes. The mirror maker used the machines only at night, when he was alone. During the day he busied himself in traditional ways and methods, perhaps because he didn't want to give his pupils any deep insights into the secrets of his art. Did he ever sleep at all? Hard to say. In Merle's eyes Arcimboldo belonged to the fixed inventory of the workshop, just like the oak doors and the high windows with their dust-encrusted panes on which generations of apprentices had scratched their initials.

Arcimboldo walked over to one of the devices, adjusted a switch, and then turned to her. Behind him the machine spurted out three clouds of steam in short bursts. "So now, tell! Where were you?"

Merle had considered all the long way back over what she wanted to say to Arcimboldo. The decision had not been an easy one for her. "I don't think you're going to understand me."

"Don't worry about that. I only want to hear the truth."

She took a deep breath. "I've come to thank you. And so that you know that I'm all right."

"That sounds as though you intend to leave us."

"I'm going away from Venice."

She had reckoned with all possible reactions to this news, such as that he would laugh at her, scold her, or lock her up. But not with the sorrow that now darkened his eyes. No anger, no malice, only plain regret. "What has happened?"

She told him everything. Beginning with her meeting with Serafin, about the fight in the deserted house, the vial with the Flowing Queen, and about Serafin being taken prisoner. She described the robes and faces of the three traitors to him, and he nodded in annoyance at each individual, as if he knew exactly who was the one involved. She spoke of the voice in her head and, a little ashamed, of the fact that she had drunk the contents of the vial.

After she'd finished, Arcimboldo sank dejectedly onto a wooden stool. With a cloth he blotted the sweat from his forehead, blew his nose into it forcefully, and threw it into the stove opening. Both watched as the material was consumed by the flames. They were quiet, almost a little reverent, as if what was burning there was something else: a memory, perhaps, or the thought of what might have been—without the Egyptians, without traitors, and without the poison spell that had driven the Flowing Queen out of the canal.

"You're right," said Arcimboldo after a while. "It's no longer safe for you here. Not anywhere in Venice. But in you the Flowing Queen can leave the lagoon, for you were born here and so are a part of her."

"You know more about her than you've ever told us," she declared.

He smiled sadly. "A little. She was always an important

part of my work. Without her there can be no more magic mirrors."

"But that will mean that . . ."

"That sooner or later I must close the workshop. So it is. The water of the lagoon is a component of my art. Without the breath of the Flowing Queen that goes into every mirror, all my talents are useless."

Apprehension closed around Merle's heart. "What about the others? Junipa and Boro and . . ." There was a lump in her throat. "Must they go back to the orphanages?"

Arcimboldo thought briefly about it, then shook his head. "No, not that. But who knows what will happen when the Egyptians invade? No one can say ahead of time. There will perhaps be fighting. Then the boys will certainly want to fight on the side of the defenders." He rubbed both hands over his face. "As if that would do any good."

Merle wished that the Flowing Queen would give her an answer to that. A few reassuring words, something or other! But the voice inside her kept silent, and she herself didn't know how she could have cheered the mirror maker.

"You must keep on taking care of Junipa," she said. "That you must promise me."

"Certainly." But his agreement didn't sound quite as convincing as Merle wanted it to be.

"Do you think she's in danger from the Egyptians? Because of her eyes?"

"No matter where the Empire has invaded, the first to suffer under them have always been the sick, the wounded, and the weak. The Pharaoh puts healthy men and women into his factories, but the rest . . . I can give you no answer about that, Merle."

"But *nothing* must happen to Junipa!" Merle could no longer understand how she'd thought of going away without saying good-bye to Junipa. She had to see her, as quickly as possible. Perhaps she could even take her with her. . . .

"*No,*" the Flowing Queen weighed in. "*That is impossible.*"

"Why not?" Merle asked rebelliously. Arcimboldo looked up, since he assumed she was speaking to him. But when he realized that her look was directed inward, he knew whom she was addressing.

"*The way we must go is hard enough for one alone. The old man has promised to take care of your friend.*"

"But I—"

"*It will not work.*"

"Don't interrupt me!"

"*You must believe me. Here she is safe. There, outside, she will only bring you into unnecessary danger. Both of you.*"

"Both of us?" retorted Merle acidly. "*You,* you mean!"

"Merle!" Arcimboldo had stood up and taken her by the shoulders. "If you are really speaking with the Flowing Queen, you should adopt a different tone."

"Bah!" She took a step back. Suddenly there were tears in her eyes. "What do you know anyway? Junipa is my friend. I can't just run out on her!"

She took another step and rubbed angrily at her eyes. She didn't want to cry. Not here, not now.

"You aren't running out on me," said a voice behind her, very gently, very softly. Merle whirled around.

"Junipa!"

In the dark of the open door the silvery eyes were sparkling like a pair of stars that had just wandered there from heaven. Junipa walked forward. The yellow flames of the stove fire flickered over her thin features. She was wearing her white nightgown, with a red shawl over it.

"I couldn't sleep," she said. "I was worried about you. Eft came to me and said that I'd find you here."

Dear, good Eft, thought Merle gratefully. She'd never show it openly, but she knows exactly what's going on in each of us.

Relieved, she hugged Junipa. It felt good to see her friend and to hear her voice. It seemed as though they had been separated for weeks, although she'd left Junipa at the festival just a few hours before.

When Merle let go, she looked Junipa straight in the

eyes. They unsettled her no longer; she'd seen worse in the meantime.

"I listened at the door," Junipa confessed with a shadow of a smile. "Eft showed me the best way to do it." She pointed over her shoulder, and there, in the dark of the corridor, stood Eft, who raised an eyebrow but said nothing.

Merle couldn't help it: She laughed, although it wasn't at all how she was feeling. She no longer had herself under control, just laughed and laughed. . . .

"You heard everything," she chortled finally. "Both of you?"

Junipa nodded, while Eft's eyes suggested a smile, but otherwise she remained stock-still.

"Then you certainly think I'm crazy."

"No," said Junipa earnestly. And Eft said softly, "The one touched has come home to take leave. The way of the hero takes its beginning."

Merle didn't feel like a hero, and that this all might be the beginning of something . . . she didn't want to think about that at all. But in her heart she of course knew that Eft was right. A leave-taking, a beginning, and then a journey. Her journey.

Junipa grasped her hand and held it fast. "I'm staying here with Arcimboldo and Eft. You go wherever you must go."

"Junipa, do you remember what you told me, on the very first night?"

"That I was always just a millstone around people's necks?"

Merle nodded. "But you most certainly are not! And you wouldn't be either, if you'd come with me!"

Junipa's smile outshone the cool silver of her eyes. "I know. Much has changed since that night. Arcimboldo can use my help, especially if it really should come to a fight of Venetians against Egyptians. The boys would be the first to join the resistance."

"You have to stop them."

"You know Dario," Arcimboldo said with a sigh. "He won't let anyone keep him out of an ordinary scrap."

"But a war isn't a scrap!"

"He won't see it that way. And Boro and Tiziano will go with him." The mirror maker looked very old and gray, as if the admission of his powerlessness cost him great strength. "Junipa will be a valuable help to us. In all things."

Merle wondered if Arcimboldo perhaps loved Eft the way a man can love a woman. Did he see in Junipa the daughter he and the mermaid would never have?

But who was she anyway that she was trying to evaluate the feelings of another? She'd never had a family, didn't know what it was like to have a father and a mother. Perhaps Junipa would find that out anyhow, if she gave Arcimboldo and Eft a chance.

It was right to go alone. Only she and the Flowing

Queen. Junipa's place was here, in this house, with these people.

She pressed her friend to her once more, then embraced Arcimboldo, and finally also Eft. "Farewell," she said. "We'll all see each other again, sometime."

"Do you know the way?" Junipa asked.

"I will show her," said Eft, before Merle could answer at all. Arcimboldo agreed with a nod.

Merle and the mermaid exchanged a look. Eft's eyes gleamed, but perhaps that was only due to the hard contrast with the shadow that the edge of the mask cast over her features.

Junipa grasped Merle's hands one last time. "Good luck," she said, her voice thick. "Take good care of yourself."

"The Flowing Queen is with me." The words were out before Merle could even form the thought of speaking them. She wondered if perhaps the Queen had helped to reassure Junipa.

"Come now," Eft said, and she led the way down the corridor with quick steps.

After a few yards Merle looked around once, back to the door of the workshop. There stood Junipa, beside Arcimboldo. For an irritating moment Merle saw herself standing there at the side of the mirror maker, his arm on her shoulder. But then her likeness turned back into the girl with the mirror eyes, dark hair became blond, her stature still smaller, more vulnerable.

Eft led her out to the inner courtyard, led her straight over to the well, led her down into the depths.

The inside of the well felt like something living, and in spite of the coolness of the stone it grew warm around Merle, and she thought: *Yes, this is how it can begin. This is how it can truly begin.*

7

Through the Canals

MERMAIDS! A THRONG OF MERMAIDS!

In the gray-green darkness, a silvery twinkle shone
from their tails like the flickering of fireflies on a summer
night. Two of them were holding Merle by the hands and
pulling her along with them through the canals.

Eft had climbed down into the well along with her.
Only very gradually had it become clear to Merle that the
gentle murmur around her legs did not come from the
water itself. Something was moving around her in the
water, whirling rapidly, touching her with featherlight fingers, more delicately even than a dog's nose sniffing a

stranger, very carefully, very lightly. She had the feeling the touches reached deep under her skin, as if someone were reading her spirit.

Eft spoke a few words in the strange language of the merfolk. Alien and mysterious, they echoed from the walls of the well shaft, penetrating deep below the surface to the ears of those who understood and knew what was to be done.

A pale hand appeared out of the water in front of Merle and handed her a globe of veined glass. It appeared to be a kind of helmet. Eft helped her to invert it over her head and to fasten the little leather band firmly around her neck. Merle wasn't at all afraid anymore, not in this place, not among these creatures.

"*I am with you,*" said the Flowing Queen. For her this was a homecoming to her kingdom, imprisoned in Merle's body and yet protected by it from the Egyptian sorcerers' poison.

Eft had remained behind in the well, and now Merle was swimming underwater in a swarm of mermaids through the canals. Where were they taking her? Why was she able to breathe inside the glass globe? And why did the mermaids give off a comfortable warmth so that Merle didn't freeze in the icy water?

Questions upon questions, and new ones kept adding to them, an army of doubts forming in her head.

"*I can give you answers to some,*" said the Flowing Queen.

Merle didn't dare speak, for fear of using up the air in the glass helmet.

"*You do not have to say it for me to hear it,*" said the Flowing Queen in Merle's innermost self. "*I thought you had understood that much already.*"

Merle took pains to formulate her thoughts into clear sentences.

"How long can I breathe under this thing?"

"*As long as you want.*"

"Does Eft use it too when she climbs down into the well at night?"

"*Yes. But it was not created for her. It comes from a time when the merfolk still commanded some of the old knowledge, from ancient times when the water was everywhere and the multiplicity of life in the oceans was immeasurable. Some of that knowledge has remained, buried in the old cities under the sea, in deep trenches and folds on the sea bottom. In those days, countless years ago, expeditions were sent out from the cities from time to time, and sometimes they returned with treasures like this helmet.*"

"Is it technology or magic?"

"*What is magic but technology that most men do not understand—not yet or no longer?*" The Queen seemed to be amused at her own words for a moment, then became serious again. "*But you are not entirely wrong. From your point of view it is a work of magic rather than technology. What looks to you like glass is in reality hardened water.*"

"Arcimboldo said that he used the water of the lagoon for producing his magic mirrors. And that he can only work it when you are contained in it."

"He uses a similar process. Externally his mirrors look as if they consisted of ordinary glass. But in truth their surface is an alloy of hardened water. Centuries ago, in the era of the suboceanic kingdoms, craftsmen worked with water the way you humans today work with wood and metal. Another time, another knowledge! Arcimboldo is one of the few who know how to handle it today—even though his cunning is only a shadow of the suboceanic craftsmen's. And Arcimboldo spoke the truth: It was my presence that made the waters of the lagoon what they were. Without me they will not harden."

Merle nodded thoughtfully. All the Flowing Queen's explanations led to one thing. She hesitated before she directed the thought to the Queen: "Are you a suboceaner? One of the old people under the sea?"

The Queen was silent for a long time, while the shimmering fish tails of the mermaids danced around Merle in the darkness.

"I am old," she said at last. *"Infinitely older than all the life under the sea."*

There was something in the Flowing Queen's tone that made Merle doubt her words. What she said was certainly no lie—but was it the whole truth? Merle knew that the Queen at this moment was reading her thoughts and so also knew her doubt. But for some reason the Queen didn't address it. Instead she changed the subject:

"Before, you wanted to know where the mermaids are taking us."

"Out of the lagoon?"

"No, that they cannot do. The danger would be too great. If an Egyptian lookout were to discover a whole swarm of them under the surface, he would follow them. We cannot risk that. Too many merfolk have died at the hands of men already—I will not ask them to now give their lives for their oppressors as well."

Fascinated, Merle's eyes followed the slender bodies swarming around them and safely guiding them through the deep canals. A reassuring warmth came from the hands of the two mermaids who were gently pulling her through the water.

"They are taking us to the Piazza San Marco," said the Queen.

"But that's—"

"The center of the city. I know."

"And there we'll run straight into the arms of the Guard!"

"Not if I can prevent it."

"It's my body, don't forget! I'm the one who has to run away. And be tortured. And killed."

"There is no other way. There is only one way by which we can leave the city. And to do that, someone must help us."

"In the Piazza San Marco, of all places?"

"We have no other choice, Merle. We can only meet him there. There he is . . . well, he is being held prisoner."

Merle choked on her own breath. Right beside the Piazza San Marco lay the old Doge's palace, the former residence of the Venetian princes and today the domicile of the city councillors. The dungeon of the palace was notorious, as was the one under its lead roofs, and the extensive prison on the other side of the canal, too, which could only be entered from the palace, over the Bridge of Sighs. Whoever crossed that bridge never saw daylight again.

"In all seriousness, you intend to free a prisoner from the Doge's dungeon so that he can help us leave Venice? We might just as well jump from the nearest high tower!"

"That is closer to the truth than you think, Merle. Because the one who will help us is not imprisoned in the dungeon but in the Campanile."

"The highest tower in the city!"

"Indeed."

The Campanile stood on the Piazza San Marco and towered over all of Venice. Merle still did not understand what the Queen was driving at.

"But there's no prison in there!"

"Not for ordinary criminals. Do you remember the legend?"

"What's your friend's name?"

"Vermithrax. But you know him rather as the—"

171

"The Ancient Traitor!"

"The same."

"But that's only a story! An old wives' tale. Vermithrax never really lived."

"I think he would be of another opinion."

Merle closed her eyes for a few seconds. She had to concentrate, make no mistakes now. Her life depended on it.

Vermithrax, the Ancient Traitor! He was a figure of myth and sayings; people used his name as a curse. But a living, breathing creature—never! Magic spells and mermaids, all that was reality, a part of her everyday world. But Vermithrax? That was as if someone told her he'd had lunch with God.

Or drunk the Flowing Queen.

"All right," said Merle in her thoughts with a sigh, "you're saying, then, that the Ancient Traitor is being held prisoner in the Campanile on the Piazza San Marco, right?"

"My word on it."

"And we're simply going to go to him, free him, and . . . then what?"

"That you will see when we are with him. He still owes me a favor."

"Vermithrax owes you something?"

"A long time ago I helped him."

"That obviously brought him far—straight into prison!"

"Your mockery, my dear, is superfluous."

172

Merle shook her head in resignation. One of the mermaids looked over to make sure everything was all right. Merle gave her a brief smile. The woman returned it with her shark's smile and turned her eyes forward again.

"If he's been held there all these years, how come no one knows about it?"

"*Oh, everyone knows it.*"

"But they think it's a legend!"

"*Because they want it that way. Perhaps many tales and myths would turn out to be true if only anyone had the courage to look in a well for a golden ball or cut the thorn hedge around a castle.*"

Merle thought it over. "He's really up there?"

"*That he is.*"

"How do you intend to free him? He'll certainly be heavily guarded."

"*With a little luck,*" the Queen replied.

Merle was just about to start an answer when she sensed that the mermaids were rising toward the surface. Above her, Merle could make out the keels of gondolas, rocking gently on the waves; they lay next to each other lined up in rows. Merle knew where they were. This was the gondola landing area at the Piazza San Marco.

The water around the gondolas had taken on an orange glow. *Daybreak,* Merle thought with relief. *Sunrise.* Her mood rose a little, even though the light would make their way to the Campanile more difficult.

"*Too early,*" countered the Flowing Queen. She sounded concerned. "*Too early for sunrise.*"

"But the light!"

"*It is shining toward us from the west. The sun comes up in the east.*"

"What is it then?"

The Flowing Queen was silent for a moment, while the mermaids stopped uncertainly several yards under the surface.

"*Fire,*" she said then. "*The Piazza San Marco is on fire!*"

8

Messenger of Fire

THREE YARDS ABOVE THE GROUND, THE LION OPENED ITS paws and let him drop. Serafin arched his back in the air and landed safely on his hands and feet, thanks to thousands of similar leaps from high windows, roof balustrades, and terraces. He might no longer be a master thief of the Guild, but he hadn't lost his skills.

In a flash he righted himself, slightly bent forward, ready for battle, when two guardsmen pointed their rifles at him and thus banished any thought of self-defense. Serafin expelled his breath sharply; then he stretched and relaxed his muscles. He was a prisoner; it might be smarter not to act too obstreperous. He would need his powers later, when they brought him before the jailer and his torturers. No need to wear himself out on a few guardsmen.

Resignedly he held out both arms so they could put on the hand irons. Yet the men didn't do it but kept him in check with their rifles. Only a boy. Not worth the trouble.

Serafin suppressed a smile. He wasn't afraid of them. So long as he was still outdoors, outside the dungeon, and far from the Bridge of Sighs, that last walk of the condemned, he had no fear. His self-confidence was a protective shield that he held upright in order not to think of Merle—though he wasn't entirely successful.

Nothing must have happened to her! She was alive and safe! These words became a credo that he repeated in his innermost thoughts.

Concentrate on your surroundings! he said to himself. *And ask yourself questions—for instance, why did we land just here and not in the prison courtyard?*

This was amazing, in fact. The lion had thrown him down on the edge of the Piazza San Marco, where the two guardsmen were already waiting for him. Now they were joined by two more. All four wore the black leather of the Councillors' Guard, ornamented with rivets, which gleamed in the light of some fire beacons marking the shore very close by.

The Piazza San Marco—St. Mark's Square—stretched out in an L-shape in the center of Venice. One end was bounded by the water. The entrance to the Grand Canal was very close by, while on the opposite bank the towers and roofs of the island of Giudecca rose against the night sky.

The piazza was surrounded by splendid buildings. The most impressive was the Basilica of St. Mark, a massive monster of domes and towers. Venetian seafarers had brought together the gold ornaments and the statues from all over the world centuries before. Some called it the house of God, others the pirates' cathedral.

Beside the basilica stretched the facade of the Doge's palace, where no prince had reigned for a long time. Today the city councillors determined the policies of the city, with sumptuous feasting and drinking.

Serafin and his guards were situated on the opposite side of the piazza, at the end of a long arcade, not very far from the water. The nearby columns shielded them from the view of the vendors who, careless of the early hour and the darkness, had already begun to set up their meager displays in the piazza. It was a wonder any trade at all was possible after so many years of siege.

Serafin briefly weighed an attempt to run and plunge into the water. But the guardsmen were quick shots. He wouldn't even make half the distance before their bullets hit him. He must wait for a better opportunity.

Meanwhile, he'd figured out why the lion had brought him here and not to the prison courtyard. His guards were under the command of the three councillors who were working clandestinely for the Empire and had betrayed Venice. The other councillors must not learn of it. But a prisoner who was set down in the prison by a flying lion of the Guard would doubtless attract attention. That was exactly what the traitors must avoid, and so they wanted him to go the last portion of the way on foot. That way he would pass through as an ordinary criminal whom the guardsmen had picked up by chance, and especially since some of them would recognize him as a former master thief of the Guild.

And if he cried the truth aloud? If he told anyone on his path, anyone here on the piazza, what he'd seen? Then he could—

His head was brutally jerked backward. Hands shoved coarse material in his mouth, pulled the edges over his chin and nose, and knotted the ends at the back of his head. The gag was so tight that it hurt. Also, the taste was anything but pleasant.

So much for his—admittedly not very well thought-out—plan.

With their gun barrels the men poked him out from the shadows of the arcade into the piazza. A peculiar smell hung in the air. Possibly it was wafting over from the palace dungeons.

Others also seemed to be aware of the stench. A few

vendors looked up in irritation from their work on their stands, sniffing the air and making faces.

Serafin tried to get a look at his guards. But when he turned his head to the side, someone slammed a rifle butt into the small of his back. "Eyes forward!"

The traders' stands were arranged in two rows to form a shopping street that ran from the water's edge toward the Basilica of San Marco. Serafin's path crossed it in the middle of the piazza. Now he could see more clearly some of the men and women who were unloading their goods there in the light of the torches and gas lanterns. There might still be more than an hour left till sunrise; but then they would be all prepared for the buyers.

Serafin observed that increasingly fewer salespeople were busy with their stands. Some had grouped together, gesticulating wildly in the air and wrinkling their noses. "Sulfur," he heard over and over. "Why sulfur? And why here?"

He must have been mistaken. The stench was not coming from the dungeon.

They now passed the second shopping row and left the stands behind them. There were still about a hundred yards to the narrow side entrance to the Doge's palace. Other guardsmen were standing watch to the right and left of it. Among them was a captain of the Guard, with the symbol of the flying lion decorating his black uniform. Frowning, he observed the approach of Serafin and his escort.

The talk of the dealers at Serafin's back grew louder, more excited, more confused. Serafin felt as though there were a sudden trembling in the air. His skin began to prickle.

Someone screamed. A single, sharp cry, not even particularly loud. The captain of the Guard at the gate turned his gaze from Serafin to the center of the piazza. The smell of sulfur was now so strong that it hit Serafin in the stomach. Out of the corner of his eye he saw that his guards were holding their noses; the stench was much stronger for them than it was for him. The gag over his mouth and nose protected him from the worst of it.

One of the men stopped and vomited. Then a second.

"Stop!" commanded one of the soldiers. After a brief hesitation, Serafin turned around.

Two of his guards were doubled over and coughing and spitting vomit on their shining polished boots. A third was holding his hand over his mouth. Only the fourth, the one who'd ordered him to stop, was still holding his weapon pointed at Serafin.

Beyond the guardsmen Serafin saw the groups of dealers spring apart. Some of them were staggering around blindly, stamping through puddles of vomit. Serafin glanced back at the side door of the Doge's palace. There, too, the guards were battling with their nausea. Only the captain was still standing up straight; he was holding his nose with one hand. Alternately he breathed through his mouth and screamed orders to which no one was paying any attention.

In silence Serafin thanked his guards for the gag. He felt sick too, but the material kept the worst of the sulfurous fog away from him.

While he was considering whether this was the opportunity he'd been waiting for, a deep rumbling began. The ground trembled. The rumbling grew louder and increased to a thundering.

One of the stands in the center caught fire. Panicked dealers started a wild Saint Vitus's dance around the flames. A second wall of planking flamed up, then a third. Like the wind, the flames rushed along the shopping street, even where the individual stands stood far away from each other, as if the fire might have reached over to them on its own. There was no wind blowing that could have fanned the flames, yet they kept on spreading. The air was still except for that imperceptible trembling that raised the hairs on Serafin's forearms.

The captain of the Guard looked over at the seething waters, scanning for enemy gunboats or fire catapults. Nothing, no attacker. Serafin followed his eyes to the sky. There, too, only darkness, no sunbarks of the Empire.

The two rows of booths were now ablaze, a flickering beacon that cast the facade of the palace and the basilica in firelight. The screaming dealers made no attempt at all to save their goods. In their panic they fell back to the left and right to the edges of the piazza.

Serafin drew in a deep breath—sulfur, still more sulfur!—and then he ran. He was ten paces away before one of his guards noticed his disappearance. It was the one who'd vomited first; he was just wiping a hand over his lips. With the other he held his rifle and was waving it wildly in Serafin's direction. Now his comrades also looked up and saw their prisoner escaping. One of them pulled his rifle around, aimed, and fired. The bullet whistled past Serafin's ear. Before the man could shoot a second time, a new wave of sickness overwhelmed him. A second man fired, but his bullet came nowhere near Serafin. Way before its target, the shot drilled a scar in the pavement, a golden crater in the flickering light of the fire.

Serafin ran as fast as he could, although he was soon out of breath. Nevertheless, he didn't pull down the gag. He stormed over to the basilica and only dared to turn around once he was there. No one was following him. His guards were busy with themselves, one supporting himself on his rifle like a crutch. Some vendors were also crouching on the ground, far from the flames, their faces buried in their hands. Others had sought protection behind the columns of the arcade and stared numbly over at the flickering inferno that was consuming their possessions.

But the thundering sounded once more, this time so loud that everyone clapped their hands over their ears.

Serafin took cover behind a flower tub, one of the many that flanked the basilica. It would certainly have been more sensible to flee and disappear into one of the alleyways. But he couldn't run away now. He had to see what happened next.

At first it seemed as if all the burning dealers' booths collapsed in on themselves at once. Only then could Serafin see the true extent of the catastrophe.

Between the flickering rows of stands, exactly along the lane between them, the ground had opened. The fissure extended for a length of 100 or 120 yards. It was broad enough to swallow the stands along its edges.

Serafin stopped breathing, incapable of thinking of anything else, not even of his flight. The guardsmen had drawn together, just in front of the gate of the palace, and there they stood like an indignant herd of geese, yelling in wild confusion and waving their weapons, while their captain tried in vain to reestablish order.

Serafin crouched lower behind the flower tub until only his eyes peered over the edge.

Flames were flickering within the fissure. At first they seemed to burn evenly, then they moved gradually from both ends toward the middle, and there they pulled themselves together into an unbearably bright ball of flame.

A figure peeled itself out of the firelight.

It floated upright and bore something around its head that at first sight looked like a halo. The appearance was reminiscent of the representations of Christ on altarpieces, images as he ascended to heaven after his death, the hands crossed gracefully. But then Serafin saw that the figure had the face of a newborn, fleshy and swollen. The halo revealed itself to be a sort of circular saw blade, with teeth as long as Serafin's thumbs; it was attached to the back of the creature's head and appeared to be fused with skin and bone. The crossed hands were gigantic chicken claws, gray and scaly and segmented. The creature's plump body ended not in legs but in something long, pointed, that was wound with wet bandages; it looked like a trembling reptile's tail, which was prevented by the bandaging from thrashing around uncontrollably. The creature's swollen eyelids slid back like night snails and exposed pitch-black eyeballs. Also, the blubbery lips opened, revealing teeth filed to a point.

"Hell presents its greetings," intoned the creature. Its voice sounded like a child's, only louder, more penetrating. It echoed over the whole piazza.

The guardsmen raised their rifles, but the messenger from Hell laughed at them. He was now hovering six feet over the fiery crack, and still its flames bathed him in garish flickering light. Tiny tongues of fire danced up and down along the bandages of his lower body, without burning the material.

"Citizens of this city," cried the emissary so loudly that his voice even carried over the crackling. "My masters have an offer to make you." Green spittle poured from the corners of his mouth, spread itself into the folds of his double chin, collected on his crop, and dropped down below. The heat of the flames evaporated the drops as they fell.

"We wish," he said, and he bowed, with a crooked grin, "to be your friends from now on."

Something shook the world.

Just a moment before, the swarm of mermaids had been quietly floating in the water several yards under the surface. Then an earsplitting bang had sounded, and a shock wave seized them and whirled them around in confusion, as if an angry god had hit the sea with a fist. Merle saw the gondolas over them being thrown against each other like paper boats; some were wedged together, others broke into pieces. Suddenly an invisible force tore her away from the two mermaids holding her hands. First she was sucked down deeper below, and then spat up again into a dense jumble of gondola pieces. She opened her eyes wide, saw the sharp keels rushing toward her like black sword blades, was about to scream—

The round helmet of hardened water took the blow. A hard jolt went through Merle's body, but the pain was bearable. The water was as roiled as if a hurricane were storming over the surface. Suddenly a mermaid's hands grasped her by the waist from behind and swiftly maneuvered her under the gondolas and through to the pilings of a nearby boat landing, only a few yards away. The mermaid's face was strained. It was costing her all her strength to withstand the alternating play of pressure and suction. Merle reached the pier and before she could react, she was catapulted to the surface, in her head the Flowing Queen's scream, *"Hold on tight!"*

She threw open her arms and clung to a slimy pile of the landing stage, slipping down it a little ways until her thrashing feet found a toehold. In no time she clambered up onto the steps, collapsed onto the dock, and coughed up saltwater.

The surface of the water around the landing was still turbulent, but it seemed to be quieting gradually. Merle took off the helmet, saw a hand stretching out to her from the waves in farewell, and threw the sphere into the water. Delicate fingers closed around the edge of the neck opening and pulled the helmet into the depths. Merle watched a swarm of bright bodies shoot away under the water.

"I feel something . . . ," the Queen began slowly, but then she fell silent again almost immediately.

Merle turned and looked over through dripping strands of hair to the piazza.

At first she saw only the fire.

Then the figure. She saw it as clearly as if every detail, every horrible detail, had burned into her retina within the space of a second.

". . . be your friends from now on," she heard the creature saying.

She picked herself up and ran onto the pavement. But there she stood still. She hesitated. Guardsmen were gingerly gathering around the hovering creature, way beyond its reach, yet still close enough to reach it with their bullets.

Hell's messenger paid no attention to the soldiers but directed his words to his audience behind the columns of the arcade and around the edges of the piazza.

"Common folk of Venice, Hell offers you a pact." Luxuriating, he allowed the words to reverberate. The echo transformed his child's voice into a grotesque squeal. "Your masters, the councillors of this city, have rejected our offer. Yet hear it yourselves and come to your own decision." Again he allowed a pause, punctuated by commands of the captain of the Guard. A second, then a third troop hurried forward as reinforcements, accompanied by a dozen riders on stone lions.

"You fear the wrath of the Pharaoh's kingdom," the messenger continued. "And that rightly. More than thirty years long you have warded off the Empire. Yet very soon now the mummy armies of the Pharaoh will launch a great blow and sweep you from the face of the earth. Unless it should happen . . . yes, unless it should happen that you have powerful allies on your side. Allies like my masters!" A pant worked its way through the fleshy lips. "The hosts of our kingdom are a match for those of the Empire. We can protect you. Yes, that we can."

Merle appeared to be spellbound by the disgusting appearance of the fiery figure. More and more people were streaming to the edges of the piazza from all directions, lured by the flames, the noise, and the prospect of a gigantic spectacle.

"*We have no time to waste,*" said the Flowing Queen. "*Quick, run to the Campanile!*"

"But the fire . . ."

"*If you run past on the left, you will make it. Please, Merle—this is the best possible moment!*"

Merle ran. The tower rose in the inner corner of the L-shaped piazza. She had to run along the entire length of the fiery fissure, behind the messenger from Hell, who was floating over the flames with his face toward the palace. The stench of sulfur was overpowering. The messenger continued, but Merle scarcely heard him. At first, going along with the offer from the princes of Hell might seem appealing—but just looking at the nauseating creature was enough to make it clear that such a pact would take the Venetians from frying pan to fire. True, it might succeed in beating the Empire and keeping it out of the lagoon. But what new governors would seize the palaces of the city instead of the sphinx commanders? And what sacrifices would they require?

Half the distance to the Campanile was behind her before Merle realized that the entrance was unguarded. The tower guards had joined the troops in front of the

Doge's palace. At least a hundred rifle barrels were now pointed at the messenger, and new ones were being added every minute. The lions on the ground, all wingless and of granite, pawed angrily, their claws scratching furrows in the pavement of the piazza. Their riders were having trouble keeping them in check.

"From every inhabitant of the city a drop of blood," cried Hell's messenger into the crowd. "Only one drop from each, and the pact is sealed. Citizens of Venice, think! How much blood will the Empire demand of you? How many of you will die in fighting around the lagoon, and how many dead will the hosts of the Pharaoh later claim?"

A young boy, seven years old at the most, tore himself loose from his horrified mother and ran on his short legs past the soldiers up to the messenger.

"The Flowing Queen protects us!" he cried up to the creature. "We don't need your help!"

The panicked mother tried to run after him, but others held her fast. She struggled, flailed around her, but she could not get free. She cried the name of her child over and over again.

The boy looked defiantly up at the messenger once more. "The Flowing Queen will always protect us!" Then he simply turned around and ran back to the others without the messenger's hurting him at all.

Merle had felt a pain in her chest at the child's words. It was a moment before she realized that it wasn't her own feeling. It was the pain of the Flowing Queen, her despair, her shame.

"*They are relying on me,*" she said tonelessly. "*They are all relying on me. And I have disappointed them.*"

"They don't have any idea of what has happened."

"*They will soon find out. At the latest when the Pharaoh's war galleys anchor in the lagoon and the sunbarks spray fire from the sky.*" She was silent for a moment, then added, "*They should accept the messenger's offer.*"

Merle almost stumbled over her own feet in fright. Only twenty more yards to the tower.

"What?" she cried out. "Are you serious?"

"*It is a possibility.*"

"But . . . Hell! I mean, what do we know about it?" And she added quickly, "Professor Burbridge's exploration experiences alone are enough to . . . oh, well, wish them to the Devil."

"*It is a possibility,*" the Queen said again. Her voice was unusually flat and weak. The little boy's words seemed to have touched her deeply.

"A pact with the Devil is never a possibility," contradicted Merle, gasping for air. Running and arguing demanded too much of her stamina. "The old stories have already told us that. Everyone who's gotten himself into something like that is the loser in the end. Everyone!"

"*Again, they are only stories, Merle. Do you know whether anyone really ever tried it?*"

Merle looked back over her shoulder at the messenger in the midst of the flames. "Look at him! And now don't give me wise sayings, like 'You shouldn't judge a person by his looks'! He isn't even a human being!"

"I am not one either."

Staggering, Merle reached the door of the Campanile. It was standing open. "Listen," she gasped, exhausted, "I don't want to insult you, but Hell—" She broke off, shaking her head. "Perhaps you really aren't human enough to understand about that."

With that she gave herself a shake and entered the tower.

Serafin could have seen Merle running on the other side of the piazza, but his eyes were firmly fixed on the messenger— and on the ever-increasing crowd of soldiers gathering in front of him.

The part of the Piazza San Marco directly in front of the basilica was now also filled with people who had hurried there from everywhere to see what was going on. Some might already have heard that a messenger from Hell had appeared, but probably they hadn't believed it. Now they could see the truth with their own eyes.

Serafin kept fighting the urge to just run away. He'd only escaped prison by a hair, and now with every minute he spent here, the danger increased that someone would recognize him and take him prisoner. It was dumb, so dumb to hide here behind the flower tub while the Guard were looking for him!

But the soldiers had other concerns at the moment, and Serafin, too, pushed out of his mind the danger he was in. He must see with his own eyes how this matter ended, he must hear what the messenger had to say.

And now he caught sight of something else: Three men had come out of the palace. Three councillors in splendid robes. Purple, scarlet, and gold. The traitors. The councillor in gold ran up to the captain of the Guard and was talking excitedly to him.

The flames flickered higher for a moment, caressing the body of the messenger with their glowing tongues and illuminating the smile that divided his jellylike features.

"One drop of blood," he cried. "Think carefully about it, citizens of Venice! Only one drop of blood!"

Merle was rushing up the steps of the Campanile. She was gasping for air. Her heart pounded as though it were going to burst in her chest. She couldn't remember when she had ever been so exhausted.

"What do you know about the Ancient Traitor?" the Flowing Queen asked.

"Only what everyone knows. The old story."

"He never really was a traitor. Not the way they tell it."

Merle had trouble getting enough breath to speak; even listening was giving her problems.

"I will tell you what really happened. Back in that time when Vermithrax was turned into the Ancient Traitor," the Flowing Queen went on. *"But first you should know what he is."*

"And ... what ... is ... he?" Merle gasped, as she took step after step.

"Vermithrax is a lion. One of the old ones."

"A ... lion?"

"A flying and talking lion." The Queen stopped speaking for a moment. *"At least he was when I saw him last."*

Merle stopped in astonishment. She had a terrible stitch in her side. "But ... lions don't talk!"

"Not any that you know. But earlier, a long time ago, many years before the revival of the Pharaoh and the era of the mummy wars, all lions could talk. They flew higher and faster than the great sea eagles, and their songs were more beautiful than those of men and of the merfolk."

"What happened?" Merle started moving again, but she wasn't able to manage more than a weary dragging forward. She was still dripping wet and completely exhausted and although she was sweating, her entire body shivered.

"The stone lions and the people of Venice have been allies since time immemorial. No one knows anymore how this happened originally. Perhaps they were creatures from a distant corner of the world? Or the work of a Venetian alchemist? It doesn't matter. The lions served the Venetians

as fighters in many wars, they accompanied their ships on dangerous trade routes along Africa's coast, and they protected the city with their lives. In thanks, their faces soon appeared on all arms and flags of the city, and they were given an island in the north end of the lagoon as a home city."

"If the lions were so strong and powerful, why didn't they build their own city?" Merle could hardly hear her own words, so weakly did they pass her lips.

"Because they trusted the citizens of Venice and felt bound to them. Trust was always an important part of their nature. The wanted it no other way. Their bodies might be of stone, their flight fast, and their songs full of poetry, yet no one had ever seen a lion build a house. They had long accustomed themselves to existence among men who loved roofs over their heads and the comfort of a city. And that, I fear, was the reason for their downfall."

Merle paused briefly at a narrow window that looked out on the piazza. She was alarmed when she saw that the numbers of soldiers and guardsmen had multiplied within the last few minutes. Obviously the councillors had pulled together the uniformed services from all quarters, from the night sentries to the highly decorated captain. There must be hundreds. And they were all pointing their rifles and revolvers, even brandishing unsheathed sabers, at the messenger from Hell.

"Keep on going! Hurry!"

After Merle, sighing, had turned to the stairs again, the Queen continued her story: *"It could not go well. Humans are not created to exist peacefully with other creatures. It happened as it must. It began with fear. Fear of the strength of the lions, of their powerful wings, their fangs, and their mighty claws. More and more, men forgot how much the lions had done for them, yes, that Venice had them alone to thank for her dominant position in the Mediterranean. From fear grew hatred and from hatred the desire to finally subjugate the lions—for do without them they could not and would not. Under the pretext of preparing a festival of gratitude for the lions, they induced them to gather on their island. Ships transported countless numbers of cattle and swine there, slaughtered and gutted. The slaughterhouses had received the order to put everything they had in their storerooms at the disposal of the festival. In addition there was wine from the best Italian grapes and clear well water from the rocks of the Alps. For two days and two nights the lions enjoyed themselves unrestrainedly on their island. But then, gradually, the sleeping potion with which the treacherous Venetians had painted the meat and with which they had laced the water and the wine took effect. On the third day there was no longer a single lion on his feet in all the lagoon; all had fallen into a deep sleep. And again the butchers went to work, and this time they took from the lions their wings!"*

"They . . . just . . . cut off—"

"*Cut off. Indeed. The lions noticed nothing, so power-ful was the sleeping potion in their blood. Their wounds were tended to, so that hardly any died, but then the Venetians left them on the island, in the certainty that the weakened lions were prisoners. Lions fear the water, as you know, and the few who tried to leave the island by swim-ming drowned in the currents.*"

Merle felt such revulsion that she stopped moving again. "Why are we going to such trouble to save the city? After all that the Venetians have done to the lions and the merfolk! They don't deserve anything better than for the Egyptians to invade here and raze everything to the ground."

She felt the Queen smiling gently, a wonderful warmth in the area of her stomach. "*Don't be so bitter, little Merle. You are also a Venetian, just like many others who do not know all that. The treachery against the lions is long ago, many generations.*"

"And you really think people today are wiser?" Merle asked scornfully.

"*No. They probably never will be that. But you cannot condemn anyone for a crime that he himself is not respon-sible for.*"

"And what about the mermaids, then, that they har-ness before their boats? Eft said that they all would die."

The Flowing Queen said nothing for a moment. "*If

*more of you knew of that, if more might know the truth . . .
perhaps then there would not be such injustice any longer."*

"You say that you are no human—and yet you are
defending us. Just where do you get this damned goodness?"

"Damned goodness?" repeated the Queen with amusement. *"Only a human could use those two words in the
same sentence. Perhaps that is one of the reasons I still have
hope for you. But do you not want to hear how the story of
the lions continues? We are almost to the top of the tower.
Before we get there you should know what role
Vermithrax played in all this."*

"Go on."

*"The lions only recovered slowly, and there were fights
among them as to how to proceed. It was clear they were
prisoners on their own island. They were weak, the pain in
their shoulders threatened to kill them, and they were
despairing. The Venetians offered to supply them with food,
as long as the lions were willing to serve them as slaves. After
long debate, the lion folk agreed to it. Some of them were
transported to another island, where scientists and
alchemists began to undertake experiments with them. New
generations of stone lions were bred until finally they
became what they are today—not animals but also not exact
likenesses of their noble forefathers, a race of lions who were
born without wings and had forgotten their singing."*

"And what about Vermithrax?" asked Merle. "Or the
lions who can still fly even today?"

"When the Venetians began their treachery, there was a small troop of lions outside the lagoon, spying out the lands to the east for the humans. On their return home they found out what had happened and they roared with rage. But in spite of their anger there were too few of them to offer the Venetians more than a skirmish. So they decided to go away, instead of choosing certain extinction fighting a superior force. There were not more than a dozen, but they flew the entire way across the Mediterranean to the south, and farther still into the heart of Africa. There they lived for a while among the lions of the savannahs, before they realized they were only accepted out of fear rather than as equals. The stone lions retreated farther, high into the mountains of the hot countries, and there they remained for a long time. The injustice of the Venetians became history, then myth. But finally, several hundred years ago, there was a young lion by the name of Vermithrax. He believed all the old legends, and his heart was heavy with grief at the fate of his people. He made the decision to return here in order to pay the citizens of Venice back for their crime. But only a few wanted to join him, for meanwhile the mountains had become homeland to the descendents of the refugees, and hardly any felt pleasure at the thought of heading off into the unknown distance.

"So it happened that Vermithrax made his way to Venice with only a handful of companions. He firmly *believed that the oppressed lions of the city would join his side and their tormentors would go down in defeat. But Vermithrax started with a serious error: He underestimated the power of time."*

"The power of time?" Merle asked wonderingly.

"Yes, Merle. Time had slowly healed the wounds, and, worse still, had made the lions submissive. The old urge for comfort had overcome the silent, wingless race of lions. They were content with their existence as servants of the Venetians. None of them remembered the life of freedom anymore; the capabilities of their forebears had long been forgotten. Hardly any were willing to put their lives on the line for a rebellion that was not theirs. They obeyed the orders of their human masters rather than rebelling against them. Vermithrax's attack on the city cost many lives and left an entire district in rubble and ashes, but in the long run it was finally doomed to failure. His own people stood against him. It was lions who vanquished him, those lions he would have freed and who now of their free will had become the accomplices of men."

"But then they were really the traitors, not he!"

"All a question of point of view. To the Venetians, Vermithrax was a murderer who had fallen upon them from a foreign sky, killed countless people, and tried to stir up the lions against them. In their view, what they did was completely justifiable. They killed most of the attackers, but they left a few living to allow the scientists to breed a

new generation of flying lions. No one remembered any-more how it had been when the lions had wings, and so it seemed alluring to the humans to have winged lion ser-vants who could carry great burdens or, in war, could attack the enemy from the air, the way Vermithrax had done during his attacks on the city. A small number of new lions arose, a cross of the free, winged lions returning home from Africa and the will-less, loyally devoted slaves of Venice. What came out of it you know: the flying lions on which the bodyguards of the city councillors ride today. You have already made their acquaintance."

"And Vermithrax?"

"For Vermithrax they invented a particularly subtle, cruel punishment. Instead of killing him, they imprisoned him in this tower. He must suffer his fate here in the airy heights, and nothing is worse for a flying lion than to be robbed of his ability to fly. For Vermithrax, who had floated free over the broad grasslands of Africa for many years, it was doubly cruel. And so his will was broken—not through the defeat but through the betrayal of his fellow lions. He did not understand the indifference in their hearts, their doglike devotion, and the carelessness with which they had placed themselves under the command of men against him. The knowledge of this betrayal was the hardest of all punishments for him, and so he decided that it was time to put an end to his life. He waved away the food they brought him, not for fear of poison but in the

hope of dying quickly. But Vermithrax, this rebel and rowdy, was probably the first of his race who had to learn that a creature of stone needs no nourishment. Certainly, stone lions also feel hunger and, indeed, eating is one of their favorite activities—but food is not a necessity of life for them. So Vermithrax is still housed in this tower today, over us, under the roof. From there he can look out over the city and is still a prisoner." The Flowing Queen paused, and then she added, *"To be honest, I do not know what condition we are going to find him in."*

Merle was approaching the last landing. Light fell through a window onto a mighty door of steel. The surface shimmered bluish. "How did you meet Vermithrax?"

"When he led his companions here from Africa several hundred years ago, he thought that he must do the same as men in one thing, in order to be equal to them—he must overcome the inborn fear lions have of the water. His forefathers had become slaves because they could not deal with the waters of the lagoon. They had become prisoners on their own island, and Vermithrax did not want to fall into the same trap as they had. As soon as he saw the lagoon before him, he therefore took heart and plunged into the waters, defying death. But before this challenge even the most daring among the lions must capitulate. The water and the cold numbed him, and he was in danger of drowning."

"And you saved him?"

"I explored his mind as he sank into the deep. I saw the

boldness of his plan and admired his strong will. A plan like that should not have come to grief before it had ever begun. So I called the merfolk to pull him back to the surface and bring him safely to the shore of an uninhabited island. I also introduced myself, and while he returned to himself again and gathered strength, we had long discussions. I will not say that we became friends—for that he understood too little what I really was, and I believe he feared me because I—"

"Because you are water itself?"

"I am the lagoon. I am the water. I am the source of the merfolk. But Vermithrax was a fighter, a hothead with an indomitable will. He showed me respect, and gratitude, but also fear."

The Flowing Queen fell silent as Merle, exhausted, stepped onto the highest landing of the stairs. The steel door of the tower room was three times as high as she was and almost twelve feet wide. Two bolts the length of a man were fastened across the outside.

"How shall we—," she began, but she broke off as the noise on the piazza increased from one moment to the next. She ran to the barred window and looked down.

From here she had a breathtaking view over the front part of the piazza and the fiery fissure opened down its middle, and for the first time she saw that it ended just a few yards before the water. Had the crack continued on into the sea, Merle and the mermaids would have been drawn right into the flames by the suction of the water.

But it wasn't this realization that froze the blood in her veins. It was the catastrophe that was beginning down below.

Three winged lions zoomed down from the roof of the Doge's palace, whipped on by the screams of their riders. The City Council had made its decision: No more dealings with the princes of Hell, once and for all.

Before the messenger could react, the three lions were upon him. Two rushed past him on the left and right, missing him by a hairsbreadth, and were through the flames too quickly for their riders to come to any harm. But the third lion, the one in the middle of the formation, seized the messenger in its open jaws, managing to grab him in the middle of his fat body, snatched him away from the flaming fissure, and carried him off. The messenger shrieked, a dreadful succession of sounds, inconceivably high and shrill for human ears. He was hanging horizontally in the lion's jaws, his bandaged, wormlike lower body twisting like a fat maggot. All over the piazza people cowered; even soldiers let their weapons fall and pressed their hands over their ears.

With the messenger in his mouth, the lion flew a tight curve over the roofs. Then he shot down toward the soldiers gathered in front of the palace. Over their heads, he let the screeching creature drop like a rotten piece of meat.

"Merle!" cried the Flowing Queen in her thoughts. *"Merle, the door! . . ."*

But Merle could not take her eyes off the spectacle. The soldiers sprang apart, just quickly enough to avoid the messenger's falling on their heads. Screaming, he hit the ground among them, robbed of all his loftiness, only a monstrous thing whose gigantic chicken claws thrashed ceaselessly in the air while the worm projection of his lower body drummed in panic on the pavement.

"Merle! . . ."

For a few heartbeats, stillness reigned over the entire piazza. The people were silent, forgetting to breathe, unable to grasp what was happening before their eyes.

Then a triumphant shout went up. The mob had tasted blood. No one thought of the consequences any longer. Almost four decades of isolation and fear of the world outside cleared the way.

Words formed from the shouting, then a shriller, more thundering speech-song:

"Kill the beast! Kill the beast!"

"Merle! We have no time!"

"Kill the beast!"

"Please!"

"Kill the beast!"

The gash the messenger's fall had opened in the formation of soldiers closed in a wave of pressing bodies, flashing blades, and twisted faces. Dozens of arms rose and fell, striking with sabers, rifle butts, and bare fists at the creature on the ground. The messenger's screaming became a whimper, then was silenced altogether.

"The door, Merle!"

When Merle turned around, in a daze, her eyes fell again on the two powerful bolts. So huge!

"You must open it now," entreated the Queen.

From the other side of the steel came the roar of a lion.

9

The Ancient Traitor

THERE WAS NO POINT IN QUESTIONING THE MATTER ANY longer. Merle had undertaken a task. The decision had been made when she drank the contents of the vial, and perhaps even earlier, when she left the lantern festival with Serafin. An adventure—that was what she'd wanted.

It was surprisingly easy to slide back the lower bolt on the door. At first she applied her whole weight against it, but then the gigantic steel bolt slid to the left as if it had just been oiled the day before.

The second bolt was somewhat more difficult. It was fastened a good handsbreadth above Merle's head, too high for her to put her whole weight against it. It took a long time before she finally succeeded in moving it a little bit. Sweat was pouring down her face. The Flowing Queen was silent.

There—the bolt slid to the left. Finally!

"You have to push both doors in," the Queen instructed. She didn't sound really relieved yet. Soldiers were going to be turning up again soon. They had to have Vermithrax freed by that time.

Merle hesitated only long enough to draw a breath. Then she leaned with both hands against the steel doors. With a metallic grinding, the two sides of the door swung inward.

The Campanile's tower room was bigger than she'd expected. In the darkness she could make out the outlines of the jumble of beams that supported the high point of the roof. Far, far above her fluttered pigeons. White bird droppings covered the floorboards like fine snow; it was so dry and dusty that Merle's feet stirred up small clouds with each step. The stale air smelled acrid with the pigeons' excrement. The inhabitant of this attic prison, on the other hand, possessed no scent of his own, nothing that could be differentiated from the stone all around him.

It was very dark. A single shaft of light fell through a window halfway between the floor and the lower timbers of the tower roof. Outside, the sun was finally rising. Bars as thick as Merle's thighbone cut the light into slices.

The walls were covered with a network of steel grating too, as if people were afraid that otherwise the prisoner could tear the walls apart. Even the high roof beams were covered over with gratings.

The light that came in through the window moved like a bundle of gleaming ropes through the tower room and pooled in the center of the floor. On each side of the yellow spot of light, the darkness was total; the opposite wall was not discernible.

Merle felt small and lost under the high arch. What should she do now? she wondered.

"*You must greet him. He must know that we come in peace.*"

"He won't recognize you if you don't speak to him yourself," retorted Merle.

"*Oh yes, he will.*"

"Umm . . . hello?" she said softly.

Pigeons rustled in the joists.

"Vermithrax?"

Rustling sounded. Beyond the sunbeams. Deep in the darkness.

"Vermithrax? I'm here to—"

She broke off as the shadows gathered into something solid, substantial. There was a swishing sound followed by a strong gust of wind—wings that had been folded together, stretching. Then steps, soft, like the padding of cats' paws, not so heavy and jarring as those of the other lions. Animal, and yet placed with deliberation. Cautious.

"The Flowing Queen is with me," she blurted. Probably Vermithrax would laugh at her.

A silhouette, higher than a horse and twice as wide, detached itself from the darkness. In a moment he was standing there in the light, his head bathed in the glow of the morning sun.

"Vermithrax," Merle exhaled softly.

The Ancient Traitor looked at her from proud eyes. His right paw extended murderous claws—and immediately withdrew them again. A flash of quick, hundredfold deaths. Each of his paws was as big as Merle's head, his teeth as long as her finger. His mane, although of stone, rustled and waved at every movement like silky fur.

"Who are you?" His voice was deep and possessed a slight resonance.

"Merle," she said uncertainly. And then again, "I am called Merle. I'm a student of Arcimboldo."

"And bearer of the Flowing Queen."

"Yes."

Vermithrax took a majestic step toward her. "You have opened the door. Are soldiers waiting outside to kill me?"

"At the moment they're all down in the piazza. But they'll be here soon. We have to hurry."

He remained standing there, and now the light illuminated his entire body.

Merle had never before seen a lion of obsidian. He was

raven black, from his nose to his bushy tail. A slight gleam showed on his flanks, the slender back, and his lion's face. The hair of his enormous mane appeared to be constantly in motion, an imperceptible rippling, even when he was holding his head still. His opened wings soared over him, each almost nine feet long. Now he folded them casually together, completely silently. Only a draft of wind again.

"Hurry." Lost in thought, he repeated her last word.

Merle felt impatience rising in her. Lion more or lion less, she didn't want to die just because he couldn't decide whether to trust her.

"Yes, hurry," she said firmly.

"Hold out your hand to him."

"Are you serious?"

The Queen didn't answer, and so with a heavy heart, Merle moved toward the obsidian lion. He awaited her, motionless. Just as she stretched out her hand to him, he raised his right paw in a gliding movement, high enough for it to rest under Merle's fingers.

From one heartbeat to the next a change took place in him. His expression became gentler.

"Flowing Queen," he murmured, scarcely audibly, and inclined his head.

"He can feel you?" Merle asked, without saying it aloud.

"Stone lions are perceptive creatures. He already felt my presence when you opened the door. Otherwise you would have been dead long ago."

Again the lion spoke, and this time his dark eyes fixed on Merle—for the first time, really on *her*. "And your name is Merle?"

She nodded.

"A beautiful name."

There's no time for that now, she wanted to say. But she only nodded again.

"Do you think you can ride on my back?"

Naturally she'd suspected that it would come to that. But now, when a ride on a real stone lion—and in addition, one who could speak and fly—was immediately before her, she felt her knees as weak and fragile as an air bubble.

"You need have no fear," said Vermithrax loudly. "Just hold on tight."

She walked up to him hesitantly and watched as he lay down.

"*Get on with it,*" urged the Queen gruffly.

Merle gave a soundless sigh and swung onto his back. To her amazement the obsidian felt warm beneath her and appeared to fit the form of her legs. She sat as securely as if in a saddle.

"Where shall I hold on?"

"Grab deep into my mane," said Vermithrax. "As deep and as firmly as you can."

"Won't that hurt you?"

He laughed softly and a little bitterly, but he didn't

answer. Merle took hold. The mane of the lion felt neither like real fur nor like stone. Firm, and yet flexible, like the branches of an underwater plant.

"If it comes to a fight," said the lion, looking fixedly over at the door, "bend as deep as you can over my neck. On the ground I'll try to protect you with my wings."

"All right." Merle tried to keep her trembling voice under control, but she succeeded only with difficulty.

Vermithrax began to move and glided to the door in a feline motion. In a flash he was out through the gap between the doors, onto the upper landing of the staircase. He carefully evaluated the width of the stairwell, nodded in satisfaction, and spread his wings.

"Couldn't we run down the steps?" Merle asked worriedly.

"Hurry, you said." Vermithrax hadn't finished speaking when he rose gently in the air, glided over the banister, and plunged steeply into the depths.

Merle let out a high scream as the rushing air pressed on her eyelids and she almost catapulted backward off the lion's body. But then she felt a steady pressure on her back—Vermithrax's tail tip pressed her into his mane from behind.

Her stomach seemed to turn inside out. They fell and fell and fell. . . . The ground in the center of the stairwell was filling her entire field of vision when, with a shake, the obsidian lion righted himself again, swept just over the bottom of the tower, and with an elementally powerful roar, shot out the door of the Campanile, a black streak of stone, larger, harder, heavier than any cannonball and with the force of a hurricane.

"Frrreeeeeeeeeee!" he screamed triumphantly in the morning air, which was still impregnated with the sulfurous vapors of Hell. "Free at last!"

Everything went so fast that Merle scarcely had time to notice any details, not to mention put them together into a logical succession of experiences, pictures, perceptions.

Men were bellowing and running here and there. Soldiers eddied around. Officers shouted orders. Somewhere a shot cracked, followed by a whole hail of bullets. One glanced off Vermithrax's stone flank like a marble, but Merle was not hit.

In a low-level flight, barely nine feet off the ground, the black obsidian lion rushed across the piazza with her. Men parted and ran, screaming. Mothers grabbed their children, whom they'd just let go free after the death of the messenger.

Vermithrax let out a deep growl, like a rockfall in the tunnels of a mine; it was a moment before Merle realized that this was his laugh. He moved with astonishing grace, as if he'd never been imprisoned in the Campanile. His wings were not stiff but powerful and elastic; his eyes not blind but sharp as a hawk's; his legs not lame, his claws not dull, his spirit not dulled.

"He lost the belief in his people," declared the Queen in Merle's thoughts, *"but not the belief in himself."*

"You said he wanted to die."

"That was long ago."

"Live and live and live," roared the obsidian lion, as if he'd heard the words of the Queen.

"Did he hear you?"

"No," said the Queen, *"but he can feel me. And sometimes perhaps even what I am thinking."*

"What *I'm* thinking!"

"What we are thinking."

Vermithrax rushed away over Hell's fissure. The flames were quenched, but a gray wall of smoke divided the piazza like a curtain. Vaguely Merle could see that stone and rubble were filling the crack from below and gradually closing it. Soon only the ruptured pavement would be a sign of the event.

More bullets whistled around Merle's ears, but strangely, during this entire flight she had no fear of being hit. Everything went much too fast.

She looked to the left and saw the three traitors standing in the bunch of guardsmen, in the middle a puddle of slimy secretions that flowed from the body of the messenger.

Purple. Gold. And crimson. The councillors had recognized who was sitting on the back of the lion. And they knew that Merle shared their secret.

She looked forward again, saw the piazza drop behind and the waves rushing under her. The water glowed golden in the dawn, a promising highway to freedom. To their right lay the island of Giudecca, but soon they also left its roofs and towers behind them.

Merle let out a shrill cry, of fear no longer, merely a vent for her euphoria and relief. The cool wind sang in her ears, and finally she could breathe deeply again, a boon after the horrible smell of sulfur in the piazza. Wind stroked her hair, flowed across her eyes, her spirit. She melted with the air, melted too with Vermithrax, who bore her over the sea, forty or fifty feet over waves of liquid fire. Everything was dipped in red and yellow, even she herself. Only Vermithrax's obsidian body remained black as a piece of night that was rushing forward in flight from the light.

"Where are we flying?" Merle struggled to speak over the noise of the wind but wasn't sure she was succeeding.

"Away," cried Vermithrax boisterously. "Away, away, away!"

"*The siege ring,*" the Flowing Queen reminded them. "*Keep in mind the Egyptian heralds and the sunbarks.*"

Merle repeated the words for the lion. Then it occurred to her that Vermithrax had been locked up in the Campanile for so long that he could know nothing of the rise of the Empire and the Pharaoh's war of annihilation.

"There is war," she explained. "The whole world is

at war. Venice is besieged by the armies of the Egyptians."

"Egyptians?" Vermithrax asked in surprise.

"The kingdom of the Pharaoh. He's got a circle around the lagoon. Without a plan we won't get through it."

Vermithrax laughed at the top of his lungs. "But I can fly, little girl!"

"So can the sunbarks of the Empire," retorted Merle, her cheeks reddening. Little girl! Bah!

Vermithrax made a slight turn and looked back over his shoulder. "You make your plan! I'll worry about them back there!"

Merle glanced back and saw that they were being followed by half a dozen flying lions. On their backs sat black figures in leather and steel.

"The Guard! Can you lose them?"

"We'll see."

"Now, don't be reckless!"

Again the lion laughed. "We two will understand each other well, brave Merle."

She had no time to find out whether he was making fun of her. Sharp whistling sounded in her ear—rifle bullets whizzing past them.

"They're shooting at us!"

Their pursuers were about a hundred yards behind them. Six lions, six armed men—no doubt in the service of the traitors.

"Bullets can't hurt me," cried Vermithrax.

"Well, wonderful! Not you, maybe. But they can *me*!"

"I know. That's why we—" He broke off and laughed threateningly. "Here's a surprise for you."

"He's crazy!" If Merle had spoken aloud, her voice would have sounded resigned.

"Perhaps a little."

"Do you think I'm crazy?" asked the lion cheerfully.

Why lie? "You were locked up in that tower for too long. And you know nothing about us people."

"Did you not reproach me for the same thing?" the Flowing Queen interjected. *"Do not oversimplify."*

Vermithrax cut a sharp turn to the right in order to avoid another gun salvo. Merle swayed on his back, but the bushy tip of the lion's tail pressed her firmly into his mane.

"If they keep on shooting so wildly, they'll soon use up their ammunition," she bellowed into the wind.

"They are only warning shots. They want us alive."

"What makes you so sure?"

"They could have hit us long ago if they had wanted to."

"Does Vermithrax know that?"

"Of course. Do not underestimate his intelligence. These aerial maneuvers are harmless games. He is having fun with it. Possibly he only wants to find out if he has forgotten anything in all the years."

Merle's stomach began to feel as if hands were tearing it in different directions. "I feel sick."

"That will pass," replied Vermithrax.

"All right for you to say."

The lion looked back. "There they are."

He'd allowed their pursuers to get closer. Four were just behind them still, but two now flanked them on either side. One of the riders, a white-haired captain of the Guard, looked Merle in the eye. He rode on a quartz lion.

"Give up!" he cried across the gap between them. He was about thirty feet away. "We're armed and outnumber you. If you keep flying in this direction, you'll fall into the Egyptians' hands. We can't allow that—and you can't wish it."

"Which councillor do you serve?" Merle called.

"Councillor Damiani."

"He is not one of the three traitors," said the Queen.

"Why are you following us?"

"I have my orders. And, dammit, that beast under you is the Ancient Traitor, girl! He laid half of Venice to rubble and ashes. You can't expect we'll simply let him go."

Vermithrax turned his head to the captain and inspected him with obsidian eyes. "If you give up and turn around, I'll let you live, human."

Something strange happened. It wasn't the reaction of the guardsman that astounded Merle, but that of his lion. With Vermithrax's words the winged creature awoke from the indifference with which it usually carried out the orders of its human master. The lion stared over at

218

Vermithrax, and for a long moment its wingbeats became more excited. The captain also noticed this and pulled on the reins in irritation. "Quiet, now." His lips formed the words, but the wind snatched them away.

"The lion cannot understand why Vermithrax talks," declared the Flowing Queen.

"Talk with the lion," cried Merle into the obsidian lion's ear. "That's our chance."

Vermithrax abruptly let himself drop down thirty feet. The length of two men now lay between his paws and the churning sea. The closer they came to the waves, the more keenly Merle perceived their speed.

"Now!" roared Vermithrax. "Hold on tight!"

Merle clutched even deeper in his wind-tossed mane as the obsidian lion speeded up with a series of quick wing-beats, then made a 180-degree turn, climbing at the same time, and suddenly flew at their pursuers.

"Lions," he called over the water in a thundering voice. "Listen to me!"

The six winged lions of the Guard hesitated. The beats of their wings slowed. They hung almost motionless in the air; thus their rumps sank down, moving from the horizontal almost to the vertical. Girths and buckles creaked as the six riders were raised up in their security harnesses. None of them had expected this maneuver. The lions were acting on their own will, and the guardsmen were not used to that.

The captain called out to his men, "Aim at the girl!"
But in this position the gigantic heads of their lions were
in the soldiers' way, and none of them could aim with only
one hand and hold on to the mane with the other.

"Listen to me!" cried Vermithrax once more and
looked from one lion to another. He too was floating in
place, his wings beating unhurriedly up and down.
"Once, I returned to this city in order to free you from
the yoke of your oppressors. For a life in freedom. For
an existence without compulsion and orders and battles
that were never your own. As much air under your
wings as you want! Hunting and fighting and, yes,
speaking again, when you wish! A life like that of your
forefathers!"

"*He is using your language,*" said the Flowing Queen.
"*The lions no longer understand their own.*"

"They're listening to him."

"*You have to ask for how long.*"

The six riders bellowed helplessly at their lions, but
Vermithrax's voice easily overrode theirs. "You hesitate
because you have never before heard that a lion speaks the
language of men. But do you not also hesitate because
there is a lion who is ready to fight for his freedom? Look
over at me and ask yourselves: Do you not see in me your
own selves again?"

One of the lions spit sharply. Vermithrax started,
almost imperceptibly.

"*He grieves,*" explained the Queen. "*Because they could be like him and yet they are still only animals.*"

Other lions joined in the spitting, and the captain, who'd grown up with the lions and spent his entire life with them, smiled with the certainty of victory.

"Rebel against your masters!" Vermithrax bellowed angrily. The mood tipped from one moment to the next without Merle's understanding the reason for it. "Don't take orders anymore! Throw your riders into the sea, or carry them back to the city! But let us go in peace."

The lion that had been the first to spit extended the claws of its front paws threateningly.

"*It is no use,*" said the Flowing Queen with a sigh. "*It was worth the try, but it is pointless.*"

"I don't understand," thought Merle bewilderedly. "Why wouldn't they listen to him?"

"*They fear him. They are afraid of his superiority. For many, many years no lion in Venice has spoken. These ones here have grown up in the belief that they are superior to all other lions by means of their wings alone. But now another one comes along who is even more powerful than they. They cannot grasp that.*"

Merle felt the anger rising in her. "Then they're just like us people."

"*Well, well,*" retorted the Queen. She sounded amused. "*Out of the mouths of babes . . .*"

"Don't make fun of me."

"No, excuse me. I did not intend to."

Vermithrax spoke softly over his shoulder. "We're going to have to run for it. Get ready."

Merle nodded. Her eyes wandered over the six guardsmen. None of them had yet succeeded in aiming his rifle. But that would change as soon as the lions were horizontal again; as soon as they flew forward again.

"And—go!" roared Vermithrax.

What happened then went so fast that only looking back later did Merle realize how very close to death she had been.

With a roar and powerful wingbeats Vermithrax sped forward, under and past the formation of six guardsmen, steeply up behind them, upside down over them and away.

Merle squealed in horror. Even the Queen cried out.

But Vermithrax turned over and Merle sat right side up again, clutching his mane, still not quite grasping how she'd survived the last seconds safe and sound. The moment during which the sea had suddenly been over her head had been short and not really dangerous—Vermithrax was too fast and had too much momentum for Merle to have been able to lose her grip. Nevertheless . . . he could at least have warned her!

Again they shot over the water's surface, this time toward the south, where the islands of the lagoon were fewer and small in comparison to those up in the north.

Thus they were voluntarily ruling out a whole string of good hiding places, and Merle earnestly hoped that Vermithrax's decision was the right one. He had a plan, she told herself.

"*I do not think so,*" said the Queen demurely.

"You don't?" Merle did not put the question aloud.

"*No. He does not know his way around.*"

"How reassuring."

"*You must tell him what he should do.*"

"I?"

"*Who else?*"

"So you can blame me when we land in Nowhere!"

"*Merle, this affair depends on you, not on Vermithrax. Not even on me. This is your journey.*"

"Without my knowing what we're planning?"

"*You already know that. First: Leave Venice. And then: Find allies against the Empire.*"

"Where?"

"*What happened in the piazza was at least something like a first spark. Perhaps we can get the fire to kindle.*"

Merle made a face. "Could you please express yourself a little more clearly?"

"*The princes of Hell, Merle. They have offered to help us.*"

Merle had the feeling of losing sight of the ground underneath her again, though Vermithrax was flying in a straight line toward the horizon.

"You really intend to ask Hell for help?"

"*There is no other way.*"

"What about the Czarist kingdom? People say they've also stopped the Pharaoh's troops there."

"*The Czarist kingdom is under the protection of the Baba Yaga. I do not think it is a good idea to ask a goddess for help.*"

"The Baba Yaga is a witch, not a goddess."

"*In her case that is one and the same, unfortunately.*"

Before they could get into the subject more deeply, Vermithrax uttered an alarmed shout: "Look out! Now things are going to get unpleasant!"

Merle quickly looked over her shoulder behind them. Between the black feathered wings she saw the open mouth of a lion, and underneath, its outstretched claws. It shot toward them from behind. The target of its attack was not Vermithrax but she herself!

"They wanted it this way," the obsidian lion growled sadly. He whirled around in midflight, so that Merle once again had to hold on with all her might so as not to be thrown from his back. She saw the eyes of the attacking lion widen, an animal reflection of its rider's—then Vermithrax ducked away under the paws of his opponent, turned half to the side, and slit its belly open with a well-aimed blow of his claws. When Merle looked around again, lion and rider had disappeared. The waters of the lagoon turned red.

"They bleed!"

"Just because they are stone does not mean that their insides are any different from those of other living creatures," the Queen said. *"Death is dirty and stinks."*

Quickly Merle turned her eyes away from the red foam on the waves and looked forward, at the outlines of isolated islands approaching. Behind them lay the mainland, a dark stripe on the horizon.

Soon there were two more lions gaining on them. Vermithrax killed the first just as swiftly and mercilessly as his previous opponent. But the other learned from the carelessness of its companion, avoided the slash of the obsidian claws, and tried to reach Vermithrax's underside. Vermithrax cried out as one of the claws grazed him. At the last moment he avoided the deadly blow. Roaring angrily, he flew in an arc, rushed straight at his astonished foe, closer, closer, closer; did not swerve; did not yield; only at the very last second pulled up and swiped the face of the other lion with his rear paws. Stone splintered, then lion and rider disappeared.

Merle felt tears on her cheeks. She didn't want all this death, and still she could not stop it. Vermithrax had urged the lions of the Guard to let them go. Now the only thing left for him was to defend their very lives. He did it with the strength and determination of his people.

"Three left," said the Flowing Queen.

"Must they all die, then?"

"Not if they give up."

"They'll never do that. You know that."

On one of the three surviving lions rode the captain of the Guard. His white hair was tossed by the wind; the expression on his face betrayed uncertainty. It lay on him to order a retreat, but Merle saw by looking at him that he would not even consider that possibility. Capture. If necessary, kill. Those were his orders. For him there was no alternative.

It went fast. Their opponents had not the shadow of a chance. The captain was the only one left, and again Vermithrax bade him retreat. But the soldier only spurred his lion harder. With a lightning move he shot at Merle and Vermithrax. For a brief moment it looked as though the lion of the Guard had in fact succeeded in landing a hit with its claws. But Vermithrax flew an avoidance maneuver that again brought Merle into a dangerous slanting position. At the same time he began the counterattack. The eyes of his enemy showed comprehension, but not even the recognition of defeat was enough to make him turn back. Vermithrax screamed in torment as he dug his claws into the flank of the other; then he turned quickly so that he needn't look as lion and rider plunged into the water.

For a long time no one said a word. Even the Flowing Queen was silent, stricken.

Below them appeared islands with ruins of old fortifications still standing, defenses that people had erected against the Empire. Today they were nothing more than ribs of stone and steel. Cannon barrels rusted in the sun, frosted by the salty winds of the Mediterranean. Here and there forgotten tent poles stuck up out of the swampy wilderness, hardly distinguishable from the three-foot-high reeds.

Once they flew over a section where the water looked lighter, as if a formation of wide sandbanks extended below it.

"*A sunken island,*" said the Queen. "*The currents carried away its walls long ago.*"

"I know it," said Merle. "Sometimes you can still hear its church bells ringing."

But today the ghosts themselves were silent. Merle heard nothing but the wind and the soft rushing of the obsidian wings.

10

Sunbarks

THE LIGHT OF THE MORNING SUN WASN'T STRONG ENOUGH
to brighten the Canal of the Expelled. Its light flowed
golden over the upper stories of the houses but ended
abruptly twenty-five feet above the ground. Below that,
eternal dusk reigned.

The solitary figure hurrying from doorway to doorway was glad of it. He was on the run, and the half-light
suited him perfectly.

Serafin stole along the fronts of the empty buildings,
continually casting glances behind him to the entrance of
the nearest canal. Anyone following him would appear

there first, or in the sky above, on a flying lion. However, Serafin thought that was improbable. After everything that had happened in the Piazza San Marco, the Guard presumably had more important things to do—following Merle, for instance.

He'd recognized her on the back of the black beast that had charged out of the tower of the Campanile like a thunderstorm. At first he hadn't believed his eyes, but all at once he was entirely certain: It was Merle, without a doubt. But why was she riding on a winged lion, and moreover, the biggest one Serafin had ever seen? The explanation had to be that it was because of the Flowing Queen. He could only hope that nothing happened to Merle. After all, he was the one who'd gotten them into all this. Why did he always have to stick his nose into things that didn't concern him? If they hadn't followed the lions to the house where the traitors were meeting with the envoy . . . yes, what then? Possibly the galleys of the Pharaoh would already be tied up at the Zattere quay and the canals would be reflecting the annihilating fire from the sunbarks.

In the hubbub and panic in the piazza he'd had no trouble ducking into one of the alleyways. However, it wouldn't be long until the Guard had brought in the information that a former master thief of the Guild was living in the house of Umberto. By afternoon, at the latest, soldiers would be looking for him on the Canal of the Expelled.

Yet where else should he go? Umberto would throw him out if he knew what had happened. But Serafin remembered what Merle had told him about Arcimboldo. Contrasted with Umberto, the mirror maker seemed to be a gentler master—even if Arcimboldo, after all the tricks they'd played on him, probably wouldn't be too happy to speak to a weaver boy. It was a risk that Serafin accepted.

The boat Arcimboldo used once a month to take the new mirrors to their buyers lay tied before the door of the mirror workshop. No one knew exactly who his customers were. But who cared about a few magic mirrors? To Serafin, it all suddenly seemed unimportant.

The front door was standing open. Voices sounded from the inside. Serafin hesitated. He couldn't simply walk in there. If Dario or one of the other boys ran across him on the way, it would be the end of all secrecy. Somehow he must manage to catch the mirror maker alone.

He had an idea. He cast a cautious look at the workshop over on the opposite bank. No one was visible behind the windows. Good. There wasn't a soul in front of Arcimboldo's at the moment either.

Serafin detached himself from the shadows of a doorway and ran. Swiftly he approached the boat. The hull was shallow and elongated. More than a dozen mirrors were hanging in a wooden frame construction at the stern. The narrow spaces between them were padded with cotton blankets.

Other blankets lay in a great heap in the bow. Serafin moved a few to one side, crouched down beneath them, and pulled them over his head. With a little luck no one would notice him. He would make himself known to Arcimboldo when they were under way.

It took a few minutes, but then there were voices. Among them, muffled, he recognized that of Dario. The boys brought a last load of mirrors onto the boat, fastened them securely in the support, and then went back on land. Arcimboldo gave a few instructions, then the boat rocked a bit more strongly, and finally it was under way.

Soon afterward Serafin peered out from under his cover. The mirror maker was standing in the other end of the boat and sculling like a gondolier with an oar in the water. The boat slid unhurriedly down the canal, bent away, went farther. Occasionally Serafin heard the traditional warning calls of the gondoliers crying out before they approached crossings. But most of the time it was utterly silent. Nowhere in the city was it so quiet as in the side canals, deeply embedded in the labyrinth of the melancholy district.

Serafin waited. First of all, he wanted to see where Arcimboldo would land. The gentle rocking was so soothing, it made him sleepy. . . .

Serafin awoke with a start. He'd nodded off. No wonder, under the warm covers and after a night in which he'd never closed an eye. The growling of his stomach had awakened him.

When he looked outside through a gap in the covers, he was more than a little astonished. They'd left the city and were gliding over the open water. Venice lay a great distance behind them. They were heading north, toward a maze of tiny swampy islands. Arcimboldo stood unmoving at the oar and looked out, stony-faced, over the sea.

Now would be a good opportunity. Here outside, no one would see them together. But now Serafin's curiosity won the upper hand. Where was Arcimboldo delivering the mirrors? People no longer lived here since the outbreak of the war; the outer islands were abandoned. Umberto suspected that Arcimboldo sold his mirrors to the rich women of society, the way the master weaver sold his garments. But in this wasteland? They'd even left the lion island far behind them. Only the wind whistled over the gray-brown waves; sometimes a fish could be seen.

Another half hour might have passed before a tiny island appeared. The mirror maker headed for its shore. In the far distance, high over the mainland, Serafin thought he saw small strokes against the sky: the Pharaoh's reconnaissance aircraft, sunbarks, powered by the black magic of the high priests. But they were too far away to be dangerous to their boat. No bark dared venture so deeply into the realm of the Flowing Queen.

The island was about 200 yards across. It was overgrown with reeds and scrubby trees. The wind had pressed tree crowns and knotty branches pitilessly toward the ground. In earlier times such islands had been popular locations for isolated villas erected by noble Venetians. But for more than thirty years no one had come here anymore, never mind lived here. Islands like these were little slivers of no-man's-land, and their mistress was the foaming sea alone.

Ahead of the boat appeared the opening of a small waterway, which wound its way to the interior of the island. On both sides the trees grew densely crowded together, their branches touching the water. Multitudes of birds sat in the branches. Once, when Arcimboldo dipped his oar a bit too forcefully, gulls exploded from the brush and fluttered excitedly over the tips of the trees.

After a last bend, the creek fed into a small lake, which formed the heart of the island. Serafin would have liked to bend forward to see how deep the water was, but it was too risky. Arcimboldo might be sunk in thought, but he certainly wasn't blind.

The mirror maker let the keel of the boat run gently onto land. The hull scraped over the sand. Arcimboldo shipped the oar and went onshore.

Serafin rose up just far enough to see over the railing to the shore. The mirror maker was crouching before a wall of thicket. He drew something in the sand with his index finger. Then he stood up, parted the thicket with his hands, and disappeared into it.

In a flash Serafin shook off the blankets and left the

boat. He made an arc around the strange sign that Arcimboldo's finger had left in the sand and ducked between the plants into damp dusk. He could still see Arcimboldo, a vague shape behind leaves and branches.

After a few more steps he discovered the mirror maker's goal. In a clearing rose the ruins of a building that looked like the pleasure palace of a Venetian nobleman. Only the foundation walls were standing now, darkly black with the burned-on soot of a fiercely hot fire that had left the mansion in rubble and ashes a long time ago. The plant world had long since begun to reconquer its kingdom: Broad fans of vines were climbing over the stones; grass was growing from the jagged tops of walls; a tree leaned out of a window opening like a skeleton with a bony arm outstretched in greeting.

Arcimboldo approached the ruin and disappeared inside. Serafin hesitated, then hurried from his hiding place and took cover behind a wall. Crouching, he stole along it to a burned-out window opening. He carefully raised his head until he could just see over the wall.

The inside of the ruin was an intricate labyrinth of hip-high remains of walls. An unusually large amount of stone was gone, entire walls completely toppled. The old roof tiles formed hills, from which vigorous weeds sprouted. A normal fire would never have been strong enough to cause such destruction. This looked more like the result of an explosion.

Arcimboldo strode through the ruins and kept looking alertly around him. The thought that other people could be stopping at the island made Serafin uneasy. What if they saw him? Possibly they might then leave him marooned here, far away from all the boat routes in the middle of the lagoon.

Arcimboldo bent and again wrote something on the ground with his finger. He turned himself around as he did so, so that the sign in the dust formed a circle. Only then did he right himself again, turning toward the center of the ruin.

"Talamar," he called out.

Serafin didn't recognize the word. It might be a name.

"Talamar!" Arcimboldo repeated. "The wish is fulfilled, the magic worked, the agreement kept." It sounded like a charm, like a magic spell. Serafin was trembling with excitement and curiosity.

Then he noticed the smell of sulfur.

"Talamar!"

The stench was wafting over from the ruin. The source was a place that lay hidden behind the blackened stump of a wall.

There was a hissing sound. Serafin hurried away, along the outer wall, until he came to a window that had a better view of the source of the stench.

It was a hole in the floor, similar to a well. The edge was irregularly mounded up, like that of a crater. This is where the detonation that destroyed the building must have occurred. Serafin couldn't make out how deep the opening was. The hissing grew louder. Something was approaching.

Arcimboldo bowed. "Talamar," he said once more, now a call no longer but a humble greeting.

A spindly creature crept out of the hole on long legs. It was almost human but its joints appeared to bend into wrong angles, which gave it a dislocated, morbid appearance. It moved on all fours—and with its abdomen upward, like a child making a bridge. This made its face upside down. The creature was bald and blind. A wreath of thorny iron tendrils lay close around the eye area like a blindfold. A single spiky loop had escaped and ran crookedly over the face of the creature, straight across the toothless mouth. Where the thorns touched the lips, a broad, bulging scar had formed.

"Mirror Maker," the creature called Talamar whispered, and then repeated Arcimboldo's words: "The wish is fulfilled, the magic worked, the agreement kept. At the service of Darkness forever and ever."

"At the service of Darkness forever and ever," the mirror maker said also. With that, the ceremony of greeting was complete. "I am bringing the order of thirteen mirrors according to the wish of your master."

"He is also yours, Mirror Maker." Despite the unclear speech, the tone of the creature sounded wary. Talamar turned himself with a complicated movement of his angled limbs until his head hung over the edge of the opening. He uttered a string of shrill sounds. In a flash a crowd of black creatures no larger than baby monkeys poured out of the sulfurous shaft. They were blind, like Talamar himself, their eye sockets empty. They bustled hurriedly away. Soon afterward Serafin heard them busy at the boat.

"There's bad news," said Arcimboldo, without stepping outside the circle. "The Flowing Queen has left the lagoon. The water has lost its power. I won't be able to produce any more mirrors until she returns."

"No mirrors?" shrieked Talamar, waving one of his spindly arms. "What are you babbling about, old man?"

Arcimboldo remained calm. No single quiver betrayed any fear or unease. "You understood me, Talamar. Without the Flowing Queen in the waters of the lagoon, I can produce no more magic mirrors. The most important ingredient is missing. That means no more orders." He sighed, his first expression of feeling in the presence of the creature. "Perhaps that won't matter anymore anyway, when the Empire takes possession of the city."

"The masters offered you help," whispered Talamar. "You killed our messenger and turned down our support. You bear the responsibility for this yourselves."

"Not we. Only those who rule over us." Arcimboldo's tone became contemptuous. "Those damned councillors."

"Councillors! Fiddlesticks! All nonsense!" Talamar

gesticulated wildly. The movements made him look still more alien, still more frightening; as always he was standing upside down on all fours. Now Serafin noticed that the creature's heart was beating in a small glass box that was fastened to its stomach with straps—a knotty, black muscle like a pulsating heap of excrement. "Fiddlesticks! Fiddlesticks!" he kept thundering. "Mirrors must be here, more mirrors, more mirrors! So my master wishes."

Arcimboldo frowned. "Tell him that I would gladly do business with him. Lord Light was always a good customer." He said it with a cynical undertone that Serafin understood very well, but Talamar didn't notice at all. "But as long as the Flowing Queen is gone, I can produce no mirrors. Besides, the Egyptians will close my workshop—provided they leave one stone on top of another at all."

Talamar was getting more and more excited, beside himself. "That will not please him. Will not please him at all."

"Do you by any chance fear the anger of your master, Talamar?"

"Fiddlesticks, fiddlesticks! Talamar fears nothing. But you shall fear him, Mirror Maker! You shall fear Talamar! And the anger of Lord Light!"

"I can change nothing about that. I have done business with you so that the workshop would survive. Without your gold I must have closed it long ago. And what would have happened to the children then?" The old man shook his head sadly. "I could not let that happen."

"Children, children, children!" Talamar made a dismissive gesture. But then he distorted his raw lips into a grin. The steel vine over his mouth stretched and pulled the loops over his eyes tighter. "What about the children? You have done everything you were told to do?"

Arcimboldo nodded. "I have taken the two girls into my house, as was the wish of your master." He hesitated. Serafin could see that he was weighing whether to continue, but then he proceeded to keep Merle's disappearance to himself.

Talamar's head swung forward and back. "You have fulfilled all the wishes of the master?"

"Yes."

"And they are also the right girls?"

"All was accomplished to Lord Light's satisfaction."

"How can you know that? You have never met him."

"If it were otherwise, you would have told me, wouldn't you, Talamar?" Arcimboldo grimaced. "It would have been a special joy to you if I were to fall into disfavor with Lord Light."

The creature let out a cackling laugh. "You can supply no more mirrors. The master will be angry." Talamar considered briefly and then a horrible grin split his features. "As recompense we will collect on another contract. Earlier than planned."

Arcimboldo had made every effort to show no weakness before Talamar, but now he could no longer conceal his consternation. "No! It's too early. The plan—"

"Has been changed. Effective immediately."

"That lies outside your authority!"

Talamar neared Arcimboldo until his skinny fingers almost touched the drawn circle. "My authority is Lord Light! You have no right to question it, human! You will obey, nothing else."

Arcimboldo's voice suddenly sounded weak. "You want the girl?"

Talamar giggled. "The girl with the mirror eyes. She belongs to us. You have known that from the beginning."

"But she was supposed to remain with us for years!"

"The change has been initiated. That must be enough. Lord Light will take personal care of her."

"But—"

"Recollect yourself, old man: At the service of Darkness forever and ever! You have sworn an oath. The wish must be fulfilled, the magic worked, the agreement kept. You break the agreement if you supply no more mirrors. For that we take the girl. And remember that sooner or later she would have fallen to us anyway."

"Junipa is only a child!"

"She is the mirror girl. You have made her into that. And as far as the other is concerned—"

"Merle."

"In her there is great strength. A strong will. But not so much power as in the other one. Therefore bring us the mirror girl, old man. Your creature, and soon ours."

Arcimboldo's shoulders sagged. He looked at the ground. He was beaten; defeat was inescapable. Serafin felt pity for him, in spite of all he'd heard.

The column of black monkey creatures returned. Every three bore one of the mirrors over their heads; it looked as though they were carrying fragments of the blue sky over the island. One after the other they marched into the hole, along a path that snaked down the walls of the shaft like a screw thread. Soon not a single mirror could be seen any longer. Arcimboldo and Talamar were again standing alone on the rim of the Hell hole.

"At the service of Darkness forever and ever," yelped the creature.

"Forever," whispered the mirror maker dejectedly.

"I will await you here and receive the mirror girl. She is the most important part of the great plan. Do not disappoint us, old man."

Arcimboldo gave no answer. Silently he watched as Talamar crept back into the hole on his angled limbs, like a human spider. Seconds later he was gone.

The mirror maker picked up the bundle of coins that Talamar had left on the floor and took his leave.

Serafin was waiting for him in the boat.

"You listened to it all?" Arcimboldo was too weak to

show real surprise. Heaviness lay in his movements and his voice. His eyes showed apathy and dejection.

Serafin nodded.

"And—what do you think of me now?"

"You must be a desperate man, Mirror Maker."

"Merle has told me of you. You are a good boy. If you knew the whole truth, you could perhaps understand me."

"Tell it to me."

Arcimboldo hesitated, then he climbed into the boat. "Possibly I shall do that." He went past Serafin, tossed the bag of gold carelessly on the planks, and took up the oar. With tired thrusts he maneuvered the boat along the waterway in the direction of the open sea.

Serafin sat between the empty supports for the mirrors. Small, wet footprints covered the wood.

"Will you do it? Hand over Junipa, I mean?"

"It's the only way. It has to do with much more than my life." He shook his head dejectedly. "The only way," he repeated tonelessly.

"What will you tell Junipa? The truth?"

"That she is a chosen one and always was. Just like Merle—and yet in an entirely different way."

Serafin took a deep breath. "You have truly a lot to tell, Mirror Maker."

Arcimboldo held his gaze for a few seconds longer, then he looked out toward the lagoon, far away, farther still than the landscape, farther than this world.

A gull planted itself on the railing beside Serafin and looked at him with dark eyes.

"It has grown cool," said the mirror maker softly.

After a while Merle thought of the mirror again, the mirror in the pocket of her dress. While she held on to Vermithrax's mane with one hand, she pulled it out of her pocket with the other. It had survived the flight from Venice unharmed. The mirror surface of water gleamed silvery in the late-morning light and sloshed back and forth without a single drop leaving the frame. Once a foggy flicker whizzed across it, only briefly, then was gone again. The phantom. Perhaps a creature from another world, another Venice. What would that look like? Did the people there fear the Pharaoh's kingdom just like the inhabitants of this world? Did sunbarks there also circle in the sky like hungry raptors? And were there also a Merle, a Serafin, and a Flowing Queen there?

"*Perhaps,*" said the familiar voice in her head. "*Who knows?*"

"Who, if not you yourself."

"*I am only the lagoon.*"

"You know so much."

"*And yet I possess no knowledge that reaches beyond the boundaries of this world.*"

"Is that true?"

"*Certainly.*"

Vermithrax joined in. His booming voice drowned out the rushing of his wingbeats. "Are you speaking with her? With the Queen?"

"Yes."

"What's she saying?"

"That you are the bravest lion the world has ever seen."

Vermithrax purred like a house cat. "That's mighty nice of her. But you don't have to flatter me, Merle. I owe you my freedom."

"You don't owe me anything at all," she said with a sigh, suddenly downhearted. "Without you I'd probably be dead."

She stuck the water mirror back in her pocket and carefully buttoned it in. A piece of another world, she thought numbly. So close to me. Perhaps Serafin was really right in what he said about the mirror pictures in the canals.

Poor Serafin. What had become of him?

"There ahead!" cried Vermithrax. "Left of us, to the south!"

They had all three known that there would come a moment when they would face the military power of the Pharaoh. Yet so much had happened since they'd left the Campanile, the fears of the siege ring had become distant and diffused for Merle.

But now it had come to the point. In a few moments they would be flying over the ring. It was still a blurry line on the horizon, but it was inching nearer and nearer.

"I'm going to have to climb to a higher altitude," explained Vermithrax. "The air will become thinner, so don't be afraid if you find breathing a little difficult."

"I won't be afraid." Merle tried to give her voice a firm ring.

The gigantic obsidian wings of the lion bore them higher and higher, until the sea beneath them became a uniform surface, without waves, without currents.

Far ahead of them Merle saw the war galleys of the Pharaoh, tiny as toys. The distance could not obscure the fact, however, that the ships had enough destructive power to easily take the insufficient Venetian fleet within hours. The same ships had already—at the beginning of the great mummy war—set loose the first scarab swarms in all the leading countries. The thumb-size eating machines of chitin and malice had rolled inexorably over the continents. First the harvests fell victim to them, then livestock, and finally people. The scarabs were followed by the mummy armies, umpteen thousands snatched from their graves by the high priests of the Pharaoh, furnished with weapons, and sent out to battle, will-less and incapable of feeling pain.

The great war had lasted for thirteen years; then its out-come was decided—as if there'd ever been any doubt about it. The Egyptian Empire had enslaved the people and its armies marched on nearly every street in every part of the earth.

Merle bent deeper over the mane of the stone lion, as if that might protect her from the danger that threatened them from below, from the surface of the sea.

The hulls of the galleys were painted golden, for the indestructible skin of the Egyptian desert gods was also of gold. Each galley had three masts with a multitude of sails. Two rows of long oars projected from the flanks of the hull. In the stern of each ship there was a high construction with an altar on which the high priests in their golden robes performed sacrifices—animals, ordinarily; but also, some whispered, humans.

Small steamboats crossed between the galleys and were used for reconnaissance, provisioning, and pursuit. The siege ring was some fifteen hundred feet wide and extended across the water in both directions to the coasts on either side. There sat diverse arrangements of war machines and foot soldiers, thousands upon thousands of mummy soldiers, who waited, without will of their own, for the signal to attack. It was only a question of days before the Egyptian commanders would receive the final confirmation: Without the Flowing Queen, Venice was helplessly awaiting its downfall.

Merle closed her eyes in despair, before Vermithrax's voice suddenly snatched her from her thoughts. "Are those the flying ships you've spoken of?" He sounded both puzzled and fascinated at the same time.

"Sunbarks," Merle confirmed wryly, as she looked

ahead over the fluttering mane. "Do you think they've discovered us?"

"Doesn't look like it."

Half a dozen slender shapes crossed some distance ahead of them. Vermithrax was flying higher than they were; with a little luck they would pass the barks without the captains noticing them.

The sunbarks of the Empire gleamed golden like the galleys, and since in the sky they were closer than the powerful battleships on the sea, the gleam of their keels was brighter many times over. They were three times as long as a Venetian gondola, roofed over, and provided all around with narrow, horizontal window slits. How many men were behind them was not visible from the outside. Merle estimated that a bark held places for ten people at most: a captain, eight crew members, and the priest whose magic held it in the air. In sunshine the slender flying ships were lightning quick and featherlight to maneuver. When the sky was cloudy, their speed slowed and their movements became clumsy. Finally, by night they were next to unusable.

But on this morning the sun was beaming brightly in the sky. The barks glistened like predators' eyes in front of the hazy background of water and land.

"We'll be over them any minute," said Vermithrax.

Merle's breathing became faster. The obsidian lion had been right: The air up here was thin and caused a pain in her chest. But she said nothing aloud; she was only thankful that Vermithrax was strong enough to take them up so high and over the Egyptians.

"We have almost made it," said the Flowing Queen. She sounded tense.

The sunbarks were now directly under them, glittering blades that soared in wide arcs around the lagoon. No one on board was thinking about the flight of a single lion. The captains were concentrating their attention on the city, not on the airspace above their heads.

Vermithrax sank lower again. Merle felt grateful as her lungs filled more quickly with air. But her eyes were still fixed, spellbound, on the barks, now rapidly falling away behind them.

"Can they see us from the galleys?" she asked hoarsely. No one gave her an answer.

Then they had crossed the ring of warships.

"Made it!" the Flowing Queen exulted, and Merle repeated her words.

"It would have been ridiculous not to," growled Vermithrax.

Merle said nothing. But after a while she spoke again. "Didn't you notice anything?"

"What do you mean?" asked the lion.

"How still it was."

"We were flying too high," Vermithrax said. "Sounds don't travel so far."

"*Yes, they do,*" contradicted the Queen, without Vermithrax's being able to hear her. "*You are right, Merle. Complete stillness prevails on the galleys. Deathly stillness.*"

"You mean—"

"*Mummy soldiers. The ships are crewed by living corpses. Just like all the war machines of the Empire. The cemeteries of the conquered lands offer the priests an inexhaustible stock of supplies. The only living men on board are the high priests themselves and the captain.*"

Merle sank into a deep silence. The idea of all those dead who were fighting in the service of the Pharaoh made her even more anxious than the thought of what lay ahead of them.

"Where are we flying?" she asked after a few minutes. They'd gone around the Pharaoh's armies in a large arc and now finally were gliding toward land.

"I'd like to see my homeland again," boomed Vermithrax.

"No!" said the Flowing Queen, and for the first time she availed herself of Merle's voice. "We have another goal, Vermithrax."

The lion's wingbeats became irregular for a moment. "Queen?" he asked uncertainly. "Is that you?"

Merle wanted to say something, but to her horror, the will of the Flowing Queen overcame her own and suppressed her words. With crystalline sharpness it was borne in on her that from now on her body no longer belonged to her alone.

"It is I, Vermithrax. It has been a long time."

"That it has, Queen."

"Will you help me?"

The lion hesitated, then nodded his mighty obsidian head. "That I will."

"Then listen to what I have to say. You too, Merle. My plan affects each one of us."

And then Merle's lips spoke words that were completely foreign to her—places and expressions and over and over a single name: Lord Light.

She didn't understand what it had to do with her, and she wasn't even sure whether at that moment she wanted to know any more about it at all. For the time being nothing could faze her, nothing frighten her. They'd broken through the siege ring, that was all that counted. They'd escaped the grasp of the greatest army the world had ever seen. Merle's relief was so overpowering that all the Flowing Queen's dark prophecies and plans bounced off her as though they had nothing to do with her at all.

Her heart was beating furiously, as if it wanted to burst in her chest, the blood was rushing in her ears, and her eyes were burning from the headwind. Never mind. They'd escaped.

Several times she looked back and saw the rows of galleys and swarms of sunbarks becoming smaller and finally merging entirely into the blue and gray of the horizon— only grains of sand within a world that was too great to look on any longer at all the wrong that the Egyptians had done to it without taking action.

Something was going to happen, Merle could feel that suddenly. Something big, something fantastic. And in a flash came the awareness that this was only the very beginning, mere child's play in comparison to what lay ahead of them.

And then, very gradually it dawned on her that Fate had prepared a special role for her in all of it. She herself and the Flowing Queen, perhaps even Vermithrax.

Although the Queen was still speaking through her, although her lips were moving unstoppably and articulating strange words, Merle permitted herself the luxury of closing her eyes. A rest. Finally. She wanted simply to be alone with herself for a moment. She was almost surprised that she succeeded, in spite of the guest she was harboring.

When she looked again, they had reached the mainland and were flying over scorched fields, bald mountain ranges, and burned villages, and for a long, long time none of them spoke a word.

Lord Light echoed in Merle's thoughts. She hoped the words would provoke the voice inside her to a reaction, an explanation.

But the Flowing Queen was silent.

Merle's fingers curled more deeply into the lion's obsidian mane—something to hold firmly to, a good feeling among so many bad ones.

In the distance they saw the peaks of mountains, far, far away on the horizon. The land stretching to there from the sea had once been full of people, full of life.

But now nothing was living here anymore. Plants, animals, people—nothing.

"They are all dead," said the Flowing Queen softly.

Merle felt the change taking place in Vermithrax even before she stretched out a hand and felt dampness and realized that the obsidian lion was weeping.

"All dead," the Queen whispered.

And then they were silent, looking toward the far peaks ahead of them.

The Stone Light

Contents

1

Son of Horus

FAR BELOW, THE LANDSCAPE, LOOKING LIKE A SEA OF ashes, steadily passed beneath the wings of the obsidian lion. Vermithrax's pitch-black stone body glided along under the thick cloud cover, almost weightless. The girl on his back had the feeling that if she simply stretched out her arm, she could touch the puffy undersides of the clouds.

Merle was clutching the flying lion's mane with both hands. Vermithrax's long coat was of stone, like his entire body, but for some reason Merle didn't understand, his fur felt soft and flexible—only one of the countless marvels the stone lion concealed in his mighty obsidian body.

The wind at this height was bitterly cold and cutting. It effortlessly penetrated Merle's coarse, calf-length dress. The skirt had hiked up and uncovered her knees, so her legs were exposed to the wind. The goose bumps on her legs had come to seem just as matter of course as her growling stomach and the earaches she was having from the height and the cold air. At least her heavy leather shoes protected her feet from the cold, a feeble consolation considering their desperate situation and the empty countryside that was moving along a hundred yards below them.

Two days had passed since Merle had escaped from her native city of Venice on Vermithrax's back. Together they'd broken through the Empire's siege ring and were flying north. Since then they'd seen nothing beneath them but ravaged wilderness. Empty, ruined cities of jagged remnants of burned-out walls; abandoned farms, many burned down or ground to dust under the heels of the Egyptian army; villages in which only stray cats and dogs were still alive; and, of course, those places where the soil looked as if it were turned inside out, churned up, and devastated by powers that were a thousand times greater than any ox-drawn plow.

Only Nature resisted the brutal power of the Empire, and so it happened that many fields were sparkling with springtime green, blooming lilac bushes rose over the deserted walls, and trees wore dense, succulent foliage.

The strength and life in all these plants stood in mocking contrast to the abandoned farms and settlements.

"How much farther?" Merle asked glumly.

Vermithrax's voice was deep as a well shaft. "Before another full day passes."

She said nothing in reply but waited for the ghostlike voice inside her to make itself known, as it usually did when Merle needed comfort or just a few cheering words.

But the Flowing Queen was silent.

"Queen?" she asked boldly. Vermithrax had long ago gotten used to the fact that Merle occasionally spoke with someone he could neither see nor hear. He could easily tell when her words weren't addressed to him.

"Did she answer?" he asked after a while.

"She's thinking," came out of Merle's mouth, but it wasn't she who spoke the words. The Flowing Queen had once again made use of Merle's voice for herself. For the time being, Merle tolerated this rudeness, even though she was silently angry about it. At the moment she was glad that the Queen was at least showing a sign of life.

"What are you thinking about?" Merle asked.

"About you humans," the Queen said and then changed into her mind-voice, which only Merle could hear. *"How it could come to this. And what would bring a man like the Pharaoh to . . . do something like this."* She didn't have a hand of her own to gesture toward the wasteland on the ground, but Merle knew very well what she meant.

"Is he one, then? A human being, I mean? After all, he was dead until the priests brought him to life again."

"The mere fact that a man rises from the dead still need not mean that he engulfs all the countries in a war such as the world has not seen for a long time."

"For a long time?" Merle mused. "Was there ever a war in which someone succeeded in conquering the entire world?" Except for Venice, whose hours were numbered, only the Czarist kingdom had withstood the attacks of the Empire for three decades. All other countries had long since been overrun by mummy armies and scarab swarms.

"People tried. But that was thousands of years ago, in the time of the suboceanic cultures."

The suboceanic cultures. The words resounded in Merle's ears long after the Queen's voice was silent. After she'd freed the Flowing Queen from the hands of an Egyptian spy, she'd first assumed that the strange being was a survivor of the suboceanic kingdoms, which, according to the stories, had once been inconceivably powerful. But the Queen had denied that, and Merle believed her. It would have been too simple.

No one was able to see through a being like her completely, not even Merle, who was closer to the Queen than anyone else since their joint flight from Venice.

Merle snatched herself from her thoughts. Thinking about Venice meant thinking about Serafin, and right now that simply hurt too much.

She peered out over Vermithrax's black mane. Before them rose the rocky crags of high mountains. The landscape had been hilly for some time, and now it was rising ever more steeply. Soon they would reach the mountains. Supposedly their destination lay only a little bit beyond them.

"There's snow down there!"

"What did you expect?" asked the obsidian lion with amusement. "Look how high we are here. It's going to be quite a bit colder before we get to the other side."

"I've never seen snow," Merle said thoughtfully. "People say there hasn't been any real winter for decades. And no summer. Spring and fall just melt into one another somehow."

"Apparently nothing changed at all while I was locked up in the Campanile." Vermithrax laughed. "The humans are still always complaining from morning till night about the weather. How can so many heads busy themselves with so many thoughts about something they can't influence at all?"

Merle couldn't think of an answer. Again the Queen made use of her voice. "Vermithrax! Back there, at the foot of this mountain . . . what is that?"

Merle swallowed, as if she could just choke down the unwelcome influence that was controlling her tongue. She immediately felt the Queen withdraw from her mouth, a feeling as if, for the blink of an eye, all the blood left her tongue and her cheeks.

"I see it too," she said. "A flock of birds?"

The lion growled. "Quite large for a flock of birds. And much too massive."

The dark shadow floating like a cloud over part of the mountain's flank was sharply outlined. It might be several thousand yards away yet, and in comparison to the huge rock giant in the background, the thing darkly silhouetted against the slope didn't seem particularly impressive. But even now she suspected that this impression would change if they were to come nearer to it. Or if the thing came to them.

"Hang on!" cried Vermithrax.

He lost altitude so abruptly that Merle felt as if her insides were being expelled through her ears. For a moment she felt like throwing up. She was about to snarl at the obsidian lion when she saw what had prompted him to undertake the maneuver.

A handful of tiny dots were whizzing around the large silhouette, bright spots that glowed in the light of the setting sun as if someone had sprinkled gold dust over a landscape painting.

"*Sunbarks,*" said the Queen in Merle's mind.

Now they've got us, Merle thought. They've blocked our way. Who would have guessed we're still so important to them? Granted, she was the bearer of the Flowing Queen, the protecting spirit who lived in the waters of the lagoon and who saved Venice from the Egyptian conquerors. But that was past now. The city was irrevocably in the tyrants' power.

"*It must be coincidence that we are meeting them,*" said the mind-voice of the Flowing Queen. "*It does not look as though they have noticed us.*"

Merle had to agree she was right. The Egyptians couldn't have overtaken them so quickly. And even if they'd succeeded in alerting a part of their armed forces, they certainly wouldn't have been waiting for the fugitives so very visibly on the snow field of a glacier. "What are they doing here?" Merle asked.

"*The big thing must be a collector. One of their flying mummy factories.*"

Vermithrax now shot away over the top of a dense forest. Occasionally he had to avoid towering firs and spruces. But otherwise he was heading straight toward their adversary.

"Perhaps we should avoid it," Merle said, trying not to sound too anxious. But in truth her heart was racing. Her legs felt as if they belonged to a rag doll.

So that was a collector. A real, actual collector. She hadn't ever seen one of the Egyptian airships with her own eyes, and she would gladly have missed out on the experience. She knew what the collectors did, even *how* they did it, and she was only too painfully aware that each collector was under the command of one of the dreaded sphinx commandants of the Pharaoh.

Quite a dark outlook.

And yet it got worse.

"That is really a *crowd* of sunbarks flying around it," said Vermithrax tonelessly.

Merle, too, could now make out that the golden dots were nothing other than the smallest flying units of the imperial fleet. Each of the sickle-shaped sunbarks had places for a troop of mummy soldiers, besides the high priest whose magic held the bark in the air and in motion. If the Egyptians should become aware of Vermithrax and his rider, the setting of the sun would be their only chance: The darker it grew, the clumsier the barks became until, at night, they finally became completely unusable.

But the side of the mountain was still flooded with bloody red; in the west, the sun was only half sunk behind the peak.

"Avoid it," said Merle again, this time more urgently. "Why aren't we making a wide arc around it?"

"If I am not mistaken," said the Queen through Merle's mouth, for the words were also addressed to the lion, "this collector is on the way to Venice, to take part in the great battle."

"Assuming there is one," said Merle.

"They will give up," said Vermithrax. "The Venetians were never especially courageous. Present company excepted."

"Thank you very much."

"*Vermithrax is right. There will probably not be any fighting at all. But who knows how the armies of the Empire will fall on the city and its inhabitants? Venice has led the Pharaoh around by the nose for more than thirty years, after all.*"

"But that was you!"

"*To save you.*"

They had now come to within just a few hundred yards of the collector. The sunbarks were patrolling at a great height over them. The barks glowed red as the light of the sinking sun caught their golden armor. Merle's only hope was that from above, the obsidian lion was invisible in the shadows among the treetops.

The collector was massive. It was in the form of a pyramid whose top point was cut off. Framed by a crenellated battlement, there was an extensive observation platform with several superstructures, which were arranged so that they were higher toward the middle and created a kind of point. Merle made out tiny figures behind the battlement.

The forest grew thinner as the land rose slightly. Now they could make out deep furrows in the forest floor, a labyrinth of protective trenches, which still, after all the years, had not been completely grown over. At one time a bitter battle had raged in this place.

"*Here men are buried,*" said the Queen suddenly.

"What?"

"The land over which the collector hovers—there must have been a large number of dead buried there during the war. Otherwise it would not be hovering so steadily in one place."

In fact, the massive body of the mummy factory was hanging completely motionless over a meadow on which the high grass bent in the evening wind. In another time, this could have been an idyllic picture, a place of rest and peace. But today the collector cast its threatening shadow over it. It floated just high enough over the meadow for a Venetian palazzo to have found room under it.

"I'm going to land," said Vermithrax. "They'll see us without the tree cover."

No one contradicted him. The obsidian lion set himself down at the edge of the forest. Merle felt a hard jolt as his paws touched the ground. Now for the first time she became conscious of how very much her backside hurt from the long ride on the stone lion's back. She tried to move, but it was almost impossible.

"Do not dismount," said the Queen. *"We might have to take off again in a hurry."*

Lovely prospect, Merle thought.

"It is beginning."

"Yes . . . I see that."

Vermithrax, who knew no more about the Empire and its methods than what Merle and the Queen had told him after they freed him from his tower prison in the middle of the Piazza San Marco, let out a deep snarl. His mane stiffened. His whiskers suddenly stood out as straight as if they'd been drawn with a ruler.

It began with the leaves of the trees around them withering so fast that it seemed as if the autumn had decided to carry out its work a few months too early and within a few minutes. The foliage turned brown, curled, and gently fell from the branches. The fir tree under which they'd taken shelter lost all its needles, and from one moment to the next, Vermithrax and Merle were covered with a brown mantle.

Merle shook herself and blinked up toward the collector. They weren't directly beneath it, Heaven forbid, but they were near enough to be able to see its entire underside.

The gigantic surface was suddenly covered with a network of crisscrossing dark yellow glowing stripes, with multifold angles and following no recognizable pattern. A round area in the center, half as large as the Piazza San Marco, was all that remained dark. Merle had to clutch Vermithrax's obsidian mane more tightly when suddenly the ground trembled, as in a strong earthquake. Very close by, several trees were uprooted and tipped over, tearing out other trees as they fell and crashing to the ground in the midst of a thick cloud of flying dirt and needles. The air was so filled with dry splinters and bits of the withered foliage that, for a moment, Merle found it hard to breathe.

When her eyes stopped tearing, she saw what had happened.

The field over which the mummy factory hovered was gone. The soil was churned up as if by an army of invisible giant moles. The glowing net was no longer attached to the underside of the collector, but was unraveled into an immense number of glittering ropes of light and hooks, no one formed like the next. They were all aimed downward, approaching the ravaged ground and pulling something out of it.

Bodies. Gray, fallen-in corpses.

"So that's how they get their mummy soldiers," whispered Vermithrax, and his voice was faint with the horror of it.

Merle pulled at his mane. She had averted her eyes, could no longer look at what was taking place before her. "Let's get out of here!"

"*No!*" said the Flowing Queen.

But Vermithrax had the same feelings as Merle. Just get away from there. Away from the suction of the collector before they themselves ended on one of the glittering hooks and were pulled up into the mummy factory, where slaves and machines would turn them into something that was satisfied by a *different* kind of life, of submissiveness and obedience and the will to kill.

"Hold on!" he roared. The Queen objected loudly in Merle's voice, but the obsidian lion paid no attention to her. In no time his wings raised them into the air. In a daring stratagem, he turned to the east, against the fast-approaching darkness. At the same time he shot forward, careless of all the sunbarks and high priests who might become aware of them at this moment.

Merle clung so tightly to Vermithrax's coat that her arms vanished up to the elbows in his mane. She bent deep over his neck, to offer less wind resistance, but also to avoid the shots of the Egyptians. She hardly dared look up, but when she finally did, she saw that half a dozen sunbarks had detached from their formation around the collector and taken up the chase.

Vermithrax's plan was as simple as it was suicidal. He had surmised that in the massive body of the collector there must be weapons that could easily shoot a flying lion from the sky. But if he got close to the vicinity of the sunbarks, the commanders on board the collector would perhaps think twice about shooting at a target in the midst of their own people.

It wouldn't work, Merle thought. Vermithrax's plan would have been a good one if they were dealing with ordinary opponents like the ones the winged lion knew from his own times, when he was not yet a prisoner of the Venetian City Guard. But the sunbarks were occupied by mummy soldiers, each of them only too easily replaced, and they would even sacrifice one or two priests.

Vermithrax cursed when he came to the same conclusion.

Only a little way ahead of them, a wooden bolt the length of a man whizzed through the air past them, fired from one of the ports in the collector body. The mummy factory itself was too cumbersome for a pursuit, but its weapons were vicious and long-range.

Merle felt sick, worse than ever as Vermithrax kept doubling back and maneuvering turns that she would not have believed possible for his heavy stone body. Up and down, often in such quick succession that Merle soon lost any feeling for over and under. Even the Queen was silent with concern.

Once, Merle looked back. They were now almost at the level of the observation platform. Several figures stood behind the battlement. Merle could see their robes and their grim faces. High priests, she guessed.

Among them was one who caught her eye especially. He was a good head taller than the others and wore a ballooning cloak that looked as if it were woven of pure gold. His hairless skull was covered with a network of gold-colored filaments, like a jeweler's engraving on a brooch.

"The Pharaoh's vizier," whispered the Flowing Queen in her head. *"His name is Seth. He is the highest priest of the cult of Horus."*

"Seth? Isn't that the name of an Egyptian god?"

"The priests of Horus have never been known for their humility."

Merle had the feeling that the eyes of the man were boring into her forehead across the distance. For a heartbeat it seemed to her that the Queen groaned in pain inside her.

"Everything all right?" she asked.

"*Look away! Please . . . not into his eyes.*"

At the same moment a whole swarm of bolts rushed over their heads. Two of them struck sunbarks that were quite close to the lion. Smoke billowed from one as it went down in a tailspin of jerky spirals. The other fell like a stone and smashed on the ground in showers of steel splinters. The rest of the sunbarks pulled back a little so as not to be caught in the hail of shots from the collector.

This was the chance Vermithrax had been waiting for.

With a wild cry he plunged down. On his back, Merle screeched as the ground shot up toward them. She already saw them lying smashed beside the debris of the bark.

But a few yards over the rocks, Vermithrax pulled out of the dive, swept across the ground and the edge of a wall of rock, then sank down deep again, behind the wall and out of the collector's line of fire. Now they had to deal only with the four remaining barks, which would follow them over the rock wall at any moment.

The Flowing Queen had recovered from the penetrating eyes of the vizier. "*I know now why I chose Vermithrax for our flight.*"

"Because you had no other choice." Merle hardly

heard her own words; the headwind tore them from her lips like scraps of paper.

The Queen laughed in her mind, which was a strange feeling, for it seemed to Merle as though she herself was laughing, entirely without her own effort.

The lion flew across a labyrinth of ravines before he discovered one that was broad enough to hide in. Shots were striking to the right and left of them, steel bullets this time, fired from barrels in the noses of the sunbarks. But none came close enough to them to be dangerous. Stone fragments were raining on them from all sides. Sparks flew when ricocheting shots skidded over the rock walls and ate furrows in the stone.

The ravine was not deep, with hardly more than twenty feet or so to the surface level. It narrowed as they went farther into it, the walls just far enough apart so that Vermithrax could fly through at a lower height. Two sunbarks had followed them into the rocky labyrinth, while the other two were gliding over the maze of ravines and lurking, in case the obsidian lion surfaced again. It wasn't difficult for Vermithrax to fly around sharp corners and curves, while the long sunbarks had to slow down before each bend in order not to crash against the rocks.

Beneath them the gorge filled with water, the blind arm of a brook or mountain lake. Vermithrax followed its course, and soon they were racing over the surface of a river. The rock walls were farther apart now, offering the sunbarks enough room to maneuver. But Vermithrax's lead was still too big, and the two barks overhead had not yet discovered the ravine.

"*We cannot keep flying so low if we want to get to the other side of the mountain.*"

"We have to survive first, don't we?"

"*I am only trying to plan things, Merle. Nothing else.*"

It was hard for Merle to concentrate. Not at this speed, not with death hanging over her. They might have escaped the collector, but the sunbarks were still after them.

"Vermithrax!" She bent toward the lion's ear and tried to talk over the noise of the wind. "What do you have in mind now?"

"Sundown," he replied shortly. His tone revealed that he was more exhausted than she'd realized. In fact, it hadn't occurred to her at all that a creature like Vermithrax could also just run out of breath.

The river under them grew faster. Merle saw that the water no longer glowed red, as it had a few minutes before, but only reflected the shadowy rock walls. Also, the sky had lost its glow and changed to violet blue.

She felt like screaming with relief. Vermithrax was right, his plan had worked. He'd outsmarted the Egyptians. The sunbarks had vanished. Merle imagined the sickle-shaped flying ships going back to the collector at a creeping pace, crippled by the failing daylight, as useless as pieces of iron salvage.

The stream became faster, wilder, and above all louder, and soon a crown of white foam rose up before them, spreading across the entire span of the water. Behind it there was nothing but darkness.

With a jubilant cry, Vermithrax raced out over the waterfall, which crashed to the ground about a hundred yards below. The obsidian lion maintained his level so that Merle could look out over the country at the foot of the mountain, over forests and fields slumbering in the darkness of the falling night. The lion slowed his wing beats, but he continued flying forward unswervingly. Merle stared silently at the landscape passing below for a long time before she again addressed the Queen.

"What do you know about this Seth?"

"Not much. Followers of the cult of Horus recalled the Pharaoh to life over thirty years ago. Since then they appoint the high priests of the Empire. That means that Seth has been their leader since then."

"He didn't look that old."

"No. But what difference does that make?"

Merle thought about how she could make clear to someone who was timeless like the Queen that a human being's exterior should give information about his age. When it didn't, it could mean two things: Either the person was not showing his true face or, though he might look like a human, in reality he was not one. At least not a mortal.

When Merle showed no sign of answering the question,

the Queen went on: *"The Horus priests have much power. In truth, they are the ones who steer the fortunes of the Empire. The Pharaoh is only their puppet."*

"That would mean that Seth, if he is the leader of the priests of Horus and in addition the vizier of the Pharaoh, that he also—"

"Is the true ruler of Egypt. Indeed."

"And the world."

"Unfortunately."

"Do you think we'll meet him again?"

"You should pray that it does not happen."

"Pray to the Flowing Queen? The way all Venice is probably doing right now?" She was immediately sorry for the words, but it was already too late.

In the hours that followed, the Queen was silent and withdrew herself into the farthest corner of Merle's consciousness, wound into a cocoon of her cool, alien, godly thoughts.

They crossed the mountains a little bit farther to the east without meeting an adversary again.

At some point, it must have been after midnight, they saw the other side before them in the gray icy light of the stars, and now finally Vermithrax allowed himself a stop to rest. He landed at the top of an unapproachable needle of rock, just wide enough for him to lie down and for Merle to climb from his back.

She ached all over. For a while she despaired of ever being able to walk again at all without every step, every bone, every muscle hurting.

In the darkness she kept looking for signs of pursuers, but she could discover nothing suspicious. Only a predatory bird circled in the distance, a falcon or a hawk.

No sound came from the broad lands at the foot of the mountain, not once the cry of an animal or the fluttering of the wings of birds. Her heart shrank, and apprehensiveness overwhelmed her. With alarming certainty she realized that there was nothing alive down there anymore. No human beings, no animals. The Egyptians had even abducted the dead, to man their galleys, sunbarks, and war machines.

She lowered herself down at the edge of the tiny plateau and stared out into the night, lost in thought. "Do you think Lord Light will help us?" It was the first time in hours that she'd addressed the Queen. She didn't really expect an answer.

"*I do not know. The Venetians treated his messenger badly.*"

"But they didn't know what they were doing."

"*Do you think that makes a difference?*"

"No," said Merle dejectedly. "Not really."

"*Exactly.*"

"All the same, Lord Light did offer to support Venice in the fight against the Empire."

"That was before the Body Guard killed his messenger. Besides, it is not in the nature of humans to enter into a pact with Hell."

Merle grinned mirthlessly. "I've heard entirely different stories about that. You really don't know much about us humans."

She leaned back and closed her eyes.

In the year 1833, the English explorer Charles Burbridge had discovered that Hell was anything but an old wives' tale. It existed as a real, subterranean place in the center of the earth, and Burbridge had led a series of expeditions there. He was the only one to return from the last one. Many of the things he saw and experienced were documented and, up to the beginning of the great war, were taught in school. But there was no doubt that this was only a fragment of his actual discoveries. According to the rumors, the remainder were too dreadful, too shocking, for him to reveal them in public. Therefore, after Burbridge's last expedition, no one else had dared the descent. Only since the outbreak of the war had new signs of life come up from below, which finally climaxed with Lord Light, the storied ruler of Hell, offering the Venetians his support in the battle against the Pharaoh. But the City Council, in its arrogance and self-satisfaction, refused his help. Merle herself had become a witness when Lord Light's messenger was murdered in the Piazza San Marco.

And now Merle, the Flowing Queen, and Vermithrax were on their way to ask Lord Light personally for help, in the name of the people of Venice, not its city councillors. But it was questionable whether—even if their mission were successful—they'd be in time. And who could say anyway that Lord Light wouldn't do exactly the same to them as had been done to his messenger in Venice?

But the worst thing was that there was nothing else left for them to try except to climb down into the abyss on Burbridge's trail. And none of them, not even the Queen, had any idea of what they would find down there.

Merle opened her eyes and blinked over at the sleeping Vermithrax. She was dog tired herself, but she was still too excited to be able to rest.

"Why is he helping us?" she whispered thoughtfully. "I mean, you're the Flowing Queen and somehow a part of Venice—or the other way around. You want to protect what belongs to you. But why Vermithrax? He could simply fly back to his relatives in Africa."

"*Assuming he would still find them there. The Empire has not only spread to the north.*"

"Do you think the other talking lions are dead?"

"*I do not know,*" said the Queen sadly. "*Perhaps. Possibly they have just moved farther on, so far away that the Egyptians will not find them for the time being.*"

"And Vermithrax knows that?"

"*Perhaps he surmises it.*"

"Then we're all he has, right? His only friends." Merle stretched out a hand and gently stroked one of the lion's stone paws. Vermithrax purred gently, turned on his side, and stretched all four feet toward her. His jowls fluttered each time he took a breath, and Merle could see that his eyes were twitching under the lids. He was dreaming.

She pulled her dress more closely around her body to protect her from the cool wind, then snuggled up close to Vermithrax. Again he purred blissfully and began to snore softly.

The Queen is here, she thought, because she and Venice belong together in some sort of way. One can't exist without the other. But what about me? Really, what am I doing here?

Her closest friends, Junipa and Serafin, her master Arcimboldo, and the mermaid Eft, they were all still in Venice, where they were exposed to the dangers of the Egyptian invasion. Merle herself was an orphan. She'd been found in a basket on the canals as an infant and had grown up in an orphanage. Today the thought that she had no parents who might have been concerned about her was, for once, a comforting one.

Still, it wasn't that simple. Sometime she'd find out what sort of people her mother and her father had been. Sometime, most certainly.

Lost in thought, she pulled the magic hand mirror

from her pocket. The surface consisted of water that could never leave the mirror, no matter how she held it. Sometimes, when Merle thrust her arm inside it, she could feel her fingers enclosed by those of a gentle, warm hand. The water mirror had lain beside her in the basket when she'd been found. It was the only thing that bound her to her parents. The only clue.

There was something else in the mirror: a milky veil, which constantly flitted over the surface. The phantom had escaped from one of Arcimboldo's magic mirrors and settled itself in the small hand mirror. Merle would have been glad to establish contact with it. She only wondered how. Serafin had told her that the phantoms in Arcimboldo's mirrors were humans from another world who'd succeeded in crossing to this one—without, however, realizing that they appeared here only as phantoms, blurry hazes trapped inside mirrors.

Serafin . . . Merle sighed inaudibly.

She'd hardly begun to know him and then they were separated by the Body Guard of the city councillors. They'd spent only a few hours together, wearing, dangerous hours, in which they'd snatched the crystal vial with the essence of the Flowing Queen from the Egyptian spy. And although they knew so little of each other, she missed him.

She fell asleep with the thought of his smile, of the roguishness in his eyes.

In her dreams it seemed to her that she heard the scream of a falcon. She was awakened briefly by a gentle draft of air on her face, the scent of feathers, but there was nothing anywhere near them, and if there had been, it concealed itself in the darkness again.

2

The Master Thief

THE TOWER CLOCKS OF VENICE HAD STRUCK MIDNIGHT long ago. Deep darkness lay over the city and the waters of the lagoon. The streets were empty, nothing was stirring except stray cats hunting their prey, untroubled by the threat of the Empire.

It was quiet on the bank of the narrow canal, alarmingly still. Serafin sat on the stone curbing and let his feet dangle. The soles of his shoes were a mere handsbreadth above the water. The alley between houses that he'd followed here was narrow and dark; it dead-ended at the water's edge.

Not so many hours ago he'd come here with Merle and shown her the reflections on the surface—reflections that might not really be there and were only to be seen between twelve and one o'clock at night. They showed the houses on the bank of the canal, and yet they weren't reflections of the reality: Some of the windows mirrored in the water were illuminated, although in reality the buildings were abandoned and dark. Now and again something moved, such as the reflections of pedestrians who didn't exist at all—not in *this* Venice, the city in which Serafin and Merle had grown up. Instead, there were rumors that a second Venice existed in another world, and perhaps even a dozen or a hundred of them.

Feeling melancholy, Serafin crumbled bits of a small loaf of bread into the water, but no fish came to receive the unexpected delicacies. Since the Flowing Queen had been driven from the waters of the lagoon by the poison of the Egyptian high priests, one rarely saw fish swimming through the canals. Instead of them, algae now thrived in the waters, and Serafin wasn't the only one who had the feeling that it was growing worse with each passing day. Dark green strings, amorphous and twisted, like wet spider-webs. It could only be hoped that they didn't really come from one of the great sea spiders, which no one had ever seen but were rumored to be living in the Mediterranean in the ruins of the suboceanic kingdom, there where the water was deepest.

Serafin felt miserable. He knew that Merle had escaped from Venice on the back of a stone lion, and for all his confusion, he was still grateful for that. At least at the moment, she was in no danger from the Egyptians—provided she'd been able to get past the siege ring of the Empire without being caught by the sunbarks.

It wasn't the impending invasion that caused his concern either. The fear of the Egyptians went deep, certainly, but in a peculiar way that frightened him, he'd resigned himself to it. The capture of Venice was inevitable.

No, something else was gnawing at him, hardly letting him sleep and making him restless all day long. His stomach felt like a hard ball that wouldn't let him take any nourishment. He had to force himself to take each bite, but even that didn't always succeed. The crumbs of bread on the water below him were his evening meal.

He was concerned about Junipa, the girl with the mirror eyes. And of course about Arcimboldo, the magic mirror maker on the Canal of the Expelled. It had been Arcimboldo who'd taken Junipa and Merle from the orphanage and made them apprentices in his workshop. Arcimboldo who—as Serafin had learned shortly before—had entered into an agreement to soon surrender Junipa to Lord Light, the master of Hell.

Serafin had demanded explanations from Arcimboldo, and the magic mirror maker had answered most of his questions.

Arcimboldo seemed to be a beaten man. For years he'd secretly supplied Lord Light with his magic mirrors. Time after time, he'd met with Talamar, Lord Light's courier, to hand over new mirrors. And one day Talamar had made a special proposal, to which, after a long hesitation, Arcimboldo had agreed. He should restore sight to the blind Junipa, of course with the help of his magic mirrors. A noble gesture on his part, and since then, Junipa learned a little faster each day how to manage with her new powers of sight.

But that wasn't all.

Lord Light had not directed Arcimboldo's attention to Junipa out of altruism. Serafin had had to probe for a while before the mirror maker finally told him everything.

"Junipa can also see in the dark with her new eyes," Arcimboldo explained over a glass of tea, while the moon shone through a skylight in the workshop. "Merle has probably told you that already. But it doesn't end with that."

"End?" asked Serafin with irritation.

"The magic mirror glass with which I replaced her eyeballs will give her the power to look into other worlds at any time. Or better: through the *mirrors* of other worlds."

After a long silence, Serafin finally found words again. "Such as the ones that are reflected in some of the canals around midnight?"

"You know about those? Yes, into those, and also

others. Junipa will look through her mirrors at those who live there, and they'll never know it. She'll observe kings and emperors making important decisions in their mirrored halls, and she'll see when fully laden ships are reflected in the waters of distant oceans. That is the true power that her mirror eyes give her. And it is she whom Lord Light is after."

"Control, isn't it? That's what he's all about. Not only does he want to know what's going on in this world—he'll only be satisfied when he knows everything. About all worlds."

"Lord Light is curious. Perhaps we should say 'thirsting for knowledge'? Or 'interested'?"

"Unscrupulous and vicious," said Serafin angrily. "He's exploiting Junipa. She's so happy that she can see after a life of blindness—and she has no idea what's behind it."

"She does," contradicted Arcimboldo. "I've spoken with her. She now knows what power she will have at her command in time. And I believe she has accepted it."

"Did she have a choice?"

"Lord Light gives none of us a choice. Not me, either. Had I not taken his gold, the workshop would have closed long ago. He's bought more magic mirrors than anyone else since the Guild expelled me. Without him I'd have had to send all my apprentices back to the orphanages. Merle and Junipa wouldn't even have come here." The little old man shook his head sadly. "Serafin, believe me, my own fate is not the issue here at all. But the children . . . I couldn't allow that."

"Does Junipa know where she's going to go?"

"She suspects there's more behind it. Even that she won't be staying here with us for long. But she knows nothing of Talamar and Lord Light. Not yet."

"But that can't be allowed to happen!" Serafin exclaimed, almost overturning his tea. "I mean, we simply can't allow her to . . . to go to Hell. In the truest sense of the word."

To that Arcimboldo had said nothing, and now Serafin was sitting here on the canal and looking for a solution, for some sort of way out.

If Venice had been a free city and there had been no Egyptians threatening it, perhaps he might have been able to flee with Junipa. He'd once been one of the most skillful master thieves in Venice, of whose existence most of the city's citizens had no inkling at all. But the Empire's siege ring enclosed them on all sides, a hangman's noose of galleys, sunbarks, and umpteen thousand soldiers. There was no way out of the city, and to hide from Hell *and* the Egyptians somewhere in the alleys was a futile undertaking. Sooner or later they'd find them.

If Merle were still in Venice, together they might perhaps have found a solution. But with his own eyes he'd seen her fly over the Piazza San Marco on the back of a stone lion—over the lagoon, out of the city. And for reasons he didn't know himself, he doubted that Merle would be back soon enough—if ever—to save Junipa from her fate.

Where was Merle? Where had the lion taken her? And what had become of the Flowing Queen?

The reflection of the other world faded as a clock in a nearby church tower struck one, followed by quite a few others. The hour after midnight was past, and with it the lighted windows on the water vanished abruptly. Now the waves reflected the dark housefronts only very vaguely, unlit, a reflection of the reality.

Serafin sighed softly, stood up—and suddenly bent forward again. There was something in the water, a movement. He'd seen it clearly. Not a reflection, from this or any other world. Perhaps a mermaid? Or a big fish?

Serafin saw a second movement, and this time it was easier to follow it with his eyes. A black silhouette glided through the canal, and now he discovered a third. Each was about fifteen feet long. No, fish were certainly not *that* big, even if these were shaped something like sharks. They came to a point in front, but the width was the same along the rest of their length, like a thick tree trunk. Serafin saw no fins, either, as far as he could make out in the dark water.

The last silhouette slid along just under the surface, not so deep as the others, and now the moonlight broke over its surface. No doubt about it—metal! With that, there was really no more doubt about where they came from. Only magic could move objects of iron or steel through the water like feathers. Egyptian magic!

Serafin ran. The surrounding houses came right down to the water, so he couldn't run directly along the canal. He had to take a roundabout way to follow the three vehicles. He quickly ran back through the blind alley, went around several corners, and finally came to a piazza that he knew only too well. Forty steps away from him, a little bridge led over the canal into which he'd just scattered his supper. In a narrow house on the left, he and Merle had met the three traitors from the City Council and the Egyptian spy. Here they'd thwarted the delivery of the Flowing Queen.

Now the house stood there abandoned and inconspicuous. No one would have supposed that the invasion of the Empire had begun precisely here, behind boarded-up windows and a gray, crumbling façade.

On the bridge stood a figure in a long, dark cape. Its face was hidden under a deep hood.

For a moment Serafin had a sense of walking through an invisible door into the past. He'd already seen this same man once, at the same hour of the night, in the same place: the Egyptian envoy, the spy, from whom they had wrested the crystal vial containing the Queen. Merle had burned his hand with the help of her magic mirror, while Serafin had set a horde of angry street cats on his neck.

But now the man was here once more, and again he was hiding himself under a hooded cape like a street robber.

Serafin overcame his shock quickly enough not to be discovered. He swiftly pressed himself against a house-front. The moon was illuminating the opposite side and a large portion of the narrow piazza; but the part through which Serafin was moving lay in deep shadow.

Protected by the darkness, he approached the bridge. The envoy was waiting for something, and after Serafin's recent discovery, there was little doubt as to what that was. In fact, there now sounded a hollow metallic sound, which was irregularly repeated. Something was striking against the wall of the canal under the bridge.

Something was coming alongside.

The envoy hurried to the foot of the bridge and from there looked into the water. Meanwhile, Serafin was still thirty feet away from him. He hid behind a small altar to the Virgin Mary that someone had attached to the house wall a long time ago. Very likely, no offerings had been placed there for a long, long time. In recent years most people had prayed to the Flowing Queen; nobody believed in the power of the Church anymore, even though there were still some holdouts who attended church as a matter of form.

Serafin watched the envoy move back a few steps, away from the edge of the canal. He was making room for six men climbing up the narrow steps from the water.

Men? Serafin bit his lower lip. The six figures had been men once. But today they bore no likeness to their former selves.

Mummies.

Six mummy soldiers of the Empire with faces dried up and fallen in, so that they resembled each other like twin brothers. Any characteristics that might once have differentiated them had vanished. Their faces were those of skeletons, covered with gray skin.

All six wore dark outfits that glittered metallically in the moonlight now and then. Each held a sword such as Serafin had never seen before: The long blade was curved, almost half-moon-shaped, but the edge—unlike that of a scimitar—was on the inside of the curve, which led to a completely different way of wielding it. Egyptian sickle swords, the feared blades of the imperial mummy soldiers.

There must have been room for two of them in each of the strange vehicles in the water. They had sat in them one behind the other, as in a hollow tree, unable to move. But mummies, Serafin thought cynically, probably didn't have to scratch at all; that would only have peeled the desiccated skin from their bones.

So that was what the Egyptians made of the dead. Slaves without will or mercy who sowed death and destruction. Presumably there were similar scenes playing out all over Venice at this moment. The invasion had begun.

But there was a difference between being conquered by flesh-and-blood opponents and by . . . something like that. You could talk with humans, ask for mercy, or at least hope that they retained a portion of their humanity. But with mummies?

Serafin could no longer bear the idea of a Venice emptied of all life, in which an inhuman Pharaoh ruled. He knew that it would be best for him to keep still, not move, not even breathe, but that was impossible. At last, when it became clear to him that the Egyptian envoy had command of the six soldiers, he could not creep away. He had to do something, had to act. Even if it was madness.

He let out a sharp whistle. For a moment nothing happened. But then the envoy whirled around so fast that his dark cloak billowed out. His hood slid back for a moment, long enough so Serafin could see what the cats had done to him. The spy's face was furrowed with crusted wounds, not harmless scratches but deep gouges, which would soon scab over to an ugly wasteland of scars. And the man knew whom he had to thank. He remembered the sound that had set the cats on him.

He remembered Serafin.

The envoy called something in a language that Serafin didn't understand and pointed toward the altar, as if his eyes could see through the massive stone. Faster than Serafin would have thought possible, the mummies began moving, their sickle swords raised. One of them stayed behind, near the envoy. The man pulled his hood up again, but first he threw Serafin a hate-filled look in which there was a promise—of pain, of misery, of long torture.

The mummies had covered half the distance. Serafin had just leaped from his hiding place when the cats finally came.

Thirty, forty, fifty stray cats, from all directions, from all openings, from the roofs and out of the sewers. And with every second there were more, until the piazza swarmed with them.

The envoy shrieked and retreated backward up the bridge, while he ordered one of the other soldiers back with a shrill command so that he could keep the cats from getting at him. But the other four mummies paid scarcely any attention to the animals, who fell on them from all sides. Claws sank into the paper skin. Teeth bit into clothing and armor, snapped at fingers, and tore dusty scraps from cheeks and arms.

None of it stopped the mummy soldiers.

They kept single-mindedly on their way, stamping through a sea of fur and claws, each hung with a dozen cats like living Christmas tree decorations. The sickle swords whistled through the air and in blind rage struck their victims, some on the ground, some in mid-leap. Meowing and shrieking echoed and reechoed from the houses. But the animals learned quickly. More and more often they fastened themselves to the sword arms of the soldiers, until the mummies sagged under the weight.

Serafin was immobilized with horror. Not for long, only for a few instants. It was enough for him to realize that the cats were sacrificing their lives for him. With all the danger that threatened him, he couldn't permit that. Cats were the friends of the master thieves, their allies, not their meek slaves. He hesitated a moment, then let out a new succession of whistles. Immediately the wave of cats surged back; only those who were biting and hooked into mummies stayed a few seconds longer. Then they also gave up, let themselves drop, and whisked away.

Serafin's command meant that the cats should run away, back to wherever they had come from. But they didn't obey. They fell back from the mummies for only a few yards, stopped at the edge of the piazza, and watched their opponents with glowing eyes.

Meanwhile, Serafin had run to the other side of the piazza. From there he looked back and saw the cats clumped in front of the buildings like a wave of fur. He also saw that the mummy soldiers were hard on his heels.

The cats waited for him to call them to attack again, but he didn't have the heart to. Nearly a dozen animals lay dead or dying in the lane that the four mummy soldiers had plowed. The grief that overwhelmed Serafin at this sight shook him even more strongly than fear for his life.

Ten more yards and the four soldiers would reach him. Silently they rushed toward him. In the background, up on the bridge, stood the envoy, his arms crossed, barricaded behind his two guards.

"The cats!" cried a light voice suddenly out of the shadows behind Serafin. "They should pull farther back!"

Serafin whirled around. A torch burned in the recess between the houses, but he couldn't recognize who was holding it. He whistled again, moving toward the source of the light as he did so.

This time the cats obeyed. In the wink of an eye, they climbed the houses and windowsills, drainpipes and steps, wooden beams and balustrades.

"Watch out!" bellowed a second voice, this time from the left.

Serafin turned and ran. The mummy soldiers had almost reached him. He looked back over his shoulder—and saw two garish tongues of flame leap out of the street openings in the direction of the mummies. There was a crackling snarl, then the four mummies were alight. Flames licked over their dried-out bodies, sprang from one limb to the other, ate along under the steel of their armor. One soldier sank to its knees, while the other three still ran on. Two struck wildly about themselves, as if they could drive off the flames with their sickle swords. But the third rushed straight at Serafin without stopping, its weapon raised, ready to deal the deadly blow.

Serafin was unarmed except for his knife, which he tore from his belt. He knew he hadn't a chance with it.

Nevertheless, he stood there as if his boots had taken root. He'd been a master thief of the Guild, the youngest ever, and had learned that you don't run away from an opponent. Not if others were ready to risk their lives for you. And as he saw it, not only had the cats done that, but also the mysterious helpers who came to his aid with their fire breath.

Now he saw three figures leap out of the recesses on both sides of the street. Two flung their torches to the ground, while the third rushed at one of the burning soldiers with his drawn saber. Very briefly the idea flitted through Serafin's mind that he knew this face, all three faces, but he had no time to make sure.

The burning mummy threw itself at him like a demon, a towering column of fire, from which the razor-sharp blade of the sickle sword struck at him. Serafin avoided the blow and at the same time tried to put some distance between himself and his opponent. He could perhaps escape the sword, but if the flaming creature fell on him, he would burn miserably.

Out of the corner of his eye he saw the fighter with the saber strike the head of his mummy foe from its shoulders, with an elegant turn that showed either long practice or enormous talent. The two others had also drawn their blades and fought with the remaining mummies, nowhere near so skillfully as their leader, but the fire assisted them. It consumed the undead soldiers with such speed that they literally fell apart before they could become dangerous. Serafin's adversary, too, in spite of all its determination, became ever weaker, its movements more uncontrolled, until its legs gave under it. Serafin took a few steps backward and watched as the mummy was consumed by flames like a heap of straw.

"Watch out!" cried a voice.

Serafin looked hastily around. The two bodyguards of the envoy had rushed forward, followed by their master. They rushed at his saviors. Serafin's eyes were tearing from the smoke of the numerous fires. He still could not clearly see who was standing with him. Earlier he had seen their faces . . . but no, that was impossible.

He quickly ran around the first fire, jumped over the second, and lifted a sickle sword from the ground. One of the mummies had lost it before it was entirely burned up. The grip was warm, almost hot, but not so bad that he couldn't hold it. The weapon felt clumsy to him, the balance of the blade with a will of its own. But he wouldn't allow others to fight for him while he stood by doing nothing. He grabbed the weapon with both hands and rushed into the fight.

The leader of the three rescuers sprang skillfully forward and back, avoided sword blows, and inflicted numerous wounds on one mummy soldier. Then the saber flashed through the defenses of the soldier in an explosion of blows and thrusts and beheaded it. Again, dust billowed out in all directions, but no blood flowed. The torso collapsed. Serafin quickly realized that this was the best way to conquer a mummy: The magic of the Egyptians affected the dead brain; without skulls they were ordinary corpses again.

And then, when he finally recognized who'd saved him, he didn't believe his eyes. He would have expected anyone else, but not *him*.

The two other fighters had their hands full to keep the last mummy off their necks. Serafin supported them with the heavy sickle sword as well as he could, while the leader pressed forward, avoiding a revolver shot from the envoy, pursuing him to the bridge and there striking him down with slashing saber blows.

Finally the last mummy also fell. Serafin looked across the plaza, his breath rattling. The traces of dead cats were clearly to be seen in the flickering light of the fire. He swore to himself never again, under any circumstances, to ask the cat folk for help. He had used them selfishly, without considering, and bought his life with those poor creatures lying there in front of him.

One of his fellow fighters laid a hand on his arm. "If what I've heard about the friendship of thieves with the cats is true, they made their decision themselves."

Serafin turned and looked Tiziano in the face. Arcimboldo's former apprentice smiled crookedly, then bent and wiped the dust off his saber blade on the uniform of a mummy torso. Boro, the second fighter, walked up next to him and did the same thing.

"Thanks." Serafin himself thought it could have sounded a little heartier, but he was still too astonished that it was they who'd come to help him. Although Tiziano and Boro had probably never been bad fellows at the bottom of their hearts—at least that's what Merle thought; her problem was much more that they were too closely allied with Dario. Dario was the oldest of Arcimboldo's apprentices and Serafin's archenemy from the time he'd given up master thievery, and the two hated each other's guts. One time Dario had even attacked Serafin with a knife in Arcimboldo's workshop on the Canal of the Expelled.

And of all people, Dario, who was more detestable to him than almost anyone else, whom he considered underhanded, lying, and cowardly, this same Dario now came straight across the piazza to him, carelessly shoving his saber back into its sheath, the saber with which he'd just saved Serafin's life.

Dario bowed to Serafin, looked him over, then grinned. But it didn't seem especially friendly, only arrogant and unmitigatedly insufferable. Entirely the old Dario.

"Looks as if we came just in time."

Tiziano and Boro exchanged looks that seemed embarrassed, but neither of them said a word.

"Many thanks," said Serafin, who still could think of nothing better. To deny the help he'd desperately needed from the three would have been foolish and transparent — and besides, it was just the sort of answer Dario would have given in his situation. Instead, and in order to differentiate himself even more strongly from his former adversary, he added a compliment with a sincere smile: "You can handle a saber really well. I wouldn't have expected it of you."

"Sometimes you can be wrong about others, hmm?"

"Very possibly."

Boro and Tiziano gathered up their torches and rubbed them on the housefronts until the flames were extinguished. Now for the first time Serafin noticed the bulbous flasks they wore at their belts. There must be a fluid in there they'd used to spit fire. Certainly he'd heard that Arcimboldo's apprentices had left the magic mirror workshop two days ago in order the join the resistance fighters against the Empire. But he was astonished at how fast they'd learned to handle the flames. On the other hand, it was possible that they'd learned it earlier. He knew much too little about them.

"I thought you'd have turned tail sooner," Dario said. "Thieves aren't fighters, are they?"

"Not cowards, either." Serafin hesitated. "What do you want with me? You certainly didn't cross my path by accident."

"We were looking for you," Boro said. Dario repaid him with a dark side glance. But the sturdy youth took no notice of him, wholly in contrast to the past. "Someone wants to see you."

Serafin raised an eyebrow. "Oh?"

"We're not mirror makers anymore," said Dario, before one of the others could come forward again.

"Yes, I'd already heard that."

"We've joined the rebels."

"Sounds fabulous."

"Don't get funny."

"Your performance was quite impressive. You just polished off six of those . . . brutes."

"And the fellow in the cape," said Dario.

"And the fellow in the cape," Serafin repeated. "I wouldn't have been able to deal with them alone. Which perhaps means that I wouldn't be a particularly good rebel, right?"

They all knew better, for although Serafin wasn't a skillful fighter with a saber, like Dario, as a former master thief he possessed a whole list of other talents.

"Our leader wants to speak with you," said Dario.

"And I was thinking that was you."

Dario's look grew as dark as the empty eye sockets of a mummy soldier. "We don't have to be friends, no one's asking that of you. You should just listen. And I think you owe us that, don't you?"

"Yes," said Serafin. "I guess I do."

"Good. Then just come with us."

"Where?"

The three exchanged looks, then Dario lowered his voice conspiratorially. "To the enclave," he whispered.

3

Lilith's Children

Merle saw the statues even from a distance, and they were bigger than anything she had ever seen in her life. Very *much* bigger.

Ten figures of stone—each at least four hundred feet high, although that was a rough estimate, and they might actually have been even a little higher—standing around a gigantic hole in the landscape. That was what it was, in fact: a hole. Not a crater, not a deep valley. The closer they came to the opening, the clearer it became that it had no bottom, as if a divine fist had simply smashed a piece out of the earth's crust like a splinter from a glass ball. The hole had an irregular shape and must have been larger than Venice's main island.

As Vermithrax flew closer to it, the edges blurred in the moisture drifting across the landscape like a very fine drizzle. Soon Merle saw only the vast edge in front of her, as if the lion had brought them to the end of the world. The opposite side of the abyss was no longer visible. Merle was seized by a feeling of great emptiness and desolation, in spite of the Queen inside her, in spite of Vermithrax.

For hours now they'd been noticing a strange smell — not of sulfur, like the time Hell's messenger had appeared in the Piazza San Marco, but sweeter, hardly less unpleasant, as if something were decaying in the innards of the earth. Perhaps the heart of the world, she thought bitterly. Perhaps the entire world was just dying from the inside out, like a fruit on a tree in which rot and parasites had spread. The parasites were the Egyptians. Or, she corrected herself, maybe even all the people who had no better ideas than to plunge into a war of mythical dimensions.

But no, *they* were not the ones who had begun this war. And also not billions of other people. At this moment, for the first time, she became aware of the whole magnitude of the responsibility she'd undertaken: She was looking for help in the battle against the Egyptians, for help for an entire world.

In the battle against the Egyptians. There it was again.

And she was right in the middle of it. She was no better than all the others in this war.

"*Do not talk such nonsense,*" said the Queen.

"But it's the truth."

"*That it is not. No one wants more war, even more bloodletting. But the Egyptians will not let anyone talk to them. There is no other way. The fruit on the tree is help-less when it rots—but we have a choice. We can make our own decisions. And we can try to defend ourselves.*"

"And that means more war. More dead."

"*Yes,*" said the Queen sadly. "*It probably does.*"

Merle looked out over Vermithrax's mane again. To her left and right, the obsidian wings were rising and falling. The soft swishing swelled and receded, gently, almost leisurely, but Merle hardly heard it anymore. The sound had long ago entered into her flesh and blood, just like the lion's throbbing heartbeat; she felt it beneath her as if she were herself a part of this stone colossus, merged into him the way the Queen was now a part of her. She wondered if things would all come to the point when they, who had once been three, would more and more become one, just like the Egyptians, who numbered in the millions but fol-lowed only one brain, one hand, one eye—that of the Pharaoh.

Yes, said a cynical voice that wasn't the Queen's, and at the end the shining prince is waiting for you on his white horse and will carry you to his castle of flower petals.

Vermithrax's voice snatched her back to reality. "That is so . . . gigantic!"

Merle saw what he meant. The closer they came to the statues, the more titanic they seemed to her, as if they were continuing to grow right out of the soil, until the stone skulls broke through the clouds somewhere and swallowed the stars with their mouths.

"They are watchmen. The Egyptians built them," said the Queen with Merle's voice so that Vermithrax could hear too. "Here the Egyptian forces clashed with the armies of the Czarist kingdom for the first time. Look around you—everything is wasted and destroyed and uninhabited. Even the birds and insects have flown away. It is said that the earth itself finally convulsed in pain and distress, a last act of strength, to make an end of the fighting, and it swallowed all that it found on it."

"It really looks as though the ground fell in!" Vermithrax said. "Simply collapsed on itself. No earthquake could do something like that."

"There has only twice in history been something comparable. For one, the landslide that swallowed Marrakesh a few years ago—and perhaps the same powers were at work there as here—and then of course the wound that the fall of Lucifer Morningstar made in the earth."

"Morningstar?" asked Vermithrax.

"Even a stone lion must have heard of him," said the Queen. "An infinitely long time ago—so the humans tell it—a burning light from Heaven was supposed to have fallen directly to the earth. Many stories are told of its origins, but most people still believe that it was the angel Lucifer, who turned against his creator and was thrown out of Heaven by him. Lucifer fell burning to the depths, tore a hole in the earth, and thence plunged into Hell. There he rose to become ruler and the most powerful antagonist of his creator. So the angel became the devil— at least the old legends say so."

"Where is this place where Lucifer hit the earth?" Vermithrax asked.

"No one knows. Perhaps it is somewhere at the bottom of the sea, where no one has looked—except for the inhabitants of the subterranean kingdoms. Who knows?"

Merle felt her tongue loosen, and finally she herself was able to speak again. "I can't stand it when you do that."

"*Excuse me.*"

"You're only saying that."

"*I am dependent on your voice. We cannot exclude Vermithrax.*"

"But you could ask politely. How about that?"

"*I will take pains to.*"

"Do you believe that story? I mean, about Lucifer Morningstar and all that?"

"*It is a legend. A myth. No one knows how much of it corresponds to the truth.*"

"Then you have never seen that place in the sea yourself?"

"*No.*"

"But you know the suboceanic kingdoms."

"*I know no one who has seen the place with his own eyes. And no one who knows for certain whether it ever existed at all.*"

She'd never get anything more out of the Queen this way. But what did she care about the suboceanic cultures at the moment, anyway? A much more pressing problem lay directly in front of her, now stretching from one horizon to the other.

They were still some forty feet away from the edge of the Hell hole. In front of them rose one of the ten statues, more impressive than the Basilica of San Marco. It was the figure of a man with naked upper body and legs. According to the manner of ancient Egypt, he had only a loincloth wound around his hips. His skull was hairless, smooth as a polished ball. This head alone must have weighed several tons. The figure had both elbows bent and the palms laid together in front of its chest so that the arms formed a large triangle. The stone fingers were intertwined in a complicated gesture.

Merle suppressed the impulse to imitate it with her own hands; she would have had to let go of Vermithrax's mane to do it.

"*Ask him to fly past two other statues,*" said the Flowing Queen.

Merle passed the request on to the obsidian lion. Vermithrax immediately flew a loop and turned east, where the next stone giant was, a few hundred yards away. Each of these monumental figures stood with its back to the abyss, its pupilless eyes gazing rigidly into the distance.

"And the Egyptians built them?" Merle asked.

"*Yes. After the battlefield sank into the ground, the remaining armies of the Czarist kingdom used the opportunity to flee. They retreated many thousand of miles to the northeast and established a new boundary there, which they still hold today. The Egyptians went around the area and continued their advance, while their priests had these statues erected to watch over the entrance to the interior of the earth.*"

"Only symbolically, I hope."

The Queen laughed. "*I do not believe that the statues will suddenly come to life when we fly past them. In case that is what you meant.*"

"I was thinking of something like that, yes."

"*Oh, well, I have of course not been here myself before, and—*"

Merle interrupted her by clearing her throat.

"*Yes?*"

"Please hold your tongue."

"*If I had one, I would not always be needing yours.*"

"Did anyone ever tell you that you're a know-it-all?"

"No one."

"Then now is the best time to do it."

"What is a know-it-all?"

Merle let out a groan and addressed the lion. "Vermithrax, was she always like this?"

"Like what?" asked the obsidian lion, and she had the feeling that he was smirking, even though from her place on his back she couldn't see his face.

"So difficult."

"Difficult, hmm? Yes . . . yes, I think you could say that."

Again the Queen laughed inside her, but she dispensed with any remark. Merle could hardly grasp that for once the Queen did *not* have to have the last word.

The second statue was not appreciably different from the first, with the exception that the fingers were intertwined in a different way. The third figure displayed yet another gesture. Otherwise they were all as alike as peas.

"Is that enough?" Vermithrax asked.

"Yes," said the Flowing Queen, and Merle passed it on. Vermithrax flew around the statue without it awakening.

"Did you really expect that all at once it would start moving so as to catch us out of the air with its hand?"

Merle shrugged her shoulders. "I think for a long time I haven't known what to expect anymore and what not to. I also didn't think that I would free Vermithrax from his prison. Or fly over the countryside on his back. Aside from all the other things that have happened in the last few days."

She tried to catch a glimpse over the edge of the abyss, but she saw only rocks and fine, vapory veils, bathed in a reddish shimmer. She wasn't sure if that was caused by the sun, which stood high over the wasteland, or if the source of the diffuse glow was inside the earth.

"Do you think that's really Hell down there? I mean, like in the Bible or the pictures on church altars?" Her skeptical tone surprised her. Hadn't she just declared that after all their experiences there was nothing left that could astonish her?

Vermithrax didn't answer, perhaps because he was still thinking, or he had no clear opinion about it. But the Queen answered, *"What do you think?"*

"I don't know." Merle's eyes swept over the expressionless face of the nearest statue, and she wondered if the artist who had created these features would actually have made them so utterly emotionless if gravest danger lay in wait there below. "Anyway, Professor Burbridge never wrote of gigantic fires roasting the damned. Or of chains and torture chambers. I guess we should believe him. Besides—," she broke off.

"What?"

After a short pause Merle took up the thread again. "Besides, a Hell like the one in the Bible wouldn't make sense. Inflicting pain on someone for all eternity is so . . .

so unreasonable, isn't it? After all, we punish a person so he won't do something bad again. And, of course, to scare off anyone else. But if the good are incapable of sinning, and at the same time the sinners have no chance to do good because, after all, they're imprisoned forever in Hell . . . I mean, what sense would there be in it?"

The Queen said nothing to that, but Merle had the feeling that she silently agreed with her, was even a little proud of her. Emboldened, she went on: "If God is in fact infinitely good, the way it says in the Bible, then how come he sentences some people to eternal damnation? How do the two fit together, good and punishment?"

To her surprise, Vermithrax now joined in. "You're right. Why should we punish a guilty person if the punishment can't change him anymore?"

"Sounds like quite a waste, I think."

"*We might call that down there Hell,*" said the Queen, "*but I do not think it has anything to do with what your priests preach. Neither with God nor with the Devil.*"

"But?"

"*Only with our own selves. We survive, or we die. That depends on us alone.*"

"Can anyone like you actually die?"

"*But of course,*" said the Queen. "*I live and die with you, Merle. Whether I want to or not.*"

Merle grew dizzy at these words—and to her astonishment, she again felt something like pride. But at the same time she felt the invisible weight on her shoulders grow a little bit heavier.

"What do you think?" cried Vermithrax over his shoulder. "Should we try it?"

"That is what we came here for, after all."

Merle nodded. "Let's try it!"

Between her knees she felt the lion draw in a deep breath and once briefly tense all his muscles. Then he turned sharply, flew a narrow arc, and shot out over the edge.

The sweetish odor became even stronger as they found themselves over the abyss, but there was still nothing to see except the steep rock walls and a sea of mist. The reddish glow of the vapors became more intense now, as if there were a sea of lava hidden under the layer of fog, which would evaporate into hot air any minute.

Obviously the same thought was on Vermithrax's mind. "What's under the clouds?"

"May I?" the Queen asked. Merle thought she sounded slightly too ironic, too sure of herself.

"Go ahead." And before she knew it, the Queen was already speaking with her mouth. "It is only ordinary fog, nothing more. It has to do with the fact that two different levels of air density come together here. You will probably have to get used to breathing under there at first."

"What are air densities?" asked the lion.

"Just trust me." Then she withdrew into herself again.

"She says things like that all the time," Merle said to the lion.

"How do you stand it?"

Merle had a dozen caustic remarks on her tongue, but she suppressed them. Secretly—and she only reluctantly admitted to it—she was even a little glad that she had the Queen in her.

Sometimes it was good to have someone who knew all about you share everything and have an answer to many questions.

And sometimes it was a scourge.

Vermithrax began the descent. He didn't head down in a straight line but turned in wide circles. As he did so, he tilted dangerously to the side, so that after a short time Merle could feel her stomach rebel once again. She would never get used to this accursed flying.

The obsidian lion stayed close to the southern wall. The stone was dark and appeared to be full of cracks. Once Merle thought she made out a kind of groove leading down from the upper edge; it looked like a makeshift staircase or a road that someone had hewn out of the rock. But at the next turn she lost sight of the narrow ribbon again. Anyway, she had her hands full just holding on tight and keeping her eyes more or less rigidly on the back of Vermithrax's head in the hope of being able to keep her nausea and dizziness halfway under control.

The fog lay a few yards below them, smooth as a

frozen lake. Only, its center was filled with incessant motion, wafting veils that turned around themselves like lone dancers of water vapor. The red glow was brighter in some places than others. Whatever might await them down there in the depths, it wouldn't be long before they came face-to-face with it.

It had been cool high up in the air; but now, the farther down they moved, the warmer it became. Not hot, not humid, in spite of the moisture, but warm in a comfortable way. However, Merle was much too tense to be happy about it. Only a few minutes before, when Vermithrax had been circling the statues, the wind had cut through her clothes like a knife through parchment, but the cold wasn't what was occupying her mind. Other thoughts claimed her attention, concerns and speculations, premonitions, and an appropriate measure of confusion.

Then they broke through the fog.

It was only a short moment, certainly not a minute, until Vermithrax's descending flight had borne them through the layer of mist and thrust them out on the underside in a star-shaped eruption of steam and gray vapors. Merle had automatically held her breath, and now, when she tried to take in a deep breath, she was overcome with panic: It wouldn't work! She couldn't breathe! Her throat closed, her chest burned like fire, and then there was only fear, pure, instinctive fear.

But no, there *was* air, and now she filled her lungs with

it, yet it seemed to be different somehow, perhaps thinner, perhaps heavier, it didn't matter. Gradually Merle grew calm again, and then for the first time she became aware that Vermithrax had also gone into a wobble, seized by the same terror of suffocating, by the certainty that it had all been a bad, even fatal, mistake. But now his wing beats steadied, became gentler again, more regular, and the winding course of their descent stabilized.

Merle leaned forward a bit. Not too far, because she already guessed what she would see—an abyss, a bottomless abyss—but the reality exceeded her fears by a great deal.

If a term such as *depth* had ever applied to anything— pure, frightening, reason-transcending *depth*—it was this shaft into the vitals of the earth. The mist was now gone completely and replaced by a clarity that seemed to Merle wrong somehow, somehow inappropriate. She had last experienced this feeling when she swam through the Venetian canals with the mermaids, protected by a glass globe that provided her with a remarkably sharp view of the world under the water. Nonetheless, it was a sight for which the human eye wasn't created; really, everything ought to have been blurred and cloudy, a wavering curtain on her retina.

Here below, in the interior of the abyss, something similar was happening to her. This was no place for human beings, and it astonished her that still she perceived it with all her senses, took it in, if she could not also comprehend it.

The rock walls fell away vertically to the deep, but it seemed to Merle that she saw every indentation, every projection, a little more clearly than above the fog. She could also make out the opposite side better now, although she didn't at all have the impression that the walls were any closer together. Everything was bathed in red golden brightness, which came from the rock itself, from a hair-fine network of veins of glowing lines, in some places clumped, in others almost invisible.

"Impressive," said the Queen, and Merle thought that was an utterly inadequate description, a modest, empty word in the face of this marvel.

Suddenly she became aware that this place must be a facet of the real, true Hell. Something that, except for Professor Burbridge and a small number of select people, no human being had ever seen.

Then she caught sight of the tents.

"Do you see that?" Vermithrax bellowed.

"Yes," whispered Merle, "I see them."

A ways below them and about eighty yards sideways, there was a ledge in the rock wall, a protruding cliff, like the nose of a giant upside down. The upper side was flat and, estimating roughly, twenty by twenty yards wide. There were three tents on it. One was in tatters, although the poles still stuck up in the air like the branches of a dead tree. Something had slit the canvas. A knife perhaps. Or claws.

The two other tents looked undamaged. The flap at the entrance of one was thrown back. As Vermithrax neared the camp, Merle could see that the rock ledge was abandoned.

"What do we do now?" she asked.

"*You are curious, are you?*"

"Aren't you?"

"*A mind can only take in a limited amount of knowledge, and to mine, those things there make no difference.*"

Show-off, Merle thought. "Then aren't you interested in what happened to the people?"

"*It is of interest to you. That is enough.*"

Vermithrax circled several times in front of the rock cliff. Merle noted how carefully he inspected the tents and the other remains of the camp. There was a fireplace; a row of chests, which were piled behind at the rock wall; a dish right beside the burned-out campfire; also three rifles, which were leaning against the wall as if their owners had just vanished behind the rocks for a moment. Whatever might have happened to these people, they hadn't even had time to grab their weapons. An ice-cold tingle ran down her back.

Finally the obsidian lion had seen enough; he made an abrupt swerve and landed on the rock ledge, only a few yards away from the destroyed tent. Now Merle could also see that the path she'd already noticed above opened onto this plateau, and to the right of them it led on farther down into the abyss.

She leaped from Vermithrax's back, landed on both feet—and at first fell right onto her backside. Her knees were weak, her muscles stiff. It was almost an accustomed feeling by now, but it had never been so bad before—possibly also a result of the changed air conditions, just like the weariness that she now felt more strongly than in the past few days. And the rest on the plateau where they'd spent the night wasn't even six or seven hours ago.

Maybe, it occurred to her suddenly, they'd lost time in some way when they entered this other world by crossing the fog, or even earlier, when they'd passed the stone watchers. Had they in truth traveled not just a few seconds but several hours through the layer of mist?

Nonsense, she told herself, and *"Nonsense!"* said the Flowing Queen in her mind. But somehow it seemed to Merle not entirely convincing either time.

After she'd limbered up her legs and her knees would again bear the featherlight weight of her body, she began to search the tents. Vermithrax begged her to be careful, while he sniffed the rifles and rooted through the chests with nose and paws. Even the Queen warned her to be careful, which really was something totally new.

Ultimately they found little that would be useful to

them. In one of the undamaged tents Merle found a thin leather band on which dangled a dried chicken claw as a pendant. At the top, sticking out of the severed limb, were several sinews like the wires of a puppet. When Vermithrax challenged her to pull on them, the chicken's claw closed, as if all at once there were life in it. Merle almost dropped the hideous thing in terror.

"Yucky." She let go of the claw and only held on to the leather thong.

"*It is a good luck charm,*" the Queen explained.

"Oh, yes?"

"*The inhabitants of the Czarist kingdom carry them. You do know that they are under the protection of the Baba Yaga?*"

Merle nodded, although she was aware that the Queen couldn't see it, only feel it at the most.

On the other side of the plateau, Vermithrax rooted through another chest with his front paws and poked around in it with his nose.

"*What do you know about the Baba Yaga?*"

"Not much. She's a witch. Or something like that."

The Queen was clearly smirking. "*A witch. A goddess. The people have seen very much in her. It is a fact that she has protected the Czarist kingdom, as I*"—she stopped, as if pain and guilt welled up in her and in some strange way rubbed off on Merle—"*as I protected Venice.*"

"Do you know her? Personally, I mean."

"No. She is not like me. At least I guess that. But what I want to say is this: Since time immemorial the Baba Yaga has had a certain form with which the people identify her. An old woman who lives in a little house—but this house stands on two chicken legs as tall as trees and can run around on them like a living creature."

Merle swung the pendant. "Then this thing is a sort of symbol?"

"It is. The way the Christians wear a cross to protect themselves from evil, so the inhabitants of the Czarist kingdom wear such a chicken foot—at least those who believe in the protection of the Baba Yaga."

"But that would mean—"

"That these are the remains of an expedition that was sent here by the Czar."

Merle thought over what that might mean. The armies of the Egyptians had overrun the entire world within a few decades—with the exception of Venice and the Czarist kingdom. However, there had never been contact between the two, at least none of which the common folk had learned. Nevertheless, the sight of the destroyed camp filled her with a remarkable feeling of loss, as if an important opportunity had been missed here. How did it look in the Czarist kingdom? How did people there defend themselves against the attacks of the Empire? And, not least, how did the Baba Yaga protect them? All questions to which they perhaps could find answers here, if someone didn't prevent them.

"Do you think they're dead?" Merle directed the question to both the Queen and Vermithrax.

The lion trotted over placidly. "The tent wasn't slit with a knife, at any rate. The edges are too rough and frayed for that."

"Claws?" Merle asked, and she guessed the answer already. Gooseflesh crept along her arms.

Vermithrax nodded. "There are traces of them on the ground."

"They scratched the *rock*?" Merle's voice sounded as though she'd swallowed something much too large.

"I'm afraid so," said the lion. "Pretty deeply, too."

Merle's eyes slid to the obsidian lion's paws and inspected the ground. His own claws left no traces in the stone. The creatures the Czar's expedition had encountered—what kind of claws must they have?

Then she knew. The answer popped up from her memory like the head of a sleeper who unexpectedly awakens. "Lilim," she said immediately.

"*Lilim?*" the Queen asked.

"When Professor Burbridge discovered Hell sixty years ago and encountered its inhabitants for the first time, he gave them this name. The teacher in the orphanage told us about them. Burbridge named them after the children of Lilith, the first wife of Adam."

Vermithrax cocked his head. "A human legend?"

Merle nodded. "Perhaps the oldest of all. I'm surprised you don't know it."

"Every people and every race has its own myths and stories about its origin." The obsidian lion sounded a little offended. "You don't know the old lion legends, either."

"I know who Adam was," said the Queen. *"But I have never heard of Lilith."*

"Adam and Lilith were the first humans God created."

"I thought the woman was named Eve."

"Eve came later. The first time, God created Adam and Lilith, man and woman. They were alone in Paradise and were supposed to have children together, to people the world with their descendants. Anyway, they were the first living creatures at all."

Vermithrax growled something, and Merle looked inquiringly at him.

"That's typical of you humans again," he said crossly. "You always believe you are the first and best. The first stone lions had been there for a long time before that."

"That's what *your* legends say," Merle retorted, grinning.

"Of course."

"Then we aren't likely to find out which is the truth, are we? Not now, not here, and probably never at all."

Vermithrax was forced to agree.

"All the myths of origins tell the truth," said the Queen mysteriously. *"Each in its own special way."*

Merle continued, "So Lilith and Adam were destined to have children together. But whenever Lilith wanted to approach her husband, he drew back from her, filled with fear and disgust."

"Hah!" growled Vermithrax. "That certainly didn't happen to the first lions at all!"

"Anyway, Adam was afraid of Lilith, and finally God lost patience and banned Lilith from the Garden of Eden. Filled with anger and disappointment, she wandered through the desert regions outside Paradise, and there she met creatures that had nothing in common with Adam, creatures that were more alien and more gruesome and more terrifying than anything we can imagine."

"I can imagine something like that," said the lion, with a side glance at the claw marks in the rock.

"Lilith bred with the creatures and was supposed to have borne them children that surpassed even their fathers in monstrosity—the Lilim. In the legends they are the demons and monsters who wander through the forests and deserts and over the bare rocks of the mountains."

"And Professor Burbridge knew these stories," said the Queen.

"Of course. When he needed a name for the inhabitants for his papers and his scientific works, he called them the Lilim."

"Well, good," said Vermithrax. "Our Czarist friends also met a few of them. Don't you think we should avoid that?"

"Vermithrax is right," replied the Queen. *"We had better leave. We are safer in the air."* But there was something in the way she emphasized that last sentence that alarmed Merle even more deeply. For who actually said that the Lilim had no wings?

"Just a moment." She ran over to the chests that the lion had already searched. Out of the corner of her eye she'd seen a few items that were useless to Vermithrax but that she could use. She found a small knife in a leather sheath, no longer than her hand, and put it in the pocket of her dress along with the magic mirror. In addition, she discovered several tin boxes with food rations, stone-hard strips of dried meat, zwieback, a couple of water bottles, and even a few cookies. She packed them all in a small leather knapsack she'd found in one of the tents and strapped it onto her back. While she was doing that, she chewed on a piece of dried meat, which was as hard as tree bark and as tough as shoe soles, but nonetheless, she managed to swallow the shreds. In the past few days she'd had very little to eat; the rations of the Czarist expedition looked more than suitable to her.

"Hurry up," Vermithrax called to her as she was fastening the straps of her new knapsack.

"I'm coming," she said—and suddenly she had a feeling of being watched.

Her fingers let go of the leather straps, and—despite the omnipresent warmth—she shivered. Her hair was standing on end. Her heart skipped a beat once, then began racing again, so suddenly that it almost hurt.

Confused, she looked toward the back of the plateau, to the rock wall, then over at the tents and at both openings to the paths that led up and down from there. Nothing moved. There was no one there. Only Vermithrax, who stood at the edge of the cliff, tapping impatiently on the rock with one claw.

"*What is wrong?*" asked the Queen.

"Don't you feel anything?"

"*Your fear masks everything.*"

"Hurry up," Vermithrax called. He still hadn't noticed anything.

Merle dashed toward him. She didn't know what she was running from, or if there was even a reason for her fear. She had almost reached Vermithrax when a piercing, screeching sound, drawn out and painful, made her whirl around.

At first she didn't see anything. Not really. But there was *something*, a movement perhaps, a change near the place where she'd shouldered the knapsack.

"Merle!"

The rock quivered under her feet as Vermithrax sped to

her, much faster and more nimbly than she would have thought possible, a black flash of obsidian who was suddenly behind her, scooping her from the floor with one of his wings and letting her slide down a ramp of stone feathers.

"*Lilim,*" sounded in her head, and it took a moment before she realized that it wasn't her own thought but a shout from the Flowing Queen.

Vermithrax began to lift off. An instant later they were rushing out over the edge of the cliff, still in a leap, not in flight. They dropped a good yard down into emptiness before the wings of the weighty lion stabilized their position in the air, at the same time bearing them away from the abandoned camp of the Czarist expedition and the spirit of death enveloping the empty tents.

Merle started to look around, but the Queen said sharply, "*Do not do that!*"

Of course she did it anyway.

The rock wall had come alive. Then Merle realized that it wasn't the stone itself that had begun moving but something that had perhaps been there the entire time, had been lurking, or was just now creeping out of some invisible cracks and holes like the scarab swarms of the Empire.

The entire surface of what she'd taken for mere rock had dissolved and now streamed from all sides toward the rock ledge, a concentration and agglomeration so strange and bizarre that she couldn't think of any human or animal motion like it. It wasn't like the crawling of insects, even if that perhaps came closest; it was more as if the dark scales and shells billowed in grotesque zigzags on the plateau, apparently without order, completely chaotic, and yet so purposefully that within seconds the ring enclosed the rock ledge.

Under the rippling top surface, which consisted of a host of man-sized bodies, Merle saw more and more tilted strands and structures that might be limbs, many times broken and angled, spiderlike and yet so utterly different. As they moved, they left behind a track of deep scars in the rock where they'd dug in their invisible claws and slashed the stone, tangled paths like a relief by a mad sculptor.

The dark flood poured over the edges of the plateau from all directions, also down from the overhang, and buried the tents and the chests under them. The creatures concealed themselves behind their stony shells, or what Merle took to be shells, and yet any brief flash of fangs or claws was enough to fill her with sheer terror.

Faster and faster, Vermithrax hurried out into the emptiness, away from what was taking place behind them. But Merle still saw the plateau sink completely under the assault of the Lilim, swallowed up, like a stone inexorably pulled down into a vortex of quicksand.

As if by itself, Merle's hand crept into the pocket where she kept the mirror. She absently pushed her fingers through the surface, deeper into the warmth of the magic place behind it. Very briefly she thought she heard a whisper, a voice—of the phantom trapped in there?—then she thrust her arm in up to the elbow, and finally she again felt the hand that grasped hers from the other side and stroked her fingers, gently reassuring her.

4

The Enclave

THE SKY HUNG GRAY AND HEAVY OVER VENICE, foretelling the rain that would soon be pelting onto the palazzos and canals. A cutting wind, much too cool for this time of year, was blowing in from the north and whistling down the crooked streets, across deserted piazzas and the promenades along the banks of the islands. It swirled up fliers that the indefatigable resisters had distributed a few days before, after the appearance of the messenger from Hell and his offer to protect the Venetians from the armies of the Empire. The fliers were full of slogans, slogans against the city councillors and the Pharaoh and anyone else who could be blamed for the desperate situation, slogans that might have put them in prison in other times, most certainly in the pillory. But today no one cared about that anymore. Fear held all Venice under its spell, so absolutely, so hopelessly, that even the soldiers of the City Guard forgot to arrest troublemakers and insurgents.

In the very heart of this rebellion, in the secret hideout of the rebels—the enclave, as Dario had called the building— Serafin was eating breakfast.

He wasn't doing it very calmly, naturally, but not in a hurry, either, for he knew he could do nothing but wait. They would call him sooner or later and take him to their leader, the master of the enclave. Neither Dario nor any of the others had called the leader of the rebellion by name— obviously a precautionary measure. And yet the others' mysteriousness made Serafin more uneasy than he was willing to admit.

The palazzo lay in the center of Venice, hardly more than a stone's throw from a half dozen famous buildings and places. And yet there was an aura of solitude around it—solitude a little too intense for it not to be magical, thought Serafin.

The night before, on the way here, he and his three escorts had encountered traces of the invasion that was beginning all over Venice. On several canal banks they'd found the empty metal shells in which the mummy soldiers had penetrated the labyrinth of watery streets. They discovered no trace of the soldiers themselves, but they all realized that there was no going back now. The mummies were roaming through the streets, singly or in small groups, spreading fear and horror and completing the taking of the city from within. Here and there Serafin and the others had heard loud voices in the distance, also screams. Once they'd caught the sound of the clash of steel on the other side of a block of houses, but when they arrived they found only corpses, which Serafin identified as members of the Thieves' Guild.

No one understood very well what the Pharaoh had in mind with this sort of attack. His war galleys and sunbarks lay in sight of the quays of the lagoon, and it would have been easy to send soldiers on land all around the main island.

Serafin guessed that the Pharaoh was only trying to rattle the Venetians. But the lagoon dwellers could scarcely be further rattled after more than three decades of siege. And if it were pure cruelty? The macabre fun of beginning the invasion small, in order to then drive the attack to high pitch in a storm of fire and steel?

Serafin didn't understand it all, and he hoped that the master of the enclave had some answers ready for his questions.

The room into which Tiziano had led him was on the second floor of the palazzo. As with most of the old palaces, the ground floor was empty. At one time, when all these buildings had still belonged to the rich merchant families of the city, there had been merchandise and goods stored there below, in unornamented halls that every few years would be flooded by *acqua alta,* Venice's famed high waters.

But today, after so many years of isolation, there was hardly any trade in Venice, and the little that remained made no one rich. Most of the well-to-do families had fled to the mainland long ago, right at the beginning of the war, never supposing that there they would be helplessly delivered to the mummy armies and scarab swarms. No one could have foreseen that the power of the Flowing Queen would protect the city, and it was a malicious irony of fate that those who had enough money to flee were the first to fall victim to the Egyptians.

The windows and doors of the empty ground floor were walled up with large stones, apparently long before anyone ever even thought of a resurrection of the Pharaoh. The rebels had not settled into an abandoned building. Serafin assumed that the leader of the rebellion had been living here for a long time already. Perhaps a nobleman. Or even a merchant, one of the few who were still left.

Serafin shoved the last piece of bread into his mouth as the door of the bare room opened. Tiziano told him to come with him.

Serafin followed the former apprentice mirror maker through corridors and suites, up a staircase, and under an archway. He didn't see another soul the entire time. It seemed as though all were strictly forbidden to enter the apartments of the master of the enclave. But at the same time, Serafin had the feeling that the atmosphere of the corridors and high rooms had altered, a scarcely noticeable shift of reality to something different, confusing. It wasn't that the light changed, or the smell—everything here smelled moldy and of damp stone—no, it was the way his surroundings *felt,* as if he were perceiving with a new sensory organ that had only been waiting to finally be activated.

At Tiziano's bidding he stopped before a double door, almost three times as tall as he was.

"Wait here," said Tiziano. "You'll be called in." He turned to go.

Serafin grabbed his shoulder. "Where are you going?"

"Back to the others."

"You aren't staying here?"

"No."

Serafin looked mistrustfully from Tiziano to the door, then back again. "This isn't some trap or something?" He felt a little foolish as he voiced this suspicion, but he couldn't forget his old quarrel with Dario. He believed his—former?—archenemy was capable of any meanness.

"What would be the sense of that?" asked Tiziano.

"We could just have left you to the mummies, couldn't we? Things would have taken care of themselves."

Serafin still hesitated, then he nodded slowly. "Sorry. That was ungrateful."

Tiziano grinned at him. "Dario can be quite a pain, huh?"

Serafin couldn't help smiling back. "You and Boro, you've noticed that?"

"Even Dario has his good sides. A few of them. Otherwise he wouldn't be here."

"That probably goes for all of us, I guess."

Tiziano gave an encouraging nod toward the door. "Just wait." With that, he finally turned and walked briskly back the way they had come. The thought sizzled through Serafin's head that he'd never find his way back alone. The interior of the enclave was a first-class maze.

The right half of the door was swung open by an invisible hand, and at once he was enveloped in something light and soft, which played around his body like a hundred gentle fingers, light as a feather, almost bodiless. Surprised, he took a step backward. It was only a filmy silk curtain that a draft was blowing against him.

"Enter," said a voice. A woman's voice.

Serafin obeyed and pushed the curtain aside, very carefully, because he had the feeling that the delicate tissue could tear between his fingers like spiderwebs. Behind that, barely six feet away, a wall of curtains bellied out, all of the same material and in the same light yellow, which reminded him of the color of beach sand. He remembered to close the door behind him before he began to move. Then he ventured deeper into that labyrinth of silk.

He passed one curtain after another, until he gradually lost all orientation, even though he'd only been going straight the entire time. How far behind him was the door? A hundred yards, or only ten, fifteen?

Gradually he was able to make out shapes behind the silk, angled silhouettes, pieces of furniture perhaps. At the same time the damp, moldy smell of Venice was overlaid with an exotic scent, a whole explosion of smells. They reminded him of the strange spices he'd once stolen from a merchant's storeroom, years before.

On the other side of the curtain lay another world.

The ground was strewn with sand, so high that his boots sank into it without hitting any firm ground. The ceiling was hung with lengths of dark blue material, which provided a sharp contrast to the surrounding lightness, like an evening sky over the desert. And then he realized that this was exactly the impression that all this was supposed to awaken: the illusion of a desert landscape, completely artificial, and yet so different from anything that one could ever find in Venice. There were no painted dunes, no statues of camels or Bedouins; nothing here was real, and still it all seemed as convincing as an actual visit to the desert— at least to Serafin, who'd never left the lagoon.

Several islands of soft cushions were piled up in the center of this wondrous place. The spicy smell came from bowls, from which hair-thin columns of smoke were curling up. Between the cushions was a pedestal of coarse sandstone and on it, heavy and blocky, stood a round water basin of the same material. The surface was a good three feet in diameter and was stirring slightly. Behind the basin stood a woman, only her upper body visible. She had thrust her right arm into the water up to the elbow. At first Serafin thought she was stirring it, but then he saw that she was holding her arm completely still.

She looked up and smiled. "Serafin," she said, and he found it quite astonishing how melodious his name sounded when such a creature spoke it.

She was beautiful, perhaps the most beautiful woman that he'd ever seen—and as the messenger boy of Umberto, who wove magic fabrics for Venice's noblewomen, he'd encountered many a beauty. She had smooth, raven-black hair, so long that the ends disappeared behind the edge of the sandstone vessel. Her slender body was clothed in skintight material, napped like fine fur and of the same yellow as the curtains. Large, hazelnut brown eyes inspected him. Her lips were full and dark red, although he was certain that she wore no makeup. The skin of her face and her left hand, resting on the edge of the basin, were dark, not black like one of the Moors, of whom there were several in Venice, but tanned dark by the sun.

And then, in a flash, he knew.

She was an Egyptian.

He knew it with absolute certainty, before she directed another word to him or could introduce herself. The leader of the rebellion against the Egyptians was an *Egyptian.*

"Have no fear," she said, when she noticed that he recoiled a step. "You are in safety. No one here will do anything bad to you." A spark of regret burned in her eyes as she took her right arm out of the water and laid it in front of her on the stone rim. Neither hand nor arm was wet. There was no trace of water beading on her skin or on the strange material of her clothing.

"Who are you?" He had the feeling he was stammering terribly. He had every reason to.

"Lalapeya," said the woman. "I don't believe you know the language from which this name comes."

"Egyptian?" He felt brave, downright daring, when he said this one word.

Her laugh was very clear, almost melodic. "Egyptian? Oh no, absolutely not. This name was already old when the first pharaohs mounted their golden thrones many thousands of years ago."

And with that she came out from behind the basin in a strange, flowing movement that disconcerted Serafin and confused him—until he saw her legs.

She had four of them.

The legs of a lioness. The *lower body* of a lioness.

Serafin started back so violently that he got tangled up in one of the silken curtains, lost his balance, and fell over backward, pulling a torrent of yellow silk with him.

When he had finally freed himself, she was standing directly in front of him. If he stretched out an arm, he could touch one of her paws, the soft yellow fur that covered her and that he'd just taken for a tight-fitting dress.

"You— You are . . ."

"Certainly not a mermaid."

"A sphinx!" escaped him. "A sphinx of the Pharaoh!"

"The last part is not true. I have not met the Pharaoh, ever, and I regret it most deeply that some of my people serve him."

Serafin tried to get to his feet, but he only partially succeeded, and when he again pulled back from her, one foot dragged the pulled-down curtain with him, two, three paces away.

The lion paws carried the sphinx after him in an elegant motion. "Please, Serafin. I've shown you so that you know whom you're dealing with. But it wasn't urgently necessary."

"What— What do you mean?"

She smiled, and it made her look so pretty that it almost pained him to see the animal part of her body at the same time. "What do I mean? Oh, Serafin! *This,* of course."

At the sound of the words, her image blurred before his eyes. At first Serafin thought that the sand was billowing up from the ground, but then he realized that it was more than that.

She wasn't only blurred in his perception—her entire body seemed to dissolve for one second and reconstitute itself, not a flowing transition but an explosion-like whirl, as she dispersed in a cloud of tiny little parts, then in the same breath put herself back together as something new. Something different.

Her face and the slender upper body remained unchanged, but now they no longer grew out of the body of a lion but continued naturally into narrow hips and long, brown legs. The legs of a woman.

Her fur had vanished. Without replacement.

"Allow me?" Naked, she bent over, fished up the curtain at Serafin's feet, and with a lightning twirl, covered her nakedness. The yellow settled around her figure like a dress; no one would have guessed that the stuff had just been hanging from the ceiling as a curtain; on her it looked as natural and perfectly fitting as the most expensive fabric from Umberto's workshop.

Serafin had tried to turn his eyes away, but she left him no time for that. Instead, the image of her completed body kept shining before his eyes as if it had burned into his retina. Like light spots after one has looked at the sun for too long.

"Serafin?"

"Uhh . . . yes?"

"Is this better?"

He looked down her, down to her narrow feet, which stood half covered in soft sand. "It doesn't change anything," he said, having to force out every word. "You're a sphinx, no matter what shape you assume."

"Of course. But now you don't need to be afraid of my claws anymore." Pure roguishness gleamed in her eyes.

He made a great effort to ignore her scornful undertone. "What are you doing here?"

"I lead the counterattack."

"Against the Pharaoh?" He laughed and hoped that it sounded as humorless as it was meant to. "With a few children?"

She rubbed her right foot over her left; he almost believed she felt the embarrassment she intended to convey. Only almost. "Are *you* a child, Serafin?" The way she raised her eyes was a bit too coquettish to be accidental.

"You know exactly what I mean."

"And you know, I think, what *I* mean." All at once her tone became sharper, the emphasis harder. "Dario and the others might be just fifteen, sixteen, or seventeen years old"—with which she indirectly confirmed what he already suspected: that there were no grown-ups among the rebels—"but they are skillful and quick. And the Pharaoh will underestimate them. That is perhaps our strongest weapon: Amenophis's vanity."

339

"You said that you don't know him."

"Not in his current form. But I know how he was earlier, in his first life."

"How long ago was that?"

"Far more than three thousand years."

"You are *three thousand* years old?"

She laughed again, but only briefly. "A few thousand more or less."

Serafin pressed his lips together and said nothing more.

Lalapeya continued: "Amenophis's vanity and arrogance are the reason I've only chosen boys like you. Do you think I'd have found no men larger and stronger than anyone here in this house? But it would have been pointless. The Egyptians will put every grown man under arrest today and deport them afterward. A handful of children, on the other hand . . . Now, I think the Pharaoh will first grapple with the more important things. What color to make his suite here in Venice, for example. At least that is what the earlier Amenophis would have done."

"You really intend to fight the Egyptians with Dario and the others?" She might be right in what she said, but nonetheless he believed she was making it too simple.

"I am no warrior."

Yes, he thought, that's obvious, or is it? Then he remembered her razor-sharp lion's claws and shuddered.

"But," she went on, "we have no choice. We must fight, for that is the only language Amenophis understands."

"If only a fraction of what they say about the Empire is true, the Pharaoh can snuff out Venice in a few minutes. What are a few rebels supposed to do to him?"

"You shouldn't believe everything you hear about the power of the Egyptians. Some of it is true—but some also depends on skillfully spread rumors and on the power of illusion. The priests of Horus are masters of deception."

"It's hopeless in spite of all that. I've seen the mummy soldiers. I've seen how they fight."

The sphinx nodded. "And how they die."

"Through luck, nothing else."

Lalapeya expelled a great sigh. "No one here is thinking of going against the mummy soldiers in the field. At least not the way you imagine it."

"What, then?"

"First I must know if you'll help us." She took a step toward him, on the soft feet of a dancer. It was impossible to resist her charm.

"Why me?"

"Why you?" She smiled again, and her voice sounded a little gentler. "I think you underestimate what a reputation you have. A master of the Thieves' Guild at thirteen, the youngest Venice has ever seen. No one can climb up a housefront faster or more skillfully. No one can slip past any guard more quickly. And no one is braver when it comes to carrying out a task at which all before him have failed."

Lalapeya's words made him uncomfortable. She didn't need to flatter him, and that meant that she was appealing to his honor. Her words also came very close to the truth. And yet all that lay an eternity ago, in another life.

"I was thirteen then," he said. "And today—" He paused. "And today," he went on, "I'm no longer what you said. I left the Guild. I no longer steal. I'm an apprentice to the master weaver Umberto, that's all."

"Nevertheless, you stole the Flowing Queen from the Egyptians."

He stared at her, wide-eyed. "You know about that?"

"Of course." But she didn't provide an explanation, and that made him suspicious again. When she noticed, she quickly added, "You and the girl, Merle."

"What do you know about Merle?"

Lalapeya hesitated. "She has left Venice."

"On a stone lion, yes, I know," he said impatiently. "But where is she now? Is she all right?"

"Nothing has happened to her," said the sphinx. "More than that I don't know."

He had the strong feeling that she was lying, and he made every effort to let her feel it. At the same time, he could see that her decision was firm and she wouldn't tell him more. Not at the moment. If he were to remain for a while, however, he might succeed in getting more out of her, about Merle and the Queen and—

He winced when he realized that he'd fallen into her trap. He'd swallowed the bait.

"I'll help you," he said, "if you tell me more about Merle."

Lalapeya seemed to weigh the offer. "I'd prefer that you did it because you agreed to the necessity."

He shook his head. "Only for Merle."

The sphinx's eyes, her brown, profound eyes, moved over his face, checking to see if he spoke the truth. He was nervous, although he knew that she'd find nothing different; he meant every word just as he'd spoken it. For Merle he'd even go to Egypt, if he had to, and thumb his nose at the Pharaoh. And perhaps break his skull on the best mummy soldier of all. But after all, it was the attempt that counted. Somehow.

"Are you in love with Merle?" asked Lalapeya after a while.

"That's none of your business." The words were already out before he realized what he was saying. "And anyway it has nothing to do with this," he added hastily.

"You needn't be ashamed of it."

He was about to reply but then swallowed the answer and asked instead, "Do you know Merle?"

"Perhaps."

"Oh, come on—what kind of an answer is *that*?"

"The truth. I'm not sure if I know her." Her eyes showed a flash of shock when she realized that possibly she'd betrayed too much. With noticeable control, she said, "I'm not accustomed to being interrogated." But her smile showed that she wasn't angry with him.

Serafin freed himself from her look and walked a few steps back and forth, as if he were weighing whether he really wanted to remain here any longer. His decision had already been made long before. Where could he have gone? Umberto's weaving workshop stood empty, the master had fled God knew where. Serafin had long ago turned his back on his former friends from the Thieves' Guild. And back to Arcimboldo, Eft, and Junipa? Something told him that maybe this would be the right way. But could he somehow protect Junipa from Lord Light better if he joined the sphinx and her odd crew?

Finally he came to a stop. "You must tell me what you have in mind."

"We will not make war on the Egyptians. That would in fact be presumptuous and suicidal. The war will be directed against Amenophis himself."

"Against the Pharaoh?"

When she nodded, the strange desert light flickered over her black hair like tiny flames.

"You want to kill *him*?" asked Serafin, aghast. "An assassination?"

"That would be one way. But it wouldn't be enough. Amenophis isn't an independent ruler. Also, he's ruled by those who have called him back to life. At the moment, anyway."

"By the priests?"

"By the priests of Horus, yes. For centuries they had lost their meaning, had shrunk to a secret cult long forgotten by almost everyone. Until they awakened the Pharaoh in the pyramid of Amun-Ka-Re to new life. With that they gave new strength to a weak, vegetating country. A new leader. A new identity. That and their magic were the two means with which they created the Empire. They're the ones who pull the strings, not Amenophis."

"But that makes everything even more hopeless."

"Where the Pharaoh is, there also are the heads of the priesthood, above all Seth, his vizier and grand master of the Horus cult."

"In all seriousness, you intend for us to go to Heliopolis, into the city of the Pharaoh, and there . . . *eliminate* . . . not only him but also his vizier and perhaps a whole legion of his priests?" He emphasized the word *eliminate* as if it were the idea of a small child, for that was how sensible he thought this whole crazy idea was.

"Not to Heliopolis," said the sphinx very quietly. "Amenophis and Seth will soon be here. Here in Venice. And if I'm not deceived in everything, they will establish their quarters in the Doge's Palace."

Serafin gasped. "The Pharaoh is coming here?"

"Certainly. He won't miss the moment of his greatest

triumph. This is not only a victory over a single city—it is a victory over the Flowing Queen and all she stood for. His triumph over the past and also over his own death. Aside from the Czarist kingdom, there's no one else in the world who can withstand him."

Serafin rubbed a hand over his forehead and desperately tried to keep pace with the sphinx's explanations. "Even if it were true that the Pharaoh is coming to Venice . . . to the Doge's Palace, for all I care . . . what would that change? He'll be hidden behind an army of bodyguards. Behind his mummy soldiers. And, don't forget, behind the magic of Seth and the other priests."

Lalapeya nodded slowly, and her smile was as loving as if she were speaking with a young kitten. "That's why I want you to help us."

"I should break into the Doge's Palace?" Serafin rolled his eyes. "While the *Pharaoh* is there?"

The sphinx didn't have to answer him. He already knew that was exactly what her plan was. But she said something else that touched him more deeply than any slogan or any promise: "For Merle."

5

In the Ear of the Herald

THERE WAS NO DAY IN HELL. AND NO NIGHT.

After the long descent, Vermithrax had set down on a rock shaped like a hatbox; a human could have climbed down the steep walls only with appropriate equipment. Of course they all—the obsidian lion as well as Merle and the Flowing Queen—knew that basically it made no difference where they camped if they had to deal with opponents like the Lilim.

"Maybe down here there aren't creatures like those up there," said Merle, without great conviction.

"*Possibly a few of the most dangerous ones live up*

there, as guards of the entrance, so to speak." The Queen's voice was firm, her enthusiasm undampened. Nevertheless, Merle had the feeling that she was only trying to bolster her courage and didn't completely believe what she said herself.

At least they agreed that there must be a great number of different kinds of Lilim. The messenger Lord Light had sent to the Venetians had had nothing in common with the creatures in the rock wall.

"Which doesn't mean, however, that the others are less terrible or fast." The obsidian lion licked his wings with his stone tongue. "On the contrary, perhaps we've only met the most harmless so far."

"Thanks a lot, Vermithrax," said Merle bitterly, and she had the feeling that the Queen was thinking exactly the same thing. "A joker like you is enormously helpful at the moment."

The lion didn't even look up. "I'm only saying what I think."

Until then Merle had been sitting cross-legged on the rock beside Vermithrax. Now, with a sigh, she let herself sink back until she felt the smooth stone at her back. She crossed her arms behind her head and looked up, there where, in her world, the sky had been.

An expanse of speckled red spread before her eyes, at first still resembling a layer of clouds in the light of the setting sun: a rock ceiling that extended infinitely in all directions, a few thousand yards over them. The network of glowing red veins that had run through the walls of the rock shaft also appeared in the interior of Hell in dirty orange.

Anyway, *Hell* . . . the term seemed to Merle to be ever more unsuitable for the place they'd found at the end of the shaft. A desolate rock landscape formed the bottom of this underground kingdom—at least the part where they were—and, like the ceiling, it was shot through in many places with glowing veins, some as fine as hairs, others as broad as Vermithrax's legs. The stone felt warm, but not really hot anywhere, and the wind blowing down here smelled of tar and the strange sweetness that Merle had noticed at the edge of the abyss.

The ceiling toward which she was gazing likewise consisted of rock, but for the human eye, its great height reduced the structure to spots of light and dark, dipped in the shimmering red of the fire veins.

Merle didn't really know what to think about all this. On the one hand, the environment was impressive and fear-inspiring because of its immeasurable size; but on the other hand, she told herself that this was nothing but a gigantic cavern in the bowels of the earth, perhaps a whole system of caverns. It had nothing to do with the Hell talked about in the Bible. However, and this was the catch, this might change suddenly as soon as they actually bumped into more Lilim—and they expected to at any time.

Even now, at rest, Vermithrax was alert, his body tense.

However, Merle now realized that Professor Burbridge had called this place Hell only for lack of a better name. He'd pulled the myth over the reality like a mask, to make it more understandable for the general public.

"Vermithrax?"

The obsidian lion turned from his wings and looked over at her. "Hmm?"

"Those creatures, up there on the rock wall, they looked as if they were made of stone."

The lion growled agreement. "As if the rock wall itself had come to life."

"Isn't that a strange coincidence?"

"You mean because *I* am of stone?"

She rolled onto her stomach and supported her chin in both hands to be able to look Vermithrax in the eyes. "Yes, somehow. I mean, I know that you have nothing to do with them. But yet, it is strange, isn't it?"

The lion sat up so that he could look at Merle but keep his eyes on the area around the rock at the same time. "I've already thought about that."

"And?"

"We simply know too little about the Lilim."

"How much do you lions know about yourselves? For instance, how come your mane is stone, but all the same it feels soft to the touch? And why does your tongue move although you're made of obsidian?"

"It's stone inspirited with a soul," he said, as if that were answer enough. When he saw that Merle wouldn't be content with that, he went on, "It's stone, but it's also flesh or hair. It has the structure and the strength and the hardness of stone, but there's also life within it, and that changes everything. That's the only explanation I can give you. There have never been scientists among us lions who've investigated all these things. We're not like you humans. We can accept things without taking them apart and snatching the last secret out of them."

Merle thought these words over while she waited for the Queen to express herself. But the voice inside her was silent.

"And the Lilim?" Merle asked finally. "Do you think they're also made of stone with a soul?"

"To me, those creatures didn't look as if they possessed a soul. But there are men who say the same thing about us lions. So then, who am I to judge the Lilim?"

"That sounds quite wise."

Vermithrax laughed. "It isn't at all difficult to pass uncertainty off as wisdom. Your scholars and philosophers and priests have been doing that since you humans have existed." After a short pause he added, "The leaders of us lions too, by the way."

It was the first time Merle had heard him say something disparaging about other lions, and she had the feeling that it had cost him great effort. In fact, the lion folk differed much more from humans than she'd thought until now. Perhaps, she carried the thought further, the relationship of lions to Lilim was even closer than to humans. She wondered if this idea should frighten her, but she felt nothing but curiosity about it.

It came right down to the fact that *everything* down here frightened her somehow, even the rock on which she lay and the mysterious warmth that rose from inside it. She had the feeling it could explode at any moment, like the volcanoes she'd heard of. But she suppressed this uncomfortable thought too, like so many others.

"What should we do when we've found Lord Light?" She put the question to no one in particular. That was what had busied her on the long flight into the abyss, the question of the goal of her mission. Slowly her eyes traveled over the cheerless rock desert extending in all directions. The landscape didn't look as though anyone could live here voluntarily, certainly no prince or ruler like the mysterious Lord Light.

"The Queen must know that," said Vermithrax. He was master of the art of letting his voice sound completely indifferent, even if he was presumably as stirred up inside as Merle was herself.

"*We will ask him for help*," said the Flowing Queen.

"I know that." Merle got to her feet, walked to the edge of the mesa, and let the warm, humid wind waft to her nose. Vermithrax called to her to be careful, but she

had the feeling she had to sense the dangers of this environment with her own body in order to be sure that she
wasn't dreaming it all.

The steep wall fell away at her feet, 175 to 200 feet
deep, and Merle grew dizzy. Strangely, she felt that was
almost a good feeling. A true, actual feeling.

"I know that we've come here to ask him for help," she
said finally. "For Venice and for all the others. But how do
we do that? I mean, what will he think when a girl on a
flying lion appears before his throne and—"

"*Who says he has a throne?*"

"I thought he was a king."

"*He rules over Hell,*" said the Queen patiently. "*But
here below is rather different from the upper world.*"

Merle couldn't take her eyes off the rough rock land.
She saw no great difference from wildernesses she'd seen
in drawings and engravings. A desert people like the
Egyptians might feel quite comfortable down here.

Then a thought came to her, and it hit her like a blow
in the face. "You *know* him!"

"*No,*" said the Flowing Queen tonelessly.

"How do you know that he has no throne, then? That
he isn't like other rulers?"

"*Only a surmise.*" The Queen was seldom so tight-
lipped.

"A surmise, eh?" Her voice now sounded reproachful
and angry, so that even Vermithrax looked over at her in

confusion. "That's why you knew so precisely where to find the entrance," Merle burst out. "And that down here everything is different from up above. . . . But there, for once, you were mistaken. It's not so different at all. For me, anyway, it looks like an ordinary grotto." She'd never seen a grotto with her own eyes, but that didn't matter now. She had no better argument.

"*This* grotto, *Merle, has an area that is probably as large as half the planet. Perhaps it is even much larger. And how else would you describe the Lilim if not as 'different'?*"

"But that wasn't what you meant before," Merle said with conviction. She'd had enough of being put down in each of her discussions. It was a remarkable feeling to argue with someone you couldn't look in the eye and whose voice wasn't real. "I don't understand why you aren't honest with me . . . with us."

Vermithrax was brushing his whiskers with his paw, but he wasn't missing a word. He could only guess at the course of the conversation from what Merle said.

Again she thought that it simply wasn't fair that only she could hear the Queen. And had to argue with her on her own.

"*I have heard rumors about Lord Light, things the mermaids have picked up. That is all.*"

"What sort of rumors?"

"*That he is no ordinary ruler. It is not about power with him.*"

"What else?"

"That I cannot tell you. I do not know."

"But you have a surmise."

The Queen was silent for a moment. Then she said, *"What can a ruler of an entire kingdom concern himself with, if not with power? And furthermore, how great could his influence over his subjects be then? The Lilim in the rock wall did not look as if they would take any orders out of pure humility."*

"So what does he concern himself with?" Merle asked doggedly.

"With knowledge, I think. He likes ruling this world, but above all, I think, he investigates it."

"Investigates? But—"

A loud exclamation from the lion interrupted her. "Merle! Over there!"

She whirled around and almost lost her balance. For an instant the edge of the steep cliff was dangerously close, the rocks leaped toward Merle's feet. Then she caught herself again, turned hastily away from the drop, and followed Vermithrax's look with her own eyes.

At first she detected nothing at all, only empty red over the breadth of the wasteland. Then she realized that the lion's predator's eyes were sharper than her own. Whatever he'd caught sight of must still be beyond her range of sight.

But it wasn't long until she saw it. And whatever it was, it was coming nearer.

"What is that?" she exclaimed, breathless and suddenly oppressed with a flood of horrible pictures; fantasies of flying Lilim, thousands of them, danced in her mind.

Yet it wasn't thousands, but only three. And although they were floating high over the rocks, they possessed no wings.

"Are they . . ."

"Heads," said Vermithrax. "Gigantic heads." And after a moment he added, "Of stone."

She shook her head, not because she doubted his words but because it was the only reaction that seemed appropriate. Heads of stone. High in the air. Of course.

But after a while she could see them for herself. She saw the heads coming nearer, and quite fast—faster than Vermithrax could fly, of that she was sure.

"Come on, mount!" bellowed the lion, and before she could think of a good argument against it, she was already leaping onto his back, curling her hands into his mane, bending over, and pressing her upper body firmly to his obsidian coat.

"What is he going to do?"

"What are you going to do?"

"Look at them. They aren't alive." Vermithrax's paws pushed off the rock, and seconds later they were already hovering three feet above the hatbox mesa.

"They are not alive," Merle repeated to herself and then added more loudly, "So what? What does that mean?"

"That means they aren't Lilim. At least, not dangerous ones."

"Oh, yes?"

"*Wait*," said the Queen. "*Perhaps he is right.*"

"And if he isn't?"

She received no answer. She would probably not have heard it anyway, for now the three heads were close enough to see details.

They were human heads, without any doubt, and they were hewn out of stone. So high up in the air there were no fixed points by which to gauge their size, but Merle guessed that each was at least fifty yards high. Their faces were stiff and gray, the eyes open, but without pupils. The stone hair, formed like a helmet, lay close to the head and left the ears free. The powerful lips were open a crack, but what from afar Merle had thought was an entrance to the head's inside showed itself up close to be an illusion, which was supposed to create the impression that the heads were speaking.

Now they also heard voices.

Words streamed over the plain like a swarm of birds, fluttering and restless, a language that Merle had never heard in her life.

The heads were still about half a mile away and were approaching in an arrow formation, one head at the point, the two others behind and to the right and left.

"Those voices . . . is that *them*?"

"I don't know whether those are their voices, but

they're coming from inside them," said Vermithrax. Merle noticed that he had his ears pricked. Not only could he see better than she could, he also heard much more and was able to distinguish sounds and where they came from.

"What do you mean? They're not their voices?"

"Someone else is speaking out of them. They aren't alive. Their stone isn't—"

"Inspirited with a soul?"

"Precisely." Vermithrax fell silent and concentrated completely on his flight. Merle had thought they would flee from the heads, but the lion had until now kept himself still in the air at a point that lay straight across the flight path of the foremost stone head. To her boundless horror, she now realized that Vermithrax was turning— not away from the heads, but toward them. He actually was intending to fly into them.

"Vermithrax! What are you doing?"

The obsidian lion did not answer. Instead he made his wings fan up and down even faster, maneuvered himself a little farther to the left—and waited.

"What do you—"

"*He is planning something.*"

"Oh?" Merle would probably have turned red with fury if her fear hadn't driven all the blood from her face. "They're coming right at us!"

The uncanny voices blared louder and louder over the wasteland and were echoed back from the rock walls and towers of stone. It seemed to Merle as if she were dangling in fireworks of strange words as a multitude of different sounds exploded around her like colored fountains of flame. Even if she'd had command of the strange language, she wouldn't have understood anything at all, so loud, so shrill were the syllables coming out of this nearest head. A piercing whistling started in Merle's ears before the heads came level with them.

Vermithrax shook his head, as if trying to drive the noise out of his sensitive ears. His muscles tensed. Abruptly he rushed forward to the front head, at the last moment laid himself on an angle, bellowed something incomprehensible to Merle—probably a warning to hold on especially tight—and dived through under the ridge of the right cheekbone. Merle saw the huge face rush by her like a wall of granite, too big to take in with one look, too fast to perceive more than the weight, the size, the sheer force of its speed.

She called Vermithrax's name, but the wind tore the syllables from her lips and the voices of the flying heads overwhelmed any sound.

So suddenly that her fingers gave way and her entire body was pulled backward, Vermithrax smashed his claws into the stone ear of the head and pulled himself along. At the same time his wings stopped beating, bent inward, and caught Merle before she could plunge down into the deep. The tips of the feathers pressed her down onto his back with the force of a giant fist, while Vermithrax did his best to absorb the brutal jolt that went through them both at the first contact with the head.

Somehow he succeeded. Somehow he found a grip. And then they were sitting in the ear of the gigantic head and rushing with insane speed across the rocky country.

Merle needed a while before her breathing had grown calm enough for her to be able to speak again. But even then the thoughts flitted around in her head like moths around a candle flame, wild and nervous, and she had trouble giving them a clear direction, had trouble grasping what had just happened. Finally she clenched a fist and struck Vermithrax. He didn't seem to even feel it.

"Why?" she bellowed at him. "Why did you do that?"

Vermithrax climbed over a stone bulge deeper into the ear. It opened around them like a cave, rocky, dark, a deep funnel. Astonishingly, the noise here inside was dulled; for one thing, because it was now only a single voice that they heard, for here they were shut away from the racket of the two other heads; for another, because the voice of the head was directed to the outside.

Vermithrax let Merle slide from his back and lay down between two stone bulges, exhausted. He panted, his long tongue hanging down to his powerful paws.

"The probability is fifty-fifty," he brought out between two deep intakes of breath.

"What probability?" Merle was still angry, but gradually

her anger was overwhelmed by relief that in spite of everything they were still alive.

"Either the head is taking us to Lord Light, or it's taking us in exactly the opposite direction." Vermithrax pulled in his tongue and put his head down on his front paws. Merle became conscious for the first time how very much he'd exhausted himself with the leap to the flying head and just how closely they'd slid past death.

"This head here," said Vermithrax wearily, "is announcing something. I don't understand the words it's broadcasting, but it's always the same over and over again, as if it had a message. Perhaps it's a kind of herald."

"A message from Lord Light to his people?"

"Possibly," said the Flowing Queen. *"Vermithrax could be right."*

"What else?" asked the lion.

Merle rolled her eyes. "How should I know? Down here everything is different. These things could be who knows what!" As she spoke, she looked around the stone cave. It seemed so incredible: They actually had a firm seat in a gigantic ear.

"These heads are dead objects," said Vermithrax. "This is an important difference from the Lilim. Someone built them. And he did it for a certain purpose. Since Lord Light just happens to be the ruler of this place, it must have been he."

"And why fifty-fifty?"

"Possibly the head is on the way to its master because it's fulfilled a mission—or it's just begun its journey and is going away from Lord Light. One of the two."

"That means we can only wait, doesn't it?"

The lion nodded, which looked strangely clumsy, since his nose still lay on his paws. "Looks like it."

"What do you think?" Merle asked the Queen.

"*I think he is right. We could probably wander through Hell for months without finding a trace of Lord Light. But this way we have at least a chance.*"

Merle gave a sigh, then she edged closer to the lion and stroked his nose. "But next time, you tell me beforehand, okay? I really want to know *why* you're almost killing us all."

The lion growled something—was it a yes?—and nestled his fist-sized nose into Merle's hand. Then he purred blissfully, thrashed his tail a couple of times, and closed his eyes.

Merle remained sitting beside him a moment longer, then she levered herself up on wobbly knees and climbed to the outer stone bulge of the giant ear.

Impressed, she looked down. The mournful landscape was flying along a thousand feet below them, so monotonous that there was nothing, but nothing at all, that she could have fastened her eyes on. Probably they were going too fast anyway. She doubted that Vermithrax could have kept up even half as much speed over a long period.

"What a desolate place!" she whispered with a groan. "Did Lord Light ever try to plant something here? I mean, to add a little color. A little variety."

"Why should he? Nothing lives here. At least nothing that could value such efforts. Or do you think that the Lilim in the camp up there would be happy about a few flowers?"

"You don't have to make it sound so ridiculous!"

"I do not mean to at all. Only, you must use other measures in this world. Other terms, other concepts."

Merle was silent and leaned back. But then a thought came to her that made her sit right up again.

"If these heads are something like flying machines, like the sunbarks of the Empire, then there must be someone in them, mustn't there? Someone who steers them!"

"We are alone."

"Are you sure?"

"I would feel it. And Vermithrax, too, I think."

Merle stretched out on the hard stone, observed the slumbering obsidian lion for a while, then looked out over the landscape of Hell. What a strange place! She tried to remember how Professor Burbridge had traveled through it, but she couldn't think of anything. After all, she hadn't really read any of his books; her teacher in the orphanage had talked about a few passages, but most of what she'd heard were synopses at second hand. Some descriptions, that was all. Now she regretted that she hadn't been more interested in it at the time.

On the other hand, she remembered quite clearly the dangers of Hell that Burbridge had recounted in his reports. Gruesome creatures, which waited for the unsuspecting behind every stone and every . . . yes, tree. She was certain that the talk had been of *trees*—trees of iron, with leaves like razor blades. Well, here anyway, in this part of Hell, there appeared to be no plants, either of iron or of wood.

She also recollected very well stories of barbarous creatures that moved in huge packs over the plain, landscapes that were wrapped in everlasting fire, mountains that folded their wings and flew away, and ships of human bones that sailed over the lava oceans of Hell. All those were pictures that had stuck in Merle's mind, so greatly had they impressed her at the time.

And now there weren't any of those.

She was disappointed and relieved at the same time. The Lilim in the rock wall were murderous enough for her taste, and she could perfectly happily do without hordes of cannibals and gigantic monsters. However, she felt a little cheated, as if now, after years, all the infernal pictures had turned out to be just wild stories.

But Hell was gigantic, and so there might be different landscapes and cultures down here, as there were up on the earth. If a traveler from another world were set down somewhere in the Sahara, he'd certainly be disappointed if people had told him beforehand about the splendid palaces of Venice and its many branching canals. Even more, he probably wouldn't be able to believe they existed at all.

Merle climbed back to the outermost swelling of stone and looked out at the rocky ground rushing past way below them. No change, no trace of life. Oddly, she felt no drafts of wind, no suction, which there really should have been at this speed.

A little bored, especially after all she'd been through, she turned her gaze behind them, to the second stone head, which was following them at some distance. From here she couldn't see the third, which was on the other side.

Suddenly she started up, her sluggishness vanishing at one stroke.

"That isn't . . . ," she began, but she forgot to end the sentence. Then, after a moment, she asked, "Do you see that too?"

"*I see through your eyes, Merle. Of course I can see him.*"

Between the lips of the second head there was a man.

He was perched behind the lower lip and lay with his upper body and arms stretched out over the stone, apparently lifeless, as if the mighty head had half swallowed him and then had forgotten to swallow the rest. His arms dangled back and forth, his head lay on one side, face turned away. He had very long, snow-white hair, and Merle would have taken him for a woman, if he hadn't suddenly turned his head and looked over at her. He looked out at her between the white strands, which covered his features like fresh-fallen snow. Even at this distance she could see how narrow and wasted his face looked. His skin had hardly any more color than his hair; it was as pale as that of a corpse.

"He is dying," said the Flowing Queen.

"And so we should just look on while he does it?"

"We cannot get to him."

Merle thought it over; then she made a decision. "Maybe yes."

She sprang back inside the ear, shook Vermithrax awake, and pulled the tired, ill-humored lion with her to the edge of the stone ear. The white man had now turned his face away again and was hanging over the lip of the head like a dead man.

"Can we get over there?" The tone of her voice made it clear that she would not accept a no.

"Hmm," said Vermithrax gloomily.

"What's that supposed to mean . . . hmm?" Merle waved her arms and gesticulated wildly. "We can't simply let him die over there. He needs our help, you can see that."

Vermithrax growled something unintelligible, and Merle waved her hands more and more furiously, appealed eloquently to his conscience, and finally even said, "Please." At last he murmured, "He could be a danger."

"But he's a human being!"

"Or something that looks like one," said the Queen with Merle's voice.

Merle was much too excited to reprimand her for this breach of their agreement. "In any case, we can't just stay sitting here and watching." She added emphatically, "We can't, can we?"

The Queen wrapped herself in silence, which in a certain way was also an answer, but Vermithrax replied, "No, probably not."

Merle let out her breath. "You intend to try it?"

"*Try what?*" asked the Queen, but this time Merle just ignored her.

Vermithrax looked calculatingly from the edge of the ear across the gulf to the second stone head. "The head isn't flying exactly behind us, but at an angle. That makes it more difficult. But perhaps . . . hmm, if I pushed off hard enough and so got out far enough and then simply let myself fall back, I could maybe hook onto him again and—"

"Simply! Did you just say 'simply'?" asked the Queen through Merle's mouth.

Stop it! Merle thought.

"*But it is madness. We do not know who or what he is and why he is in such a condition.*"

"If we keep sitting around here, we'll never find out either."

"*Perhaps that would be better.*" But the Queen's tone revealed that she'd accepted her defeat. She was a fair loser—perhaps also an offended one—and once more she lapsed into silence.

"It will be difficult," said Vermithrax.

"Yes." As if Merle didn't know that.

"I can't just stand there in the air until its face rams into me—that would kill me. I can only try again to jump up sideways, on the ear or on the hair somewhere. And then from there I have to climb around the head to reach the man."

Merle took a deep breath. "I can do that."

"You?"

"Certainly."

"But you have no claws."

"No, but I'm lighter. And more agile. And I can hold on to the smallest unevenness." She didn't really believe that herself, of course, but somehow she thought it sounded plausible.

"Not a good plan," said Vermithrax, unimpressed.

"Just get me over there, I'll take care of the rest. I've had enough of sitting around on your back the whole time"—she smiled fleetingly—"I mean, nothing against your back, but I simply can't be so . . . inactive. I never was particularly good at that."

The lion pulled up his lips, and it took Merle a moment to recognize that as a grin. "You're quite a brave girl. And a completely crazy one."

She beamed at him. "Then we'll do it?"

Vermithrax ran the point of his tongue over his finger-length canine teeth. "Yes," he said, after another long look over the gap, "I think we'll simply give it a try."

"*Simply*," said the Queen with a groan. "*There it is again.*"

6

Junipa's Fate

"WHAT'S THAT SUPPOSED TO MEAN," DARIO ROARED, "you want to leave again right away?"

Serafin held his glare easily. It had never particularly impressed him when someone yelled at him. Usually, loudness was just a sign of weakness. "It means exactly what I said. That I have to leave once more before the attack. And don't worry, *General* Dario: I'm not planning to desert your army of heroes."

Dario was boiling with rage, and he looked now as if he were sorry he had no more than two fists he could clench. "That's not the way it works here," he said sharply, less loudly but no less angrily. "You can't just leave for a few hours while we're getting ready to go to the Doge's—"

Serafin interrupted him. "Perhaps *you* have to get yourselves ready. *I* don't have to. You *asked* me"—he emphasized the word with special relish—"to help you because you know that I'm the only one who has a ghost of a chance to get into the palace. You know, Dario, the rules are very simple: I'll try to get into the palace, and whoever follows me will do exactly what I say. If not, he either stays here or is probably a dead man within the first few minutes." He chose such dramatic words intentionally, because he had the feeling Dario could best be managed that way. Besides, he'd really had enough of this discussion even before it began.

"With all due respect to your instincts," said Dario, controlling himself with difficulty, "but—"

"Excuse me: My instincts are all you have." Serafin pointed to the small group of rebels who'd gathered in the dining room of the enclave: a dozen boys his age, some even younger, most of them from the street. They were practiced in fending for themselves, stealing, and outwitting the City Guard. Some of them were still wearing the ragged clothing in which they'd grown up, and others who'd clothed themselves anew from the inventory in the sphinx's house looked dandified in their colorful shirts and trousers. Most of those things looked as if someone had collected them for a masquerade ball; it was only after a while that Serafin realized the clothes must actually have come from various previous centuries and been preserved over time in the sphinx's boxes and trunks. Once again he wondered how long Lalapeya had been living here in Venice. She'd given him no answer to that.

Dario had had the wit to choose his new trousers and shirt in velvety purple, dark enough to melt into the night. The others who'd been less careful in their choice of clothes would stay here. They didn't know it yet, but Serafin would make sure of it. He couldn't burden himself with breaking-in companions who weren't engaged with their whole mind.

"You haven't got your mind on this," Dario said, as if he'd read Serafin's thoughts in order to use his own arguments against him. "How can we rely on you if your mind is on something else all the time?"

"And that's exactly the reason why I intend to leave again now." Serafin paid no attention to the silent faces listening attentively to every word exchanged between him and Dario. "To clear my head for what we have ahead of us, I have to take care of a certain matter. I can't allow it to distract me."

"And what matter of world-shaking importance would that be?"

Serafin hesitated. What was it that Dario was after? Not, as he'd originally thought, to make a fool of him in front of all present. Also, not to question his leadership qualities (and Serafin would have been the first to agree with him there: He'd never been a good leader, always a loner). No, Dario was curious. Perhaps he even guessed what Serafin had in mind. And was ashamed.

Lalapeya, thought Serafin. She told him. And now he's trying to make me look bad in front of the others because he feels bad himself. Really, he's not abusing me but himself.

"I'm going to the Canal of the Expelled," he said, observing every movement of Dario's face, every trace of emotion that went beyond anger. In an instant, Dario's features were a singular admission of guilt.

"What could you want there?" Dario asked softly. His tone was very different from a few moments before. A murmur went through the line of rebels.

"I intend to go to Arcimboldo's magic mirror workshop," Serafin said. "I have to check on him, and on Eft. And above all, on Junipa." He lowered his voice so much that only Dario could understand him. "I have to get her away from there. Someplace where she's safe. Otherwise she won't survive the coming days. And probably not Arcimboldo, either."

Dario stared at him, eyes narrowed, as if he could look through him to his inmost being. "Someone wants to kill Arcimboldo?"

Serafin nodded. "I'm afraid that's what it's going to boil down to. I can't imagine that he'll actually surrender Junipa. And if he refuses, they'll kill him."

"Surrender? Who to? The Egyptians?"

Serafin grabbed Dario by the upper arm and led him away from the others, through a door into the next room where they could talk undisturbed. "Not the Egyptians," he said.

"Who else?"

Serafin looked thoughtfully out the window. It was dark outside. They were going to invade the palace later this very night. Their spies had reported that the Pharaoh had installed himself there a few hours ago. Before then, Serafin had to take care of Junipa, Arcimboldo, and Eft. Next to that, everything else, even the fight against the Egyptians, paled to meaninglessness.

Serafin gave himself a shake and looked Dario in the face. He knew with certainty: He had no more time to explain the circumstances to Dario.

"Just come with me."

"Are you serious?"

Serafin nodded. "You can handle a saber well. Much better than I can."

Dario's distaste for allying himself with his old archenemy still burned in his eyes. But there was also something else: a trace of relief and, yes, of gratitude. For Serafin had made it easy for him, enabling him to go along without having to ask. That was what surprised Serafin the most. Dario *wanted* to go with him and had from the very beginning. Only he hadn't been able to bring himself to say it, not to Serafin.

"And the others?" asked Dario.

"Will have to wait."

"Lalapeya?"

"She too."

Dario nodded. "Then let's get going right now."

Back in the dining room, Dario gave the surprised Tiziano the order to take over command until they were back. Tiziano and Boro exchanged irritated looks, then grinned, and Tiziano nodded proudly. The other boys wanted to know what Dario and Serafin were going to do, but when Boro promised them all a second portion of supper, their interest flagged, and they turned to the steaming dishes. Serafin smiled when he saw that. All their lives, they would be street children at heart and hungry for any meal.

After carefully surveying the street, Serafin and Dario left the enclave through the main entrance. The sphinx's palazzo was in the Castello district, in the middle of Venice, but tonight there wasn't a single inhabitant on the street.

The mummy soldiers' random attacks had now turned into organized patrols—Venice had fallen into the enemy's hands without a battle, without any intervention from the City Guard. The traitorous city councillors had seen to it that the city would capitulate as soon as the Queen was gone and the enemy troops had moved closer. In the past few nights, the mummy troops' attacks on civilians had gone a step further to crush the citizens' fighting spirit.

Most had simply given up: the city and themselves. Now it was only a question of time until the first would be dragged from their houses and carried off to the boats.

The two boys kept close to the façade of the palazzo as they set out. In a whisper, Serafin asked about the walled-up windows of the ground floor, but Dario didn't know what was hidden behind them. No one ever entered the lower floor, that was law. There weren't even doors.

It wasn't far to the Canal of the Expelled, barely fifteen minutes at a run. Yet they had to detour several times when they heard the clink of steel or the sound of rhythmic steps, but never voices, coming from around a bend. Once, they were only a few steps away from one of the mummy patrols, as they pressed themselves into a niche, hoping the Pharaoh's slaves wouldn't sense them. A cloud of dust rose to Serafin's nose as the bony figures marched past them.

After some minutes they reached a small intersection. Here the Canal of the Expelled branched off from a broader waterway. Serafin's heart gave a leap when he saw the deserted bridge and the empty sidewalks. At this very spot, not too long ago, at the lantern festival, everything had begun for him and Merle. The thought filled him with sorrow and fear. Where was Merle now?

Nothing had changed on the Canal of the Expelled. Almost all the houses on the cul de sac had been empty for a long time, doors and windowpanes destroyed. Only the two workshops, their gray façades staring at each other across the water like the faces of old men, had been occupied, until recently. But now Umberto's weavers had left their house, and the windows of the magic mirror workshop were also dark.

"Are you sure they're still here?" asked Dario, as they approached Arcimboldo's workshop. They checked again and again to be sure no one was following them. Serafin kept an eye on the sky for flying lions, although in the darkness he could see almost nothing. If there were something dark and massive sweeping across the stars, it was too fast for his tired eyes.

"You must know Arcimboldo better than I do," he said. "I didn't have the impression he's a man who'd abandon his house and crawl into a hole somewhere."

Dario returned his look with a spark of anger, but then he realized Serafin's words were not an attack. He nodded slowly. "Perhaps we shouldn't have left him and Eft behind." He hadn't forgotten what he owed to Arcimboldo.

Serafin laid a hand on his shoulder. "He knew that you'd go. He said so to me. And I believe he even wanted that a little."

"He spoke to you about it?" Dario looked at him. "When?"

"Not long ago. I was with him outside in the lagoon, after you loaded the mirrors into the boat."

"The last delivery . . ." Dario's voice sounded thoughtful suddenly, as his eyes strayed to the entrance of the mirror workshop. "He never told us where he took all the mirrors. Or who he sold them to." He started and stared at Serafin. "Do these happen to be the people we're supposed to protect him from? Are we here on account of them?"

Serafin was about to tell him the whole story right then and there: how he'd watched Arcimboldo hand his magic mirrors over to Talamar, the courier from Hell, and how Talamar had demanded the girl Junipa for his master, Lord Light. The girl with the mirror eyes.

But then he kept silent and just nodded briefly.

"What kind of people are they?" Dario asked.

Serafin sighed. "If we're unlucky, we'll meet one of them tonight." He was about to move on, but Dario held him back.

"Come on, spit it out."

Serafin looked from Dario to the dark workshop, then back to Dario again. It wasn't easy for him to tell the truth. Dario wouldn't believe him.

"Hell," he said finally. "Arcimboldo was selling his mirrors to Lord Light for years. To one of his couriers."

"Lord Light?" Dario's voice was quiet, as if this news didn't really surprise him. Then he nodded slowly. "The Devil, that is."

"That remains to be proven," said Serafin. "No one has

ever seen Lord Light." But he was only trying to make it sound better, he knew that.

"And Arcimboldo obeyed him?" Dario asked.

A lone gust of wind brushed Serafin's face and made him shiver. Again he looked up at the night sky. "He didn't only make the mirrors for him. He also took Merle and Junipa into his house on Lord Light's orders."

"But . . . ," Dario began, then shook his head. He'd never liked the two girls, but he didn't go so far as to blame them. "Tell the rest," he begged.

"There isn't more to tell. Junipa was blind, you know that, and Arcimboldo implanted the mirror eyes at Lord Light's request."

"Those damned eyes," whispered Dario. "They're creepy. Like ice. As if a cold wind were blowing out of them." He stopped, and then after a moment he added, "Why? What do Hell or Lord Light get out of it if Junipa can see again?"

"No idea." Serafin noted the doubt on Dario's face. But for some reason he didn't want to try to explain about the power the mirror eyes gave Junipa. "Arcimboldo only did what they commissioned him to do. To save the workshop and also you apprentices. He was afraid he'd have to send you back to the orphanage if he refused Lord Light's commissions. He was only concerned about you." Serafin hesitated a moment, then he said, "And he was glad to be able to help Junipa. He said she was so happy to finally be able to see."

"And why are we here now?"

"Talamar, Lord Light's errand boy, has demanded that Arcimboldo surrender Junipa to him. But I think he knew Arcimboldo would refuse to do it. He gave him a deadline. And therefore we have to get your master, Junipa, and Eft to safety before—"

"Before this Talamar comes for the girl," Dario ended the sentence. "And punishes Arcimboldo for his disobedience."

"Then you're still with me?" Serafin hadn't forgotten what happened when Dario went after him with a knife that time in the mirror workshop. Then, Dario had used Junipa as a shield. On the other hand, Serafin felt that he was dealing with a different Dario today, one who was straighter with other people—and with himself.

"Sure." Dario drew his saber, a decisive but also a slightly useless gesture. "No matter who we have to deal with. And if the Pharaoh and Lord Light are inside there toasting each other, we'll just show them both where to go."

Serafin grinned and started moving. Together they covered the last few yards to the workshop. The sign over the door, ARCIMBOLDO'S GLASS FOR THE GODS, appeared even more unreal than ever. On this night the gods were farther away from Venice than ever before.

A soft thumping sounded as the mirror maker's empty boat struck the canal wall behind them, making Serafin and Dario jump. Something had disturbed the calm water. Perhaps only the wind.

Still no lions in the sky.

The front door was open. Dario cast a surprised look at Serafin, but he merely shrugged. It was only after they'd cautiously entered that they saw the reason: The door lock was broken—in fact, it was smashed, splintered like the wood of the oak door, which had been thrown against the wall with such force that the plaster was missing in several places.

On the alert, Dario peered into the darkness.

Serafin whispered only one word: "Talamar."

He didn't know what made him so sure. It could just as well have been mummy soldiers who'd forced their way into the house. But he sensed the breath of Lord Light's slave like a bad smell that fouled the air. Like something that singed the hairs on the back of his neck and made all the roots of his teeth suddenly start aching. The presence of something bad through and through, perhaps even more evil than the power that had sent it here.

"Talamar," he said once more, louder this time, more grimly.

Then he ran, despite Dario's warning, despite even the darkness that seethed in the entry hall like a black brew in a witch's kettle. He tore up the stairs, turned off at the second floor, and recoiled when he saw hectic movements flit over the walls to the right and left of him. But it was only his own image that flitted through a tremendous number of mirrors on the walls everywhere.

Dario was running directly behind him when a deafening shriek sounded. Dario increased his pace, almost pulling past Serafin.

Who had screamed? Man, woman, or girl? Or maybe something else entirely, not in torment but in shrill, blazing triumph.

Through the corridors, from all directions at once, came the whisper: "The wish is fulfilled, the magic worked, the agreement kept."

The boys turned the corner, straight into the corridor that led to the high double doors of the workshop. Arcimboldo's shop floor resembled the laboratory of an alchemist in olden days rather than the room of a craftsman. His magic mirrors consisted of silvered glass, magic, and the essence of the Flowing Queen.

But the caustic vapors that met them now had nothing to do with alchemical substances or magic. They were the breath of damnation, of the black pestilence Talamar. Serafin knew it, felt it with every nerve, with every fiber. His senses cried alarm. His mind screamed to him to turn around.

But he ran on, raised his saber high, opened his mouth in a scream of rage and helplessness—and flew through the open door into the laboratory, rushed through clouds of acrid smoke and sour steam, stumbled, and came to a stop, hardly able to breathe. And *saw*.

Eft lay in a corner, maybe dead, maybe only unconscious. In the pallid fog that filled the room, it wasn't possible to see if she was still breathing. She wore no mask,
but her face was turned away.

Something was moving in the mist, like a giant spider with four legs. Limbs bent out of line, as if someone
had put a rag doll together wrong. A body whose belly
faced up, and an upside-down face, the pointed chin facing the top, the malicious eyes at the bottom. Like a
human child making a bridge; and yet far removed from
any humanity.

The messenger from Hell was pulling something
behind him with one hand, a motionless bundle. A body.

Junipa.

Serafin hesitated only a moment to make sure that
Dario saw the same thing he did, then dove through the
caustic mist at Talamar so fast that Hell's messenger could
scarcely react. Instead of avoiding him, the creature
dropped Junipa, raised an arm—in a distorted movement
that had nothing in common with anything earthly—and
turned away the saber blade with his naked skin, hard as
stone, as impervious as the horn shell of an insect. The
blade rebounded with a sickening thudding sound, and
Serafin was almost thrown to the ground by his own
momentum. He caught himself at the last moment, took
two steps back, and then stood, legs astride, ready for the
next exchange of blows.

A shrill laugh rang from the creature's twisted mouth; his eyes searched, explored, discovered the second opponent.

Dario had learned from Serafin's mistake. Instead of engaging Talamar on a straight line, he made a step toward the beast, whirled around, sprang to the right, then to the left, and finally leaped clear over his antagonist in an acrobatic jump, turned in the air, and using both hands, drove the saber into the body of Hell's courier from above.

Talamar groaned as the tip scratched his skin. He shook himself as if it were an insect sting, spit out a string of staccato sounds, then merely wiped the blade aside. The tip had penetrated scarcely a finger's breadth, too little to weaken him or seriously wound him at all. Dario snatched the saber back before Talamar could grab it, landed on both feet, staggered briefly, then retrieved his balance and called out to Serafin something that was swallowed up in the creature's angry bellowing.

But Serafin understood it anyway.

Dario now was standing on Talamar's right side, while Serafin was still on his left. They could take the messenger from Hell in a pincer movement if they managed skillfully. If they dealt fast enough.

Talamar was quite capable of speaking the language of the Venetians—Serafin had heard it himself—but the sounds that he now uttered hurt Serafin's ears. It was as if the sounds were something living, sent out to weaken Talamar's opponents and destroy their concentration.

Serafin forced himself to be calm. His eyes sought the motionless figure of Junipa, half buried under Talamar's body, and he believed he saw a metallic flash, a reflection in her eyes. They were open. She was watching him. And yet Junipa could not move, as if Talamar had laid a spell on her. Her limbs were rigid, her muscles frozen. But she was breathing, he now saw very clearly. She was alive. And that was what counted.

Dario let out a whistle. Serafin looked up, nodded to his companion. And both attacked at the same time, letting the sabers whirl and rain down on Talamar's armored skin.

Steel bounced on horn. Without success.

Talamar screamed again, not in pain, but in rage. Then he went on the counterattack.

He had recognized Dario as the most dangerous foe, and so he favored him with his first thrust. The claws on Talamar's fingers, no shorter than a dagger blade and just as sharp, flashed forth and back, darting, whirling blurs, and then Dario cried out, staggered back, and bumped against a workbench. With great presence of mind he threw himself backward, although losing his saber in the process, slithered across the top of the bench, and plunged to cover behind it. Just in time, for Talamar's claws drove behind him, imprinting five deep scars in the wood.

Serafin used the moment while the creature was distracted. He didn't know how to penetrate Talamar's armored skin, but his instinct told him that he should direct his attacks to the creature's head. His saber cut through the gray mist, drove the vapors away from Talamar's features, and for the first time uncovered his entire face. In one tiny instant, almost frozen in time, Serafin saw the steel thorn vine that ran like a band over Talamar's eyes; saw the individual tendril that had loosened itself from the others and led diagonally across the creature's mouth.

Then the blade of the saber struck Talamar's face—and bounced off again.

The scream that now came from the creature's throat sounded agonized and uncontrolled, and for the first time Serafin had the feeling of being dangerous to Talamar in spite of everything, yes, even being able to kill him.

Instead of retreating and recovering strength for a new attack, Serafin pursued him immediately, thrust the saber forward, felt how he struck resistance—and saw the blade shatter into a thousand splinters.

Talamar hauled back and dealt a blow that would have killed Serafin had it been better aimed. But though the claws only grazed him, they dug deep scratches into his right cheek. Serafin staggered and clattered to the floor. He fell so hard that it knocked the wind out of him, and when his vision cleared again, Talamar was gone.

Junipa had also vanished.

"Serafin?"

He looked up and saw Dario stand up behind the workbench, gather his saber from the floor, and then stare incredulously at the five deep gouges in the top of the workbench. It didn't take much imagination to visualize what would have been left of him if the blow had actually struck him.

"Here!" Serafin cried, but it sounded like an inarticulate wail, not like a word.

"Where is he?" Dario staggered over to him. He was supporting himself on his saber like a crutch. His face was contorted in pain and a bruise like an exotic plant bloomed under his left eye.

"Gone."

"Where?"

Serafin picked himself up before Dario reached him. He was still holding the hilt of the saber in his hand. He stared at it in disbelief, and then carelessly threw it aside. The metal hilt clattered on the wooden floorboards, skittered a ways away, and was then taken up by a hand, which pulled it abruptly from the billows of mist like a hungry animal.

"Eft!" Serafin bent forward and helped the woman to her feet. "I thought—"

She didn't let him finish. "Where's Arcimboldo?"

Serafin looked around, saw only Dario, who shrugged, and then he shook his head. "I don't know."

Eft pushed his hands away and struggled forward, her

upper body bent over, and dragged herself through the caustic fog, which was burning in Serafin's lungs like liquid fire.

"He must . . . be here . . . somewhere."

Serafin and Dario again exchanged looks; then they fanned out and searched the interior of the workshop.

After a short while, they were certain that neither Talamar and Junipa nor Arcimboldo were there. Instead they stumbled on an opening in the floor, with charred edges, jagged, like a star that a child might have drawn on the floor with unskilled fingers.

For a moment, Serafin thought that the hole led directly to Hell.

But after his eyes grew used to the darkness, he saw at the bottom of the opening the floor of the story below. He would have jumped down then and there, but Eft held him back.

"Leave it," she said. "He's gone."

"And Junipa?"

"He took her with him."

"We have to stop him!"

She shook her head. "He's fast. He could be anywhere by now."

"But . . ." Serafin fell silent. Whatever he intended to say was wiped away at one blow. They had failed. Talamar would take Junipa to Lord Light. The girl was lost.

"*Master!*" Dario's voice sounded muffled through the

mist, probably from a room nearby, but even at a distance, the despair in his call lost nothing of its intensity.

Serafin ran, but Eft was even faster. She had a cut on her head, with blood running down to the corners of her mouth, just in front of her ears. Her broad mermaid's mouth was open a little, and Serafin saw the shine of the rows of sharp teeth inside. But he had no time to think about that.

He followed her through the mist, through an open door.

Arcimboldo had kept his magic mirrors in the storeroom. Most were gone—he'd handed them over to Talamar on the last delivery. Only a few still hung on their hooks or leaned against the wall, work ordered by his few Venetian customers.

The old man was lying facedown on the floor. His left arm was stretched out close to his body, unnaturally turned, as if it had been broken behind his back or dislocated. His right hand clutched a hammer. Nearby lay the remains of a mirror, jagged shards that he'd obviously struck out of the frame himself.

A question shot through Serafin's mind, even before the shock of grief. Had Talamar succeeded in getting into the workshop through a magic mirror? And had Arcimboldo destroyed the entrance with the hammer?

Dario crouched beside his master but didn't dare to touch him, either out of respect or fear of the truth.

Eft pushed the boys aside and rolled Arcimboldo onto his back. Then they all looked into his dimmed eyes, half-covered with strands of the wild white hair lying around his head like wet wool.

With a gentle movement of her hand, Eft closed the old man's eyes. Her fingers were shaking. She lifted Arcimboldo's upper body, pressed it close to her, and laid the back of his head carefully in her lap. With trembling hands she pushed his hair back, stroked his cheeks.

Dario looked up for the first time. Looked into Eft's face.

He uttered a gasp, and for a moment it looked as if he would draw away from her. But then he had himself under control again. He gave one quick look at Eft's legs—no fishtail, Serafin could read in his thoughts—then took the hand of his former master and pressed it firmly.

Serafin felt out of place. He hadn't known the magic mirror maker well, but he'd liked him. He would have paid his respects to the dead, but he feared that any gesture would seem shallow and false. The two had so much to be grateful to Arcimboldo for, their grief must be infinitely deeper. He bowed briefly, turned around, and went back to the workshop.

He didn't have to wait long before Dario joined him.

"Eft wants to be alone with him."

Serafin nodded. "Yes, of course."

"She said we should wait for her."

Dario perched on the edge of a table. His gaze was turned inward. It astonished Serafin that Dario wasn't in more of a hurry to get back to the enclave, in spite of everything; the attack on the Pharaoh still had to take place tonight, and it did not lie in Dario's power to change this plan.

"What is she going to do?" Serafin asked.

"I think she intends to go with us."

"To the enclave?"

Dario nodded.

Perhaps that wasn't such a bad idea. Eft was old, over a hundred, he guessed, perhaps even older, but her appearance was that of a woman in her thirties. She was slender and lithe, and it wouldn't have surprised him if she knew how to handle a blade.

"You didn't know it, did you?" Serafin asked.

"That she's a mermaid?" Dario shook his head. "No. Of course we wondered why she always wore those masks. She never let anyone see her whole face, only from the nose up. A disease, we thought, or an accident." He shrugged his shoulders. "Who knows, maybe we also did suspect it a little. Tiziano made a joke about it one time, what if . . . but no, I didn't know. Not really."

They left the workshop and sat outside in the hall, on the floor, their backs against the wall, Serafin on one side and Dario on the other. Both had their knees drawn up and looked down the corridor. Dario's saber lay at his feet.

The quiet was broken by the clicking of a door lock, as Eft locked the workshop from the inside. The last thing Serafin saw was Arcimboldo's body, which Eft had laid out on a workbench, half-concealed behind the billowing clouds of mist.

"What's she doing?"

Dario looked over at the double doors as if he could see through the wood. "No idea. We have to wait."

Serafin nodded his agreement.

And so they waited.

One hour. Possibly even two or three.

They didn't speak much, but when they talked, there was nothing of the old enmity between them, only respect and something that might someday become friendship.

But they'd paid a high price for it. Arcimboldo was dead, Junipa abducted.

Much too high a price.

The thought of having still to invade the Doge's Palace after all this and carry out an assassination of the Pharaoh was suddenly so unreal, so utterly and completely insane, that Serafin quickly repressed it.

The corrosive mist had slowly dissipated when the door lock clicked a second time. But now another smell took its place.

Something was burning. Fire in the workshop!

Serafin and Dario awakened from their trance and sprang up. Eft came toward them. Something gleamed in her hands. At first Serafin thought it was a blade, but then he made out a mask of silvery mirror glass. Eft pressed it to her as if it were something unspeakably costly, more than only a keepsake that she had taken in remembrance.

Behind her the workbench was burning.

A column of black, greasy smoke billowed up, was trapped under the roof, and then crept along to the door like the advance front of a swarm of ants.

"Let's go," said Eft.

The two boys exchanged uncertain looks, then Serafin looked inside the workshop again. The flames dancing around Arcimboldo's laid-out body concealed the destruction they were wreaking. Something about the profile of the dead man seemed strange to him, as if the face of the old man were now smooth as a ball.

His eyes traveled again to the silvery mask in Eft's hand. The features were thin and haggard. The face of an old man.

"Let's go," said the mermaid once again, her free hand pulling the edge of a neckerchief over her mouth until she looked like a robber who was preparing for his last big holdup.

Dario nodded, and Serafin joined the two of them as they hurried quickly down the corridor. He looked back over his shoulder once more, but now he saw only smoke and flames billowing out into the passage in thick plumes.

Moments later the three were running along the Canal of the Expelled, away from Arcimboldo's pyre.

Flames were now shooting from several windows, and dense smoke spread over the water.

7

The Pharaoh

Behind the golden dome of the Basilica of San Marco rose a falcon, larger than any animal on earth, higher than the highest tower, mightier than the statues of the pharaohs at home in Egypt.

He drew himself up to his full height of more than a hundred man-lengths, with round black eyes and a beak as large as the hull of a boat. His plumage was of pure gold and stood out against the night sky as if it were in flames.

Horus, the falcon god.

He unfolded his wings like golden sails and laid them on both sides of the façade of the basilica, around its rich

Byzantine carving and ornamentation, around its pediments and windows and reliefs. The tips of the wings met in front of the portals, slipped over one another, until the entire basilica was caught in its embrace, concealed as if behind a curtain of glowing, gleaming lava.

The falcon god laid claim to what was his.

He showed everyone who now possessed the power in Venice that the city was now only a part of Egypt, a part of the Empire, a fief of the old gods.

Standing on a roof opposite was Seth, highest of the high priests and the Pharaoh's vizier. His head was slightly bent and his arms crossed over his upper body. Sweat stood in shining beads on his forehead, and his golden robe was soaked with it. At this moment he *was* the falcon, the absolute master of this illusion.

Seth held the illusion upright for a minute longer, then spread his arms apart with a quick movement and sharply expelled air through his mouth and nose.

The towering falcon dissolved in a fountain of glittering spangles that sank to the Piazza San Marco around the basilica as if the stars themselves were plunging from the sky.

Applause sounded from the rows of priests gathered in the piazza below him. Only the mummy soldiers, of whom several dozen were scattered all over the piazza, stood unmoved, staring straight ahead out of dead, sunken eyes, some even out of empty eye sockets.

But Seth required no rejoicing, no applause to know the extent of his talent. He was conscious of his power, of every tiny aspect of his godlike abilities. The golden falcon god was nothing more than a skillful illusion, a symbol of the victory of the Empire, like the others that time after time sent the Pharaoh into naive raptures. The toys of a child.

What a waste, Seth thought disapprovingly. Of power, respect, and credibility. He, the highest priest and second man of the Empire; he, the venerable Seth; was wasting his energy on Amenophis's whimsies. And everyone in the priesthood, as well as his closest confidants, knew that he had no other choice. Not in times like these, when the sphinx commanders were winning more and more influence and power and pushing the priesthood out of the ruler's favor. It was worth it to make the Pharaoh happy—at least until the power of the priests of Horus was no longer threatened by the accursed sphinxes.

Seth snorted. Here the Empire was, celebrating its greatest victory, the conquest of Venice after more than three decades of siege, and it was primarily Seth's victory, his personal triumph over the Flowing Queen—and yet he could not rejoice in it. His satisfaction was only external, nothing more than a masquerade.

The sphinxes were to blame for that. And, of course, the Pharaoh himself.

Amenophis was a fool—a silly, narcissistic coxcomb

on a throne of gold and human lives. The priests of Horus had chosen him and made him into the figurehead of the Empire because they believed him weak, pliant, and easy to influence. Only a child, they'd said, and they exulted when they succeeded in waking him to new life in the stepped pyramid of Amun-Ka-Re.

He was their handiwork, their puppet, they'd believed. And in certain ways that applied today.

But only in *certain* ways.

Silently, Seth allowed a long cloak to be placed around his shoulders and accepted a cloth that one of his inferior priests handed to him. He used it to pat the perspiration from his bald head, from the spaces in between the golden wires that had been countersunk into his scalp as ornament, but also as a means for concentrating his spiritual power. The other priests had the network tattooed into their skin in color, but his own was of pure gold, worked by the smiths of Punt, deep in southern Africa.

Seth walked into the stairwell with measured steps, followed by his priests. Numerous mummy soldiers had been stationed around for his protection. Remarkably numerous. Seth wondered who had given the order for it. Certainly not he.

As he entered the piazza below, a priest adept came up to him, bowed three times, kissed his hands and feet, and begged permission to deliver a message from the Pharaoh:

Amenophis wished to see Seth, right now, in his new chambers in the Doge's Palace.

Internally boiling with rage, Seth left the adept and his subordinates, crossed the piazza, and entered the palace. Amenophis summoned him like one of his body slaves. He, the highest among the priests of Horus, the spiritual head of the Empire. And that in front of the assembled priesthood. Through the mouth of a lowly adept!

Seth entered the palace through the richly decorated Porta della Carta, a masterpiece of gothic stonework. On the other side of the great interior courtyard, he mounted a splendid staircase in the shadow of two huge statues of gods. Mars and Neptune looked coldly down on him. Seth would have them pulled down as soon as possible and replaced with Horus and Re.

Through wide corridors and several anterooms he finally reached the door behind which some rooms had been arranged as the personal domicile of the Pharaoh. Appropriate to the status of a ruler, the rooms were on the top floor of the palace, just under the attic. Above them, in earlier times, prisoners had been locked into tiny cells under the lead roof. But today, so far as Seth knew, the dreaded rooms stood empty. He would inspect them later and decide whether it would be a suitable place to incarcerate the rebels among the city councillors.

Not all the city councillors had taken part in surrendering the Flowing Queen. Amenophis had ordered the three instigators executed the evening before, publicly, in the Piazza San Marco. He was grateful to them for their help but suffered around him no one whose word could not be trusted. The other councillors had been confined somewhere in the palace since then, separated from their bodyguards. Most of the soldiers had been imprisoned at the same time. Later an attempt would be made to enlist them on the side of the Empire; Amenophis was fascinated by the powerful bond between the soldiers and their stone lions. And kindling the Pharaoh's interest above all were the winged stone lions, who were only at the disposal of the Body Guard of the City Council.

Seth, on the contrary, thought that it would be better to kill all lions, right away, however difficult such an undertaking might be—even if it were necessary to sacrifice a few dozen mummy soldiers for each lion. It was a mistake to let them live. Amenophis might see in the lions only animals that would be suitable to tame and use for his own purposes; but Seth was of another mind. The lions were not dumb creatures who let themselves be trained at will. He could feel the divinity in them, their intelligence, their ancient knowledge. And he wondered if, in truth, the sphinx commanders were not behind the Pharaoh's decision as well. They were half lion themselves, and it was obvious that they knew more about the Venetian lions than they were admitting.

Was there any relationship between the sphinxes and

the stone lions? And if yes, what significance did it have in the intrigues of the sphinx commanders?

Seth had no time to pursue the thoughts any longer. One of the Pharaoh's lackeys had already reported his arrival. Now he asked Seth to enter.

The Pharaoh was resting on a divan of jaguar skins. He wore a white robe of human hair, shot through with gold threads. One hundred slave women had worked on it for almost a decade. Amenophis possessed several dozen of these robes, and often he would rip up a just-finished one if he didn't like the curve of a line or a detail of the pattern.

The Pharaoh smiled as Seth approached him. Amenophis awaited him alone, and that was more than unusual. Ordinarily the Pharaoh was surrounded by his tall soldiers from the Nubian desert, whose sickle swords had already polished off so many would-be assassins.

Strange too was that the makeup on the Pharaoh's face was even more garish than usual. But that could not conceal that his face was that of a child not yet thirteen years old, the age at which, more than three thousand years ago, the boy pharaoh had been poisoned. After the Horus priests reawakened him, he'd no longer aged. Amenophis had ruled for more than thirty years now, but he still always looked like a spoiled, snot-nosed child.

But that characterization didn't even begin to include all his bad characteristics. Seth had often speculated as to whether the ancient poison had been mixed by his predecessors, by Horus priests who could no longer tolerate the moods of this cruel dwarf.

Secretly he felt that possibly Amenophis asked himself the same question—which might be one of the reasons why recently the Pharaoh had been freeing himself more and more aggressively from the influence of the priesthood and turning to the sphinxes.

"Seth," said Amenophis, waving a casual greeting to him with his right hand.

The high priest bowed deeply and waited until the Pharaoh indicated that he rise. This time Amenophis took an especially long time over it, but Seth allowed the affront to pass over him without reacting. Sometime the conditions would alter, and then it would be he, Seth, to whom the Pharaoh had to creep. A really uplifting thought, which wrested a pleased smile from him.

Amenophis bade him come closer.

"You wished to see me, Re?" The Pharaoh preferred to be addressed by the name of the sun god.

"More precisely, we wanted *you* to see something, Seth."

The priest raised an eyebrow. "What could that be?"

Amenophis lolled on the jaguar divan and smiled. The golden color under his left eye had run, but he didn't look as if he had reason to weep. What would Amenophis have been laughing himself to tears about?

Seth felt increasingly uneasy.

"Re?" he asked once more.

"Go to the window," said the Pharaoh.

Seth went over to one of the high windows. From here he could look out on the now darkened Piazza San Marco. As always, it was illuminated by countless torches and fire-basins, but the scenery in the glow of the flames had changed.

Mummy soldiers were driving the priests together, several dozen men in long robes, not far from the place where, a few days before, the messenger from Hell had torn open the paving. A powerful sphinx was overseeing the arrest, which was taking place in uncanny silence. Among the prisoners Seth recognized his closest confidants, men with whom he had planned the resurrection of the Pharaoh and carried it out. Men who warned him and had trusted him when he brushed off their worries. What a fool he'd been!

For now his priests were going to pay for his stupidity, of that there was no doubt.

Very slowly and with as much dignity as he could muster, Seth turned around to the Pharaoh.

Amenophis was no longer alone. Utterly soundlessly, two sphinxes had come to his side on velvety lion feet. Their upper bodies were those of men, their underbodies belonged to mighty lions. Both had sickle swords that any ordinary man could hardly have lifted.

"Why, Re?" asked Seth softly and so under control that he surprised himself. "Why my priests?"

"The priesthood of Horus has discharged its duty," said Amenophis lightly, without losing his smile. "We thank you and yours, Seth. You were a great help to us, and we will not forget that."

The Pharaoh loved to speak of himself in the plural. But at the moment it almost seemed to Seth that Amenophis actually meant himself and his new advisers, the sphinx commanders.

"That is betrayal," he squeezed out.

"Of whom?" Amenophis's eyes widened in feigned astonishment. "Not of the Pharaoh. Also not of the gods."

"We have made you what you are." Seth now dispensed with the deferential address. "Without us you were only another body in the old graves, only a mummy in your sarcophagus, so hated by those who poisoned you that they didn't even put any gold in the grave with you. Everyone knew that. Why otherwise, do you suppose, did the grave robbers never try to invade your crypt?" He laughed derisively. "They knew what they'd find there. Only the corpse of a cocky child, whose cries for play and amusement even his closest intimates could no longer stand. Only the body of a dumb boy who—"

One of the sphinxes took a gliding step toward Seth, but Amenophis held him back. "Seth," he said, restrained, though his eyes showed the priest how very much his words had enraged him. "Silence. Please."

"I say the truth. And your new . . . *lapdogs* will soon

realize that as well." He'd intended to irritate the sphinxes, but he knew they wouldn't be drawn in. One grinned wearily, the other didn't change expression. It had been foolish to attempt to disconcert them, Seth knew that, too.

"We do not intend to kill you," said the Pharaoh. His lips drew into a malicious smile. "Not *you.*"

"What do you intend, then?" Seth looked out again at his corralled priests. The swords of their guards gleamed in the torchlight.

Amenophis smirked. "First—their deaths. And after that, your attention."

Seth turned around, and again a sphinx took a threatening step forward. This time Amenophis did not restrain him.

"It is not necessary that they die," said Seth. He looked for a spell, an illusion, with which he could surprise the Pharaoh, but he knew it was pointless. The sphinxes' magic was equal to his, and they would turn any attack aside. If not these two, then one of the others, who were without question watching from behind the walls.

"Not necessary?" Amenophis repeated in his childish voice. He stroked his index finger over the golden coloring on his face and regarded the tip of his finger with interest. It shimmered like an exotic beetle. "We will make you an offer, Seth. You should not turn it down. We know very well that we have you and your priests alone to thank for this victory. It was you who found a way to drive the Flowing Queen out of the water—wherever she's holed up now. So do not think that we feel no gratitude."

"Yes," Seth managed with difficulty to say. "I see that."

Amenophis stretched his finger with the gold paint on it toward one of the sphinxes. The creature came forward and, his face expressionless, allowed the Pharaoh to smear two golden streaks over his cheeks. War paint.

"We are the ruler of the Empire, the only, the greatest, the most powerful," said Amenophis. "Is that not so?"

"So is it, Re," answered the sphinx devotedly.

The Pharaoh released him with a wave, and the creature again took up his post next to the divan.

"You spoke of an offer," said Seth.

"Ah. We knew that it would interest you." Amenophis stroked the palm of his hand over the jaguar skins. "We want more of these."

Seth swallowed in bewilderment. "I should . . . hunt jaguars for you?"

The childish Pharaoh broke into shrill laughter. "Oh, Seth, you dumbbell! No, of course not. We think we will find another who can provide us with a pair of these exquisite little animals, won't we?" He was still laughing, but now he gradually calmed himself. "It concerns the following, Seth. Our new advisers . . . our friends . . . in their infinite wisdom had a vision."

Everyone knew that sphinxes did in fact have access to

ancient wisdom. Seth would have given his right hand to find out what game they were playing. It made him half-crazy not to be able to see through them.

"A vision of our death," Amenophis went on.

"The priests of Horus would not have allowed you ever to die."

"Well answered. But we both know that you are lying. Sometime our person would have become wearisome to you. And who would then have taken our place on the throne? You yourself, Seth? Yes, we almost believe that would have been possible."

Seth had to control himself not to spit at his feet. "So what do you want?"

"The sphinxes are of the opinion that the power that could be dangerous to us is not of this world. At least not on the surface."

"Hell?"

"Indeed. The prophecy of the sphinxes predicts that something will come out of Hell and annihilate us. Is that not completely enchanting?" He laughed again, but this time it didn't sound so arrogant. "And who rules over Hell?"

"Lord Light."

"That outlaw! That filth! But yes—Lord Light. He has already tried to agitate the Venetians against us. Our honorable traitors were able to prevent that, by giving the order to kill the messenger from Hell. But Lord Light will give himself no rest, we know that, and the prophecy of the sphinxes confirms it." His eyes narrowed. "On the other hand—we will *not* die, Seth. No matter what Lord Light is hatching against us—he will not conquer us. Because we will pull the evil out by the root."

Now it was Seth's turn to laugh. In fact, he laughed so loud and so ringingly that Amenophis looked at him as though he doubted his high priest's understanding.

"You want to kill Lord Light?" Seth got out. His voice sounded too high, and he urgently needed air. "Is that your intention?"

"Yes—and no. Because *you* will kill him, Seth. Not we."

"That's suicide."

"That depends on you."

Seth shook his head. He had expected something, but not that.

His eyes traveled to the two sphinxes. They must know what madness this proposal was. If it was just about getting him out of the way, why were they making this farce out of it instead of ending him with their swords?

He found the answer himself, and it disturbed him deeply: because they believed what the Pharaoh was saying. Amenophis hadn't lied. The vision wasn't an invention. The sphinxes *feared* Lord Light.

He got hold of himself and asked, "What exactly did the sphinxes see?"

"Nothing," said one of the two, speaking unbidden for the first time. Amenophis let it happen without reprimanding the sphinx.

"Nothing?"

"Our visions do not reach us in the form of pictures," said the sphinx, with great seriousness. "They are feelings. Impressions. Too cryptic to give concrete advice."

Seth burst out laughing again, a trace too shrilly. "One of you had a . . . bad feeling, and therefore you want to kill Lord Light? Risk a war with Hell?" He paced excitedly back and forth a few times, then stopped again. "That is completely mad!"

The sphinx ignored his last words. "Something will come out of Hell and destroy the Pharaoh. That is the prophecy. And you will keep it from coming true."

The Pharaoh made a motion with his hand. Something rustled behind an opening in the paneling, and Seth felt someone rush past him. A little later a short trumpet signal sounded.

Seth whirled around to the window and saw the mummy soldiers approaching the corralled priests with sickle swords raised.

"Stop it!" Seth's voice sounded toneless.

A second hand signal, a new trumpet signal. The soldiers froze in motion.

For a moment there was silence. Even in the piazza below, everything seemed to have quieted.

"I will do as you wish," said Seth.

"We know that." The Pharaoh smiled charmingly. "We never had any doubt of it. These priests are like your own children."

"A high priest accepts his responsibility. A Pharaoh should do so also."

Amenophis waved him off. "Twaddle! You will set out today."

"Why I?"

"Because you are devotedly loyal to us, of course. Why else?" Amenophis looked genuinely surprised. "Because we can rely on you. No one else would keep his word in such a circumstance. But you, Seth, you will do it. We know that. And you will accomplish this matter quickly."

Seth's hatred threatened to overpower him, yet he remained outwardly calm. "How shall I get from here to Axis Mundi?"

"A friend will take you to Lord Light's city," said the Pharaoh. "Right up to his throne."

The door swung open and in walked the biggest sphinx that Seth had ever seen. He had long, bronze-colored hair that fell far down his back and was bound into a ponytail as thick as Seth's arm. The musculature of his upper body, in no way inferior to his lion legs, was more powerful than any Seth had ever seen in a human being. And his face was unusual: It was covered over with light brown hair, like the remains of a mane—really inconceivable for the beardless sphinxes. The pupils of his eyes were slits. The eyes of a predatory cat.

The creature smiled at Seth, exposing yellow canine teeth, while it casually twitched its flanks and unfolded gigantic wings, leathery, but covered with a furry down.

This is impossible, Seth thought. Sphinxes don't have wings. And their eyes and teeth are like those of men.

But this thing was something different. It exuded strength and cruelty like a bad smell.

"Iskander," said Amenophis, and—incredible!—he bowed in the direction of the beast. Turning to Seth, he said softly, "Your companion."

8

Winter

V ERMITHRAX PUSHED OFF FROM THE EDGE OF THE giant ear.

Merle lost her orientation immediately. Right, left, up, down—all blurred into one, a whirling vortex of red light and rocks. The head rushed on over them; they were caught up in its airstream, tumbled, almost overturned— and then for a brief moment they held stable in the air.

Only for a few seconds.

Then Vermithrax let out a roar, threw himself to one side, actually did a somersault, and came straight back to horizontal again before Merle could lose her grip and fall.

Her heart raced so loudly that it filled her entire mind, thumping painfully in her skull. No room left for clear thoughts.

Then the second head was upon them, and the world turned into chaos. The obsidian lion roared again, then a jolt went through his body, which continued through Merle's bones, muscles, and joints like the blow of a hammer. It felt as if she'd been seized and thrown headfirst against a stone wall.

When she returned to her senses, she was lying beside Vermithrax behind the external bulge of one ear, bedded in something that at first she took to be ashes. Then she recognized black down. Bird feathers, she would have assumed in the upper world. Here below they might come from Heaven knew what sort of creatures.

With her luck they were probably carnivores that had especially chosen this ear for their hibernation.

There were a strikingly large number of feathers. And they smelled of tar, like the wind that blew across the desert of Hell.

"There is no one here," said the Flowing Queen in her head. *"Not here in the ear."*

"Are we there, where we . . . where we wanted to be?"

"Not we—where you *wanted to be!"*

Hairsplitting, thought Merle. "Is this the second head?"

"Yes," answered Vermithrax instead of the Queen. "It worked. Just right."

Merle picked herself up. Her head was still pounding, as if someone had locked her under a bell tower on Christmas Eve. She staggered, and Vermithrax tried to support her with his lion tail. But she shook her head, waited a moment, then managed to stay on her legs through her own strength.

This was something she had undertaken. And she would carry it through to the end.

"How heroic."

Merle ignored the comment. She had to climb out of the ear and down the side of the gigantic stone jaw along to the mouth. And all that perhaps to find a dying man whom no one could help anymore.

Nevertheless, she would try.

Vermithrax was breathing hard. He looked exhausted, his eyes glassy. In spite of that, he perceived what Merle had in mind.

"Rest up for a moment."

"Then I'll probably come to my senses and think differently about it." Merle's voice trembled slightly, but at once she had herself under control again.

The lion tilted his head and scrutinized her piercingly. "Once you get something into your head, you don't abandon it so easily."

Merle wasn't sure if she should feel flattered. She felt the obsidian lion's good will. He wanted to give her courage. And, to be honest, she needed a whole lot of it.

"Better now than later," she said, and she began to climb over the parapet, over the first bulge of the ear.

"*Are you certain you want to do this?*" asked the Queen.

"You aren't going to try to talk me out of it, are you?"

"*It is your decision alone.*"

"Indeed." She knew that the Queen could force her to stay here, by taking control not only of her tongue but also of her whole body. Yet she did not do that. She respected Merle's decision, even if she didn't approve of it.

Without any word of farewell—for she avoided even thinking of the word farewell—she climbed to the outside of the ear. The stone was large-pored, full of scars and cracks. Some of them might have belonged to the structure of the stone by nature, others clearly stemmed from collisions with . . . yes, with what? Flying stones? Lilim claws? Bird beaks as hard as steel?

You don't want to know that. Not really. Don't get distracted.

The fastest way to the corner of the stone head's mouth was straight across its cheek, a deep hollow under the prominent cheekbones. She wondered if the face might have been modeled on the face of a particular person. If so, he was either old or undernourished. No one she knew had such deep cheeks, not even the hungry children in the orphanage.

"*Do not look down,*" said the Flowing Queen.

415

"I'm trying as hard as I can not to."

Her hands and feet sought holds and found them amazingly quickly. Actually, it wasn't half so difficult as she'd thought. She followed the advice of the Queen as well as she could and kept her eyes firmly fastened on the stone wall. Sometimes, when she had to take care to place her feet on a secure projection, she couldn't avoid seeing a small section of the ground rushing past, infinitely far below her. Her heart beat like crazy and her stomach convulsed into a hard knot that lay like a stone on her intestines.

One of her fingernails broke as she shoved her right hand into the next recess. She might have half the distance behind her already, but she couldn't be certain. As long as she stared only at the stone, she couldn't judge proportions. What if she'd only covered a few yards? Much less than she thought?

Onward. Ever onward.

Only a little bit more.

Very slowly she turned her head and looked along the rock wall. The corner of the mouth wasn't far away. If she could only manage to get over the stone lower lip, she'd be safe for the time being.

Provided the man in the mouth was as well disposed toward her as she was toward him.

And if he wasn't as weak as he looked?

If he attacked her?

416

She shook off the thought, concentrated on her hands and feet again.

Yet as hard as she tried to repress it, she couldn't avoid seeing her situation in her mind's eyes: She was hanging on the side of a fifty-yard-high stone head, high over the rocky wasteland, and this head was moving forward at such an insane speed that the landscape under her blurred to a single whirl.

And all that for a stranger about whom she knew nothing. He might be dangerous, even a murderer, perhaps a true slave of Lord Light. Nevertheless, she was putting her life on the line for him. And not just her own. For if she believed the Flowing Queen, the fate of Venice depended on her.

The realization struck her unprepared, and she lost her hold. Her left hand slipped off, only her right clung on to a stone outcropping that was so narrow it wouldn't have held a flowerpot. She panicked and began to kick. Her feet slid over the edge of a recess and then hung free over the abyss for a moment.

"That does it," said the Flowing Queen drily.

Merle tensed her muscles—and pulled herself back up a little. She got hold of a projection with her left hand again, found a stop under her feet. And pulled herself on.

"Not bad."

"Many thanks for your support," Merle pressed out between her teeth.

A few yards farther, then she reached the corner of the mouth.

"You did it."

"That sounds as though you didn't think I would."

"Do you really believe I would have let you go, then?"

Those words confirmed Merle's fear: The Queen could take control over Merle's body if she wanted to. That wasn't a good thought, but it also wasn't one she was prepared to worry about at the moment.

She was able to grab a crack in the lower lip and pull herself toward it. Gathering all her strength once more, she sought a hold and heaved herself over the lip into the mouth of the stone head.

With a gasp she rolled over the bulge, suddenly grabbed emptiness, slipped down, fell . . . and landed on a hard surface.

At least there were no teeth to spear her. Not even a tongue. Only a hollow space, like a grotto. The back part lay in complete darkness. Impossible to make out what was back there. A tunnel deeper into the interior of the head? Or simply a back wall?

Merle raised herself and looked along the inside of the lip.

The man had changed his position. Not on his own, it appeared to her. He had slipped and, like her, fallen on the floor of the mouth cavity. There he lay in the middle of the flood of his white hair, as if he were in a puddle of milk.

But he was breathing. He even groaned softly.

Merle crawled closer to him on her hands and knees. Her heart pounded in her ears. She considered whether to wait a moment. Catch her breath, rest. She could hardly feel her arms from the strain. If he were really to attack, she was hardly in a condition to defend herself.

What was she doing here, anyway?

"Hello?" she asked carefully.

He was lying on his side with the back of his head toward her. His white hair was spread about him like a star, long strands that—if he were standing upright—must reach almost to his hips. His left hand was concealed under his body, but he had the right arm outstretched. The fingers were long and bony. Merle could clearly recognize the veins under the pale skin, blue lines like ink that had run on a white piece of paper.

"Hello?"

The fingers of the right hand twitched, curled to claws, clenched to a fist. Then they slackened again.

Merle took a deep breath, summoned all her courage, and moved slowly around the man. She had to decide which she would rather have at her back, him or the darkness at the back of the mouth cavity. She decided for the darkness and kept her eyes on the stranger.

She was grateful that the Flowing Queen remained silent. Merle didn't need her taunting remarks to know how absurd her behavior was. How mad.

"Are you injured?"

As she moved forward, she could gradually see more of his face.

His eyes were open and staring at her. His gaze followed her steps.

Merle got goose pimples. "You're awake," she stated. "Why don't you say anything?"

His lips trembled uncontrollably, giving the lie to the clear look of his eyes. Or was he just putting on an act for some reason? Was he waiting for her to bend over him?

Did everyone have Lilim claws?

His movements might be playacting. The skin quivered slightly, as if something were crawling along underneath it. He frowned and at the same time looked quite pitiful.

A trick?

"He cannot do anything to you."

The Flowing Queen's words surprised her. Merle had expected a warning from her, at the very least.

"Are you sure?"

"He is debilitated. Just about to die of thirst, it appears."

Merle remembered her knapsack and the provisions from the expedition's camp that she'd packed in it. The bundle was so firmly strapped to her back that she'd almost forgotten it. Now she took it off, opened one of the water flasks, smelled it—who knew when it had been filled fresh?—and approached the man with it.

"Should I?"

"That is why you came, after all."

Merle nodded silently, then she shoved her left hand under the man's head, lifted it, and dropped water onto his cracked lips. His white hair felt strange, oddly light, although it was thick and full. The eyes, which seemed so disquietingly alert and clear, observed Merle with such intensity that they could have belonged to another man, completely separate from the rest of his weakened body. This blazing, profound look irritated her. Frightened her a little.

Merle pressed the top of the flask closer to his lips, tilted it back again, waited until he'd swallowed, guided the flask to his mouth again. She did the same thing four or five times, and each time she let him drink a little more.

Finally he signaled with a shake of the head. Enough.

She wiped the top of the flask off on her skirt and carefully screwed it closed. She might have to make do with her water supply for much longer. Merle had only two bottles; this was the first—and it was almost empty. They had only the one left.

She put the bottle back in her knapsack.

"Thanks," came from the man's lips. She hadn't seen him speak, as if he'd moved neither tongue nor jaw, but she could hear him clearly.

"I . . . thank you." He used her language, with an almost unnoticeable accent.

Merle helped him to sit up. She leaned him with his back against the inside of the stone lip. Again she noticed how light his hair was, almost as if it weren't even there. It felt like flower petals.

"What's your name?" she asked him.

"Winter."

Flower petals—or snowflakes.

"Winter? What else?"

"Just Winter."

She examined him in irritation, then she grinned. "I'm Merle. Just Merle."

He was weak, his hands trembled slightly. But Merle needed only to look into his eyes to see that he was wide awake. He saw and heard her clearly, and he was thinking about it. Hard.

"What are you doing here?" he asked.

That didn't sound particularly polite, and he must have noticed that Merle frowned. Despite that, he didn't ask for pardon but repeated his question several times.

"*We should not have bothered about him,*" said the Flowing Queen demurely.

Merle thought for the first time that the Queen was probably right. But she wouldn't admit it. Probably the Queen had read it in her thoughts anyway.

"We're just passing through," she said hastily, which sounded quite silly, in view of the circumstances. But nothing better came to her in a hurry.

Winter smiled. His eyes blazed. But he didn't question her words.

"Just as I am," he said.

"Where are you going?"

"There's only one destination here down below."

Here down below, he'd said. That must be a sign that he came from above, from her world.

"And what's that?" she asked innocently.

"Axis Mundi."

"Axis—what?"

"*Axis Mundi,*" said the Flowing Queen. *"The axis of the world."*

"The city of Lord Light," said Winter. "I take it that you're both also on the way there."

So he knew that Merle wasn't alone. She remembered how he'd stared when she'd still been in the front head.

As if he meant to confirm her thoughts, he said, "That was quite brave before, of you and your lion."

"He is not *my* lion."

"Oh?"

"Only my friend."

"*Your* friend?" He smiled again, and this time the corners of his mouth also twitched. "You humans are strange creatures. One and the same word, and nevertheless you take offense at it. My lion, my friend . . . remarkable, isn't it?"

"Then you're not human?"

"I am winter."

"Now it is coming," murmured the Queen.

But Winter was silent, giving no further explanation.

"Do you come from above?"

"Yes."

"Why are you here?"

"I'm on a hunt."

"For what?"

"For someone."

"How long have you been down here already?"

"A long time."

"Longer than a year?"

"I don't know how long a year is."

"But you just said you came from above."

"For me there are no years. Only winter."

"He is crazy," said the Flowing Queen.

"When you say winter, do you mean the season?"

"I am winter."

"Yes, I understood that. But you said that you—"

He leaned forward with a jerk, so fast that she flinched and instinctively drew back a little. He didn't bother about that but just bent a little farther toward her.

"I am the ice. And the snow. And the cold."

Merle suppressed a grin. "You are *the* winter?"

He nodded, obviously satisfied, and leaned back again.

"Like the summer? The fall?"

Again he nodded.

Wonderful, she thought. Really grand. Someone like this is just what we were missing.

"*You see,*" said the Queen.

"I hate it when you say that," growled Merle.

"*I know.*"

Winter's eyebrows drew together. "What do you mean?"

"I was talking to myself."

"Do you do that often?"

"Don't say that it's a sign of . . . hmm, confusion. I guess *you* shouldn't be a judge of that."

Winter's face twitched again. Suddenly he burst into peals of laughter.

Merle frowned. "What's so funny?"

"You."

"Heartfelt thanks."

"You don't believe me."

"Whatever you say." She was gradually losing all her shyness of him. She hoped that it wasn't simply a sign of increasing apathy. If she made the mistake of feeling that nothing mattered to her, she could just as well jump out and down right now.

She felt that Winter would stay with his assertion. A living season. Of course.

Ultimately, it didn't matter at all.

"This thing here, this head," she said. "Do you know what it is?"

"A herald. It reports news in the breadth of Hell to Lord Light."

"Do you understand what it's saying?"

"I haven't given it a thought."

"You're traveling in it and haven't thought about whether you understand it?"

He shrugged. "No."

Mere noticed something. From far away, the voices of the heads had been clearly audible. Before, in the ear of the first one, they'd sounded dull and blurred. And now, in the mouth, of all places, she could hardly get more than a distant mumble. Shouldn't the words have been deafening right here? The source of the voice must be somewhere else, perhaps in the bottom, in the stump of the neck. That they weren't heard better here must mean that there was no connection between the neck and the mouth. She found that reassuring.

"Who directed you here?" she asked.

"I myself. And others."

"*Well, well,*" said the Flowing Queen.

"What kind of others?"

"Lord Light's subjects. I've met many of them. I've crisscrossed this country. I was everywhere—except in Axis Mundi." He snorted softly. "I should have gone there right off."

"Why didn't you?"

"There were . . . signs that the person I'm looking for wasn't staying there. But it's the last possibility."

"Who are you looking for, then?"

Winter hesitated, then he smiled. "Summer."

"Who else?"

"Summer?" Merle asked, blinking.

Winter's eyes misted dreamily. "My beloved Summer."

Merle couldn't think of anything to say to that. She had saved a madman from dying of thirst.

"Is this head . . . this herald on the way to Axis Mundi?"

"On the direct path."

"Are you sure?"

He nodded. "I know this country, I've traveled it. And I've seen many things. The heralds only join up into a group when they're on the way back to their master."

So Vermithrax had been right. She was sorry that he wasn't here. He'd be worried about her, so alone in the head's ear.

"When are we going to reach the city?"

"Very soon now. The heralds are going faster and faster. Not much longer and they'll be silent. Then it's not much farther."

Good. That was something, anyway.

Merle dug in her knapsack. "Are you hungry?"

"Winter doesn't eat."

"But Winter drinks," she said snippily. "At least it looked a lot like that."

"What would Winter be without water? There would be—"

"No ice, no snow—I understood." She swallowed a sigh and began to gnaw on a piece of jerky; it felt horribly tough between her teeth.

Winter watched her eating for a while, then he bent toward her again. "May I have some more water?"

"Help yourself."

"You are becoming close friends now, eh?" said the Flowing Queen acidly.

Merle handed the opened bottle to Winter. They would find water in Axis Mundi, at least she hoped so.

"Winter?"

He set down the bottle. "Yes?"

"This Summer, is he . . ."

"She," he said emphatically. "Summer is feminine."

"Oh, nice. Summer . . . Is she a . . . hmm, person like you?"

He smirked. "You mean, does she look like a human?"

Merle nodded.

"Yes, she does," he said. "When she wants to. Just as I do."

"Where do you know her from?"

"There are only four of us. One should assume that we occasionally cross paths, don't you think?"

Spring, summer, fall, and winter. It occurred to Merle that she herself had just been thinking a few days before that there was no real summer and winter anymore, that spring and fall ran unnoticeably into each other.

No wonder, she thought cynically, if they're both running around down here.

"And now you're looking for her? Did she go away?"

"Vanished. From one day to the next."

"You're in love with her." A statement, not a question. Now that she'd accepted his remarkable story, it was easier and easier for her to speak seriously with him about it. It was a piece of absurd theater into which she'd walked onstage a little late.

"In love with . . . Pah!" He let the word drive between them like an ice crystal. "Never before has there been a stronger love. Never a more magnificent day than that one when Winter put his arms around Summer for the first time."

"*He* is *a human,*" said the Flowing Queen.

"That sounds quite . . . romantic."

Winter stared sadly up through the open stone mouth to the heaven of Hell. "Up there, in the upper world, I can touch nothing without its turning to ice." His hand reached out like a snake and grasped Merle's leg. She shrank back. "If I were to touch you so, you wouldn't even have time to be afraid. You would stiffen to ice on the spot."

Coolly she brushed his hand off. "Oh, yes?"

"That is my curse. My eternal sorrow."

He's putting on an act, Merle thought, but he has no experience with the public. "And down here?" she asked politely.

"Nothing." He shook his head as if he could not grasp it himself. "No ice, not even a breath of cold. Here I'm nothing, almost like a human."

"Thanks."

"I didn't mean it that way."

"Of course not."

Winter sighed and twirled a strand of white hair between his bony fingers. "I do not speak with humans often. I only notice too late when I've wounded one of you."

"And Summer?"

His eyes again took on that dreamy glow, which amused her and at the same time made her a little sad. "Summer is like me. And yet quite different."

"One often hears something like that about couples in love," she said with precocious wisdom.

"*You are thinking of Serafin,*" the Queen butted in.

"I am not!"

"*And how!*"

Winter's eyes narrowed. "*That* is your conversation with yourself?"

Merle shook her head hard, in the slight hope that the Queen in her head would get dizzy from it—but she knew that was nonsense. "It's all right."

"There is someone there." Winter did not take his eyes off her. "In you. I can feel him."

Merle was startled. Did he really feel the presence of

the Flowing Queen in her thoughts? His look was so serious, as if he'd just accused her of a betrayal.

"*He knows,*" said the Queen.

Instinctively Merle slid away from him a little. He made no move to follow her. Perhaps he was still too weak. But his eyes remained firmly fastened on her, sticking to her eyes like pincers.

"There's no one there," she said unconvincingly. "Tell me more about Summer."

"Summer can touch no human, just like me."

"What would happen?" She knew the answer already, before he said it, and with satisfaction she thought that perhaps she could see through him a bit. His madness followed certain firm rules.

"Everything that is touched by Summer must burn," he said.

Merle nodded. She could fill in the rest of the story. "And therefore it's possible for you two to touch each other without the other freezing stiff or going up in flames. Right? The effects cancel each other out."

Winter tilted his head to one side. "How do you know that?"

"I have"—she almost said *imagination*—"guessed."

He sighed again. He was beginning to overdo it with his suffering expression. "She was the first creature I could ever touch without fear. It was just the same for her. We were made for each other."

"*Yes,*" said the Queen peevishly, "*they all say that.*"

"And you think she's here? In Hell?"

"She was abducted."

Who abducted a being that could set anyone on fire who touched her? But Merle didn't want to quarrel with him.

Instead she stood up, climbed up to the stone bulge of the gigantic lip, and looked out over it into the distance. Actually, she only wanted to keep him from staring at her again with his dark, bottomless eyes.

Her breath stopped.

"Winter?"

She heard a rustling as he carefully stood up and appeared beside her.

"Is that it?" she asked tonelessly.

Out of the corner of her eye, she saw him nod.

"Axis Mundi," he said.

Many miles ahead of them rose a wall of rock, reaching from the ground to the ceiling of Hell. It could have been the end of this subterranean world had there not been a wide gap there. What lay behind it was not discernible.

However, she clearly saw the two gigantic stone figures that flanked the opening. Figures of humans. Each of the figures must be at least five hundred yards high, possibly even higher. They stood well forward, at the edges of the gap, the faces turned toward each other. But they were holding themselves strangely crooked, the upper bodies bent forward. Their arms were intertwined with each other, as if they were going to wrestle.

"The Eternal Fighters," said Winter softly.

"Is that what they're called?"

He nodded. "People tell about them everywhere. Lord Light had them erected. See how they're standing? It's said that on Lord Light's orders they come to life to continue their fight. And grind up everything that's in the gap."

Now for the first time it became clear to Merle that the two figures formed a gate. The city must lie just behind it, on the other side of the rock wall.

"Is that the only entrance?"

"The only one that's known."

"Then perhaps there are others?"

"None that anyone knows of."

Merle rolled her eyes but said nothing. Instead she looked out over the wasteland to the feet of the fighters. Dark, seething lines moved through the rock desert like ant trails. Thousands upon thousands of Lilim!

They were coming and going between the feet of the fighters, endless caravans that were taking the road toward Axis Mundi or were leaving it.

"They all have to go between the statues' legs," she said with a shudder.

"That's the idea. It creates respect."

"It will create respect in *me* when we fly through there."

Winter twisted one corner of his mouth, perhaps a thin smile. "As long as they aren't wakened to life, nothing can happen to us."

"Have they ever? Become living?"

He shrugged. "Quite often, if you believe the legends in the outer regions. But the closer one comes to the city, the fewer of these stories there are. Apparently no one has yet seen it with his own eyes."

"A good sign, I guess."

"*It could also mean,*" said the Queen, "*that all are dead who have seen it.*"

Silently the heads raced toward the center of Hell. The closer they came to the two stone giants, the more breathtaking those became, true mountains in the shape of men.

But why humans? Why had Lord Light not created them on the model of the Lilim?

Or were there Lilim who looked like humans?

Again she inched away from Winter a little, unnoticeably, she hoped. He did notice it, however. In his eyes she could read that he knew what she was thinking. He knew her fear. But he didn't defend himself. Said not a word, turned his head, and looked again toward the fighters.

When he changed his position, it was as if he and his shadow were moving in different directions. Only for a moment. Perhaps an illusion.

Merle again turned her eyes toward the gate of Hell's city.

9

Axis of the World

THEY WEREN'T THE ONLY ONES IN THE AIR APPROACHING the gap in the rocks. Merle could now distinguish creatures swarming around the stone colossi like mosquitoes, a multitude of dark dots. They were too far away to make out any details.

Merle and Winter took cover behind the stone bulge. Merle hoped that Vermithrax had also withdrawn deeper into the ear. She worried about him. He was alone and had no one to explain to him what was going on outside.

"He is doing well," the Queen said reassuringly.

The first head, which was diagonally in front of them,

sank into the shadows of the gigantic legs. From above, Merle could see the giant feet on the ground, mighty ovals of rock, around which snaked the Lilims' route of march. Still, she wasn't able to see the creatures in detail, so tight was the throng, so great the distance.

The heralds raised their flight path considerably, until they were soaring above the stone knees of the colossi. Merle lost sight of the columns deep below them and instead looked up at the gigantic bodies of the fighters. From close up, they could just as well have been bizarre rock formations; their proportions were discernible only from a distance. The stone thighs, between which the heralds were flying, became great walls, too big to measure.

The sight took Merle's breath away. The thought that these huge things were created artificially, with sweat and blood and endless patience, was beyond her power of imagination.

What did the workers who'd hewn these figures out of stone look like? Like men? Or instead, like the watchers in the abyss, roachlike creatures that had eaten the superfluous rock instead of cutting it away?

Despite the heralds' speed, it took quite a while until they had the fighters behind them. The gap in the rocks was somewhat deeper than Merle had thought, and it had a slight bend, which made it impossible to see the end of it. The rock walls moved past them on the left and right, and there Merle saw flying Lilim, coming toward them or flying in the same direction. They all seemed to avoid the heralds in wide arcs, as if they were afraid of the giant stone heads.

No Lilim appeared to be like the other. Some resembled the pictures that men had made of the inhabitants of Hell for thousands of years: horned, scaly beings that sailed on arching wings. Others were similar to oversized insects, clicking and rattling in black shells of horn. But the greater part were like nothing Merle had ever seen. With most, the extremities could be determined, sometimes also something that might be a face, eyes, jaws, teeth.

"They all look completely different," she said, fascinated.

Winter smiled. "After a while you'll discover that there are repeating patterns. They're just not so easy to recognize as with humans or animals. But when you get used to the sight, you see them right away."

At some point the gap came to an end. Before them opened a grandiose panorama.

Axis Mundi.

The city of Lord Light, the center of Hell.

Merle had received a foretaste of real size when she saw the watchers at the abyss and then the two fighters in the rock gap. But this was pure madness: a view that could be apprehended only if she turned off her reason and simply *looked*—merely observed rather than tried to understand. For this place did not let itself be truly understood.

The city looked like a sea of tortoise shells, shoved

over and under one another, some tilted, others broken. Domes of rock stretched among towers, minarets, and pyramids, under bridges and paths and grillwork. No area was unbuilt, all spaces were inhabited. The rock walls between which Axis Mundi spread out like a coral reef were lined with houses and huts; the towers infested with whole tribes of insectoid Lilim; the ledges, which, like the bones of an elephant graveyard, rose above the buildings, covered with swarming life; and even in the thousands of columns of smoke that disappeared under the ceiling nested dark, fluttering creatures.

Enthroned at the center of this hodgepodge of inconceivable diversity was a dome that was broader and higher than all the others. The heralds headed toward it, and Merle guessed that they were approaching the holy of holies, the triumphal temple of Lord Light, the center of Axis Mundi, of Hell, and perhaps of the whole world, merged into one mighty edifice.

It would be a while yet before they arrived there, so far was the road from the rock gap, over roofs, spires, and gables. Merle used the time to examine the chaos below them more carefully. Once, a few years ago, in the streets of Venice, she'd seen a beggar whose entire face was infected by a proliferating ulcer that looked like the top of a cauliflower. From above, Axis Mundi reminded her of that sight, a grotesque work of tumors, entwined and distorted like melted muscle tissue.

And then there was the smell.

A spice dealer might perhaps have been able to recognize the individual odors in this abominable mixture of scents of all kinds. But in Merle's nose, the stink worked like a poison that etched itself into her mucous membranes.

The view over the city and the vague idea of what might live down there was enough to cast her into deep despair. Whatever had they been thinking of to come here? That Lord Light resided in a golden tower and would receive them with open arms? How should they find help here for their city, for their friends?

This was Hell, after all—true, at least in some respects, to the horrors that Professor Burbridge had evoked in his reports. And some things, she had no doubt, were certainly even worse.

"Do not let it frighten you," said the Flowing Queen. *"We have nothing to do with all that down there. It is Lord Light who interests us, not this scum."*

He is one of them, Merle thought.

"Possibly."

He will not help us.

"He offered it once, and he will do it again."

Merle shook her head silently, before she noticed that Winter was again looking at her suspiciously.

"Is that his palace?" she asked.

Winter's hair was being whirled around in the headwind

439

like a snowstorm. "I've never been here. I don't know."

The stone head kept on toward the monstrous dome, and now Merle noticed that the entire building appeared to be shining, from the inside out. In a different way from the subterranean lava strands, which provided light to all Hell, the dome glowed with no tinge of yellow or red, at once much brighter and yet duller.

"Before you ask—I do not know what sort of light that is," said the Queen.

Winter's dark expression had brightened. "That could be she."

Merle looked at him with wide eyes. "Who? Summer?"

He nodded.

The Queen groaned.

Merle had a suspicion what the light might mean. Until now she hadn't thought about why Lord Light bore this name at all. What if it was a description rather than a name?

"I am sorry to have to disappoint you," said the Flowing Queen quickly. *"In earlier times, the master of Hell was named Lucifer, and in your language that means nothing other than 'bringer of light.' Lord Light is a name humans have given him. Furthermore, quite a new one."*

Light bringer, Merle thought. Someone who brings the light—and maybe even imprisons it under a dome?

Winter's behavior changed. He no longer brooded or

confused Merle with dark hints. Instead, he ran back and forth along the lip, casting excited looks toward the dome and chewing on his lower lip like a nervous boy. Merle grinned stealthily. And *he* claimed not to be human?

A few hundred yards before the giant dome, the heads changed direction. Instead of flying straight toward the vault, they now approached an interconnected construction of rectangles and towers rising at the side of the dome. Merle noticed that everything here, every building, even the giant dome vault, consisted of smooth stone. Nothing was built of masonry and mortar. Every elevation within the city looked as if it had grown, as if someone had worked the rock and stretched it, the way the glass blowers on Murano worked their gatherings of glass; as if someone possessed the power to force the rock to an alien will.

The heralds glided through an opening that reminded Merle of the mouth of a giant fish. In comparison to this door, the stone heads seemed like pebbles. Beyond the opening was a broad hall, where a good dozen stone heralds were resting in several rows on the floor; they looked like remains of ancient statues in an archeologist's storeroom.

First the front head sank into a free place, then their own. Its bottom struck the ground with a murderous jolt that knocked Merle and Winter off their feet. The noise was deafening. The stone quivered for a while afterward from the force.

Merle fought her way up, still quite dizzy and deaf from the impact. Fearfully she looked down. She'd almost expected that Lilim would hurry toward the head from all directions, like harbor workers to unload a newly arrived ship. But the floor around the herald remained empty. At first.

A powerful shadow appeared before the mouth opening, then Vermithrax shot across them, much too fast and with wing beats that created a real storm. He was just able to decrease his speed enough not to smash against the gums of the mouth cavity. Snorting, he landed on the floor and whirled around, all predator, all fighter from head to paws.

He approached tensely, keeping his eyes on Winter. Without looking at Merle, he asked her, "Are you all right?"

"We're all fine and dandy."

A silent duel of gazes between Vermithrax and Winter was under way. Merle was glad not to be standing between them, lest the quantities of mistrust and tension now in the air strike her like lightning.

"Vermithrax," she said soothingly, "Winter is on our side." Still, as she spoke, she wasn't at all sure of that anymore. Perhaps it was pity. Or naive confidence.

"Your name is Winter?" asked Vermithrax.

The white-skinned, white-haired man nodded. "And yours Vermithrax." He said the lion's strange name without hesitation or a trace of mispronunciation, as if he'd already known him for a long time. And in fact, he did add, "I have heard of you."

The obsidian lion threw Merle a questioning look, but she raised her hands defensively. "Not from me."

"Your story is an old and well-known one," said Winter to the lion, "and indeed, all over the world. I have heard of it in many places."

Vermithrax raised an eyebrow. "Yes?"

Winter nodded. "The most powerful of the stone lions of Venice. You are a legend, Vermithrax."

Merle automatically wondered why, then, she'd never heard the whole story about Vermithrax's uprising against the Venetians. The Flowing Queen had been the first to tell her of it.

"You come from above?" asked the lion.

Winter nodded again.

In order to cut short the menacing interrogation, Merle joined in and told Vermithrax everything she'd learned about Winter. The story sounded even more incredible from her mouth. Vermithrax remained hostile, and she could hardly blame him. Perhaps it had been a mistake to tell about Winter's unhappy love for Summer. With that she'd strained his credulity to the utmost—and beyond.

"*Merle,*" said the Flowing Queen suddenly, "*we must get away from here. Quickly.*"

Vermithrax was just about to take another threatening step toward Winter, when Merle leaped between them.

"Stop it now! Right this minute, you two!"

Vermithrax stopped, finally turned his eyes from Winter, and looked at Merle. The expression in his eyes became gentler at once. "He could be dangerous."

"What is most dangerous are the Lilim, who are coming from all sides," said Merle, but it was the Flowing Queen who spoke out of her.

Are you sure? Merle thought.

"Yes. They will soon be here."

Vermithrax made a leap and landed on the edge of the stone lower lip. "You're right."

Winter also climbed the stone bulge, nimbly followed by Merle. A horrified sound escaped her throat, and she quickly reassured herself with the thought that it must have been the Flowing Queen. Of course she knew better.

Countless Lilim were approaching the herald, absurdly comical figures with too many limbs, sharp-edged horn shells, and eyeless heads. The majority bustled along flat on the floor, while others went upright, if also bent forward, as if by the weight of their horny bodies. Some others ran on long, skinny legs, as if they were on stilts, and their arms stood out at angles like the legs of daddy longlegs. Those were the ones that horrified Merle most, for they moved fast and with agility, and Merle had to think involuntarily of giant spiders, even if that over-simplified the matter—and prettified it.

"They haven't discovered us yet," said Winter, as he

leaped back behind the lip. Vermithrax and Merle followed him.

The lion waved Merle over with a scraping of his paws. "Get on!"

She cast a glance at Winter and hesitated. "What about him? There's room enough on your back for two."

Vermithrax looked anything but happy. "Do we have to?"

Merle looked over at Winter once more, then she nodded. "Very well. Hurry up!"

Merle climbed up onto the lion's black back. Winter followed her after a short hesitation. She felt him take a place behind her and try to find the best position. There was just time enough for him to grab on tight, for Vermithrax unfolded his wings and lifted them into the air with one powerful motion.

They shot out between the herald's lips just as the first angled leg of a Lilim pushed over the edge.

Vermithrax rushed out into the hall. On the floor below, the Lilim turned their heads, some as ponderously as tortoises, others swiftly and with malicious eyes. Some let out shrill animal sounds, others articulated words in a strange language. Over her shoulder Merle saw a whole flood of creatures climbing to the chin of the herald and streaming into the mouth cavity. But the ones with the long limbs remained behind and stared up at Vermithrax. One gave out a succession of high, sharp sounds, and at once the direction of the stream of Lilim changed. Like angry ants they swarmed out to all sides.

Merle clung to Vermithrax's mane, while he climbed as high as possible, up to just below the ceiling of the hall. Her fingers got hold of something that didn't belong there. When she pulled out her right hand, she saw that something had caught in Vermithrax's coat, one of the black feathers from the ear of the herald. Only it wasn't a feather at all: It was a tiny black crab, so fine-limbed that she'd taken its limbs for down. It didn't move, was obviously dead. So they hadn't lain on the leavings of Lilim in the ear but on Lilim themselves. The thought caused her such revulsion that for a moment it even masked her fear. She had the feeling that her entire body must be crawling. Shuddering, she cast a last look at the dead crab thing and then flung it into the void.

Winter had tried at first to cling to the flanks of the lion, but now, when that hold wasn't enough, he put an arm around Merle's waist from behind. She had the feeling he shrank from the touch; perhaps out of fear she still might freeze to ice.

"*They were expecting us,*" said the Queen.

"But how did they know that we're here?" Merle no longer cared if Winter overheard her.

"*Perhaps they could sense one of you.*"

"Or you."

The Queen didn't say anything to that. Perhaps she was considering that idea, in fact.

The obsidian lion flew over the rows of giant heads and kept heading toward the door through which the heralds had entered. It must be a good fifteen hundred feet to it from where they were. From up here the hall looked even more gigantic.

"Vermithrax!"

Merle flinched when she heard Winter's cry.

Their enigmatic companion pointed his long fingers above them. "There they come!"

The obsidian lion flew faster. "I see them too."

Confused, Merle looked toward where Winter was pointing. She'd expected flying Lilim, flying beasts like those they'd seen in the rock crevice and over the city. But what she saw now was something different.

The Lilim who'd taken up their pursuit didn't fly— they were clambering along under the ceiling!

They were the same ones she'd already seen down there on the floor, long-legged, spiderlike, and yet many times stranger than all that she knew from the upper world.

And they were inconceivably fast.

Vermithrax decreased his altitude a little again, so that the creatures couldn't reach him from above with their long legs. But they now seemed to be coming from everywhere, as if they'd already been lying in wait, invisibly merged with the rock ceiling. Merle watched as some of them apparently appeared from nowhere. They'd been up there the whole time and now detached themselves from the flat stone surface, their long limbs outstretched, and from one heartbeat to the next, they launched into darting motion.

"There ahead!" she yelled to override the sound of the flight and the screeching of the Lilim. "They're in front of the door now!"

The entire ceiling over the hall's exit had awakened. A carpet of dry bodies twitched and shoved and tumbled up there, over and under one another, like an army of daddy longlegs, none of them smaller than a human and some almost twice as large. Many stretched single limbs downward, trembling and twitching, to reach Vermithrax in the air.

The lion remained relaxed. "If we fly low enough, they won't get us."

Merle was about to say something, and she felt that the Queen was getting ready to speak in her thoughts as well, but then they both kept silent and left it to Vermithrax to carry them to safety.

Winter was the only one who objected. "That way won't work."

Merle looked over her shoulder. "What do you mean?"

She saw his eyes widen. His grip around her upper body became firmer, almost painful. "Too late!"

She looked ahead again.

The entire ceiling was now in motion, a boiling mass of bodies and eyes and spindle-thin legs.

In front of them one of the Lilim plunged into the depths, a whirling tangle of limbs, too far away to be dangerous to them. Merle's eyes followed its fall, a hundred, a hundred fifty yards down, and she was certain that the creature would shatter on the floor. The thing landed, remained lying there for a moment, rolled up like a ball — then put out its legs and ran hectically here and there as if nothing had happened, forward and back, in a circle, until finally it stopped below, waiting, and stared up at them.

"*No,*" whispered the Queen, and Merle grasped what Winter had meant by "too late."

Around them the Lilim began falling from the ceiling like ripe fruit. A spider leg with a sharp hook on the end grazed Vermithrax's left wing and pulled out a handful of feathers. The obsidian lion went into a brief wobble, but then flew on, ever faster, toward the mighty door.

The Lilim fell. More and more pushed off from the ceiling and plunged. Vermithrax was compelled to fly daredevil avoidance maneuvers. Merle bent forward until her face almost touched his mane. She couldn't see what Winter was doing behind her, but she figured he was also pulling his head in.

It was as if they'd been caught in the middle of a bizarre rain shower — with the difference that it was raining living creatures, gigantic spider animals, only one of which would have been enough to put an army to flight. But here they were falling by the dozens, finally by the hundreds.

Vermithrax hadn't a chance.

A Lilim's body crashed on the lion's back end, slid off, and with its whirling limbs might have pulled Winter down with it, had he not swiftly slid closer to Merle and taken cover. So the hook on the Lilim's leg just tangled in Winter's long hair and pulled out a strand. Winter didn't even seem to notice it.

A second Lilim smashed onto Vermithrax's left wing, and this time they almost all crashed. At the last moment, Vermithrax got his ponderous body under control again— until the next Lilim fell in front of him and scratched his nose with its hook. Vermithrax bellowed with pain, shook his head so hard that Merle almost fell off, opened his eyes again and saw another creature, which struck at him with its legs as it fell, a whirling black star of horn and teeth and knife-sharp hooked claws.

The next fell right on Merle.

She was torn from Winter's grasp, slipped sideways, and fell into the abyss. She heard Vermithrax bellow above her, then Winter, then both together, and while she still fell she thought coolly that she would die now, finally and without any way out.

She felt something clawing around her, limbs like dry

branches, which pressed against her legs, her upper body, even against her face; it felt as if she'd run into a low-hanging branch in the dark. Her back was pressed against something soft, cool, a body, hairy and moist like a sliced peach.

The impact was bad.

But much worse was when she realized *what* had saved her.

The Lilim had closed around her like a protective ball, the way spiders do just before they die. It had turned in the air and had landed on its back. Merle could see the ceiling of the hall through the latticework of its limbs, an inferno of plunging bodies in which she saw no trace of the obsidian lion. But her vision was blurred anyway, her mind hardly in a position to process the images.

She'd fallen more than three hundred feet to the ground, and she had survived. The shock struck deep, if not deep enough to completely paralyze her. Her mind grew clearer with every breath, forming the beginnings of thoughts out of the confusion in her head.

The first thing that came into her mind was doubt as to whether she should in fact be grateful that she was still alive. She felt the damp, sticky underside of the Lilim at her back, the bristly hairs sticking through her clothing like dull nails. She saw the hairy, lath-thin limbs over her, cramped, motionless.

"*It is dead,*" said the Flowing Queen.

Merle needed a moment before she took in the meaning of the words.

"*If it had landed on its feet like the others, it would have survived. But it landed on its back in order to protect you.*"

"To protect . . . me?"

"*It does not matter why—in any case, you should try to free yourself from its grasp before rigor mortis sets in.*"

Merle pushed with all her strength against the enclosing limbs. They squeaked and snapped, but they would not be moved. Merle had not only to battle with her revulsion but also with the trembling of her arms and legs. Her head might have realized that she was still alive, but the rest of her body appeared to be just a bit later getting ready. Her muscles trembled and twitched under her skin like fish in a trap.

"*Hurry!*"

"All right for you to talk." Anyway, her voice was the old one again. Perhaps a little shrill, perhaps a little breathless. But she could speak.

And curse. Loudly.

"*That was pretty good,*" said the Flowing Queen, impressed, after the flood of swear words from Merle's mouth had dried up.

"Years of practice," gasped Merle as she pushed aside the last Lilim leg. She made a great effort not to look down as she put both hands on the damp, soft mass at her back and pushed herself up. Somehow she succeeded in freeing herself of the cadaver's embrace and springing to the floor between two branch-limbs.

Her feet gave out and she fell. Not from exhaustion this time.

Around her hundreds of Lilim stood and stared at her, teetering on their long legs and sharpening their hooked claws on the ground. They'd encircled Merle and their dead comrade, but they came no nearer, as if something were holding them back. Perhaps the same command that had made the Lilim sacrifice himself for Merle.

The Queen anticipated the upshot of this realization: *"They are not going to do anything to you. Someone intends something else for you."*

For us, Merle wanted to say, but finally her voice failed her. She turned her eyes up to the roof and saw that no more Lilim were falling to the floor. The ceiling was still in motion, but the swarming was gradually decreasing and the creatures again melted into the rock, became invisible.

Vermithrax, she thought.

"He is alive."

Merle looked around the hall, but she could see no farther than the second or third row of the Lilim army. "Certain?"

"I feel him."

"You're only saying that to calm me."

"No. Vermithrax is alive. Just like Winter."

"Where are they?"

453

"Here somewhere. In the hall."

"The Lilim have them?"

"I am afraid so."

The thought that the obsidian lion had been forced by the Lilim to land or even fall made her heart miss a beat. But the Queen said he was alive. Merle didn't want to question that. Not here, not now.

The circle of Lilim had closed to about three feet around them. Although the spider creatures predominated, there were also some others among them, pressed flat to the ground or two-legged or without limbs altogether, a seething, swarming, whispering chaos of claws and spines and spikes and eyes.

So many eyes.

And movement everywhere, a ferment of iridescent surfaces, shiny with dampness, like a mess of algae and flotsam in the waves.

"Someone is coming."

Before Merle could ask how the Queen knew that, the wall of Lilim parted. The front ones fell silent, some sank their heads in respect—or what Merle took for respect.

She had expected a commander, a kind of general, perhaps an animal, bigger than all the others, something that far surpassed the others in strength and cruelty and pure repulsiveness.

Instead she saw a little man in a wheelchair.

He was being pushed by something that had a distant

resemblance to a knot of glowing ribbons, which were in constant motion, turning in and around one another and still moving forward as they did so. It was only when they came closer that she realized that it wasn't one creature but innumerable ones: a multitude of snakes, which moved together like a single organism, linked together and controlled. Its heads moved alertly back and forth, and its bodies shimmered in unimaginable colors, more beautiful than anything Merle had seen since her flight from Venice.

The man in the wheelchair examined Merle without any emotion. No smile, also no malice. Only blank, empty features—the interest of a scientist who was looking at a new but not especially fascinating species under a magnifying glass.

The coldness in his eyes made Merle shudder. They made her far more anxious than the thousand-headed army of monstrosities.

Was that by any chance Lord Light? Was the lord of Hell actually this little man with the dead facial features?

"*No,*" said the Flowing Queen.

Merle would have loved to ask what made her so sure, but the man in the wheelchair left her no time. His voice was old and squeaky, like the creaking of hardened leather.

"What to do, what to do?" he murmured, more to himself than to anyone else.

Then: "I know, I know."

He doesn't have all his marbles, Merle thought.

The man gave the mass of snakes behind his wheelchair a sign, and immediately the bands billowed around and turned the chair, shoving it back in the direction from which it had come.

"Bring her to me," growled the man with his back to Merle. "Bring her into the Heart House."

10

The Assault

There were seven of them.

Too many, Serafin thought as they pushed through the
darkness. Way too many.

Five boys, including himself and Dario. In addition,
two slender figures, two women. Larger than some of the
boys—*rebels*, he chided himself, full of cynicism—but
smaller than he was.

Eft had the kerchief over her face again, although he
wasn't sure why. Presumably they'd be seeing worse
things this night than a mermaid's mouth. But she insisted
on her masquerade, though he didn't believe she was

ashamed of her origin. She was a mermaid and always would be. The human legs Eft bore instead of her *kalimar*, her scaly tail, were only external. In her veins flowed the salty sea, the water of the lagoon.

The second woman was Lalapeya. The sphinx had taken her human form, and now his having seen her with her lion body seemed to Serafin almost like a bad dream. Each diminution of her perfection, each tiny blot seemed absurd in consideration of such perfection. He had to forcibly remind himself that this, too, was just part of her magic. The magic did not end with her external change; she manipulated the thoughts of all those who looked at her, just as she appeared to manipulate everything that happened around her.

And Serafin still wondered whether what they were doing was right. Why was he going along with Lalapeya? What was it that made him and the others do what she wanted?

Not *all* the others. Eft withstood the sphinx's magic. Serafin suspected that Eft saw Lalapeya in her true form sneaking through the tunnels, a creature half lion, half human, moving forward on the velvet paws of a predator. He'd already noticed, too, that Lalapeya made less noise, less even than he did. It might look as though she was walking on human feet—but the truth was something else.

The sphinx was no human and would never be one. Why was she so interested in Venice and its inhabitants?

What made her incite a gang of street boys to assassinate the Pharaoh? The *Pharaoh*! Serafin simply could not understand why he'd let himself in for this.

"Eft," he whispered in the half-dark of the underground canal.

She looked at him over the edge of the scarf covering her mouth. She nodded once, very briefly.

"Do you feel it too?" he asked.

Again she nodded.

"What is it?" He rubbed his hand over his right arm. The hairs were standing on end, and his skin was crawling, as if he'd grabbed hold of an anthill.

"Magic," said Eft.

"Sphinx magic, worked by the commandants of the Pharaoh," said Lalapeya, who suddenly stood beside the mermaid, as if someone had poured the darkness into the shape of a young woman.

Eft threw her a side glance, but she said nothing.

"Sphinx magic?" Serafin asked. He kept hoping that the other boys didn't notice his uncertainty. But Dario, at least, perceived it and stopped next to him.

Serafin raised a hand and brought the entire troop to a halt. He and Dario and the two women formed the lead. So far. Tiziano, Boro, and little Aristide, whom they'd chosen because of his agility and adroitness, had followed without a single objection, question, or doubting look, along those secret canals that only a handful of other master thieves

besides Serafin knew of—canals that extended under piazzas and streets and were nevertheless just above the water
level. In some places the ground was damp, in others the
water was ankle deep; for the most part, however, the
secret paths were dry. Dry enough for a group of assassins.

Murder, Serafin thought. That was the word that until
now he'd avoided the way stone lions avoided water. He
was a thief, one of the best, but certainly no murderer.

"What does that mean: sphinx magic?" he asked, turning this time to Lalapeya.

He knew that the others shouldn't have been listening,
but his conscience forbade him to leave them in the dark.
If they were running straight into a magic trap, each of
them had the right to know about it. They were doing
what they did with free will, not from a sense of obliga-
tion. They were doing it for themselves, not for the city or
even the citizens, who'd never given a damn about the
begging street children.

For themselves. For each one of them.

For me, thought Serafin.

On the faces of the boys he read something more: for
Lalapeya. That made him almost more uneasy than the
magic crawling on his skin.

"Sphinx magic is worked by—," began Lalapeya, but
she was interrupted by Serafin.

"Worked by sphinxes. Yes, you said that already. But
what are they doing?"

Tiziano and Aristide stared at him wide-eyed. No one had ever spoken to Lalapeya so disrespectfully.

But she didn't bother about that. Smiling, she looked at Serafin, holding him fast with her eyes, and continued, "Such magic may mean all possible things. It can kill someone who comes under its influence, and do it in more ways than humans can imagine. It can also be harmless and merely warn someone that they know of him."

"Then do they know that we're here now?" asked Dario in alarm. Even in the dark, Serafin could see how much Dario was sweating. Serafin's forehead was also damp, and every few steps he'd run his hand over his face so that the trickles didn't run into his eyes.

"They would know—if I hadn't blocked the magic," said the sphinx, and now her smile grew a little wider. She looked stunning.

A relieved murmur went through the group of boys, but Serafin was still tense. "I can still feel the magic on my skin."

"That means nothing. Those are only the discharges in the air that occur when two spells run up against each other. Mine on theirs. That itching you all feel is only an aftereffect of the spells, not the spell itself."

They went on their way again, but soon, somewhere under the Church of San Gallo, in a columned undercroft full of spiderwebs and forgotten statues of saints, Serafin held Eft back. She carried Arcimboldo's mirror mask with her in a knapsack of hard leather. Serafin shrank from coming too close to the strange relic, so he laid his hand on Eft's arm, not on her shoulder. As she slowed, he quickly pulled his fingers back. She stopped now, a few steps away from the others.

"Do you trust her?" he whispered.

"Yes." The cloth over the mermaid's mouth stretched and puffed out with each breath and even more when she spoke.

"Completely?"

"She is Lalapeya." As if that were reason enough.

"You knew that she was a sphinx, didn't you? From the beginning."

"I see her in her true form. She cannot deceive me."

"Why?"

"The mermaid folk and the sphinxes have been related to each other since ancient times. Not many remember that today, but many thousands of years ago there were close ties. With the loss of the magic, we mermaids have also lost our meaning and power, while the sphinxes—at least some of them—have always understood how to fit themselves to new circumstances."

"Like Lalapeya?"

Eft shook her head decidedly. "Not her. She has been what she is today for a long time."

"But—"

She didn't let him finish. "She is older than most of the

other sphinxes, even if she doesn't look so to you humans. She knows how it was earlier, and she honors the old relationship." Eft was quiet for a moment; then she said, "She gave us a secret place for our dead."

The cemetery of the mermaids, thought Serafin, enthralled. An ancient legend. No one knew where it was. Many had sought it, but he knew of no one who had found it. "Lalapeya established your cemetery?"

Eft nodded. "Long ago. We are in her debt, even if she has never asked us for anything."

"What is she doing in Venice?"

"She was already here when the city did not yet exist. The question should be: What is the city doing in a place that was under Lalapeya's protection for thousands of years?"

"Thousands of years . . ." Serafin let the words melt on his tongue. He cast a look toward the sphinx, to the girlish young woman who led the procession at Dario's side.

"She never tried to drive the humans away, although that would have been her right," said Eft. "Her duty, some of us even said. This here, this night, Serafin . . . this is the first time that Lalapeya has intervened in the fate of Venice. And she must know very precisely why."

Serafin stared at the mermaid and had trouble holding her piercing gaze. "Do you know it too?"

Eft's scarf quivered as she smiled with her shark's mouth. "Maybe."

"That isn't fair."

"There's a knowing that is not meant for humans. But just believe me when I say to you that she knows what she's doing." Her eyes narrowed. "She made mistakes earlier. Now she is fulfilling her destiny."

A thousand questions burned on Serafin's lips, but Eft hurried on again to reach the front of the troop. He hastened to keep up with her.

"What is she? Some kind of a guard?"

"Ask her yourself."

"But a guard of what?"

Eft pointed forward. Reluctantly he followed her eyes and discovered that Lalapeya was looking back at him over her shoulder. She smiled, but it looked sad. He simply did not know what to make of her. Nevertheless, he asked no further questions for the moment, not even when he was walking beside her again and making every effort not to look at her. He was quite aware that she was looking over at him every now and then.

He took the lead and went on ahead alone, a few steps in front of the others. He again concentrated on the matter he knew more about than anyone. He sought the best way to get through the city in concealment, as he had done countless times in the past.

At length he had them all stop under a round hatch in the ceiling of the tunnel and gave them to understand that from here on they mustn't make a sound.

With Dario's help he opened the hatch and climbed up. Above the exit stood a round staircase, which led through all the floors of the Doge's Palace. The steps were narrow and had a much-needed banister: a few posts holding an old handrail. In earlier days, criminals were sometimes led to condemnation on these circular stairs, but today they were rarely used. The thick dust on the floor and the handrail showed that the last usage had been a long time ago.

Serafin was quite certain that the Egyptians wouldn't know of this staircase. Not yet. The Pharaoh's body-guards would get busy with the plans of the palace, no question, but he doubted there'd been enough time for that yet. For that reason too, the attack had to take place as soon as possible, this very night.

He loosed a rope from his belt, fastened it with a few quick flicks of his wrist to the lowest banister post, and helped the others climb out. He was in suspense as to how Lalapeya would come up—perhaps with the spring of a lion—but then she climbed the rope just like anyone else, with her hands and feet, if with a little less effort than the others. With her it almost looked playful, which once more earned her the admiration of the boys. The climb was most difficult for Eft, who, in spite of all her agility, had no practice in rope climbing.

Silently and swiftly they ran up the spiral staircase. The Pharaoh's chambers were on the upper floor, but Serafin was only too aware that he mustn't take the easiest approach. What they desperately needed was an advantage, and they wouldn't gain that by the shortest route.

He led the group past the entrance to the upper floor, still higher, to the end of the stairs, where the steps came up against a plank door. The wood was darkened with age, the mountings corroded by rust.

As Serafin had expected, the door could be opened without difficulty. The heavy latch, as long as his lower arm, yielded with a grating sound, and the door swung slowly inward. Wordlessly Serafin directed his comrades through the opening into a dusky half light.

He'd explained the exact route to the others at the enclave—however, only as far as this staircase. The last part of the plan he'd kept to himself.

All the same, each of the others guessed where they were—there was only one place in the Doge's Palace that was higher than the top floor. In past centuries, many thousands of prisoners had lost their lives up here in the dreaded lead chambers under the roof, herded into tiny cells, in winter half-frozen, in summer subjected to the heat of the sun beating down on the lead roofs; they might just as well have been imprisoned in ovens.

Each of them, even the most uneducated street boy, knew the stories of the prisoners' sufferings. Serafin would have been just as impressed as the others if this had been his first visit up here. At the beginning of his thieving career, he and a few friends had made a game of sniffing around in the Doge's Palace under the noses of the City Guard.

"No one can hear us up here," he said to the others. "The ceilings are thickened, because of the screams in the olden days."

"What do you have in mind?" Tiziano asked.

Serafin grinned, before Eft's dark look reminded him that this wasn't a game, unlike that time when he was dancing around under the noses of the City Guard. "We're going to invade the Pharaoh's rooms from above," he said. "That's the only way that's pretty sure not to be guarded."

Dario raised an eyebrow. "*Pretty* sure?"

Serafin nodded.

"And you think no one's going to hear when we break open the ceiling?" asked Boro. "And what with, anyway? With our bare hands?"

"No," said Serafin. "There's a narrow staircase behind the paneling, leading from the cells in the top floor. The Doges used the secret passageway when they wanted to watch the torture without being seen."

"Torture" wasn't a word that raised the mood, and so no one asked any more questions. They were depressed enough; their fear was too consuming.

Serafin led them through dusty passageways, so narrow that they had to go single file. They passed cells standing open, from which came a horrible smell, even though it had been ages since anyone was imprisoned here.

Outside there was a soft warmth, like spring, and still, under the lead roofs they all had trouble breathing. The stuffy air from the lead chambers filled their lungs like hot water. Only Lalapeya, whose people came from the great deserts, remained untouched by it. She and Eft whispered with each other a few times, but Serafin didn't understand what they said.

Finally they came to an empty room, which had once served as a torture chamber. Serafin stopped by a narrow iron door with a grated window in it. The door was closed, but it took only a few moments for him to unlock it with the tip of his dagger. Behind the door, narrow steps led steeply downward, apparently inside a wall.

"These steps end behind the paneling of a salon on the floor below," he whispered. "From now on, not another word! And get ready for the big fireworks."

"Serafin?" Tiziano held him back by the arm as he was just about to move forward.

"What?"

"If we make it . . . I mean, in case we survive this business, how do we get out of here again?"

Serafin took a deep breath, not because of the bad air, but because he'd been afraid somebody would ask this question. At the same time, he was glad to finally get it behind him. He threw a quick look at Lalapeya, but she only nodded encouragingly and left the speaking to him—and with it the reponsibility.

Serafin sighed. "You all know that it won't be over when the Pharaoh is dead. His guard will attack us, and it's also only too possible that within a few seconds it will be swarming with mummy soldiers down there as well. Not to mention the priests of Horus and"—another glance at Lalapeya—"the sphinx commanders."

Boro let out a hoarse laugh. It was supposed to sound hard-boiled, but everyone saw through him. "We're as good as dead."

Serafin shrugged. "Perhaps. Also perhaps not. Our speed counts. If we get the chance to retreat, we'll do it the same way. Up these stairs, through the lead chambers, and down the spiral staircase again to the secret tunnels."

"And then?"

"Then we run."

"No," contradicted Eft. "That won't be necessary. Down below we'll have help. You remember the old landing under the Calle dei Fuséri, don't you? The basin we just saw there?" The boys nodded. "Help is waiting for us there. From there on we can flee."

Dario let out a soft whistle between his teeth. "Mermaids?"

Eft didn't answer, but they all knew that he was right. On the steps they drew their weapons. Each had a revolver with six shots, as well as a pouch full of ammunition. In addition, Serafin, Dario, Boro, and Tiziano carried sabers. Eft had only a small knife, no longer than her thumb, but it was sharper than any blade Serafin had ever seen.

Lalapeya was unarmed. Serafin was sure that she possessed other means of defending herself. She was a sphinx, a being of pure magic. It was she who'd brought them all together. And she was—he hoped—the key to the downfall of the Pharaoh.

At the foot of the stairs they came up against another door, higher this time, the rear side of a wall panel. There was no latch, no lock. It was secured by a secret mechanism on the outside.

Lalapeya stepped back, slipped behind the line of boys. It had been arranged so. She needed time to work her magic against the Pharaoh, time the others were supposed to gain for her.

Serafin and Dario exchanged looks, nodded to each other, then with their combined strength they kicked against the wood. With a dull thud, the door burst out of the wall and crashed flat on the floor on the other side. Dust welled up, and for a moment the thunder of the impact resounded in Serafin's ears.

With a wild yell, Serafin and Dario stormed forward, over the wooden door, out into the room, followed by the others. Eft was beside them, then Tiziano, then the rest behind him.

Instantly mummy soldiers confronted them, as if they'd only been waiting for the intruders. The mummies were posted to the right and left in front of a closed double door that led into a room beyond. The two doors were ornamented with inlays of gold leaf; they glimmered in the light of several gas lamps. It looked as though the gold vines were moving over the wood like snakes, a confusing play of reflections.

Tiziano was the first to fire a shot at one of the mummy soldiers. He hit him in the shoulder, but then a second shot in the forehead stopped the soldier.

The boys now fired out of all barrels. Boro had to avoid the stroke of a sickle sword. The blade grazed his skull and tore a piece of skin from his head. At once there was blood running down his face, but nevertheless he whirled around, took aim, and fired. The bullet went astray and drove into the golden portal with a crack. Dario was immediately beside him and struck the mummified head from the soldier's shoulders.

Serafin raced to the next door. The first hurdle was overcome.

In a flash, Eft was at his side. He was just about to push open the door when a roar sounded. It rang through the main entrance to the room, which led out into a broad corridor. Reinforcements were on the way. Priests of Horus, if they were unlucky. Or, much worse, sphinx commanders.

Serafin waited no longer, rammed the right door in, and sprang through it, revolver drawn. He had no practice in handling firearms, but he hoped that his talent—or his luck—would be enough not to miss the Pharaoh and his vizier.

In the center of the second room was a divan of jaguar skins. Serafin could only make out the outlines; the center was blocked by four sphinxes, gazing at him with dark looks. They carried mighty sickle swords, much bigger than those of the mummy soldiers. Their lion bodies did not move, were stiff as statues, but one of them whisked away a few flies with his tail.

He's shooing flies, thought Serafin in shock, while for us it's a matter of our lives. That's how seriously he takes us: nothing more than a heap of blowflies.

At that moment Serafin lost all hope.

It happened very abruptly and without any warning. It had nothing to do with the danger from the sphinxes or that they had obviously expected the rebels—

(Betrayal!)

—but only with this one swish of the lion's tail, this one, tiny, apparently unimportant gesture.

Blowflies, went through his mind again. Nothing more!

Behind him a yell rang out, and out of the corner of his eye Serafin saw a dozen or more mummy soldiers pushing through the broken door. Boro and Tiziano were standing against them, splitting the skulls of the foremost soldiers with powerful blows of their sabers. Gray dust boiled up and settled like a veil of fog over the fighters.

A strange feeling of timelessness, of intolerable sluggishness, came over Serafin. It seemed to him that the battle was taking place underwater. All movements seemed to become slower, more lethargic, and for a moment a cry of jubilation rose in his throat.

Lalapeya's magic! Finally it was coming to their aid!

Right afterward the disappointment could scarcely have struck him harder. It was no spell. No magic guile. It was only himself, his own senses that slowed, as his mind retreated into deepest shock for a few seconds. Shock — and brutal recognition.

They were fighting for a lost cause. Dario vanquished one mummy soldier after another, with absolutely balletic ease, but he had no chance against the superior strength. Sooner or later he would succumb to the onrush of opponents.

Serafin warded off the attack of a mummy soldier who suddenly appeared behind him. Nothing of all this had the unpleasant taste of reality now. Everything seemed unreal, artificial, simply wrong, even his own fighting. It seemed to him that he was observing their defeat from the outside, and so he finally recognized the mistake with which they had begun, he himself, and Eft, and also the others.

They'd been betrayed.

And Lalapeya was nowhere to be seen.

Serafin let out a shriek that made even the mummy soldier pause. At the same time he struck in self-defense, first splitting the sickle sword, then the gray skeletal head. Eft brought down a second, and now the four sphinxes began to move. Through the gap between them Serafin saw that the jaguar divan was empty. And there was no trace of the vizier.

"Lalapeya!" he bellowed in a fury of rage, but no one answered. Dario threw him a look that seemed strangely empty to Serafin, as if an unseen hand had wiped every dream, every spark of hope from his eyes.

Eft seized Serafin's arm and pulled him back into the first room. Tiziano stood there, his revolver drawn. He was shooting in blind fury all about him, until Dario knocked the weapon out of his hand with his fist, for fear the bullets would hit one of them.

No trace of Lalapeya. Anywhere.

More mummy soldiers streamed into the room through the first door and blocked their escape route. Frantically Serafin looked around him. His eyes fell on Boro, who tore a small bottle from his belt and drank it empty in one pull. His cheeks stayed full, he didn't swallow the contents. Then he snatched a matchbox from his pocket, kindled a flame in the palm of his hand, and spit the fluid across it in the direction of the mummy soldiers. His hand turned red first, then black, but he didn't bother about it; he also paid no attention to Dario and Aristide, who were just able, with a daring leap, to get to safety before the fire licked over them and struck the line of advancing mummy soldiers.

"Out of here!" bellowed Eft as a wall of flame shot up behind her, a chaos of reeling, flaming bodies, who spread the fire to one another, until the front part of the room had turned into a flaming hell.

"Back!" cried Serafin, but Boro didn't obey. He continued to spit his flaming breath at their adversaries. He stopped only when the fire had almost reached him. With a quick glance he evaluated the situation, saw his friends, saw the saving door to flight, and finally started moving.

Too late. One of the sphinxes bounded through the door to the inner room without coming close to the fire on the other side of the room and reached Boro just as he was about to turn to the secret door. The sickle sword, as long as a small tree, rose up and struck.

Serafin screamed and was about to plunge into the room as it filled again with attackers. And then he was being pulled along by Dario as together they rushed behind Eft up the narrow stairs, followed by Tiziano and Aristide. Reaching the top, Serafin cast a look back and saw that the sphinxes were standing at the entrance to the stairs and shouting angrily: The passage was too narrow and the ceiling too low, so their sphinx bodies wouldn't fit through the door. If they'd tried anyway, it would have been an easy matter to strike them from the upper steps.

But none of the fugitives thought of that. Even Serafin, who'd experienced more daredevil escapes than all the others together, felt only panic, icy horror. He saw himself storming through the lead chambers like a stranger, out into the round stairwell and down the steps. If anyone had been waiting for them there, he would have had fairly easy game: Only Dario and Serafin still carried sabers. Tiziano held his revolver in his hand, without noticing that it was opened and all the bullets had fallen out of the cylinder. Aristide, at the end, was unarmed, and he pressed both palms of his hands over his ears as he ran, as if he could thus shut out the world outside.

One after the other they leaped through the trapdoor into the deep. No one took the time to pull the cover back over the opening; the Egyptians would find out anyway which path they had taken.

"To the landing place," cried Eft, gasping.

No one asked for Lalapeya. She wasn't with them, and all guessed why. Now, as they ran behind one another through the darkness of the secret pathway, with their feet splashing in puddles and having to take care not to bang their heads on the low ceiling and support beams, the thought came to Serafin for the first time that he ought to have been able to prevent it. Everything that had happened. It had lain in his hands. If he'd followed his instinct; if he hadn't let himself be drawn into this suicide mission; and if he hadn't believed Eft when she said to trust Lalapeya; yes, if he'd followed his feelings in all this only once, one single time, then Boro would still be alive now.

He had felt wrong. Serafin had known, he had known deep in his heart that this was no game, none of his master thievery. He'd been flattered that the sphinx had chosen him in particular to get her into the palace. And he'd fallen for it, for each one of her lies.

He looked up and met Eft's dark eyes. The mermaid was staring at him, enigmatically as always. She pulled the scarf from her face and bared her shark's mouth. "Wait still, before you pass judgment on her," she said. Without the scarf or mask, her voice sounded more hissing, each *S* a little sharper.

"Not . . . pass judgment?" he repeated, disbelieving. "You surely aren't serious."

But Eft didn't answer, only turned and ran on behind the others, who'd taken the lead.

Serafin went faster until he'd caught up with the mermaid again. How had she meant that? How could she ask that he not judge Lalapeya for her betrayal? Boro lay dead on the upper floor of the Doge's Palace and they themselves might not survive the next few hours. For all that, he should *not pass judgment on her*?

Had he still had the wind and the strength, he would have laughed out loud. And he would much rather have screamed at someone, Eft perhaps, or one of the others, to give vent to his helpless anger, and even to hurt someone, no matter whom, as he himself was hurting.

"Let go of it," said Eft as they bent under a low beam. "It doesn't help anything."

It took a moment before it became clear to him that the same thoughts must be going through her head, the same hatred, the same disappointment.

They'd all been betrayed. Lalapeya had led them to their doom.

They reached the underground landing with the last of their strength. A broad canal ran parallel to the path for a little way. A boat was floating on the waves, now and again knocking hollowly against the stonework. It was unusually made, larger and rounder than an ordinary rowboat and in no way comparable to the long, slender gondolas.

"A sea turtle," said Eft. "Or, rather, its shell. What's left after it has lain on the sea bottom for a while."

The sea turtle shell floated on its back. It was several yards in diameter and was hollowed out like a giant soup dish.

Beckoning them frantically, Eft urged, "Get in, hurry!"

Dario hesitated. "Into a sea turtle?"

"Yes, damn it!" Eft's eyes were angry. "We haven't time!"

The group climbed into the shell among algae and the encrusted remains of earlier sea dwellers, touching them as little as possible.

Eft was the last to climb into the floating bowl of horn and sit down on the bottom with them. Serafin felt the warty surface of the shell through the thin material of his trousers, but he didn't care. He felt gutted, his insides frozen to ice.

All at once, heads rose from the water around their vessel, only just up to the eyes—large, beautiful eyes. Then the mermaids showed the rest of their faces. In the darkness their teeth shone like slivers of moon floating on the water.

There were eight, enough to drag the heavy sea turtle shell through the labyrinth of canals out into the open water. Aristide was talking to himself and unable to take his eyes off the mermaid who was next to him in the water, although in the dark, hardly more was visible than a wide fan of hair, which now moved slowly forward. The shell began to move along with the mermaids, an unusual but effective raft, on which the survivors now glided through the darkness. A slight odor of dead fish and algae hung in the air.

Serafin's eyes sought Eft. The mermaid had turned away and was supporting herself with her lower arms on the edge of the shell. Expressionless, she stared into the dark water. It was clear how very much she longed to be gliding through the cold stream with her sisters with a scaled tail instead of legs.

The mermaids pulled and pushed them around a multitude of turns and bends, through low tunnels and open waterways that ran between façades without windows, through hidden gardens and, once or twice, even through waterways in the interiors of abandoned buildings. Serafin soon lost his bearings. Not that he wasted too much thought on that.

He could think only of Lalapeya, of what she'd done to them. He didn't understand her reasons. Why did she just call a rebellion into life in order to rub it out so thoughtlessly?

Wait still, Eft had said, *before you pass judgment on her.*

He would have liked to ask her what she meant by that, but this wasn't the time. None of them was in the mood to talk. Perhaps it would have been better, maybe it would have freed them from a part of the burden and grief. But no one cared about that at the moment. They all brooded silently to themselves, with the exception of Aristide, who kept on murmuring soft, disconnected sentences and staring, wide-eyed, into emptiness.

It was one thing to hear about mummy soldiers and sphinxes and what a sickle sword could do to a human being—but it was something entirely different to see a friend die, in the certainty that he gave his life for yours.

Serafin wasn't sure whether they would defend

themselves if someone were to attack them now. It wasn't the way it was in stories, where heroes took on another fight as they were on the run and with a breezy remark on their lips.

No, it wasn't like that at all.

They'd given everything they had, and they'd lost. Boro was dead. It would be a long time before the survivors could get over that. Even Eft, brave, hard, grim Eft, was oozing grief from all her pores like sweat.

From some of the rooflines, Serafin realized that they were crossing the Cannaregio district toward the north. If the mermaids intended to take them out of Venice, this was the best way—somewhere to the north lay the mainland. But he had no illusions about that: The Egyptians would spot them on the open water. Even if the siege ring no longer existed—after all, the city was taken—there must be enough patrols out to discover them within the shortest possible time.

But he didn't voice his objections. He was too exhausted and more than grateful to entrust his life to others; perhaps they'd go about it more responsibly than he had himself.

Soon he could make out a tunnel opening that led out to the open sea. A velvety night sky still hung over the lagoon, but the stars gave enough light to sprinkle the water's surface with points of light and to provide an overpowering feeling of breadth. A fresh night wind blew across the water toward them and penetrated the tunnel. It felt easier to breathe now.

The sea turtle shell pushed unhurriedly out of the tunnel opening. Before them, several hundred yards away, San Michele, Venice's cemetery island, rose from the dark wilderness of water. The ochre-colored wall that enclosed the angular island seemed gray and dirty in the icy light of the stars, as if it had been erected from the bones of those who lay buried on the island. The dead had been buried here since time immemorial, thousands and more thousands of names engraved on gravestones and urns.

In the darkness over the island, a collector hovered silently.

Dario let out a hoarse curse. He was the only one who made a sound. Even Aristide stopped talking to himself.

The collector cut a dark triangle in the diadem of the star picture. Colossal and threatening, the mighty pyramid hung a few dozen yards over the island. By day there would certainly have been sunbarks swarming around it, but now darkness ruled, and without light, the barks couldn't take off.

The mermaids pushed the sea turtle shell eastward, noticeably faster than in the maze of tunnels and canals. The headwind drove into the faces of the five passengers. Eft pulled the pins out of her long hair and shook it out. It fluttered wildly around her like a black flag at her back, a pirate queen on the search for booty.

But although they all had to hold on tight, they couldn't take their eyes off the collector over the cemetery island. They guessed what it was going to do there.

"Can they really do that?" murmured Tiziano, shocked.

"Yes," said Dario dazedly. "They certainly can do that."

Aristide began to mutter softly again, incoherent stuff that robbed Serafin of his last shred of nerve. But he was too tired to lash out at the boy. Not even the sight of the collector could pull him out of his lethargy. They had just been unable to save the living; what did the dead matter to him?

"My parents are buried over there," said Dario tonelessly.

"So are mine," whispered Tiziano.

Aristide groaned; perhaps it was words, too.

Eft sent Serafin a look, but he ignored her. To not think. To not look back. I don't want to know all that.

On the underside of the collector a glowing network of lines and hooks appeared, flamed suddenly in the darkness, and solidified, a storm of lightning bolts that all appeared at the same time and did not die out.

"It's starting," Tiziano said.

The first light-hook detached itself from the black and drove down soundlessly, disappearing behind the wall of the cemetery island. None of the five had ever witnessed a collector at work, but they knew the stories. They knew what would happen.

More and more glowing lines were sent down from the underside of the collector, creating a jagged, multi-angled trellis between the flying pyramid and the island of San Michele.

Serafin could no longer bear the horror on the faces of his companions. He turned away. His own father had disappeared before he was born, and his mother had been killed in an accident when he was twelve; her body had never been found. But he felt his friends' sorrow and horror, and it hurt him almost as much as if he'd had relatives or friends buried on San Michele himself.

His eyes wandered over to the shores of Venice. The coastline of the Cannaregio district moved ever more quickly past them, while the eight mermaids moved the sea turtle shell faster and faster over the dark waves. Now and again one of them appeared over the edge of the shell, but most of the time they stayed underwater, invisible in the dark.

Serafin saw mummy soldiers on the shore walls and patrolling along the Fondamenta, but they paid no attention to the collector in the sky over the cemetery island or to the sea turtle shell.

And there was something else.

The sky over the roofs lit up, a narrow edging of light, like Saint Elmo's fire over the roofs and gables. It was too early for sunrise, and furthermore, it wasn't the right part of the sky: In the east the sky was still deep black.

Fire, thought Serafin. The fire in the mirror workshop had probably set the entire district on fire. He wouldn't allow the idea close enough to him to really be frightened, but nevertheless, he looked over at Eft to see if she'd also noticed the strange glow.

Over her shoulder he saw that the light-net of the collector had enclosed the entire island. Clouds of dust and earth rose behind the walls.

Eft was also no longer looking toward San Michele. She was looking back at the city, and her eyes gleamed, as if someone had lit candles in their cavities. Only a mirror image. The reflection of a new, glittering brightness.

Serafin whirled around. The Saint Elmo's fire over Cannaregio's rooftops had spread to a glowing inferno.

And yet—there were no flames! No conflagration! Serafin had never seen anything so beautiful, as if the angels themselves were sinking into the lagoon.

Then he discovered something else.

The mummy soldiers on the shore were no longer patrolling: Some lay motionless on the ground, others drifted in the water. Someone had extinguished them in a moment, quickly, like a deadly wind gust that had strafed the shore.

Only a single figure now stood on the Fondamenta on the bank, not far from the opening of a canal: the outline of a powerful lion with the upper body of a young woman. She had both arms raised to the sky and her head laid back. Her long hair floated on the wind like a billow of smoke.

"It is she," said Eft. No one except Serafin heard her. The other boys still stared spellbound at the collector and the island.

Serafin felt all the hate and rage in him force their way out. He saw Boro before him as he'd stood in the middle of the sea of flames just before the sphinx reached him. And now Lalapeya, who'd caused all this, was standing there and working some magic to hold up the fugitives.

"Serafin!" cried Eft. But it was too late.

He'd shoved his saber into his belt, and before anyone could stop him, he made a headlong dive into the water. It closed over him, sealing his eyes and ears with oppressive silence and darkness. He wasted no more than a quick thought on the mermaids who floated all around him in the water; also gave no thought to the collector or San Michele or any of his friends.

He thought only of Lalapeya.

He surfaced, gulped some air, and swam away as fast as he could—and that was amazingly fast, considering his exhaustion, which now fell away from him like a bundle of rags. Blurrily, he saw the shore come closer, only a few yards more. He had the feeling he wasn't alone, that there were bodies to the right and left of him, even under him.

But if the mermaids really were following him, they made no attempt to stop him.

His hand struck cold stone, slippery with algae and sewage. The walled bank was almost seven feet high; he would never in his life be able to climb up there without help. Still filled with anger, he looked around him, saw the body of a mummy soldier floating nearby in the water, and then, a little farther to the left, he spotted a boat landing. He swam over with a few strokes and climbed into one of the tethered rowboats. A powerful disturbance arose in the water behind him as one of the mermaids under the surface made a U-turn and returned to the turtle shell.

Once in the boat, Serafin looked around. He'd been driven off course and was now a good two hundred yards away from Lalapeya. The sphinx had entwined both hands over her head, and the light was gathering there, creeping down from the roofs along the façades like something living, a glittering, sparking carpet of brightness, flickering like a fog illuminated from the inside out. A beaming aureole surrounded Lalapeya's hands, spread along her arms to her body, and finally enveloped her entirely.

Serafin didn't wait to find out where all this was leading. He couldn't permit the sphinx to do something to the others with the help of her magic. She'd already caused too much suffering. And this was probably the last opportunity he'd have to pay her back.

He pulled out his saber, sprang from the boat to the pier, and ran to the bank. His steps sounded hollow on the wood, but Lalapeya didn't notice him. It was as though she was in a trance, entirely concentrated on the annihilating blow. In the supernatural light she looked like a vision of a Madonna with the lower body of a monster, a blasphemous caricature from the pen of a medieval miniature painter, overwhelmingly beautiful and horrible at the same time.

Only once, very briefly, did Serafin look across the water to the sea turtle shell. Eft had gotten up and was standing erect in the shell. She called something over to the bank, perhaps trying to draw Lalapeya's attention to her. But the sphinx didn't react.

The other boys had noticed what was happening, and their eyes swung back and forth between the nightmare spectacle on the cemetery island and the occurrence on the shore. Dario waved at Serafin with his saber, perhaps cheering him on, perhaps something else?

Still thirty yards to the sphinx. Now twenty.

The glow intensified.

Serafin had almost reached her when Lalapeya abruptly turned her head and looked at him. Looked at him out of her dark brown, exceedingly beautiful eyes.

Serafin did not slow. He merely let the saber drop — against his will? — then pushed off from the ground with outstretched arms and sprang at Lalapeya.

Her girl's face contorted. She snapped her eyes wide open. Even in her pupils there flickered a supernatural glow.

Serafin broke through the wreath of brightness, was able to grab her upper body, and swept her off her lion legs. In a heap of arms and legs and predator's claws they crashed to the ground, rolled over and over, suddenly plunged into emptiness, and splashed into the water. A knife-sharp claw grazed Serafin's cheek, another tore his clothing and perhaps the skin under it, yes, he was bleeding, there was blood in the water. Then he saw Lalapeya's face, heard as she let out a piercing scream, now only a young woman with wet, stringy hair, no supernatural appearance anymore, and the light had vanished too.

He saw her thrashing with her arms and fought against the urge to simply press her under the water until it was all over, to pay her back for everything: her betrayal, the death of Boro, the way she'd used him.

But he didn't. It occurred to him that she couldn't swim and would go under if he didn't help her. He was tempted to leave her to herself, but suddenly he searched in vain for the hatred in his heart that had just now driven him from the sea turtle shell and to the shore. It was as if his anger had blown away and left nothing but emptiness.

"Serafin!" she screamed, her voice distorted by the water that pushed across her lips. "Help . . . me. . . ."

He couldn't see her lion's paws under the surface

anymore and was afraid her claws would shred him if he came too close to her. But he was indifferent even to that. He launched himself, glided over, and grabbed her from behind. He felt how she struggled under the water, and she hit against him, this time with human legs. She couldn't swim, either as human or sphinx, but the heavy lion's body would have pulled her down faster than her light girl's figure. He laid an arm around her chest from behind and tried to keep them both above water somehow, but he sensed right away that he wouldn't manage for long. In her panic she was resisting and threatened to pull him under.

Hands seized both of them from underneath and drew them out onto the water, toward the sea turtle shell, which floated in the darkness like half a skull. The mermaids didn't show themselves, stayed under the surface, but there must have been at least two, perhaps more. Serafin floated on his back, Lalapeya pressed in front of him, still in his arm. She'd stopped kicking, she wasn't moving at all, and for a moment he thought she was dead, drowned in his embrace—and wasn't that what he'd wanted when he ran at her like a berserker? Hadn't he intended for her to die and so discharge a part of her blood guilt?

Such thoughts seemed absurd to him now, and he sighed with relief when she moved and in vain tried to turn her head.

"Why did you . . . do that?" Her voice was mournful

and she sounded as if she were crying. "Why did you . . . stop me?"

Why?

A dozen answers shot through his head. But suddenly, in a flash, he was aware that it was *he* who had betrayed — not others, but he himself.

While the mermaids dragged them to the shell of the sea turtle, he discovered finally what Lalapeya had seen before him. And he realized that her magic had never been aimed at them, never at Eft and the boys, but always only at the collector.

The gridwork of fixed light flashes that bound the underside of the collector with San Michele were now a single quivering jumble of straight and crooked beams, hooks, curves, spikes, and loops. But they hadn't aimed at the dead Venetians who were buried by the umpteen thousands on the cemetery island.

It was something else that they sought and had found. Something altogether different.

The mermaids pushed Serafin and Lalapeya out of the water; Eft, Dario, and Tiziano pulled them in. The shell boat tilted and would probably have capsized if the mermaids hadn't held it steady in the water. Only Aristide crouched unmoving in his place and stared over at the cemetery island; he talked ceaselessly to himself and his fingers curled into claws; it looked as though he wanted to scratch out his eyes.

The others crowded close together in the center of the turtle shell, and while the mermaids went silently back to their work and drew the shell farther to the east, away from shore and toward the open sea, the six passengers looked at the island.

San Michele's walls had cracked. In many places wide pieces wobbled and collapsed, followed by uprooted cypress trees, which bent to one side like black lance tips and bored into the water. The entire island seemed to break apart, great cracks opened up, and seawater flowed in, undermining graves and chapels and causing the clock tower of the church to fall.

Something that had lain under the island, under the graves and crypts and the small cloister, was being pulled into the open by the light-hooks of the collector, in a chain of dust explosions and whirls of loose soil. Something that was half as large as the island itself.

The body of a sphinx.

A sphinx larger than any creature Serafin had ever heard of. Larger than a whale, greater than the sea witches in the bottomless depths of the Adriatic, greater even than the legendary giant kraken in the abyss of the oceanic trenches.

Half lion, half human, though both seemed out of order, the arms and legs too long, the face too small, the eyes too far apart. Hands as large as warships, with fingers too many and too long, and lion paws with extended claws of yellow horn and bone. The travesty of a sphinx and yet of an absurd grace, hideously distorted, almost a caricature, and yet with a grotesque elegance.

The gigantic cadaver lay on its side, the face turned toward the city, and floated against the underside of the collector, borne by hundreds of hooks of light. It *was* a cadaver, although it showed no trace of decay; there was no doubt that it was dead, and had been for perhaps centuries.

What was Lalapeya guarding? Serafin had asked Eft, just a few hours before.

What was she guarding?

Now, finally, he saw it before him, and he realized that her attack on the palace, the assassination attempt on the Pharaoh, had been nothing but a diversion. Something that would give Lalapeya time to destroy the collector and defend the grave of her charge.

Eft looked over at Serafin and placed her hand on his, but he wouldn't be comforted.

Boro had died for a dead sphinx.

No, he corrected himself: for a dead god.

A god of the sphinxes.

And with this thought, this realization, he collapsed and wept on Eft's breast. He saw that Lalapeya was also weeping, perhaps for other reasons, and then the sphinx god disappeared inside the collector, and somehow, through a chink in the defenses of Serafin's mind, crept the certainty that their enemies now had at their disposal a weapon overshadowing all that had existed previously.

Yet at the moment, it didn't matter. At the moment, all that counted was his despair.

Lalapeya sat down beside him and took his hand, but she felt cold and lifeless, somehow dead.

11

Heart House

WHEN MERLE AWOKE, SHE WAS ALONE.

Her first movement was to the water mirror in the pocket of her dress. Good. They hadn't taken it away from her. She had the distinct feeling, as she pressed the oval through her dress, that it had missed the touch of her hand.

She wasn't certain how long she'd been lying in the dark, in an unsettling silence, with only the pulsing of her heartbeat and the whispering of her own confused thoughts in her ear. The darkness awoke with her, breathed with her. Alone in complete darkness, alone with herself. Thousands of questions, thousands of doubts, and even more fears.

Where was Vermithrax? What had become of Winter? So alone.

Only then did it dawn on her what was so unusual about this aloneness. She no longer felt the Flowing Queen!

"I am here," said the voice in her head, and it seemed a hundred times louder than usual. *"Do not worry."*

"You didn't say anything. I thought you were gone."

"Did that make you happy?"

"Not here."

"Oh, when it becomes serious, then I am good enough."

"I didn't mean it that way, as you very well know." Merle felt over the ground on which she lay. Cold stone, cut, polished smooth. A prison cell, she guessed. *Bring her into the Heart House,* the old man in the wheelchair had said. From that, she'd imagined something else. No, to be precise, she hadn't imagined anything at all.

"You have slept."

"How long?"

"Hard to say. I have certain abilities, of course, but a built-in clock is not among them."

Merle sighed. "Since we've been down here . . . in Hell, I mean . . . since then I've lost all sense of time. Because it never gets dark. Have we been here now for a day or two, or perhaps even a week?"

"*I do not know.*"

"Then tell me where we are. Or don't you know that, either?"

"*In the Heart House, presumably.*"

"Oh?" Merle rolled her eyes in the dark.

The Queen was silent for a moment, then she said, "*We will find out right now. They are coming to get us.*"

Merle was just about to ask how the Queen knew that when she heard thumping steps, then the grating of an iron lock. A column of light suddenly appeared in the darkness, grew broader, opened to a door. Remarkable silhouettes, jagged and full of points, appeared in the door frame, looking like exotic plants, perhaps many-armed cacti, but then they appeared to dissolve and put themselves together anew. Possibly it was only happening in Merle's head and, yes, the first sight was probably a deception, an image that fear painted for her.

She'd just come to terms with this thought when the Queen said, "*Shape changers.*"

"You really know how to cheer a person up."

"*I knew that you would be glad to have me with you sometime.*"

"In your dreams."

"*I cannot dream. Only when you dream.*"

A hand seized Merle, and she was led through the door into the light, out onto a grating walkway that ran along a rock wall. On one side of the walk were doors of steel at regular intervals, on the other yawned an abyss.

The outlook was shocking in its breadth. Obviously they were on the inside of the gigantic dome they'd seen on the flight into Axis Mundi. The rock wall curved slightly as it continued upward. High over Merle its contours dissolved into reddish yellow mist. Dozens of grating ledges ran along it. Other walkways, floating unsupported over the abyss, led out into the glowing mist, where they met other walkways, crossing them or joining with them and thus forming a broad network of traversable iron tracks, innumerable miles long.

Red-gold brightness shone up from the base of the dome, many times refracted by mist, which drank the light so that its real source could not be seen. As the light illuminated the entire base of the dome, it seemed to Merle as though she were standing over a sea of lava. But she had already guessed that the solution of this riddle wasn't so simple, for no heat came from the light. Even the mist that billowed in the dome felt rather clammy and uncomfortable. And then something else dawned on her: Although the dome consisted of rock, it had looked from the outside as if *it* was what was giving off the light. Therefore the brightness from the ground must be coming *through* the rock, yet at the same time it wasn't strong enough to blind Merle. It was almost as if the light in the depths was illuminating the stone so that the dome itself was glowing.

It was strange. And thoroughly unreal.

Her new companions also fit right in. The shape changers—if that in fact was what they were—had made an effort to assume human forms. And the effort had succeeded. Not the form of just any human, but that of Winter—which was even more ironic, since he'd insisted that he wasn't human at all.

However, their faces seemed plump, unfinished somehow, as if they were swollen. Their bodies were white, but they hadn't taken the trouble to imitate the structure or form of Winter's clothing. Also, their eyes looked as if they were painted, blind like the pupils of dead fish.

If they'd hoped to decrease some of Merle's fear through this weird masquerade, they achieved exactly the opposite effect.

They escorted her silently along the walkways and at each crossing indicated with a wave which direction to turn. They led her crisscross over the walks, out over the glowing chasm, until they finally came to a platform situated at a junction of several walkways.

On the platform stood a small house.

It didn't fit here. Its walls were half-timbered, and it had a steep, red-shingled roof. A weathercock rose from the pointed gable. The windows were subdivided into bull's-eye panes, and beside the wooden door, to make the idyll perfect, someone had placed a bench, as if the inhabitant of this little house came outside from time to time to smoke a leisurely pipe. The house radiated the coziness of a fairy tale. As she came closer, Merle caught sight of a carved sign over the door: WALK IN, BRING HEART IN! Little hearts and flowers were worked around the letters, without skill, as if by the hand of a child.

One of her guards pushed her up to the door; the other stayed back at the edge of the platform. Someone opened the door from the inside, and then Merle was led in, under the sign with the inscription, which now, on second reading, gave her gooseflesh, for some unexplained reason. Wasn't it supposed to read "bring luck in"? For a moment she had the feeling that her heart was beating a few beats faster, as if under protest, so hard that her chest hurt.

Inside the house, someone had attempted to maintain the romantic look of the outside but had woefully failed at it. To be sure, there were structural beams here, too, and even a rustic cupboard with flower inlays, but there were other objects that wouldn't fit into the deliberate quaintness of the scenery.

The operating table, for example.

The ground floor of the Heart House consisted of a single room, which in a wondrous way appeared to be much more extensive than the outside of the house. An optical illusion, Merle decided.

"*Perhaps,*" said the Flowing Queen.

In the back part of the room, only scantily concealed behind a jumble of beams that stabilized the building, were various metal trays, with scoured surfaces, on which instruments were spread out, carefully arranged on black cloths and scrupulously polished. Steel flashed in the omnipresent glowing light coming in through the bull's-eye windows.

The door closed behind Merle. She whirled around and saw who'd opened it to her. The snakes who'd been pushing the old man's wheelchair in the herald's hall glided toward her in a single motion and, immediately in front of her, puffed up into a pear-shaped figure at least a head taller than she was. The creature bent forward until its upper surface was only a finger's breadth away from Merle's nose, a shimmering mass of intertwining bodies. Finally the snake nest flowed and spread sideways and, as an ankle-high carpet, moved into the rear of the room, where it towered itself up again, this time into a pointed form like a sugarloaf. There the creature stayed and waited.

Merle wanted to turn and flee, but the shape changer barred her way. He now looked less like Winter, instead becoming something else too repugnant when Merle gave him more than a fleeting glance.

"*I cannot help you,*" said the Flowing Queen.

Good to hear, thought Merle.

"*I am sorry.*"

So am I.

"*I know I brought you here, but—*"

Be quiet. Please.

"Is that she?" cried a voice.

If the snakes gave an answer, Merle couldn't hear it. But right after that the voice ordered, "Bring her down here."

The snakes glided over to Merle again. She avoided their touch and voluntarily went to the opening in the floor out of which the voice had come. Although Merle had heard him only once before, she recognized the old man again right away.

"To me, to me," he cried.

Merle reached the opening and climbed down a spiral staircase into a room whose floor and walls consisted of steel mesh. Light from the depths flooded through it from all sides. Through the mesh under her feet she could look into the glowing abyss, the same as on the outside, on the walkways. For the first time, she became so dizzy that she had to remain standing at the foot of the stairs, holding on tightly to the handrail.

In the center of the spiral staircase was a round disk, which could be moved to the upper floor with a block-and-tackle mechanism; the wheelchair for which it had been built was empty. Its owner was moving through the cage room underneath the house on crutches. The crutches ended in palm-sized wooden feet, wide enough not to get stuck in the wire mesh.

Wide glass cylinders, almost ten feet tall, were distributed around the walls. There were at least fifteen or twenty of them, Merle estimated. Each of the cylinders was filled with a fluid, which shimmered golden, like honey, in the light of the dome. In the fluid, caught like ancient insects in amber, floated creatures that had once been alive. None of them were human.

Merle had to force herself to turn her eyes away from the grotesque forms, but she looked at them long enough to recognize that they all had one thing in common: All displayed a deep cut—mostly in the center of the body—that was sewn with thread and crossed stitches. Operation scars. There where the chest was in humans.

Heart House, Merle thought, and shuddered.

"Look around," the old man said, as he shifted his weight to the right and pointed with the left crutch in a trembling swing around the room that took in all the glass cylinders and creatures. "My work," he added softly, in a whisper, as if he didn't want to awaken the creatures in the containers.

"Who are you?" asked Merle, all the while taking pains to look only at him.

"My name?" He let out a cackling laugh that seemed phony to her, and she couldn't help wondering if he was only acting his madness. The crazy scientist, nothing but a role. But one he fancied himself in. And that was at least as unsettling as true madness.

He said nothing more, and Merle asked her question

again. She noticed as she did so that he'd gotten her to speak exactly like him: He had the habit of repeating his sentences, as if first he had to make sure of the sound of it, in order to then say it again, the second time more clearly.

"Most here—at least those who can speak—just call me the surgeon," said the old man. "Just the surgeon."

"Are you a doctor?"

He grinned again. His whole face seemed to dislocate when he did. What she had taken for gray skin was in reality beard stubble, reaching up to beneath his eyes. "But certainly a doctor, certainly."

He was trying to frighten her. That might mean that in truth he wasn't so dangerous as he pretended—or also very much worse: a madman *and* a role-player.

"These creatures here"—Merle pointed to a cylinder without looking into it—"are they all your . . . patients?"

"Early examples," he said, "from a time when my technique had not yet matured. Not matured. I've saved them to remind me of my mistakes. Otherwise one so easily becomes cocky, you know. So cocky."

"Why are you showing me this?" She'd noticed that neither the shape changer nor the snakes had accompanied her down the stairs. She was alone with the old man. But somehow she couldn't believe that he was careless. He felt very secure. And for good reason, certainly.

"I want you to have no fear of me."

Ha-ha, she thought.

"He is playing with you," said the Queen.

It had come to my attention.

"Then go along with it. Make the better move. Checkmate him."

Hopefully he won't take my Queen first.

"Very witty."

"What do you want of me?" Merle asked the old man.

He smiled warmheartedly, and it almost looked real. "You must have patience. Patience."

Merle made a great effort not to show her fear. If he was giving her the opportunity, she must try to find out as much as possible. "When the Lilim caught me, you ordered them to bring me here right away. But then you imprisoned me first. Why?"

He dismissed her question with a careless wave. "I had to do it." With a grin, he added, "Had to do it."

Instinctively, Merle looked about her, letting her eyes travel slowly over the creatures floating in the cylinders.

"No more here," he said. "No more here."

"Where are my friends?"

"In safety."

"You are only saying that."

"Nothing has happened to any of them. Although the lion fought like"—he giggled—"well, like a lion."

"When can I see them again?"

The surgeon put his head on one side as if he really had

to think about the answer. "We will wait. Patience. You will soon learn to have patience."

"What do you want of me?" she asked a second time.

"That's simple," he said. "I am going to exchange your heart. For a better one. One of stone."

"But—"

"It will go quickly," he interrupted her. "My mistakes with these unfortunate creatures here were way back. Today that is not a problem anymore. I may be old, but I learn more with each new heart. Each heart."

Merle's pulse sounded so loud in her ears that she could hardly understand his words anymore. Instinctively she shrank back against the banister and held on to it tightly.

"Soon you will have forgotten everything. Forgotten everything, believe me."

This is fun for him, Merle thought, full of loathing. That's why he brought me down here: He wants me to see what he does. And he wants me to ask for the details.

He confirmed her fear. "Just ask, just ask! The faster your heart beats, the easier the operation is. Your heart is strong, isn't it? So strong."

She hesitated, then she said, "You are human, aren't you? I mean a real . . . not a shape changer or something like that."

"But certainly."

"Do you come from above?"

"Why do you want to know that?"

She quickly sought an answer that would satisfy him and that would lead to further talk.

"I've been to many doctors," she lied. "And there's nothing I'm more afraid of than doctors in the upper world, believe me." Perhaps it would help if he supposed she was a little naive.

"*Good idea,*" said the Flowing Queen.

"I was also a doctor in the upper world," the old man declared with self-satisfaction. "In the upper world I was a doctor, just so. Many were afraid of me. That is nothing of which you need be ashamed. Not ashamed."

"How long have you been down here?"

"Many years. So many."

"And what brought you here?" When she saw that he was becoming suspicious, she quickly added, "I mean, were you a criminal or something like that? Did you experiment with people? Then I'd at least know why I'm so terribly frightened."

He regarded her for a moment, then he nodded imperceptibly. "Experiments, yes. But no crime. I was a scientist. I am still a scientist. As we all are."

"Are there more humans down here?" Merle asked the old man.

He thumped with his crutch on the floor mesh twice, three times; then he smiled. "Interrogating me, hmm? But now that's enough. We will begin. Will begin."

Merle took a backward step up the stairs, but her feet slipped on something soft, slippery. She lost her balance, pitched forward to avoid cracking her back on the sharp metal steps, and skidded flat on the floor. When she looked up, the snake nest was pulling together behind her; a part of it still covering the stairs like an oil film, shimmering in all the colors of the rainbow.

"No!" she cried out, sprang to her feet, and whirled to the old man. He was sick, weak, and scarcely bigger than she. She would attack him rather than let him implant a stone heart in her.

"Too late!" said the Queen.

Merle felt it at the same moment. Her legs grew cold as the seething snake carpet climbed up her, faster than she could react. In a flash a solid layer of gleaming snakes covered her legs, her trunk, kept slithering farther, up to her shoulders and from there along her arms until the cool, intertwining creature enclosed her entire body like a skin-tight suit. They left only Merle's head untouched.

She tried to resist, but it was in vain. Involuntarily she moved forward, began climbing the steps. The snakes controlled her arms and legs, moving them like a puppet's.

Merle tried to turn her head and succeeded to some degree, although her legs continued to walk up the stairs. "Stop that!" she bellowed at the surgeon, who had just lowered himself into his wheelchair. "Call off these brutes."

The old man only smirked, turned on a switch, and

was pulled up by the block and tackle in the center of the spiral staircase, slowly enough so that Merle could keep pace with him.

At the top she moved directly to the operating table, lay down flat on her back, and bellowed and cursed so plentifully that the surgeon threatened to order the snakes to crawl into her mouth. At that she fell silent and looked on helplessly at what was happening to her.

Some snakes loosed themselves from the middle of her body and disappeared to the right and left under the table-top. Merle tried to arch herself, and the result was pitiful, hardly more than a twitch in her middle body.

Steel bands were closed over her wrists and ankles, then the rest of the snakes also withdrew, crept and slithered from the table and gathered together on the floor in the pear-shaped form of the nest.

Merle pulled and rattled on her bonds.

"Very good, very good," said the surgeon. "I think we will anesthetize you first. Is your heart really beating fast enough?"

Merle screamed a whole torrent of curses at him, the worst she could think of, and after the years in the orphanage there were quite a number. She didn't care if the snakes crawled over her face. She was indifferent to anything at all, if only this disgusting man might be struck by lightning on the spot.

The surgeon gave the snake nest a wave, and soon it

began to smell unpleasant behind her head, sharp, biting, like some of the chemicals in Arcimboldo's workshop. The anesthetic was being prepared.

The sharp smell became stronger. She turned her head, as well as she could, to look behind her, and out of the corner of her eye made out the seething of the snakes. They swelled toward her like a dark wave.

Merle's perceptions grew muddled. Her surroundings revolved, flowed into one another.

Snakes bustled in the background.

Merle's heart hammered in her chest.

The surgeon came closer, his face swelled, filled her field of vision, filled the world.

His flesh and that of the snakes, glowing like the colors on the palette of a painter.

His grin.

"Stop!"

The world rotated again, a world of yellow teeth and gray hair.

"Stop, I said!"

The smell grew weaker. Her surroundings changed. The face of the old man lost its distinctness, pulled back.

"Release her at once!" Not the voice of the surgeon, also not her own. Someone else.

The iron cuffs on her hands and feet snapped back, and suddenly she was free. No more chains and no more snakes holding her.

With the disappearance of the biting fog, she could see the room again. The white ceiling, the wooden beams, everything back in place.

Two voices were arguing with each other in the background. One belonged to the surgeon. The other was that of the stranger who'd saved her.

Saved?

Perhaps.

"Merle?" asked the Flowing Queen, sounding as dazed as Merle herself.

I am here, she thought, even though she felt as if someone else had taken over thinking for her. Indeed, where else would she be?

"You are all right." Not a question, a statement.

All right. Yes.

The argument broke off, and now someone was bending over her face. Not the surgeon. But the man was at least as old.

Scientist, as we all are, the surgeon had said.

As we all are.

"Are you Lord Light?" asked Merle weakly.

"Yes," said the man. He had thick, gray hair.

"You are a human," she stated, and thought she was dreaming, was almost convinced of it.

Lord Light, the ruler of Hell, smiled. "Believe me, Merle, the human is a better devil than the Devil."

His face withdrew, then she only heard his voice.

"And now, please, stand up and come with me."

12

Lord Light

THE SURGEON REMAINED BEHIND IN THE HEART HOUSE. Merle cast a last look at the man in the wheelchair as Lord Light pushed her out onto the platform, one hand on her shoulder, not in an unfriendly way, yet firmly. The surgeon stared, first at her, then at Lord Light, his small, narrowed eyes blazing with hate and fury.

"You needn't fear him anymore," said her companion, as they stepped from the platform onto one of the grating walkways.

Lord Light, hammered in her head. He's Lord Light. Only a man.

"The surgeon can do nothing more to you," he said.

Her hand moved to her chest, feeling for the quick pulsing of her heart.

Lord Light noticed it. "Don't worry, it's still the old one. Stone hearts don't beat."

Examining him from the side, she thought he looked like a scholar—which he doubtless was, if the surgeon had told the truth.

He wore a black frock coat, narrowly cut, with a flower of red glass on the lapel. His trousers were also black, and his pointed patent leather shoes gleamed. The golden chain of a watch hung in a semicircular loop out of his jacket pocket, as if the shape were mimicking the dark circles around his eyes. Merle had never seen such dark circles, as dark as if they were painted. Nevertheless, he didn't act tired or exhausted, quite the contrary. He radiated a liveliness that belied his age.

Merle couldn't take her eyes off him. This man, of all people, was supposed to help her free Venice? An old man who walked along beside her in his frock coat as if they were going on a Sunday walk together?

"*Ask him his name,*" said the Flowing Queen. "*His true name.*"

Merle ignored her. "Where are my friends?"

"No one has harmed a hair of them. The lion has raged continuously since the Lilim took him prisoner, but he is well. He survived the crash in the Hall of the Heralds without injury."

They walked side by side along a grill walkway, then down a long set of stairs and across other walks. "I want to see him."

"You will."

"When?"

"Soon."

"How is Winter?"

Lord Light sighed softly. "Is that his name? Winter? He's a strange fellow. To be honest, I can't tell you how he is."

"What do you mean?"

"He's fled."

"What?" She stopped, a hand on the railing of the grill walkway. At some distance she saw several figures peel away from the light clouds, no larger than matchsticks, with too many arms and legs; at a crossing they turned off and quickly disappeared again in the glowing mist of the dome.

"He escaped," said Lord Light, turning to her. She felt the impatience in his voice, but still he didn't pressure her. "I had a long conversation with him. And then he was gone."

"*A long conversation?*" asked the Queen suspiciously.

"He was weak," said Merle incredulously. "Sick, I think. When we met him, he could hardly stand on his own."

"Well, at least he could *free* himself on his own."

Merle looked past him, down into the glowing depths.

She wondered why she had no fear of Lord Light. "That's impossible. You're lying to me."

"Why should I do that?"

"Perhaps you've killed him."

"Without a reason?"

She hesitated briefly as she tried to find a logical argument. She was very close to saying something dumb like, "But you're the lord of Hell! You're mean, any child knows that. You don't need a reason to kill someone." But then she thought about it a moment longer and whispered, "It simply can't be. He was much too weak."

Lord Light began walking again and bade her follow him: He wanted to show her something, and it was a long way there. Merle wondered why he didn't simply call over some flying monstrosity to carry them to their destination; but that didn't fit him. Neither did he fit the picture of Lord Light she'd made for herself.

Should I ask him now, she wondered, whether he'll help us? But somehow this prospect suddenly seemed a mistake to her. The dimensions of this world-within-the-world made her business shrivel to blurry insignificance.

But that was why they'd come, wasn't it?

Wasn't it?

Instead of an answer, the Queen said once more: *"Ask him his name."*

This time Merle obeyed, before the Queen could take over her voice.

"What's your name?" she asked. "I mean, Lord Light surely isn't your true name—at least not if you really are a human being."

Humor gleamed in his eyes when he looked down at her. "Have you any doubt that I'm human?"

"I don't know." That was sincere. "I just saw shape changers, after all, and they—"

"Then you also saw how pitifully badly they can imitate a human being."

"How about with magic, then?"

"I'm no magician, only a scientist."

"Like the surgeon?"

He shrugged. "If you like."

"Then tell me what your name is."

Laughing, he raised both hands as if he had no other choice but to give in to her persistence. He cleared his throat—then he told her his name.

Merle stopped in her tracks. She stared at him, openmouthed. "Seriously?"

The clouds of mist prevented his laugh from echoing into the distance. "I have of course been down here for quite a while now, but I haven't forgotten my name, believe me."

"Burbridge?" she repeated. "*Professor* Burbridge?"

"Sir Charles Burbridge, honorary chair of the National Geographic Society, First Explorer to Her Majesty the Queen, discoverer of Hell, and its first and probably only cartographer. Professor of geography, astronomy, and biology. And an old man, I'm afraid."

Merle exhaled through her clenched teeth. It sounded like a whistle. "You *are* Professor Burbridge!"

He smiled, now almost a little embarrassed. "And something more than that," he said mysteriously. But then he went on again, this time without telling her to come along. He knew that she'd follow him.

Merle trotted wordlessly along beside him as he knocked dust from the left arm of his coat with his hand. Shaking his head, he said, "You know, one can teach these creatures to build all this here, whole cities, steam engines, and factories—but one is doomed to failure if one tries to impart to them anything so basic as a sense of fashion. Look at this here!" He held out his sleeve and she had to force herself to look very closely. "See it?" he asked her. "Cross-stitch! They sew such a piece of clothing with cross-stitch! Absolutely inexcusable."

Merle thought of the creatures in the Heart House. Cross-stitch. She shuddered. "Where are you taking me?"

"To the Stone Light."

"What is that?"

"You'll soon see."

"Is Vermithrax there?"

He smiled again. "He should be, anyway. Provided he hasn't tricked these blockhead guards like your other friend." A grin. "But I think not."

Silently they went down more steps, followed endless walkways. Merle had the feeling that soon they would have crossed the entire dome. Yet wherever she looked, she never saw the curving wall anywhere; they were still somewhere in the center of the light dome. Also, the Heart House had disappeared over them.

The Stone Light.

She got gooseflesh, without understanding why.

She kept wanting to ask him for the help his messenger had offered to the Venetians, wanted to fulfill her mission—but she had the feeling that for a long time it hadn't been about that anymore. Not about Venice. Not about her.

Did we *really* come here about that? she asked in her thoughts and received no answer. The Queen had been notably quiet since the Lilim had taken Merle into their power, almost as if she were afraid someone would notice her. But was that the only reason?

"The surgeon," said Merle after a long while, "can he do that, really? Put a stone heart in a human?"

"Yes, he can."

"Why does he do it?"

"Because I ordered him to."

Merle's stomach lurched, but she didn't let it show. She'd been taken in by him and his friendliness. It was time to remember who he was and what he represented down here.

"The messenger I sent to you up in the Piazza San Marco," he said in a conversational tone, "he had a stone heart. One of the first that actually functioned. And the same with many others upon whom I rely. The stone makes it easier to control them."

"They haven't wills of their own anymore?"

"Not like you and me. But it's a little more complicated."

"Why do all that? The Lilim appear to obey you anyway. Or does each of them have a stone heart?"

"Bah! Control their leaders and you control the whole bunch. You know, down here everything seems gigantic and immeasurable. But in truth, the threads all run to small centers, as in a knot. Or even a heart. Get it on your side, and the rest is child's play."

He was walking more slowly now, almost sauntering, a nice old man who wouldn't harm a fly.

Bah, she thought, Devil take him! Then it occurred to her that *he* was the Devil.

"But why?" she asked again.

He took a deep breath, looked at his spotlessly shining shoes, then out into the mist. "Why did I come here and build all this? Why did I write books full of lies about Hell so that no one would dare to think of coming down here? For science, naturally! What else?"

"You became the ruler of Hell in order to study it?" She remembered that the Flowing Queen had once suggested something quite similar—and wondered again if she hadn't even *known* it.

The Queen remained obdurately silent.

"Several of us came here," said Burbridge. "I and a handful of colleagues from different faculties. Medical men like the surgeon, but also aestheticians, geologists, and biologists, such as me, even a philosopher. . . . He made the mistake of debating with a Lilim about Plato's cave allegory. The Lilim didn't agree with him. He didn't agree with the Lilim, either, by the way." He wore an amused smile, but it almost looked a little sad. "We had to learn a great deal. Adapt to new things and fundamentally change ourselves—not only our preoccupations and opinions but also ourselves. Our consciences, for example. Our ethics."

Merle nodded, as though she knew exactly what he was talking about. And basically, she saw through what he intended to say quite well: that he, no matter how one looked at it, had done the right thing. As if he personally had made the sacrifices that this madness had cost.

Suddenly she felt he was nothing more than false and a glib liar. She despised him almost more than the surgeon. The old man in the wheelchair had at least been honest, to her, but also with himself.

Burbridge, on the other hand, was a hypocrite.

She had always hated men like him when she was still living in the orphanage and had learned to know more of his type than she liked: administrators, priests, teachers. Even some of those who came to take children away with them.

She felt sick. Not from the height, and not from fear. Only from him and his nearness.

"You don't share your research results with anyone. You've served up a quantity of nonsense to the world above and kept for yourself everything you've actually found out down here. What's the point of that?"

"Tell me, Merle, you're curious too, aren't you?"

"Certainly."

"Then imagine your curiosity like a glass of water. And now take a whole barrel of it. Then you know how it looks in the heart of a scientist. Of a true scientist!"

Rubbish, she thought. Just talk. He and his researcher friends could probably outdo each other in lying.

"Will we be there soon?" she asked, to change the subject.

"Look down below. You'll be able to see it right now."

"The Stone Light?"

He nodded.

"How can a light be stone?" she asked.

He grinned and again looked terribly friendly. "Perhaps it always has been, and you just haven't noticed until now."

She looked over the handrail down into the abyss. He was right. The mist gradually dissolved. Vaguely she could make out something down there like a dark star, massive gray beams that ran out from a bright central point in all directions. But it wasn't until they'd gone down another long staircase that she saw that these beams were walkways, which opened onto a round grill walk in the middle. It had a diameter of about 150 yards, and only a single walkway cut straight across the center like a lone spoke.

The grill circle floated high over the glowing bottom of the hall, which now, as they came closer, turned out not to be a smooth surface but a mighty dome, like the upper quarter of a ball, which lay buried in the rock. Its size couldn't even be guessed at, but it must cover the entire base of the rock dome. The circular mesh walkway was located exactly over the center of this curvature, suspended over its highest point; there were no columns or supporting structures, the walkway alone held it in the air.

"That down there," said Burbridge, "is the Stone Light."

"It looks like a piece of the moon." She imagined that someone had cut the moon into slices like a loaf of bread; after that, they'd laid one of the two heels on the ground and erected the dome over it.

Burbridge continued, "Think of a gigantic, glowing ball, which has fallen from the sky at some point, broken through the outer crust of the earth, and drilled down here into the bottom of Hell. What you see there is a part of it, which still shows above the rock. The Morning Star, Lucifer, the fallen angel. Or simply the Stone Light."

"Did you have the dome built over it?"

"Certainly."

"Why? What does the Light do, then, except to illuminate?"

For the first time the Flowing Queen made herself heard again: *Are you still playing naive, or are you really?*

Be quiet, thought Merle. To her surprise, the voice obeyed without contradiction.

As they walked farther, down ever deeper, toward the light and the round grill pathway, Burbridge circled the entire interior of the dome with a wave of his hand. "When I came here for the first time, this place was a holy place for the Lilim, and they feared it. None of them dared to approach it voluntarily. They avoided this place as well as they could. I was the first to show them how one could put the power of the Light to use."

"But Axis Mundi, the city," said Merle, "it must be much older than the sixty or seventy years since you discovered Hell." Even as she spoke, it dawned on her how old Burbridge must in fact be, and she wondered if he had the Light on the bottom of the dome to thank for that.

As he walked, the professor absentmindedly stroked the handrail with one hand. "There was already a city on this spot when humanity was still crouching in its caves. The Lilim once possessed a highly developed civilization— not *technically* highly developed; rather, more comparable to our Middle Ages. But they possessed a social structure and their own culture, they lived in cities and large communities. However, that was all long past when I came down into Hell. The few who'd survived the decline in the course of eons lived as loners in the vastness of the rock deserts, some also in tribes and packs. But there was no civilization anymore. That was all long declined and forgotten. Together with this city."

Merle gradually understood. "Was the city already here when the Morning Star—or the Stone Light— crashed down here?"

Burbridge nodded. "It was the center of the old Lilim culture. The Stone Light destroyed large parts of that and made it uninhabitable for thousands of years. When I came, the Lilim told a whole heap of legends about the ruins of the city. Some maintained that the Light made them deformed, and they became caricatures of themselves—to the human eye at least."

"And is that true?"

Burbridge shrugged. "Who knows? More than sixty years ago, when I made my first visit here, there was no trace left of it at all. I discovered the Light and recognized that its energy could be useful for a whole list of things. But I knew, naturally, that I would need helpers, countless helpers, and that men couldn't be considered for it."

"Why not?"

"What do you think would have happened if I'd gone

back to the surface and reported what I'd stumbled on here? They would have thanked me, of course, pinned all sorts of orders on my lapel, and sent me home. And then they'd have appointed others to make use of this place. First the British Crown, then perhaps the Czar. They would have hired experts, wouldn't have needed me for it anymore—a brilliant, but also very young scientist!" Grimly he made a gesture of dismissal. "No, Merle, what I needed then was my own kingdom, with its own subjects and workers. I and some of my colleagues, in whom I'd confided, succeeded in uniting a majority of the Lilim through simple things, a few technical tricks, playthings from the magic hat of the colonial masters of all ages. The Lilim might look like beasts to our eyes, but at bottom they are no different from the natives that the Spaniards and Portuguese found in South America or the French in Indonesia. With a little energy they can be manipulated and controlled."

"With force, you mean."

"That too, yes. But not only and not primarily. As I said, a little technology, a few simple trinkets can work wonders here. And when we finally got to the point where they were serving us, and we could make use of the power of the Stone Light, we were also in a position to offer greater wonders. The flying heralds, for example. Or other powers that at first sight appear to be magic, like the destruction and boring through rock on a large scale. And, naturally, the hearts of stone, which keep an organism alive *and* control it."

"Isn't that magic?"

"Well, yes, depending on the point of view. It certainly has something of magic, and, to be honest, I doubt that the surgeon himself understands what he's doing. The real work is taken over by the heart—the Stone."

Merle wiped the sweat from her forehead, although down here, despite the closeness to the Stone Light, it wasn't really warm. She looked up at the glowing dome. "It's the same. Exactly the same."

"What do you mean?" he asked in surprise.

"The Stone Light. The Morning Star. The ball down there in the ground. It's just like a giant heart that beats in the center of Axis Mundi."

He agreed with her enthusiastically. "I'm very happy that you got this idea yourself. You're right on the mark. My own theory is that the Morning Star—wherever it came from—functioned like a heart that for an infinitely long time was on the hunt for an organism that it could drive. Until it finally landed here. The world of the Lilim can, exactly like any society, be compared with a large living thing. At one time, the city on whose ruins we erected Axis Mundi was the center of this world. When it was destroyed, the Lilim culture fell because it didn't know how to use the power of the Light. But today, thanks to our help, the Lilim are doing better. With the Stone Light,

I've given their people a new heart, and now the organism of this society is growing and thriving to something still bigger, better."

"Do the individual Lilim see it that way?"

Burbridge's euphoria cooled. "They're like ants. The individuals don't count, only the people is of any significance. The individual may suffer grief, or pain, or exhaustion, but the whole draws on it and profits from it."

Merle snorted. "*You* profit from it. Not the Lilim."

He examined her carefully, and suddenly his eyes showed disappointment. "Do you really see it that way?" When she didn't answer, he straightened and walked on faster. It was obvious that he was angry. Without turning around, he continued, "What profit am I supposed to get out of it? Wealth, perhaps? Bah, I wouldn't even have a chance to enjoy it. What else? Luxury? No. Freedom? Hardly, for my life hasn't belonged to me for a long time, but to this world. Power? Perhaps, but that means nothing to me. I'm no megalomaniacal dictator."

"You've already given the answer yourself."

"Oh?"

"You do it for science. Not for the Lilim, perhaps not even for yourself. Only for science. That's another form of power. Or megalomania. For your investigations will never help anyone, because no human will learn of them."

"Perhaps yes. Sometime."

It was pointless. He wouldn't understand. And it

didn't matter anymore. "One thing you must still tell me."

"Just ask."

"Why are you telling me all this? I mean, I'm only some girl."

"Only some girl?" His left eyebrow twitched up, but he still didn't look at her. "Perhaps you'll understand everything soon, Merle."

Once more she thought of her mission, of help for Venice. But in her mind she saw the city like a floating island moving ahead of her in the sea, ever farther away, toward the horizon, toward forgetting.

Burbridge himself no longer showed the least interest in it. And there could only be one reason for that. Because he'd long had what he wanted.

Only some girl . . .

It all was a tangle of confusion to her.

The grill ring over the Stone Light was now barely a hundred yards below them. The walks became wider, and more and more often they went through passages and tunnels in which powerful machines rumbled. Flues spouted clouds of fumes and smoke, which mixed with the ever-present mist and made breathing more difficult. At the sides of the walkways, steel gears as big as houses engaged with each other, or chains and belts moved over or under them and led to other wheels and machines. The closer they came to the bottom of the dome, the more the constructions on both sides of the walkways resembled the insides of those steam factories on some of the islands in the Venetian lagoon; Merle had learned to know two of them when the administrator of the orphanage had tried to place her there as a worker.

She wondered where the Lilim were who served all these machines. There were no workers anywhere, of any kind; it was as if the installations were completely deserted. And yet many of the machines were running at high pressure, and in some passageways the sound was deafening.

It was only after a while that she discovered that the machine tunnels weren't deserted at all. Sometimes she saw a shadow between the apparatus, or something scurried across the ceiling at lightning speed. Several times, loops and angled pipes she'd taken for parts of machines suddenly moved; in truth, individual Lilim were hiding there, pulling in their limbs at the last minute.

"*They are hiding,*" said the Flowing Queen, but when Merle said the words out loud, Burbridge only nodded, brought out a short "Yes," and fell into silence again.

They're afraid of him, she thought.

"*Or of you,*" said the Queen.

What do you mean?

"*You are his guest, are you not?*"

His prisoner.

"*No, Merle. A prisoner would be in chains or locked up;*

one does not have conversations with prisoners. He treats you like an ally."

At last they left the tunnels and the smoking flues behind them and entered the bottom level. There were no more structures on the walkways leading to the star-shaped grill circle. Again, only thin iron railings separated them from the alluring vortex of the abyss.

Even from afar, Merle saw that they were being awaited on the round walkway. The grill circle rested like a crown over the center of the Light, thirty or forty yards over the curve. All around stood figures, grouped at narrow intervals along the railings. Figures with human proportions. They stood completely motionless, like statues, and as she came closer, Merle saw that their bodies were of stone.

"They're waiting for something," said the Queen.

They are only statues.

"No. That they most certainly are not."

Merle had already seen that a single walk went straight through the grill circle, from one side to the other. In its center, and thus in the exact center of the dome, there was a little platform, just big enough to offer places for several people. At the moment it was empty.

On a rope from the platform dangled the body of an Egyptian.

He wore golden robes, which were torn and charred in many places. His head was shaved bald. A golden pattern covered his scalp like a net.

She had seen this man just once, and that only from a distance. However, she recognized him at once.

Seth.

The vizier of the Pharaoh. The superior of the priests of Horus.

His body was twisting slightly, sometimes with his face toward Merle, sometimes his back. They'd hanged him with a coarse rope, which seemed strangely archaic in a place like this. She would have supposed that Burbridge would have more elaborate techniques at his disposal for putting a man to death.

Seth. The second man of the Empire. Burbridge had had him hanged like a street thief. As much as his death relieved her, it horrified her as well.

Always, when the dangling dead man turned his face toward her, his lifeless eyes skimmed over her. The same look as that time when he'd stared at her from the tip of the collector. A chill ran up her back like ice-cold fingertips.

"The Pharaoh sent him to kill me," said Burbridge. He sounded detached, almost a little astonished. "One could almost think Amenophis wanted to get rid of him. Seth never had a chance down here."

"Where did you catch him?"

"Over the city. He came far. But not far enough."

"*Over* the city?" she asked.

Burbridge nodded. "He flew. Naturally, not he himself." He pointed upward. "Just look up there!"

Merle's gaze followed his hand. She discovered two cages, which were hanging on long chains from a steel beam high over the mesh circle. The first cage was over the right half of the circle, the other over the left. It looked as if at any moment the chains would let them down—only there was nothing on which they could have been placed. Under them was only the glowing, curving upper surface of the Stone Light.

In one cage a mighty sphinx ran back and forth, back and forth, like a predator missing the freedom of the jungle for the first time. Powerful wings lay folded on its back. Merle hadn't known that there were winged sphinxes at all.

In another cage, very much calmer, almost relaxed, sat—

"Vermithrax!"

The obsidian lion awakened from his trance and moved his face closer to the cage bars. At this distance she couldn't see details, but she felt the sorrow in his gaze.

The sphinx saw that Vermithrax moved and snarled at him across the glowing abyss.

"*No reproaches, please,*" said the Flowing Queen, but not even she could stop the quavering of her voice.

We brought him here, thought Merle. After all the years in the Campanile he was finally free, and now he's a prisoner again.

"*You can do nothing about it.*"

The Queen intended to reassure her, but Merle would not accept it. They both bore the guilt for Vermithrax's fate.

She turned to Burbridge with trembling lips. The quivering of her cheeks betrayed that she was close to tears. But she still had herself under control. She wanted to scream at him, call him names. But then she pulled all her thoughts together and looked for the right words.

"Why are you friendly to me, but you imprison my friend?" she asked, controlling herself with difficulty.

"We need him. More than the sphinx, even."

Merle's eyes went to the sphinx, who, half predator, half human, was rampaging in his cage, frantic with fury. The steel box swung back and forth, but its strong chain was equal to the burden. Merle's eyes quickly turned back to Vermithrax. His long obsidian tail hung down between the bars of the cage and twitched slightly.

We have to free him, she thought.

"*Yes.*" This time the Flowing Queen had no objections. No suggestions either, however.

"An experiment," said Burbridge, "for which we've waited a long time."

"What . . . are you planning to do with them?" Merle asked.

"We're going to dip them in the Stone Light."

"What?" Merle stared at him.

"I've thoroughly considered whether I should show

you this, Merle. But I think it's important for you to understand. That you grasp what goes on down here. And why this world is the better one."

Merle shook her head dumbly. She understood nothing. Nothing at all. Why her especially?

"What's going to happen to him?" she asked.

"If I knew that, it wouldn't be necessary to try it," replied Burbridge. "We're not experimenting with this thing for the first time today. The first attempts were failures."

"You burn living creatures, only to see—"

"Don't you feel it?" he interrupted her. "The Stone Light gives off no heat. It cannot burn anyone. Including your friend."

"Then why do you want to dip Vermithrax in it?"

He grinned triumphantly. "In order to see what happens, of course! The Light changes every living creature, it *binds* itself with it and makes something new out of it. The stone hearts are part of the Light, small fragments, and they take the body's own will away from it. Afterward we can do what we want to with them. That has shown itself to be quite practical, especially with the resistant Lilim."

So, not all the Lilim had readily placed themselves under his rule. There were rebels. Potential opponents.

Merle and Burbridge were now standing at the inner railing of the round grill walk. Quite nearby was the first of the motionless stone figures that flanked the entire circle.

"We tried it with the golems," Burbridge continued. "Statues, bodies, hewn out of stone. We let them down into the Light on the chain and when we pulled them up again, they were *alive*."

Merle's eyes flicked over the endless line of stone figures. They had human shapes, certainly, but their proportions were too massive, their shoulders too broad, their faces smooth as balls.

The professor twisted the corners of his mouth. Then, loudly, he called out a word in a language Merle didn't understand.

All the stone figures made a step forward at the same time. Then they went stiff again.

He turned to Merle again with a smile. "Stone that becomes alive. A good result, one could say. In any case, a combat-effective one."

Was that supposed to be a threat? No, she thought, he didn't need to scare her with a stone army.

"And now," he said, "we come to a new attempt. A second experiment, one could say. Your friend consists of stone that is already living *before* he comes into contact with the Stone Light. What do you think might happen when we dip the obsidian lion into the Light? What will become of *him*?" There was a spark in Burbridge's eyes, and Merle realized that it was a part of the scientific curiosity he'd spoken of earlier. But it was a cold and calculating gleam. It had an alarming similarity to the Stone Light, and for the first time she wondered whether possibly she might be speaking not with Burbridge himself but with something that had gained power over him.

A heart on the hunt for a body, he'd said. One like his own? Was that the way the Light organized and directed whole societies and peoples? By giving a new heart to its leader first of all?

"We must get away from here," said the Flowing Queen.

Really?

"I feel something!"

Two figures approached over one of the walks to the circle.

One was a bizarre creature that looked like a human walking on all fours—but its chest and its face were pointed upward. Around its head, eyes, and mouth were wound thorny vines of steel.

The second figure was a girl with long, white-blond hair.

Impossible! Absolutely impossible!

And yet . . .

"Junipa!"

Merle left Burbridge standing and ran up to the two of them.

The creature took a step back and let the two girls fall

into each other's arms. Merle no longer kept back her tears.

When they pulled away from each other, Junipa smiled, her mirror eyes glowing in the light of the Stone Light. Very deep inside, very briefly only, Merle was horrified at this look; but then she realized that the mirror fragments only reflected the flickering brightness that was all around them.

"What are you doing here?" she asked breathlessly, asked it again, and yet again, shaking her head, laughing and crying at the same time.

Junipa took a deep breath, as if she must pull all her strength together to speak. She held Merle's hands, and her fingers now closed about them even more strongly, as if she never again wanted to let go of her friend, her confidante from the first days in Arcimboldo's mirror workshop.

"They have . . ." She fell silent, started over: "Talamar abducted me." With a wave at the grotesque thing behind her, she added, "He killed Arcimboldo!"

"*We must get away,*" said the Flowing Queen. "*At once!*"

Merle stared at Talamar, saw the steel vine, which had distorted the face into a wasteland of scars. "Arcimboldo?" she whispered, disbelieving.

Junipa nodded.

Merle wanted to say something, anything—"*That's*

impossible! He can't be dead! You're lying!"—when a scream sounded behind her.

A scream of fury.

A scream of hate.

"Must get away from here!" said the Flowing Queen once again.

Merle whirled around and looked back, across the few yards to Burbridge and to the edge of the round grill walkway.

At first look, nothing had changed. The professor still stood there, his back to her, looking into the center of the circle. The golem guards were stiff as before. The sphinx rampaged in his cage, while Vermithrax sat motionless, gazing into the deep. Not at Merle and Junipa, and not at Lord Light.

The lion was looking down at the narrow walk that cut through the middle of the circle. At the platform in the center.

That platform from which the dead priest of Horus had been dangling.

The end of the rope now hung empty over the abyss. It was frayed, as if it had been bitten off.

Seth stood on the platform—*alive!*—with both arms raised and again uttered a scream.

"Iskander," he roared into the light-flooded emptiness.

The cage of the sphinx exploded as if the bars were glass.

And then Iskander descended on them.

13

The Fighters Awaken

THINGS HAPPENED TOO FAST FOR MERLE TO SEE IT ALL AT first. Only a little later did she succeed in grasping most of it, a movement here, a blur there, underscored by a cacophony of noise and screams and the rushing of powerful wings.

The sphinx shot out of the cloud of steel and iron fragments into which his prison had changed from one minute to the next. He raced down, faster than the remains of the cage plunging down around him, and reached the platform in no time.

Seth was waiting for him. He sprang agilely onto

Iskander's lion back, screaming out a string of orders in Egyptian. Immediately, the sphinx launched himself from the platform, stormed onto the round path and, with a single, clawed blow, beheaded three of the golem guards that stood in his way. Burbridge threw himself to the ground behind them, while other stone soldiers on both sides stomped forward to protect their master.

Carried on by his swing, Iskander had to fly a loop in order to renew the attack on Lord Light.

When the cage burst, Merle had instinctively thrown herself on Junipa and pulled her to the ground with her. She halfway expected that Talamar would tear her friend away from her. But instead, the creature jumped nimbly over Junipa and raced over to Burbridge and the golem soldiers, with the intention of defending Lord Light with his life.

Unexpectedly, Merle and Junipa were left unguarded.

Not that it was of much use to them. All they could do was lie flat on the ground, Merle protectively over Junipa, who, though only a year younger, seemed to her at that moment like a child who must be shielded.

"Too late!" whispered the Flowing Queen in her thoughts, but what she meant by it wasn't clear to Merle yet.

She lifted her head, first made sure that Junipa was all right, and then looked back at Burbridge. She was lying about ten yards from the place where the walkway entered the circle; ten yards from the place where Burbridge was taking cover behind a bunch of golem soldiers, while the sphinx with his rider—

Dead! Seth had been dead!

—flew in for a new attack. Two other stone men burst under a blow from Iskander's claw, while Seth bellowed further orders in Egyptian, clasped both arms around Iskander's half-human upper body, and kept his eye on the light-filled mist of the dome.

Merle didn't know how he'd managed to survive the execution, and perhaps it was better so. He was a high priest of Horus, one of the most powerful magicians in the Empire, and he must know how to raise the dead. Possibly that had been in his plan from the beginning: lull Burbridge into security and then be able to strike totally unexpectedly.

And he understood about striking, no doubt about it.

More golems shattered into pieces, proving that every-thing that Lord Light had expected of them had been in error. They might offer protection from humans and Lilim, but not against the anger of a sphinx, whose power and strength and cruelty were legendary among the peoples of the world.

Iskander was, as Merle saw at once, no ordinary sphinx. He was bigger, stronger, and in addition to that, winged. His long, bronze-colored hair had loosed itself from his neck and whirled wildly around his head, a net of fluttering strands like the tentacles of a bizarre water plant. He had claws not only on his lion feet but also on both hands of his human torso, and they were long and sharp enough to break even stone. Merle didn't like to imagine what would happen if they landed on soft flesh, muscles, skin, and bone.

Her eyes sought the second cage, in which Vermithrax was still imprisoned. The obsidian lion was no longer sitting there quietly but vainly trying to bend the bars apart with his paws. To no avail. Iskander's cage had been destroyed by Seth's magic, not by the muscular power of the sphinx, and Vermithrax's prison remained untouched by it. The steel box shook and jerked as Vermithrax ran around in it angrily, throwing himself against the bars repeatedly and bellowing something to Merle that she couldn't understand over the noise of the fight.

Why didn't any Lilim come to Burbridge's aid? He'd trusted in the strength of the golem soldiers. But wouldn't he have guessed what the sphinx was capable of doing?

Merle thought of the empty machine tunnels, the anxious creatures who took shelter from their master behind steel and smoke.

Only a single Lilim was ready to go to his death for Lord Light.

Talamar dared a desperate maneuver. When Iskander shot down once again from high altitude, the grotesque creature jumped from one of the railings and threw himself at the sphinx. Iskander crashed against him, lost his orientation for a moment, smashed into the opposite railing, and lost his rider. Seth was slung from the sphinx's back and thumped onto the walkway.

Talamar hung with his limbs entwined around Iskander's body and was carried high up with him, depriving him of sight: Talamar's scrawny body clung before the sphinx's chest and face. Iskander was confused for a moment. Then he seized the Lilim with both hands, tore him to pieces, and flung him into the abyss. Talamar's remains fell into the deep in a red cloud and disappeared in the glow of the Stone Light.

Iskander let out an angry scream, licked the Lilim blood from his claws as he flew, and ignored the calls of his master. Seth had pulled himself up to the railing with his unwounded arm; the golden grid inlaid in his scalp was sprinkled with damp red. Again and again he roared orders up to Iskander, but the sphinx didn't obey.

The winged creature screeched in wild triumph, shot away over Seth, and flew in a wide arc. His eye fell on Vermithrax and recognized in him a worthy opponent. He rushed at the obsidian lion's cage with brutish fury, leaped on it, fastened himself to the bars, and tore at them. Iskander was no ordinary sphinx. He was something artificial, bred through the black arts of the Pharaoh and his priesthood, a cross of several beasts, and Merle wouldn't have been surprised if somewhere in him there were also the traces of a Lilim.

Iskander rattled the bars of the cage again, while Vermithrax struck at him from inside. He wounded the sphinx on his legs and paws, but the pain only made Iskander angrier. The cage danced wildly on its chain, swung wide back and forth, twisted and circled, and the sound of grinding iron came down to the round walkway over the Light.

Merle and Junipa clung to each other; neither could do anything, and even the Flowing Queen stormed in Merle's thoughts in fear for Vermithrax's life.

Injured, Seth was still leaning against the railing, looking frantically from Iskander to Burbridge. The professor appeared very briefly behind the wall of his remaining golem soldiers to assess the situation, then took cover again and sent two golems in Seth's direction. The stone giants hurried forward with rumbling steps. The priest of Horus tried to hurl a magic spell against them, but when he opened his lips, only blood came out, red foam, which ran over his chin and soiled his chest.

"Iskander!" he cried in a long, drawn-out howl into the ever-present brightness. At the same moment the golems reached him, were about to seize him—and then suddenly Seth was gone, and a mighty falcon shot forward, wobbling, between the giant soldiers, turned a groggy circle over Burbridge, and then rushed upward, disappearing without a trace into the mist of light in the dome.

The sound of a metal grinding and rending alarmed Merle and Junipa and drew their eyes up to the cage.

Vermithrax had succeeded in splitting Iskander's face with a well-placed slash between the bars. The blow had torn a hand-sized piece of skin from the sphinx's head like old wallpaper. But Iskander's roar of pain was no different from the sound of his insane rage; his tearing and shaking grew even stronger.

The grinding sound came again, followed by shrill poppings.

Merle screamed. Junipa's hands dug into Merle's arms like pincers, clutching as hard as she could.

The chain parted, and for a fraction of a second the cage appeared to float in the nothingness, held like a cocoon by an invisible spiderweb.

Then it plunged.

The roaring of the obsidian lion was mixed with that of the sphinx. Iskander pushed himself off the cage just in time, before it could carry him with it to the depths. His wings whipped the air and caused a maelstrom in the haze of light. He wavered and swayed, then stabilized his position and looked down to where the cage was becoming ever smaller.

Merle tore herself loose from Junipa, rushed to the railing, and looked into the abyss.

"*Oh, no,*" whispered the Flowing Queen, over and over again.

The cage rotated as it fell, like a child's building block. Inside it, Vermithrax was hardly still recognizable, only a black blur, which became smaller and smaller as it fell toward the brightness. Then the cage paled in the glowing mist over the curved surface; the chain, which had fallen behind it like an iron tail, vanished last of all.

Merle did not utter a sound.

The Queen was also silent.

When Merle finally turned around, with trembling knees and hands that were scarcely able to hold on to the railing, Junipa was beside her. Junipa with the mirror eyes, out of which the glow of the Stone Light looked at her with its own intelligence. The impression vanished just as soon as Junipa bent toward her and the reflection vanished from the mirrors.

Now Merle saw herself in them, with teary eyes and shining cheeks, and she was infinitely grateful when Junipa pulled her friend toward her, held her, and murmured soft words of sympathy in a tone that was soothing and cheering at the same time.

A resounding crash. The two girls whirled around.

Iskander was not being stopped by the obsidian lion's fate. Again he shot toward the catwalk in a nosedive, but this time he didn't rush away over the golems but landed among them. Blows that might have felled trees struck him from all sides, and already the skin under his fur was turning dark red. But he raged further among his antagonists. For every blow that struck him, he delivered several more, shattering golem soldiers in all directions. Splinters of stone flew everywhere, striking Merle and Junipa, and yet they had no choice, except to watch what happened next.

Now other Lilim were approaching from somewhere, winged creatures like those Merle had seen between the gigantic statues at the gate of Axis Mundi. But they were still far away, hardly more than tiny points in the brightness above.

Burbridge sprang among the stone soldiers shattering around him, both arms held protectively over his head, bent, now only a panicked man who feared for nothing but his life.

If the Stone Light had been in him, it had abandoned him now. Or was waiting to find out for itself how it was for a human to die. The search for new experience. Knowledge that made it easier for it to consume the next human, the next organism—or to become consumed by it, as a new heart, a new center of all things.

Iskander's power was ebbing, but his strength was still terrible enough to obliterate the last golem. Finally Burbridge stood alone on a heap of rubble, some parts still appearing human, others nothing but fragments of stone and sand.

Iskander hauled back for a deadly blow, when something shot up from the depths behind him, glowing bright like a meteor, only bigger, with a shape that resembled a lion. A deep roar overwhelmed Iskander's scream of rage and echoed back from the distant dome walls.

The sphinx turned, his movements slower than before, weakened by his battle and his own rage. And he recognized Vermithrax. Saw the light in which the obsidian lion was bathed, no, that shone through him, as if he himself had turned to light, light of stone, not hot, not cold, only different, strange, and fearsome.

Vermithrax seized Iskander by the head, tore him from the walkway, pulled him into the air, flung him up, and thus broke his neck.

The sphinx's wings fluttered one last time, held him in the emptiness for a moment, and then he would have plunged—had not the flying Lilim arrived at that moment. They caught up the body and carried it quickly away.

Burbridge laughed.

Laughed and laughed and laughed.

Vermithrax didn't bother with him; instead he rushed over to Merle and Junipa and landed beside them on the walkway. The grill rattled under his paws, as if his weight had multiplied at one stroke.

"Come," he cried in a voice that sounded a little more rumbling than before, "get on!"

His body was no longer black. He glowed, as if someone

had poured lava into the shape of a lion, and he was bigger, his feathered wings wider, his head heavier, his teeth and claws longer. In the midst of her relief, Merle wondered if that was all the Light had done or whether there were other changes, ones that she couldn't see now, which might appear later when no one was thinking about it anymore. She remembered the spark in the professor's eyes and saw a dissimilar, brighter glow in Vermithrax's eyes, two beaming points like stars implanted in his face.

But she was also happy, so happy, and she hugged the glowing lion's head and patted his nose before she sprang on his back with Junipa and held on tight.

"He is still the same old Vermithrax," said the Queen in her head, and at the moment, Merle believed her. *"Still the same old Vermithrax."*

Vermithrax took off and rushed over the bunch of Lilim clustered around the dead sphinx. They let go of Iskander's body; not much was left of him. Burbridge bellowed orders, and one of the Lilim shot over to him and waited until his master sat down on him—a serpentine creature that bore some likeness to a dragonfly, spiraled like a corkscrew, with massive wing shells like those of a beetle, three on each side, and a head that looked like a swirl of teeth.

The Lilim rose up, placed itself at the head of the flying pack, and took up the pursuit of Vermithrax. Burbridge yelled something, but his voice was too shrill to understand.

So they rushed after the glowing lion, the first living creature of stone that had been dipped in the glow of the Stone Light.

"*They are afraid,*" said the Flowing Queen. "*They are afraid of Lord Light, but also they are afraid of Vermithrax and what he is now.*"

What is he, then? Merle asked in her thoughts.

"*I do not know,*" said the Queen. "*I thought I knew much, but now I only know that I know nothing.*"

Junipa was sitting behind Merle and had flung both arms around her, holding on desperately and trying frantically not to look down into the abyss. Vermithrax was mounting more and more steeply, and it cost Merle all her strength to cling to his glowing mane. It was lucky that Junipa was thin, almost emaciated; it was all that allowed Merle to keep both their weights on Vermithrax's back.

Vermithrax was faster than before, as if the Light had doubled the strength of his wings. But he lost a portion of his valuable head start when he was compelled to circle under the highest point of the dome before he discovered an opening to the outside, a sort of gate, which was guarded by two winged Lilim. Both drew back anxiously when they saw him coming toward them, a beaming fury, a living, breathing, roaring comet.

Vermithrax bore Merle and Junipa out of the haze of light, broke out of the brightness with them, and shot out into the eternal red dusk of Hell. After the extreme glitter of the interior of the dome, the diffuse lava light of the rock ceiling over Axis Mundi seemed to Merle dark and uncanny. Her eyes needed a while to get used to it.

She imagined how Vermithrax must be affecting the Lilim who'd gathered in streets and on piazzas: a glowing tail of light against the rock sky, a creature that hadn't yet been seen in Hell.

She glanced back and saw again the growing swarm of their pursuers, which shot out of the dome not even a hundred yards behind them, pulling a thin veil of light along with them before it paled and dissolved into glowing dust.

Lord Light sat on the back of the foremost Lilim, with fluttering coattails and streaming hair, his face twisted; some blows of the sphinx had grazed him and torn red furrows in his hair and clothing.

"*He wants Vermithrax,*" said the Queen. "*More than anything else, he wants Vermithrax.*"

And as if Junipa had heard the words in Merle's head, she contradicted the Queen: "He wants you, Merle. He's after you." After a moment she added, "And after me. My eyes."

"Your eyes?" cried Merle over her shoulder, while deep below them the towers and roofs and domes of Axis Mundi moved past and Vermithrax neared the gap in the rock wall.

"Yes. He ordered Arcimboldo to implant them in me."

"But why you?"

"You know how I began to see with the mirror eyes? First only outlines and shapes, then your faces, and then everything? And how I began to even see in the dark? I can *always* see, no matter where and when, whether I want to or not."

Merle nodded. Of course she remembered that.

"It didn't stop with that," Junipa said.

"How do you mean?"

"I can see even farther." She sounded sad. "Always farther. Through things and . . . other places."

Merle looked back at the Lilim. Vermithrax had increased the distance again, but the number of pursuers had grown to fifty or sixty.

"Other places?" she repeated.

"Into other worlds," said Junipa. "That's the reason why Lord Light needs me. I'm supposed to look into other worlds for him . . . into worlds that need a new heart, he said."

Merle shivered and thought of Winter. She was suddenly overcome with remorse because she hadn't thought about him the whole time. He'd fled, Burbridge said. In silence she wished him the best of luck. He'd been going through Hell alone before they met him, and he'd probably manage from now on.

"Where are we flying?" she roared into Vermithrax's glowing ear.

In front of them the gap now yawned, like a chasm in the rocks of Hell. "Out of the city, first," cried the lion. "And then we'll see where our leader takes us."

She didn't understand. "Our leader?"

Vermithrax's mane vibrated as the powerful lion head nodded. "Look straight ahead!"

Merle peered forward over the glowing head. The gap was darker than its surroundings, and it was hard to make out anything in it. There were a few flying Lilim, but most turned aside when they saw Vermithrax coming toward them.

But then Merle saw what he meant: a tiny dark dot that was flying some distance ahead of them. She just caught sight of it before it disappeared behind the first bend of the rock gap. It looked like a bird, like a—

A falcon!

"We'll hope that Seth knows how we're going to get out of here," cried Vermithrax.

"*Quite possible,*" said the Queen, and finally she sounded like herself again. "*Perhaps we really will manage it.*"

The walls of the rock gap grew rapidly toward them along both sides. Vermithrax rushed between them at breakneck speed. Projections, ledges, and spines blurred in the corners of Merle's eyes to a brown-red fog.

They had almost reached the last curve when a shudder ran through the rock walls, a shaking and explosion, followed by dust and an avalanche of rubble that plunged down to the bottom to the right and left of them. The vibrations appeared to come toward them, as if the structure of the rock walls were falling in waves, which rolled toward them, grinding and thundering. The rockfalls became stronger, ever more pieces broke out of the rock with such force that they were carried far out into the pass. Sometimes Vermithrax made a swift turn to the side in order to avoid them, but even he couldn't prevent his riders from being repeatedly struck by small stones, which smacked painfully against them like shots.

The end of the gap came into view in front of them, and their worst fears were confirmed.

The gate to the city was impassable.

The Eternal Fighters were alive—awakened, as all here was awakened, by a light of stone.

The two mighty statues had begun their wrestling, bent forward and wrapped around one another like two children in a fight over a toy. Their wrestling was so dogged, they were so evenly matched, that their positions changed constantly. Again and again, they crashed against the rock walls in the narrow mouth of the gap and caused further tremors. Merle saw a Lilim hit by a piece of stone and thrown down into the depths. Some barely caught themselves, others crashed against the walls or to the ground.

But the stream of pilgrims and travelers between the

feet of the rock giants were getting the worst of it. The endless ribbon was frayed. In panic, those who'd managed to get inside the gap streamed forward, plunging and stumbling over one another, pulling themselves up, running on two, four, and more legs; some emitted screams that sounded almost human, others high whistles, scratchy growls, or sounds for which there are no words and no descriptions.

Even if the two battling stone giants did not completely fill the gap, anyone daring to run between them ran the danger of being ground up on the spot. It was suicide to fly through the gate.

"I'm going to try it," cried Vermithrax.

Merle looked over her shoulder again, nodded encouragingly to Junipa first, then looked at their pursuers. The Lilim were relentlessly on their heels. Vermithrax was flying more slowly on account of the fighters, and the Lilim had caught up to them a little. Lord Light still rode at their head. She wondered how he'd succeeded in waking the fighters from a distance. Before, when it had looked as if the sphinx would kill him, Merle had assumed that the Stone Light had withdrawn from Burbridge. But now it appeared to be back, perhaps stronger than ever; there was no doubt that the Light, with its power over stone and rock, had called the Eternal Fighters to life. Suddenly Merle had the thought that possibly this whole place, perhaps the whole of Hell, was already possessed by the

Stone Light. And she wondered if it hadn't been a mistake to look at the Egyptian Empire as the greatest danger for the world. Perhaps they'd deluded themselves; perhaps the Pharaoh or even Lord Light or Hell were not the ones who were the worst threat to them all. Perhaps an entirely different war was taking place here in concealment. The Stone Light strove for more. First Hell. Then the upper world. And then, with Junipa's help, all the other worlds that might exist somewhere behind the walls of dream and imagination.

Vermithrax suddenly pulled in his wings and let himself drop. Something gigantic rushed away over them and cracked with deafening thunder against the rock wall—the elbow of a fighter as big as a church tower.

Junipa's hold around Merle's waist was so tight that she could hardly breathe, but it didn't matter, for she was almost forgetting to breathe with the tension. Stone splinters rattled down on them, and it was thanks to Vermithrax's speed alone that they weren't struck by any of the larger pieces. Suddenly everything else was meaningless. They dove into the middle of the fight between the two titans, and now saw nothing more but high stone walls and ramparts that relentlessly shifted, grinding and cracking, rubbing against each other and sometimes slowly, sometimes with lightning speed, moving toward or away from them. Vermithrax flew hair-raising maneuvers to avoid the bodies of the fighters, his wingtip sometimes touching the curve of a muscle here or the crest of a rib there.

Then, just as abruptly as the fighters had popped up, they were behind them. Vermithrax carried the two girls out of immediate danger, past the edges of the rock gap, and out into the breadth of the plain, high over the heads of scattered Lilim hordes, who flowed fan-shaped in front of the fighting place of the stone giants and sought their safety in flight.

"Have we made it?" asked Junipa in Merle's ear. The words sounded breathy, tired, and feeble.

"At least we're out of the city." Was that any ground for relief? Merle didn't know, and she was sorry that she couldn't be more encouraging for Junipa.

Before Lord Light's swarm reached the fighters, the two titans froze, closely intertwined with one another as before. The flying Lilim, headed by the one carrying Lord Light, shot unhindered between the bodies. The fighters had crushed hundreds of Lilim under their feet, and the survivors were still fleeing in all directions; it would be a long time before anyone dared to come here again. Yet Merle saw a few Lilim stop on the ground and gesticulate toward the red sky with a multitude of the most various limbs at Lord Light and his companions. Then Vermithrax strengthened the beat of his wings, and his speed became so fast that Merle had to blink to keep the headwind from making her eyes burn.

The falcon had flown through the rock gap and the bodies of the fighters much more quickly than Vermithrax. But now Vermithrax caught up again and soon was staying just in sight of the bird. He was their only chance. On their own, they'd never find the gateway they'd used to enter. No one could have committed to memory the route the heralds had used, and so they knew neither where to find that entrance nor how long it would take to get there.

Seth must know another way out of Hell.

Merle had hundreds of questions she would have liked to put to Junipa. But they were both completely exhausted. Her curiosity could wait.

The wasteland seemed even more monotonous to her now than during their flight with the heralds. The jagged rock fans and fissures, the cracks in the ground, the pointed rock promontories, and long-solidified lava glaciers repeated themselves over and over and over again, as if they had in truth been flying in circles for an eternity. Only small variations, differing formations here and there, confirmed to Merle that they were always going straight ahead, that Seth wasn't fooling them.

At some point, long after Merle's sense of time had failed and she was having trouble not losing her grip with weariness, an outline peeled itself away from the red glow on the horizon. At first she thought it was a wind spout, perhaps of a cyclone. Then she realized that it was massive and didn't move from the spot.

A column. Miles high, so that it linked the floor of Hell with the ceiling.

As they approached they could make out openings, irregularly arranged, but all the same size. Windows.

"That's no column," whispered Merle in astonishment. "That's a tower!"

"The falcon is heading straight for it," said Vermithrax.

"Is that the exit?" asked Junipa, her voice weak.

Merle shrugged her shoulders. "Seth at least seems to think it is. Anyway, he's led us here."

"*Yes,*" said the Queen, "*but not us alone.*"

Merle didn't have to look back to know that the Queen spoke the truth. The swarm of Lilim was still behind them, flying just as tirelessly as Vermithrax and the priest of Horus.

"This could become exciting," she murmured.

"And shortly," said Junipa, who, unlike her, had looked back.

Now Merle couldn't resist either and looked behind them.

The Lilim were barely fifty yards away.

She could see Burbridge's smile.

14

Flotsam

THE SEA TURTLE SHELL DANCED ON THE WAVES LIKE AN autumn leaf sailing down from a tree. Serafin's stomach had been cramped for hours, as if he were actually falling, an endless drop into an uncertain chasm, and something in him seemed to be tensing for the impact—for *something* that would put an end to the monotony.

He'd already been looking out at the unchanging sea for so long that he saw its image when he closed his eyes: a sky hung with clouds, and under it the gray, wavy desert of the sea, stirred up but not stormy, cold but not icy, as if the water itself couldn't decide what it wanted. There was no land to be seen anywhere. Their condition hadn't grown any more hopeful a while ago, when the mermaids who'd been pulling them had vanished without a trace. They'd dived away from one moment to the next, and he had only to look into Eft's eyes to read how perplexed she was.

Eft sat between Dario and Tiziano in one of the horn segments of the sea turtle shell, holding the knapsack containing Arcimboldo's mirror mask pressed firmly against her. Serafin grieved with her, certainly, but in spite of all that, he'd have appreciated it if she'd pushed away her despondency for a while and given a few thoughts to the future. The immediate future.

It didn't look good. Not by any means.

Aristide had given up babbling to himself, though. Serafin had been afraid that either Dario or Tiziano would throw the boy overboard, but by daybreak, Aristide had finally grown quiet. Now he stared numbly ahead of him, didn't answer when spoken to, but nodded occasionally or shook his head if someone asked him a question.

But strangest of all was the way Lalapeya was behaving. The sphinx, in her human form, crouched half over the edge of the shell and let her hand dangle in the water up to her wrist. Someone—Serafin thought it was Tiziano—had remarked that perhaps Lalapeya hoped to catch a fish for breakfast, but no one laughed. And anyway, by now the time for breakfast was long past.

The sphinx's silence filled Serafin with anger, almost more than the situation into which Lalapeya had brought them. After endless hours on the water, first in darkness and now in the bright daylight, she still hadn't considered it necessary to explain the experiences of the night to them. She brooded to herself, gazed into emptiness—and let her hand hang in the water as if she were only waiting for someone underneath to grab it.

But whoever she might be waiting for refused her the favor.

"Lalapeya," said Serafin for the hundredth time, "what happened on San Michele? How long had that . . . that thing been lying there?"

He thought, She will say "a long time."

"A long time," she said.

Dario shifted backward and forward against the horn wall at his back, but he didn't find the comfort he was seeking. "That was no ordinary sphinx."

"Oh, really?" Tiziano made a face. "As if we hadn't noticed that ourselves."

"What I mean," said Dario sharply, staring angrily at his friend as he spoke, "is that it wasn't just a *large* sphinx. Or a *gigantic* sphinx. That thing lying buried under San Michele was . . . more." The appropriate words failed him; he shook his head and was silent again.

Serafin agreed with him. "More," he said shortly, and after a pause: "A sphinx god."

Aristide, confused, silent Aristide, looked up and said his first words in many hours: "If it was a god, then it was an evil one."

As if Lalapeya had suddenly awakened from a trance that had carried her far from the boys and the sea turtle shell, even from the sea, she said: "Not evil. Only old. Unimaginably old. The first son of the Mother." She took her hand out of the water, stared at it for a long moment, as if it belonged to someone else's body, then went on, "He was already lying under there before there was Egypt—and I mean the *ancient* Egypt! At a time when other powers ruled the world, the suboceanic cultures and the lords of the deep and—" She broke off, shook her head, and began again: "He lay there a long time. At that time no humans lived in the lagoon, and he was brought there so that no one would disturb his rest. He *was* a god, at least by your measures, even if at that time no one called him that. And they wanted to be sure that he would remain there undisturbed forever. Therefore, guards were put in place to watch over him."

"Guards such as you," said Serafin.

The sphinx nodded, looking infinitely beautiful in her grief. "I wasn't the first, but that isn't important. I watched the lagoon for so long that I gave up counting the years. I came here when there was still no city, no houses or fishermen's huts at all. But then I watched men come, take possession of the islands, and settle there. Perhaps I ought to have prevented it, who knows? But I always liked you humans, and I saw nothing wrong with your living there where *he* lay buried. I did what I could to protect his honor and rest. It was I who saw to it that San Michele would also become a cemetery for you humans, too. And I took pains to be a friend to the mermaids, for they are the true masters of the lagoon—or at least they always were until the humans made a sport of catching them and killing them or hitching them before their boats."

Eft had been listening attentively for some time, and now she nodded in agreement. "You gave us the cemetery of the mermaids. A place that the humans could not find. To this very day."

"I've only done what I could do best," said Lalapeya. "I've watched the dead. Just as I have done for thousands of years. And it was easy. At first I had only to be there, only wait. Then it was time to build a house, finally a palace, all in order not to attract attention, to give no one reason to mistrust." She dropped her eyes, and for a moment it seemed as if she were about to put her hand into the water again, almost mournfully, guiltily. "When the lagoon was still uninhabited, the loneliness didn't bother me. That only came later, when all the others turned up, the mermaids and the humans. And naturally, the Flowing Queen. I had to see how it was to have friends, to trust others. Therefore I gave the mermaids a place for their dead, but they avoided me too."

"We honored you," said Eft.

"Honored!" Lalapeya sighed softly. "I wanted friend-ship and instead I got honor. One has nothing to do with the other. I was always lonely and would have remained so, if not . . ." She fell silent. "When the great war began, when the Egyptians conquered the world, I knew that it was time to act. I heard that they possessed the power to awaken the dead and to enslave them—and then finally I understood that I, without knowing it, had been awaiting this moment down all the ages. Everything suddenly made sense. If the Egyptians succeeded in making the *god,* as you called him, be their tool . . . if they actually succeeded in that, yes, then they would truly be masters of the world."

"But where do the sphinx commanders come into it?" asked Dario.

"I no longer doubt that the Pharaoh has been merely a puppet of the sphinxes for a long time," said Lalapeya thoughtfully. "The commanders are young, in comparison to me and some others of my people, and they have no respect for the old laws and customs anymore. They rec-ognized the power that the god would give them. Had it not been for the Flowing Queen, they would have reached their goal much earlier."

Serafin nodded slowly. So that was it. The sphinxes had worked in the background all those years to make the old god of their people into their slave. For that, they first needed the Pharaoh, then the priests of Horus with their power to subjugate the dead. Not much longer and they would rule the Empire with the help of the old god.

Lalapeya continued. "So I began to take precautions. All the millennia, all the waiting . . . now finally I realized that it hadn't been for nothing. And so I tried all that was in my power." She dropped her eyes. "And I have failed. Such a long time, and then a defeat. The son of the Mother is lost."

Serafin had said not a word. But now he had to accept the responsibility: Her failure wasn't her fault. He was the one who'd prevented her from stopping the collector; he'd wrecked all that she and her predecessors had been awaiting for eons.

But that also didn't change the fact that Boro had had to sacrifice his life.

Serafin didn't feel guilty. He wanted to, but he could not. They had both made mistakes, Lalapeya and he, and now they must both bear the consequences.

"We're dying of thirst," said Tiziano, as if Lalapeya's confession hadn't taken place at all. Perhaps he hadn't been listening to her.

Serafin stared at the sphinx and now she returned his look, and for a fleeting moment he thought he'd seen those eyes once before, but not in her.

"Land!" Dario's voice shattered the silence. "There's land over there!"

All looked in the direction he was pointing. Even Lalapeya.

Tiziano leaped up, and at once the shell began to rock and tip, and suddenly water splashed over the edge, an entire wave, and then they were sitting up to their ankles in wetness.

"Sit down, damn it!" Dario raged at him.

Tiziano, completely in thrall to his euphoria over the light-colored mound in the distance, stared at him for a moment as if he didn't understand what Dario wanted of him. But then he sank back into his place without taking his eyes off the gray hump that had broken through the surface of the sea some distance away, like the hump of a whale.

The mound must have been visible for quite a while before Dario had discovered it, but its color was hardly any different from that of the sea or the sky.

"That isn't land," said Serafin, and no one contradicted him.

There was tense silence for a while, then Dario said aloud what all were thinking: "A fish?"

And Aristide: "A whale?"

An icy shiver ran down Serafin's back. He shook his head. "If it is one, then it's no longer alive. The thing doesn't move. Eft?"

When she looked at him and he looked into her eyes, he immediately wished that he'd kept back the question. But it was too late for that now.

"You won't want to hear it," she said softly.

"*I* want to hear it," said Dario in irritation.

"Me too," Tiziano added quickly.

Serafin was silent.

Eft didn't take her eyes off him as she said, "We're sinking."

"What?" cried Tiziano in horror. Again he leaped up but was immediately pulled back into his place by Dario.

"That's only a little water," said Dario quickly, letting a little of the saltwater on the floor run through his fingers. "Not bad. And I don't know what that has to do with that thing out there—"

"We're going under," said Eft once more. "Have been for quite a while now. Very, very slowly. We can't stop it. And the only place we can go is that thing over there." She pointed to the light-colored elevation in the sea without looking toward it herself.

"Why didn't you say anything before?" Serafin asked.

"What difference would it have made?"

Aristide looked frantically from one to the other. "We're sinking? Really?"

Dario closed his eyes for a moment and took a deep breath. "That's what she said, yes."

"Hairline cracks," said Serafin, and for the first time he examined the water level inside the sea turtle shell. They'd all been wet through since they'd left Venice, and no one had paid any attention to the dampness on the bottom of the horn shell. But now it dawned on him that they had in fact been sitting in water before Tiziano had almost caused the shell to capsize.

"Hairline cracks?" Tiziano splashed around in the dark water, as if he could feel them with his bare fingers and stop them.

Dario became very calm. "Good. So we're going under. But up there ahead is land . . . or something like it. And you, Eft, know exactly what it is."

She nodded. "If everything doesn't deceive me, it's a body. And a very special one, at that. The mermaids sensed it, so they swam away. They were afraid."

"A . . . a body?" stammered Tiziano. "But . . . that thing is at least . . . at least seventy, eighty yards long. Isn't it?" When no one answered, he said once more, louder this time, "Isn't it?"

Now they floated nearer to the light gray mound. And gradually, very gradually, Serafin distinguished an outline.

"The cadaver of a sea witch," said Eft.

Serafin's heart beat faster.

"Sea witch," repeated Aristide, and now it was he who was about to stand up. Dario pulled him back with such force that Serafin briefly considered remonstrating with him.

He let it go and turned to Eft. "How long do we have?"

She slowly moved her right hand through the water

inside the sea turtle shell. "Three hours. Maybe four. Possibly the shell will break apart sooner."

"Can we reach land in that time?"

"I haven't the least idea where we are."

Serafin nodded. Nothing could surprise him anymore. "So we have to leave the shell?"

"Yes."

"And climb up on that thing?"

"She's dead," said Eft. "She can't do anything more to anyone."

"One moment!" Dario rubbed the palm of his hand across his eyes, then massaged his temples with a slow movement. "You're suggesting in all seriousness that we climb onto a dead *sea witch*?"

Eft sniffed the wind. "She hasn't been dead long. She'll float for a few days."

"Longer than three or four hours," Serafin heard himself agree, even if he couldn't grasp that he was accepting this madness.

"I'm not going up there," stammered Aristide.

Tiziano said nothing.

"I'm certainly not going up on that." Aristide's voice sounded higher now, almost panicked.

"She can't be dangerous for us anymore," said Serafin soothingly. "And she's our only hope."

Tiziano came to his aid. "Imagine it's a dead fish. Then you'd probably even eat it."

Aristide stared at Tiziano for a long moment, speechless, then his features contorted, and his voice was a shrill howl. "You're all completely crazy! Completely mad!"

Dario ignored him. "The current is driving us straight toward it. Just a few minutes." When Aristide tried to protest again, Dario silenced him with a look that could have turned him to stone. His eyes narrowed as he again looked over at the floating body of the sea witch. "Is that her face there?"

All stared at the place he indicated.

"Yes," said Eft. All at once she turned pale and said nothing more. No one except Serafin noticed it. But he asked no more questions; there was time for that when they were sitting safely on the corpse.

The wind turned, and from one breath to the next it stank as terribly as the Venetian fish market on a summer day.

The witch was floating on her back. As far as Serafin could see from here, she had the body of a gigantic old woman—as far as the hips. From there her body continued into a powerful fish tail, such as the mermaids had, only the witch's was as long as a ship. Her hair floated like a gray carpet of algae, spread out in a fan on the waves. They'd have to be careful the sea turtle shell didn't catch in it; if they were forced to leave the shell while it was in the middle of this flood of hair, they'd be hopelessly tangled in the long strands and drown.

Serafin expressed this thought aloud, and immediately they all tried to propel the shell with their hands and steer it in another direction, toward the scaly tail, where it would be simplest to climb onto the sea witch. Even Lalapeya helped, though Serafin wasn't certain if she was merely taking the opportunity to dip her hands into the water again to feel for heaven knew what.

Only two yards.

Only one.

The turtle shell bumped against the witch's fish tail. The scales were as large as wagon wheels, overlaid with seaweed, slime, and algae that had settled into the cracks. The stink took their breath away. The boys swallowed and fought with their nausea until their noses and stomachs gradually got used to it. Only Eft and the sphinx seemed to be immune to it.

No one wanted to be the first to lay a hand on the scaly tail. Even Eft, deathly pale, stared at the dead witch, although Serafin suspected that she had other reasons for that. Later, he said to himself. Not now. Not one single worry more.

He took heart, grasped Dario's shoulder, balanced a long moment in the rocking shell, and then grabbed the edge of a scale with his right hand. The scabby horn plates were arranged like roof tiles, overlapping one another, and offered enough grip for fingers and feet. Had there not been the horrible stench, Serafin would almost have felt at home: In his lifetime, he'd already climbed up and down so many roofs that climbing a fish tail was child's play.

Once on top, he turned and looked along the curve to the sea turtle shell. From here it was even more clearly visible how low the shell already lay in the water. Eft's estimation had been more than generous. Serafin doubted that the shell would have stayed afloat for more than an hour longer.

He couldn't help the others, could only watch as, one by one, they climbed over the edge of the shell, grabbed onto the scales with trembling hands, and tried somehow to get a grip on the slippery surface. The tangle of dead water plants was as slippery as soft soap, but somehow they all finally succeeded in reaching the highest point of the bulge of the tail. Eft was the last to leave the shell. Serafin and Dario reached down to pull her up.

The sea turtle shell rocked for a while longer beside the body, then it was seized by a current and carried away. Aristide and Tiziano watched it go, but Serafin's attention was now entirely devoted to the gigantic body on which they were stranded.

He'd overcome the nausea, but the disgust remained. Never in his life had he seen anything so repellent. He stood up carefully and managed several steps over the rounded top of the fish tail in the direction of the upper body.

A hand was placed on his shoulder from behind.

"Let me go first," said Eft, walking ahead of him and taking over the lead. The others, including Lalapeya, stayed back on the tail. As long as the cadaver lay quietly in the water, nothing could happen to them there, and for a moment Serafin enjoyed the quiet at the side of the silent Eft.

As soon as they'd left the scales, the consistency of the surface under them changed. The belly of the witch was soft and spongy; with every step the indentations around Serafin's soles filled with fluid. He'd often walked through Venice's piazzas when markets there had been dismantled; then the pavement was overflowing with an ankle-deep layer of rotten fruit and vegetables—this felt very similar under his feet.

They meandered through the hollows between the ribs. Water had collected in long puddles, with all kinds of small animals darting about in them.

From here Serafin could make out the witch's chin, a pointed triangle above several broad swellings. Behind it the nostrils were visible, two cave openings under a sharp ridge of skin and cartilage.

A wide scar divided the chin, overgrown by proud flesh. Eft saw it and stopped.

"What's wrong?" Instinctively, Serafin looked all around him. There was no threat of danger, at least nothing he could name.

Eft's face, despite the taxing walk, was chalk white.

"Eft," he said imploringly, "what's the matter?"

"It is she."

He frowned and at the same time felt his stomach lurch. "She?"

Eft didn't look at him as she spoke, only stared at the ugly scar, which was as long as a team of horses. "The witch who took my kalimar from me."

"Your scaled tail?"

She nodded. "I begged her to do it, and she gave me the legs of a human for it."

"Why?"

Eft took a sharp breath in, then out. Then she told Serafin the story of her first great love; of the merchant's son who'd sworn everlasting faithfulness but then had shamefully betrayed her; of the witch's warning that she could of course change Eft's legs but not her broad mermaid's mouth with the needle-sharp teeth; of how a few men had beaten her half to death while her lover looked on; and how Arcimboldo, at that time still a boy, had found her, cared for her, and taken her in.

"Merle knows the story," she said finally. "She was the first after Arcimboldo to whom I told it. You're the second." Her tone remained expressionless with these words; they were not meant as a distinction, not as a warning, only as a declaration.

Serafin looked from her over to the gray landscape of the witch's face. "And now that she's dead, that means—"

"That I must forever remain what I am today," she said with a thick voice. "Not human, not mermaid."

He looked for a solution, a few hopeful words. "Couldn't another witch—"

"No. The magic of one witch can only be undone by her alone." Her eyes mirrored the bleak sea. "By her alone."

He felt helpless and wished he hadn't come with her, had left her alone with her sorrow.

"It cannot be changed." She didn't sound really collected, but she was trying hard. "We'll go back to the others."

Dejected, he trotted along beside her and imagined how this gigantic creature once had lurked in the depths of the sea, a hideous giantess who hunted for fishing boats and merchant ships—and, in passing, plunged a mermaid in love into unhappiness. He admired Eft's courage: She'd left her home, had swum out into the open sea, into unknown regions, which alone must be creepy for mermaids, and had *begged* a sea witch for something. He knew very well he wouldn't have done it. Not for all the love in the world.

Not even for Merle?

He quickly repressed the thought, but it was hard. He still couldn't imagine what had happened to her. The uncertainty gnawed at him, even when he really wasn't thinking of Merle at all—or other things were more pressing. Surviving, for instance.

The others were sitting where Serafin and Eft had left them. Only Lalapeya had stood up and removed herself from the boys a little, in the direction of the broad tail fin, which floated on the waves like the sail of a sinking ship. She stood alone down there, her arms crossed, and looked out to sea, out into the emptiness.

Dario got up when he saw Serafin and Eft and came to meet them. He was about to say something, perhaps to ask what they'd done, when suddenly Aristide let out a cry.

All faces turned in his direction.

It had not been a call, only an inarticulate sound, born of fear and sheer helplessness.

"What—" Dario fell silent. He saw it too. Just like all the others.

The water surface on both sides of the tail was no longer empty. Heads had appeared, narrow women's faces with long hair that floated, shimmering, on the waves.

Eft took a step forward, hesitated only a moment, then called out in the language of the mermaids. Immediately all the faces in the water turned in her direction. A remarkable chatter arose, sounds of surprise when the mermaids looked into Eft's features, recognized the sharp-toothed mouth, and obviously asked why one of their people walked on legs like a human being.

"I guess those aren't the ones who brought us here?" Serafin's statement was expressed as a question, but he expected no answer.

Eft climbed down over the curve of the tail until the water lapped at her feet. One of the mermaids came closer, and then minutes passed while the two of them spoke with each other in the language of the ocean, entirely without gestures, only with words and tones and strange syllables.

Finally Eft came back to Serafin, and together they went to Dario, Tiziano, and Aristide. Lalapeya also joined them.

"To make it short," said Eft, "there was a fight between two enemy sea witches. The older one lost—we're standing on her right now. The other, a young witch, although she's older than we all are—excluding Lalapeya, of course"—Eft gave the sphinx a half-hearted smile—"the younger therefore claims this part of the undersea as hers."

Undersea. Serafin was hearing this term for the first time, and it called up pictures of the suboceanic kingdoms, images that no human had ever seen and yet everyone knew in his imagination. Images from legends, from fairy tales, from ancient myths.

"We've intruded on her territory." Eft looked nervous, although she sounded calm. "And now she wants to speak with us. Not with all of us. But she wants two of us to go with the mermaids to speak with her and give an account of ourselves."

A murmur ran through the group. Only Serafin and Lalapeya were silent.

"To be honest," said Eft, "I'm really astonished. Sea witches aren't known for dealing with humans. They eat them or do far worse things with them. But they don't talk with them. At least not until today."

"Eat them," Tiziano repeated softly, and Aristide turned ashy.

"What do you suggest?" asked Lalapeya.

"We obey," said Eft. "What else?"

Dario looked out at the good dozen heads dancing on the waves like flotsam. "They couldn't come up here, could they?"

"No," said Eft. "But they could pull the cadaver under. Or ask a hungry whale to eat it out from under our feet."

Dario blanched.

"I'll go with them." Eft's decision was firm. "They have diving helmets with them."

Lalapeya sighed. "I'll go with you."

"No," said Eft. "Not you."

And then she looked Serafin firmly in the eye.

He looked down at the water, then back at the friends—Dario, Tiziano, Aristide—who were staring at him, and finally he again met Eft's gaze.

"I?" He wasn't even certain if he asked the question aloud or if it was merely echoing in his head.

And again images: a mighty shadow, eighty, a hundred yards long; a white body that gradually separated itself from the night-black darkness; eyes that had seen more than fish in the depths; in them infinite wisdom, infinite guile.

Slowly Serafin nodded.

15

Friends

Winds smelling of tar swept around the sides of
the tower and whistled in openings and cracks, singing
with the voices of the lost. For the first time, Merle
thought that perhaps this *was* the Hell of the Bible and not
merely a hollow space in the interior of the earth: the truth
of the myths under a crust of rock and sand and dusky
light.

The tower had three walls, which gradually tapered
toward the top, like a mighty lance point that someone
had planted in the wilderness. Its edges were correspond-
ingly sharp. When Merle looked inside through one of the

windows, she could make out steps of stone in the half-dark. She wondered how angular a staircase with a triangular base would have to be and was glad that Vermithrax was taking them up on the outside.

The obsidian lion stayed close to the wall, only a few yards away from the dark stone. Merle saw insects zigzagging over it and other, larger creatures whose skins matched the background like chameleons; they remained motionless, sunbathing reptiles in a land without sun.

"Merle," said the Flowing Queen, *"do me a favor and look at the falcon. I want to know exactly where he is flying."*

She dutifully turned her eyes upward. The bird shot up close to the tower wall, much more steeply than Vermithrax could. The lion had to take care not to get too vertical or he ran the danger that Merle and Junipa would fall off his back. Also, Merle's arms would hurt even more from the burden, because she had to hold Junipa's additional weight.

For various reasons, the Lilim at their heels were also not flying up the wall any more steeply than Vermithrax. Most of them had broad wings, which bore them forward with great speed; but when it was a matter of climbing upward, they fluttered like the fully fed doves on Venice's Zattere quay.

Earlier, before they'd reached the tower, Burbridge had called something to Merle and Junipa, but they couldn't understand him because of the screaming winds and the noise of many pairs of wings. His smile confused her and frightened her more than she wanted to admit. It wasn't a smile confident of victory, or of premature triumph—no, she almost had the impression that he was again showing his friendliness and kindliness.

Stay with me, I am your friend. Give up, and everything will be fine.

Never in this life!

She could only vaguely estimate how high they were by now. The rocky wastes had long ago melted to a uniform orange; details were no longer discernible. At this height, the tower walls measured around a hundred yards from one corner to the other, and at that, they were only half as wide as those down at the bottom. Merle estimated that they had about half the ascent behind them, at least a mile and then some. The idea of falling off Vermithrax's back at this height was anything but uplifting, and she was aware that her hands instinctively dug deeper into his glowing mane. At her back, Junipa was more silent than ever, but at the moment that was all right with Merle. She wasn't in the mood to talk. Anyway, her breathing was so fast, it was as if she was carrying the others up, not Vermithrax.

"Merle! The falcon!"

The Flowing Queen's cry cut through her thoughts like an axe. It would have made her wince if her muscles hadn't cramped into hard knots long since.

She looked up just in time to see the falcon fly outward, away from the tower, in a gentle arc, turning as he flew, and then, exactly horizontal, disappear into one of the window openings.

Vermithrax reacted immediately, if also quite a bit less nimbly. He moved away from the wall of the tower, turned in a broad spiral, and followed the bird inside. His wings were too wide, and he had to land on the windowsill.

"Pull your heads in!"

He squeezed through the opening as Merle and Junipa pressed as close to him as possible in order not to crack their skulls. But finally they were through, and immediately the glowing body of the lion filled the tower with light.

It was the staircase that Merle had correctly discerned from the outside. It was broad enough to offer room for an army and, because of the triangular form of the tower, even more angled than she'd imagined. The steps were of differing heights; some were slanted, others even curved. They weren't created for humans but for something that had longer and *more* legs. The walls were covered with strange signs, with lines and circles and loops.

"Those are not signs," said the Flowing Queen, as Vermithrax took off again and now began flying up over the steps, a dizzying ascent that almost turned Merle's stomach. Back and forth, in a wide left-hand curve, now

and again interrupted by daredevil maneuvers when a wall appeared unexpectedly behind a curve and Vermithrax only narrowly escaped a collision.

"What do you mean, not signs?" asked Merle.

"They are tracks."

"Things ran along the walls?" She thought of the barbs on the legs of spiders, remembered the Lilim in the Hall of the Heralds, and shuddered. "How old is this tower?"

"Very old. It comes from a time when the lords of the depths were at war with the suboceanic kingdom."

"It's time you told me about that."

"Now?"

"No." Merle pulled her head in between her shoulders as Vermithrax came alarmingly close to the ceiling. "Not now," she said. "But sometime, you won't be able to get out of it anymore."

The Queen was quiet again, but Merle realized why a moment later. Behind them the noise had grown loud, as Burbridge and the Lilim followed up the stairs. The humming of insect wings and the slow rushing of leathery wings echoed from the walls and rebounded a hundredfold on the steps and edges; it sounded as though Burbridge's troops had gained unexpected reinforcements.

"They're going to catch us." Junipa's words were not directed at anyone except herself, but Merle heard them nevertheless.

"No," she countered, "I don't think so." And in fact,

she was suddenly no longer afraid of Lilim. As long as she didn't have to see Burbridge's smile, now concealed behind a corner of the stairwell, the Lilim were, in her mind, only a crowd of clumsy monsters, who were no match for either Vermithrax's strength or his skill. In truth, it was Burbridge alone whom she feared. Burbridge and the Light in him.

The same Light that now also caused Vermithrax to glow, that penetrated him, filled him, that made him bigger, stronger, and more dangerous.

More monstrous?

Perhaps.

Seth—or the falcon he'd become—was no more to be seen, but now there was no further doubt that he was seeking the fastest way up, to an exit used millennia before by those beings the Queen had termed the lords of the depths. The enemies of the suboceanic cultures. The ancestors of the Lilim, whose kingdom had perished when the Stone Light smashed their city.

The farther they got from the floor of Hell, the cooler it became. Perhaps it was because of the shadows inside the tower, Merle thought; perhaps also because of the sweat on her skin and the powerful headwind blowing through her clothing and hair. A look at Junipa's narrow hands on her waist showed Merle that she had gooseflesh too. Of course, Vermithrax was glowing like a powerful lantern, but the glow gave no warmth at all, just like the light inside the dome. He'd bathed in the Stone Light, and no one knew yet what consequences that would have for him and for them all.

"Do not think about it," said the Queen. *"Not now."*

I'm trying not to.

Another corner, another turn of the stairs. Steps in the most unusual forms, which repeated at certain intervals, as if the higher ones were made for large creatures, the lower ones in between for smaller ones. Before Merle's eyes arose the picture of a seething mass of beings shoving and squeezing themselves up the steps, while creatures with many bent stilt-legs stalked over them, and other, still stranger creatures ran along the walls and ceiling effortlessly.

She shivered, and this time the cold wasn't the reason.

"What will he do with us if he catches us?" she asked the Queen, before she realized that she'd spoken the words aloud.

"The same as with me," said Junipa.

Merle felt the Queen's amazement, but still the voice inside her said nothing. Waited.

"What do you mean?" she asked, this time turning directly to Junipa.

"I said, he'll do the same thing to you as he did to me."

Was the throbbing and whirring of wings behind them closer? Or was it only a trick of the acoustics that made it sound louder, more threatening?

"I understood that," said Merle. "But what exactly . . . I mean, if you don't want to talk about it, I could—"

"No." The Queen sounded unusually firm. "She should say it."

But it wasn't necessary for Merle to repeat the question.

"You can feel it if you want," Junipa said softly. Her hand moved from Merle's waist to her right underarm, as if Junipa wanted to loosen its hold on the lion's mane.

"Feel?" asked Merle.

Vermithrax flew a loop. The girls on his back were thrown to the left, and Merle almost lost her grip. She dug her hands into the mane and pressed her knees to the lion's flank. Her heart stopped for a moment.

"Later," she got out between clenched teeth.

Junipa said nothing more, and the Queen also remained silent.

"We must be getting to the top soon!" Vermithrax's words rebounded from the walls, rumbling through the stairwell like rolls of thunder. His light beams passed over the walls like an army of fluttering ghosts.

They'd lost sight of the falcon a long time ago. If there was an exit up there, and Seth reached it first and perhaps attacked them from the front . . .

"Do not think of anything like that," said the Queen.

Merle shivered more and more. The cold was increasing, not only inside her.

"Not much farther!" Vermithrax beat his wings faster, his loops around the sharp bends became ever more head-long.

"They're catching up," Junipa whispered into Merle's ear.

Merle looked back, but she couldn't make out any-thing in the shine of Vermithrax's body. The stairwell at their backs was empty. The sounds of those coming up from below, however, betrayed clearly that their pursuers hadn't given up.

"They're catching up." Once more. Still softer.

Merle shook her head. "I don't think so."

"Yes. Soon."

You can feel it, Junipa had said.

Merle was worried, and all of a sudden, not only because of Burbridge and his Lilim.

An icy wind blasted against them, made her hair flut-ter, and poked a thousand needle pricks through her cloth-ing. Behind them, in the depths, an angry yell sounded.

"What was that?"

"*Only wind,*" said the Queen.

"I mean the yell."

"*Lord Light.*"

"But why?"

"*Perhaps his Lilim cannot take the cold.*"

"Seriously?"

"*I do not think it is ever cold in Hell. They are not used to it.*"

The ice-cold wind was now blowing down steadily from above.

"How far now, Vermithrax?"

"It's getting lighter. There's an exit over us somewhere."

Lighter? She saw only the light that streamed from the lion. It felt as if they were riding on a meteor through the dark shaft. His light flitted over the coarse walls, producing wandering shadows and awakening the furrows and scratches to life; like the creatures who'd left them behind, the tracks appeared to crawl over the walls on spindly legs.

When Merle looked more closely, she realized that the light was reflected, as if the walls were covered with glass—or with ice.

In fact, there were ice ferns on the stone.

From one minute to the next, the cold seemed to her to become even more severe.

In her mind, she turned to the Queen: I take it you don't know where this exit leads either?

"No."

Not into everlasting ice, I hope.

"I do not believe that we have flown so far. Not in such a short time."

Was she deluding herself or was the fluttering of wings from the deep becoming fainter? She heard Burbridge's angry bellow once again, but the shaft behind them remained empty.

Junipa's hands clenched.

"We've just made it," said Merle to cheer her up.

She felt Junipa nod; her chin struck against Merle's shoulder.

The steps under them were now evenly coated with a thin layer of ice. Vermithrax's glow made the surface sparkle in a variety of colors.

Junipa's hands clenched even more tightly around Merle's waist, pressing painfully into her side. She trembled pitifully.

"Not so tight," Merle called behind her. "That hurts."

Junipa must not have heard her, for the pressure remained the same, even increased.

"There, ahead!" Vermithrax glowed even brighter for a moment as the steps fell away under them and they rushed out into a broad hall. The ground plan was triangular, like that of the tower. The slanting walls met high above them at a point in the half-dark, beyond Vermithrax's light.

They'd reached the tip of the tower.

Rubble formed mountains and valleys on the floor of the hall. At some time there'd been a ramp here, but now only the remains of it were discernible. It had led to an opening to the outside, which from afar looked strangely irregular, until Merle realized that it had once been very much wider and today was closed except for a slanting hole. The cold inside the hall was noteworthy; here, too, ice glittered on the rubble and walls.

In front of the opening, under a gray, cloudy sky, there was a balustrade, half destroyed and without railings. But it was wide enough for Vermithrax to be able to land on it. From there they would, hopefully, be able to see what awaited them outside.

The beat of the Lilim wings had faded. Perhaps the Queen was right: The cold had forced them to give up. It was also possible that the sound was merely lost in the breadth of the hall.

Merle tried to wrench herself out of Junipa's painful grip, but the girl's hands were clenching her sides desperately. "Not so tight," she cried once more, again without result.

While Vermithrax was mounting to the balustrade, Merle looked over at the entrance to the stairwell. From above, she could see that a heavy stone slab lay over it, as large as a Venetian piazza. A broad crack had split it from one side to the other; that was the opening through which they'd flown out into the hall. Someone had done everything imaginable, presumably a long, long time ago, to bar the Lilim's way to the upper world. In vain.

The crack gaped like a black mouth in the floor of the hall. Still, none of their pursuers were to be seen.

"We've—"

—shaken them, she was about to say. At that very moment, Junipa pulled her backward.

Merle's stiff, frozen fingers lost their grip on Vermithrax's mane, the Queen screamed something in her thoughts, the obsidian lion's back slid away under them, and then they fell.

Fell down into the darkness.

For a moment Merle believed that she'd fallen through the crack straight back into Hell. But they were way too far away from the stairwell. Instead, the fall ended after a few moments on a slope of loose rubble, a remnant of the ramp, about half the height of the hall. Merle fell flat on her back. It felt as if her back had smashed to pieces. Then she tumbled onto her side, rolled a few yards, and was stopped by a flat piece of stone. It was under an overhang of ruins, so that she couldn't be seen from above.

Junipa landed beside her, cracking against the stone like a bundle of loose bones. But in contrast to Merle she didn't cry out. Didn't utter a sound.

You can feel it. . . .

Merle looked up, peered out through the gap under the overhang, and discovered Vermithrax, glowing like a star in the darkness, much too far away. He flew a loop and looked for her. She tried to call him, but only a croak came from her lips. There was sand in her mouth, grit between her teeth. Her breath steamed white, like smoke. The ground under her was so cold that for a moment she was afraid that her palms would freeze to it. She wasn't used to such cold, not at this time of year, especially not after the warmth of the inner earth.

Junipa.

Merle looked searchingly around for her friend, intending to creep to her to help her. She shrank in horror as Junipa suddenly stood beside her and looked down at her impassively. Her mirror eyes reflected nothing but darkness; they looked like empty holes.

Junipa was bleeding from a wound on her knee, and her palms were scraped, but she seemed not to feel the pain.

Just stared at Merle.

Stared with black mirror shards. With eyes that saw through everything. *I should look into other worlds for him. Into worlds that need a new heart.*

"We must get away from here," said Merle, levering herself up.

Junipa shook her head. "We wait."

"But—"

"We wait."

"*Do you not understand yet?*" asked the Queen.

Of course Merle understood—but she didn't want to admit it. Impossible. Not Junipa.

"*That was no accident,*" said the Queen. "*She did it on purpose.*"

The obsidian lion flew another loop in the darkness and passed the opening through which Merle was able to look out under the overhang. He'd never find her under here, unless somehow she managed to crawl out from underneath it.

But there stood Junipa, right in her way.

"Let me through," said Merle. Her right ankle hurt and hardly bore her weight.

Junipa didn't move. Just stared.

"Let me through."

It was dark under there; the only shimmer of light came from the opening high over them and from Vermithrax. He now called Merle's name, and this time she answered him. But she doubted that her voice made it out from under the overhang all the way up to the lion above.

Junipa took a step toward her. The darkness in her eyes came nearer.

"What did they do to you?" asked Merle.

"You can—"

"Feel it, yes, I know. But I want you to say it to me."

Junipa briefly tilted her head, as if she were considering what Merle meant by that. Then she began to open the placket of her dress. Her flat chest, bony like all the rest of her, shone silvery, as if her entire body had begun to turn into a mirror. But that was only a deception. Only her white, smooth skin.

"Here," she said.

In the darkness, the scar was hardly more than a line, a shadow.

Cross-stitch.

Merle's voice sounded as far away as the rushing of Vermithrax's wings. "You were in the Heart House."

Junipa nodded.

"But why don't I see anything? The wound . . ."

Junipa buttoned her dress again. "A heart of Light heals all wounds." It sounded memorized, a line from a bad poem. But then Merle saw that the wounds on Junipa's knees had closed. Now only a dark spot and a few stripes of dried blood remained.

She looked for rage inside her, for hatred of Burbridge, of the surgeon, of the whole accursed brood. But instead there was only sadness and infinite pity for Junipa. A blind orphan girl in whom cold mirror glass had been set for eyes, and now, on top of it, a new heart. A heart from the Stone Light. She was manipulated and changed at someone else's discretion. And in so doing, he took from her all that was *her own self*.

"*You cannot help her,*" said the Queen.

She is still my friend.

"*Lord Light controls her. Just as the Stone Light controls him. Or them both.*"

She is my friend. I cannot give her up.

"*Merle.*" The voice of the Queen sounded imploring but also sympathetic. "*You cannot rip the heart out of her chest again.*"

Not I. But perhaps someone else. We must try it.

"*You intend to take her with you?*"

Merle gave no answer. Instead she grasped Junipa's hands and was surprised that the girl let it happen. Perhaps a good sign. "Junipa, listen. You don't need to obey him. No matter what he threatens you with. We will find a way to help you."

"Threaten?" Junipa frowned, not understanding. "But he doesn't threaten me at all."

Merle took a deep breath. In the distance she saw Vermithrax's light gliding over the hall walls. But she didn't want to call him for fear of losing Junipa completely. At least Junipa had kept on talking with her and hadn't tried to grab her. Perhaps there was more of the old Junipa still in her than the Queen believed.

Merle forced herself to smile. "Let's get out of here."

"We wait," said Junipa.

"Junipa, please."

The girl drew her arms back, looked blankly from one hand to the other for a moment, then came toward Merle.

With a cry Merle reeled back and crashed against rock. Junipa grabbed her arm, but she was able on her side to grab Junipa's wrist. Merle's instinct commanded her to let go, withdraw, run away, and call out to Vermithrax; the Flowing Queen was also talking at her, pleading with her to give Junipa up, to flee, to get them to safety.

But the girl in front of her was her best friend. And she couldn't help what had happened to her.

Merle wriggled out of Junipa's hold. It wasn't a serious attack, not one that was supposed to injure her. Junipa wanted to hold her, perhaps only for a few seconds, a few minutes. Long enough for Burbridge's Lilim to overcome the cold and retrieve their victims. She couldn't see the crack from here, didn't know if Burbridge was already in the hall. But then she saw Vermithrax's light again and told herself that he wouldn't be there over her if the enemy were already in the vicinity.

Suddenly she received a blow from Junipa that knocked her to her knees. She immediately sprang up again and flung her antagonist against the rubble. Junipa's head cracked on the hard stone and bounced back like a volleyball—then she collapsed and lay motionless. Before Junipa could get up, Merle slid her knapsack from her back, looked for something, anything with which she could defend herself, threw water bottle, mirror, hen's claw carelessly on the ground. And gave up.

What had she expected? To be able to snatch Junipa from this nightmare with cold water? Slowly Merle turned to her, in the certainty of defeat, sensing that Junipa wouldn't give up, not before Burbridge had achieved his goal. And was corrected.

For Junipa still lay stretched on the ground, motionless and with no sign of life. Her mirror eyes were open. They stared into Merle's little hand mirror, which was lying before them on the rocks.

Merle bent for the mirror and the claw and shoved both into her pocket, then she ran, leaping over rubble and fissures, finally emerging from under the overhang. She waved both arms and bellowed Vermithrax's name as loudly as she could, and after a few seconds, she saw the light turn toward her. The obsidian lion shot down out of the darkness. His glow illuminated her surroundings, creating shadows behind angled pieces of debris.

"Where's the girl?" he asked as he landed next to her.

"Wait!" Merle stormed back under the overhang and came back with Junipa a moment later, carrying her like a child in both arms, with wheezing breath and a pain in the small of her back. Junipa was moving her lips, but Merle didn't understand what she was saying.

"We have to take her with us." She was about to say something else, but now her mouth opened without her help, as the Queen took it over. "She belongs to Lord Light! She has betrayed us!" Merle would have liked to bellow with rage, but she couldn't even do that as long as the Queen was controlling her tongue. She pulled all her will together, balled her anger like a fist—and discharged it with a wild yell.

She felt the Queen's astonishment. Her deep uncertainty. Felt how she withdrew, deeper into her interior, shocked at Merle's sudden strong-mindedness.

Don't you do that again! Merle thought furiously. Not ever again!

And she thought, We never once asked him . . . for help for Venice, for Serafin and Junipa and all the others . . . never once asked. In truth, you never intended to, right?

You wanted to be sure you were right about something. That's why we came down here. Was it about Burbridge? Or the Stone Light? No, she thought icily: Basically it was always only about *you*.

Contempt and a deep sense of injury were suddenly her only feelings. And at the same time she realized that the secret around the Flowing Queen was much larger, much more incomprehensible than she could grasp at this moment.

The Queen was silent and Vermithrax, surprised, allowed Merle to load Junipa onto his back. Then she climbed on behind her, wedged the lifeless Junipa backward between her and the lion's neck, curled her hands into Vermithrax's mane, and gave him the signal to take off.

The obsidian lion rose with a mighty flap of his stone wings and flew up to the opening.

Junipa's lips moved more and more vehemently, but Merle dared not put her ear closer to the girl's face, for fear it could be a trick to force her to Burbridge.

But then, very briefly, she did think she understood something that sounded like a word. Something that didn't belong here at all.

"Grandfather," said Junipa.

And then, more clearly: "He is your grandfather."

Merle stiffened.

"*He is not,*" said the Queen. "*She is lying. He is lying.*"

Junipa's eyes opened slowly, and in the mirror eyes Merle saw herself, lit from below by the light of the lion, white as a ghost.

Junipa's features slept, only her eyes remained open, looking through Merle, the shadows, the world. Somewhere into the land of lies, the land of truth.

"Grandfather," murmured Merle.

"Do not do that! That is exactly what he intends. Burbridge is only using her; he invents lies to weaken you."

Merle stared a moment longer into the mirror eyes, at her two white likenesses, then gave herself a shake.

"It wouldn't change anything," she said, but in her head the thoughts were buzzing like a swarm of hornets. "Grandfather or not, he's to blame for what happened to Junipa . . . and all the others."

The Queen must have been feeling what was going on in her, but she restrained herself and kept quiet.

Vermithrax had almost reached the destroyed balustrade when Merle spoke a thought out loud. "Why can he control Junipa but not Vermithrax? Vermithrax has much more of the Stone Light in him than she does."

The lion landed on the broken ledge not far from the opening to the outside. A drifting of snow had blown in and trailed off into ever-thinning white on the dark stone, like feathers from a burst down cushion.

"It doesn't rule me." Since his bath in the Light, the

voice of the lion sounded even more awe-inspiring. "It is mine, but I am not its."

His eyes said: Not yet.

Perhaps it was only an illusion, vanished in a blink. Please, please, please, thought Merle.

Behind him wings whirred in the darkness, slowly, torpidly, and as Merle and Vermithrax looked around, Burbridge on his Lilim hovered in the half dark. The spiral body of the creature wavered and trembled, its eyes glittered even more than before, and Merle saw that it was coated with ice.

You were right, she thought. The Lilim is freezing.

"*Of course,*" said the Queen.

The creature came no nearer, held itself in the air with difficulty, barely twenty yards away from them, and on a level with the balustrade.

Burbridge only looked at her. All the friendliness had departed from his features. The rest of his Lilim troops had not come with him. It must be clear to him that he was running the danger of being attacked by Vermithrax.

However, he was here.

"Merle," he said to her. "Do you know your name? I can tell you your name."

Whose name did he mean? The name of the Flowing Queen? But what—

A gust of wind made the snowdrift swirl up. White flakes, frozen hard like glass splinters, drove over the ragged edge of the balustrade down deeper into the darkness. The Lilim trembled and pulled back.

Burbridge said nothing more, only slowly shook his head. Merle had the feeling that the gesture had nothing to do with the Lilim. Only with her.

Then he kicked the creature in the flanks, and the slender body turned heavily and sank back into the deep, to the crack in the floor, and through it into the stairwell.

Merle detached her gaze from the abyss and looked again into the face of the unconscious Junipa. Her lids were closed now, but through two tiny cracks there was a shimmer of silver. Merle's hand wandered to Junipa's chest. No warmth, no heartbeat. But for a moment she had the impression that light streamed through her fingers, a fan of brightness. However, it paled before she could be certain it wasn't an illusion.

She would help Junipa. Somehow she would help her.

What could Burbridge have meant? *Your name . . .*

Vermithrax bore her outside.

Glowing brightness awaited her, as if the Stone Light had also seized the upper world. But it was only the white of the landscape and the white of the sky. Snow clouds covered the sun. The plain that stretched far below them was buried under a deep layer of snow.

"Winter," whispered Merle.

"In the middle of summer?"

"Winter. He's here."

The Queen hesitated. *"You think . . . ?"*

"He spoke the truth. He arrived here before us."

They stood high over the icy plain, and the wind bit painfully into Merle's face. She'd long since been frozen through and thought it couldn't get worse. But now she felt that the cold would kill her if she couldn't warm up at a fire soon. Her hands shoved themselves into the pockets of her dress on their own. Her right hand touched the oval frame of the mirror, but it was also cold as ice. Only the water inside felt reassuringly warm, as always.

She'd assumed they were standing on a mountain, several dozen yards over the plain. But now as she looked around, she realized that was wrong. The snow-covered surface was smooth, but it was no balustrade as on the inside of the hall.

It was a step. The incline, as she looked down, consisted of a dozen such steps, each several yards high.

"Merle!" Vermithrax's voice made her look up. "On the horizon."

Blinking, she followed his gaze, blinded by the endlessness of the snow. After her eyes had become somewhat accustomed to the brightness, she made out shapes in the distance. Too pointed and symmetrical for mountains. They were constructed of the same steps as those on which they stood.

Merle turned her head and looked up behind her. The stepped incline grew narrower above, ending in a point.

"*Pyramids,*" said the Queen.

Merle could scarcely breathe for cold, but also because she realized where they were.

Egypt.

And the desert was three feet deep in snow.

Merle's hand felt for the water mirror, slid in, into gentle, comforting warmth. And while her eyes kept skimming over the ice, over to the snow-covered pyramids, slender, feminine fingers grasped her own inside the mirror, clasped them, stroked them.

Mother, thought Merle numbly.

The mirror phantom murmured, whispered, murmured.

And somewhere, on the tail fin of a floating sea witch, the sphinx Lalapeya crouched by the water, her hand plunged deep into the sea, and shed silent tears.

The Glass Word

Contents

1

Ice and Tears

THE PYRAMIDS ROSE OUT OF DEEP SNOW.

Around them stretched the Egyptian desert, buried under the mantle of a new ice age. Its sand hills were frozen stiff, its dunes piled high with drifts of snow. Instead of heat waves, ice crystals danced over the plain in swirling wind gusts that revolved a few times and feebly collapsed again.

Merle was crouching in the snow on one of the upper steps of the pyramid, with Junipa's head resting in her lap. The girl's mirror eyes were closed, the lids trembling as though behind them a few beetles were struggling to get free. Ice crystals had caught in Junipa's eyelashes and eyebrows and made them both seem even lighter. With her white skin and her smooth, pale blond hair she looked like a porcelain doll, even without the hoarfrost that was gradually covering both girls: fragile and a little sad, as if she were always thinking of a tragic loss in her past.

Merle was miserably cold: Her limbs trembled, her fingers shook, and every breath she took felt as if she were sucking ground glass into her lungs. Her head ached, but she didn't know if it was because of the cold or what she'd endured on their flight out of Hell.

A flight that had brought them straight here. To Egypt. In the desert. Where the sand and dunes were buried under a three-foot-deep layer of snow.

Junipa murmured something and frowned, but still she didn't open her eyes. Merle didn't know what would happen when Junipa finally awoke. Her friend was no longer herself since her heart had been replaced with a fragment of the Stone Light when she was in Hell. In the end Junipa had tried to turn Merle over to her enemies. The Stone Light, that incomprehensible power in the center of Hell, held her firmly in its grip.

She was still unconscious, but when she woke up . . . Merle didn't want to think about it. She'd fought with her friend once, and she wouldn't do it again. She was at the end of her strength. She didn't *want* to fight anymore, not against Junipa, not against the Lilim down below in Hell, and also not against the henchmen of the Egyptian Empire up here. Merle's courage and determination were exhausted, and she only wanted to sleep. She leaned back, relaxed, and waited for the frosty wind to rock her into an icy slumber.

"No!"

The Flowing Queen roused Merle from her stupor. The voice in her head was familiar to her and at the same time infinitely strange. As strange as the being who'd installed herself inside her and ever since had accompanied her every thought, her every step.

Merle shook herself and marshaled her last reserves. She *must* survive!

She quickly raised her head and looked up at the sky.

A bitter battle was still raging up there.

Her companion, Vermithrax, the winged lion of stone, was engaged in a daredevil air duel with one of the sunbarks of the Egyptian Empire. Vermithrax's black obsidian body had glowed ever since his bath in the Stone Light, as if someone had poured him from molten lava. Now the lion traced a glowing trail in the sky, like a shooting star.

Merle watched as Vermithrax again rammed the wobbling sunbark from above, fastened himself to the sickle-shaped aircraft, and remained sitting on top of it. His wings settled on the left and right of the fuselage, which was about three times as long as a Venetian gondola. The craft rapidly lost altitude under the lion's mighty weight, rushing toward the ground, toward the pyramid—and toward Merle and Junipa!

Merle finally snapped out of her trance. It was as if the cold had laid an armor plate of ice around her, which she now burst with a single jerk. She leaped up, seized the unconscious Junipa under the arms, and pulled her through the snow.

They were on the upper third of the pyramid. If the sunbark's crash shattered the stone, they hadn't a chance. An avalanche of stone blocks would pull them with it into the interior of the structure.

Vermithrax looked up for the first time and saw where the bark's tumbling flight was heading. The air resounded with a sharp crack as he pulled his wings apart and tried to steer the bark's descent. But the vehicle was too heavy for him. It continued on its downward course, straight toward the side of the pyramid.

Vermithrax roared Merle's name, but she didn't take the time to look up. She was pulling Junipa backward along the stone step. She had to pull her foot out of deep snow with every step, and she was in constant danger of stumbling. She knew that she wouldn't be able to stand up again once she fell down. Her strength was as good as used up.

A shrill howling pierced Merle's ears as the sunbark came nearer—an arrow point aimed at her by Fate; there was hardly any doubt that it would knock her into kingdom come.

"Junipa," she gasped out, "you have to help me. . . ."

But Junipa didn't move, though behind her closed lids there was twitching and trembling. But for those signs of life, Merle might as well have been dragging a corpse through the snow, for Junipa no longer had a heart to beat. Only stone.

"Merle!" Vermithrax roared again. "Stay where you are!"

She heard him, but she didn't react and had taken two more steps before the words got through to her.

Stay where she was? What the devil—

She looked back, saw the bark—so close!—saw Vermithrax on the fuselage with outspread wings, which the headwind was trying to blow backward, and recognized what the lion had realized a moment before she did.

The sunbark wobbled even more, swerved from its original trajectory, and was now rushing toward the opposite edge of the pyramid's side, just where Merle had been trying to get herself and Junipa to safety.

It was pointless to turn around. Instead, Merle let go of Junipa, threw herself over her, buried her face in her arms, and awaited the impact.

It took its time—two seconds, three seconds—but when the crash came, it felt as if someone had struck a gong right beside Merle's ears. The vibration was so great that she was sure the pyramid was going to collapse.

The stone was shaken a second time when Vermithrax came down beside them, more falling than landing, snatched up both girls in his paws, and carried them into the air. His body was cool, despite the glow he gave off.

His precaution turned out to be unnecessary. The pyramid was still standing. Occasional clumps of snow broke from the edges and slid one or two steps deeper, to be dispersed in blinding clouds of crystals, momentarily wrapping the incline in a fog of ice. Only after the avalanche had settled could Merle tell what had become of the bark.

The golden sickle lay on one of the upper steps, only a little beyond the place where Merle and Junipa had cowered seconds before. The vehicle had landed sideways, close to the wall of the next step up. From the air, Merle could see only a little damage, a hole in the upper side that Vermithrax had torn in the fuselage.

"Put us down again, please," said Merle to the lion, breathless certainly, but at the same time so relieved that she felt new strength streaming through her.

"Too dangerous." The lion's breath formed white clouds in the ice-cold air.

"Come on. Don't you want to know what was in the bark?"

"Absolutely not!"

"*Mummy soldiers,*" the Flowing Queen interjected in Merle's mind, inaudible to the two others. "*A whole troop of them. And a priest who held the bark in the air with his magic.*"

Merle cast a look over at Junipa, who was dangling in Vermithrax's second paw. Her lips moved.

"Junipa?"

"What's up?" asked Vermithrax.

"I think she's waking up."

"*Once again, just at the right moment,*" the Queen bleated. "*Why do these things always happen just when one does* not *need them?*"

Merle ignored the voice inside her. No matter what it might mean for them all or whether they'd have more trouble because of it, she was glad that Junipa was coming to herself again. After all, she'd been the one who knocked Junipa unconscious, and the thought continued to pain her. But her friend had left her no choice.

"*If she still is your friend.*" It wasn't the first time that the Flowing Queen had read her thoughts; the bad habit had begun way back.

"Of course she is!"

"*You saw her. And heard what she said. Friends do not behave that way.*"

"That's the Stone Light. Junipa couldn't help it."

"*That changes little about the fact that she may try to do you harm.*"

Merle didn't answer. They were floating a good ten yards over the nearest pyramid step. Gradually Vermithrax's firm grip began to hurt.

"Set us down," she asked him once more.

"At least the pyramid appears to be stable," the lion agreed.

"Does that mean we can look at the bark?"

"I didn't say that."

"But there's nothing moving down there. If there are really mummies in there, they must be—"

"*Dead?*" the Queen asked pointedly.

"Out of action."

"*Maybe. Or maybe not.*"

"Those are just exactly the sort of remarks we need," said Merle caustically.

Vermithrax had made his decision. With gentle wing beats he brought Junipa and Merle back to secure ground—as secure as four-thousand-year-old pyramids situated over an entrance to Hell are.

He first set Merle down on one of the stone steps. After she was able to stand, she carefully took Junipa from Vermithrax's grasp. Junipa's lips were still moving. Weren't her eyes open a crack now? Merle thought she saw the mirror glass under the lids.

Slowly she let her friend down into the snow. She was burning to run over to the bark, but she had to take care of Junipa first.

She gently stroked Junipa's cheek. When her frozen fingers touched the skin, it was as if ice met ice. She wondered how long it would be before the first frostbite showed.

"Junipa," she whispered. "Are you awake?"

From the corner of her eye she saw Vermithrax's glowing body tense, noticed the mighty muscle cords that clenched under the obsidian-like fists. The lion was ready to respond to an attack immediately. And his distrust was directed not toward the sunbark alone. Junipa's treachery had made him just as mistrustful as the Queen, only he didn't show it so openly.

The girl's eyelids fluttered, then opened hesitantly. Merle saw her own face reflected in the mirror shards Junipa had for eyes. She hardly recognized herself. As if someone had shown her a picture of a snowman, with ice-encrusted hair and blue-white skin.

We need warmth, she thought with alarm. We'll die here outside.

"Merle," came weakly from Junipa's chapped lips. "I . . . You have . . ." Then she fell silent again and clutched the hem of Merle's dress. "It's so cold. Where . . . are we?"

"In Egypt." Although she said it herself, it seemed as absurd to Merle as if she'd said "On the moon."

Junipa stared at her with her mirror eyes, but the gleaming glass betrayed none of her thoughts. When the magic mirror maker Arcimboldo had implanted them in her and made the blind girl see, Merle had found the gaze of the mirrors cold; but the feeling had never been as appropriate as it was now, in the middle of this new ice age.

"Egypt . . ." Junipa sounded hoarse but no longer as indifferent as she had inside the pyramid, when she'd tried to talk Merle into remaining in Hell. A breath of hope rose in Merle. Had the Stone Light lost its power over Junipa up here?

From the direction of the bark came a metallic sound, followed by creaking.

With a threatening growl, Vermithrax whirled around. Again the ground trembled under his feet.

At the side of the bark—in the wall now facing skyward—a section of the metal snapped outward and stood there for a moment, trembling like an upright insect's wing.

Vermithrax pushed protectively in front of the girls, blocking Merle's view. She almost put her neck out of joint in order to see between his legs.

Something worked itself out of the opening. Not a mummy soldier. Not a priest.

"*A sphinx,*" whispered the Flowing Queen.

The creature had the upper body of a man, whose hips merged into the body of a lion, with sand-colored fur, four muscular legs, and razor-sharp wild animal claws. He appeared not to be aware of Vermithrax and the girls at all, he was so battered by the crash. Blood was flowing into his fur from several contusions; a gouge in his head was particularly deep. After several attempts, he managed to climb feebly out of the hatch, until in the end he lost his balance, rolled over the edge of the bark's fuselage, and fell. He crashed onto the next lower step, as hard as a full-grown buffalo. His blood sprinkled the snow. He lay there, unmoving.

"Is he dead?" asked Merle.

Vermithrax stamped through the snow up to the bark and looked down at the sphinx. "Looks pretty much like it."

"Do you think there are more inside?"

"I'm going to look." He approached the bark in stalking position, low to the ground and with mane on end.

"If the bark was only a scout, what was a sphinx doing on board?" asked the Queen. *"Normally a priest is available for such tasks."*

Merle didn't know too much about the hierarchy of the Egyptian Empire, but she did know that the sphinxes ordinarily occupied the most important positions. Only the high priests of Horus stood between them and Pharaoh Amenophis.

Vermithrax climbed onto the fuselage as agilely as a young cat. Only the soft scratching of his claws on the metal betrayed him. But if there were actually anyone still alive inside, their voices would have warned him long before.

"Why a sphinx?" asked the Queen once more.

"How should I know?"

Junipa's hand felt for Merle's. Their fingers closed around each other's. In spite of the tension, Merle was relieved. At least for the moment, it appeared that the

Stone Light had lost its influence over Junipa. Or its interest in her.

Vermithrax, still prowling, covered the last distance to the open hatch. He pushed his gigantic front claws to the edge of the opening, stretched his neck forward, and looked down.

The attack they were all expecting did not come.

Vermithrax walked all around each part of the hatch that was not obscured by the open cover. He looked into the interior from all sides.

"I am so cold!" Junipa's voice sounded as if she were far away in her thoughts, as if her mind had still not processed what had happened.

Merle pulled her closer, but her eyes remained fixed on Vermithrax.

"He will not go inside there," said the Queen.

What do you want to bet? Merle thought.

The obsidian lion made an abrupt leap. His powerful body just fit through the opening, and as he disappeared inside, its outline glowed. From one moment to the next, their surroundings became gray and colorless. For the first time Merle became conscious of how very much his brightness had made the icy surface around them sparkle.

She waited for a noise, the sound of battle, cries and roars and the hollow crashing of bodies banging against the bark's fuselage. But it remained quiet, *so* quiet that now she began to really worry about Vermithrax.

"Do you think something's happened to him?" she asked the Queen, but then she saw Junipa shrug her shoulders wearily because Merle had spoken the question aloud. Of course after all she'd been through, Junipa had probably forgotten what had happened to Merle. Who could really believe that the Flowing Queen—a legend, an incomprehensible power of whom the Venetians whispered reverently—would one day be living in Merle's mind?

So much had happened since then. Merle wanted nothing more than to tell Junipa of her adventures, of her journey through Hell, where they hoped to find help against the overwhelming Empire. But instead they'd found only sorrow and danger and the Stone Light waiting for them. But Junipa, too. Merle was burning to find out her story. She wanted to rest somewhere and do what she'd done with her friend before, night after night: talk with each other.

A metallic *clang* sounded from inside the bark.

"Vermithrax?"

The lion did not answer.

Merle looked at Junipa. "Can you stand up?"

A dark shadow passed over the mirror eyes. It took a moment for Merle to realize that it was only the reflection of a raptor that was flying over their heads.

"I can try," said Junipa. She sounded so weak that Merle had serious doubts.

Junipa struggled to her feet; heaven only knew where she got the strength. But then Merle remembered how the fragment of the Stone Light in Junipa's chest had healed her wounds in seconds.

Junipa stood up and dragged herself closer to the bark along with Merle.

"Do you mean to climb down there after him?" the Queen asked in alarm.

Someone has to see about him, Merle thought.

Secretly the Queen was just as worried about Vermithrax as Merle was, and she didn't conceal this feeling especially well: Merle felt the Queen's unrest as if it were her own.

Just before she reached the farthest tip of the curving fuselage she looked down at the lifeless sphinx two yards deeper in the snow. He had lost still more blood. It fanned out like an irregular red star, pointing in all directions. The blood was already beginning to freeze.

Merle looked up at the hatch again, but the fuselage of the bark was too high and they'd come too close to be able to see the opening now. It wouldn't be easy to climb up on the smooth surface.

A loud *crack* made them jump, yet it instantly resolved their fears.

Vermithrax was again perched on the fuselage. He had catapulted out of the hatch in one leap and was looking down at the girls with gentle lion eyes.

"Empty," he said.

"Empty?"

"No human, no mummy, and no priests."

"*That is impossible,*" said the Queen in Merle's thoughts. "*The Horus priests would not allow the sphinxes to go on patrol alone. Priests and sphinxes hate each other like poison.*"

You know a whole lot about them, Merle thought.

"*I have protected Venice from the Empire and its powers as long as I could. Do you really wonder that I learned at least a little about them from experience?*"

Vermithrax unfolded one wing and lifted first Merle, then, hesitantly, Junipa beside him on the golden fuselage of the bark. The lion pointed to the hatch. "Climb inside. It's warmer inside there. At least you won't freeze to death."

He had scarcely finished speaking when something gigantic, massive rose up from the emptiness beside the wreck and landed on the fuselage behind the girls with a wet, thumping sound. Before Merle realized it, Junipa's hand was snatched from her own.

She whirled around. Before her stood the wounded sphinx, holding Junipa in his huge hands. She looked even more fragile than before, like a toy in the claws of that beast.

She didn't scream, she only whispered Merle's name, and then she was utterly silent.

Vermithrax was about to shove Merle to one side to better get at the sphinx on the bark. But the creature shook his head, with effort, as if every movement cost him hideous pain. Blood dripped from his head wound onto Junipa's hair and froze solid.

"I'll tear the child to pieces," he got out with difficulty, in Merle's language, but with an accent that sounded as if his tongue were swollen; perhaps it actually was.

"*Say nothing.*" The voice of the Queen sounded imploring. "*Let Vermithrax deal with it.*"

But Junipa—, Merle began.

"*He knows what to do.*"

Merle's eyes fastened on Junipa's face. The girl's fear seemed to freeze on her features. Only the mirror eyes remained cold and detached.

"Don't come any nearer," said the sphinx. "She will die."

Vermithrax's lion tail thrashed slowly from one side to the other, back and forth, again and again. A shrill squeal sounded as he extended his claws and the points scratched on the fuselage.

The sphinx's situation was hopeless. In a fight he wouldn't have been able to do anything against Vermithrax. And yet he armed himself in his own way: He held Junipa in his grip and used her like a shield. Her feet were dangling twenty inches off the surface.

Merle noticed that the sphinx was not standing securely. He had bent his right foreleg just enough that the ball of the paw no longer touched the snow. He was in pain and in despair. That made him unpredictable.

Merle forgot the cold, the icy wind, even her fear.

"Nothing's going to happen to you," she said to Junipa, not certain whether her voice would reach her friend. Junipa looked as if with each breath she was pulling back into herself a little deeper.

Vermithrax took a step toward the sphinx, who evaded him, grasping his hostage tightly.

"Stay where you are," he said in a strained voice. The glow of the obsidian lion was mirrored in his eyes. He didn't understand who or what was standing there before him: a mighty winged lion, who shone like freshly wrought iron— never before had the sphinx seen such a creature.

This time Vermithrax obeyed the demand and halted. "What is your name, sphinx?" he asked in a growl.

"Simphater."

"Good, Simphater, then consider. If you harm a hair of the girl, I will kill you. You know that I can do it. So quickly that you won't even feel it. But also slowly, if you make me angry."

Simphater blinked. Blood was running into his left eye, but he hadn't a hand free to wipe it away. "Stay where you are!"

"You already said that."

Merle saw how every sinew and muscle in the sphinx's arms strained. He changed his grip, grabbed Junipa by both her upper arms, and held her out in the air.

He's going to tear her apart, she thought in a panic. He'll simply break her in two!

"*No,*" said the Queen without any real conviction.

He's going to kill her. The pain is driving him mad.

"*Sphinxes can tolerate much more pain than you humans.*"

Vermithrax radiated endless patience. "Simphater, you're a soldier, and I won't try to lie to you. You know that I can't let you go. Nevertheless, I have no interest in your death. You can fly this bark, and we want to get away from here. That's very convenient, don't you think?"

"Why the bark?" said Simphater with irritation. "We fought up there. You can fly. You don't need me."

"I don't. But the girls. A flight on my back in this cold would kill them in a few minutes."

Simphater's blurry eyes wandered over Merle and the lion, then hovered over the dazzling white of the endless snow fields. "Did *you* do that?"

Vermithrax raised an eyebrow. "What?"

"The ice. It doesn't snow in this desert . . . it never did before."

"Not we," said Vermithrax. "But we know who is responsible for it. And he is a powerful friend."

Again the sphinx blinked. He seemed to be weighing whether Vermithrax was lying to him. Was the lion just trying to make him unsure? His tail switched back and forth, and a drop of sweat appeared on his forehead, despite the icy cold.

Merle held her breath. Suddenly Simphater nodded

almost imperceptibly and set Junipa down gently. She only realized what was happening to her when her feet touched the golden surface of the bark. Stumbling, she ran over to Merle. The two embraced each other, but Merle did not go below. She wanted to look the sphinx in the eye.

Vermithrax had not moved. He and Simphater stared at each other.

"You are keeping your word?" asked the sphinx, sounding almost astonished.

"Certainly. If you get us away from here."

"And do not try any magic tricks," Merle added, but now it was the voice of the Queen who spoke out of her. "I know the sphinx magic, and I will know if you try to use it."

Simphater stared at Merle in surprise and seemed to be asking himself whether he'd underestimated the girl at the lion's side.

No one was more astonished at her words than Merle herself, but she made no attempt to deny the Queen the use of her tongue—even though she'd found out that she could do it.

"No magic," said the Queen, once more through Merle's mouth. And then she added some words to it, which belonged neither to Merle's vocabulary nor to that of any other human being. They belonged to the language of the sphinxes, and their import seemed to impress Simphater deeply. Once more he eyed Merle suspiciously, then his expression changed to one of respect. He lowered his head and bowed humbly.

"I will do what you desire," he said.

Junipa looked confused, but Vermithrax knew well who spoke from Merle. Better than any human he sensed the presence of the Queen, and Merle had asked herself more than once what constituted the bond between the spirit creature inside her and the obsidian lion.

"You get in first," he said to Simphater, pointing to the hatch.

The sphinx nodded. His paws left red impressions in the snow.

A shrill cry resounded over the icy plain, so piercing that Merle and Junipa put their hands over their ears. The scream reverberated over the landscape, out to the scattered snow pyramids in the distance. The ice crust cracked, and at the edges of the steps above and below the bark, icicles broke off and bored six feet deeper into the snow.

Merle knew that sound.

The cry of a falcon.

Simphater froze.

Over the horizon appeared the outline of a gigantic raptor, many times higher than all the pyramids, feathered in gold and with wings so huge it looked as if he intended to embrace the world. When he spread them, they triggered a raging snowstorm.

Merle watched as the icy masses of the plain were whipped and whirled up to them as a white cloud wall; just before they reached the pyramid they lost their strength and collapsed. The gigantic falcon opened his beak and again let out the high scream, still louder this time, and now all around them the snow was in motion, trembling and vibrating as if there were an earthquake. Junipa clung to Merle, and Merle instinctively clutched at Vermithrax's long mane.

Simphater lapsed into utter panic, shrank back with wide eyes, lost his balance on the smooth fuselage of the sunbark, and skittered over the edge into empty space, this time with much greater momentum than before. The next pyramid step did not stop him; he fell farther down, his long legs snapped, his head cracked several times on ice and stone, and the sphinx finally came to rest at the foot of the pyramid, many steps and yards below them, twisted so unnaturally that there could be no doubt that he was dead.

The falcon screamed for a last time, then he closed the wings in front of his body the way a magician closes his cape after a successful magic trick, hid himself behind them, and dissolved.

Moments later the horizon was empty and all was as before—with the exception of Simphater, who lay lifeless in the snow below them.

"Into the bark, quickly!" cried Vermithrax. "We must—"

"Leave?" asked someone above them.

On the next higher step stood a man, unclothed despite the cold. For a moment Merle believed she saw fine feathers on his body, but then they faded. Perhaps an illusion. His skin had once been painted golden, but now only a few smeared stripes of color were left. A fine-meshed netting of gold had been implanted in his bald scalp. It covered the entire back of his head and reached forward to his eyebrows, looking like the pattern of a chessboard.

They all recognized him again: Seth, the highest of the Horus priests of Egypt, personal confidant of the Pharaoh and second man in the hierarchy of the Empire.

He had flown out of the underworld in the form of a falcon after his failed attempt to assassinate Lord Light, the ruler of Hell. Vermithrax had followed the bird, and so they found the pyramid exit that brought them back to the surface.

"Without me you would have gotten nowhere," said Seth, and yet it didn't sound half as fear-inspiring as he probably intended.

The sight of the icy desert disconcerted him, just as it did all the others. At least he didn't appear to be freezing, and Merle saw that the snow under his feet was melting. Not without reason was Seth counted the most powerful magician among the Pharaoh's servants.

"Into the bark!" whispered Vermithrax to the girls. "Hurry up!"

Merle and Junipa rushed over to the hatch, but Seth's voice halted them again.

"I don't want to fight. Not now. And most certainly not here."

"What then?" Merle's voice trembled slightly.

Seth seemed to be considering. "Answers." His hand included the breadth of the icy plain. "To all this."

"We know nothing about it," said Vermithrax.

"You claimed something different before. Or were you trying to deceive poor Simphater in his last moments? You know who's responsible for this. You said he was your friend."

"We are not interested in a quarrel with you either, Horus priest," said Vermithrax. "But we are not your slaves."

The priest was an enemy like no other, and it was not Vermithrax's way to underestimate his opponent.

Seth smiled nastily. "You're Vermithrax, right? Whom the Venetians in ancient times called traitor. You left your folk of the talking stone lions behind in Africa a long time ago to go to war against Venice. Don't give me that thunderstruck look, lion—yes, I know you. And as for your not intending to be slaves: I have no desire to have a servant like you. Your kind is too dangerous and unpredictable. A painful experience we had to suffer with the rest of your people too. The Empire has ground their cadavers to sand in the corpse mills of Heliopolis and scattered them on the banks of the Nile."

Merle couldn't have moved, even if she'd wanted to. Her limbs were frozen; even her heart seemed to stand still. She stared at Vermithrax, saw the anger, the hatred, the despair in his glowing lava eyes. He'd been driven by the hope of one day returning to his people ever since she'd known him.

"You lie, priest," he said tonelessly.

"Maybe. Perhaps I am lying. But perhaps not."

Vermithrax crouched to spring, but the Queen called through Merle's mouth, "Don't! If he is dead, we will never get away from here alive!"

For a moment it looked as though there was nothing that could hold Vermithrax back. Seth even took a step backward. Then, however, the lion got control of himself, but he maintained his ready-to-spring stance.

"I will find out if you spoke the truth, priest. And if the answer is yes, I will find you. You and all who are responsible for it."

Seth smiled again. "Does that mean that we can now set personal feelings aside and come to the nub of our business? You tell me what is going on in Egypt—and I will take you away from here in the bark."

Vermithrax was silent, but Merle said slowly, "Agreed."

Seth winked at her, then looked again at the lion. "Have I your word, Vermithrax?"

The obsidian lion drew his front paw over the metal of

the bark. It left behind four finger-wide furrows, as deep as Merle's index finger was long. He nodded, only once and very grimly.

Ground to sand in the corpse mills, echoed again in Merle's thoughts. An entire people. *Could* that be at all true?

"*Yes,*" said the Queen. "*This is the Empire. Seth is the Empire.*"

Maybe he's lying, she thought.

"*Who knows?*"

But you don't believe it?

"*Vermithrax will find out the truth sometime. What I believe is unimportant.*"

Merle wanted to go to Vermithrax and embrace his powerful neck, reassure him, and weep with him. But the lion stood there as if turned to ice.

She motioned to Junipa and climbed after her down into the interior of the bark.

2

Undersea

SERAFIN AND EFT FOLLOWED THE MERMAIDS DOWN INTO the depths of the ocean.

Both wore diving helmets, transparent spheres that fastened around the neck with a leather band. But what looked like glass was actually hardened water, a legacy of the suboceanic kingdoms, which had collapsed thousands of years before. When Serafin hesitated to entrust his life to the sleek sphere, Eft explained to him that Merle had also swum through the canals of Venice using such a helmet; it was how she'd escaped the henchmen of the Empire.

Serafin had taken a few deep breaths before he put the helmet over his head, only to discover immediately that it wasn't necessary—he could breathe without difficulty under the hardened water, which nevertheless felt like glass. The sphere didn't even steam up on the inside. And after he'd survived the first moments of doubt and rising panic, he got used to it astonishingly quickly.

He and Eft had shaken hands with all the companions, even Lalapeya. The sphinx was continuing to maintain her human form. Then they'd climbed down to the mermaids in the water. Serafin's clothing became sodden with water right away, but not one drop came through the leather band at his neck. He was convinced that the helmets were magic; and if ancient techniques were in fact the reason behind them, they'd long been forgotten, along with their masters.

He'd pictured their descent into the sea witch's kingdom as a fantastic journey through the deep, breathtaking views over coral reefs, intertwining plants, and unknown creatures. Swarms of millions of fish, shimmering and colorful and of piercing beauty.

Instead they were greeted by darkness.

The light from the surface vanished after a few yards. First the surroundings turned dark green, then black. He could no longer see Eft, nor the two mermaids who drew them steeply downward by their hands. The pressure on his body hurt, but nothing more seemed to harm him, which contradicted practically all the theories he'd heard about diving to such depths. It was really naive to ascribe all this to the effect of the helmet, he knew that only too well, but what other choice did he have?

The wall of blackness around him was complete; he couldn't even see his own arms. He might as well have been able to float down bodiless. And perhaps it was exactly that: You gave your body to the coat check at the entrance to the kingdom of the sea witch the way you would elsewhere divest yourself of top hat and coat. It irritated him—no, in truth it frightened him terribly—that he and Eft could no longer see the mermaids, although he kept on feeling their hands. And what if that was only his imagination? What if he'd been floating down alone for a long time, into an abyss of cold and darkness and God knew what sort of creatures?

Don't think about it. Don't drive yourself crazy. Everything is all right. Everything will turn out well.

He called up the memory of Merle's face, her smile, the courage and flash in her eyes, the brave expression around her lips, and her untamable wild hair. He simply had to see her again. For that he would even put up with meeting a sea witch.

Under him—in front of him?—over him?—diffuse lights appeared in the blackness. As they came closer they looked like, yes, like *torches.*

Soon he realized that his guess was very close to the

truth. At wide intervals there were globes hanging in the sea, not firm ones, like his helmet, but wavering, constantly changing their form: air bubbles. And in the bubbles burned fire.

Fire in the deep sea, dozens, hundreds of fathoms under the surface!

By the gleam of the torches he could now make out his companions again, pale apparitions with long hair, women whose hips extended into lithe, scaly tails. Even behind the curtain of floating clouds of particles and inky strands of shadow, their faces would have been of flawless beauty—had it not been for their broad mouths, stretching from one ear to the other and studded with a quantity of razor-sharp teeth. Yet it wasn't the shark's jaws of the mermaids that drew his gaze again and again but their strikingly beautiful eyes.

The air bubbles with flames licking at their curves were now more frequent, and soon he saw the bottom of the sea. The ground was rocky, with extreme variations in height. The light bubbles bobbed gently up and down on bizarre fish bones and spikes, awakened to life by invisible currents, while the deep clefts and canyons lost themselves in blackness. Soon he could recognize that the surfaces of the undersea mountains themselves were covered with structures, ruins of walls, of buildings, of streets and alleys. Whether this place had at one time lain above the water or its inhabitants had lived here like fish remained uncertain. It was clear that this city had been abandoned a long time ago.

If it had been a part of the suboceanic kingdoms, that took away a little of its mystery, Serafin thought—whoever had lived here couldn't have been very much different from ordinary men, for their requirements were the same: walls to hide behind, streets in order not to lose their way, protection behind stone and metal.

The sea witch resided on a cliff, high over the sunken rock country.

She twined like a white worm in the darkness, fire bubbles dancing around her like fireflies—and yet, bafflingly, she escaped their glow, as if her skin were able to protect itself from reflecting the light.

She blew out an air bubble, as large as the freight hold of a trading frigate. She beckoned Serafin and Eft with thin, slender-boned hands. Her long hair floated around her head like a forest of water plants, waving and floating, without ever sinking back onto her shoulders.

She was as large as a mighty tower, even larger than her rival's corpse, which Serafin and the others had discovered on the surface. Her face united the beauty of the mermaids with the menace of a giant octopus.

The air bubble wafted toward Serafin and Eft. Just before it reached the two of them, the mermaids left their sides and whisked away with a few skillful flicks of their scaled tails. Serafin tried to avoid the bubble, but it touched him and drew him inside it. With a gasp he slid down its curve and came to lie at the bubble's deepest point. A moment later Eft landed beside him. She still wore the small knapsack with Arcimboldo's mirror mask on her back, from which nothing and no one could separate her. The straps were fastened so tightly that they cut into her shoulders.

The face of the witch appeared out of the darkness. She formed her lips into a kind of pucker, with which she sucked the bubble toward her. Her gigantic features came closer and closer, finally were as big as a house. Serafin tried to shrink back, but his hands and feet found no hold on the slippery bottom of the bubble. He could only sit there and wait as they steadily approached the witch's mouth.

"She's going to suck us in."

"No, I don't think so." Spellbound, Eft's eyes were fixed on the mighty face, terrible and beautiful at the same time.

"Sea witches are man-eaters," he said doggedly. "Every child knows that."

"Carrion-eaters, that's the difference. They eat dead men, not living ones."

"And who's to keep her from fixing that little flaw with a snap of her fingers?"

"If she wanted to kill us, she could have done it on the surface. But she's just vanquished another sea witch and taken over her kingdom. Maybe she's in a good mood—as far as you can say such a thing about a sea witch."

The face was now about ten yards away. A dozen fire

bubbles slid forward and flickered around the witch's head like a crown. Serafin stared only at her lips, full and dark, no broad slit like the mouth of the mermaids. Behind the lips, teeth gleamed brightly, long and sharp as fence posts.

The wall of the bubble bent in under the witch's features—nose, mouth, and eyes broke in and suddenly were directly in front of Serafin and Eft. The witch had pulled the bubble over her face like a mask. Water ran over her white-gray skin, broad rivulets flowing from the bridge of her nose down to the corners of her mouth and to her chin.

She had the face of a young woman, enlarged to absurdity as if under a magnifying glass. To look her in the eyes was to look so quickly from right to left that Serafin became dizzy, they were so far apart.

Eft had given up any attempt to stand. She remained sitting and did her best to indicate a bow. Serafin gathered that the same was expected of him, and so he did it.

The sea witch looked down at them, a wall of mouth and eyes and grisly teeth. "I welcome you to the under-sea." Her voice was not as loud as Serafin had feared, but the smell that came across her lips pressed him back against the bubble wall like a hot squall. Within seconds the inside of the bubble smelled like a slaughterhouse in the Calle Pinelli. The odor even came through the diving helmet. "What has brought you into my realm?"

"A flight," said Eft straight out.

"From whom?"

"You know what times we live in, Mistress. And from whom men flee."

The witch nodded only slightly, but the movement made the entire bubble tilt and threw Serafin and Eft together. One of the gigantic mouth corners rose in amusement. "The Egyptians, then. But you are no human."

"No. However, I live among them."

"You have the mouth of a mermaid. How can the humans ever accept you as one of their own?"

"I was young when I left the water. I did not know what I did."

"Who took your tail from you?"

"You must smell her scent on me."

Again the witch nodded, and again Serafin and Eft slithered around like insects that a child has trapped in a jar. "I killed her. She was old and stupid and full of evil thoughts."

Serafin thought of the corpse of the witch on the surface. He was amazed at the words of the creature before him. He couldn't have imagined that a sea witch could label something like that evil at all. Or would want to. *They are carrion-eaters,* Eft had said. But did that make them bad by nature? Men also ate dead meat.

"I was never a servant to your rival," Eft said to the witch. "It was a business deal. She was paid for exchanging my scaled tail for legs."

"I will believe that. When she died, she had no servants left. Even some of the other witches feared her."

"Then it was good that you conquered her."

The witch made an encircling movement deep under Serafin and Eft with her tree-size hands. "You know who once lived in this kingdom?"

Eft nodded. "The suboceaners were powerful in this area of the undersea."

"There is still an enormous amount to discover. The ruins of the suboceanic cultures are full of riddles. But I would have a greater compulsion to find them out if I did not have to worry about the Egyptians."

"Why should a being like you have to fear the Pharaoh?"

The witch allowed herself a real smile for the first time. "You need not flatter me, mermaid-with-legs. True, I am powerful here in the undersea. But that which gives the Egyptians power could also become dangerous to me sometime. And yet I do not fear for myself only. The Empire has almost exterminated the mermaids. We sea witches are born to rule, but over whom shall we rule if our subjects become ever fewer? Someday there will be no more mermaids, and then our hour has also come. The sea will become an empty, dead kingdom, full of fish with no understanding."

"Then hatred of the Egyptians unites us," said Eft.

"I do not hate them. I recognize their necessity in the course of things. But that does not mean that I will come to terms with them. With all the anger and the sorrow they have caused me." For a moment the gaze of the huge witch eyes was turned inward, lost in thought and heavy with care. Just as quickly her attention returned to the here and now. "What will you do if I let you go?"

Serafin had remained quiet for the entire time, and now, too, he thought the most reasonable thing was to leave the talking to Eft. She knew best how to deal with such a being. "The humans who are with me will die of thirst on the wide sea," said Eft. "And I do not want to go on alone. I would rather die."

"Great words," said the witch. "You mean them seriously, don't you?"

Eft nodded.

"What is your goal?"

Yes, thought Serafin, *what really is our goal?*

"Egypt," said Eft.

Serafin stared at her. The witch noticed it.

"Your companion is of another opinion?" The question was formulated as if it were addressed to Eft, but in fact the witch was now looking at Serafin, and she was expecting that he would give an answer.

"No," he said uncertainly. "By no means."

Eft gave him the shadow of a smile. Turning to the witch, she said, "Our only choices are hiding or fighting. I will fight. And I am sure my friends will choose the same course once they have the opportunity to think about it."

"You intend to attack Egypt?" asked the witch scornfully. "You alone?"

Serafin thought of the small troop waiting for them on

the surface of the water. He guessed that Dario, Aristide, and Tiziano would join them. But Lalapeya? She was a sphinx, even if she'd assumed the form of a human. Already, in Venice, she'd taken a stand against her people and so against the Empire, but the defeat had worn her out. He wasn't sure that she was ready to carry on the fight now. Or what sort of a reason she might have for it.

Anyway, what did that really mean, "fight"? What would that look like? The witch was right: At best they were six—against the combined power of the Pharaoh and the sphinx commanders.

Again the witch put the question to Eft: "You want to attack Egypt?"

Eft smiled, but the effect was grim. "We will find ways to injure them. Even if it's small things: a raid here, a dead priest there. A leaking ship, perhaps a dead sphinx once in a while."

"Nothing of that will even reach the ear of the Pharaoh," said the witch, "not to mention worry him."

"That doesn't matter. The act counts, not the result. You must understand that, Mistress. Did you not speak of exploring the ruins of the suboceanic kingdoms? What's your purpose in that? They will not rise again in their old glory. No result—only the will to do it. Just as with us."

"Are you speaking of obsession?"

"I would call it dedication."

The witch was silent, and the more minutes that passed,

the more convinced Serafin became that Eft had adopted the right tone. At the same time, it was clear to him that the mermaid had meant every word seriously. That frightened him a little, but he also admired her determination. She was right. He would go with her, no matter where.

"What is your name?" asked the witch finally.

Eft told her. Then she added, "And this is Serafin, the most skillful of the master thieves of Venice. And friend of the mermaids."

"You are mad, but you are also brave. That pleases me. You are a strong woman, Eft. A dangerous woman, for others and for yourself. Be careful that the scales don't tip too much to your side."

It had never occurred to Serafin that sea witches could be wise. Behind the fearsome facade there was far more than the bestial hunger for human flesh.

"Does that mean you are letting us go?" Eft spoke matter-of-factly, without any emotion.

"I am not only letting you go, I am going to help you."

The witch's words might have impressed Serafin, but that didn't mean he wanted her for a companion. No, not at all.

But the witch had something else in mind. "My hand-maidens will take you back to your companions. Wait there for a while. Then you will find out what I mean."

And that was what happened.

The face of the witch withdrew from the bubble and sank into the darkness. Serafin discerned its warped outlines in the shadows one last time before the fire bubbles all around went out and the titanic being became one with the darkness.

They returned the way they had come. As they broke through the surface and saw the light of day over them, Serafin uttered a thankful sigh. Perhaps he wasn't the first human who'd survived an audience with a sea witch, but certainly one of the few. He'd learned as he listened to her, and his picture of the world had become yet a little more faceted, livelier, more varied. For that he was grateful to her.

Dario and the other boys helped them out of the water, up onto the floating corpse of the old sea witch. *Full of evil thoughts,* cried a voice from the deep into Serafin's mind, and now he found it even a little more disgusting to place his feet on the dead flesh of the corpse and to support himself on his hands while climbing up onto it.

Lalapeya awaited them on the ridge of the lifeless scaled tail. The sphinx did not smile, but she acted relieved. It was the first time since their flight from Venice that Serafin saw anything in her expression other than grief and sorrow.

They took turns reporting what had happened and were not interrupted by the others one single time. Even when Eft told what goal she'd named to the witch, no one argued.

Egypt, then, thought Serafin. And in an absurd, nightmarish way, it felt *right.*

An hour or two later the water began to boil, and something mighty rose from the sea.

3

The Heart of the Empire

THE SUNBARK FLEW LOW, FOLLOWING THE COURSE OF THE frozen Nile. It was buffeted by the winter winds, but at least no snow was falling, which could have forced them down.

Merle gazed out through the window slits. Below them the land lay dazzlingly white. The once green banks of the Nile hardly contrasted with the desert anymore—everything was buried under a thick layer of snow. Here and there a frozen palm grove protruded from the ice, and sometimes she saw ruins of huts, the roofs crushed by the weight of the snow.

Where are all the people? she wondered.

"Frozen to death, perhaps," the Queen said in her thoughts.

Only perhaps? Merle asked.

"If the Pharaoh had not already incorporated them into his mummy armies."

You think he would have completely wiped out his own people to fill his army?

"You must not think of the Pharaoh as an Egyptian. He was a devil, even when he was alive more than four thousand years ago, but he has not been a human since the high priests awakened him. Whether the people who lived here on the Nile were ever his own is no longer of any consequence. Probably he saw no difference between the people here and those in all the other lands he conquered."

A land without people? But then who is he waging this war for?

"Not for the Egyptian people, that is certain. Perhaps not even for himself. You must not forget the influence of the priests of Horus on him."

Junipa was leaning on the wall of the bark beside Merle, her knees drawn up and her arms around them. Merle felt that Junipa was observing her, sometimes openly, sometimes covertly. Seth had fallen into a kind of trance after the bark's takeoff, which was probably necessary to steer the flight. Merle had observed him for a long while; then she'd decided to use the opportunity to tell Junipa everything that had happened since they'd parted

646

at Arcimboldo's in Venice. The girl with the mirror eyes listened, passively at first, then with increasing interest. But she said nothing, asked no questions, and now Junipa was sitting there, and Merle could virtually feel what was going on in her friend's mind, as if Junipa were waiting for a sign of the Flowing Queen.

Merle's eyes wandered over to Seth, who sat on a pedestal in the front part of the bark, his face turned toward the inner space. A vein stood out on his forehead and disappeared beneath the golden network. Nevertheless, Merle thought she felt him groping toward her with invisible feelers. Once before, at their first encounter, she'd had the feeling that he was looking straight into her interior—and that he saw who was hidden there.

She wondered whether the Queen shared her perceptions, but this time she received no answer. The thought that even the Flowing Queen could be afraid of the most powerful of the Horus priests frightened her.

Seth was steering the bark by the power of his thoughts. The golden vehicle floated almost one hundred feet over the pack ice of the Nile, not very fast, for the cover of snow clouds over them was unbroken and no sunbeam pierced it. The diffuse daylight was enough to keep the bark in the air, but it wasn't strong enough to speed it up.

Merle had assumed that there would be strange equipment inside the bark and a sort of console like the ones in the steamboats that crossed the Venetian lagoons. But there was nothing like that. The interior was empty, the metal walls bare. They hadn't even installed benches—comfort was of no value to the undead mummy troops usually transported in the barks. The airship had all the charm of a prison cell.

Vermithrax stood right in front of Seth and kept his eyes on the priest. He'd folded his wings, but his claws were extended the entire time. His lava glow filled the interior of the bark with radiant brightness, which was reflected from the metal walls. The golden glow burned in Merle's eyes, even penetrating through the lids; she felt as if she'd been enclosed in amber.

Junipa had her eyes closed, but Merle knew that she could see anyway. With her mirror eyes she looked out through the lids, in the light as well as in darkness, and if Professor Burbridge had told the truth, she was also able to see into other worlds with them. That was more than Merle could imagine. More than she *wanted* to imagine.

The task of telling Seth the truth about the new ice age had fallen to Merle, of course. Vermithrax would rather have had his eyeteeth pulled than to fulfill a wish for the hated priest.

And so Merle had told the story of Winter, the mysterious albino whose life she'd saved in Hell. Winter, who'd insisted he was a season become flesh, searching for his missing love, Summer. She'd vanished years ago, he said, and since then there'd no longer been any real summer in the world, no July heat and no brooding sun in August. In Hell, Winter was only an ordinary human, but he'd told how on the surface he brought ice and snow with him, under which he buried the land. Winter could touch no living creature without freezing that being to ice in an instant. Only Summer, his beloved Summer, withstood this curse and nullified it with her singeing heat. Only those two could lie in each other's arms without killing one another, and it was their fate to belong to each other forever.

But now Summer was gone and Winter was searching for her.

Professor Burbridge—or Lord Light, as he was called as the ruler of Hell—must have given Winter a clue that lured him here to Egypt for the first time in thousands of years. In his wake, snowstorms had smoothed out the dunes and deadly ice lay over the desert.

There was no doubt that Winter had been here. Just like Merle, he'd left Hell through the steps inside the pyramid. But where did his path lead? Toward the north, apparently, for Seth was steering the bark northward, and as yet there was no end to the snow.

Seth had listened to her report and not interrupted her once. What was going on in his head remained his secret. But he'd kept his word: He'd gotten the bark into the air and so saved their lives. He'd even succeeded in producing a dry warmth inside the airship, which came from the gold layer on the walls.

"*He knows more about Winter than he is admitting,*" said the Queen.

Where do you get that? Merle asked in her thoughts. Her ability to speak soundlessly with the Queen had improved markedly in the days since their descent into Hell. She always found it easier to form the words with her lips, but she'd gotten quite good at the other way too, when she concentrated.

"*He is the second man of the Empire, the deputy of the Pharaoh,*" said the Queen. "*If the Egyptians have something to do with Summer's disappearance, he must know about it.*"

Summer is here?

"*Well, Winter is in Egypt. And he will have a good reason for it.*"

Merle looked over at Seth once again. With his closed eyes and relaxed facial expression he had lost something of his external menace. All the same, she did not for one second harbor the illusion that he could have anything else in mind except killing them all at the end of their journey. Their lives would depend on Vermithrax's getting to him first. The battle between the lion and the priest was unavoidable.

Seth's words had hit Vermithrax in a place that was vulnerable, despite all his strength. The words had sown doubt in him, doubt in that one bright spot that had given him hope of a better future. The reunion with his people, whom he'd long ago left behind somewhere in Africa, had always been the goal for Vermithrax, the end point of his journey. And now he was nagged by the fear that Seth might have spoken the truth, that the talking stone lion people had been extinguished by the Empire.

Merle turned to the Flowing Queen again: Do you think that's true?

"*The Empire would be capable of it.*"

But the lions are so strong. . . .

"*Other peoples were too. And they were more numerous than the free lions. Nevertheless, every single one of them was killed or enslaved.*"

Merle looked out the window. Who were they fighting for, actually, if there was no one left out there in the world? In an absurd way, that linked them to the Pharaoh: They were all engaged in a battle whose real goal they had long lost sight of.

Seth opened his eyes. "We'll be there soon."

"Where?" asked Merle.

"At the Iron Eye."

"What's that?" Merle had assumed that he was taking them to Heliopolis, the Pharaoh's capital city. Perhaps even to Cairo or Alexandria.

"The Iron Eye is the fortress of the sphinxes. From there they watch over Egypt." His tone was disparaging, and for the first time it occurred to Merle that Seth might be ruled by other motives than the absolute will for power. "The Iron Eye is in the Nile delta. It will come into sight soon."

Merle turned to her window slit again. If they were that far north, they must already have flown over Cairo. Why hadn't she seen anything of it? The snow was piled high, but not high enough to bury a city of millions of people.

It must be, then, that someone had leveled Cairo. Had there possibly been some resistance by the Egyptian people after the Pharaoh and the priests of Horus had seized power? The idea that Cairo and all its inhabitants had been annihilated took Merle's breath away.

Junipa's voice snatched her from her thoughts. "What do you want with the sphinxes?" she asked the priest.

Seth looked at Junipa for a long moment, expressionless. Then he smiled suddenly. "You are a clever child. No wonder they put the mirror eyes in you. Your friends were probably asking themselves what *they* were supposed to do in the Iron Eye. But you ask what drives *me* there. And that's just what it comes down to, isn't it?"

Merle wasn't sure she understood what he was talking about. She glanced at her friend, but Junipa did not betray what was in her mind by any emotion. Only when she spoke again did Merle understand where she was going— and that in fact she was right about it.

"You don't like the sphinxes," Junipa said. "I can see that."

For a fraction of a second Seth appeared surprised. Then he immediately had himself under control again. "Possibly."

"You are not here because the sphinxes are your friends. You are not going to ask the sphinxes for help, to kill us."

"Do you really believe I need help for that?"

"Yes," said Vermithrax; it was the first time he'd spoken in hours. "I certainly do believe that, utterly."

The two antagonists fixed each other in a stare, but neither went any further. Not here, not now.

Again it was Junipa who eased the tension. Her gentle, infinitely relaxed voice groped for Seth's attention. "You tried to kill Lord Light, and you returned from Hell into a land that has turned into a desert of ice. Why didn't you make your way to the court of the Pharaoh first or to the temple of the Horus priests? Why straight to the stronghold of the sphinxes? That is quite remarkable, I think."

"And what, in your opinion, might all that mean, little mirror maiden?"

"A fire in your heart," she said enigmatically.

Merle stared at Junipa before her eyes met those of the obsidian lion. For a moment, amazement drove the coldness out of Vermithrax's eyes.

Seth tilted his head. "Fire?"

"Love. Or hate." Junipa's mirror eyes glowed in the golden shine of the lion. "More likely hate."

The priest was silent, thinking.

Junipa spoke again: "Vengeance, I think. You hate the sphinxes, and you are here to destroy them."

"By all the gods!" murmured the Flowing Queen in Merle's mind.

Vermithrax was still listening intently, and his eyes moved from Junipa back to Seth. "Is that true?"

The priest of Horus paid no attention to the lion. Not even Merle, whom he'd observed constantly before, appeared to have any importance for him now. It was as if he were alone in the bark with Junipa.

"You are actually an astonishing creature, little girl."

"My name is Junipa."

"Junipa," he repeated slowly. "Quite astonishing."

"You're no longer the right hand of the Pharaoh, are you? You lost everything when you didn't succeed in killing Lord Light down there." Junipa thoughtfully turned a strand of her white-blond hair between thumb and forefinger. "I know that I'm right. Sometimes I see not only the surface but also the heart of the matter."

Seth sighed deeply. "The Pharaoh betrayed the Horus priests. He gave me the commission to murder Lord Light. The sphinxes prophesied to Amenophis that someone would come out of Hell and kill him. Therefore he intended that I should kill Lord Light—and best that I

654

should also die while doing it. Amenophis had all my priests taken prisoner and threatened to kill them if my mission was not successful."

"Now," said Vermithrax with pleasure, "you are ruined. My congratulations."

Seth glared at him, but he made no reply. Instead he continued, "I am certain that Amenophis already knows that Lord Light is still alive." He lowered his eyes, and Merle almost wished she could feel pity for him. "My priests are now dead. The cult of Horus exists no more. I am the only one left. And the sphinxes have taken our place at the side of the Pharaoh. It was planned thus from the beginning: We should awaken Amenophis again and lay the foundations of the Empire. The sphinxes are the ones who are now harvesting the fruits of all our labors. They waited in the background until the time was ripe to draw the Pharaoh to their side. They got him to betray us. The sphinxes used Amenophis, and they used *us*. We were manipulated without knowing it. Or, no, that's not right. Others warned me, but I threw their advice to the winds. I didn't want to believe that the sphinxes were playing a false game with the Empire. But it was always going toward one thing: The Empire conquers the world, and the sphinxes take over the Empire. They made us into their tools, and I was the most gullible of all, because I closed my eyes to the truth. My priests had to pay the price for my mistake."

"And now you are on the way to the sphinxes to avenge them," said Junipa.

Seth nodded. "*That*, at least, I can do."

"*My heart is quite heavy,*" the Queen remarked sarcastically.

Merle paid no attention to her. "How do you intend to annihilate the sphinxes?"

Seth appeared a little shocked at his own openness. He, the most powerful of the Horus priests, destroyer of countless lands and slaughterer of entire peoples, had openly spoken his thoughts to two children and an embittered stone lion.

"I don't know yet," he said after a moment of thoughtful silence. "But I will find a way."

Vermithrax snorted scornfully, but not as loudly as he would probably have done *before* Seth's avowal. The priest's candor had surprised him, too, even impressed him a little.

Nevertheless, no one made the mistake of considering Seth an ally. If it meant an advantage for him, he would sacrifice all of them at the first opportunity. This man had extinguished tens of thousands with a wave of his hand, had burned cities to the ground with a brief command, and desecrated the cemeteries of entire nations in order to make the bodies into mummy soldiers.

Seth was no ally.

He was the devil himself.

"*Good,*" said the Flowing Queen. "*And I was beginning to think he was going to wind all of you around his finger with his entertaining little tragedy.*"

Merle grasped Junipa's hand. "What more do you know about him?" she asked, disregarding Seth's blazing look.

The mirror eyes reflected Vermithrax's golden glow with such intensity that Merle's image in them glowed like an insect in a candle flame. "Seth is a bad man," said Junipa, "but the sphinxes are infinitely worse."

Seth gave a slight, scornful bow.

"That will look good on your tombstone," said Vermithrax grimly.

"I will order that it be chiseled out of your flank," returned the priest.

Vermithrax scraped one of his paws across the floor but refused to be drawn into another battle of words. He preferred a battle with sharp claws to such subtleties.

Merle regarded Junipa with growing concern for a long moment, but then her eyes strayed to the window—and beyond it the monstrosity that rose over the delta of ice.

"Is *that* the Iron Eye?"

Seth didn't look out, keeping his expressionless gaze on Merle. No one needed his confirmation. They all knew the answer.

Junipa also pressed her face against the narrow glass. Ice patterns had formed around the edges of the windows, finely branching fingers that reached toward her mirror eyes.

It looked like a mountain, a pointed cone of ice and snow, an unnatural pucker in the flat landscape, as if someone had bunched the horizon together like a piece of paper. As they came closer, Merle could make out details. The image in front of them was pyramid-shaped, but with steep slopes, cut off at the top as if someone had struck off the point with a scythe, and there, in place of the point, peeling itself out of the snowdrifts, was a collection of towers and gables, balconies, balustrades, and arcades of columns. Whatever was hidden in the interior of the Iron Eye, that up there was the *true* eye. It seemed to Merle like the crow's nest of a gigantic ship, which could look out over the country and perhaps the entire Empire. The colossus—was it of steel or stone, or really made of iron?—appeared to Merle functional, without decoration, without any useless flourishes. But the upper buildings with which the fortress culminated sparkled in fantastic elegance: playful buildings with much decoration, narrow bridges, and extravagantly framed windows. If there was a place where the sphinxes really *lived*—not reigned, not commanded—then it was there at the tip of the Iron Eye.

The fortress was high, perhaps higher than the sky; but no, it was just that the cloud cover was hanging so gray and heavy over it, as it had everywhere on their journey. All-powerful the Iron Eye might be, but not supernatural, not heavenly.

He is a bad man, but the sphinxes are infinitely worse.

Merle heard Junipa's words about Seth once more, a whispering echo in her thoughts.

The bark circled in a wide arc around the whole area. Merle was not sure what Seth was intending by that. Did he mean to impress them with a final glorification of his magic powers? Or did he want them to see the power of the sphinxes along with the fortress? A warning?

Finally he guided the bark toward one of the countless openings in the south side of the eye, horizontal slits in the snow-covered white of the steep side. As they approached, Merle could see a whole squadron of sunbarks inside.

A dozen reconnaissance craft circled around the fortress, keeping the frozen arms of the river delta under surveillance. Yet their movements were sluggish, the cloudy sky having robbed the dreaded sunbarks of their agility. The birds of prey had turned into lame ducks.

"What are you going to do now?" Merle asked.

Seth closed his eyes again, concentrating on the landing. "I must land the bark in the hangar."

"But they'll see us when we disembark."

"That's not my problem."

Vermithrax took a step toward Seth. "It could easily become yours."

Once more the priest opened his eyes, but his gaze was directed toward Junipa, not at the lion who threatened him. "I could try to land up on the platform. The patrols will see it, but if we have any luck, we would already have disappeared between the buildings by that time."

"Why is he risking his life for us?" the Queen asked mistrustfully.

"That's a trick," growled Vermithrax also.

Seth shrugged, now with his eyes closed again. "Do you have a better suggestion?"

"Take us away from here, now," said the lion.

"And the truth you are seeking?" Seth smiled. "Where else will you find it?"

Vermithrax was silent then. Merle and Junipa said nothing more either. They had the choice between being set down in the snow again or hiding somewhere in the Iron Eye until they'd agreed on a reasonable plan.

Just before the hangar opening, the bark swerved, rose, and floated upward in a broad spiral. Merle tried to keep the patrols in sight, but her vision was limited by the narrow window slits, and she could make out only a single flying sickle in the distance. Finally she gave up. She had to resign herself to the fact that at the moment her life lay in Seth's hands alone.

The bark needed several minutes to reach its target. Merle turned to the other side of the airship so that she could look at the buildings more closely. Thick caps of snow lay on all the roofs, balconies, and projections, and the vacant edge of the platform was so deeply snowed in that Merle questioned whether they could leave the bark at all there. It would be next to impossible to run away from their opponents in the deep snow.

Seth let the sunbark sink to the ground. It landed gently on the snow, accompanied by the crunching and snapping of the icy crust. The first buildings were more than twenty yards away from them. Through the window slits Merle saw narrow, deep lanes between the buildings. Considering the numerous roofs and towers, there must be a real labyrinth of lanes and streets in there.

Involuntarily Merle thought of Serafin. Of how, as a master thief, he would have known how best to move inconspicuously through such a maze of streets.

Of how very much she missed him.

"Get out of here!" Seth's voice wiped Serafin's face from her thoughts. "Quick, *get moving!*"

And then she ran. With Junipa by the hand. Occasionally without her too. Then with her again. Stumbling. Freezing. Without daring to look up, for fear she might see a bark diving down at her.

Only when they'd taken cover behind a wall, one after the other and even Seth and Vermithrax almost harmoniously side by side, did Merle dare breathe again.

"What now?" The lion was staring tensely at the edge of the platform, where the glittering snow field ended abruptly in front of the gray of the cloud background.

"You can go where you want to." Seth cast a sideways look first at Merle, then at Junipa. It didn't escape Merle how piercingly he kept examining Junipa, before in the bark and now here outside, and she didn't like it at all.

Junipa herself didn't notice. She had placed a hand flat on the wall of the building, and now a suppressed groan came from her throat. With a jerk she pulled her arm back and stared at her palm—it was red as fire, and on the palm glowed droplets of blood.

"Iron," said Vermithrax, while Merle bent over Junipa's hand worriedly. "The walls are actually made of iron."

Seth smiled to himself.

The lion sniffed a finger's breadth away from the wall. "Don't touch! The cold will make your skin stick to it." And then he seemed to remember that Junipa had already made exactly that mistake. "Everything all right?" he asked in her direction.

Merle had used her sleeve to blot the blood from Junipa's hand. It wasn't much, and it didn't keep flowing. Junipa was lucky. Except in a few places where the thin outer layer of skin had peeled off and was still stuck to the iron, she wasn't injured. In a normal person it would have taken one or two days until she could clench her fist again, but Junipa carried the Stone Light in her. Merle had seen with her own eyes how quickly Junipa's wounds healed.

"It'll be all right," she said softly.

Seth shoved Merle aside, took Junipa's hand in his, whispered something, and then let it go again. Afterward the redness paled, and the edges of the shredded skin had closed.

Merle stared at the hand. Why did he do that, she thought. Why is he helping us?

"*Not us,*" said the Flowing Queen. "*Junipa.*"

What does he want from her?

"*I do not know.*"

Merle wasn't sure she wanted to believe her. The Queen still had too many secrets from her, and if she thought about it carefully, new riddles were constantly appearing. Merle didn't even take the trouble to hide these thoughts from her invisible guest. The Queen might as well know that she didn't trust her.

"*Seth is playing a double game,*" said the Queen. Again mistrust rose in Merle. Was the Queen trying to divert attention from herself?

The priest had turned away from the little group and hastened, stooping, through the snow to a door that led into the interior of the building: a high tower with a flat roof, whose upper surface was covered with a bizarre pattern of ice tracery. At first look, it wasn't possible to see that under the crust of frost was concealed polished metal.

"Wait!" Vermithrax called after the Horus priest, but Seth acted as if he hadn't heard the lion. Just before the door he stopped and looked behind him briefly.

"I don't need the extra baggage of children and *animals.*" The way he emphasized the word was an open challenge. "Do what you want, but don't run after me."

Merle and Junipa exchanged a look. It was too cold out

here, the wind was as cutting as broken glass. They had to get inside the fortress, no matter what Seth thought about it.

With two sliding steps Vermithrax was beside the priest and shoved him aside, a bit more roughly than necessary. When he noticed that the door was barred, he pushed it in with a blow of his paw. Merle realized that the lock had broken and the door was made of wood. Only the outer surface was overlaid with a reflective metal alloy. Perhaps the walls were made the same way and were not really of massive iron, as she'd supposed until now. She wasn't at all sure if ordinary iron could reflect like that; probably it was some other metal. Real iron existed only in the name of the fortress.

"That was certainly discreet," Seth observed mockingly as he walked past Vermithrax into the interior of the building. Beyond lay a short corridor, which led into a stairwell.

Everything was silvery and reflective, the walls, the floor, the ceiling. Inside, the mirrors were no longer of metal but of glass. They saw themselves reflected in the walls of the passages, clear as glass, without any noticeable distortions. Since the mirror walls on both sides of the corridors lay opposite each other, their likeness continued into infinity, a whole army of Merles, Junipas, Seths, and obsidian lions.

Vermithrax's glow shone in the multiplication as brightly as a sun, a whole chain of suns, and what had been quite useful to them up till now—a constant source of light, entirely without lamps or torches—became a treacherous alarm signal to anyone who approached them.

The stairs were wider than in a human building. The intervals had to fit the four lion paws of a sphinx, and the height of the individual steps was also enormous. For Vermithrax, however, the unusual dimensions were an advantage, and so he took Merle and Junipa on his back and observed with satisfaction how Seth was soon sweating with exertion.

"Where are we going, actually?" Merle asked.

"*I would like to know that too,*" said the Queen.

"Down," retorted Seth, who was walking in front.

"Oh?"

"I didn't ask you to come with me."

Vermithrax tapped him on the shoulder with the tip of his wing. "Where?" he asked with emphasis.

The priest stopped, and for a few instants such fury blazed in his eyes that Merle felt Vermithrax's muscles tense under his coat. She wasn't even sure if it actually was only fury that raged in the priest's head: Perhaps it was magic—black, evil, lethal magic.

But Seth laid no spell on them. Instead he glared at Vermithrax for a moment longer, then said softly, "Soon it will be swarming with sphinxes up here. Someone will notice that we landed on the platform. And I don't want to be here when that happens. Farther down it's easier to hide. Or do you think in all seriousness that sphinxes are dumb enough to overlook thousands of lions who shine like the full moon and perhaps have as much intelligence?" And with that he pointed to the endless line of Vermithrax's reflections all around them in the stairwell.

Before the obsidian lion could reply, Seth was on his way again. Vermithrax snorted and followed him. As they rocked quickly downward, Merle observed herself and Junipa in the mirrors. It gave her a headache and made her dizzy, and yet she could not escape the fascination of this apparent endlessness.

She remembered again the magic water mirror in her pocket and the mirror ghost who'd been trapped inside since the beginning of her journey. She pulled the shimmering oval out and looked at it. Junipa was looking over her shoulder.

"You still have it," Junipa stated.

"Sure."

"Do you remember how I looked into it?"

Merle nodded.

"And I wouldn't tell you what I saw in the mirror?"

"Are you going to tell me now?" asked Merle.

They both looked for a moment longer at the wavering surface of the water mirror, at their own wobbling faces.

"A sphinx," Junipa said softly, so that Seth could not hear her. "There was a sphinx on the other side. A woman with the body of a lion."

Merle let the mirror sink, until its cool back touched her thigh. "Seriously?"

"I don't make jokes," said Junipa sadly. "Not anymore, not for a long time."

"But why—" Merle broke off. Until now she'd believed that the hand that reached for hers on the other side of the water mirror when she shoved her fingers into it belonged to her mother. The mother she had never known.

But—a sphinx?

"Perhaps it was something like a warning?" she said. "A sort of look into the future?"

"Perhaps." Junipa didn't sound convinced. "The sphinx was standing in a room full of billowing yellow curtains. She was very beautiful. And she had dark hair, just like you."

"What are you trying to say?"

Junipa hesitated. "Nothing . . . I think."

"Yes, you are."

"I don't know."

"Do you really think my mother was a sphinx?" She swallowed and tried to laugh at the same time, but it failed miserably. "That's just nonsense."

"What I saw *was* a sphinx, Merle. I didn't say it was your mother. Or anyone else you had to know."

Merle regarded the mirror in silence; it had accompanied her all her life and she had always guarded it like the apple of her eye. Her parents had laid it in the wicker basket in which she'd been set out on Venice's canals as a newborn. It had always been the only link to her origins, the only clue. But now it seemed to her that its reflection was a little darker, a little stranger.

"I shouldn't have said anything," said Junipa, downcast.

"Yes, you were right to."

"I didn't want to frighten you."

"I'm glad I know." But what did she know, really?

Junipa shook her head behind Merle's shoulder. "Perhaps it was only some old image. Neither of us has any idea what it means."

Merle sighed, but as she was about to put the mirror away, she again remembered the ghost trapped inside, a milky film that rushed back and forth over the watery surface. "Do you think it could be that phantom from Arcimboldo's mirrors?"

Gently she touched the surface with her fingertip. Not deep enough to poke through the surface. Very, very gently.

"There is someone here," said the Flowing Queen.

Silence.

"Everywhere," said the Flowing Queen, and for a moment she sounded almost panicked. *"He . . . he is here!"*

"Here?" Merle whispered.

Vermithrax noticed that something was happening on his back and briefly lowered his head, without, however, looking back so as not to make Seth aware of the two girls' activity.

"Hello?" Merle whispered.

A syllable sounded in her mind, then the sound blurred, whispering and hissing.

Was that you? she asked the Queen, although she already guessed the answer.

"*No.*"

She tried again, with the same experience. The voice from the mirror was too unclear. Merle knew why: Her fingers had poked too deeply into the water of the mirror. It was impossible while they were going down the stairs to stay still enough—but that's exactly what seemed to be needed to hear the voice of the ghost. She was angry with herself for not having tried it sooner. But when? Since her flight from Venice she hadn't ever had a single quiet moment, no real breather.

"Later," she whispered, drew out her finger, and let the mirror disappear into the buttoned pocket once more. To Junipa she said, "It won't work here. It's too wobbly."

"Something's not right," Seth said at the same time.

Vermithrax slowed. "What do you mean?"

"Why aren't we meeting anyone?"

"It's said that the sphinx population isn't very large," said Merle with a shrug. "At least, someone told us that."

"That is true," said Seth. "No more than two or three hundred. They don't reproduce anymore."

"*They never have,*" said the Queen.

How do you know so much about them? Merle asked.

"*Old reports.*" For the first time Merle felt very clearly that the Queen was lying.

Seth went on, "But there are still enough left to populate their own stronghold."

"If the barks are being piloted by sphinxes these days, a whole lot of them must be gone," Merle said.

"But even if you take away the ones who are in Venice or at the court in Heliopolis, there must still be far more than a hundred in the fortress. It's unusual for everything to be so dead."

"Maybe we should be glad about it instead of pulling a long face," suggested Vermithrax, who by nature had to oppose everything that came from Seth.

The priest lowered his voice. "Yes, perhaps."

"Anyhow, there were patrols outside," said Merle. "So the sphinxes must be in here somewhere."

Seth nodded and went on. They might now have gone some one hundred and fifty feet downward, but still there was no end to the stairs. A few times Merle managed to look over the railing, but only more and more mirrors shimmered up at her from below. It was impossible to see the bottom of the staircase.

And then, unexpectedly, they got to the end.

The stairwell opened into a large room, mirrored like all the others in this fortress. The walls consisted of countless mirror surfaces like the faceted eye of an insect.

"I wonder who polishes them all," Merle murmured,

but she was only covering up the fear that the surroundings aroused in her. The room might be approximately round and empty, but the mirrors reflecting each other a thousand times made it impossible to determine its dimensions clearly. They might just as well be going through a mirror labyrinth of narrow corridors. Vermithrax's glow, beaming back at them from all directions, didn't make things any easier, and it constantly blinded them. Only Junipa was not disturbed by it; with mirror eyes of her own, she looked through the brightness and the illusion of the multiplications.

Someone yelled something.

For a moment Merle thought Seth had cried out. But then she realized the truth: They were surrounded.

What at first look appeared to be hundreds of sphinxes who approached them from all sides was soon revealed to be only one.

The dark-haired man with the lower body of a sand-yellow lion was broader in the shoulders than any of the harbor workers on the Venetian quays. He wore a sword lance as long as a man, its blade reflecting Vermithrax's golden glow. It looked like a torch.

Seth stepped forward and said something in Egyptian. Then he added so that all could understand, "Do you speak the language of my . . . friends?"

The sphinx nodded and weighed the sword lance in his hands for a moment, without lowering the point. His eyes kept darting uncertainly toward Vermithrax.

"You are Seth?" he asked the Horus priest in Merle's language.

"It is so. And I have the right to be here. Only the word of the Pharaoh weighs more heavily than mine."

The sphinx snorted. "The word of the Pharaoh commands that you be taken prisoner as soon as anyone sees you. Everyone knows that you have betrayed the Empire and are fighting on the side"—he hesitated—"of our enemies." His short pause was probably due to the fact that he couldn't imagine what enemies of the Empire were left after decades of war.

Seth bowed his head, which might have seemed submissive to the sphinx but in truth was preparation for—yes, what? A magic blow that would shred his opponent?

Merle was never to find out, for at that moment the sphinx received reinforcements. Behind him, through an almost invisible opening between the mirrors, a troop of mummy soldiers appeared. Their images multiplied in the walls like a chain of cut paper dolls being drawn apart by invisible hands.

The mummies wore armor of leather and steel, but even that could not conceal that these undead soldiers were specimens with uncommonly robust proportions. Their faces were ash gray, with dark rings under the eyes, but they did not appear as wasted and half decayed as other mummies of the Empire. Perhaps they hadn't been dead so long when they were snatched from their graves to serve in the Pharaoh's armies.

The soldiers moved into place behind the sphinx. Their mirror images made it hard to say how many there really were. Merle counted four, but perhaps she was wrong and there were more.

The air over the golden network that covered the back of Seth's head shimmered the way it does on an especially hot summer day.

Horus magic shot through Merle's mind, and at the same time she had to think that his magic could just as well be directed at them and not against their enemies.

At the same moment the mummy soldier in front raised his sickle sword. The sphinx looked back over his shoulder, visibly irritated by the appearance of the soldiers but at the same time grateful for their support. Then he turned again to Seth, Vermithrax, and the girls on the back of the lion. He now grasped that the Horus priest had not bowed to honor him, saw the boiling air over Seth's skull, raised his lance, about to launch it at the priest—

—and was felled from behind by the mummy soldier's sword blow.

Instantly the soldiers leaped over the sphinx lying on the ground and struck at him from all sides. When there was no more life in him, their leader turned slowly around. His eyes passed over Vermithrax and the girls, then fastened on Seth.

The network on the priest's skull glowed, and fireballs like balls of pure lava appeared in Seth's hands.

"No," said the mummy soldier. His voice sounded astonishingly alive. "We don't belong to them."

Seth hesitated.

"Let them alone, Seth," cried Merle. She didn't suppose the priest would pay any attention to her, but for some reason he still didn't throw the fireballs.

"They are not real," said the Queen in Merle's head.

The mummies?

"Not those, either. But I meant the fireballs. They are only illusion. The Horus priests understand that better than anyone: about lies, about deceit. And, in addition, about alchemy and the awakening of the dead."

Then he can't burn up the soldiers at all?

"Not with this playacting."

Merle let out a deep sigh. She watched the foremost mummy soldier raise his left hand and rub his face with it. The gray disappeared, the dark eye rings smeared.

"We are no more dead than you are," he said. "And before we all slaughter each other, we should at least find out if it would not be more reasonable to work together." The man spoke with a strong accent, his *r*'s sounding strangely hard and rolling.

Seth's fireballs went out. The air over his skull quieted.

"I think I know who they are," said the Queen. *"Merle, do you still remember what you found in the*

abandoned tent in the abyss of Hell? Before the Lilim appeared and destroyed everything?"

Merle needed a second or two before she realized what the Queen was getting at. The chicken's claw?

"Yes. Do you still have it?"

In my knapsack.

"Tell Junipa to get it out."

A moment later Junipa was fumbling with the fastenings of the knapsack.

"Who are you?" Vermithrax asked, and he took a threatening step forward. Seth stepped aside, becoming cautious and perhaps realizing that his illusions were inferior to the fangs and teeth of the lion.

"Spies," said the false mummy soldier.

Junipa fished the chicken's claw on its little leather band from Merle's knapsack and handed it forward to her.

The mummy soldier spotted it at once, as if Merle had waved a glowing torch at him.

"Spies from the kingdom of the Czar," he said, smiling.

4

Pirates

SERAFIN WAS STANDING IN FRONT OF A ROUND PORTHOLE and watching the wonders of the sea bottom move past them. Swarms of fish sparkled in the semidarkness. He could make out undersea forests of bizarre growths and things that might perhaps be plants, perhaps animals.

The submarine that had taken them aboard on the sea witch's orders was gliding, raylike, through the deep, accompanied by dozens of fire bubbles such as they'd already seen at the witch's side. The glowing spheres were drawn along to the right and left of the boat like a swarm of comets, covering the sea bottom with a flaring pattern of light and dark.

Dario walked over to him. "Isn't this incredible?"

Serafin acted as if he'd been snatched from a deep dream. "This boat? Yes . . . yes, it really is."

"You don't sound especially enthusiastic."

"Have you seen the crew? And that madman who calls himself the captain?"

Dario gave him an amused smile. "You haven't figured it out yet, have you?"

"What?"

"They're pirates."

"Pirates?" Serafin uttered a soft groan. "How do you get that?"

"One of them told me while you were moping around here for hours at a time."

"I was thinking about Merle," Serafin said quietly. Then he frowned. "*Real* pirates?"

Dario nodded, and his grin became wider. Serafin wondered what made his friend so enthusiastic about the fact that they'd fallen into the hands of a band of robbers and murderers. Romantic dreams of piracy, perhaps; the old stories of noble freebooters who crossed the oceans of the world proudly and with no respect for authority.

The news didn't surprise Serafin especially. Dario's discovery fit right into the picture. What sort of an ally might they expect from a sea witch? Besides, Captain Calvino commanded his crew with a harshness that bordered on cruelty. And the sailors themselves? Recognizable as cutthroats, even from a distance, dark fellows with wild hair, dirty clothing, and innumerable scars.

Just terrific. Fantastic. Out of the frying pan, into the fire.

"They pay for the witch's protection with corpses," Dario said with relish.

"And I thought we'd all seen enough corpses," Serafin blazed at him.

Dario flinched. The memory of their flight from Venice and Boro's death was still fresh in his mind, and the comment obviously pained him. Serafin regretted his sharp retort: Dario's enthusiasm for the pirates was nothing but a masquerade behind which he hid his true feelings. Indeed, underneath it, he was suffering like all the others over what had happened.

Serafin laid a hand on his shoulder. "Sorry."

Dario managed a troubled smile. "My mistake."

"Tell me what else you found out." In a burst of harsh self-criticism, he added, "At least you were smart enough to find out more about our new 'friends,' instead of just staring stupidly out the window."

Dario nodded briefly, but then his grin was replaced by an uneasy look. He stepped up next to Serafin at the porthole, and both turned their faces to the glass.

"They collect the bodies of their victims in a space in the back part of the boat. But to be honest, I'm not sure there are any ships left up on the surface that could be robbed by pirates. They certainly wouldn't dare attack the Egyptian war galleys, and as far as I know, there hasn't been any trade to speak of in the Mediterranean since the beginning of the war."

Serafin nodded. The Empire had cut all the trade routes. In the deserted harbors there were no more customers for merchants. Like all the others, the traders, together with the crews of their ships, had landed in the mummy factories as slaves.

Dario cast a guarded look back into the room: They were in one of the narrow cabins, along whose bronze-colored walls ran a maze of pipes, artfully worked into extravagant decorations, similar to the plasterwork in Venetian palaces, with the single difference that the patterns here were made of metal and wood. Not for the first time, Serafin wondered whom Captain Calvino had seized the boat from. He most certainly had not designed it himself, for he did not appear to be the kind of man who appreciated beauty. And along with all the functionality of the undersea boat, it was obvious that someone with taste and an understanding of art had been at work here.

Besides the two boys, there were also two sailors in the cabin. One of them was pretending to be asleep in his berth, but Serafin had seen him blink and look in his direction several times. The second man let his legs dangle over the side of his bunk as he whittled the figure of a mermaid from a piece of wood; wood shavings fell into the empty berth below him. There were eight empty beds, and the boys knew that there were several of these crew quarters aboard the boat. Captain Calvino had quartered Serafin and Dario in this cabin, Tiziano and Aristide in another. Eft and Lalapeya were lodged in a double cabin at the end of the central passageway, which ran like a spinal column through the entire boat; it wasn't far from the captain's cabin.

At this hour most of the crew members were carrying out their duties in the labyrinthine spaces of the submarine. It was obvious that the two men in the berths had been placed there to keep an eye on the passengers, even if they took pains to appear uninterested. No one kept the boys from wandering around the boat, and yet they didn't take a step that was not observed. Captain Calvino might be an unscrupulous slave driver, but he was no fool. And not even the sea witch's unequivocal order to transport his guests to Egypt unharmed kept him from openly conveying his displeasure with that order.

In a whisper, Dario relayed what he'd learned: "The sea witch has placed the boat under her protection for as long as Calvino provides her with the flesh of corpses. They collect victims of shipwrecks and drownings all over the Mediterranean and bring them to the sea witch. The fellow I spoke with told me they dive around under the battlefields of the great sea wars all year long and catch the dead in nets. Appetizing job, eh? Oh, well, anyway, that's what they do, because piracy isn't going so well anymore.

No one, not even this madman Calvino, wants to get mixed up with the Egyptians. And if he isn't fishing bodies out of the water, he carries out commissions for the witch. Like getting us to Egypt."

"Do you know how they got this boat?"

"They said Calvino won it, together with the crew, in a dice game. No idea if that's true at all. If it is, you could probably figure he cheated, that so-and-so. Have you seen how he stares at Lalapeya?"

Serafin smiled. "To be honest, I'm not the least bit worried about her." The idea that Calvino might have the sphinx brought into his cabin was simply irresistible: Picturing the captain's dumb face when the sphinx took her true form and showed him her lion's claws was worth gold.

"Have you spoken with Tiziano and Aristide?" asked Serafin.

"Of course. They're wandering around in the boat somewhere and sticking their noses into everything that's none of their business."

Serafin's guilt deepened. The others had immediately started to become familiar with their new surroundings. Only he was spending valuable time indulging in his melancholy thoughts. The uncertainty over what had become of Merle troubled him more strongly the longer they were under way. But he mustn't let himself lose sight of the most important thing: to bring them all out of this story safe and sound.

"Serafin?"

"Umm." He blinked as Dario's face came into focus in front of him again.

"You aren't responsible for anyone here. Just don't talk yourself into that."

"I'm not."

"I think you are. You led us when we went into the Doge's palace. But that's long past. Out here, we're all in the same"—he grinned crookedly—"in the same boat."

Serafin sighed, then managed a weak smile. "Let's go up to the bridge. I'd rather look Calvino in the eye than sit around here not knowing if he's just given the order to cut all our throats." As they went to the door together, he called to the two men in the berths, "We're just going out for a few minutes to sabotage the machinery."

The sailor with the whittling knife stared in surprise at his comrade, who acted as if he were just awakening from a deep sleep with an unconvincing yawn.

Serafin and Dario made their way quickly down the passageway. Everywhere the sights they saw were similar: pipes and steam ducts, artfully integrated into the richly decorated walls and ceilings and thick with verdigris; oriental carpets torn by heavy boots; the curtains in front of some portholes gnawed by mildew and dampness; and chandeliers missing single crystals and even arms, fallen off at some time and never replaced. The former glory of the boat was long gone to ruin. Wooden moldings were gouged and spoiled with childish whittlings, some actually broken by fighting fists. Here and there glass doors were missing from cupboards and partitions. The ceilings and floor coverings were full of wine and rum spots. On some of the murals, the pirates had blackened teeth and added mustaches.

The bridge was in the top of the submarine, behind a double-sectioned window that looked out into the ocean deep like a pair of eyes. Captain Calvino, clothed in a rust red morning coat with a golden collar, was walking back and forth in front of the windshield, his hands clasped behind his back, arguing excitedly with someone who was blocked from Dario and Serafin's view by a column. Half a dozen men were working at wheels and levers, which, like most everything aboard, were made of brass; one man sat on an upholstered saddle and was pedaling furiously on a couple of pedals, which drove heaven knew what kind of a machine.

The two boys walked slowly up to the small platform in the front part of the bridge. Calvino did not interrupt his furious pacing for one second. As they approached, they discovered who was with him and quite obviously needling him to a white heat.

Eft saw the two boys at the same time. Her wide mermaid mouth was not covered by its usual mask. The knapsack in which she preserved Arcimboldo's mirror mask hung over her shoulder, as always, for Eft never let her precious possession out of her sight for a moment.

"I know boats like this," she said, now turning to Calvino again. "And I know how fast they can be. Faster anyway than what you're trying to fool us with here."

"I've already told you a thousand times, and I'll tell you once more," thundered the captain. The scar that split his lower lip and reached down to his Adam's apple showed white against his flushed face. "The Egyptians control the sea, and for a long time they haven't been content to just search for prey on the surface. To go faster, we have to go up, and I will not take that risk. The sea witch's commission says to take you and these children to Egypt—mad enough, by Neptune!—but she said nothing about the matter of being in such a hurry. So you will kindly leave it to me to decide what speed we travel at."

"You are a stubborn old goat, Captain, and I'm not the least surprised that you've let this marvel of a boat run down this way. We should probably consider ourselves lucky if we get to Egypt at all before your garbage heap of a tub breaks apart."

Calvino whirled around, came close to Eft, and stopped about six inches away from her. He stretched his scarred face toward her threateningly. Serafin was sure that Eft was now able to smell the remnants of meals in his dark beard. "You may be a woman or a fishwife or the devil knows what, but you will not tell me how to run my boat!"

Eft remained unimpressed, although she must also have seen the saber that dangled from the captain's belt.

Calvino had wrapped his right hand around the grip in his rage, but he hadn't yet bared the blade. He would doubtless go to that length soon if Eft didn't back off. What, by all the saints, was she doing, anyway? Did it matter at all whether they reached Egypt today or tomorrow or the day after?

Eft assumed her most charming smile—which in a mermaid looks about as friendly as the open arms of an octopus. Her shark's teeth gleamed in the light of the gas lamps. "You are a fool, Captain Calvino, and I will tell you why."

Serafin noticed that the crew members on the bridge pulled their heads a little deeper between their shoulders. They well knew what a storm was going to break over them any moment.

But Calvino was silent, possibly because he was much too flabbergasted. No one had ever dared to speak to him in that tone. His lower lip trembled like the body of an electric eel.

Eft pressed on. "This boat, Captain, was already worth a fortune before the war, more than you and your cutthroats could imagine in your wildest dreams. But today, now that there's no more sea travel, the boat is of such unimaginable worth that not even the treasuries of the suboceanic kingdoms would have been enough for it."

Now she's overdoing it, Serafin thought, but at the same time he saw that Calvino was frowning and listening carefully. Eft was a little closer to her goal: She'd made him curious.

"You've been on board too long, Captain," she continued her harangue, and now the sailors were unmistakably pricking up their ears. "You've forgotten how things look in the world up there. You and your people have let this boat and its art treasures go to ruin while you sail through the world's oceans and look for lost treasure. Yet you'll find the greatest treasure of all here, right under your behind, and you have nothing better to do than turn it into a scrap heap without equal and look on while your crew ruins it a little more day by day."

Calvino's face was still hovering a few inches away from hers, as if frozen in space. "The greatest treasure of all, you say?" Now his voice sounded softer and more controlled than before.

"Certainly—as long as you don't care that it's rotted like an old piece of plank on the shore of some island or other."

"Hmm," said Calvino. "You think I'm . . . untidy?"

"I think," Eft said in a friendly voice, "you are the biggest slob between here and the Arctic Circle, and that in every respect. All the more difficult for me to point out to you your obvious *mistakes!*"

Oh my, oh my, oh my, Serafin thought.

Dario sucked in his breath audibly. "Now she's gone completely crazy," he whispered to his friend.

Captain Calvino stared, wide-eyed, at Eft. His

thumbs nervously polished the pommel of his saber, while his thoughts doubtless circled around murder and manslaughter; around fishwife filet; around a paperweight made of the jaws of a mermaid.

"Captain?" Eft tilted her head and smiled.

"What?" The word rose growling out of his throat like sulfur vapor from a volcano crater.

"I haven't by any chance offended you, have I?"

Two sailors whispered to each other, and before the two knew it, Calvino was beside them and barking at them with such a gigantic explosion of epithets that even Serafin and Dario, both former street boys from the alleys of Venice, blushed to the tips of their ears.

"Someone should write this down," Dario said out of the side of his mouth.

Calvino started, and his eyes fell on the boys. For a moment it looked as though he was going to let loose his fury on them, too, but then he swallowed his vituperations and turned again to Eft. Dario let go of his breath.

The outburst of rage had calmed the captain a little, and he could now look Eft in the face again without stabbing her with his eyes at the same time. "You are . . . impertinent."

Eft was obviously suppressing a grin, which was probably a good thing, for that is not a beautiful sight in a mermaid. "This boat is an unparalleled disgrace, Captain. It stinks, it's dirty, and it's neglected. And if I were you—and thanks be to the Lords of the Deep I'm not—I'd make sure that my men brought it into line in a hurry. Every pipe, every picture, every carpet. And then I'd lean back for a moment and enjoy the idea of being one of the richest men in the world."

Serafin watched the words seep into Captain Calvino's consciousness and spread their entire import. One of the richest men in the world. Serafin wondered if Eft knew what she was talking about. On the other hand, you'd have had to be a fool not to recognize what value this submarine had. In times like these it was priceless—if also, and Calvino might overlook that in his greed, *literally* beyond price, for there was no one left who could have bought it.

But presumably the captain would not have sold his boat for any price in the world anyhow. Much more, it was the knowledge of the value of his vessel, the sudden recognition of his wealth, that roused his enthusiasm. He'd been aboard for too long, and as so often happens when one has something around day after day, he'd forgotten how valuable it was.

He looked at Eft for a few seconds longer, then whirled on his heel and snarled a series of orders to his subordinates, who immediately began to relay the captain's wishes to the crew through a speaking tube that reached to the farthest corner of the submarine.

Clean up, the command was. Clean and dust. Remove rust and polish. And then, Calvino ordered, the art treasures that had collected in one of the lower cargo areas over the course of the years should be distributed to the walls and the remaining sound glass cabinets. And woe to him who still dared to do anything to them with charcoal or knife tip!

Finally Calvino gave the former mermaid a crooked grin. "What's your name?"

"Eft."

He bowed gallantly, overdoing it a little, but his good will was evident. "Rinaldo Bonifacio Sergio Romulus Calvino," he introduced himself. "Welcome aboard."

Eft thanked him and then, no longer able to suppress her grin—the captain seemed to be a little frightened by it—she shook his hand and finally went over to the two boys. Serafin and Dario were still standing there with mouths agape, unable to grasp what had just happened.

"How did you do that?" Serafin asked softly as they left the bridge, followed by Calvino's benevolent gaze at Eft's backside.

Eft winked at Serafin. "He's only a man too," she said with satisfaction, "and I still have the eyes of a mermaid."

Then she hurried ahead to supervise the work of cleaning up.

They reached Egypt the next day.

Nothing had prepared them for what they saw as the submarine rose to the surface. Ice floes floated on the open sea, hundreds of yards away from land. The closer they came to the white coastline, the more obvious it became that winter had descended on the desert. No one understood what had happened, and Calvino had his men pray three Our Fathers to protect them all from tritons and sea devils.

Serafin, Eft, and the others were just as mystified as the captain and his crew, and even Lalapeya, the silent, secretive Lalapeya, declared without being asked that she had not the least idea what was going on in Egypt. Without doubt, such an outbreak of winter had never happened before. Ice floes along the desert coast, she explained, were about as usual as polar bears dancing on the tips of the pyramids.

Captain Calvino gave the order to measure the thickness of the ice layer at the bank. Barely more than three feet, it was soon reported to him. Calvino growled ill-humoredly to himself and then conferred with Eft on the bridge for a whole hour—as with every conversation between the two, there was a lot of shouting, terrible curses, and finally a yielding captain.

Shortly afterward Calvino had the boat dive, and they ran into the Nile delta beneath the ice sheet. The great river and its tributaries were not deep, and it required some skill to maneuver the boat between the ice and the river bottom. Sometimes they heard sand grinding under the hull, while the fin-shaped upper projections of the boat's hull scraped along the ice layer. It would be a miracle, raged Calvino, a goddamn miracle if no one noticed them with all this racket.

Most of the time they moved forward at a walking pace, and Serafin began to wonder where they were heading, anyway. The witch's commission had been to set them down on the coast—and now Calvino was voluntarily taking them farther inland, and furthermore, under conditions that were worse than any of them could have imagined. Eft's influence on him was amazing.

The interior of the boat was already gleaming in many places. Everywhere there were sailors busy with cloths and sponges and sandpaper, painting and varnishing, tearing up old carpets and replacing them from the resources of the overflowing storage holds. Many of the stowed objects had lain there for decades, some perhaps since the privateering expeditions of the previous owner, long before the beginning of the mummy war. Even Calvino appeared surprised at what came to light, art treasures and magnificent handwork, such as hadn't been seen for a long time. He became more and more aware, Eft told Serafin, that he'd been imprisoned for too long in the brass world of the submarine and had forgotten to value the beauties of the upper world. Which of course didn't keep him from roaring around like a berserker, screaming at his men, and handing out draconian punishments for overlooked dirt streaks and flakes of rust.

Serafin had a vague feeling that Eft liked the pirate captain. Not the way she'd worshipped Arcimboldo, and yet . . . there was something between the two of them, an absurd love-hate that amused Serafin and at the same time disconcerted him. Was it possible for two people to come closer under such circumstances? Had it been that way with him and Merle? The recognition that they'd spent less time together than Eft and Calvino during the short journey filled his mind. He began to doubt that Merle thought of him as often as he thought of her. Did she miss him? Did he mean anything to her anyway?

A horrible grinding and cracking brought his musings to an abrupt end. It didn't take long before Calvino bellowed out of the speaking tube and, with a string of oaths, informed them of what had happened.

They were stuck. They had run aground in the pack ice of the Nile and could go neither forward nor backward. The iron fins of the submarine had eaten into the ice cover like a saw blade and plowed a lane for a distance of several dozen yards, then became hopelessly wedged in.

Serafin feared the worst and hurried to the bridge. But there stood Calvino and Eft calmly beside each other in front of the windshield of the boat, looking out into the waters of the Nile beneath the ice layer. The witch's fire bubbles had remained back at the coast, but the vague light beams that shimmered through the ice were enough to reveal the most important thing. Through the windshield it looked as if the submarine was stuck under the white ceiling of an indistinct hall. Icicles as thick as tree trunks hung down in front of the window.

It turned out that Captain Calvino was by no means as undisciplined in an emergency as Serafin would have expected. He took account of all the facts, conferred with

Eft, and then gave the order to open the upper hatches of the boat, so that the passengers could climb out.

Climb out? thought Serafin in horror. Had that really been Eft's advice? To simply set them down in the middle of this desert of ice?

An hour later Eft and Lalapeya, Serafin and Dario, Tiziano and Aristide stood ready at the hatch, enveloped in the thickest fur clothing that could be found in the pirates' storage hold. Calvino remembered that the things came from a grounded schooner whose crew he'd annihilated at the beginning of the war. The ship had been on the way to Thule in Greenland, there to load heaven-knew-what in exchange for the warm clothing on board. The jackets, boots, and trousers did not fit any of them—Lalapeya, especially, with her petite body, was at a disadvantage—but they would be enough to protect them from freezing to death. Finally, each put on a shapeless fur cap and slipped both hands into padded mittens. From the weapons room the pirates handed each of them revolvers, ammunition, and knives. Only Lalapeya refused weapons.

Calvino stayed behind with his men to watch the boat and to try to free the top fin from the ice. He thought that it would take many hours, perhaps even days, and the fear of being discovered by the Egyptian sunbarks was clearly written in his face. Although Eft did not ask him to, he promised to wait for three days for a sign of life before he returned to the open sea.

"Where are we going, anyway?" Tiziano morosely said aloud what they'd all wondered a dozen times already.

Eft stood beneath the open hatch that led to the outside. The white circle framed her head like a frozen halo. Her eyes were fixed on Lalapeya, who looked anything but happy in her much-too-large fur clothing. Serafin also inspected the sphinx, and once more he wondered what moved her to keep on accompanying the desperate group. Was it really only hatred for the Empire? The loss of the dead sphinx god who had rested for centuries under the cemetery island of San Michele and whom she had tried in vain to protect from the Empire?

No, thought Serafin, there was something else, something unspoken, which none of them knew anything about. He could feel it as clearly as if the eyes of the sphinx were saying it to him.

"Lalapeya," said Eft. Her words sounded almost festive. "I take it you know where we are. Perhaps you've known the whole time that the first part of our journey would end here."

Lalapeya said nothing, and as much as Serafin tried, he still found no answer in her silence. She confirmed nothing, denied nothing.

Eft went on, "Not far from here, in the middle of the Nile delta, is the fortress of the sphinxes. The mermaids have no name for it, but I think there is one. The captain knows this place, and if the onset of winter has done nothing worse than cover everything with snow and ice, it must be two or three miles from here, at most."

"The Iron Eye sees your living, sees your strivings, sees your dying," Lalapeya recited, and the words sounded to Serafin like a saying from a distant past. The sphinx had passed entire epochs alone in Venice, but she had not forgotten the culture of her people. "The Iron Eye—that's the name you're looking for, Eft. And yes, I can feel it. The closeness of other sphinxes, many in one place. It's suicide to go there." But the way she said it, it didn't sound like a warning but like a confirmation of something that was unavoidable anyway.

"What are we going to do there?" asked Aristide.

"It's the heart of the Empire," said Lalapeya instead of Eft. "If there is a spot where one can injure it, it's there." She said nothing of a plan, perhaps because there was none. The stronghold of the sphinxes, no one doubted, was impregnable.

Eft shrugged, and Serafin thought again about what she had said to the sea witch: that they had to begin somewhere if they wanted to oppose the Empire. That a victory could also lie in small things. Her words had never been out of Serafin's head since then.

But what would it help if they all died doing it? It was as if they were going to run against a wall of their own free will in spite of the certainty that they couldn't even inflict a scratch.

He was just about to give voice to his doubts when he felt Lalapeya gently touch his hand. Without anyone else noticing it, she bent toward his ear and whispered, "Merle is there."

He stared at her, dumbfounded.

Lalapeya smiled.

Merle? he thought, but he didn't dare to put the question. If Dario and the others knew of it, they would accuse him of being involved in this business only because he wanted to see Merle again, not because he believed in their higher goal. *Good,* he thought, *they should follow their higher ideals*; he, anyway, knew why he was *really* doing it, and his motives didn't seem to him any less honorable than theirs. They came out of himself, from his heart.

Lalapeya nodded to him, barely noticeably.

Eft's voice made them both look up at the hatch. Serafin had the feeling he was perceiving everything blurrily, the surroundings, Eft's speech, the presence of the others. Suddenly he was burning to climb up to the outside.

Merle is there, he heard the sphinx say again and again, and the words flitted through his head like moths around a candle.

Eft had not stopped speaking, giving instructions for how to manage in snow, but Serafin scarcely listened.

Merle is there.

At last they set out.

696

5

Back to the Light

"I CAN FEEL IT. WITH EVERY STEP. EVERY TIME I TAKE A breath." Junipa kept her voice low so no one except Merle could hear her. "It's as if there's something in me . . . here, in my chest . . . something that pulls on me and drags me as if I were on a rope." Her mirror eyes turned to her friend like the signal fire of a lighthouse: silvery light behind glass. "I try to resist it. But I don't know how long I'll be able to do it."

"And you can remember everything that happened in the pyramid?" Merle was holding Junipa's hand and stroking it gently. They were sitting in the farthest corner of the Czarist spies' hiding place.

Junipa swallowed. "I know that I tried to stop you. And that we . . . that we hit each other." She shook her head in shame. "I am so sorry."

"You couldn't help it. It was Burbridge."

"Not him," Junipa contradicted. "The Stone Light. Professor Burbridge is just as much under its control as I am—as long as he's down there, anyway. Then he's not the scientist he used to be anymore, only Lord Light."

"And it's better for you up here?"

Junipa considered for a second before she found the right words. "It feels weaker. Maybe because it's stone and can't penetrate the stone of the Earth's crust. At least not completely. But it isn't gone. It's always with me, all the time. And sometimes it hurts quite a lot."

Merle had seen the scar on Junipa's chest after they climbed out of Hell, the incision through which Burbridge had had a new heart inserted—a splinter of the Stone Light. It was now reposing, cold and motionless, in her chest cavity, keeping her alive as her real heart had done before, like a glowing, sparkling diamond. It healed her wounds in a very short time and lent her strength when she was exhausted. But it also tried to force her under its control.

When Junipa said that it hurt, she didn't mean the pain of the operation, the scar. She meant the pressure to betray Merle another time—the fight against herself, the inner strife between her gentle ego and the icy power of the Stone Light.

And as much as the thought pained Merle, she had to be wary of what Junipa did. It was possible that she'd suddenly stab them in the back a second time.

No, not Junipa, Merle thought bitterly. The Stone Light. The fallen Morning Star in the center of Hell. Lucifer.

She was silent for a moment, and then she spoke about a thing that had been on her mind for a long time. "What you said there, in the pyramid . . ."

"That Burbridge claimed to be your grandfather?"

Merle nodded. "Do you know if that's true?"

"He said it, anyway."

Merle looked at the ground. She opened the buttoned pocket of her dress and pulled out the water mirror, stroking the frame with the tips of her fingers. Her other hand felt for the chicken's foot, now dangling on a cord around her neck, absently playing with the small, sharp claws.

"More soup?" asked a voice behind them.

The two girls turned around. Andrej, the leader of the Czarist spy troop, had sketchily washed the gray color from his face and wore just a part of his mummy armor. He was a tough, grim man, but the presence of the girls brought out a friendliness in him that seemed to amaze his four comrades.

On the other side of the low-ceilinged room, the men were still standing around Vermithrax, their wooden soup bowls in one hand, the other repeatedly stretching toward the obsidian lion's glowing body.

They didn't know that he'd plunged into the Stone Light. In contrast to Junipa, it had gained no power over him. Merle found that strange, but so far she hadn't been able to observe anything disquieting. Since then Vermithrax had been stronger, even a little bigger than before, but aside from his body's lavalike glow, he had not changed. He was the old, good-natured Vermithrax, who now, despite all his concern for his people and his hatred of Seth, was enjoying the admiring attention the Czarists offered him. He basked in their questions, their timid touching, and the respect in their faces. They'd all heard of the stone lions of Venice, even of the few that were able to fly. But that one of those lions was able to speak like a human and, in addition, radiated light like one of the icons in the churches of their homeland—that was new and fascinating to them.

Junipa refused the soup that Andrej offered them, but Merle let him fill her bowl again. After all the days of nourishing herself on tough dried meat, the thin broth seemed like a delicacy to her.

"You do not have to be afraid." Andrej misunderstood the fact that they were sitting in a corner, separated from the others. "The sphinxes will not find us here. We have been here almost six months, and so far they have not once noticed that we exist."

"And you don't find that strange?" Merle asked.

Andrej laughed softly. "We have asked ourselves that a thousand times. The sphinxes are an ancient race, known since the beginning of time to be wise and clever. Do they only observe and tolerate us? Do they feed false information to us? Or are they simply indifferent that we are here because we have no chance of sending our knowledge home anyway?"

"I thought you had carrier pigeons?"

"We did indeed. But how many pigeons can one keep in a place like this before someone notices them? The birds were used up after the first weeks, and there was no way of sending us new ones. Therefore we are only collecting—in our heads, not on paper, nothing is written down—and soon we will return to our homeland. Thanks be to the Baba Yaga."

He gave the girls an encouraging smile, and then he went back to the others. He respected the wish of the two of them to be alone.

"He's strange, don't you think?" said Junipa.

"Very nice," said Merle.

"That too. But so . . . so understanding. Quite different from what you'd expect from someone who secretly traveled halfway around the world and has been hiding in his enemy's stronghold for half a year."

Merle shrugged. "Perhaps his mission has helped him to keep his sanity. He must have seen a lot of bad things." She indicated the other spies with a somber nod. "All of them."

Junipa's eyes wandered from the Czarists over to Seth, who was sitting near the entrance, leaning up against one of the mirror walls. In his bound hands he held a drinking bowl. His ankles were also bound. Had Andrej known who his prisoner really was, he would probably have struck off his head without hesitation. Even if Vermithrax might have agreed thoroughly with that, Merle thought it was wrong. Not because it was unreasonable and quite certainly not because it was undeserved, but she hoped that Seth could still be useful to them. And this time the Flowing Queen shared her opinion.

"Are you going to try it again?" asked Junipa, when she saw Merle's fingertips moving from the frame of the water mirror over the surface.

Merle only nodded and closed her eyes.

Her fingers touched the lukewarm water as if they were lying on glass, without breaking through the faint rings. The murky phantom on the surface brushed against the ends of her fingers. Merle still had her eyes closed, but she could feel him, his frantic rushing back and forth over the water.

She heard his whispers, distorted and much too far away for her to be able to understand them. She must somehow bind the phantom to herself, like a piece of iron to a magnet.

"The word," she whispered to Junipa. "Do you still remember the word?"

"What word?"

"The one Arcimboldo gave us when we had to imprison

702

the phantoms in the magic mirrors for him." Their old teacher had opened the door through one of his mirrors for them that time in Venice. They had entered the magic mirror world and found the mirror phantoms inside: beings from another world who wanted to cross into this one and then were stranded in Arcimboldo's magic mirrors as spirit-like shadows. The spirits moved almost invisibly and as lightly as wind gusts in the glassy labyrinths of the mirror world, yet they were forever barred from returning or from a further journey into a physical existence. With a magic word the girls had bound them and brought them back to their master, who had let them go into the reflections in the water of the Venetian canals.

"Hmm, the word," murmured Junipa thoughtfully. "Something with *intera* or *intero* at the beginning."

"*Intrabilibus* or something like that."

"Something like it. *Interabilitapetrifax.*"

"*Childish rubbish,*" scolded the Queen.

"*Intrabalibuspustulens,*" said Merle.

"*Interopeterusbilibix.*"

"*Interumpeterfixbilbulus.*"

"*Intorapeterusbiliris.*"

Merle sighed. "*Intorapeti*—wait, say that again!"

"What?"

"What you just said."

Junipa thought for a moment. "*Intorapeterusbiliris.*"

Merle exulted. "Almost! Now I remember:

Intorabiliuspeteris." And she said it so loudly that for a minute even the conversation between the Czarists and Vermithrax on the other side of the room stopped.

"Seth is watching us," Junipa whispered.

But Merle neither bothered about the Horus priest nor paid attention to Junipa's warning. Instead she said the magic word impatiently a second time, and now she suddenly felt a tickling that crept from her right hand up to her elbow.

"Merle!" Junipa's voice became imploring.

Merle blinked and looked at the mirror. The phantom flickered like a circular billow of fog around her fingertips.

"*It worked,*" said the Flowing Queen. She also sounded concerned, as if she were not pleased that Merle was making contact with the phantom.

"Hello?" asked Merle tonelessly.

"Brbrlbrlbrbr!" said the phantom.

"Hello?"

"Harrlll . . . hello."

Merle's heart beat faster with excitement. "Can you hear me?"

Again the strange muttering, then: "Of course. It was you who couldn't hear *me.*" He sounded fresh and not at all ghostly.

"Did he say something?" asked Junipa, and Merle realized that her friend couldn't hear the phantom. Neither could the others in the room, who'd now resumed their conversation and paid no more attention to what Merle was doing. With the exception perhaps of Seth. Yes, he was very definitely observing her. A shudder ran down her back.

"Can you help me?" she asked straightaway. She had no time for verbal sparring. At any moment Andrej could signal them to come for a discussion of their situation.

"I've been wondering when you'd ever get around to that," said the phantom snappishly.

"You will help me?"

He sighed like a mulish little boy. She wondered if that's exactly what he'd been before he became a phantom: a boy, perhaps even still a child. "You want to know what's behind your water mirror, don't you?" he asked.

"Yes."

"Your friend is right. If you call someone who's sometimes a woman and then again a woman with lion's legs a sphinx, then she'd probably be a sphinx."

Merle didn't understand a word. "Could you be a bit clearer?"

Again the phantom sighed. "The woman on the other side is a sphinx. And, yes, she is your mother." When Merle took in her breath sharply, he added, "I think so, anyhow. Now are you satisfied?"

"What's he saying?" whispered Junipa excitedly. "Tell me!"

Merle's heart was racing. "He said the sphinx is my mother!"

"He said the sphinx is my mother," the phantom

mimicked, mocking her. "Now, do you want to know more, or not?"

"*He is an ill-bred brat,*" commented the Flowing Queen. The phantom didn't seem to be able to hear her, for he didn't react to that.

"Yes," said Merle, her voice wobbling, "yes, of course. Where is she now? Can you see her?"

"No. She doesn't have a wonderful mirror like the one in which you're holding me prisoner."

"Holding you prisoner? You jumped into it yourself!"

"Because otherwise the same thing would have happened to me as the others."

"Did you know them?"

"They were all from my world. But I only knew my uncle. He didn't want me to come with him, but then I sneaked into his workroom at night and jumped into the mirror after him. He looked really dumb when he noticed it." The phantom giggled. "Oh, well, and then *I* looked dumb when I realized what had happened to us."

"*Jawing,*" the Queen said, "*nothing but jawing.*"

"Let's talk about my mother again, all right?"

"Sure," said the phantom. "Whatever you want."

"Where is she now?"

"The last time I saw her she was sitting on a dead witch in the middle of the sea." He said it as matter-of-factly as if he'd seen her cooking.

"In the sea?" Merle asked. "Are you sure?"

"I *know* how the sea looks," he replied spitefully.

"Yes . . . yes, sure. But, I mean, what was she doing there?"

"Holding one hand in the water and creating a magic mirror out of it. So she could hold your hand. Remember?"

Merle was terribly confused. "So can you only see her when she holds one hand in the water?"

"Just like you."

"And you hear her too?"

"Both of you."

"But then why can't I hear her?"

"We could change places anytime," he retorted snippily.

Merle thought for a while. "You must tell me what she says. Does she know how to speak with you?"

"She very quickly tumbled to the fact that there's someone in the mirror besides her little daughter. And she was polite enough to ask me my name first."

"Oh . . . what's your name, then?"

"I've forgotten."

"But how—"

"I said that she asked, not that I could give her an answer."

"How can anyone forget his name?"

"How can anyone suddenly become a dust mark on a mirror? No idea. The only thing I can remember are the last few seconds in my uncle's room. Everything before that is gone. But I have the feeling that it's gradually coming back. Sometimes I remember details, faces, even tunes. Perhaps if you carry me around for a few more years in your musty pocket, then—"

This time it was she who interrupted him. "Listen. I'm sorry about what happened to you, but I can't do anything about it. No one forced you to run after your uncle. So—do you intend to help me or not?"

"Yes, yes, yes," he said, drawling.

"If you can talk with"—Merle hesitated—"my mother, then you can pass on to her what I say. And the other way around."

"A sort of translation, you mean?"

"Exactly." Now he's got it, she thought, and even the Queen sighed somewhere deep in her thoughts.

"Guess I could probably do that."

"That would be very nice."

"Then will you take me out of your pocket sometimes?"

"If we ever get away from here in one piece, we might find a way to get you out of this mirror."

"*Do not be too generous with promises you may not be able to keep,*" said the Queen.

"That won't happen." The phantom sounded a little sad. "I can't take on a body in your world. Everyone said that."

"Maybe not a body. But a larger mirror. How about the sea?"

"Then I'd be something like a sailor, wouldn't I?"

"I suppose."

"Hmm . . . I guess that would be all right." And then he began to sing a song, quite tunelessly, something about fifteen men on a dead man's chest. Quite nonsensical, Merle thought.

"We'll try," she said hastily, so that he'd stop the howling. "Promise."

"Merle?" Suddenly he sounded serious.

"Yes?"

"Merle . . ."

She was breathing faster. "What is it?"

"She's here again. Your mother, Merle . . . she's here with me."

"What the devil is she doing?" Dario shifted crossly from one foot to the other. The snow crunched under the soles of his boots, and Serafin thought that Dario's teeth would soon crunch just as much, from fury, if Lalapeya didn't stand up that instant and go on.

The sphinx was crouching on the bank of the frozen Nile, between blocks of fractured ice whose edges had shoved over and under one another. The boys had taken shelter in a dead palm grove only a few yards away. The palm fronds had long since broken off under the burden of snow, and all that remained were just a few slanting trunks sticking out of the white wasteland like fingers. The boys among the dead trees made splendid targets from the air. Eft was not with them; she stood below on the bank beside the sphinx, looking down at her worriedly.

Serafin couldn't stand it any longer. "I'm going down to them."

He looked at the Iron Eye one more time; it rose above them like a gray wall, an incomprehensibly high monstrosity. You could have taken it for a mountain, if it hadn't risen so smoothly and abruptly out of the icy plain. The twilight helped to veil the true nature of the fortress.

Somewhere behind the snow clouds the sun was going down. At least they soon wouldn't need to fear the barks any longer. But certainly there were other guards outside, here at the foot of the Iron Eye. Guards who were still fast and deadly at night.

Dario murmured something as Serafin clomped away, but he made no move to follow him. That was quite all right with Serafin. He wanted to speak with Eft and the sphinx alone.

But when he finally looked over Lalapeya's shoulder and saw what she was doing, the words remained stuck in his throat.

A hole gaped in the ice at the water's edge. It looked as if a predator had scratched it with its claws. So close to the Iron Eye, the ice was much thinner than the place where the boat had gotten stuck. Twelve inches, Serafin estimated, at most. That must be because of the warmth radiating from the fortress. It had certainly become warmer, but the temperature was still way below freezing.

Lalapeya was crouching in the snow, bent forward, her arm plunged into the water up to the elbow. Her hand was motionless in the ice-cold stream. The sphinx had shoved back the sleeve of her fur coat; her naked lower arm was slowly turning blue. Nevertheless she made no move to withdraw the hand. Only now did Serafin notice that she was whispering something to herself. Too softly. He couldn't understand what she was saying.

Distressed, he turned to Eft, who'd stepped up beside him. "What's she doing?"

"She's speaking with someone."

"Her hand will freeze."

"It probably already has."

"But—"

"She knows what she's doing."

"No," he said angrily, "obviously she doesn't! We can't burden ourselves with dragging her into the fortress half-frozen." He reached out his hand to pull Lalapeya back by the shoulder, away from the water.

But Eft halted him, and the hissing that suddenly came from her shark mouth made him flinch. "It's important. Really important."

Serafin staggered back a step. "She's crazy. Both of you are crazy." He was about to turn away and go back to the others. But again Eft held him back.

"Serafin," said the mermaid imploringly, "she's speaking with Merle."

He stared at her dumbfounded. "What do you mean?"

"The water helps her do it." Eft waved Serafin a few steps farther away and there—on the bank of the frozen Nile—Serafin now learned what was special about Merle's water mirror.

He folded his arms over his chest and rubbed his upper arms under the fur, more from nervousness than from cold. "Is that the truth?" he asked with a frown. "I mean, are you really serious?"

Eft nodded.

Serafin lowered his voice. "But what does Merle have to do with Lalapeya?"

The mermaid showed her teeth: a smile. "Can't you figure that out?"

"No, damn it!"

"She's her mother, Serafin. Lalapeya is Merle's mother." Her fearsome grin grew wider, but her eyes remained human and wondrously beautiful. "Your friend is the daughter of a sphinx."

Merle listened with concentration to the phantom's words while at the same time she struggled not to let her trembling fingers dip too far into the reflection. She mustn't let the connection to him break off now, she had to hear what the sphinx—her mother—had to say to her.

"She says you must go to Boerbritch," the phantom repeated.

"Burbridge?" Merle asked.

"You should go to him, only there are you safe. Safer anyway than in the Iron Eye."

"But we just got away from Burbridge, out of Hell! Tell her that."

A while passed, then the phantom brought back the answer. "She wants me to tell you that you should meet him in his mirror room. You and your friend. She should guide you there."

"Junipa guide me into a mirror room?"

"Yes. Wait, that's not all . . . ah, now. She should take you to him. There you will be safe."

Merle still didn't understand. "Safe from whom? From the sphinxes?"

Again a pause, then: "From the Son of the Mother, she says. Whatever that means."

Merle growled in annoyance. "Would you be so good as to *ask*?"

While the phantom obeyed, the Queen chimed in. *"I do not know if that is such a good idea, Merle. Perhaps you should—"*

No, Merle thought decidedly. You stay out of this. This is my affair alone.

The voice of the phantom reported back. "The Son of the Mother. That seems to be something like a name for . . . yes, *the* forefather of the sphinxes, as it were, their oldest ancestor. A kind of sphinx god, I guess. She says he is on the way here, or is even in the fortress. She is not sure. And she says that the sphinxes are going to try to awaken him to life again."

Merle was startled when the Queen uttered a strange sound. How much do you know, really? she thought for the hundredth time.

"The Son of the Mother," whispered the Queen. *"Then it is true. I felt him but I thought it was impossible. . . . By all that is holy, Merle, you must not do what she asks. You must not go away from here."*

You could have told me about that before, Merle thought bitterly. You ought to have trusted me.

The phantom went on, "She keeps saying the same thing, Merle. That your friend must take you to Burbridge, before it's too late. That you should go into his mirror room and should wait there for him if necessary. She says he can explain everything to you, about you, about her, and about your father."

"Ask her who my father was."

The pause grew longer. "Burbridge's son," said the phantom finally. "Steven."

Steven Burbridge. Her father. The thought felt strange and frightened her.

"What is her name?"

"Lalapeya," said the phantom.

Merle felt her fingers begin to tremble. She bit her lips and tried to pull herself together. It was all so confusing and so overwhelming at the same time. Had the sphinxes not been her enemies from the beginning? Were they not the true rulers of the Empire? If her mother was actually a sphinx, then her people had plunged the world into ruin. But Merle was not like them, and perhaps Lalapeya wasn't either.

"Merle," the phantom interrupted her train of thought, "your mother says that only Junipa can guide you. That is very important. Only Junipa has the power to use the glass word."

Merle was as dizzy as if she'd been whirling in a circle for hours. "The glass word? What's that supposed to be?"

"One moment."

Time passed. Much too much time.

"Hello?" she asked after a while.

"She's gone."

"What?"

"Lalapeya took her hand out of the water. I can't hear her anymore."

"But that's—"

"Sorry. Not my fault."

Merle looked up and for the first time was aware of Junipa again, who sat in front of her, filled with concern. "I should guide you? He said that?"

Merle nodded, numb, as after a nightmare. She ought to have been celebrating. Now she knew who her parents were. But it changed so little. Really, nothing at all. It only confused her even more, and it frightened her.

In a whisper, she told Junipa everything. Then she looked up and saw that Seth had not taken his eyes off them. He smiled icily when their eyes met. She quickly looked away.

"I know what he meant," Junipa whispered tonelessly.

"Really?"

Junipa was breathing shallowly, her voice sounded hoarse. "Through the mirrors, Merle. We should go through the mirrors." She smiled sadly. "That's what Arcimboldo gave me these eyes for, after all, isn't it? I can not only *see* with them. They're also a key, or at least a part of one. Burbridge told me everything: why he gave Arcimboldo the commission to take me out of the orphanage and so forth. I was supposed to look into other worlds, but I can also go there."

"Even back to Burbridge?" Merle whispered. "Back to Lord Light?"

Junipa's smile seemed even more downcast, but somewhere in the gleam and glitter of her eyes was also something else: a faint, shy triumph.

"Everywhere," she said.

"But why—"

"Why didn't we do that long ago? Because it isn't so

simple. I need something for it, the same thing with which Arcimboldo opened the door in the mirror that time in the workshop."

Merle saw the scene flash before her: Arcimboldo, as he bent before the mirror and moved his lips. How he soundlessly formed a word.

"The glass word," said Junipa, as she let the sound of the syllables melt on her tongue. "I didn't know they called it that."

"And you don't know how it sounds?"

"No," Junipa said. "Arcimboldo was murdered before he could tell me."

Good God, Serafin thought, when Lalapeya pulled her right hand out of the water. It was gray up to the wrist, almost blue, and looked as if it were made of wax. It hung at the end of her arm as if it no longer belonged to her body. Lifeless, as if it were dead.

The sphinx's features were twisted with pain, but still the fire of her willpower burned in her fawn-colored eyes.

"Eft," she said, paying no attention to Serafin.

Eft quickly bent toward her and was about to help Lalapeya to stand, but she'd misunderstood the sphinx: Lalapeya was not asking for help.

"Merle needs . . . the word," she said doggedly.

Eft shook her head. "We must look after your hand. If we could somehow manage a fire—"

717

"No." Lalapeya looked pleadingly at Eft. "First the word."

"What does she mean?" asked Serafin.

"Please!" The sphinx sounded tearful.

Serafin's eyes fastened on Eft. "What word?"

"The glass word." Eft looked at the ground, past Lalapeya, as if she saw something in front of her in the snow. But there was only a shadow there, and she stared at it as if she were asking for advice.

"Merle and Junipa must go to Burbridge," said Lalapeya. "Junipa has the *sight*, she is a guide. But to open the door, the door of mirror glass, she needs the glass word." The sphinx held her deadened hand pressed firmly to her chest with her healthy left one. Serafin had never had frostbite himself, but he'd heard that it was just as painful as being burned. It was astonishing that Lalapeya didn't collapse.

"I don't know the word," said Eft hesitantly.

"You, no. But he."

Serafin stared at the two women, his eyes wide. "He?" And then he understood. "Arcimboldo?"

Lalapeya didn't answer, but Eft nodded slowly.

"Merle has a right to the truth. I don't have enough strength . . . to tell her everything. Not here." Lalapeya looked down at her inert, waxy right hand. "But the word . . . that I can tell her." Her gaze became entreating. "Right now, Eft!"

Eft hesitated a moment longer, and Serafin, who felt terribly helpless in his ignorance, would have liked to have taken her by the shoulders and shaken her: Do it now! Do something! Help her!

Eft sighed deeply, then nodded. Swiftly she loosened her knapsack and pulled out the mirror mask: a perfect replica of Arcimboldo's features in silvery mirror glass. Eft had made it after the mirror maker's death, and Serafin had the dark suspicion that this was Arcimboldo's real face, taken from the corpse and changed by mysterious magic into glass.

Eft handed the mask to Lalapeya.

"Will he speak with me?" the sphinx asked doubtfully.

"With anyone who puts it on."

Serafin looked from one to the other. He didn't dare disturb them with questions.

Lalapeya regarded the wrinkled features of the mirror master for a few seconds, then turned the mask and inspected the inside. Uncertainty flashed in her eyes for a moment, then she pressed the glass to her face with her left hand. The mask remained stuck, even though she took her hand away. The interior seemed in some miraculous way to fit Lalapeya's narrow features; the glass fitted over her face without overhanging the sides.

Serafin watched breathlessly, almost expecting to hear Arcimboldo's voice speak. He felt distaste for the idea; it seemed to him undignified, like the tired old tricks of a ventriloquist.

A minute passed, during which none of them moved. Even those left behind in the palm grove were silent, although they couldn't see exactly what was going on in front of them. Serafin guessed that the boys felt it anyway, just as he did himself. One could feel the magic, which radiated in all directions through the ice and cold, perhaps even into the river, where it induced the fins of the frozen fish cadavers to flutter. The hairs on the backs of Serafin's hands were standing up, and for the same reason he felt a gentle pressure behind his eyeballs, as with a bad cold. But the feeling passed as quickly as it had come.

Lalapeya placed her sound hand over the mask with fingers spread and effortlessly pulled it off. Underneath, her face was unscathed, not even reddened. Eft sighed when the sphinx returned her glassy mirror shell to her.

"That was all?" asked Serafin.

Eft shoved the mask back into her knapsack. "You wouldn't say that if *you* had had it on your face."

Lalapeya bent over the opening in the ice again.

"No," whispered Serafin. But he didn't hold her back. They all knew that it was the only way.

Lalapeya plunged her sound left hand into the water. Serafin thought he could feel the cold creeping up it, the blood leaving her lower arm, and the skin turning white. Sphinxes were creatures of the desert, and the icy cold must hurt her terribly.

Again minutes passed in which nothing moved, in which the frost itself held its breath around them and the icy wind came to a standstill over the plain. Lalapeya's face grew paler and paler while she exposed her hand to the cold and the flesh gradually went dead. But she didn't pull it back; she waited patiently and felt under the ice in the darkness for an answer to her silent call.

Then the corner of her mouth twitched: the fleeting shadow of a smile. Her eyelids closed as in a deep, deep dream.

She whispered.

A tear flowed from the corner of her eye and turned to ice.

"What sort of a word is *that* supposed to be?" yelped the phantom.

"Magic words are always tongue twisters," Merle explained. "Most of them, anyway." She said it as convincingly as if she had actually heard more than two of them in her life.

The phantom grew more heated. "But such a word!" He had needed five attempts before he was certain that he had said it right, just as Lalapeya had said it to him on the other side.

Merle had to confess that she still couldn't keep it in her head. Compared to that, she spoke the magic word for the mirror phantoms as easily as a nursery rhyme.

But Junipa nodded and that was the main thing. "I can say it. It's quite simple." She said it, and it sounded perfect.

She *is* a guide, thought Merle, impressed and at the same time a little disturbed. Whatever it might mean—she actually was one!

"Tell my mother—," she began, but the phantom interrupted her.

"She's gone again."

"Oh."

For the first time the phantom sounded as if he felt a little pity for Merle's situation. "Don't be sad," he said gently. "She'll be back again. Most certainly. This business was quite . . . difficult for her."

"What exactly do you mean by difficult?"

"You'll worry yourself unnecessarily."

If the phantom had intended to soothe Merle with that, he achieved exactly the opposite. "What's wrong with her? Is she sick? Or injured?" she asked in alarm.

So the phantom told her what Lalapeya had undergone in order to produce the contact. And that she thus might lose both her hands.

Merle pulled her fingers back and let the mirror sink. For a moment she stared into emptiness.

Now she no longer doubted that the sphinx was her mother.

"Merle?"

She looked up.

Junipa smiled encouragingly. "Do you want to try it? I mean, right now?"

Merle took a deep breath and looked around at the others. The spies were still standing beside Vermithrax. He was telling them in his full-toned lion's voice about their adventures in Hell. At another time Merle would perhaps have been concerned that he was telling too much—especially as Seth was listening intently from his corner—but at the moment she had other things on her mind.

"Can you do it, then?" she asked Junipa. "Here?"

Junipa nodded. Merle followed her eyes to the mirrored wall and saw her own reflection crouching depressed on the floor, her fist clenching the handle of the water mirror.

"The mirrors," she whispered, shoving the water mirror into her pocket and buttoning it and touching the ice-cold wall with her other hand. "That's it, isn't it? That's why everything is made of mirrors here. The sphinxes have made a doorway. They want to pull down the walls between the worlds with their fortress. First they conquer this world, and then the next, and then another and—" She broke off as she realized that this was the same plan the Stone Light was following. Where was the connection? There must be a connecting link between the sphinxes and the Light.

"*Let it be*," said the Flowing Queen. Merle had almost

723

forgotten her, she'd been so silent during the past few hours. *"What if you do not like the answer?"*

Merle had no time to think over the Queen's words. Junipa had stood up and extended her hand in invitation.

"Come," she said.

On the other side of the room, Seth raised an eyebrow.

Andrej also looked at them. Merle smiled at him.

"I can stop you," said the Queen.

"No," Merle said, and knew that it was the truth.

Then, hand in hand with Junipa, she stepped in front of the wall. She saw the reflections of the men, saw how they all turned around in amazement.

Junipa whispered the glass word.

They entered the mirror, plunging wonderingly into a sea of silver.

6

Her True Name

MIRRORS AND MIRRORS AND MIRRORS. A WHOLE WORLD of them.

A world among the mirrors. Behind them, between them, beside them. Lanes and tunnels, all of silver. Reflections of reflections of themselves.

And right in the middle of it: thousands of Merles, thousands of Junipas.

"As if we were traveling back through time," said Merle.

Junipa didn't let go of her hand, leading her like a child through the strange environment. "What do you mean?"

"How long has it been since Arcimboldo sent us behind the mirror to catch the phantoms?"

"I don't know. It seems to me as—"

"As if it were years, right?"

"An eternity."

"That's what I mean," Merle said. "When we go back to Venice—and someday we will do that, won't we?—so, when we go back to Venice, a lot of things there will probably be different. Almost certainly. But here, nothing has changed at all. Only mirrors, mirrors, mirrors."

Junipa nodded slowly. "But no phantoms."

"No phantoms," Merle confirmed.

"At least, not here."

"Is the mirror world actually its own world?" Merle asked.

"It's more a place in the midst of all the other worlds. Or better, sort of a saucer with many worlds lying around it, like the universe around the planets. You have to go through the saucer to get into the next world. Arcimboldo explained it to me, but he also said that it would take many years to grasp only a fraction of it. Longer than one life. Or many lives. And Burbridge thinks this is too big for the comprehension of a human being. 'Too little, really,' he said."

"*Too little, really,*" the Queen repeated in Merle's thoughts. Was she of the same opinion? Or did she see everything quite differently? As she had so often in recent days, she remained silent.

Merle thought about Vermithrax, whom she'd left behind on the other side of the mirror. The obsidian lion would certainly be terribly concerned about her. We should have let him in on it, she thought. We ought to have told him what we were going to do. But how would they have done that without letting Seth and the Czarists know about it?

Poor Vermithrax.

"He knows you," said the Flowing Queen. *"He knows that you will come through somehow. Better worry about yourself instead of him."*

Merle was about to contradict her when the Queen added, *"And if you are only worrying about Vermithrax, he will reproach himself for the rest of his life if something happens to you."*

That's mean, she thought angrily. And terribly unfair.

But the Queen had already subsided into her brooding silence again.

The girls went farther through the labyrinth of mirrors, crisscross, in a crazy zigzag, and the longer they were under way, the more Junipa blossomed. Over and over again, where Merle expected a pathway, there was only a new wall of glass and another one to the right of it and to the left of it, but nevertheless, Junipa found the narrowest crack between them, the loophole, the needle eye in this glittering, flashing, sparkling infinity.

"The sphinxes must have been here," said Merle.

"Do you really think so?"

"Just look around. The Iron Eye is a replica. Mirrors everywhere, reflecting themselves. Over and over, reflecting oneself to oneself. The Iron Eye is a copy of this, a reflection of the mirror world, as it were. Only much clearer, much . . . *more rational.* Here everything appears to be so random. If I go to the right, am I really going to the right? And is left actually left? Where's up and down and front and back?" She was going to stop at what she thought was a dead end in front of her, but Junipa pulled her on, and they passed the place without encountering any resistance. To Junipa, the path appeared to be obvious, as if her mirror eyes had picked out a pathway. To Merle it was a miracle.

She regarded her friend from the side, letting her eyes slide over the girl's delicate profile, the sweep of her milky-white skin. She stopped at the mirror shards in her eyes.

"What do you see?" she asked. "I mean, *here* . . . how do you know the right way?"

Junipa smiled. "I just see it. I don't know how to explain it. It's as if I'd already been here before. When you go through Venice, you know the way too, without having to look for particular spots, for signposts or things like that. You simply go and eventually you get there. By yourself. It's the same thing for me here."

"But you were never here before."

"No, I wasn't. But maybe my eyes were."

She was silent for a while until Merle took up the conversation again. "Are you angry at Arcimboldo?"

"Angry?" Junipa laughed brightly, and it sounded sincere. "How could I be angry at him? I was blind and he gave me sight."

"But he did it on Lord Light's orders."

"Yes and no. Lord Light, Burbridge . . . he ordered Arcimboldo to take us out of the orphanages. And the business with the eyes was also his idea. But that isn't the only reason Arcimboldo did it. He wanted to help me. The two of us."

"Without him we wouldn't be here."

"Without him the Flowing Queen would be a prisoner of the Egyptians or dead. Just like us and the rest of Venice. Have you ever considered it from that angle?"

Merle was of the opinion that she had regarded it from every possible angle. Naturally they were only free because Arcimboldo had taken them to be his apprentices. But what was this freedom worth? Basically they were prisoners like all the others—worse, even, they were prisoners of a fate that left them no choice except the way they had taken. It would have been so comfortable to stop, lean back, and say to themselves that someone else would settle the whole thing. But that wasn't the way things were. The responsibility was theirs alone.

She wondered if Arcimboldo had possibly foreseen

this. And if that was why he'd engaged in the trading with Lord Light.

"We'll be there soon," said Junipa.

"So fast?"

"You can't measure the paths here with our measures. Each of them is a shortcut in its own way. That's the point of the mirror world: to get quickly from one place to another."

Merle nodded, and suddenly she had the feeling that everything Junipa was telling her wasn't so weird at all. The more fantastic the things on her trip had turned out to be, the less astonishing they seemed to Merle. She couldn't help wondering how long ago it had been. When had the old world come apart for her and turned into something new? It wasn't at the moment when the Queen entered into her, but yet it was that same night, when she said good-bye to the old Merle for the first time and opened the door to the new one; when she'd left the festival with Serafin and let herself fall into that completely unlooked-for moment; when she'd become a little more comfortable with the idea of being grown up soon.

"There it is," said Junipa. "In front of us."

Merle blinked, saw only herself in the mirror at first, and thought acidly that it was the perfect reflection of her brooding: always only herself, herself, herself.

"*Your self-pity is so unbearable sometimes,*" the Flowing Queen said. And after a pause she asked, "*Don't you have a smart answer?*"

You're really right.

Junipa grasped her hand more firmly and pointed to a spot in the silvery infinity. "That's the door."

"Oh, really?"

"Does that mean you can't see it?"

"Someone forgot to screw on the doorknob."

Junipa smiled. "Just trust me."

"I do that all the time."

Junipa stopped and turned to her. "Merle?"

"Um?"

"I'm glad you're here. That we're going through this business together."

Merle smiled. "Now you sound entirely different from before, in the Iron Eye. Much more . . . like yourself."

"Here between the mirrors I can't feel the Stone Light anymore," said Junipa. "It's as if I had an entirely normal heart. And I can see better than you or probably anyone else. I think I belong here."

And perhaps that was the truth; perhaps Arcimboldo had in fact created her eyes out of the glass of the mirror world. *Junipa is a guide,* Lalapeya had said. And weren't guides always natives of the place? The thought sent shivers down Merle's spine, but she made an effort not to show it.

"Don't let go of my hand," said Junipa. Then she whispered the glass word tonelessly and the two of them took the decisive step together.

Leaving the mirror world was accomplished just as unspectacularly as entering it. They went through the glass as if they were passing through a soft breeze, and on the other side they found—

"Mirrors?" Merle asked before she realized that this was by no means the same place from which they'd started.

"*Mirrors?*" the Flowing Queen asked as well.

"Burbridge's mirror room," said Junipa. "Exactly as your mother said."

Behind them someone cleared his throat. "I'd hoped you'd find the way here."

Merle whirled around, even faster than Junipa.

Professor Burbridge, Lord Light, her grandfather—three completely different meanings in one person. He walked up to them but stopped a few steps away. He didn't come too close, as if he didn't want to make them nervous.

"Don't worry," he said. "In here I'm only myself. The Light has no power over me in the mirror room." He sounded older than outside in Hell. And he looked that way too: He was much more bent now, and he acted frail.

"In this place I am not Lord Light," he said with a sad smile. "Still only Burbridge, the old fool."

The mirror out of which they'd walked was only one of many, arranged in a wide circle. Most were still in the glued frames that Arcimboldo had placed around the magic mirrors when he supplied them to his customers.

The mirrors that Arcimboldo had sold to Lord Light were arranged on the walls, maybe a hundred, maybe two hundred of them. Some were also lying on the floor like puddles of quicksilver, others hung flat beneath the ceiling.

"They keep the Stone Light away from here," Burbridge explained. He wore a morning coat similar to the one he'd had on at their first meeting. His hair was disheveled and he looked untidy, as if his dapper appearance before was only a semblance that the Stone Light had kept in place. All that faded in here. The pouches under his eyes were heavier, his eyes lay deeper in their sockets. The veins showed dark on the parchmentlike backs of his hands. Liver spots covered his skin like the shadows of insects.

"We're alone." He'd noticed that Merle kept surveying the room mistrustfully, for fear of the Lilim, Burbridge's creatures. He appeared to be telling the truth, in fact.

"My mother sent me." Suddenly it didn't feel at all difficult to use that word. It sounded almost matter-of-fact: *my mother.*

Burbridge raised an eyebrow in surprise. "Lalapeya? How I hated her in the old days. And she me, no doubt about that. And now she's sending you here, of all places?"

"She said you could explain everything to me. The truth about me and my parents. About Lalapeya . . . and about Steven."

Burbridge had been standing in the center of the room at her arrival, as if he'd expected her coming.

"It is because of the mirrors," the Flowing Queen said. *"If the mirrors really protect him, then perhaps he is safest in the center where their looks meet."* Arcimboldo had said something similar to her once: "Look into a mirror, and it looks back at you. Mirrors can see!"

"It is no coincidence," the Queen continued, *"that Burbridge named the capital city of Hell Axis Mundi, the axis of the world. The same way that symbolically marks the center point of Hell, this place here is the axis of his existence, his own center, the place where he is still always himself, without the influence of the Light."* After a short pause, she added, *"Most are on the search for their center their entire life long, for the axis of their world, but only the fewest are aware of it."*

Burbridge again took two steps in the girls' direction. The movement had nothing threatening about it.

Is *he* my axis? Merle asked in her thoughts. My center?

The Queen laughed softly. *"He? Oh, no. But the center is often that which stands at the end of our search. You have sought your parents, and you are perhaps on the point of finding them. Perhaps your family is your center, Merle. And Burbridge is, for good or evil, a part of it. But sometime you will perhaps seek other things."*

Then is the center something like that happiness that one always seeks but never finds?

"It can be happiness, but also your downfall. Some seek their entire lives for nothing but death."

At least they can be certain that they'll find it sometime, Merle thought.

*"Do not joke about it. Look at Burbridge! The Stone
Light has kept him alive for decades. Do you not think he is
ready for death? And if he will find it anywhere, it will be
here, where the Light cannot get at him. At least not yet."*

Not yet?

*"The Light will know of our presence. And it will not
look on much longer without taking action in spite of all
this."*

Then we must hurry.

"Good idea."

Merle turned to Burbridge. "I must learn the truth.
Lalapeya says it's important."

"For her or for you?" The old man seemed amused
and at the same time desperately sad.

"Will you tell me about it?"

His eyes slid over the endless round of mirrors.
Arcimboldo's legacy. "You perhaps don't know much
about Lalapeya," he said. "Only that she is a sphinx, isn't
that so?"

Merle nodded.

"There is also a piece of the Stone Light in Lalapeya,
Merle. As in you yourself, for you are her child. But I'll
get to that. First the beginning, yes? Always the beginning first . . . A long time ago the sphinx Lalapeya
received the task of protecting a grave. Not just any

grave, it goes without saying, but the grave of the first ancestor of all the sphinxes. Their progenitor and not, as many believe, their god—although he easily could become that, if his old power awakens again. They call him the Son of the Mother. After his death thousands upon thousands of years ago, the sphinx people laid him to rest in a place that later was to become the lagoon of Venice. At that time there was nothing, only gloomy swamps, into which no living thing strayed. They set watchers, a long line of watchers, and the last of them was Lalapeya. In that time, during Lalapeya's watch, it happened that men settled in the lagoon, first building simple huts, then houses, and finally, over the course of the centuries, an entire city."

"Venice."

"Quite right. The sphinxes ordinarily avoided humans; in fact, they outright hated them, but Lalapeya differed from the others of her people, and she decided to leave the men and women alone. She admired their strong wills and their determination to wrest a new home from the wet, desolate wasteland."

An axis, thought Merle in sudden comprehension. A center of their small, sorrowful human world. And the Queen said, *"It is so."*

"Over the centuries the lagoon took on the form that you know today, and Lalapeya abided there all that time. Finally she was living in a palazzo in the Cannaregio district. And there my son met her. Steven."

"Who was Steven's mother?"

"A Lilim. Naturally not one like the ones you've come to know. Not one of those barbaric beasts, and not a plump shape changer, either. She was what people in the upper world call a succubus. A Lilim in the shape of a wonderfully beautiful woman. And she *was* beautiful, believe me. Steven grew into a child who carried the inheritance of both parents in him, mine as well as hers."

This thought made Merle's head spin. Her mother was a sphinx, her father half human, half Lilim. What was she herself, then?

"I often brought Steven here as a child," said Burbridge. "I told him of the Stone Light, what it was doing to us, what it was making of us. Even then, as a little boy, he resisted this idea. And when he was older, he went away. He told no one of it, not even me. He took a secret gateway, which ended in the lagoon, and he felt the influence of the Light fall away from him. He must have thought he could live as a quite normal human being." Burbridge lowered his voice. "I myself had lost this dream a long, long time ago. When I was still able to flee, I didn't want to. And today I cannot. The Light would not permit it. Steven, on the other hand, was unimportant to it, yes, perhaps it was even glad that he was gone—always provided that it thinks at all like a human, of which I have some doubt.

"So Steven went to Venice and remained there. He met

Lalapeya, perhaps by chance, although I rather believe that she sensed where he came from. He was, like her, a stranger in the city, a stranger among your people. And for a while they were together."

"Why didn't they stay together?"

"What neither had thought possible happened. Lalapeya became pregnant and brought you into the world, Merle. Steven . . . well, he went away."

"But why?"

"You must know him to understand that. He couldn't bear it when anyone held him fast anywhere, when anyone subjected him to firm . . . firm obligations. I don't know how to express it. It was the same as in Hell. He hated the Stone Light because it rules us all and only rarely allows one's own thoughts. He felt himself constricted again by Lalapeya and her child, again limited in his freedom. And I think that was the reason he went away."

Merle's lower lip trembled. "What a coward!"

Burbridge hesitated a moment before he answered. "Yes, perhaps he is one. Just a coward. Or a rebel. Or a disastrous mixture of both. But he is also my son and your father, and we should not pass judgment on him hastily."

Merle saw it entirely differently, but she remained silent so that Burbridge would tell her the rest. "Lalapeya was in despair. She had detested me from the beginning. Steven had told her everything about the Light and about my role in the world of the Lilim. Lalapeya blamed me for

Steven's disappearance. In her anger and her grief she wanted nothing more to do with Steven, and also not with her child, in whom she saw a piece of Steven."

Junipa grasped Merle's hand.

"Is that why she put me out on the canal?"

Burbridge nodded. "I think she's regretted it many times. But she hadn't the strength to make herself known to her daughter. She was still always the watcher of the forefather, the Son of the Mother."

Merle thought of the water mirror, of the many times when she'd pushed her hand in and was touched by the fingers on the other side. Always tenderly, always full of warmth and friendship. It didn't go with what Burbridge said: Lalapeya had made herself known to her, even if in the unique, mysterious way of a sphinx.

"Lalapeya must have known that you were living in the orphanage. Probably she was observing your every step," Burbridge went on. "It was harder for me. It took years, but finally Arcimboldo located you on my orders and took you to him." His eyes sought Junipa and found her half-hidden behind Merle. "Just like you, Junipa. Even if for other reasons."

Junipa made a face. "You made me into a slave. So that I could spy on other worlds for the Stone Light."

"Yes," he said sadly, "that too. That was *one* reason, but it wasn't mine; rather, it was the Light's. I myself wanted something different."

Merle's voice became icy when she understood. "He used you, Junipa. Not for himself, but for me. He wanted you to bring me here. That was the reason, right, Professor? You had the eyes put into her so that she could show me the way to the mirror room."

Again Burbridge nodded, visibly affected. "I couldn't have you brought here by the Lilim—that would only have made the Light aware of you. When you finally came into Hell of your own free will with the lion, you were in the kingdom of the Light. And how little power I possess there you have already seen, when the Lilim took you prisoner. I wanted to spare you all that. Junipa was to have brought you here through the mirrors, as she did today, into this room, where you are safe from the influence of the Light." He paused a moment and wiped his forehead. Then he turned to Junipa. "The business with your heart . . . that was never planned. Not I but the Light arranged that. I couldn't prevent it, for at that point I was also under the Light's influence. It was hard enough to resist it when I fetched Merle out of the Heart House." He shook his head sadly and looked at the floor. "It would have killed me for that if it were not dependent on me. It has made me into the master of Hell, and the Lilim respect and fear me. It would be difficult to find someone to take my place. And it would take a long time to build him up to what I am today." The shadow of a bitter smile flitted across his face. "But that has always been the fate of the Devil, hasn't it?

He can't simply quit like some captain of industry or abdicate like a king. He is what he is, forever."

Merle only looked at him while her thoughts whirled in circles, faster and faster. She caught herself trying to give her father a face, a younger version of Burbridge, without the wrinkles, without the gray in his hair and the weariness in his eyes.

"I must be grateful for the moments in which I can still be myself. But they are becoming ever fewer, and soon I will only be a puppet of the Light. Only then will I really deserve the name of Lord Light," he said cynically.

Was he actually expecting her to commiserate with him? Merle simply couldn't make him out. She looked into herself for hatred and contempt for everything that he'd done to her and Junipa and perhaps also to her father, but she wasn't able to find any shred of it.

"I wanted to see you, Merle," said Burbridge. "Even when you were still a little child. And I had so hoped the circumstances would be different. You should have met *me* first, not Lord Light. And now it has happened the other way around. I cannot expect that you will forgive me that."

Merle heard his words and understood their sense, but it didn't matter what he said: He remained a stranger to her. Just like her father.

"What happened to Steven?" she asked.

"He went through the mirror."

"Alone?"

Burbridge looked at the floor. "Yes."

"But without a guide out there he will become—"

"A phantom, I know. And I am not even sure if he didn't know that too. But I have never given up hope. If it is possible to look into other worlds, perhaps one could find him."

Junipa was staring at him with her mirror yes. "Was *that* what you wanted? For me to look for him?"

He lowered his eyes and said nothing more.

Merle nodded slowly. Suddenly she put all the pieces together. Junipa's mirror eyes, her lessons in the mirror workshop with Master Arcimboldo: Burbridge had determined her course since she'd left the orphanage.

"But why the messenger who offered to protect Venice from the Egyptians?"

"It was you I wanted to protect. And Arcimboldo, because I needed his mirrors."

"Then the business with the drop of blood from every Venetian wasn't anything but—"

This time it was Junipa who interrupted her. "He wanted to keep up appearances. And the picture people have of Hell. He's still Lord Light, after all. He has—" she said it very matter-of-factly—"duties."

"Is that true?" Merle asked him.

Burbridge sighed deeply, then nodded. "You can't understand that. This wrestling between me and the Light, the strength of its power . . . how it forces its thoughts on one and changes all that goes on in one. No one can comprehend that."

"*Merle.*" The Flowing Queen ended her silence, speaking gently but urgently. "*We must get away from here. He is right when he speaks of how powerful the Stone Light is. And there are things that have to be done.*"

Merle pondered briefly, then thought of something else. She turned to the professor again. "In the pyramid, when we were flying away from you . . . you said something there, you know a name. I didn't understand what you meant by that. Whose name?"

Burbridge came closer; he could have touched her with his hand now. But he didn't dare to. "*Her* name, Merle. The name of the Flowing Queen."

Is that true? she asked in her mind.

The Queen gave no answer.

"What would it change if I knew what she's named?"

"It isn't only her name," he said. "It has to do with who she really is."

Merle inspected him penetratingly. If it was some kind of a trick, she didn't understand what he was driving at. She tried to move the Queen to an explanation, but she seemed to be awaiting Burbridge's.

"Sekhmet," he said. "Her name is Sekhmet."

Merle dug into her memory. But there was nothing, no name that even resembled that one.

"Sekhmet?"

Burbridge smiled. "The ancient Egyptian goddess of the lions."

Is that so?

Hesitantly the Queen said, "*Yes.*"

But—

"In the old temple ruins and in the graves of the pharaohs she is depicted as a lioness. Ask her, Merle! Ask her if she was a lioness of stone."

"*More than that. I was a goddess, and yes, my body was that of a lioness. . . . At that time most of the gods still had their own bodies and wandered over the world like all other creatures. And who can say if we were really gods. We could not, in any case, but the idea pleased us and we began to give credence to the talk of the humans.*" She paused. "*Finally we also were convinced of our own omnipotence. That was the time when the humans began to hunt us. For the images of the gods are much easier to misuse for human purposes than the gods themselves. Images have no will and no desires. Statues stand for nothing but the goals of the rulers. So it has ever been. The word of a god is, in truth, only the word of the one who erected his statue.*"

Merle exchanged a look with Junipa. Her friend could not hear the Queen. In the mirror eyes Merle saw her own exhausted face and was afraid of herself.

How long ago was that? she asked the Queen in her mind.

"Eons. Further back than the family tree of the Egyptians extends. Others worshipped me before, peoples whose names are long forgotten."

"Is she telling you the legend?" Burbridge asked. "If not, I will do it. Sekhmet, the mighty, wise, all-knowing Sekhmet, was impregnated by a moonbeam and then bore the first sphinx, the progenitor of the sphinx people."

The Son of the Mother! flashed into Merle's mind. Why didn't you tell me that?

"Because then you would not have done what you have done. And what would it have changed? The dangers would have remained the same. But would you have faced them for an Egyptian goddess? I have never lied to you, Merle. I am the Flowing Queen. I am the one who protected Venice from the Egyptians. What I once was before—what role does that play?"

A big one. Perhaps the biggest of all. Because you've brought me here. You know what the sphinxes are planning. Have probably always known it.

"We are here to stop it. The Son of the Mother must not rise again. And if he does, I am the only one who can oppose him. For I am his mother and his lover. With him I bred the people of the sphinxes."

With your own son?

"He was the son of the moonbeam. That is something different."

Oh, really?

Again Burbridge spoke. "Sekhmet can do nothing about it," he said, surprisingly defending the Queen, even if he could only guess what she was telling Merle. "What she thought was a moonbeam . . . was in truth something else. It was a beam of the Stone Light, when it plunged down to the Earth. Did it find its target intentionally? And why Sekhmet in particular? I don't know the answers to that. Probably the Light foresaw that its plunge deep into the interior of the Earth would bury it and that it would be hard to influence the creatures on the surface. Therefore—and this is only my theory as a scientist—I think that therefore the Light impregnated the lion goddess intentionally so that it could found its own race. A race of creatures that bore in them a piece of the Light, possibly without being aware of it. A people, in any case, that sometime could be taken over by the Light in order to carry out its orders on the surface. As the Lilim do in the interior of the Earth." Weary and worn out, he broke off. At the end his voice had sounded weaker and weaker, increasingly older and rougher.

You heard him, Merle said to the Queen.

"*Yes.*"

And?

The Queen seemed to hesitate, but then Merle heard the voice in her head again. "*It was I who killed the Son of the Mother. I felt too late that he bore the Light in him. It was too late because the people of the sphinxes were*

*already born. I could only hinder him from rising to be
their ruler. But as it has turned out, I only achieved a post-
ponement. The sphinxes have become what I always
feared."*

Then you went to the lagoon—

*"In order to watch him. Just like Lalapeya and those
who came before her. Nevertheless, there was a great difference: The sphinxes worshipped him and kept watch to
keep anyone from desecrating his grave. I, on the other
hand, watched him to prevent his resurrection. Lalapeya
was the first one who guessed what he had in him. She had
no information, of course not, but she felt it. Especially
when she learned that the sphinxes were behind the
Egyptian Empire and saw the resurrection of the Son of the
Mother as the highest of their goals."*

Merle understood. This was the connection she'd been
seeking, the connection between the sphinxes and the
Stone Light. The Pharaoh, the Horus priests, they'd all
been tools in the hands of the sphinxes.

The war, the destruction of the world, had that all not
been important, really? Had it always been only about
Venice and what was buried beneath it?

*"With the prospect of world domination, the sphinxes
made the Horus priests and the Pharaoh compliant. But
their most important goal was always the lagoon. And I
was the only one who could keep them away from there."*
Her voice faltered for a moment, as if she'd lost power

over it. Then she added more collectedly, *"I failed. But I have come into the stronghold of the sphinxes in order to set things right. With you, Merle."*

You wanted to go there from the beginning?

"No. In the beginning I thought that we would find help in Hell. I wanted to draw the Lilim into the war against the Empire. But I did not know how great the Stone Light's power over Burbridge already was. We have lost valuable time because of that. The Son of the Mother is already in the Iron Eye, I can sense him. Even Lalapeya cannot stop that. That is why she is there."

What will happen when he awakens?

"He will be for the Stone Light on the surface what Burbridge was here below—only incomparably more cruel and determined. He has more sphinx magic than anyone. There will be no doubt about him and very certainly no mirror room into which he withdraws from the influence of the Light. The Light will saturate the world as water does a sponge. And then it will stop for no one."

Merle's eyes sought Junipa, who had been watching her with curiosity and concern. If the Son of the Mother grasped power and brought the Empire under his control, Junipa would again fall under the control of the Stone Light. Like everyone else. Like Merle herself.

Burbridge and Junipa both knew what was going on in Merle's head. They couldn't hear the dialogue between her and the Queen, but they were observing Merle carefully, her features, each of her movements. Junipa was holding Merle's hand as tightly as before, as if she could somehow support her that way, help her to take in all the new information and process it.

The information and the Queen's admission had bowled her over, but she still summoned up the strength to concentrate on the most important things: on the Queen, on Junipa, and on the Son of the Mother.

And then there was Burbridge, who stood facing her, a heap of misery, an old man who looked as if he desperately needed a chair because he was hardly able to stand on his own.

"You must go," he said. "The Stone Light tolerates it sometimes when I withdraw here. But not often, and certainly not for as long as today."

Merle gently detached herself from Junipa, walked forward firmly, and for the first time held out her hand. He took it, and tears came to his eyes.

"What will it do?" she asked softly. "To you?"

"I am Lord Light. I will always be that. It will perhaps destroy these mirrors. But that is not bad. We have met, and I no longer need them. I have said to you what there is to say . . . or at least the most important things. There are other things that I feel and think and—" He broke off, shook his head, and began again. "I cannot withstand the Light much longer. It will strengthen its hold." Now the tears overflowed and rolled down his cheeks. "If we ever see each other again, I will finally have become him whom you met in Hell. The man who allowed Junipa's heart to be exchanged. Who rules the Lilim people like a despot. And who surrendered his free will to the Stone Light."

Merle's throat was tight. "You could come with us."

"I am too old," he said, shaking his head. "Without the power of the Light I would die."

Yet that's what you want, isn't it? Merle thought. But she didn't say it aloud. The thought hurt, even if she didn't want to admit it. She didn't want him to die. But she also didn't want him to be forever what humanity had long seen him as: the Devil, Satan in person.

He seemed to guess what she was thinking. "The Light has enveloped my soul. I'm too weak to go to my death of my own will. I've held out too long for that, fought too long. I could ask you, but that would be cruel and—"

"I can't do that!"

"I know." He smiled and looked strangely wise as he did so. "And perhaps that's best. Every world needs its devil, this one too. It needs the specter of evil in order to recognize why it's so important to defend the good. In certain ways I'm only fulfilling my duty. . . even the Stone Light does that. And someday people will again fear Hell as that which it's been all these millennia: a phantom, something that one may perhaps believe in but doesn't hold for real. Legends and myths and transfigured rumors, far, far from the daily life of human beings."

"But only if we succeed in stopping the sphinxes," said Junipa.

"That is the prerequisite." Burbridge pulled Merle to him and embraced her. She returned the gesture without thinking about it. "This story down here is not yours, my child. You are the heroine of the story up there. In Hell there are no heroes. Only those who are wrecked. It is not Lord Light who is your enemy. Your opponents are above: the sphinxes, the Son of the Mother. If you succeed in stopping them, it will be a long time before the Stone Light wins power on the upper surface again. If its loyal followers up there are destroyed, it is beaten in your part of the world. And as for this old man, it's best if you forget him again. For a few hundred or a few thousand years. The Light and I . . . Lord Light, I should say . . . we have enough to do in Hell. We need not concern ourselves with the upper world." He released her from his embrace, but his eyes continued to hold hers. "That is now your task alone."

"The Lilim won't attack the humans?"

"No. They have never done that. Not as an army, not to conquer their lands. There are individuals who've found their way up there, certainly . . . but they're only predators. There will be no war between above and below."

"But the Light will live on in Hell!"

"Powerful down here, but powerless on the surface.

Without its children, the sphinxes, it will probably need thousands of years before it dares a new attempt. Until then it is nothing but what the churches preach: the Tempter, the Evil One, the Fallen Angel, Lucifer—and for all of you, basically, as harmless as a ghost rattling its chains. If it is nothing more than a part of a religion, if it again becomes an empty expression, then it can no longer hurt anyone."

"He is right," said the Flowing Queen excitedly. *"He really could be right."*

"Go," said Burbridge once more, this time imploring. "Before—"

"Before it's too late?" Merle forced herself to smile. "I've read that somewhere."

Then Burbridge laughed and embraced her again. "You see, my child? Just a story. Nothing but a story."

He kissed her on the forehead, also kissed Junipa, then he stepped back.

The girls looked at him one last time, so they could remember the picture of Charles Burbridge, not Lord Light; the picture of an old man, not the Devil, which he would soon be again.

They departed the Hell of the Lilim through the mirror and walked back into their own world.

7

The Abduction

"THEY'RE GONE," JUNIPA SAID.

"What?"

"They're not in the hiding place anymore." Piercing the silver veil of the mirror world, Junipa was looking into the Iron Eye, into the room where they'd left the comrades. "There's no one there now," she said in distress.

"Where did they go?"

"I don't know. I have to look for them."

Merle swore because she couldn't see through the mirror herself. All she saw were blurry forms and colors, but no clear pictures. At the moment she couldn't even make out which mirror the hiding place had lain behind.

"There's . . . there's been a fight," Junipa said. "The sphinxes—they discovered them."

"Oh, no!"

"There are three men lying on the floor . . . three spies. They're dead. The others are gone."

"And Vermithrax?"

"I don't see him."

"But you can't miss him!"

Junipa turned toward her, and for perhaps the first time since Merle had known her, her voice sounded irritated.

"Be patient, will you? I have to concentrate."

Merle bit her lower lip and kept quiet. Her knees were trembling.

Junipa let go of her hand and looked around, turning in all directions among the mirrors. "The Iron Eye is so big. There are too many mirrors. They could be anywhere."

"Then take me back into the hiding place."

"Are you really sure? That could be dangerous."

"I want to see it with my own eyes. Otherwise it's so . . . so unreal."

Junipa nodded. "Stay close by me. Just in case we have to disappear again fast." She took Merle by the hand again and whispered the glass word, and they walked through a mirror as if through a curtain of moonlight.

The door of the room was shattered into hundreds of mirror fragments, which covered the floor like strewn razor blades. The wall mirrors also showed cracks in several places. One wall, to the girls' right, was completely destroyed, and it took only seconds for them to realize that this was the way Vermithrax had fled from the sphinxes. The stone wall beneath the remaining glass looked like an open mouth full of missing teeth.

"There must have been many of them," Junipa declared thoughtfully. "Otherwise he wouldn't have run away. He's much stronger than they are."

Merle had gone down in a crouch beside the three dead men. She quickly saw that the Czarists were beyond help. Andrej was not among them. Merle remembered a fifth spy, a red-haired hulk of a man, who'd looked particularly grotesque in his mummy clothing. He was also missing.

"Merle!"

She looked up, first at Junipa, who'd uttered the terrified cry, then toward the door.

A sphinx was rushing toward them, his speed hypnotic. The sight froze her. But Junipa was already beside her, grabbed her, spoke the word, and pulled her through the nearest mirror. Behind them sounded a shout of surprised fury and then they heard a shrill grinding as the massive sphinx soldier crashed against the glass. A crack appeared inside the mirror world for a moment, then it was extinguished, like a pencil stroke that someone erased from the top to the bottom.

Merle was out of breath. The knowledge of how closely they'd escaped death gradually spread through her. Her heart hammered in her chest, hard and jabbing.

Junipa's eyes remained expressionless, but her face showed how angry she was. "I told you to stay by me! That was pretty close!"

"I thought perhaps I could still help someone."

Junipa looked as if she were going to make an angry reply, but then her expression resolved into its usual gentleness. "Yes. Of course." She looked encouragingly at Merle. "I'm sorry."

They smiled shyly at each other, then Junipa took Merle by the hand. Together they walked on.

Soon Merle again had the feeling of being lost and had to rely on Junipa's sense of direction. Now and again they stopped. Junipa looked around, almost sensing, like a predator prowling for prey, touched a mirror wall once or twice, and then hurried on.

"Here!" she said finally, pointing to a mirror. It seemed to Merle that it shone a little more brightly than the others, in an orangey, fiery light.

"There he is! That's Vermithrax!"

"Wait. Let me look first." Junipa stepped forward until the tip of her nose touched the glass. When she whispered the word, the surface clouded before her lips. She shoved her face through just far enough to see to the other side, dove through her white breath on the glass as if it were a pitcher of fresh milk. Merle held her hand and had the feeling that Junipa's fingers grew colder the longer she stayed part in the mirror world, part in the Iron Eye.

She whispered her friend's name.

A wavelike shuddering ran through the mirror when Junipa pulled her face back. "They're there. All four."

"Seth too?"

"Yes. He's fighting beside Andrej."

"Really?" The idea surprised her.

Junipa nodded. "What do we do now?"

We have to go to them, Merle told herself. Have to help them. Have to stop the sphinxes from completing their plan. But how? She might be the granddaughter of the Devil, the daughter of a sphinx—but she was still only a fourteen-year-old girl. Any sphinx could kill her with a single stroke. And she didn't want Junipa to be stabbed.

"I know what you're thinking," said Junipa.

Merle stared past her at the mirror and the light behind it, at the twitching forms, too distorted for her to recognize figures in them. She knew that Vermithrax and the others were fighting for their lives over there, and yet no sound of it crossed over the threshold of the mirror world. No clattering of weapons, no cries, no panting or grim moans. The world could have been destroyed on the other side, but here behind the mirrors it would have been nothing more than pretty fireworks of color and silver.

"Something's different from before," Junipa said.

"What?"

Junipa crouched, put one hand on the glass at floor level, whispered the word, and reached through. When she pulled her fingers back, they were clenched into a fist. She held it before Merle's face and opened it.

Merle stared at what she saw in front of her. Then stretched out a finger and touched it.

"Ice," she whispered breathlessly.

"Snow," said Junipa. "It's only hard because I pressed it together."

"But that means that Winter is here! Here in the Iron Eye!"

"He can make it snow even inside buildings?" Junipa frowned. Merle had told her of Winter and his search for his beloved Summer. But she still had trouble imagining a season as a flesh-and-blood being who roamed through the mirrored passages of the Eye.

Merle made her decision. "I want to go over there."

Junipa threw the snow to the floor, where it dissolved into water as soon as it landed. She sighed softly, but finally she nodded. "Yes, we really have to do something." She thought for a moment and added, "But don't go all the way through the mirror. As long as you have an arm or a foot on the other side, the mirror will remain permeable. In an emergency, we only need to jump back."

Merle agreed, even if she hardly heard what Junipa said. She was much too stirred up, her head whirling.

Hand in hand they walked through the mirror.

Blinding brightness greeted them. A snowfield that was lengthened into infinity by the walls and the ceiling. A wave of noise and fury slammed against them, worse than anything Merle had expected. Vermithrax let out a shattering roar, while he took on two sphinxes at the same time. Andrej and Seth were fighting back-to-back. The red-haired spy lay lifeless on the floor; the blow of a sickle sword had felled him. There were several mummy soldiers in the hall. Beside them Merle counted three sphinxes. Another lay motionless in the entrance.

"Merle!" Vermithrax had seen her; he blocked the blow of a sword with his bare paw and with the other pulled his claws down the chest of the sphinx. Blood flowed into the snow and was soon covered by the body of the collapsed sphinx. The second sphinx hesitated before he resolved on a renewed attack. When he saw that his sword blow bounced off the lion's glowing obsidian body as if it were a wall, he retreated. Vermithrax made a few lunges after him but then let his opponent run.

Andrej and Seth were fighting together against the third sphinx and the three mummy soldiers. The undead were no great help to their leader, continually standing in the way or stumbling into the attack of the sphinx. Finally he also let out an angry cry and stormed away, straight across the hall and through the high door, behind which still more snow stretched.

Junipa was still standing in front of the mirror wall, half in this world, half in the mirror world. Merle had taken her advice to heart and until now had endeavored not to lose contact with the mirror. But when she saw that the sphinxes were fleeing, she was about to let go of Junipa's hand and run over to Vermithrax.

Suddenly someone seized her, tore her away from Junipa, and flung her to one side. With a scream she crashed against one of the mirrors and fell to her knees. At once her dress was sucking up ice-cold wetness.

When Merle looked up, she saw Seth. He'd grasped Junipa's hand, pushed off, and pulled her with him through the mirror wall. No glass splintered, and Merle knew the reason for it: The glass door was open as long as Junipa had not left the mirror. The glass word remained in effect for her and anyone she touched. For Seth, too.

"*No!*" Merle leaped up and ran through the snow to the mirror. But she already knew that she was too late.

Seth and Junipa were gone. Merle wanted to follow them, against her better judgment, and she struck the glass with her shoulder. The glass wall creaked, but it held.

"No!" She shouted again, kicked her foot against the glass, and hammered on it with her fists. With watery eyes she stared into the mirror, but instead of her friend and the high priest, she saw only herself, with wild, straggling hair, red eyes, and shining cheeks. Her dress was wet with snow, but she hardly felt the cold.

"Merle," said Vermithrax quietly, suddenly beside her.

She didn't hear him, drummed against the mirror again, whirled around, and sank down with her back against the glass. In despair she rubbed her eyes, but the brightness around her now blinded her even more. Light reflections formed glistening stars and circles, all clear figures blurred.

One of them was Vermithrax. Another was Andrej, whom the stone lion had dragged with him and laid down between them in the snow. Somewhere in the background lay the mummy soldiers in the midst of gray fountains of dust.

"She's gone," said the lion.

"I see that, damn it!"

"Andrej is dying, Merle."

"I—" She broke off, stared at Vermithrax, then the Czarist, who stretched out a hand to her from the ground. He whispered something in his mother tongue, and it was obvious that he saw in Merle someone other than herself.

Vermithrax nodded to her. "Take his hand," he whispered.

Merle sank to her knees and embraced Andrej's cold fingers with both hands. Her thoughts were still with

Junipa, whom she'd now lost for the second time, but she did her best to concentrate on the dying man. *Unreal* kept thundering through her mind over and over. Everything is so unreal.

Andrej's free hand grasped her shoulder, so hard that it hurt, and pulled her forward. The fingers climbed to her neck. Just as Merle was about to pull back, he was able to take hold of the leather band on which she wore the chicken's foot. The sign of the Baba Yaga. The sign of his goddess.

Merle would have liked to wipe the tears from her eyes, but she knew she mustn't let go of him now. No matter what happened around her: Andrej deserved to die in peace. He was a brave man, as were his companions; they'd taken the risk of giving up their camouflage for the girls and the lion. They could have been finished off by that first sphinx alone, but Andrej had struck him for them. Perhaps because after all the months in the Iron Eye he'd been glad to meet a living, breathing human again.

Andrej clung with one hand to the chicken's foot on her neck while he murmured words in Russian, perhaps a prayer, perhaps something else. Several times there was a word that Merle thought was the name of a woman or a girl. *His daughter* flashed through her mind. He'd told her, very briefly, after he'd led all three of them into the hiding place, about his daughter, whom he'd left many thousands of miles away.

Then Andrej died. With trembling hands she had to loosen his fingers from the pendant.

Vermithrax snorted softly.

"We have to get away from here!" he said finally, and it seemed to Merle that these seven words described their journey best. Away from Venice, away from Axis Mundi, an everlasting flight. And her destination seemed always to slide into the distance again.

Vermithrax spoke again. "The sphinxes will send out the alarm."

Merle nodded absently. She crossed Andrej's hands on his chest, without knowing if this gesture was understood in his homeland. She lightly stroked his cheek with the back of her hand before she stood up.

Vermithrax looked at her out of his huge lion eyes. "You are very brave. Much braver than I thought."

She gave a sob and began to cry, but this time she quickly got herself under control. "What about Junipa?"

"We can't follow her."

"I *know* that. But still we must do something—"

"*We must get out of here! Fast.*" At moments like this, Merle sometimes forgot that she wasn't alone in her thoughts. When the Queen abruptly cut into the conversation, she started, as if suddenly there were someone standing behind her and bellowing in her ear. "*Vermithrax is right. We have to keep them from calling the Son of the Mother back to life.*"

"The Son of the Mother can go jump in a lake!" Merle shouted angrily, so that Vermithrax heard it too. He raised an eyebrow in amazement. "Seth has abducted Junipa, and at the moment that's more important to me than some kind of sphinx god and its mother!"

That was clear, she hoped. But the Queen wouldn't be moved. If there was anything on which she was an expert, it was persistence. Nerve-deadening, pitiless persistence. *"Your world will be destroyed, Merle. It will be destroyed, if you and I do not do something to prevent it."*

"My world is already destroyed," she said sadly. "From the moment you and I met each other." She didn't mean it sarcastically, and there was no malice in her voice. Every word was sincere, honestly felt: Her world—a new, unexpected one, but *her own*—had been Arcimboldo's workshop, with all its pros and cons, with Dario and the other rowdies, but also with Junipa and Eft and a place where she felt she belonged. The appearance of the Queen had brought an end to it all.

The Queen was silenced for a moment, but then she broke into the gloomy silence in Merle's head. *"Do not blame me. After the attack of the Egyptians, nothing was the way it had been."*

Merle knew very well that she was putting blame in the wrong place. "I'm sorry," she said, and yet she didn't really mean it. She couldn't help it, not here, not today, not beside Andrej's body and in front of the mirror into which Junipa had vanished as if down a silvery throat. She could say she was sorry, but she couldn't really feel it.

"Merle," said Vermithrax urgently, "please! We have to go!"

She swung onto his back. She cast a last sorrowful look at the mirror through which Junipa and Seth had disappeared, and then it was only one among many again, a facet on the many cut surfaces of a precious jewel.

"Where are we, anyway?" she asked as Vermithrax bore her through the door of the hall, stopped in the passage outside for a moment, then turned to the right. The snow inside the building lay high, twelve to sixteen inches, and it was churned up by the paws of the sphinxes and the boots of the mummy soldiers.

"Quite a way down below the spies' room." The obsidian lion gazed ahead tensely as he spoke. "We ran down stairs almost the whole time. Andrej knew the way very well. And probably his friends did too. But I couldn't understand what they were saying."

"*Andrej knew it,*" said the Queen. "*He knew that the Son of the Mother is here in the stronghold.*"

Merle passed the information along to Vermithrax. He agreed: "Seth told us while you were gone."

"Why did he do that?"

"Maybe to keep us busy while he was thinking about how to get at Junipa."

Merle deflated a little further.

"Seth only had revenge in his head," the lion added.

"*Why not?*" said the Queen. "*If that helps us to stop the Son of the Mother.*"

Merle would have loved to take her by the shoulders and shake her, but the shoulders of the Queen were now her own, and that would have looked really silly. "Good," she said after a while, "then just tell us what we should do if we suddenly stumble on him by accident."

"*May I?*" asked the Queen, with unwonted politeness.

"Help yourself."

Immediately the Queen took over Merle's voice and told Vermithrax very briefly who and what the Son of the Mother was. And what role she herself played in this affair.

"You are the mother of the sphinxes?" asked Vermithrax in astonishment. "The great Sekhmet?"

"Only Sekhmet. That is enough."

"The lion goddess!"

"*Now he is starting that business too,*" said the Queen in Merle's thoughts, and this time Merle could not suppress a faint grin.

"Is that really true?" asked Vermithrax.

"No, I am only inventing it to keep us from getting bored in this accursed fortress," the Queen said through Merle's mouth.

"Forgive me."

"No reason to become unctuous."

"Sekhmet is the goddess of all lions," said Vermithrax. "Also of my people."

"*More than that*," whispered the Queen to Merle, before she said aloud, "If you like. But I have not been a goddess for a long time—if I ever was one."

Vermithrax sounded baffled. "I don't understand."

"Just act the way you did before. No 'Great Sekhmet' here or 'goddess' there. Agreed?"

"Certainly," he said humbly.

"Don't worry about it," said Merle, when her own voice belonged to her again. "You get used to her."

"*A little humility would probably not hurt*," said the Queen peevishly.

Vermithrax carried them down more steps, deeper and deeper, and at each landing the snow became higher, the cold more cutting.

Merle looked into the mirrors, which lengthened the white into infinity, and made a decision. "We have to find Winter."

"*We have to—*," the Queen began, but Merle interrupted her.

"Alone we have no chance anyway. But together with Winter . . . who knows."

"*He will not help us. His mind is only on his search for Summer.*"

"Perhaps one thing has something to do with the other?" Merle twisted one side of her mouth in a cool smile.

"But the fastest way—"

"At the moment I'm for the safest way. What do you think, Vermithrax?"

"Everything the goddess commands."

"A lion with principles."

Merle rolled her eyes. "I don't care. We're looking for Winter! Vermithrax, keep walking to where the snow is highest."

"You will freeze to death."

"Then we'll both freeze."

"I will try to prevent that."

"Very kind."

In the middle of a stairwell, the fourth or fifth since their leaving the hall, Vermithrax stopped so abruptly that Merle slid into his mane face-first; it felt as if she'd dived into a forest of glistening underwater plants.

"What is it?"

He growled and looked around warily. "Something's wrong here."

"Are we being followed?"

"No."

"Observed?"

"That's just it. Since the fight we haven't seen any more sphinxes and mummies."

"That's all right with me."

"Come on, Merle, don't pretend to be stupid. You know what I mean."

Of course she knew. But she'd been trying the whole time to suppress it and would have liked to be able to do it a while longer. Besides, she was in the mood to quarrel. With the Queen, even with Vermithrax. She didn't rightly understand where all this anger at everyone and everything came from. Really it was Seth who'd betrayed them and abducted Junipa. Wrong! Abducted Junipa, yes—but betrayed? He'd done nothing to surrender Merle and the others to the sphinxes. He was always pursuing his own personal ends and, looking at it objectively, he had simply seized an advantage. Junipa was supposed to take him somewhere, that much was certain. For she was the key to a fast, effortless change of location. But where? To Heliopolis? Or some other place here in the Eye?

"It's as if this whole damned fortress were dead all of a sudden!" Vermithrax also sounded irritated. His huge nose sniffed the air in the circle of the stairwell, while his eyes swept alertly around. "There must still be someone somewhere."

"Perhaps they have something to do somewhere else." For instance, with Winter, Merle added in her mind.

"*Or with the Son of the Mother,*" said the Queen.

Merle imagined the scene: a huge hall in which hundreds of sphinxes were gathered. All were staring raptly at the body on its bier. Singing hung in the air, soft murmuring. The words of a priest or a leader. Grotesque apparatus and machines were turned on. Electrical charges sparked

769

between metal balls and steel coils with many turns of wire. Fluids bubbled in glass beakers, hot steam shot out of vents to the ceiling. All was reflected dozens of times in the towering silver walls.

Then a cry, leaping like flame from one sphinx to the next. Strident masks of triumph, open mouths, wide eyes, roars of laughter, of joy, of relief, but also of barely concealed anxiety. Priests and scientists, who swarmed around the Son of the Mother like flies around a piece of carrion. A dark eyelid that slowly opened. Under it a black eyeball, dried and wrinkled like a prune. And in it, caught like a curse in a dusty tomb, an increasingly bright spark of devilish intelligence.

"Merle?"

Vermithrax's voice.

"Merle?" More urgent now. "Did you hear that?"

She came alert. "Huh?"

"Did you hear that?"

"What?"

"Listen carefully."

Merle tried to comprehend what Vermithrax meant. It was only with difficulty that she was able to free herself from the picture that her mind had conjured up: the ancient, dark eye and in it the awakening understanding of the Son of the Mother.

Now she heard it.

A howling.

Again the image of a monstrous gathering of all the sphinxes arose in her. The murmuring, the singing, the sound of the rituals.

But the howling had another source.

"Sounds like a storm," Merle said.

She'd hardly spoken when something rushed at them out of the depths of the stairwell. Vermithrax bent way over the railing; Merle had to cling tightly to his mane in order not to slide down over his head into the well.

A white wall rose up out of the mirrored chasm.

Fog, she thought at first.

Snow!

A snowstorm that seemed to come directly from the heart of the Arctic, a fist of ice and cold and unimaginable force.

Vermithrax raised his wings and folded them together over Merle like two giant hands, which pressed her firmly to his back. The howling grew deafening and finally so loud that she could scarcely perceive it as sound, a blade that cut through her auditory canal and carved up her understanding. She had the feeling that her living body was turning to ice, just like the dead gull she'd found on the roof of the orphanage one winter. The bird had looked as if it had simply fallen from heaven, the wings still spread, the eyes open. When Merle had lost her balance for a moment on the smooth roof slope, it had slipped out of her hand and a wing broke off as if it were made of porcelain.

The storm passed them like a swarm of howling ghosts. When it was over and the wind in the stairwell died down, the layer of snow on the steps had almost doubled.

"Was *that* Winter?" Vermithrax asked numbly. Ice crystals glittered on his coat, a strange contrast to his body glow, which gave off no heat and was not able to melt the ice.

Merle sat up on his back, ran both hands through her hair, and wiped the wet strands out of her face. The tiny little hairs in her nose were frozen, and for a while it was easier to breathe through her mouth.

"I don't know," she got out with a groan. "But if Winter had been in that storm somewhere, he'd certainly have seen us. He wouldn't just have run past us. Or flown. Or whatever." Dazedly she knocked the snow from her dress. It was completely frozen through, and at her knees the material was almost stiff. "It's time we found Summer."

"*We?*" said the Queen in alarm.

Merle nodded. "Without her we're going to freeze. And then it doesn't matter anymore if your son wakes up or not."

"The sphinxes," Vermithrax said. "They're frozen, aren't they? That's why there aren't any down here anymore. The cold has killed them."

Merle didn't think it was that simple. But sometimes Fate played tricks on one. And why couldn't it affect the other side once in a while, for a change?

The obsidian lion began moving again. He was trudging through high snow, but he found the steps without any trouble and walked on with amazing sure-footedness. Even a little dampness could turn the mirrored floors of the Iron Eye into slides; for the moment they almost had to be grateful for the snow, for it padded the lion's steps and kept his paws from sliding on the icy glass floor.

"In any case, the storm came from Winter," Merle said after a while. "Although I don't believe he was anywhere inside it. But this must be the right path." After pondering a little she added, "Vermithrax, did Andrej say where the Son of the Mother would be brought?"

"If he did, he said it in Russian."

And you? Merle turned to the Queen. Do you know where he is?

"*No.*"

Perhaps where Summer is also?

"*How do you fig—*" The Queen broke off and said instead, "*You really think there is more hidden in Summer's disappearance, do you?*"

Burbridge told Winter something, Merle thought. Therefore Winter is looking for her here in the Iron Eye. And if Summer had something to do with the power of the Empire?

"*You are thinking of the sunbarks?*"

Yes. But also about the mummies. And all those things that can only be explained by magic. Why didn't the priests awaken the Pharaoh a hundred years ago? Or five hundred years ago? Perhaps because they only got the strength to from Summer! They call it magic, but maybe it's something else. Machines that we don't know, that are driven with a strength that they somehow . . . I don't know, *steal* from Summer. You said it yourself: Seth is not a powerful magician. He may command a few illusions, but real magic? He's a scientist, just like all the other Horus priests. And like Burbridge. The only ones who actually understand something about magic are the sphinxes.

The Queen thought that over. *"Summer as a kind of living furnace?"*

Like the steam furnaces in the factories outside on the lagoon islands, thought Merle.

"That sounds quite mad."

Just like goddesses who bring a whole people into the world with a moonbeam.

This time she felt the Queen laugh. Softly and suppressed, but she laughed. After a while she said, *"The suboceanic kingdoms possessed such machines. No one knew exactly how they were driven. They used them in their war against the Lords of the Deep, against the ancestors of the Lilim."*

Merle could see how all the mosaic pieces were gradually fitting together into a whole. Possibly the Horus priests had stumbled on remains or drawings from the suboceanic cultures. Perhaps with their help they'd succeeded in awakening the Pharaoh or building their sunbarks. Suddenly it filled her with bitter satisfaction that the cities of the suboceanic kingdoms had fallen in ruins on the ocean floor eons ago. The prospect of the same thing happening to the Empire suddenly moved quite a bit closer.

"There's someone coming!" Vermithrax stopped.

Merle was startled. "From down below?"

The lion mane whipped back and forth in a nod. "I can sense them."

"Sphinxes?"

"At least one."

"Can you get any closer to the railing? Maybe we can see them then."

"Or they us," replied the lion, shaking his head. "There's only one possibility: We fly past them." Until now he'd avoided flying down, because the shaft in the center of the spiral staircase was very narrow, and he was afraid of breaking his wings on the sharp edges. And a wounded Vermithrax was the last thing they could bear.

However, the way things looked now, they had to try it.

They wasted no time. Merle clung to him. Vermithrax rose up and leaped over the railing and down into the chasm. They had dared such a steep flight once before, during the escape from the Campanile in Venice. But this one was worse. The cold bit into Merle's face and through her clothing, she couldn't brush away the snow particles that got into her eyes, and her heart was galloping as if it were trying to outrace her. She could hardly breathe.

They passed two windings of the stairs, then three, four, five. At the height of the sixth, Vermithrax braked his nosedive with such force that Merle thought at first they'd hit something—stone, steel, perhaps an invisible mirror floor in the stairwell. But then the lion leveled and floated with gentle wing beats in the center of the stairwell, with emptiness over and under them and in front of them—

"But that can't be—" Then Merle's voice failed her and she wasn't even certain whether she'd actually said the words aloud or only thought them.

It could almost have been their own reflection: a figure who was riding on the back of a half-human creature, which was climbing the steps on four legs. A boy, only a little older than Merle, with tousled hair and cozy fur clothing. The creature on which he sat was a female sphinx. Her arms were scantily bandaged all the way to the elbows. The four paws of her lion lower body seemed to be unharmed; she had borne her rider securely up the steps.

The sphinx was beautiful, much more beautiful than Merle had imagined her, and not even her weary, emaciated look could alter that. She had black hair falling smoothly over her shoulders down to the place where human and lion melted together.

The boy opened his eyes wide, his lips moved, but his words were lost in the rushing of the lion wings and the raging of distant snowstorms below.

Merle whispered his name.

And Vermithrax attacked.

8

Amenophis

SETH HAD LONG CEASED TO THREATEN HER WITH HIS DRAWN
sword. It was unnecessary, as they both knew. And it lacked
a certain dignity for a man like him to be pointing his sickle
blade at a girl like Junipa, half as big and very much weaker.

Junipa was sure that he wouldn't do anything to her as
long as she obeyed him. Basically, she thought, she was of
no importance to him, just like Merle and the others, just
like the whole world. Seth had built up the Empire with
sweat and blood and privation, and now he would demol-
ish it again with his own hands, or at least swing the hammer to strike the first blow.

"To Venice," he'd said, after he pushed her back into the mirror world. "Inside the palace." As if Junipa were a gondolier on the Grand Canal.

When she'd looked at him for a long moment in disbelief, a spark of doubt had appeared in his eyes. As if he weren't really aware of her capabilities.

But then she said "Yes," and nothing else. And started on the way.

He was now walking some distance behind her, almost soundlessly. Only now and then the sword in his belt struck its point against a mirror edge, and the screeching that it caused rushed like a call of alarm through the glass labyrinth of the mirror world. But there was no one there who could have heard it; or if there was, no one showed himself, not even the phantoms.

Junipa didn't ask Seth what he had in mind. For one thing, she already guessed. For another, he wouldn't have given her an answer anyway.

Before, when she'd walked into the Iron Eye with Merle, she had felt again the grip of the Stone Light. A devilish pain flamed up in her chest, just as if someone were trying to bend her ribs apart from the inside like the bars on a cage. The fragment of the Stone Light that had been inserted into her in Hell reminded her emphatically that sooner or later it would again gain power over her, when she left the mirror world or just gradually when she began to feel secure. The stone in her chest was threat and dark promise equally.

Behind the mirrors she felt better, the pain was gone, the pressure vanished. Her stone heart did not beat, but somehow it kept her alive, the Devil might know why—and indeed, *he* certainly did know.

Considering her situation, the threat of the Horus priest seemed far less dreadful to her. She could run away from Seth, or at least attempt it—but there was no outrunning the Light. At least not in her world. The Light might lose interest in her for a while, the way it did after her flight from Hell, but it was always there. Always ready to seize her, to influence her, and to set her on her friends.

No, it was good that she wasn't in the Iron Eye with Merle. She was beginning to feel sure in the mirror world. Everything in this labyrinth of silver glass was somehow familiar. Her eyes led her, let her see what no one else saw, and that made her aware how very much Seth had put himself into her hands. Perhaps he wasn't even aware of it himself.

To Venice, she thought. Yes, she would take him to Venice if he wanted it.

Just as in Hell, in the mirror world there was no difference between day and night. However, now and then the darkness appeared to descend on the other side of one of the mirrors or the morning to dawn; then the shine of the silver changed, the flickering of the colors. Their light also fell on Junipa and Seth and bathed them sometimes in one color, sometimes in another, from dark turquoise to milky lemon yellow. Once Junipa turned to the priest and saw the flaming red from a mirror gush over his face and strengthen his determined, warriorlike expression. Then again a gentle, heavenly blue covered him, and the hardness left his features.

In this place between places there were still many wonders to explore. The riddle of the colors and their effect was only one of countless mysteries.

She wasn't able to say how much time passed before they reached their destination. They didn't speak about it: It was several hours, certainly. But while behind one mirror only moments passed, behind the next it might perhaps be years. Still a secret, still a challenge.

Seth stopped beside her and regarded the mirror that rose in front of him. "Is that it?"

She wondered if the priest were filled with rage alone or whether there wasn't also a little fear, a trace of insecurity in the light of the grandeur of the environment. But Seth betrayed nothing of what was going on inside him. He hid his true nature behind anger and bitterness, and his only drive was the desire for revenge.

"Yes," she said, "behind it lies Venice. The chamber of the Pharaoh in the Doge's palace."

He touched the mirror surface with the palm of his hand, as if he hoped to be able to pass through it without Junipa and the glass word. He bent forward, breathed on it, and rubbed the cloud away with his fist, as if he were removing a spot of dirt. If there had been a spot there, it would only have been the hate in him, something that would not be simply wiped away.

Seth regarded his mirror image for a little while longer, as though he couldn't believe that the man in the glass was a reflection of himself. Then he blinked, took a deep breath, and drew his sickle sword.

"Are you ready?" Junipa asked, and she already saw the answer in him. He nodded.

"I'll take a look into the room first," she said. "You'll want to know if the Pharaoh is alone."

To her astonishment, he refused. "Not necessary."

"But—"

"You understood me, didn't you?"

"There could be ten sphinxes there standing around the Pharaoh! Or a hundred!"

"Perhaps. But I don't think so. I think they're gone. The sphinxes are on the way back into the Iron Eye or are already gathered there. They've got what they wanted. Venice doesn't interest them anymore." He laughed coldly. "And Amenophis not at all."

"The sphinxes have abandoned him?"

"Just as he did the Horus priests."

Junipa said nothing. The Pharaoh's betrayal had struck Seth more deeply than he would have thought possible. The two agreed on nothing, and yet Amenophis was anchored in his soul. Not as a human being, for Seth was indifferent to him, yes, he even despised him. But as his creation, which he'd awakened to life and which stood for all that Seth had once believed in.

What Seth was planning was far more than only the taking of another's life. It was a betrayal of himself, of his goals, of all the possibilities that his pact with Amenophis had opened to him. It was also a clean break with his own works in all the decades since he planned and supervised the reawakening of the Pharaoh.

Either way, it was the end.

Junipa took hold of his arm, whispered the glass word, and pulled him through the mirror.

At once the pressure was there in her chest again, the seeking and squeezing and dragging of the Light.

The huge room behind the mirror was empty. At least at first sight. But then she discovered the divan of jaguar skins, which emerged from the semidarkness on the other side of the room. It was night in Venice, and also here in the salon; only a weak glow came through the window. Torchlight from the Piazza San Marco, she guessed. It rested softly on the patterns of the carved panels, on the brushstrokes of the oil paintings and frescoes, on the crystal pendants of the chandeliers.

Something moved on the divan. A dark silhouette in front of a still darker hill of skins.

No one spoke.

Junipa felt as if she weren't really there, as if she were

observing the scene from a faraway place. As in a dream. *Yes*, she thought, *a great, horrible dream, and I can do nothing except watch. Not take part, not run away, only look on.*

Glass shattered behind her and tinkled onto the floor in a cascade of silver droplets. Seth had smashed the wall mirror through which they'd entered the salon. No possibility of retreat anymore. Junipa looked around hastily, but there were no other mirrors here, and she doubted she would get far enough in the corridors of the palace to find another.

Amenophis rose from his divan of jaguar skins, a small, slender figure, who moved slightly bent, as if he carried a terrible weight on his shoulders.

"Seth," he said wearily. Junipa wondered if he were drunk. His voice sounded numb and at the same time very young.

Amenophis, the resurrected Pharaoh and leader of the Empire, stepped into the half light from the window.

He was still a child. Only a boy, who had been turned into something that he might never have become without gold paint and makeup. He was no older than twelve or thirteen, at least a year younger than herself. And yet he'd commanded his armies to rule the world for four decades.

Junipa stood stock-still among the ruins of the mirror. The shards were spread wide over the dark parquet. It looked as though she were swimming in the middle of a starry sky.

Seth walked past her up to the Pharaoh. If he was looking around for guards or other opponents, he didn't betray it by any motion. He stared straight ahead at the ordinary-looking boy who waited for him in front of the divan.

"Are they all gone?" he asked.

Amenophis did not move. Said nothing.

"They've left you, haven't they." Seth's tone was without any arrogance or spiteful pleasure. A statement, nothing else. "The sphinxes are gone. And without the Horus priests . . . yes, what are you without us, Amenophis?"

"We are the Pharaoh," said the boy. He was smaller than Junipa, very slight and unprepossessing. He sounded sulky but also a little resigned, as if in his heart he'd accepted his fate. And then Junipa realized there would be no spectacular final battle between the two of them. No wild swordplay, no murderous duel over tables and chairs, no antagonists who swung through the room from the lamps and the curtains.

This was the end, and it was coming quietly and without tumult. Like the end of a serious disease, a gentle death after a long illness.

"Were all the priests executed?" asked Seth.

"You know that."

"You could have let them go."

"We had given our word: If you failed, they would die."

"You already broke your word once when you betrayed the Horus priests."

"No reason to do it a second time." The boy's smile belied his words as he added, "Even we learn from our mistakes sometimes."

"Not today."

Amenophis took a few steps to the right, to a large water basin beside the divan. He put his hands in and washed them absently. Junipa almost expected that he would pull out a weapon and point it at Seth. But Amenophis only rubbed his fingers clean and shook them briefly, so that the droplets whirled in all directions, before he again turned to the priest.

"Our armies are inconceivably large. Millions upon millions. We have the strongest men as guards, fighters from Nubia and the old Samarkand. But we are tired. So tired."

"Why don't you call for your guards?"

"They left when the sphinxes disappeared. The priests were dead, and suddenly there were only living corpses in this palace." He let out a cackling laugh, which didn't sound either real or especially full of humor. "The Nubians looked at the mummies, then us, and they realized that they were the only ones alive in this building."

He had the council murdered, flashed through Junipa's mind. *The entire City Council of Venice.*

"They left us a short time later; secretly, of course. Though we had long observed what was going on in their heads." He shrugged. "The Empire is destroying itself."

"No," said Seth. "You destroyed it. At the moment when you had my priests executed."

"You never loved us."

"But we respected you. We Horus priests were always loyal and would have continued to be, if you had not given the sphinxes preference over us."

"The sphinxes were only interested in their own intrigues, that is true."

"Insight too late."

For the first time Amenophis spoke of himself in the singular. "What shall I say?" The most powerful boy in the world smiled, but it distorted his face like his reflection on the moving surface of the water basin. "I have slept for four thousand years, and I can do it again. But the world will not forget me, will it? That is also a form of immortality. No one can forget what I have done to the world."

"And are you proud of that?" asked Junipa, her first words since her arrival. Amenophis didn't deign to answer her, not even with a glance. But suddenly something became clear to her: The two were speaking Egyptian with each other; and yet she understood what they said. And at the same time she understood what Arcimboldo had meant when he told her, "As guide through the mirror world, you are a master of all voices, all tongues. For what good would a guide be if he didn't know the language of the lands through which he led others?" How could she have guessed before what that was going to mean? It was still hard for her to grasp the whole truth now. Did that really mean that she understood each of the languages that were spoken in the countless worlds? *All voices, all tongues* echoed through her mind, and she grew quite dizzy with it.

Amenophis pulled her out of her astonishment. "Immortality is better than what you gave me," he said to Seth. "A few decades, no more. Perhaps they would have made a century. But you were already tired of me, weren't you? How long would you have tolerated me? You wanted to take my place . . . poor Seth, you were quite ill with envy and ambition. And who can blame you for that? You were the one who solved the riddles of the suboceanic kingdoms. You gave the Empire all its power. And now look at you! Only a man without hair and with a sword in his hand that he never even saw until a few days ago, much less carried."

The Horus priest was standing with his back to Junipa, but she saw him tense. Death surged from every pore.

"All illusion," said Amenophis, "all masquerade. Like the gold on our skin." He ran a finger through the smudged gold paint on his face and rubbed it between his thumb and forefinger.

"The Empire is no illusion. It is real."

"Is it? Who will tell me, then, that it is not one of your illusions? There you're a master, Seth. Illusions. Masks. Sleights of hand. Others might have thought it was magic, but I know the truth. You explored the remains of the suboceanic kingdoms as a scholar. But the learned man has become a charlatan. You know how to influence the minds of men, how to delude them. Giant falcons and monsters, Seth, those are the toys of children but not the weapons with which one manages an empire. At least the sphinxes were right about that." The Pharaoh made a skipping turn and sank back onto the divan, back into the shadows. His weary voice floated into the darkness like a bird with a lame wing beat. "Is all this illusion? Tell me, Seth! Did you really awaken me to life or am I still lying in my burial chamber in the pyramid of Amun-Ka-Re? Have I really become the conqueror of the world, or is that only a dream you have conjured up for me? And is it true that all my loyal followers have left me and I am now all alone in a palace full of mummies—although perhaps I am one myself and have never left my grave? Tell me the truth, priest! What is illusion, and what is reality?"

Seth had not moved at all. Junipa moved slowly along the wall. She had a vague hope of making it to the door before one of the two of them noticed her.

"Do you really believe that?" asked Seth. Junipa stopped. Yet the words weren't directed to her, but to Amenophis. "Do you actually think that the events of the past forty years are nothing but an illusion?"

"I know what you are capable of," said the Pharaoh with a shrug. "Not real magic like the sphinxes, but you know all about deception. Perhaps in truth I am still laid out on the sandstone block in my pyramid, and you are standing beside me, your hand on my forehead—or whatever was necessary to plant all these images in my head. With every year that has passed and with every minute of the recent days my certainty has become greater: Nothing of all this is *true*, Seth! I am dreaming! My mind is caught in a huge, unique illusion! I have played the game, moved the pieces on the board, and had my fun. Why not? In truth, there was never anything to lose."

Junipa reached the door, slowly pressed down the gigantic latch. And yes, the high oaken door swung open! A draft of cool air came from the corridor and blew through her hair. But still she did not run away. The last meeting between the Pharaoh and his creator held her fast with a macabre fascination. She had to know what happened next. Had to see it.

Slowly Seth began walking up to the divan.

"Even my death is only an illusion," said Amenophis. From the mouth of a twelve-year-old, the sentence sounded as unreal as if he were rattling off a very complicated mathematical formula. Junipa was reminded again that the Pharaoh was much older than his body made him appear. Inconceivably older.

"Only illusion," he whispered once more, as if his thoughts were somewhere else, in a place of deep silence and darkness. In a grave, in the heart of a stepped pyramid.

"If that's what you think," said Seth, and he raised the sword and let it fall on the Pharaoh.

There was no resistance.

Not even a cry.

Amenophis died quietly and meekly. Seth, who had given him his life, took it from him again. Only a dream, the Pharaoh might think as he died, only delusion induced by the priest of Horus.

Junipa pushed on the door and slipped through the crack. Outside in the corridor she took four or five steps before she became aware of the silence. Seth wasn't following her.

Uncertain, she stopped.

Turned around. And went back.

Don't do it! her mind screamed. *Run away, as fast as you can!*

Nevertheless, Junipa stepped into the doorway and looked into the room again.

Seth was lying on the floor in front of the Pharaoh's body, his face turned in her direction. His left hand was clenched into a fist, the right loosening on the grip of the sword. The sickle blade was sticking out of his body. He had driven it into his own chest without a sound.

"He was wrong," he brought out with difficulty, spitting blood onto the parquet. "Everything is . . . true."

Junipa overcame her fear, her aversion, her disgust. Slowly she walked into the room and went to the divan and the two men who, until a few days before, had together guided the destiny of the greatest and cruelest realm in human history. Now they lay before her, the one dead in a sea of jaguar skins, the other dying at her feet.

"I am sorry," Seth whispered weakly, "because of the mirror—that was stupid."

Junipa went onto her knees and looked for words. She considered whether she should say something to lessen his pain or his disappointment. But perhaps that was just what he had done: He *had* lessened his pain. He had killed the master that he himself had created, had slain the child and the father.

It is good this way, she thought, and she had the feeling that the thought floated away like a feather. Like a last illusion.

Silently she stretched out a forefinger and stroked it over the strands of the golden network that was inlaid into Seth's scalp. It felt cool and not magic at all. Only like metal that had been pressed into flesh with terrible pain. It was exactly what it looked like: a network of gold in a place where it didn't belong.

As we are all, she thought sadly.

"Don't go . . . through the palace. The mummy soldiers are everywhere. There is no one left who . . . who controls them."

"What will they do?"

"I . . . don't know. Nothing, perhaps. Or . . ." He fell silent, began again: "Don't go. Too dangerous."

"I must find a mirror."

Seth tried to nod, but he wasn't able to. Instead, trembling, he stretched out a finger. Junipa looked in the direction he was pointing. And she saw what he meant.

Yes, she thought. *That could work.*

"Fare . . . well," Seth gasped.

Junipa fixed her eyes on his. "What for? You've destroyed everything."

Seth could not answer. His eyes dulled, the lids fluttered one last time. Then a slight shudder ran through his body and he stopped breathing.

Junipa walked wearily to the water basin beside the divan. It was big enough. She bent till her mouth was over it and whispered the glass word. Then she climbed onto the marble basin, swung her legs over the edge, and let herself down into her reflection.

The stone in her chest pulled her under.

9
Sphinx Splinters

IT HAD NOT BEEN EASY.

Not easy at all.

Still, Merle had somehow managed to restrain Vermithrax before he could fly over the railing with a roar and tear the sphinx and the boy to pieces.

Now, much later, at the foot of the snow-covered stairs, the obsidian lion stopped and looked over at Lalapeya. The sphinx tilted her head, closed her eyes, and appeared to scent, the way Vermithrax sometimes did too, but in her it looked less like a wild animal. She does even that, Merle thought, with grace and beauty.

"Along there," Lalapeya said, and Vermithrax nodded. He'd come to the same conclusion.

What they both scented, Merle did not know. It was only after a while that she realized that it was the snow they were sensing, the way many animals instinctively flee an oncoming cold spell or store provisions in their burrows.

Some time had passed since the meeting on the staircase. Time in which Merle had to come to terms with the fact that the sphinx at her side was in fact her mother. And that it really was Serafin who was now sitting behind her on Vermithrax's back and had put his hands around her waist to hold on.

After the obsidian lion had understood that the sphinx on the stairs was not an enemy, he'd set Merle down on the steps. She and Serafin had fallen into each other's arms, to just stand there for a long time without words, hugging each other tightly. Merle had the feeling that he almost kissed her, but then his lips only touched her hair briefly, and all she could think of was that she hadn't washed it for days. It was crazy, really. Here they were, all trapped in this accursed sphinx stronghold, and she was thinking about washing her hair! Was that what being in love did to you? And then, *was* it being in love that was responsible for the lump in her throat and the fluttering in her stomach?

Serafin leaned close to her ear. "I missed you," he whispered. Her pulse raced. She was convinced that he must hear it, the hammering in her ears, the rushing of blood throughout her entire body. And if not that, then he doubtless felt the trembling of her legs, the trembling of every part of her.

She answered that she had missed him, too, which suddenly sounded trite and empty, she thought, because he'd said it to her first. Then she just talked straight on, said all sorts of other things, which two minutes later, thank heavens, she couldn't remember, because it was probably pretty incoherent. She was sure she sounded dumb and childish, and she didn't even know why.

And then, Lalapeya.

It was an entirely different kind of reunion from that with Serafin, most of all because it was, at least in Merle's view, not a real reunion. She had no memories of her mother, not her voice, not how she'd looked. She only knew her hands, from all the hours they had held each other's in the interior of the water mirror. But Lalapeya's hands were bandaged, and Merle couldn't touch them and reassure herself that they were the same hands she'd held before.

Not that, in all seriousness, she *had* to reassure herself. She knew that Lalapeya was her mother, knew it the moment she'd seen the sphinx on the stairs, even before she recognized Serafin on her back. That might simply have been due to appearances, to a resemblance of the eyes, a similar shape of face, or the long dark hair.

But it was far more that bound Merle to Lalapeya right off: The sphinx possessed exactly that degree of perfection that Merle sometimes imagined for herself, that beauty that she hoped she'd have when she grew up. But she was only fourteen, and a thing or two would happen in her face before it would become the firm, unchanging countenance she now saw before her above the slender shoulders of a sphinx.

She couldn't embrace Lalapeya because she was afraid of touching her injured arms, and she also wasn't sure it would be appropriate at their first meeting. So they only exchanged words. They spoke with a certain reserve, but also with scarcely concealed joy. Lalapeya was beaming despite her pain—and it was clear that she was feeling true happiness. And probably relief, too, that Merle didn't reproach her for what she'd experienced as a small child.

The Flowing Queen said not one word the whole time. Was simply silent, as if she were no longer a part of Merle. As if her spirit were already caught up in the battle with the Son of the Mother and had completely tuned out of its surroundings, even at a moment like this. Once Merle thought: She's hatching something. But then she told herself that the Flowing Queen possibly knew better than any of them what lay ahead. And then who could blame her if she didn't feel like talking?

It was Vermithrax who reminded Merle that they must be on their way. She then took great pains to explain their plan to Lalapeya and Serafin. Considering how much had happened since their last meeting, she quickly realized that she must limit herself to the most essential facts. Nevertheless she earned more than one incredulous look, and it took a while before she finally came to Winter's role in the whole story: who he was, what he was looking for, and why *they* were looking for *him.*

As they made their way down the stairs together, Serafin took over the story and told how they'd landed there. When he revealed that Eft, Dario, and the others were also in the Iron Eye, Merle could hardly believe it. Especially Dario! Her archenemy from the mirror workshop. But he'd been Serafin's antagonist even more than hers. If the two of them had now become friends, in fact, a whole lot must have happened. She burned to know the details.

"Eft is hurt," Serafin said. He told how she'd become involved in a fight with a sphinx guard at the foot of the stronghold. Eft had broken her lower leg, while Dario and Aristide had suffered severe sword cuts. None of their injuries were mortal, but after they'd tried to climb one of the staircases in the lower regions of the Eye together, the others had had to give up. Tiziano had stayed with them so that the injured weren't on their own, while Lalapeya and Serafin had continued the ascent. "I didn't want to leave them behind," he said finally, "but what were we supposed to do?"

"We could have turned around and gone back to the boat together," said Lalapeya. "But then it would all have been for nothing. So Serafin and I decided to go on alone."

"Where are they now?" asked Merle.

"In a library near the entrance," Serafin answered. "There's a gigantic library down there, incredibly huge."

Merle looked at him in disbelief. Until now she'd seen nothing but mirrors in the Iron Eye. Salons, halls, chambers of mirrors. The idea of one or even several giant libraries didn't fit into the picture she'd had of the fortress. She spoke her thoughts aloud.

Lalapeya looked over her shoulder. "To you, the sphinxes must seem a people of warriors and conquerors. You've never known them to be any different, in Venice with the Pharaoh or here. But the sphinxes are far more than that. They are a people of scholars. There are many wise heads among them, and once they gave the world great philosophers, storytellers, and playwrights. In the old desert cities there were theater arenas, where we gathered not only to watch, but also to discuss. Not all the sphinxes' arguments were carried on with weapons in those days. I can remember the great speeches, the clever debates and lectures—all at a time when the human race had more similarity to animals than the sphinxes do today. There were great minds among us, and then the artists . . . the old songs and poetry of the sphinxes possess a poetic charm that is unique."

"*She speaks the truth,*" the Flowing Queen said suddenly. "*In certain respects, anyway. However, humans were not so primitive and simpleminded as she claims.*"

Of course not, Merle thought acidly, or otherwise they'd hardly have made you into a goddess.

"*I did not seek that out,*" said the Queen. "*It is characteristic of humans not to ask those whom they worship for permission first. And, unfortunately, it is also characteristic of the gods to grow accustomed to being worshipped.*"

They were following a broad corridor a good two hundred yards wide with a high, curving ceiling, almost a kind of roofed-over street, though bigger and more imposing, when Vermithrax pointed forward with his head. "There! Do you see that?"

Merle blinked in the blinding white expanse of snowflakes, extended into a plain by the mirrors on both sides of the passage. The light was too bright for her to be able to make out anything in the distance. Serafin and Lalapeya didn't see what Vermithrax's sharp eyes had spied either.

"Sphinxes," he said. "But they aren't moving."

"Guards?" asked Lalapeya.

"Perhaps. Although I don't think that matters anymore."

The sphinx gave him an astonished look, while Merle gently scratched him behind the ear. "What do you mean?" she asked.

He purred briefly, perhaps because he enjoyed the touch, perhaps just to please her. "They're white," he said then.

"White?" Serafin repeated in amazement.

"Frozen to ice."

Merle felt Serafin's tension. He didn't like sitting inactive on the back of a lion and waiting. He itched to take matters into his own hands again. She understood him well; it didn't suit her temperament to become a victim of events either. Perhaps she'd let herself be pushed around too much since her meeting with the Queen, had done what was expected of her, not what she really wanted to. But at the same time, she had to recognize that she'd never had a choice: Her path had been predestined, and even at little crossings, a detour had been out of the question. Not for the first time she felt like a puppet who was being manipulated by everyone—worse yet, like a *child*. While basically, she never had been one. In the orphanage she'd had no time for it.

They went on, and soon Merle and the others, too, realized what Vermithrax had meant. Like a forest of statues, outlines detached themselves from the omnipresent white, hardly visible at first, then a little more clearly, finally as clear as polished glass. And in fact that's what the sphinxes resembled most: glass. Ice.

There were more than a dozen, fixed in various poses of fear and retreat. Some had tried to escape Winter's touch by running ahead of him; others had tried to fight, but the expressions on their faces showed the mood of despair, even of panic. Some had let the weapons slide from their hands, sickle swords half buried by the snow.

"What has happened here?" Lalapeya murmured.

"Winter was here," Merle said. "Everything he touches turns to ice. He told me that. Every living thing, with one exception—Summer. That's why he's looking for her. That's why they love each other."

There was a grating sound. Beside them, cracks went branching through the ice body of one sphinx, and a moment later he shattered with a crash into sharp-edged fragments. Only his four lion legs remained standing. They stuck out of the snow like road markers someone had forgotten.

For a moment none of them moved, as if they were turned to ice themselves. No one knew what had made the sphinx burst—until Serafin, cursing, pointed to a small dart that was sticking out of one of the pieces of debris.

"Someone's shooting at us!"

Merle scanned the passage, and she didn't have to look long before she discovered a sphinx who was leaning out of an archway and taking aim at them a second time. Before any of them could react, he fired. Lalapeya let out a scream as the shot grazed her shoulder and struck another ice sphinx behind her with a *clink*. Grinding and splintering, he broke apart.

More sphinxes appeared behind the sniper, but only some of them were armed. Some of them held chisels and hammers in their hands, as well as glass vessels and pouches.

They were going to examine the dead, Merle thought.

They would break off little pieces to examine them and look for a weak spot in their opponent.

Unfortunately, the troop of researchers was accompanied by several soldiers, who didn't look like the intellectual creatures Lalapeya had described before. They were big and muscular, with broad lion bodies and massive human shoulders.

Vermithrax took advantage of his wings and rose into the air with his riders. Lalapeya remained behind on the ground, but the obsidian lion had no intention of abandoning her. He rushed down onto the first adversary from above, knocked the bolt gun out of his hands, and struck him on the skull with his hind paw as he flew past. The sphinx was dead before he sank into the snow on bent legs.

The other soldiers reacted quickly: They shoved the sphinx researchers back under the arch, where they were protected from the lion's air attacks. One sprang forward and placed himself opposite Vermithrax, his sword raised, while another tried to reach the gun—obviously their only one.

Vermithrax rushed past the first sphinx—not even flinching when a sword blow bounced off his obsidian body, striking sparks—and knocked the weapon out of the sphinx's hand. The lion plunged down onto the second sphinx, seized him by the arms, pulled him high, and flung him against the mirror wall like a rag doll. The glass couldn't withstand the blow. The lifeless sphinx fell to the ground in a hail of silvery splinters and moved no more.

One of the researchers had used the opportunity to leap out of the protection of the archway and now raised the bolt gun. He was unskilled in handling weapons; his first shot whistled past Vermithrax a yard wide and punched a crack in the curved ceiling.

Meanwhile Lalapeya had hurried behind the ice statues toward the only possible path of flight: a low corridor that opened off the broad mirror street about thirty yards away. If she'd followed the street, she would have been a perfect target. She just had to break through the opening to the corridor, its lower half being blocked by a six-foot-high drift of snow. She pushed into it like a hill of flour: Powdery white exploded in all directions, and then she was out of sight.

Vermithrax flew a narrow loop under the ceiling. Merle, who was used to such maneuvers, screamed to Serafin to hold on to her tightly. He strengthened his grip with stiff, ice-cold fingers, while she did her best to clutch the glowing lion's mane. Serafin was slim and wiry, but he weighed quite a bit more than the featherweight Junipa. Merle wasn't sure how long she would be able to hold on. Her frost-stiffened fingers had lost their strength; in fact, she could hardly feel the mass of her limbs. The thick mane protected her from the cutting drafts, but that was a weak reassurance in the present situation. It was only a question of time before the two of them would tumble from Vermithrax's back and either break all their bones when they hit the ground or be spitted by one of the icy sphinx bodies.

"Did you see how many there are?" Serafin shouted into her ear over the wind and the rushing wings.

"Too many, anyway."

"But there aren't enough, are there?"

"What do you mean?"

"*I know what he is thinking,*" said the Queen, "*and he is right.*"

Serafin leaned closer to Merle, which was nice, even here, even now, and he brought his lips so close to her ear that they touched her hair. The tickling in Merle's belly increased, and that wasn't only because of Vermithrax's renewed flight of attack on the sphinxes. "Too few!" Serafin shouted again. "This is their stronghold, the most secure place of all for them. What's going on down there is destroying their world. And they only send a handful of soldiers and researchers?" Merle felt him shaking his head at her neck. "That doesn't make sense."

"Maybe," she said, "there aren't any more they can do without. It's the same reason you were able to walk into the fortress so easily."

"It wasn't *easy*," he contradicted.

Merle thought of the wounded, but nevertheless she argued, "Normally a few dozen guards would have been waiting for you, not just one. Or do you think the sphinxes would leave the Iron Eye as good as unguarded?"

Vermithrax killed a sphinx soldier with ease as he flew past him, like plucking a flower from a stem. Again the sickle swords of his adversaries struck sparks from his stone underside, but the tiny splinters they hacked out of his body didn't weaken him.

"They're too few," said Serafin. "That's just what I mean. Too few guards, and now too few to examine this catastrophe down there. It must be—"

"It must be," said Merle "that this isn't the only place in the Eye where something like this is happening!" Of course, Winter was skimming back and forth through the fortress on his search for Summer, exactly as he'd done in Hell. If he followed his courses over the world just as chaotically, it was no wonder that the seasons were so unreliable: Sometimes there was frost even in April, sometimes not, and you could never predict how the weather was going to be next week.

"*The sphinxes have surely flocked here from all over the world to witness the Son of the Mother's return to life.*"

And Winter has come over them like a storm wind, Merle thought, and imagined gigantic salons full of ice sphinxes, like workshops of a crazed sculptor.

"*It might have been that way.*"

Then Burbridge told Winter about it! Merle thought. He planned for Winter to pass through here as revenge on the sphinxes.

"And the Stone Light?"

Burbridge must somehow have managed to take Winter into the mirror room.

"Looks very much like it."

This isn't the first time all this has happened, is it?

"No. But that was perhaps not Winter. Possibly Summer freed herself that time, or someone or something else came to her aid."

The downfall of the suboceanic kingdoms!

"And the Mayas. The Incas. Atlantis."

Merle recognized none of these names, but their very sound made her shudder. While Vermithrax detached himself from the sphinxes and flew up to the passageway into which Lalapeya had vanished, she explained her conjecture to Serafin, as well as she could in the headwind. He agreed with her.

They pulled in their heads as Vermithrax swept through the low arch, whirled up the remains of the snowdrift with his claws, and finally set himself down on all fours. The passage was too narrow to fly very far. Moreover, Lalapeya was waiting for them, looking worried. Her eyes sought Merle, saw that she was uninjured, and then turned to Vermithrax. "How many are there?"

"Four left. At least. Perhaps a few more."

"There must have been an army."

"Indeed."

Merle held back a grin, but she knew that they all had

the same thought. Considering how effortless Vermithrax's fight with the sphinxes had been, Winter must have already taken a large part of the work from him.

The lion and the sphinx hurried along the passageway side by side, as their adversaries appeared in the opening behind them. The scientists had stayed behind, and two soldiers took up the chase. At their backs, on the mirror street, a deep alarm signal sounded several times: The sphinx researchers used horns to call other troops from the breadth of the Iron Eye.

"Do you know your way around here?" Vermithrax asked the sphinx.

"No. When I left my people to watch over the lagoon, there was no Iron Eye yet. The sphinxes had always been a people of the desert and of the deep caves. All this here" — she shook her head resignedly — "all this has nothing to do with what I once knew."

Although the same cold prevailed in the corridor as everywhere in the Iron Eye, the snow cover around them became thinner after a few steps, finally disappearing altogether. Cutting winds blew against them, but the winds brought no new ice. Nevertheless the mirror floor was slippery with frozen dampness, and neither Vermithrax nor Lalapeya got on as quickly as they wished. The obsidian lion could have stood against their two pursuers and in all probability vanquished them, but he feared that the two would soon be followed by a larger number of opponents. And as long as he was involved in fights, he couldn't protect Merle and Serafin from attackers.

A new passageway crossed theirs, and to the right, still more sphinxes were approaching. After a quick look, Vermithrax hurried straight on. The sphinxes couldn't miss his glow. There was no question of a hiding place, especially as there were hardly any doors, only open archways that led into broad halls, infinite rooms in this imitation of the mirror world.

They crossed open canals with frozen surfaces and filigreed bridges that appeared about to break but didn't even tremble as the weighty obsidian lion thundered across them. They came through a hilly landscape of mirror shards, waste dumps as high as houses of silvery chips and sharp pieces, and then steps went down again, and more steps, and still more steps.

The pursuers stayed on their trail the whole time, often concealed behind curves and corners, but always present as surges of noise: a tramping of lion feet on ice, a roaring of angry voices, a jumble of savage curses and commands.

And then again they were stumbling through high snow, damper and heavier than before, so high that Vermithrax sank up to his belly and Lalapeya was hopelessly stuck after a few steps. The obsidian lion swept the snow masses to the side with his wings, but it soon turned out that he couldn't get them any farther that way.

"Vermithrax," cried Lalapeya, "can you carry a third rider?"

"Two or three more, if there's room for them. But that doesn't help us much."

"Perhaps it does." And as she spoke, a change took place in her.

Merle looked on with open mouth and wide eyes, while Serafin took her hand reassuringly. "Don't worry," he whispered, "she does that a lot."

Around Lalapeya, yellow fountains of sand appeared to shoot up from the snow where her lion legs were stuck. They enveloped her in seconds, until she dissolved in them, as if her entire body had exploded in an eruption of desert dust. Just as quickly the tiny particles joined together again, and Lalapeya emerged from them. She was unchanged from the hips up, but now she had long, slender human legs, which were bare, despite the cold. The fur jacket she'd gotten from the pirates reached down to her thighs, but her lower legs were exposed to the snow without protection.

Serafin let go of Merle and slipped backward a little. "Quick, up here!" he called.

Lalapeya fought her way through the snow to them, and Merle and Serafin pulled her onto the lion between them. The sphinx couldn't use her injured arms, and if she stood much longer in the snow in her bare feet, the same thing would happen to her legs. Serafin pushed as close as possible against her, put his arms around her to Merle, and yelled, "Let's go!"

Vermithrax rose from the ground and shook the snow from his paws. He dashed away over the ice, only several yards from the mirrored roof. The walls were barely far enough apart for his gigantic wings, but somehow he succeeded in not hitting the tips and carried his riders safely over the snow. Their pursuers were left behind as they tried to stomp their way through the high snow and then had to give up.

With a triumphant roar Vermithrax shot out of a round opening at the end of the tunnel into an unevenly higher hall, where it was still snowing out of gray fog that hung beneath the ceiling like real winter clouds. The flakes were thick and fluffy. They immediately stuck to Vermithrax and his riders and drove into their eyes. The lion's glow was garishly reflected in the falling snow, like curtains of gleaming light. The visibility extended for a few yards only.

"I can't see anything!" Vermithrax lurched in flight and sneezed once, so hard that Merle was afraid the shaking would throw them all from his back. Whatever his bath in the Stone Light had done, it hadn't made him immune to colds.

The obsidian lion was having trouble maintaining his altitude. He was as good as blind in the snowstorm, and the wet snow weighed down his wings. "I have to go down," he cried finally, but they'd all realized long ago that this move was unavoidable.

They sank down with the snowflakes, deeper and deeper, but the bottom they were expecting didn't appear. What they'd taken for a hall was in reality a mighty chasm, an abyss.

"Up ahead there!" Merle yelled through the deluge of snow. Snow got into her mouth. "A bridge!"

A narrow footbridge of mirror glass spanned the infinite emptiness like a guitar string. It was hardly more than forty inches wide and had no railings; both ends lay buried in the snowstorm somewhere.

Vermithrax flew down to it, and with full confidence in the sphinxes' architecture, he landed on it. It gave a slight shudder but no sign at all that the construction wouldn't bear his weight. On both ends of the bridge, five or six yards of the snow edges loosened and tumbled into the whitish gray deep.

Vermithrax shook his wings to shake off the lumpy layer of ice that had impeded his flying. Serafin tried to pull the ends of his coat wide enough to cover Lalapeya's bare legs, but she waved him off.

"Let me down. I can walk on my own again here. Vermithrax won't be flying anymore in this snow, anyway."

"The path is too narrow," said Serafin. "If you get off Vermithrax sideways, you'll fall down into the chasm."

"What about from behind?"

Serafin and Merle looked over their shoulders at the same time. The sight of the abyss on both sides of the pathway was alarming. As a master thief, Serafin had balanced over Venice's roofs all year long without wasting more than a thought on the danger. But this was different. If he went into a slide on the wet, slushy snow, nothing could save him, not luck, not skill.

"I'll try it," he said.

"No," Merle contradicted. "Don't be silly."

He looked past Lalapeya to Merle. "Her legs will freeze if she doesn't change back. So she *must* get down."

Merle glared at him: as if she didn't know that herself. Nevertheless, she was afraid for him and Lalapeya. Although, after watching her transformation, the thought that the sphinx actually was her mother seemed even more incredible.

"Be careful," said Lalapeya as Serafin slowly slid backward.

"*Plucky,*" the Flowing Queen commented dryly.

"Just hold still!" Serafin called to Vermithrax. His voice sounded grim. Merle held her breath.

"Don't worry," replied the lion, and in fact he did not move a fraction of an inch. Even his heartbeat, which Merle could feel clearly beneath her legs most of the time, appeared to stop.

With infinite caution, Serafin slid backward over Vermithrax's hips. At the same time he grasped the lion's tail;

it gave him additional stability when his boot soles sank into the snow. For a long moment he swayed slightly and cast mistrustful glances into the abyss to the right and to the left. Finally he gave Lalapeya the sign to follow him. His feet seemed to swim in the loose slush, so uncertain was his footing on the bridge. An overhasty movement and he would slide over the edge along with a gigantic snow clump.

He let go of the lion's tail in order to free the way for Lalapeya. She nimbly slid back and off the lion, while Merle twisted her neck and worriedly watched what was going on behind her.

"*They will make it,*" said the Queen.

Easy for you to say, Merle thought.

"Take one step back," said the sphinx to Serafin, "but carefully."

Extremely carefully he moved backward, striving not to pay any more attention to the depths below him.

"Good," said Lalapeya. "And now sit down. And support yourself with your hands."

He did that. He felt sick and dizzy, master thief or not. Only when he was sitting somewhat securely in the snow did he dare take a deep breath.

Lalapeya changed into a column of whirling sand, from which, in a flash, came flesh and hair and bone. After the sphinx was standing there in her lion form again, she told Serafin to climb onto her back. He obeyed, and the color returned to his face. It reassured him a little that Lalapeya and Vermithrax had four legs that gave them more traction up here. They had their predator's genes to thank that the suction of the abyss had no power over them. Fear of heights was alien, not only to the winged Vermithrax but also to Lalapeya, as was any clumsy or superfluous movement.

Merle gave a shudder of relief when Serafin was finally sitting safely on Lalapeya's back. For a long moment she'd even forgotten the cold, which was troubling her more and more. Now she again felt the bite of the frost, the icy burden of the snow, and the severe tugging of the high wind.

"What now?" asked Vermithrax.

"We follow the path," Merle suggested. "Or does someone have a better idea?"

They moved forward on eight lion paws, not sure what to expect on the other side of the thick blizzard.

After a few steps, Vermithrax stopped again. Merle caught sight of the obstacle at the same moment.

A figure crouched in front of them on the narrow band.

A man sitting cross-legged.

His long hair was snow-white, his skin very light, as if someone had formed the motionless figure of snow. The man had his head thrown back, his closed eyes facing upward. His bony hands were clutched around his knees, the dark blue veins standing out clearly.

"He's meditating," said Lalapeya in amazement.

"No," said Merle softly. "He's seeking."

Winter dropped his head and looked over at them wearily.

10

The Only Way

It almost seemed as if he'd been waiting for them. "Merle," he said, sounding neither pleased nor annoyed. "She's here. Summer is here."

"I know."

Vermithrax had come within two paces of him.

"Don't come any closer," said Winter. "You'll all freeze to ice if you touch me."

"You killed the sphinxes," Merle said.

"Yes."

"How many are left?"

"I don't know. Not enough to oppose me."

"Do you know where they've hidden Summer?"

He nodded and pointed down into the chasm.

"Down there?" Merle was irritated to have to pull every word out of him.

Again a nod. Only then did she notice that the thick snow made a detour around him. No ice crystals caught in his hair, no flakes stuck to his white clothes. His breath didn't even come from his lips in puffs of white. It was as if Winter himself was no part at all of the season he embodied.

"I've come this far," he said, "but now I lack the power to take the last step."

"I don't understand."

"Summer is being held at the bottom of this shaft. There are no other entrances, I've searched everywhere."

"So?"

Winter smiled shyly and very vulnerably. "How am I supposed to get down there? Jump?"

She'd had the idea that of course a being like him would be able to fly if he needed to. But he could not. He'd frosted the Egyptians and the Iron Eye with a new ice age, but he wasn't able to advance to the bottom of this shaft.

"How long have you been sitting there?"

Winter sighed. "Much too long."

"*He is a whining weakling,*" grumbled the Flowing Queen. "*And all this uproar he is causing around him does not change that.*"

Don't be so unfair, Merle thought.

"Pah! A weakling." Had the Queen had a nose, she would probably have wrinkled it. *"How long can he have been here? He left Hell shortly before us."*

He's just . . . well, sensitive. He's exaggerating.

"Sensitive? He is a liar! If he succeeded in getting from the pyramid to here in the delta in such a short time and then still managed to breeze through the Eye and freeze hundreds of sphinxes . . . that is damned fast, is it not?"

Merle glanced back over her shoulder at Serafin and Lalapeya. Both were looking impatient but also uncertain, faced with the strange creature blocking their way.

She turned to Winter again. "You really can't fly?"

"Not down there. I ride on the icy winds and the snowstorms. But that's meaningless here."

"What do you mean?"

Again he sighed from the bottom of his heart while the Queen uttered an exaggerated groan. "I'll explain it to you, Merle," he said. "And to your friends if they want to hear it."

Serafin growled something that sounded like, "What else can we do?"

"Summer is at the bottom of this shaft. Her strength, her sun heat, if you will, normally rises up through the shaft. No man can approach the ground, he'd burn up in an instant."

Merle shifted her weight nervously and looked down from Vermithrax's back into the deep. She saw nothing but whitish gray chaos. And she was getting colder and colder, quite terribly now.

"My presence here in the shaft interrupts the flow of heat," he continued. "Ice and fire meet each other down there, about halfway between me and her. The snow instantly melts in the air, the cold transforms into heat. Sometimes there are thunderstorms when we meet. I could let myself be carried down there by the icy winds, but Summer is captive and doesn't have her heat under control. She is weakened and not able to cool herself down, as she usually does when we meet. Down there, the wind would turn into a lukewarm puff of air, the ice would melt, and I . . . well, imagine a snowflake on a hot plate." He buried his bony face in his hands. "Do you understand now?"

Merle nodded uncomfortably.

"Then you grasp the utter hopelessness of my situation," he proclaimed, waving his arms.

"That might not even be true," said the Queen venomously. *"This fellow has almost annihilated an entire people, and now he is sitting here crying!"*

You could easily show a little more sympathy.

"I cannot bear him."

You were certainly not everyone's darling among the gods.

"Ask him if he has ever heard the word dignity."

That I most certainly will not.

"I could do it for you."

Don't you dare!

Serafin interrupted them. "Merle, what now? We can't just keep standing here forever."

Of course not, she thought with a shiver.

Then Vermithrax spoke up. "I know a solution."

In the tense silence, only the Queen murmured sourly, "*Whatever it is, it had better be quick. We have no more time. The Son of the Mother is awake.*"

"I can fly down there and try to free Summer," Vermithrax said. "I'm stone, heat and cold can't affect me . . . at least I think not. Besides, I've survived a bath in the Stone Light, so I'll probably survive here as well. When Summer is free, I can carry Winter to her. Or her to him."

Merle's fingers clutched his mane even more tightly. "That's out of the question!"

"It's the only way."

Merle felt that the Queen was about to take command of her voice, but she pushed her roughly back. For the last time, she snapped at the Queen in her mind, back off!

"*He will endanger everything if he does that! Without him we will not get far.*"

You mean, if he doesn't do what you say, don't you?

"*It is not about that.*"

Oh, yes, that's exactly what it's about, thought Merle. You've used him, just as you've used me. You knew from the beginning that we were coming here, that we had no other choice. You've always brought us exactly where you wanted us. "And now that's the end of it!" She said the last words out loud, and everyone looked at her in puzzlement. Her face had turned red, and the heat felt almost comfortable in the ice-cold air.

"She doesn't like the idea," Vermithrax stated.

Merle shook her head grimly. "At the moment what she thinks doesn't count."

The lion turned to Winter. "What will happen when Summer is free?"

The albino made a dramatic gesture with his hands that took in the entire Iron Eye. "What always has happened. All this will lose its power. Exactly as before."

Merle pricked up her ears. "Like the suboceanic kingdoms?" Her guess was very close to the mark.

Winter nodded. "They weren't the only ones to have tried it, but their failure was the most spectacular." He thought for a moment. "How shall I explain it? They tap her strength, the strength of the sun—perhaps that describes it the best. They don't realize that they are only injuring themselves. They know of the failure of the old ones, but they try it again anyway. They are so terribly weak, and they think they are so infinitely strong." Winter shook his head. "These fools! They cannot win, one way or the other. They will destroy themselves, sooner or later, even if we do not free Summer."

"But what do they want?" asked Serafin. "Why are they doing all this?"

Lalapeya answered him. "They are using Summer to

drive the barks, the factories, and the machines with her energy. Thus they have helped bring the Pharaoh to power and conquered the world. But this world was really only a finger exercise for them, only a plaything. What is actually important to them is somewhere else."

"All the mirrors?" Merle whispered.

"Their plan is to tear down the barriers between the worlds with the Iron Eye. With their fortress they're going to move from one world to another and carry on an unprecedented campaign of conquest."

Vermithrax growled. "But that takes magic. More magic than that of an ordinary sphinx."

"The Son of the Mother," said Merle. The coming events were unreeling in her mind like the light and shadow play of a magic lantern. "*He's* the key to the whole thing, isn't he? When he awakens, the Stone Light will take control. And the Iron Eye will move through the mirror world in order to smash the gates to the other worlds." She envisioned the gigantic fortress appearing in the labyrinths of the mirror world and destroying thousands upon thousands of mirror doors. The chaos in the worlds would be indescribable. Under the direction of the Light, the sphinxes would travel through the worlds like a mob of freebooters and sow death and destruction, exactly as they'd done in her own world. In other places too they would not dirty their own fingers but help upstarts like the Horus priests and Amenophis to power. Others would do the work for them, while they sat in their fortress and waited. A people of scholars and poets, Lalapeya had said. The sphinxes *were* artists, scientists, and philosophers, but the price for their life of literature and debate was a high one. And its cost was supposed to be paid by entire worlds.

"Merle," said Vermithrax firmly, "go to your mother."

She still hesitated, even though she felt that he had made his decision. "You must promise to come back."

Vermithrax purred like a kitten. "But of course."

"Promise!"

"I promise you."

That wasn't much reassurance, maybe nothing but empty words. Nevertheless, she felt a little better.

"Just fool yourself," said the Queen nastily. *"You humans always were the greatest at that."*

Merle wondered why the Queen was being so unbearable. Perhaps because Vermithrax's plan was better than her own: free Summer, thus rob the last sphinxes of their power, and so hinder the awakening of the Son of the Mother.

And the Queen's plan? Why didn't she reveal it? Where was the catch? For there was a plan, Merle had no doubt of that.

"I am worried about him." The Queen's tone had changed abruptly. No more sarcasm, no bitter irony. Instead, real concern. *"I want to speak with him—if you will allow it."*

"Yes," Merle said, "of course." The Queen played with

her feelings as if she were a piano, knew exactly which keys she had to press when. Merle saw through her and still could do nothing against it.

"Vermithrax," said the Queen in Merle's voice. "It is I."

Serafin and Lalapeya stared at Merle, and she had to remind herself that the two knew her story, of course, but they were hearing the Queen *speak* from Merle's mouth for the first time. Vermithrax had also pricked up his ears.

"I must tell you something."

Vermithrax cast an uncertain look at Winter, who had raised himself and stood astride the path, without swaying, even without blinking. "Now, Queen? Couldn't it wait?"

"No. Listen to me." He did, and all the others did as well. Even Winter tilted his head as if he were concentrating entirely on the words that fell from Merle's lips and yet were not her own. "I am Sekhmet, the mother of the sphinxes," the Queen went on, "that you know."

At least for Lalapeya and Serafin, that was a surprise. Lalapeya was going to say something, but the Queen interrupted her: "Not now. Vermithrax is right, haste is needed. What I have to say concerns only him. After I bore the Son of the Mother and with him generated the sphinx people, I soon recognized what had happened: The Stone Light had deceived me. And it had used me. I placed compliant servants in the world for it. When it became clear to me what that meant, I decided to do something. I could not kill all sphinxes and make everything unhappen—but I could keep the Son of the Mother from being made into the slave of the Light. I fought with him, mother against son, and finally I succeeded in defeating him. I was the only one who had the power to do that. I killed him and the sphinxes buried him in the lagoon." She paused, hesitated, and then continued: "What happened then, you know. But my story does not end with that, and it is important that you learn it now. You most of all, Vermithrax."

The lion nodded thoughtfully, as if he already guessed what was coming.

"I knew that I could not watch the lagoon alone, and so from the stone of the image the humans had erected in my honor, I created the first stone lions. I created them of magic and my own heart's blood, and I think that makes them—like the sphinxes and yet entirely different from them—my children, does it not?"

The lion, unable to look Merle and the Queen in the eye as they sat on his back, lowered his head. "Great Sekhmet," he whispered humbly.

"No," the Queen exclaimed, "it is not about honoring me! I intend only that you know the truth about the origins of your people. No one remembers anymore when and how the stone lions came to be in the lagoon, and so I am telling you. The lagoon is the birthplace of the stone lions, for after the Son of the Mother was buried there, I created you as guards: I myself would watch over him, but I needed helpers, my arms and my legs and hands and claws. Thus arose the first of your people, and after I was sure that you were equal to the task, I gave up my own body and became the Flowing Queen. I could not and would not live as a goddess anymore with the shame of what I had done. I became one with the water. On the one hand that was the proper decision, but on the other it was a mistake, for with it I gave up supervision of the stone lions. My servants were strong, but at the same time trusting creatures, who got mixed up with humans." She hesitated before she went on in a bitter tone, "You know what happened. How the humans betrayed the lions and robbed them of their wings; the flight of those who escaped the treachery; and finally Vermithrax's unsuccessful attack on Venice to redress the wrong that had been done to his ancestors."

The obsidian lion was silent. He'd listened with lowered head. He and his companions were the children of Sekhmet. The stone guards of the Son of the Mother.

"Then it is right that I am here today," he said finally, lifting his head with new determination. "So perhaps I can make up for the mistake of my forefathers. They failed to guard the Son of the Mother."

"Just as I did," said Lalapeya.

"And I," said the Queen from Merle's mouth.

"But fate has given me a chance," Vermithrax growled. "Perhaps all of us. We failed then, but today we have another chance to stop the Son of the Mother. And I will be no lion if we do not succeed." He uttered a pugnacious growl. "Merle, get down now."

She obeyed, very slowly, very carefully, until Lalapeya enveloped her in her injured arms. But Vermithrax walked up to Winter. The albino touched him on the nose, scratched under his chin. Vermithrax purred. He'd been right: The frost had no effect on his stone body.

"Good luck," said Merle softly. Serafin bent down from the back of the sphinx and placed a hand on Merle's shoulder. "Don't worry," he whispered, "he'll manage it."

Winter nodded to Vermithrax one last time; then the lion let out a battle roar and leaped into the deep. After a few yards, his wings stabilized his flight, and a few moments later he was only a glowing phantom behind a curtain of ice and snow. At last he faded entirely, like a candle flame extinguished in white wax.

"He will manage it," whispered the Queen.

And if he doesn't, Merle thought. What will become of us then?

Ignoring her bandaged arms, Lalapeya embraced her daughter even more tightly and looked her in the eyes at close range.

And thus they stood for a long time, with no one saying a word.

Vermithrax felt it, he felt the Stone Light in him and yet knew that it could not harm him. He'd been able to feel it when he'd bathed in the Light, down there under the dome of Axis Mundi—nothing tangible, no clear sensation. But he'd known that there was something in him that protected him from the Light and at the same time united him with it. Now it was clear to him that it was the legacy of Sekhmet, the foremother of all stone lions and sphinxes, the Flowing Queen. She had been touched by a beam of the Stone Light, and a little of this contact had also passed over to the lions. When he'd plunged into the Light, it had recognized itself in Vermithrax and protected him. Even more: It had made him stronger than ever before. Perhaps involuntarily, but that no longer mattered.

He was Vermithrax, the biggest and most powerful among the lions of the lagoon. And he was here to do what he'd been born for. If he were to die doing it, it would only close the circle of his existence. And if Seth had told the truth, he was anyway the last of his people, the last of those lions who could fly and speak. The last free creature of his species.

He propelled himself downward with broad sweeps of his wings, flew down with the snowflakes, overtook them, shot like a comet through the middle of them into the abyss. Soon it seemed to him they were growing smaller and wetter, no longer the fluffy flakes of farther up but slushy dots, then drops. Snow turned to rain. With the onset of heat, the water evaporated too, and he entered a zone of comfortable warmth, then heat, then finally roaring fire. The air around him shimmered and boiled, but he inhaled it the same as the icy air of the high heavens, and his lungs, glowing like everything in him, sucked out the oxygen and kept him alive.

He was proven right. The Light, which had made him strong, at the same time protected him from heat and cold.

Soon it was so hot that even stone would melt to glass, yet his obsidian body withstood it. The distant walls of the shaft had long since become unrecognizable; whatever material they might be made of, it was also not of this world. Of magic mirrors, perhaps, like the rest of the Iron Eye. Or of pure magic. He understood little of these things, and they didn't interest him. He only wanted to carry out the tasks he had undertaken. Free Summer. Defeat the sphinxes. Stop the Son of the Mother.

Then he saw her.

Until now he'd not been aware that he'd almost reached the floor of the shaft. It might just as well have been a lake of fire, even more flames in this sea of heat. But the light was pure and natural, not like that one of stone that spun its net of meanness and greed in Hell. This light was the one that bore warmth, the light in whose beams Vermithrax's lion people had sunned themselves on the rock terraces of Africa.

The light of the summer.

There she lay, stretched out in a sea of glitter and flame, supported by hot air, floating over the floor like a fruit just waiting to be picked.

There were no guards, no chains. Both would have been incinerated in a second. All that held her down here and had placed her in a trance was the sphinxes' magic.

Vermithrax held himself above the floating Summer with gentle strokes of his wings and gazed down at her for a long moment. She looked as if she could be Winter's sister, tall and thin, almost bony. She didn't look healthy, not in the human sense, but that might lie in her nature. Her hair was of fire. Flames also flickered behind her eyelids, yellow and red like glowing coals. Her lips were as silky as flower petals, her skin pale, her fingernails sickles of pure fire.

She didn't have her heat under control, Winter had said. And in fact everywhere there was fire licking out of her body, her body itself seemed to waver and melt like a wax figure in the heat of August.

Vermithrax observed her a moment longer. Then he stretched out his left front paw and touched her with the greatest imaginable gentleness on the upper thigh.

His heart stopped racing.

He knew about her heat, yet he didn't *feel* it.

The Light, he thought again. *The Stone Light is protecting me. I should be grateful to it and to that accursed Burbridge.*

He pulled his paw back, waited for two or three breaths, then began a narrow loop around Summer's floating body, past the flickering fountain of her fiery locks. Her hair streamed out like an explosion of fireworks, forever frozen in time. Once, twice, he kept circling around her until he was sure that he had cut through the invisible bands of the chain spell. Then he floated cautiously beside her and tried to lift her from her bed of heat.

She lay light as a feather between his forepaws and detached from her float with a slight jerk, as if he'd pulled a nail off a magnet. At the same moment the brightness around her dimmed, the shimmering of the air faded, the surroundings grew sharper. The heat ebbed perceptibly, he could literally see it. No one, no sphinx had thought it would ever be possible that there'd be a creature who could get to her here. The Stone Light, the power *behind* the power of the sphinxes, had deprived itself of the victory.

Vermithrax rose slowly upward, clutching Summer's thin body firmly. She looked undernourished, a little like Merle's friend Junipa. But with Summer it was not a sign of too little food or illness. Who could say how a season should look, her skin, her features? If Winter was a healthy example of his kind, then probably there was nothing wrong with Summer's body.

Her mind, however, was another matter.

Although Vermithrax had severed the bonds of the sphinx spell, Summer still showed no signs of awakening. She hung in his grasp like a doll, not moving. He wondered if her eyelids were at least fluttering, as is often the case with humans who are gradually awakening from unconsciousness. But Summer was *not* human. Anyway, during the steep flight it was hard for him to lift her far enough away to be able to see her face.

They flew in an aura of warmth. The snow around them melted and gradually tapered off, the closer they came to the dizzying narrow path where Winter and the others awaited them. The power of the two seasons mutually canceled out, now that Summer was no longer hurling all her power to the outside. Vermithrax assumed that this was a sign of her recovery: Her body was again using its energy on herself, directing its power inside, endeavoring to heal.

They'd almost reached the thin bridge over the mirror abyss when Summer moved in Vermithrax's claws. She groaned softly as life gradually returned to her.

Now he flew even faster, turned a triumphal pirouette around the bridge, and let Summer glide into Winter's outstretched arms. While the two embraced—he stormily, she barely conscious, still a shadow of herself—the obsidian lion sank down and gently landed in front of Lalapeya.

The sphinx let go of Merle, and Vermithrax enjoyed it when the girl threw herself on his neck with a happy shout, buried her face in his glowing mane, and wept with relief. The boy on the sphinx's back was grinning broadly. Vermithrax winked at him, seeming extraordinarily human as he did so.

Summer was growing more alert with every second in Winter's embrace. When she opened her eyes, they'd taken on the colors of sun-glowing desert sand. The flames in her hair went out. Her narrow hands clutched

Winter's back, and she let out a sob. "It happened again," she whispered. She was now weeping quite openly, without any shame. Winter's closeness gave her support.

Vermithrax looked over at Merle, who had detached herself from him. Yet it was Serafin who put words to the question they all had: "And was that really all?"

For a moment there was silence. No more snow fell, and the winter winds around them had died down almost entirely. They stood quietly over the abyss, whose floor shone like a sea of silver below them.

"No," said Merle, and again it was the Flowing Queen who spoke out of her. "That was by no means all."

"But—" Serafin was interrupted when Merle shook her head and the Queen said, "It has happened. The sphinxes have used Summer's last energies and reached their goal."

"The Son of the Mother?" asked Vermithrax somberly.

"Yes," said the Queen through Merle's mouth. "The Son of the Mother is awake. I feel him, not far from here. And now there is only one who is a match for him."

As there had been once before. Like that other time.

Mother against son, son against mother.

"Sekhmet," said Merle waveringly, now again the mistress of her own voice. "Only Sekhmet can still stop her son. But for that—" She hesitated and sought dazedly for words, which she really already knew, because the Queen had passed them to her. "She says that for that she needs her old body."

11

The Son of the Mother

IT BEGAN WITH A SUNBARK THAT FELL FROM THE SKY somewhere over the Mediterranean. It plunged down like a dead bird struck by a hunter's shot from ambush. The golden sickle wobbled downward in narrow spirals, and the sphinx on board could do nothing to stop the dive. The bark splashed into the sea in the center of a foaming fountain. Salt water sprayed through the viewing slits and leaky weld joints from all sides. Seconds later it had vanished.

Elsewhere, similar scenes took place over land. Sunbarks full of mummy soldiers fell out of the clouds and smashed on bare rocks, on deserted fields, between the tips of deep forests. Some fell over cities, frequently in the midst of burned-out ruins, or onto the roofs of houses, inhabited or uninhabited. Some sank in swamps and broad marshes, others were swallowed by jungles or desert dunes. High in the mountains they scraped along steep walls and were torn apart on rock projections.

Where men and women were witness to the events, they broke into jubilation, without guessing that the cause of it all was a girl and her motley companions in distant Egypt. Others suppressed their joy out of fear of the mummy soldiers who were guarding them—until they noticed that a change was also taking place in them.

Everywhere in the world, mummies disintegrated into dust and dried limbs, to stained corpse flesh and rattling tools. In some places it was a matter of a few breaths, during which whole peoples were instantly freed of their oppressors; elsewhere it took hours until the last mummy soldier became a lifeless corpse.

Sphinxes tried to hold the workers in their mummy factories in check, but they were too few, most of them having long since left on the road to the Iron Eye. Nor were there any Horus priests, who might have stopped the downfall; Amenophis himself had wiped them out. As for the human servants of the Empire, their number was too small, their will too weak, and their strength too little to offer serious resistance to the flaring rebellion.

The Egyptian Empire that had taken decades to establish perished within a few hours.

On the borders of the free Czarist kingdom, it wasn't long before the defenders on the walls and palisades, in the trenches and on the towers of lonely tundra fortresses, knew the truth. They dared raids, which quickly turned into campaigns—campaigns against an enemy who suddenly wasn't there anymore, against crumbling mummy bodies and shattered sunbarks.

In many places the mighty collectors, the dreaded flagships of the Empire, plunged out of the clouds. Some into bleak no-man's-lands, a handful over cities. Some took hundreds of slaves to death with them, all extinguished by a single stroke of Fate.

Here and there a few sphinxes tried vainly to keep their flying apparatus in the sky, mustering all their sphinx magic. But their attempts were to no avail. Those who crawled from the smoking, bent steel wreckage alive were killed by their human slaves. Only a few succeeded in finding shelter in woods and caves, with no hope of ever again being able to walk safely in daylight.

The world changed. Not stealthily, not timidly. The change was like a thunder bolt out of the blue, a flash in the darkest night. What was suppressed and destroyed over decades broke out like a flower through ashes and stone, developed shoots, stretched and extended itself, bloomed to resistance and new strength.

And while life awakened anew on all continents, the snow in the Egyptian desert melted.

Winter stayed behind with Summer on the edge of the abyss, where the path ran into the wall of mirror-polished steel. Summer was still too weak to help Merle and the others in their battle.

Merle was clutching Vermithrax's mane tightly with both hands. The obsidian lion bore her swiftly through the arched passages, halls, and stairwells of the Iron Eye. Water ran down the walls around them, snowdrifts and icicles melted into streamlets and lakes.

Serafin sat behind Merle, while Lalapeya followed them through the mirrored corridors at a fast gallop.

"And is she sure," Serafin shouted into Merle's ear, "that her body is preserved somewhere in the fortress?"

"She said that."

"And she also knows where?"

"She said she sensed it—after all, it was once part of her."

The Queen spoke up again. *"That ill-bred boy talks about me as if I were not here."*

And you aren't, either, Merle retorted. At least not for him. How much farther do we have to go?

"We shall see."

That's not fair.

"I know just as little as you. The presence of my former body fills all the lower floors of the fortress, exactly like the

presence of the Son of the Mother. They must both be very nearby."

Things were coming to their conclusion—*a* conclusion. Merle had to admit that everything had gotten to be too much for her long ago. So much had happened since Seth had abducted Junipa in the mirror room, and for a long time she'd felt unable to make sense out of anything anymore. Yet Serafin and the closeness of Vermithrax and Lalapeya gave her a vague feeling of security. She wished that Winter had stayed at her side too. But he refused to leave Summer and had sunk into his own superhumanity again. The seasons would continue to exist, no matter what became of the world, which they would continue to cover with ice and heat and fall foliage. Vermithrax had risked his life for Summer, but no one thanked him for it. Merle was angry at Winter. They could have used his help—whatever the Queen was planning.

You do have a plan, don't you? she asked in her mind, but as usual with inconvenient questions, she received no answer.

As they went along they passed crystallized sphinxes, frozen to milky ice when Winter touched them during his wanderings through the fortress. Water dripped onto the mirrored floor from their bodies. Merle couldn't shake off the feeling that she'd been moving through a gigantic mirrored mausoleum for hours.

Serafin was having the same thoughts. "Very odd," he said as they passed a group of icy sphinx bodies. "They're our enemies, of course, but this . . . I don't know. . . ."

Merle understood what he was trying to say. "It feels wrong somehow, doesn't it?"

He nodded. "Maybe because it's always wrong when so many living creatures simply stop *being*." After a pause, he added, "No matter what they've done."

Merle was silent for a moment, thinking about what he'd said. She came to an upsetting conclusion. "I'm not sorry for them. I mean, I'm trying . . . but I can't be. I'm simply not sorry for them. Too much has happened for that. They have millions of human beings on their consciences." She'd almost said "billions," but her tongue hesitated to put the truth into words.

The frozen sphinx bodies whisked past them like a procession, forming bizarrely columned halls of ice cadavers. Broad puddles had already formed around some of them. The thaw created by the reunion of Summer and Winter was spreading into the lower stories.

Lalapeya had been silent the entire time. Merle couldn't get rid of the feeling that her mother was observing her, as if she were trying to make a picture of her daughter that went beyond the simple surface. As if her eyes were also examining Merle's interior, her heart. Presumably she was listening to every word that Merle said.

"*Now I know!*" the Queen burst out. "*I know why my body and the Son of the Mother are overlapping this way. Why it is so difficult to keep them separate.*"

And?

"They are both here."

In the fortress? But we've known that for a long time.

"Silly girl! In one single place. In a hall." A short silence, then: *"Directly in front of us!"*

Merle was about to warn the others, but she didn't need to. Vermithrax stopped suddenly as a knife-sharp outline emerged from the panorama of mirrors and ice, a horizontal line—they were approaching the edge of a wide balcony. And beyond it, again . . . an abyss.

The lion slowly felt his way forward, Lalapeya at his side.

"What is that?" Serafin whispered.

Merle could only guess the answer: They had stumbled on the heart of the Iron Eye, on the temple of the lion goddess.

Sekhmet's shrine. The crypt of the Flowing Queen.

Merle and Serafin leaped off Vermithrax's back and, on their knees, made their way to the edge. Serafin's hand moved over Merle's. She gave him a smile and enclosed his fingers in a firm grasp. Warmth crept up her arm, electrifying her. Unwillingly, she tore her eyes away to look down into the deep emptiness below.

On the opposite wall of the hall—for a hall it was, even if its proportions were beyond comparison with any human work of construction, any throne room, any cathedral— stood the gigantic statue of a lioness, taller than Venice's

Basilica of San Marco. It was stone, with predator's fangs bared, each tooth as long as a tree trunk. Her gaze looked dark and mean, the eyes sunk in deep shadow. On each of her claws, hewn from rock, was spitted the figure of a human, as casually as dirt between her paws.

The statue was reflected many times in the mirror walls of the temple, over and over, so that it seemed as if it were not a single statue of Sekhmet standing there but a dozen or more.

"*That* was you?" Merle exclaimed.

"*Sekhmet,*" contradicted the Queen dejectedly, "*not I.*"

"But you're one and the same!"

"*We were once.*" Her tone was bitter. "*But I was never as the sphinxes have represented me. When I was still called Sekhmet, they revered me as a goddess—but not as that thing there!*" There was loathing in her voice now. "*Since then they have apparently made a demon of me. Look at the dead in the claws. I have never killed humans. But it fits with their plans. 'Sekhmet did it,' they say, 'so we can do it too.' That is the way it is with all gods who can no longer defend themselves—their adherents shape them just as it suits them. In time, no one looks for the truth anymore.*"

"This must be the deepest point of the Iron Eye," Serafin said. "Look down there."

From all the entrances to the mighty mirror temple, streams of water were splashing and gurgling into the hall, some only small rivulets, some as wide as brooks.

Lalapeya cautiously bent a little farther forward and looked down over the edge of the drop-off. "This is all going to be flooded soon, when the snow in the upper levels is completely melted."

Vermithrax was still unable to take his eyes off the tower-high stature. "Is *that* her body?"

At first Merle had had the same thought, but now she knew better. "No, only a statue."

"Where is her proper body, then?"

"*Over there,*" the Queen said in Merle's head. "*Look to the right, past the front paws. You see that low altar? And what is lying on it?*"

Merle strained and blinked and tried to make something out. It was far away. The floor of the hall lay deep below them; the balcony ran around the upper third of the wall. Whatever the Queen intended, they could reach it only with Vermithrax's help.

Merle discovered the altar just as she was about to give up. She also saw the body that was lying on it. Stretched out on its side, with the four paws pointed toward them. A wild cat. A lioness. She was no bigger than an ordinary animal; on the contrary, she appeared to Merle much more delicate, almost fragile. Her surface was gray, as if it were dusty—or stone.

Merle pointed out her discovery to the others.

"She's made of stone," Vermithrax purred. He sounded as if he felt a little flattered.

"I was not always," said the Queen with Merle's voice so that all could hear her. "When I laid aside that body, it was of flesh and blood. It must have turned to stone over all the millennia. I did not know that."

"That could be due to the touch of the Stone Light," said Lalapeya thoughtfully.

"Yes," agreed the Queen. "Possibly."

Serafin was still holding Merle's hand. He looked back and forth from her to the slender lion body far below. It seemed to him that with every moment the gurgling was a little louder, stronger, angrier. Not all the openings in the walls were at floor level; some, like the balcony, lay dozens of yards high, and the water plunged into the space below with tremendous force. The ice on the ledge where they stood was also melting, surrounding them all with slush and shallow puddles. Here and there it was already dripping over the edge into the depths below.

"We must go down there." The Queen's voice sounded somber and ominous. And once more Merle became aware that she was hiding something from her. The last part of the truth. Perhaps the most unpleasant.

Just tell me, she demanded in her head, what is it?

The Queen hesitated. *"When the time comes."*

No! Now!

The hesitation lengthened, became stubborn silence.

What's wrong, damn it? Merle tried to sound as demanding as possible—which wasn't so easy when you were only saying the words in your head and not with your mouth.

"We cannot call everything into question now."

No one's even talking about that.

"Please, Merle. It is already hard enough."

Merle was going to argue when Serafin tugged on her hand.

"Merle!"

She whirled around tensely. "What is it?"

"Something's not right down there!"

"Absolutely not," Vermithrax agreed.

Lalapeya said nothing. She was stiff with horror.

At first everything seemed unchanged: the gigantic statue of the demonic Sekhmet; next to it, much smaller, her lifeless body on the altar; and everywhere around them the water, flowing down out of the halls and passages of the Iron Eye and covering the floor.

No new arrivals. No sphinxes far and wide.

The mirror images! The reflections of the powerful statue had begun to move. At a fleeting look it might have been because of the curtains of water that streamed down the walls and broke up and distorted the reflections. But then gentle quaking and trembling turned into loud thundering. Gigantic limbs tensed and stretched. A titanic body awakened from its rigidity.

Merle felt as if she were falling miles deep into a chasm of silver. Everything around her whirled for a moment, faster and faster. She felt sick with dizziness. Only gradually did the truth emerge from the whirlpool of impressions.

Some of the reflections were in fact from the statue, and those continued motionless. But the rest reflected a being that had only the size and part of the lion body in common with the statue.

Serafin's hand clutched Merle's fingers. He'd seen this creature once before, when the Egyptian collector's magic had pulled it from the wreckage of the cemetery island of San Michele.

The Son of the Mother—the largest of all sphinxes, hideous and misshapen like a distorted image of all those who revered him—had been in the temple the entire time. In front of the wall, seen at a distance, he had appeared to be one of the innumerable mirror images.

Now they knew better.

"Down!" whispered Lalapeya sharply. "He hasn't noticed us yet!"

All followed her direction. Merle's joints had turned to ice. Vermithrax had raised the obsidian hairs of his mane in excitement and extended all his claws, ready for the last, the greatest of all fights.

Maybe the shortest.

What gave the sphinxes refined, almost perfect looks, in the Son of the Mother looked displaced, crooked, distorted. The sphinx god measured some dozen yards from his muscular human chest to his lion hindquarters. His hands had grotesque, knotted fingers, and many too many of them; they looked almost like spiders' bodies and were big enough to mash Merle and her companions with one blow. His claws were yellow and did not retract. With every step they punched a row of three-foot-deep holes in the temple's mirror floor. The four lion legs and the two human arms were too long and had too many joints, bent and stretched by muscle cords that lay strangely wrong under pelt and skin, as if the Son of the Mother had far more of them than any other sphinx.

And then his face.

The eyes were too small for his size and glinted with the same light as that of the Stone Light. His cheekbones were unnaturally prominent, and in the wings of his nose were cavelike nostrils. His forehead resembled a steep wall of furrows and scars, stemming from forgotten battles long ago. The teeth behind the scaly lips were a wall of stalactites and stalagmites, the entry to a stinking grotto, whose puffs of breath took form as crimson clouds. Only his hair was silky and shining, full and long, and of the deepest black.

Merle knew that they were all having the same thought: There was no point in it anymore. Nothing and no one could stand against such a creature. Certainly not the delicate lioness who lay lifeless down there on the altar.

"I had forgotten how dangerous he is," the Queen said tonelessly.

Marvelous, thought Merle bitterly. Just exactly what I wanted to hear.

"*Oh,*" responded the Queen hastily, "*I can beat him! I have already done it once.*"

That was pretty long ago.

"*You are quite right there.*"

The Queen appeared to have lost some of the optimism she'd displayed recently at every mention of the battle with the Son of the Mother. The Queen was daunted, whether she wanted to admit it or not. And deep inside Merle felt a fear that was not her own. The Flowing Queen was afraid.

"What's he going to do?" whispered Vermithrax with a dry voice.

The Son of the Mother was pacing back and forth in front of the grotesque statue of Sekhmet, sometimes faster, sometimes skulking, like a hunter circling his prey. His gaze was directed toward the tiny body at the feet of the statue, the petrified lion cadaver, which seemed to disquiet him far more than the masses of water that would soon overflow the mirrored temple.

"He doesn't know what to do," Lalapeya whispered. She had pushed her bandaged hands to the edge of the balcony. She must be in pain, but she didn't show it. "Just look how nervous he is. He knows he must make a decision, but he doesn't dare to take the last step."

"What last step?" Vermithrax asked.

"To destroy his mother's body," said Serafin. "That's why he's here. He wants to erase Sekhmet for all time, so that he doesn't fare again the way he did the last time."

"*Yes,*" said the Flowing Queen to Merle. "*We must hurry.*"

Merle nodded. "Vermithrax, you must take me down there."

The obsidian lion raised a bushy eyebrow. "Past him?"

"We have no choice, do we?"

The Flowing Queen had still not said a word about how she was going to change back into her own body from Merle's. But now, like an unexpected stroke of lightning, Merle realized that obviously that was where the Queen's last secret lay. That was what she had concealed from her the whole time.

Good, Merle thought, the time has come. Tell me.

She had the feeling that for the first time, the Queen was searching for words. Her hesitation became unbearable.

Hurry up, will you!

"*When I leave you, Merle . . .*" She stopped, stuck.

What then?

"*When I leave your body, you will die.*"

Merle was silent. Thinking nothing. Suddenly there was only emptiness in her.

"*Merle, please . . .*" Again hesitation, longer this time. "*If there were another possibility somehow . . .*"

Her consciousness was swept away. No thoughts. Not

even memories, things to feel sad about. No omissions, no unfulfilled wishes. Nothing.

"*I am sorry.*"

Agreed, Merle thought.

"*What?*"

I agree.

"*Is that all?*"

What did you expect? That I'd scream and rage and defend myself?

A moment of silence, then: "*I do not know what I expected.*"

Perhaps I even suspected it.

"*You did not.*"

Yes, perhaps.

"*I . . . oh, damn it.*"

Explain it to me. Why can't I live without you?

"*That is not it. It is not the change that is the reason. It is rather that . . .*"

Yes?

"*It is true that I can leave your body without your being harmed. If I move from one living creature to another, that is not a problem. But Sekhmet's body is dead, you understand? It has no life of its own anymore. And therefore—*"

Therefore you must take one with you.

"*Yes. Something like that.*"

You intend to revive that stone corpse down there with my strength.

"There is no other way. I am sorry."

You knew that the whole time, didn't you?

Silence.

Didn't you?

"Yes."

Serafin pressed her hand again. "What are you two talking about?" His eyes were filled with concern.

"Nothing." Merle thought it sounded hollow and empty. "It's all right."

At the same moment the Queen took control of her voice and before Merle could stop her, she said, "The others have a right to know. They shall decide."

"Decide what?" Serafin straightened up mistrustfully. Lalapeya also shifted closer. "What do you mean?" she asked.

In vain Merle concentrated, trying to push back the Queen's voice, as she had once before, in Hell. But this time she was unsuccessful. She could only listen as the Queen explained to the others through her mouth what was going to happen. Must happen.

"No," whispered Serafin. "That can't be."

"There must be another way," growled Vermithrax, and it sounded almost like a threat.

Lalapeya inched over to Merle and embraced her. She was going to say something, had already opened her lips, when a light, girlish voice exclaimed, "You can't be serious!"

Merle looked up. She couldn't believe it. "Junipa!"

She detached herself from Lalapeya and Serafin, slithered

as quickly as she could away from the balcony edge through the snow and water, finally leaped up, and enclosed Junipa in her arms.

"Are you all right? Are you hurt? What happened?" For a few moments the words of the Flowing Queen were forgotten, just as her own fate was. She couldn't let go of Junipa, had to keep staring at her like a ghost who'd appeared in front of her from nowhere. "Where's Seth? What did he do to you?"

Junipa smiled shyly, but she seemed to be trying to conceal pain that was tormenting her. The grip of the Stone Light. The invisible claws that were stretching toward her heart.

The Son of the Mother continued to tramp back and forth in the hall below. He was much too deep in his hate-filled thoughts to notice the goings-on up on the balcony. And he was still hesitant to destroy the body of his mother. His heavy breathing and snorting echoed back from the walls, and the cracking and shattering of the mirror floor under his claws sounded like icebergs splitting as they bumped together.

Vermithrax was making an effort to keep his eye on the beast. But at the same time he kept looking over at the two girls. Serafin also crept away from the mirror edge to the others, gave Junipa a quick hug, and then turned to her four companions, who'd appeared behind her. The entire group had walked out of a mirror wall, on which the last ice patterns were gradually melting.

Serafin greeted Dario, Tiziano, and Aristide. Dario and Tiziano were supporting Eft, whose right leg was emergency-splinted with a piece of wood; it looked as if someone had hacked it out of a bookcase with a blade, like an oversized splinter. Eft was pressing the lipless edges of her mermaid mouth firmly together. She was in pain, but she wasn't complaining.

"She insisted on coming to you," explained Junipa, who'd noticed Serafin's look. "I found her and the others in a library."

Merle gave the mermaid a warm smile over Junipa's shoulder. For a moment the surroundings were overlaid by a scene from the past, a gondola ride at Eft's side through a night-dark tunnel. "You have been touched by the Flowing Queen," Eft had said that time. "You are something very special."

Merle shook off the image and turned to Junipa again. "What happened with Seth? I was so worried about you!"

Junipa's face darkened. "We were in Venice, Seth and I. We were with the Pharaoh."

"With the—"

Junipa nodded. "Amenophis is dead. And the Empire has collapsed."

"Has Seth—"

"Killed him, yes. After that he killed himself. But he let me go."

The Queen roused in Merle's mind. "*The sphinxes aban-doned Amenophis. That is just like them! They used the Empire to awaken the Son of the Mother. And now they want to move on. They are not content with this one world.*"

Junipa grabbed Merle by the shoulder. "You weren't really serious before, were you? What you said . . . or *she* did. Whoever."

Merle shook off her hand with a jerk. Her eyes avoided Junipa's mirror gaze, slipped past her to the others. She felt as if she'd been driven into a corner from which there was no escape.

"Without the Son of the Mother, the sphinxes have no power to leave our world," she said, now turning to Junipa again, but still trying not to meet her eyes. "And if there is only one way to beat him . . . I have no choice, Junipa. No one here has."

Junipa shook her head in despair. "That's not you talk-ing!"

"The Queen wanted all of you to know the truth, so that you could make the decision for me. But now I'm the one who is speaking. And I won't allow someone else to decide. This is my affair alone, not yours."

"No!" Junipa seized her hand. "Let me do it, Merle. Tell her she can change into me."

"What nonsense!"

"Not nonsense." Junipa's gaze was firm and full of determination. "It won't be much longer until the Stone

Light gains power over me again. I can feel it. It feels around and pulls on me. I don't have much more time."

"Then go through the mirror into another world. The Light will have no more power over you there."

"I will not allow you to die. Look at me. My eyes aren't human. My heart isn't human. I'm a joke, Merle. A mean, bad joke." She looked over at Serafin, who was listening very carefully to her every word. "Anyway, you have him, Merle. You have something to live for. But I? When you're dead I have no one left."

"That is not true," said Eft.

Merle wrapped her arms tightly around Junipa, pressing her friend to her as hard as she could. "Look around you, Junipa. These are your friends. None of them will let you down."

Serafin stood there, torn. There must be another possibility. There simply *must*.

"But you heard her," Dario chimed in. "The Pharaoh is dead. That's all that matters. The Empire is as good as defeated. And if the sphinxes really want to get out of here, so much the better for us. Why should they make out any better in other worlds than in ours? We survived, didn't we? Others will also survive. That isn't our affair. And not yours either, Merle."

She sent him a sad smile. She and Dario had never liked each other, but now it touched her that even he was trying to dissuade her from her decision. Serafin had done the right thing when he'd ended hostilities with Dario: Dario wasn't a bad fellow. Even if he didn't, couldn't, grasp what she had to do.

"*We have no more time,*" said the Flowing Queen. "*The Son of the Mother will soon overcome his reluctance and destroy my body. Then it will be too late.*"

Merle released Junipa. "I must go now."

"No!" Junipa's mirror eyes filled with tears. Merle had thought Junipa couldn't cry at all.

Merle reached into the pocket of her dress and pulled out the magic water mirror. She turned around and handed it to Lalapeya. "Here, I think this is yours. The phantom in it . . . promise me to let him go, if you get out of here safely."

Lalapeya took the mirror in her bandaged hands. Her eyes were fastened on her daughter. "Don't do it, Merle."

Merle embraced her. "Farewell." Her voice threatened to choke on her tears, but she had them quickly under control. "I always knew that you were there somewhere."

Lalapeya's face was pale and tight. She couldn't believe that soon she would again lose the daughter she had just found. "It's your decision, Merle." She smiled nervously. "That's the mistake all parents make, isn't it? They don't want to accept that their children can make their own decisions. But the way it looks, you leave me no other choice."

Merle blinked away her tears and hugged her mother

one last time. Then she walked over to Eft and the others, said good-bye to them as well, again avoided Junipa's unhappy eyes, and finally went over to Serafin.

In the background, the Son of the Mother snorted and scraped in the depths of the mirrored temple. His raging sounded ever more furious, ever more impatient.

Serafin took her in his arms and gave her a kiss on the forehead. "I don't want you to do this."

She smiled. "I know."

"But that doesn't change anything, does it?"

"No . . . no, I guess not."

"We should never have gone into that house that night. Then all this wouldn't have happened."

Merle felt the warmth that he was giving off. "If we hadn't saved the Queen from the Egyptians . . . who knows what would have happened. Perhaps then everything would be looking even worse."

"But we would have had each other."

"Yes." She smiled. "That would have been lovely."

"I don't give a damn about the rest of the world."

Merle shook her head. "You do so, and you know it. Not even Dario meant what he said before. Maybe now. Maybe even tomorrow morning. But sometime he's going to think differently about it. Just like you. Pain goes away. It always does."

"Let me go," he said urgently. "If it's possible for the

Queen to cross over into me, then she can take my life strength to awaken her body."

"Why should I say yes to you if I said no to Junipa?"

"Because . . . because then you can be there for Junipa. She's your friend, isn't she?"

She smiled and bumped her nose against his. "Nice try." Then she kissed him lightly on the lips, just very quickly, and pulled away from him.

"What he says is right, Merle," the Queen said dejectedly. *"I could cross over into him and—"*

No, thought Merle, turning around to Vermithrax. "It's time to go."

The lion's huge obsidian eyes were glistening. "I will obey you. To the end. But you should know that this is not my wish."

"You don't have to obey me, Vermithrax. I'm just some girl. You do agree to it, don't you? You know that I'm right." Vermithrax, too, had once been ready to sacrifice himself for his people. If anyone at all could understand her, he could.

He lowered his head sadly and said nothing. Merle climbed onto his back and stretched to catch a look over the edge into the chasm. She watched the Son of the Mother walk slowly up to the statue. He neared Sekhmet's laid-out body and scratched his claws more powerfully. Under the water surface the mirror floor had shattered to stars of silver glass.

Merle looked around at the others one last time as

the lion went up to the edge and unfolded his wings.

Junipa was staring up at her, weeping. She looked as if any moment she was going to run to stop Vermithrax. Merle smiled at her friend and gently shook her head. "No," she whispered.

Eft struggled to straighten up in the grasp of the two boys, disregarding her broken leg. That she, who'd been born without legs, should be put out of action by an injured leg was perhaps the most cruel twist of fate.

The boys, too, were looking sadly at Merle. Dario had his jaws tightly clenched, as if he were grinding iron with his teeth. Tiziano blinked and fought unsuccessfully against a single tear that ran down his cheek.

Lalapeya appeared strangely blurred, as if her body were caught in the transformation between human and sphinx. She did not take her eyes off her daughter, and for the first time Merle really felt that Lalapeya was no longer a stranger, no distant hand inside the water mirror. She was her mother. She had finally found her.

Vermithrax reached the edge of the balcony. His wings rose and fell twice in succession, as if he had to try first to see if they would obey him.

"*It is time,*" said the Queen in alarm. "*He is about to destroy my body.*"

Vermithrax's front paws left the floor.

Behind them someone screamed Merle's name.

On the bottom, the Son of the Mother noticed the

movement out of the corner of his dark eyes. He turned around and caught sight of the obsidian lion on the edge. A primeval bellow broke from his throat, making the mirrored walls tremble and the water on the floor churn.

Serafin sprinted behind Vermithrax. Just as the lion was about to rise into the air, Serafin also pushed off, landed with both palms on Vermithrax's rear end, and was somehow able to grab hold of his fur and pull himself up. Suddenly he sat swaying behind her. "I'm coming along! No matter where—I'm coming along!"

The Son of the Mother screamed even more loudly as Vermithrax dove steeply at him, despite the second rider on his back. It was too late for him to turn around now that the beast had become aware of them. They could only bring it to an end as quickly as possible. Somehow.

"You're crazy!" Merle yelled over her shoulder while they sped downward in a nosedive.

"That's why we suit each other, isn't it?" Serafin yelled in her ear. He could hardly make himself heard over the rushing air and the roaring of the masses of water. The world sank into noise and attack and flickering silver.

Vermithrax raced toward the Son of the Mother's mighty skull. Compared to it he was as small as an insect and yet an impressive sight, bathed in the lava glow of the Stone Light and roaring with determination and explosive energy.

High over them the others crowded to the edge of the balcony and looked down into the abyss. Their faces had taken on the color of the ice that was melting around them. It no longer mattered if the Son of the Mother caught sight of them. Whatever might happen, they no longer had any influence over the events.

The gigantic sphinx took a step back from his mother's statue, turned completely around, and stretched his open jaws toward Vermithrax. His screeching made the heart of the Iron Eye quake; the high mirror temple shook to its foundations. The water on the floor boiled and surged like a witch's cauldron. The monster's movements were astonishingly fast, considering his size, and it was clear that he would become even more dangerous when he finally regained his old dexterity. He had lain for millennia in the depths of the lagoon; at the height of his powers he would probably have killed Vermithrax with one blow.

The obsidian lion avoided the many-fingered claws and raced toward one of the walls until Merle could recognize herself and Serafin in the mirror. They grew larger and larger and finally whistled past, a garish spot of color, as Vermithrax swerved sharply in front of the wall and flew back again. The sphinx bellowed and raged. He tried to swat them out of the air like an annoying mosquito, but time after time he grabbed emptiness. Vermithrax's flying maneuvers took Merle's and Serafin's breath away, but they enabled him to outfox the Son of the Mother.

The deeper they flew, the more dangerous it became. Here the beast not only tried to catch them with his fingers but also with his powerful lion paws. Once Vermithrax was left no choice but to fly between his towering legs. They escaped the monster's long claws by only a hair's breadth. The Son of the Mother struck and kicked at them, fountains of water sprayed up and splashed around them, and the beast's angry screaming hurt their ears.

Vermithrax re-emerged on the other side of his body, near enough to the stone image of Sekhmet to be able to fly down in its shadow and, on the back side of the statue, find safety for himself and his riders from their adversary's overgrown paws and sickle-sharp claws.

"Let me get down," Merle cried into Vermithrax's ear. "I'll manage it on foot just as well. You draw him away."

Vermithrax obeyed and sank to the ground in the protection of the statue. Merle slid from his back into the meltwater, and Serafin jumped down behind her. The swirling floods were horribly cold and reached up to their knees. For a moment the chill took their breath away.

There was no time for a farewell—already shattering blows were striking the mighty statue. The Son of the Mother had finally lost any respect and on the other side was doing his best to make the statue fall. Merle wondered if perhaps he guessed what they were up to.

"*Of course,*" said the Flowing Queen. "*He can feel me, just as I do him. But he has not been back in the world of the living long enough. His feelings confuse him. He still cannot control them. Yet he feels the danger. And soon he will be his old self again. Do not let yourself be deceived by the spectacle he has just created. He is no simple-minded colossus, quite the contrary. His intelligence is sharp. When he stops behaving like a newborn, he will become* really *dangerous."*

Vermithrax winked sadly at Merle one last time. Then he shot around the side of the statue and flew toward the Son of the Mother in quick zigzags, even more daringly now, ready to sacrifice himself so that Merle could reach her goal unhindered.

She looked around and saw the altar on which Sekhmet's petrified body lay, about thirty yards away, by the side of the statue. There they would be unprotected and open to the attacks of the Son of the Mother. But if their plan worked, Vermithrax's utterly mad maneuvers would distract him from Sekhmet as well as from her.

Serafin waded through the water beside her as they sneaked along the statue's stone feet. "Please, Merle—let me do it."

She didn't look at him. "Do you think I came this far in order to turn it over to someone else all of a sudden?"

He held her back by the shoulder, and against her will she stopped, after a last look at Vermithrax, who was skill-fully luring the Son of the Mother in another direction. "This isn't worth it," he said darkly. "All of this . . . it doesn't pay to die for this."

"Let it be," she replied, shaking her head. "We have no more time for that."

Serafin looked up at Vermithrax and the sphinx colossus. She saw what was going on inside him. His powerlessness was written in his face. She knew exactly how that felt.

"Ask the Queen," Serafin tried one last time. "She can't want you to die. Tell her she can have me in your place."

"*It would be possible,*" said the Queen hesitantly.

"No!" Merle made a motion with her hand as if she wanted to wave off any further argument. "That's enough. Stop it, both of you."

She tore herself loose and now ran as fast as she could, through the water to the stone Sekhmet. Serafin followed her again. Both no longer paid any attention to the fact that the Son of the Mother had only to turn around to discover them. They were betting everything on one card.

Merle reached the altar and leaped up the few steps. Again she was astonished at how delicate Sekhmet's body was, a simple lioness, with scarcely any resemblance to the demonic goddess that the builders of the statue had made of her. She wondered who had been allowed to enter this temple and regard the true Sekhmet. Certainly only a narrow circle of initiates, chosen priests of the sphinxes, the most powerful of their magicians.

What must I do? she asked in her thoughts.

"*Touch her.*" The Queen hesitated a moment. "*I'll attend to everything else.*"

Merle closed her eyes and laid her palm between the stone ears of the lion goddess. But at the same moment

Serafin seized her lower arm, and for a second she believed he was going to stop her, if necessary with force—but he did not do that.

Instead he pulled her around, took her in his arms, and kissed her.

Merle did not resist. She had never kissed a boy, not like that, and when she opened her lips and their tongues touched, it was as if she were someplace else with him, in a place that was perhaps as dangerous as this one was, only less final, less cold. In a place where hope could take the place of despair.

She opened her eyes and saw that he was looking at her. She returned the look, looked deep inside him.

And recognized the truth.

"No!" she cried and pushed him away, confused, shocked. Incapable of believing what had just happened.

Queen? she shouted in her thoughts. Sekhmet?

She received no answer.

Serafin smiled sadly as he bowed his head and took her place beside the altar.

"No!" she cried once more. "That can't—you didn't do that!"

"He is a brave boy," said the Flowing Queen with Serafin's voice. With *his* mouth, with *his* lips. "I will not let you die, Merle. His offer was very courageous. And in the end the decision was mine alone."

Serafin placed his hand between the ears of the petrified body.

Merle leaped at him, intending to tear him away, but Serafin only shook his head. "No," he whispered.

"But . . . but you . . ." Her words faded. He had kissed her and given the Flowing Queen the opportunity to move into his body. He had really done it!

She felt her knees buckling. She sank down hard on the highest altar step, only an inch above the water.

"The change has weakened you," said the Queen and Serafin together. "You will sleep for a while. You must rest now."

She wanted to pull herself up again, to rush to Serafin again, to beg him not to do it. But her body no longer belonged to her, as if along with the Queen had also gone the strength that had kept Merle on her feet for days at a time, almost without sleep and food. Now exhaustion came over her like an insidious illness. It left Merle no trace of a chance.

Reality slid away from her, shifted, blurred. Her voice failed, her limbs could no longer bear her weight.

She saw Serafin standing before the altar with eyes closed.

Saw Vermithrax circling around the head of the raging Son of the Mother like a lightning bug.

Saw her friends up on the parapet, small as knitting needle heads, a chain of dark shadow beads.

Serafin swam before her eyes. All her surroundings dissolved. And then suddenly she saw his face before her, very pale, his eyes closed.

Her spirit cried out, in infinite pain and grief, but no sound crossed her lips.

A gray phantom whisked away above her, the feather-light spring of a predatory cat of gray stone. Water splashed. Waves struck against her cheeks.

Sekhmet, she thought.

Serafin.

The end of the world inside her, perhaps also around her.

The Son of the Mother. Sekhmet. And over and over again, Serafin.

She must sleep. Only sleep. This battle was no longer hers.

Hands seized her, growing out of the silver mirror of the water surface. Thin girls' hands, followed by others. Figures everywhere in the water.

Serafin lived no more. She knew it. Wanted it not to be true. Knew it nevertheless.

The screams of the Son of the Mother everywhere around her.

"Merle," whispered Junipa, and pulled her into the mirror world.

Darkness. Then silver.

No more screams.

"Merle." Still Junipa's whisper.

Merle tried to speak, to ask something, but her lips only trembled, her voice faded to a croak.

"Yes," said Junipa gently, "it's over."

12

Snowmelt

SOMEONE HAD LIFTED HER ONTO VERMITHRAX'S BACK. Someone was sitting behind her and holding her firmly. Serafin? No, not he. It must be Eft. With her broken leg, she couldn't walk.

Junipa was guiding them through the mirror world. She went ahead, followed by Vermithrax, who held the two riders on his back with his folded wings. His heart was racing, he was panting with exhaustion. Merle had the feeling he was limping, but she herself was too weak to say for certain. She looked wearily over her shoulder. Behind the lion walked Lalapeya in her sphinx form.

Dario, Tiziano, and Aristide brought up the rear.

Something lay across Lalapeya's back, a long bundle. Merle couldn't quite make it out. Everything was hazy, and she felt as if she were in a dream. What she never would have thought possible had happened: She missed the alien voice inside her, someone who gave her courage or argued with her; who lectured her and gave her the feeling that her mind and her body were not exhausted. Someone who questioned her, kept her alert, who always and constantly challenged her.

But now she had only herself.

Not even Serafin.

At that moment she knew what Lalapeya bore on her back. It was no bundle.

A body. Serafin's corpse.

She thought of his last kiss.

Only much later did Merle realize that their path through the silvery labyrinth of the mirror world was a flight. Those who could walk were hurrying—in front of them all, Junipa, who gained in strength and determination in this place, at last free from the Stone Light again.

As if she were in a trance, Merle thought back to that day she and Junipa had entered the mirror world for the first time. Arcimboldo had opened the door for them so that they could capture the annoying phantoms in his mirrors. Junipa had been uncertain, afraid. There was no sense of that now. She moved along the secret mirror paths as if she belonged here, as if she'd never known anything else.

Around them, again and again, individual mirrors went dark, like windows in the night. The glass in some shattered, and a cold, dark suction pulled at those hurrying past. In some passages it was as if a black shadow were eating up the walls, as one mirror after another turned dark. Some exploded as Vermithrax ran by them. Tiny shards poured over the comrades like star splinters.

The longer they were under way, however, the more rarely the mirrors burst. The memory of the dark chasms faded, and soon there were no more signs of the annihilation that lay behind them. All around them shone pure silver, flickering in the light of the places and the worlds that lay beyond them. Junipa slowed, and the entire group with her.

Merle tried to pull herself upright, but she sank forward into Vermithrax's mane again. From behind she felt Eft's hand on her waist, holding her firmly. Merle heard voices: Junipa, Vermithrax, Eft. But she understood nothing of what they said. In the beginning they'd still sounded frantic, excited, almost panicked. Now their words were quieter, then fewer, until finally all lay in deep silence.

Merle tried to look around once more, to Serafin, but Eft would not allow her to. Or was it only her own lack of strength that held her back?

She felt that her mind was fading away again, that the pictures were becoming fuzzy again, the sounds of their steps duller and farther away. When someone spoke to her, she didn't understand what was said.

Was that a good thing?

She didn't even know an answer to that.

They buried Serafin where desert had once been.

Now the broad fields of sand were drinking the melt-water, the dunes dissolved into mud, and the yellow-brown ravines became streambeds. How long would that go on? Nobody knew. It was clear that the desert would change. As would the entire country.

Egypt would become fruitful, Lalapeya maintained. For those who had resisted the Pharaoh and survived his reign of terror, this was the chance for a new beginning.

Serafin's grave lay on a rock projection, where the sand and water had bonded to firm bog. When the sun shone again and evaporated the dampness, he would be as secure here as if glass had been poured around him. The rock overlooked the desert, many miles wide in all four directions. From here one looked up and out at the blue-green ribbon of the Nile, which was still the source of all life in Egypt, and someone, perhaps Lalapeya, said it would be good that Serafin began his last journey from this place.

Merle hardly listened, although many words were spoken on this day when they took leave of Serafin. Each who had witnessed his sacrifice said something; even Captain Calvino, who'd barely known Serafin, gave a short speech.

The submarine lay at the Nile bank, securely moored in front of a palm grove, or what the frost had left of it.

Merle was the last who walked to the grave, a pit that Vermithrax had dug out of the mud with his claws. She went down on her haunches and looked for a long time at the cloth in which they'd wrapped Serafin. Utterly quiet, utterly stunned, she had taken her leave, or tried to at least.

But the true leave-taking would last months, years perhaps, she knew that.

Shortly afterward she followed the others to the boat.

Merle had thought she wouldn't have the desire to come back once more later, alone, in the evening, after the grave was filled with sand and earth, but then she did it anyway.

She came alone. She hadn't even told Junipa what she had in mind, although her friend of course guessed. Probably they all knew.

"Hello, Merle," said Sekhmet, the Flowing Queen, perhaps the last of the old gods. She was waiting for Merle at the grave, a dark silhouette on four feet, very slender, very lithe. Almost unreal, had there not been the scent of wild animal wafting from the rock.

"I knew you would come here," said Merle. "Sooner or later."

The lion goddess nodded her furry head. Merle had trouble bringing the brown cat's eyes into harmony with that voice she'd heard inside for so long. But finally she managed to do it, and then she thought that really, they went quite well together. The same teasing, even contentious expression. But also eyes full of friendship and sympathy.

"There's no happy ending, is there?" Merle asked sadly.

"There never is. Only in fairy tales, but not even there particularly often. And if there is one, then it is usually made up." No question, it was the Flowing Queen speaking, no matter from what body and under what name.

"What happened?" asked Merle. "After you were yourself again, I mean."

"Did the others not tell you?"

Merle shook her head. "Junipa brought everyone through the mirrors to safety. You and your son . . . you were still fighting."

A breeze wafted over the nighttime desert and stirred the goddess's fur. Merle hadn't noticed the difference in the moonlight—everything here was gray, icy gray—but now she saw that Sekhmet's body was no longer of stone. Serafin's vital power had made her again what she had once been: an uncommonly slender, almost delicate lioness of flesh and blood and fur. She didn't look at all like a goddess. But perhaps that made her just that much more godly.

"We fought," said Sekhmet in a throaty voice. She sounded sad, probably not only for Serafin's sake. "Fought for a long, long time. And then I killed him."

"That's all?"

"What do details matter?"

"He was so big. And you are so small."

"I have eaten his heart."

"Well," said Merle, for nothing better occurred to her.

"The Son of the Mother," Sekhmet began, then she broke off and started over: "*My* son was perhaps big and very strong and even sharp—but he was never really a god. The sphinxes revered him as a god, and his magic was strong enough to bear their fortress through the mirror world. But he was eaten away by greed and hate and by a rage for which he had long forgotten the reason." She sadly shook her lion head. "I am not even sure whether he really recognized me. He had underestimated me. I opened his flank and ate through his entrails. Just like the time before." Sekhmet sighed as if what had happened made her sorry. "That time I left him his heart. This time not. He is dead and will remain so."

Merle let a moment pass before she asked, "And the sphinxes?"

"Those your friend has left alive are scattered to the winds. But there were not many. They have seen what I have done. And they fear me. I do not know what they will do. Hide, perhaps. A few will try to advance to the Stone Light, to their father. But they pose no more danger, not today."

"What happened to the Iron Eye?"

"Destroyed." Sekhmet noted the astonishment in Merle's face and purred gently. "Not by me. I guess it could not withstand the heat and cold that was called up inside it."

"Heat and cold," repeated Merle stupidly.

"Your two friends have not been idle."

"Winter and Summer?"

Sekhmet purred agreement. "They ground the mirrors between the elements. All that is left is a mountain of silver dust, which the Nile will carry away into the sea with the passage of time." She tilted her head toward the grave. "Do you want to see him? I can bring him here."

Merle thought about it for a couple of seconds, then shook her head. "I don't want anything more to do with all that."

"What do you plan to do now?"

Merle's eyes roamed over the insignificant grave mound once more. "Everyone is talking about the future. Eft is going to stay with the pirates"—she smiled fleetingly—"or with their captain, depending on whom one believes. So she can live in the sea, even if she isn't a mermaid anymore. And Dario, Aristide, and Tiziano . . . oh well, they want to become pirates too." Now she actually had to laugh. "Can you imagine that? Pirates! They're still only children!"

"You should be one too. At least a little."

Merle's eyes met the lion goddess's, and for a moment she felt in complete harmony with her, understood through and through. Perhaps they were still two parts of one and the same being, in some way; perhaps it would never really end, no matter what happened. "I haven't been a child since I . . ." Merle sought for the right words, but then she simply said, "Since the day I drank you."

Sekhmet gave out a lion sound that might have been laughter. "You actually believed that I would taste like raspberry juice!"

"You lied to me."

"Only fibbed."

"Fibbed *considerably*."

"A little."

Merle walked over to Sekhmet and put both arms around her furry lion neck. She felt the warm, rough lion tongue lick her behind the ear, full of tenderness and love.

"What are you going to do now?" Merle tried to suppress her tears, but she choked and the two of them had to laugh.

"Go north," said the lioness. "And then east."

"You want to find the Baba Yaga."

Sekhmet nodded on Merle's shoulder. "I want to know who she is. What she is. She has protected the Czarist kingdom all these years."

"As you did Venice."

"She had more success than I. Nevertheless, we could have much in common. And if not . . . well, it is at least *something* that I can do." Sekhmet again looked Merle in the eye. "But you have still not answered my question. What are you planning?"

"Junipa and I are going back to Venice. Eft and Calvino are taking us there. But we can't stay there long."

Sekhmet's eyes narrowed to tiny slits. "Junipa's heart."

"The Stone Light is too powerful. At least in this world."

"Then you will go with her? Through the mirrors?"

"I think so, yes."

The lion goddess licked her across the face, then she touched Merle's hand gently with the rough ball of one paw. "Farewell, Merle. Wherever you go."

"Farewell. And . . . I'm going to miss you. Even if you were a real pain in the neck."

The lioness purred softly at Merle's ear, then leaped over Serafin's grave in one spring, bowed in front of the dead boy under the sand, then turned and glided soundlessly into the night.

A gust of wind carried her scent back.

Vermithrax left the next morning.

"I'm going to look for my people, no matter what Seth said."

It pained Merle to see him go. It was the third departure in a few hours: first Serafin, then the Queen, now he. She didn't want him to leave her. Not him, too. But at the same time she knew that it didn't matter what she wished or did. Did not each of them seek a new task, a destiny?

"Somewhere they are living still," said Vermithrax. "Flying, talking lions like me. I know it. And I'll find them."

"In the south?"

"Rather in the south than elsewhere."

"Yes, I think that too," said Lalapeya, who was standing beside her daughter. "Perhaps they found protection there." Lalapeya wore her human form like a dress, Merle thought. Every time she saw her mother like that, it seemed to her a little like a masquerade. She was the most beautiful woman Merle knew, but still she was always a little more sphinx than human, even in that body. Merle wasn't certain if anyone else felt that.

She turned again to Vermithrax. "I wish you luck. And that we'll see each other again."

"We will." He bent forward and rubbed his huge nose on her forehead. For a moment she was blinded by the glow that he gave off.

Junipa walked up beside him and stroked his neck. "Good-bye, Vermithrax."

"I hope we'll meet again someday, little Junipa. And take care of your heart."

"I'll do that."

"And of Merle."

"Of her too." The two girls exchanged a look and smirked. Then they both fell on Vermithrax's neck together and only let him go when he growled "hey, hey" and shook as if he had fleas in his fur.

He turned around, unfolded his stone-feathered wings, and rose from the ground. His long tail whipped up sand. The ground was gradually drying out, now that the sun was in the heavens again.

They looked after him until he was only a glowing dot in the endless blue, a meteor in broad daylight.

"Do you think he'll really find them?" asked Junipa softly.

Merle didn't answer, only felt Lalapeya's bandaged hand on her shoulder, and then they went back to the boat together, where Eft was waiting for them.

The crew had polished the submarine to a high gloss. Golden pipes and door handles flashed; glass doors were, insofar as they were available, newly replaced; and a pirate who handled brush and paint better than a saber (Calvino said) had gone about repairing one of the ruined frescoes. Gradually he would take on the painting all over the boat. The captain had allowed him an extra ration of rum (for he painted better when he was drunk, he maintained), which made the other pirates offer themselves eagerly as helpers. Some had established a workshop, and every place in the boat was scrubbed, refined, and polished. Others discovered their cooking talents and prepared a festive meal in Merle's honor that wasn't bad at all. She was grateful and ate with appetite, but still, in her thoughts, she was somewhere else, with Serafin, who now lay alone on his rock and perhaps dreamed of the desert. Or of her.

Eft sat by Captain Calvino. Arcimboldo's mirror mask lay before her on the table. Sometimes, depending on how strongly the gas flames flickered in their little copper boxes and danced on the silver of Arcimboldo's cheeks, it looked as if his features were also moving, as if he were speaking or laughing.

Occasionally Eft bent forward and appeared to whisper something to him, but that might have been only an illusion and she was in truth reaching for a bowl or pouring wine into her goblet. But then what was it that made her break into laughter unexpectedly, even when neither Calvino nor one of the others had said anything? And why did she refuse to leave the mask below deck with the other treasures?

By the end of the meal she had wrung out of Calvino the promise to mount the silver face on the bridge, above the viewing window, where it could keep everything in view and, prophesied Calvino, probably know everything better than he. Eft stroked his hand and gave him a shark smile.

"All that's missing is for her to flutter her eyelashes at him," Junipa whispered in Merle's ear. The two burst out laughing immediately afterward when Eft gave the captain a flirtatious look that broke the rough fellow's resistance once and for all.

"I guess we don't need to worry about her anymore," said Merle, while Lalapeya, sitting with the two girls in her human form, laughed—in her, even that looked a little mysterious, like everything she did or said.

After the meal Junipa withdrew into the mirror world through a six-foot-tall mirror in her cabin. Only thus could she prevent the Stone Light gaining in power and influence over her. Of course she could have taken Merle and herself to Venice that way, but the two of them were enjoying the time left with Eft and the others. Furthermore, there was a promise that Merle intended to keep.

Somewhere in the Mediterranean, about halfway between continents, Calvino made the boat surface, in response to her request. Merle and her mother climbed out of the hatch onto the hull, walked over the tangle of splendid designs in gold and copper to the bow, and from there looked out over the endless sea. The surface nearby was moving, fish perhaps, or mermaids. They'd already met several. Now that the galleys of the Empire were floating rudderless on the sea, the sea women had come out of their hiding places and sank the warships wherever they encountered them.

Merle took the water mirror from Lalapeya. She touched the surface gently with her fingertips and said the magic word. The light vapor of the mirror phantom instantly gathered around her skin.

"I want to redeem my promise," she said.

The milky ring under her fingertips quivered. "Then the time has come?" asked the phantom.

"Yes."

"The sea?"

Merle nodded. "The biggest mirror in the world."

Lalapeya gently laid a bandaged hand on her shoulder. "You must give it to me."

Merle held her fingers in the interior of the oval frame a little longer. "Thank you," she said after she thought for a moment. "You probably don't know it, but without your help—"

"Yes, yes," said the phantom, "as if anyone had ever doubted it."

"You can't wait a moment longer, can you?"

"I can feel others. Others like me. The sea is full of them."

"Really?"

"Yes." He was sounding more and more excited. "They're everywhere."

"One more question."

"Umm."

"The world you came from . . . did it have a name?"

He thought it over for a moment. "A name? No. Everyone just called it 'the world.' Nobody knew there was more than one of them."

"That's exactly how it is here."

Behind them Calvino stuck his head out of the hatch. "Are you done yet?"

"Just a minute," Merle called back. Turning to the mirror, she said, "Good luck out there."

"You too."

She pulled her fingers out, and the phantom began to rotate, fast, like a whirlpool. Lalapeya received the mirror and closed her eyes. She raised the oval to her mouth and breathed on it. Then she murmured a string of words that Merle didn't understand. The sphinx opened her eyes and flung the mirror out into the sea. It flew through the air in a glittering arc. Shortly before impact, the water left the frame, an explosion of silvery beads, which melted into the waves immediately. The mirror splashed into the sea and went under.

"Is he—"

Lalapeya nodded at the waves, which thumped splashing against the hull. What Merle had taken at first for white foam revealed itself to be something nimble, ghost-like, that formed a multitude of crazy patterns before it looked like a hand waving good-bye and then faster than lightning whizzed away in a zigzag through the waves, away, away, away into freedom.

13

La Serenissima

VENICE ON A RADIANT MORNING, VENICE LIBERATED.

Seagulls screamed over the wrecks of galleys, half-sunk along the banks of the lagoon like the ribs of bizarre ocean creatures of wood and gold and iron. Men of the City Guard were posted on most of them to protect the wreckage from plunderers. Days would pass yet before the cleanup work in the city was far enough along for anyone to attend to the costly shipwrecks in the sea.

Above an island in the northeast of the lagoon, far away from the main island, a dark column stood out against the sky. Black smoke rose from the fires that burned there day and night. The fallen mummy soldiers were carried thither on ferries and laid on pyres for their final rest. The wind stood favorable and carried the ashes out over the sea.

Over the roofs and towers of the city the guardsmen flew their rounds on silent stone lions with widespread wings. The men were vigilantly observing the activities in the streets, making sure that no mummies lay undiscovered, even in the remotest back courtyards and gardens. Calling loudly from the sky, they directed the cleanup troops, repair crews, and soldiers on the ground. Down there all differences were suspended: Everyone, whether in uniform or day laborer, whether fisherman or tradesman, was busy cleaning up the streets, clearing the remains of mummy soldiers out of houses and from piazzas, and taking down the barricades, soot-blackened witnesses to the meager resistance against the Empire.

At the broad opening to the Grand Canal, Venice's main waterway, the activity was as lively as it used to be only on feast days. Dozens of boats and gondolas darted around on the water like ants at the foot of their hill, transports in one direction or the other. Everywhere, shouting and calling and sometimes even, again at last, individual songs from the sterns of polished gondolas.

On the bank of the canal mouth, at the harbor wall of the Zattere quay, stood Merle, Junipa, and Lalapeya. They waved at the departing rowboat that had brought them to shore. Tiziano and Aristide lay to the oars, while Dario and Eft waved good-bye with arms outstretched. The sea wind tore the words from their lips. The submarine lay far outside, on the other side of the ring of wrecked galleys, but none of the three turned away until the little dinghy was entirely out of sight. And even then they remained standing there, looking out over the water to where their friends had vanished.

"Will you go back with me for a little way?" Lalapeya asked finally.

Merle looked at Junipa. "How do you feel?"

The pale girl ran one hand over the scar on her chest and nodded. "Right now I don't feel anything. It's as if the Stone Light has withdrawn for the time being. Maybe to get over the defeat of the sphinxes."

Lalapeya, who had covered her petite woman's body with a sand-colored dress from the pirates' stores, led them through an alley deeper into the confusion of streets and piazzas. "The Light will probably rest for a while. After all, it has all the time in the world."

They crossed slender bridges, narrow courtyards, and the Grand Canal on a ferry. Merle was astonished at how fast the work of cleaning up was going. The traces of the thirty-year siege could not be removed within a few days, yet all the indications of the Empire's takeover of power were already erased from the cityscape. Merle wondered what had become of the Pharaoh's body. Probably they'd thrown it in the fire along with the mummies.

A young water carrier they met along the way told

them that the City Council had again taken over the business of governing. Many councillors had been executed by the Pharaoh, among them the traitors, and now their successors were trying to restore the credibility of the regime. It was said that they'd already gotten the advice of the Flowing Queen, who had returned to the lagoon with the downfall of the Empire; all decisions of the City Council would be hers; they would follow her will and would on no account anger her. Therefore it was in the population's interest to obey all orders and not to question the rule of the councillors. The young woman beamed with confidence. As long as the Flowing Queen watched over Venice, she was not afraid. She and the councillors would see to it that everything became good again.

Merle, Junipa, and Lalapeya nodded politely, thanked her for the information, and quickly went on their way to the sphinx's palazzo. No one had the heart to tell the young woman the truth about the Flowing Queen. And what sense would it have made? No one would have believed them. No one *wanted* to believe them.

In the palazzo they found many of the boys whom Serafin had excluded from the attack on the Pharaoh. They broke into shouts of joy when Lalapeya appeared in the doorway. She had no choice but to allow them to continue to live there—provided they made themselves useful working in the district and kept the salons and the corridors clean. Merle thought the company would be good for Lalapeya;

she would no longer feel so lonely in the big old building.

In the evening they sat together in the large salon and Merle and Junipa realized that this would be their last meal in this world for a long time. That made them sad and excited at the same time.

It had long been dark when Lalapeya led them into her chamber, through a labyrinth of silk curtains to a wall with a high mirror. The silver glass sparkled like the purest crystal. On the wooden frame were carved all the fabulous creatures of the Orient, a dance out of *A Thousand and One Nights.*

"Yet another good-bye," said Lalapeya, as the girls stood before her with bulging knapsacks filled with food and water canteens. "The last, I hope."

Merle was about to say something, but her mother gently laid a finger on her lips. "No," she whispered, shaking her head. "You know where you can find me whenever you want to. I will not leave here. I am the guardian of the lagoon. If the humans do not need me, perhaps the mermaids will."

Merle looked at her for a long moment. "It was you who built their cemetery, wasn't it?"

The sphinx nodded. "It lies under the palazzo. Someone must keep watch over it. And perhaps I can teach those boys out there that there is reason to respect the mermaids or even to be their friends. I think that would be a good beginning." She smiled. "Besides . . . it will soon be summer. Venice is wonderful when the sun is shining."

"Summer!" exclaimed Merle. "Of course! What became of her and Winter?"

"Became?" Lalapeya laughed. "Those two will never change. They go on through the world again as they have from the beginning of time, undisturbed by the fortunes of humans. And now and again they meet one another and then they act as if they were humans who are in love with each other."

"Aren't they, then?" Merle asked. "In love?"

"Perhaps they are. But perhaps there is no other choice for them. Not even they are entirely free."

Junipa kept thinking about what she'd said, but Lalapeya had already turned to Merle and put the question that had burned on her lips for too long. Merle had been waiting for it for days.

"You want to find him, don't you? Steven, I mean. Your father."

"Yes, perhaps," said Merle. "If he's still alive."

"Oh, that he certainly is," said the sphinx with conviction, "somewhere behind the mirrors. You've inherited your toughness and tenacity not just from me, Merle, but also from your father. Especially from him."

"We can look for him where we want to," said Junipa, and her mirror eyes seemed to blaze with determination. "In all worlds."

Lalapeya gently stroked Junipa's cheek with the back of her hand. "Yes, you can. You'll watch out for Merle, won't you? She broods too much when she's alone. She gets that from her mother."

"I won't be alone." Merle smiled at Junipa. "Neither of us will be." And then she hugged and kissed Lalapeya and finally took leave of her. Junipa touched the surface of the mirror and whispered the glass word.

Merle followed her through the wall of silver, out into the labyrinths of the mirror world, where there was so much to see, to learn, to find. Her father. That other Venice—that of the reflections on the canal. And even, who knew, another Merle, another Junipa.

Another Serafin.

But Lalapeya stood there for a long time after the two were gone and the mirror ripples had smoothed out. At last she turned around, parted the silken curtains with her bandaged hands, and strolled through the house, which was finally full of life again.

From far below, from the kitchen, it smelled of cinnamon and honey, and through the walls she could hear the ferment of the city, the awakening to the future. In between, so far away that no human ear could have perceived it, sounded the soft singing of the mermaids, somewhere in the sea, far away from all islands; behind it the call of the sea witch; the sprouting of a flower in desert sand; the wing beats of a powerful lion prince.

And perhaps even, very far away, very vague, the voices of two girls who had just walked out into another, alien world.

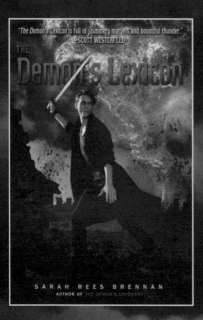

An unlikely romance.

A terrifying dream world.

One final chance for survival.

Nevermore

KELLY CREAGH